Endorsements for *Eye of the Oracle*

A wonderful epic, brimming with great characters and fantastic otherworldly places. *Eye of the Oracle* also presents the spiritual battle between good and evil, but more importantly, it shows the triumph of faith and obedience to our Creator.

—**Jason Waguespack** (Author of *Star Trek:
The Next Generation Episode Guide for Season One*)

Wow . . . pure genius! If possible, even better and more intriguing than the *Dragons in our Midst* books! I was spellbound the entire time! I'm an avid reader, and when it comes to a mind and heart-gripping book like *Eye of the Oracle*, I will read it again and again. Mr. Davis, you've outdone yourself!

—**Holli Herdeg** (Age 13)

An awesome book! *Eye of the Oracle* is a prequel to the *Dragons in our Midst* series and is a wonderful book about faith, friendship, and the battle between good and evil. After reading it my faith is stronger than ever.

—**Jonathan De Reus** (Age 14)

A worthy precursor to a spectacular series, never leaving behind the demonstration of everyone's need of love, hope, and forgiveness.

—**Chris Shupe** (Age 25)

. . . one book you definitely do not want to miss.

—**Anna Mottaz** (Age 14)

Wow! Bryan Davis is like a modern C. S. Lewis! *Eye of the Oracle* is the coolest book I have ever read! When I finished reading it, I grasped a more powerful and clearer understanding of my faith.

—**Jon Maiocco** (Age 13)

Eye of the Oracle drew me in from the first page to the last, with its vivid settings, its lively characters, and its spellbinding story. Mr. Davis has created a masterpiece, integrating high fantasy adventure with solid spiritual truths. *Eye of the Oracle* is an excellent book, a must-read for any fantasy lover!"

—**Michelle Jarvis** (Age 18)

Eye of the Oracle is definitely one of the best books I've read in a long time. It explains a lot of mysteries I wondered about in the original series. The first part of the book raised even more questions, but hang in there; everything will be answered. Just give it time—it's well worth the wait.

—**Brian Denning** (Age 14)

I LOVED this book! I could not put it down and got in trouble for reading too late on many a night. I laughed, cried, and rejoiced along with the characters as I lived with them through both their plights and joys.

—C.J. Giacomini (Age 16)

Eye of the Oracle covers the history of dragons from the days of Noah, to the Tower of Babel, to King Arthur's reign, and all the way to the 21st century events of *Tears of a Dragon*. This epic will sweep you into the land Bryan Davis has so masterfully created and make you wonder how much of it is really fiction.

—Nathan Hutchinson (Age 14)

Eye of the Oracle is an **AWESOME** book! I absolutely loved following the characters through all of their adventures and faith-finding experiences. It definitely kept me on the edge of my seat.

—Brin Lewis (Age 16)

Eye of the Oracle is a great companion for *Dragons in our Midst* and a wonderful reminder of how much God loves and provides for His children! This book will take you on exciting adventures with characters you will love! You won't want to put it down!

—Connie Wolters (Age 25)

Eye of the Oracle is astounding, both for its very well-written narrative and spiritual insight. I would recommend it to anyone looking for a good fantasy read.

—Luke Gledhill (Age 18)

I loved this book so much I got in trouble for staying up late reading it!

—Rachel Caudelle (Age 13)

I had a very hard time putting this book down, no matter how late it was. The fact that the one true God is in this story made it all the better. It is filled with so much adventure and excitement, you will love it.

—Sara Ford (Age 11)

I loved how *Eye of the Oracle* twisted and turned! It took me to another world where I could just enjoy the story and not be bothered by anything around me. It was full of suspense, action, and a dash of humor. I can't wait for the next one!

—Rebekah Hagan (Age 13)

Eye of the Oracle is amazing. Bryan Davis is a genius.

—Nicolaos Panos (Age 12)

Eye of the Oracle

Bryan Davis

LIVING INK BOOKS
Writing Worth Reading

Eye of the Oracle
Copyright © 2006 by Bryan Davis
Published by Living Ink Books, an imprint of AMG Publishers
6815 Shallowford Rd.
Chattanooga, Tennessee 37421

All Scripture quotations are taken from the King James Version.

ISBN: 0-89957-870-5
First printing—September 2006
Cover designed by Daryle Beam, Market Street Design, Inc.,
    Chattanooga, Tennessee
Interior design and typesetting by Reider Publishing Services,
    West Hollywood, California
Edited and proofread by Becky Miller, Sharon Neal, and Rick Steele

Printed in the United States of America
17 16 15 14 13 12 –W– 10 9 8 7 6 5

Library of Congress Cataloging-in-Publication Data

Davis, Bryan, 1958-
   Eye of the Oracle / by Bryan Davis.
   p. cm. — (Oracles of fire ; bk. 1)
   "Prequel series to the Dragons in Our Midst series"—T.p. verso.
   Summary: Relates the various interactions of dragons with mankind from the era before Noah's ark through the time of King Arthur and on to the present day.
   ISBN-13: 978-0-89957-870-5 (pbk. : alk. paper)
   ISBN-10: 0-89957-870-5 (pbk. : alk. paper)
   [1. Dragons--Fiction. 2. Demonology--Fiction. 3. Christian life—Fiction.
4. Supernatural—Fiction.] I. Title. PZ7.B285557Eye 2006
   [Fic]—dc22   2006026477

For those who were once blind but now see clearly, even from one world to another, Oracles who keep your eyes fixed on the One who will guide you to the final dimension—this story is for you.

For those who once lay cold and seemingly forgotten under the burden of unrelenting strife but now have found the Light that ignites an undying passion, a fire for truth, wisdom, and righteousness—this story is for you.

You are Oracles of Fire.

ACKNOWLEDGMENTS

To my faithful wife and best friend, Susie—I am amazed at your unfailing love. In my eyes, you personify grace and beauty. Thank you for reading this manuscript so many times without a single complaint.

To my AMG family—Dan Penwell, Warren Baker, Rick Steele, Dale Anderson, Trevor Overcash, Joe Suter, and all the staff—thank you for believing in these crazy stories. God is using us to change lives all over the world.

Most of all, I thank God for the inspiration, grace, and strength to conceive and create this book. Without Him, I am nothing.

Author's Note

Eye of the Oracle is the first book in the new series, **Oracles of Fire**. It is a prequel to the **Dragons in our Midst** (DIOM) series and chronicles the events that preceded DIOM. The next book in **Oracles of Fire** will be *Enoch's Ghost*, a sequel to DIOM. *Enoch's Ghost* will pick up the story where *Eye of the Oracle* and *Tears of a Dragon* end.

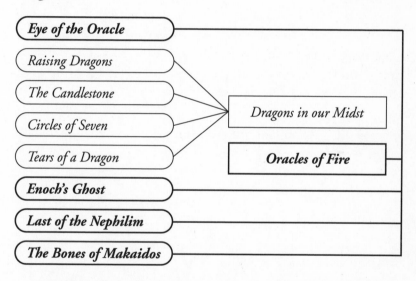

Here is how the stories line up in chronological order. The new series is boldfaced.

Readers who have not delved into *Dragons in our Midst* will have no trouble understanding and enjoying *Eye of the Oracle*. This story begins a new adventure that will lead readers into a multi-dimensional land, a fascinating journey guided by the *Oracles of Fire*.

CONTENTS

CONTENTS

BOOK 2
TRANSFORMATION

x

BOOK 3
REFINER'S FIRE

MERLIN'S PRAYER

O King of Light, so true and wise,
Who grants in troubled times
A wealth of counsel from above
And prophecy in rhymes,

I ask Thee now to pour Thy mind
In measure after measure,
For days of darkness snuff Thy light
And rob our only treasure.

An evil power snares the land
Deceiving flesh and blood,
And even kings are fooled by her
Beguiling, blinding flood.

But hast thou granted her a time
To foster lies and hate?
Dost Thou foresee what I cannot,
A day this flood abates?

A flood of murders, vengeance, wrath,
And hatefulness within
'Tis worse than forty days of rain
That purged the earth of sin.

For in this flood we must endure
And swim amidst the mire,
While kings do battle over words
And murder what they sire.

I beg you now to bring an ark,
A savior, king, a knight,
And rescue those who wait in faith
To see his sword of light.

Prepare me, Lord, to live till I
This noble son behold,
For prophets dream, but few awake
To see your plan unfold.

BOOK 1
In the Beginning

So he drove out the man; and he placed at the east
of the garden of Eden Cherubims, and a flaming
sword which turned every way, to keep
the way of the tree of life.

(Genesis 3:24)

PROLOGUE

I am a daughter of the earth, sown and rooted in the soil of the land of the dead. I am an underborn, a slave girl, a bondservant to a dark mistress of evil. For centuries I have toiled, flinching at the sound of whips, grimacing at their sting on my back, and mourning for my fellow slaves as they expired at the hands of our tormentors. One by one, they perished, and now I stand alone.

This is my story, and a story of sorrow often begins in darkness. I must lead you through the valley of the shadow of death, for only a journey through shadows will allow us to fully comprehend the beauty of heavenly light.

Alas! The darkest shadows are cast by God's very own image, rebels who stand against the holy light implanted by their creator. For those who see the light and yet raise a fist at its source are the darkest souls indeed.

You must meet these foul creatures and become aware of their sinister plots. As they hunger to steal the souls of men, you will learn to despise their dark paths and hope for the light of day to expose their evil deeds. Take heart. Though the story begins in a flood of darkness, the light of the world will guide you toward the morning star, and I will greet you on the other side of dawn.

THE SEEDS OF EDEN

Angling into a plunging dive, the dragon blasted a fireball at Lilith and Naamah. The two women dropped to the ground just as the flaming sphere sizzled over their heads. Naamah swatted her hair, whipping away stinging sparks that rained down from the fireball's tail.

With a flurry of wings and a gust of wind, the dragon swooped low. As razor sharp claws jabbed at the women, Naamah lunged to the side, and Lilith rolled through the grass. A single claw caught Lilith's long black dress, ripping it as the dragon lifted toward the sky.

Naamah jumped to her feet and helped Lilith up. The dragon made a sharp turn in the air, and, with its jagged-toothed maw stretching open, charged back toward them.

Lilith pushed a trembling hand into the pocket of her dress. "Only one hope left," she said, panting. Pulling out a handful of black powder, she tossed it over her head. "Give me darkness!" she cried.

The powder spread out into a cloud and surrounded the women. Naamah coughed and spat. The noxious fumes blinded her and coated her throat with an acrid film. A hand grabbed her wrist and jerked her down to her knees just as another flaming cannon ball passed over their heads.

"Crawl!" Lilith ordered.

Naamah scooted alongside Lilith as she scuffled over the dry tufts of grass. Sparks from the rain of fire ignited tiny blazes that illuminated their hands as they passed through the veil of darkness.

Naamah gagged but refused to cough. With a guardian dragon hovering somewhere overhead, giving any clue to their whereabouts could be fatal.

After several minutes, Lilith whispered, "I think I found the cave."

Her hands, barely visible and clutching a small bundle of sticks, crawled over a bed of gravel and then to a rocky floor. When she finally stopped, Naamah sat up and gazed into the dark cloud behind her. She squeezed fractured words through her tingling throat. "Will the dragon follow?"

"Shachar is persistent," Lilith rasped, "but she is no fool." She coughed quietly, clearing her voice. "She will not risk the possibility that we're a diversion for a more dangerous attack. If she doesn't find us soon, she will go back on patrol."

"What about her dragon sense? Won't that draw her to us?"

"I'm not sure. A dragon's danger alarm is still a mystery to me. I think since our only direct threat is to the ancient garden she patrols, her sense of protection will draw her there."

The black cloud began to dissipate, revealing the mouth of a shallow cave, barely deep enough to keep out the wind. Close to the back wall, the women found a flat stone and built a fire next to it with Lilith's collection of sticks. When the crackling flames began to rise, Lilith and Naamah sat on the stone to rest.

From her pocket, Lilith withdrew a small bundle wrapped in a black cloth. After untying a knot on one end, she produced an earthenware cup filled with herbs. "The way to Eden has yet another obstacle," she said, tossing a pinch of the herbs into the campfire. "Our task will not be easy."

Sparks flew toward the cave's low ceiling, riding on thin strings of silvery green smoke. Naamah breathed deeply of the aroma-saturated air, a pungent blend of camphor and garlic. She exhaled, tasting the herbs at the back of her tongue. "What could be more difficult than getting past a dragon?"

"There are forces in our world that dwarf the power of dragons. I have foreseen much that you don't know."

As cool, damp air chiseled away at the fire's rising warmth, Naamah scooted toward her sister, overlapping the fringes of their silky black dresses on the flat stone. Barefoot and shivering in the draft, she wrapped her arms around herself. "Didn't you know it would be this cold? We should have worn our cloaks."

"It is only temporary. The cold air is a path that leads us to the garden." Lilith pushed her long black hair off her shoulder and huddled close, her voice low. "Naamah, you must have more faith in me. My husband's arts have allowed me to see another world, the world of phantasmal knowledge. It is the realm of future possibilities, where I can see what might happen."

Naamah folded her hands. "What *might* happen?"

The bushes rustled just outside the entrance. Lilith glanced over her shoulder, her lips pressing into two pale lines as she set the cup of herbs on the cave's floor and drew a dagger from a sheath on her belt.

"Just the wind," Naamah whispered. "If it were the dragon, we would have heard her wings."

"Perhaps." Lilith's knuckles whitened as she wrung the dagger's wooden hilt. "But even the wind carries spirits who might expose our plans."

Naamah waited for the color to return to Lilith's fingers. "So . . . why are you counting on phantasmal knowledge when it can't tell you for sure what's going to happen?"

"Because our opponent is so predictable." Lilith placed her long, thin hand on Naamah's thigh. "Life is the ultimate game of chance, with millions of possible moves, so I only see what might happen. My choices and our opponent's choices mesh in a tapestry through time, and I can see where some of the threads lead if I follow one or more of the thousands of patterns that fill my eyes. So far, Elohim has reacted to my moves exactly as I expected he would."

Lilith waved the dagger over the fire. A bright, angelic creature swirled inside the rising smoke, its image warping and undulating as the draft swept it around. Inside the flames, a red dragon appeared, jets of fire blasting from its nostrils. The dragon's blaze licked at the angel's bare feet as it whipped around in the smoke's endless circles. "Our plans rest on Samyaza's shoulders, and if he fails, our doom is certain. We must prepare for that possibility."

Naamah rubbed her hands up and down her bare arms. "How can this husband of yours give you the power to see the future? I have never known a man who could see past a bottle . . . or a brothel."

"You have never known such a man, because you don't know the Watchers." She thrust the dagger back to its sheath. "Your men are all fools."

Naamah pulled the hem of her dress high above her knee. "Fools, yes, but their money spends as well as yours."

Lilith slapped Naamah's hand and yanked the skirt back down. "Your harlotry will be the death of you someday! Sister or not, I cannot protect you from yourself."

Naamah caressed her stinging hand and scowled. "You didn't call it harlotry back when we were collecting wild oats together. You've been no fun at all since you got religion with Samyaza."

Lilith grabbed Naamah's shoulder and pulled her almost nose to nose, hissing. "This *religion*, as you call it, might just save your life. If you want to survive, you had better listen to me!"

Naamah jerked away and scooted to the far edge of the stone. "I'll listen. Just don't turn me into something unearthly, like that iridescent dog you keep in your dungeon."

"That was from one of my first potions, and you know it." Lilith sighed and reached for Naamah's arm. "If Samyaza wins, then we won't have to turn into anything unearthly. If he loses . . . well, he need not know our alternate plans."

"Is that why you're so jumpy? Do you think your husband's spying on you?"

"I do feel the presence of a spy, but I doubt that Samyaza sent it."

"So what should we do?" Naamah asked.

"This spy is of no consequence. Shachar is the greater danger, but she will leave the area soon enough, and we will press on. Until then, we have time for an important step in my plan." Lilith lifted a thin cord around her neck and pulled a leather pouch from her bosom. She loosened the drawstring and carefully poured into her palm a dozen or more white crystals the size of cottonseeds, covered with tiny spikes that made each crystal resemble the head of a mace. "These are the seeds of Samyaza's power. With them we will be able to plant his potency wherever we please."

Naamah touched one with her fingertip and rocked it back and forth. "*We* will?" she asked.

Lilith poured the seeds back into the pouch but kept one in her palm and closed her fingers around it. "Our master will teach you how to use it soon enough, but first we must prepare ourselves as vessels—myself to wield the power and you to receive the planting." She picked up her cup, dropped the seed inside, and stirred the contents with a slender black root, holding the cup just above the flames as the herbs melted into a thick brew. After seven swirls, she

9

crumpled the stirrer and threw it into the mix. As purple foam rose above the brim and dribbled over the sides, she waved her hand over the top and sang in a low, mournful voice.

> O Master of the midnight skies,
> The god of darkness, light disguised,
> Provide for me the gift of flight
> And give me wings to flee my plight.
>
> Now through the waters guide my strife,
> And grant the gift of lasting life.
> Regenerate my body whole;
> For this I give my living soul.
>
> And should my husband learn my plans,
> O let his reins come to my hands,
> For strength alone cannot compare
> To woman's last beguiling snare.
>
> O let us be the farmers' hands
> To sow the seeds of fallen man.
> The giants planted here must grow
> Escaping from these lands below.
>
> In Naamah's womb prepare your soil.
> With calloused hands we'll sweat and toil.
> O make your seeds become like trees
> To trample Adam's hopeless pleas.

With both hands trembling, Lilith raised the cup to her mouth and took a long, slow drink. She closed her eyes and grimaced, a shudder crawling across her pale cheeks. After licking her lips, she rubbed some of the liquid into each of her palms, then extended the cup to Naamah.

"You must be joking!" Naamah said, squinting at the curling purple fumes. "I'm not drinking that!"

Lilith took Naamah's hand and wrapped her fingers around the handle. "Just smell it! That's all I ask. Then decide if you want to drink or not."

Naamah tightened her grip on the handle and gazed into the cup. Thick gray liquid bubbled inside. Warm vapors and a pleasant aroma bathed her senses. As she took in the delightful smell, her throat dried out, filling her with a sudden desire to drink. Her tongue clamped to the roof of her mouth, parched and swelling. It was more than a desire. She had to drink. Now!

She guzzled the liquid, then slung the cup against the cave wall and glared at Lilith. "You tricked me!"

Lilith wagged her finger. "It was for your own good."

Naamah crossed her arms over her chest and stared at the earthen shards. "I *am* going to turn into something disgusting, aren't I?"

11

"The potion does much more than that. Even if our earthly bodies die, we will be able to exist in another form. As our new bodies age, we will be able to use Samyaza's power to regenerate ourselves. But if we can get on the boat, we won't have to worry about unsavory transformations at all."

Naamah swung her head back toward Lilith and rose to her feet. "On the boat, you say?"

"Yes. The most obvious phantasmal thread leads to a terrible flood. Our enemy is building a boat that we could use to save ourselves, but the builders have a strange shield around it. Although normal humans can penetrate it, the Watchers and Nephilim haven't been able to. They want to destroy it and change Elohim's plan to flood the world. I, however, wish to find a way to get us on board in case they fail."

Naamah paced slowly in front of her sister. "I know a man who is working on a boat. He said it is very large and well-supplied."

"That would be the one," Lilith replied. "But the builders are unlikely to give away the secret of the shield."

"When he is at the market, he speaks only of supplying the boat." Naamah stopped, cocked her head upward, and smiled. "But when he visits my room, his lips become quite loose."

Lilith scowled. "Loose being the operative word." She stood and slipped her hand around Naamah's elbow. "Did this man mention the shield?"

Naamah swiveled her hips, twirling her dress slowly back and forth. "No, but if you let me sing a song to him, I can charm him into spilling his secrets."

"Oh, really?" Lilith tipped her head upward and stroked her chin. "What's his name?"

"Ham." A burning pain drilled into Naamah's pelvis. She laid a hand over her stomach but tried not to show how much it hurt. "I don't know his family name."

"I wish you had told me about this before," Lilith said, tapping her foot on the ground. "We have to find this man."

The pain stabbed Naamah again, but deeper than before, as if something had grasped her womb with sharpened claws. Still, she forced herself to keep a calm face. "If you'd let me in on your secrets once in a while, maybe I would have known you were trying to get on board."

Lilith glanced out at the bushes again and slowly turned back. "Very well. I will tell you why we are on this journey. You will soon see how all my plans tie together." She picked up a long stick and stirred the coals in their fire, creating a billowing gray plume. A new vision coalesced in the smoke, an angel standing next to a tree. The fire spewed a finger of flame through the angel's hand, making him appear to have a brilliant sword that flashed as he stood guard.

"That is the Tree of Life, and I have long coveted its fruit." Lilith pointed at the flame. "Here is our problem. One of the Cherubim protects it with a sword that creates a shield of light."

"I see," Naamah said. "Now that you have one of the Seraphim on your side . . ."

"You're way ahead of me." Lilith glanced outside and checked the brightening morning sky. "Samyaza will be there soon. I want to see him battle the Cherub and win the sword, then we can pluck the fruit at our leisure. Once he has regained his weapon, he will be invincible, perhaps even against the archangels."

Lilith arose and, bending low, sneaked out of the cave. Naamah followed close behind, pressing her hand against her belly again. Whatever that potion was, it seemed to be turning her organs inside out.

Constantly glancing at the sky, they wound their way through a dense forest, padding softly on a wide clover path until it opened into a field. Lilith halted suddenly and stooped next to a leafy bush. Naamah leaned over her, trying to follow her sister's line of sight. In the distance, a white glow arose above a thick, thorny hedge that extended as far as the eye could see.

Lilith's voice softened to a low hiss. "The hedge is Eden's boundary. The thorns are sharper than any sword, and the poison in the tips will shrivel you into a prune in seconds. The only way to enter is through the guarded gate." She skulked to the hedge and followed it toward the glow, Naamah once again trailing her. As they drew closer, a gap appeared in the hedge, and the guarded tree came into view. Stooping again, Lilith pointed at a beautiful, white-robed angel. "His sword shoots out a beam of light that can kill us even this far away. As long as he waves it over his head, it creates an almost impenetrable shield around himself and the tree."

Naamah settled quietly behind her and peered at the darkening sky. Black clouds boiled overhead. Bolts of lightning streaked jagged forks across the heavens. "Something weird is happening," she whispered.

"I didn't expect this." Lilith's brow bent downward. "Samyaza planned to come by stealth, not with a lightning fanfare."

Naamah pointed toward the top of a tall sycamore tree. "I see him."

13

A winged angel, bright and shining against the stormy back-drop, glided to the ground, his silver hair flowing in the freshening breeze. Dressed in white robes, drawn tight at his waist by a golden sash, he strode to the gate and spoke to the other angel in a booming voice. "Greetings in the name of Elohim."

The Cherub nodded, waving the sword to keep the shield in place. "May our God be glorified forever. What brings a Seraph to Eden's boundary today?"

"I have come to relieve you of your duty. You are to return to the council for a new assignment."

The Cherub glanced up at the troubled sky. "Something is amiss. I sense God's hand moving in the heavens, yet no messenger has alerted me of a change."

"I am the messenger." Samyaza held out his hand. "Give me the sword and go your way."

The Cherub lowered the sword, and the shield blinked off, but he kept the hilt firmly in his grip. "With all due respect, my liege, what is your name?"

"I am Samyaza, prince of the guardian angels." He took a step closer, bringing him within arm's reach of the Cherub. "It would not be wise to continue questioning my authority. Remember Lucifer's folly."

The sword trembled in the Cherub's hand, but his voice remained steady. "Your name is familiar to me, and you have the wings of a Seraph, but I am here by order of the Majesty on High, so I cannot abandon my post on your word alone. Only Michael can countermand the order."

Streaks of darkness shot out from Samyaza's eyes, splashing the Cherub with a sizzling, oily resin that stuck fast to his robes and spread quickly over his hands and face. The sword's light flashed on in the blinded angel's hands, sending a bright beam blazing into the sky. Samyaza lunged forward and shook the Cherub's wrist, slinging the blade under the branches.

Pushing the angel to the side, Samyaza flew toward the trunk, snatched up the sword, and stalked toward the gate. The Cherub threw himself toward the sound of Samyaza's pounding footsteps and wrapped his arms around his neck. The powerful Seraph reached back, grabbed the Cherub's hair, and heaved him toward the tree. The resin-covered angel slammed against the trunk, knocking white fruit to the ground. Samyaza marched toward him, his sword raised.

A loud clap of thunder shook the earth. Another angel, the largest yet, burst from the clouds and zoomed to the ground, landing with a drawn sword raised to strike. "Be gone, Samyaza, you wretched liar. You will not have this tree or its fruit."

Samyaza backed away, visibly trembling. "Michael! I have no quarrel with you. This was my sword before I—"

"Before you left our Lord and Master to satisfy your carnal desires." Michael helped the Cherub to his feet, and with a wave of his hand, the black resin melted away. "Take the sword and crawl back into your hole with your corrupted followers. It will be nothing more than a carving knife to you now."

Samyaza held the sword aloft, but it created no beam. Not even the tiniest spark flashed from the blade. He thrust the tip into a patch of clover and drove the sword into the ground up to the hilt, then shook his fist at Michael. "The people will follow us, not the tyrant in heaven! They want to be free of his authority, and we will teach them to follow the longings of their hearts!"

Michael waved his sword and a new, brighter shield covered the tree. As the dome swirled with radiance, the entire plot of ground ripped away from the earth, uprooting the tree and carrying Michael, the Cherub, and the fallen fruit with it. "If people want true life and freedom," Michael said as they slowly lifted into the sky, "they will look above. Like rain from the heavens, that is the source of their deliverance."

Boiling clouds swallowed the shimmering tree, and, for a moment, all was quiet. Samyaza stared at the ominous ceiling, slowly

15

turning and backing away from the garden. His wings beat the air, and, just as his feet lifted off the ground, a dragon burst out of the clouds shooting twin jets of fire from its nostrils.

Black streams surged from Samyaza's eyes, colliding with the fire. The impact created a sizzling eruption of smoky gas that spewed high into the air. The dragon pulled out of its dive and zoomed by Samyaza, smacking him with its tail before ascending again toward the clouds. Samyaza toppled, but a flurry of his wings kept him from striking the ground.

Lilith leaned over and whispered to Naamah. "Samyaza likely remembers how his master conquered the first female human. It will be interesting to see how he deals with the first female dragon."

Samyaza yanked the sword out of the ground and stabbed it at the sky. "Does the mate of Arramos only fight when she can attack by surprise?" He turned in a slow circle, his eyes darting in all directions. "Come and meet me in single combat, if you dare!"

Shachar burst out of the clouds again, and with a great beating of her wings, she landed in front of Samyaza. "I am not a dog to be baited by a bone," she roared.

The Seraph spread out his arms. "Yet, you are here, panting and drooling for the very bone you disdain."

"Only to lance a demonic abscess." She pawed the ground with her claws. "If you desire a fair fight, drop the sword and let us see who wields the greater power."

"As you wish." Samyaza bowed dramatically and released the sword.

"Step away from it," Shachar ordered. "Far away."

Samyaza marched several paces to one side and gestured toward the sword. "Satisfied?"

Shachar nodded her scaly head. "Trusting you is a fool's game, but I will risk what I must to rid the world of its greatest plague."

The shining angel flashed a wicked smile. "Since you are the aggressor, I invite your first volley."

Shachar lunged at him, her teeth bared and her nostrils flaming. Samyaza dipped under her jets and latched on to her tail as she passed over. With a mighty spin, he slung her in the direction of the sword. The dragon crashed to the ground and slid next to the hilt. As she lifted her wobbly head, her eyes seemed glazed and distant.

Samyaza zoomed to her side and grabbed the sword. With a dramatic thrust, he plunged the blade into the dragon's underbelly. Shachar let out an ear-piercing shriek and writhed in the grass. "Coward!" she screamed. "Deceiver!" She spat out a weak ball of fire, but it rolled past the towering Seraph as he backed away.

When the dragon's throes settled down, Samyaza grasped the hilt of the sword and withdrew it from her body, jumping away from a gush of fluids. He glared at the bloody blade and dropped it to the ground. "Disgusting creatures!" With a flap of his wings, he lifted into the air and disappeared in the blanket of clouds.

Shachar opened her mouth as if trying to speak. She twitched for a moment, then heaved a final sigh as her eyes slowly closed.

Lilith and Naamah ran toward the dragon. Lilith snatched up the sword and wiped the blade on the grass. "Samyaza might not be able to use this," she said, turning the blade over to clean the other side, "but if I can find the secret behind its flame, it could be a powerful weapon indeed."

She propped the blade on her shoulder and strode through the gateway, now unattended by angel or dragon. Naamah followed, gazing at the devastated garden. Knotted trees with bent crowns and twisted branches plagued the endless fields of dry grass. On one squared-off plot, leggy bushes hunkered over a tangled mess of tall weeds and thorny vines. Hundreds of thistles raised bristly heads among row after row of dwarfed fruit trees and shriveled vegetables. Naamah let out a low whistle. This was no paradise, no land of perfection, despite the claims of her childhood songs.

17

Lilith tramped down to the bottom of the hole where the tree once stood. She stooped, pinching a sample of soil and drawing it close to her eyes. "Not a trace. Not a root or seed anywhere."

Naamah noticed a glinting speck in the dirt. "Here's something!" She plucked out a smooth white pebble, barely as large as her fingertip, and handed it to Lilith. "Could this be a seed?" she asked. "It looks like a pearl."

"It could be." Lilith knelt where Naamah found the pebble and used her finger to stir the soil, a mixture of moist brown dirt and a strange white paste. "Here are two more." She collected them and slid all three into her pocket. "We'll keep them for posterity."

"Posterity?"

"Future generations. I don't know how long it takes to grow a Tree of Life, but I intend to find out."

Lilith gazed toward a path that led into a stand of skinny oaks. "The other tree should be in that direction," she said, pointing.

As she headed toward the wood, she swiped Samyaza's sword in front of her as if fending off an invisible enemy or perhaps testing its weight and balance. Naamah had to jog to keep pace with her sister. Lilith's stern expression told her it wasn't a good time to ask questions, so she just stayed at her side, taking in the sights of loss and waste in the massive garden.

After following the path through the trees, they arrived at a glade. In the center of a circle of grass, a tree, heavy with red, oblong fruit, stood tall and lush. Lilith strode right up to the nearest branch and called out, "Lucifer, my lord and master, I bring you vital information."

A fresh breeze flapped Lilith's dress as she stood in stoic silence, the tip of the sword touching the ground in front of her. The wind crawled up Naamah's legs, bringing her a chill. The pain in her stomach had settled, but a new queasiness took over. Something foul drew near, worse than a fetid carcass. Whatever it was seemed to seep through her skin and into her heart, making it slow to a few, sickening thumps.

Soon, a gentle hissing joined the shush of the wind. A long, thick snake slithered out onto the branch and rested its head near a bobbing fruit. Lilith extended her arm and pushed her hand under the serpent's belly. Bearing scales like sun-baked leather, black hexagons meshed with olive green, the snake crept along Lilith's pale arm. Its tongue darted in and out from its triangular head as it spoke in a slow, threatening cadence. "If you have come to tell me about Naamah's customer, you have come in vain. While I am in this cursed condition, my disciples sneak in through the garden's western gate. One of my agents overheard your conversation and reported the news about this boat builder."

"So that's what we heard in the bushes," Lilith said. "It *was* a spy."

The snake flicked its tongue, touching her cheek with its forked points. "I send spies on my enemies and my followers, especially followers as ambitious as you."

As the snake wrapped a coil around Lilith's neck, she lifted her chin and swallowed hard. "And how shall we use the information, my lord?"

The snake maneuvered its head in front of Lilith's eyes, wavering back and forth in a hypnotic sway. "I sent my agent to speak to my servant, Lamech, son of Mathushael. I have ordered Lamech to adopt Naamah into his family. Naamah's new brother, Tubalcain, knows Ham and will offer her to be Ham's wife."

"His wife?" Naamah said, crossing her arms over her chest. "Ham is a regular customer, but that doesn't mean I want him for a husband!"

The serpent's head shot toward Naamah, its fangs extended as it bit the empty air just inches in front of her eyes. Naamah staggered backwards, catching one of the tree's branches to keep her balance. Recoiling over Lilith's shoulders, the serpent hissed, "Either marry him or die!"

19

Naamah shivered in the tree's shadow, holding her stomach again as the fierce pain stabbed her insides.

The serpent turned its flaming red eyes back to Lilith. "Ham's father will recognize your name, so you must change it before you meet him. We cannot allow him to know who and what you are."

"Of course, my lord." Lilith kept her head tilted upward. "Do you have a preference?"

"Choose whatever pleases you. I will arrange things to make your new name work."

Lilith smiled. "As you wish, my master."

The serpent's tongue flicked again. "I have news about the sword."

Lilith lifted the blade. "The secret to its flames?"

"Yes. The sword is designed to detect the nature of the hands that grasp it. The flames shoot from the blade only if the hands are innocent and undefiled. Of course, the Cherub who guarded the Tree of Life was holy, so he was able to use the blade's protective shield over the tree."

Lilith ran a finger along the blade. "And Samyaza's hands have been deemed corrupt." She gazed at the grip, wiggling her fingers around it. "Can the sword be fooled into thinking it is being held by holy hands?"

"Perhaps. It has no thinking process of its own. It merely responds to how it was forged."

Lilith studied the etchings in the blade's silvery metal. "Who are the two dragons doing battle in the design?"

"I am one of them, and I struggle with a dragon who is to come, a warrior who will fight with me to become king of the dragons. Michael etched that symbol when he gave the sword to Samyaza and commissioned him to find and protect the holy dragon who would come to try to conquer me."

"I see," Lilith said, nodding. "So this king must have holy hands in order to defeat you."

20

"Yes. But since this usurper could be a human representative for the dragons, our goal is to corrupt every family line, whether dragon or human, with the seed of the fallen ones. But, beware. Elohim has already hatched a plan to thwart ours. I know little more than a code phrase one of my disciples overheard—'oracles of fire.' "

"That's it? No context?"

"Only that there are two of them. Perhaps a pair of angels commissioned specifically to infiltrate our ranks and destroy our work from within."

"I will watch for them." Lilith lowered the sword. "And when will you become a dragon again and leave the garden?"

As the serpent slithered along Lilith's arm, she raised her hand to the tree. It coiled around the branch, and its head turned back toward her, its voice echoing like a ghostly whisper. "When I steal the body of a certain dragon, I will be whole once more." It crawled back into the thicker foliage and disappeared.

21

Naamah ran from the tree and sidled up to Lilith, crossing her arms again. Lilith chuckled and kissed the top of her head. "Don't worry, Sister. Yours will be a marriage of convenience. We can dispose of Ham when he has served his purpose."

Naamah turned her back to Lilith, her arms still crossed. "Then *you* marry him. You seem ready to betray your husband."

Lilith grabbed Naamah's shoulder and spun her back around, her eyes turning bright scarlet. "I'm doing this for us!"

The pain from Lilith's grip made Naamah shake. As she stared at her sister's fiery eyes, she felt tears forming in her own.

Lilith slowly relaxed her fingers. Stroking Naamah's hair, she leaned close and whispered, "Lucifer has given me the means to carry out the plan that will save our lives. He knows Samyaza is not likely to cooperate, but I don't really want to betray my own husband." She pressed the tip of the sword into the grass. "I won't resort to draining his power unless I have to."

"Draining his power?" Naamah pointed at the sword. "With that?"

"No." Lilith spread out her fingers, showing Naamah her palm. Splotches of purple stained her skin from the heel of her hand to her fingertips. "My seed concoction has many uses, and absorbing potency will come in handy." Reaching up, she caressed one of the red fruits dangling from the tree. "Speaking of seeds"— she plucked the fruit—"I think these might also come in handy."

"For posterity again?"

"In a manner of speaking, yes." Lilith dropped the apple-sized fruit on the ground and chopped down with the sword, slicing it cleanly in half. Kneeling, she picked through the flesh, collecting six seeds, then, spreading out her fingers again, she let the sparkling red seeds roll around on her stained palm.

"They look like rubies!" Naamah said.

Lilith dropped them into her pocket along with the others. "Much more valuable than rubies, Sister. They are the seeds of corruption. And those who control the corrupting influence wield the power to rule the corrupted."

The Dark Side of the Rainbow

Makaidos unfurled his wings in the stiff, damp breeze. "Thigocia, I still sense danger."

"As do I." Twin plumes of smoke rose from the female dragon's nostrils. "More Nephilim?"

"I cannot tell. The danger is too far away to be sure, or perhaps my nerves are still rattled from the fight."

"It is not nervousness that troubles me." Thigocia sniffed the air and stepped on a huge blackened body lying in the midst of the grassy meadow. "The stench of this Naphil carcass is making me ill."

Makaidos tried to calm himself, but the strange beads of water sprinkling from the dark sky seemed to strum his tightened awareness. The prophets had predicted this "rain," as they called it, yet knowing it was coming merely enhanced the anxiety it aroused. Black clouds boiled over the mountaintops and streamed above their lush, orchard-filled valley, adding even more gloom to the

23

dismal skies. He breathed a stream of flames toward a nearby fig orchard, brightening the area for a brief moment. "Maybe I sense his brother lurking in the trees."

"I doubt it. I scorched his arm to the bone. He is likely running home to his demonic daddy."

Makaidos pawed the moistening soil. "Is the Oracle safe?"

Thigocia unfurled her wing. A lanky old man with thin, frazzled white hair and a ragged beard tripped over her pinion and tumbled to the grass. The man rose to his feet and brushed dirt from his knee-length robe. "If I can avoid killing myself," he said, "I should survive, at least until the deluge."

Makaidos nudged the dead giant's body with his clawed fingers until it rolled faceup. The Naphil flopped its arm on the ground with a heavy thud. Makaidos pricked the arm with a spine on his tail. No reaction, not even a twitch from his massive, six-fingered hand.

"Are you making sure he's dead?" the Oracle asked.

"Yes. I have never been able to kill any of the Nephilim before, so I thought they might be immortal. But when I saw dark mist streaming from this one's mouth, I hoped his foul soul was being dragged to the abyss."

"I torched the other giant," Thigocia said, "but it barely fazed him, and we both still feel an evil presence." Keeping her wing over the old man's balding scalp, she gazed into his eyes. "Can the Ovulum see beyond our senses? Is danger on the horizon?"

The Oracle held up a shining orb, egg-shaped and about the size of a large pear. As it rested in his palm, scarlet halos emanated from its smooth, glassy surface, painting his withered face in their glow. The rings of color radiated all around the entire company, creating an umbrella of light. "A Watcher is lurking," he said, "but the Ovulum cannot tell me how close he is."

He mopped his forehead with his sleeve and breathed out a long sigh. "The king chose well to have you two guard me. I had

24

my doubts about the female's experience, but she has certainly proven me wrong."

"We are both honored to serve the children of Adam. And you are right about Thigocia." Makaidos swished his tail toward her. "My father believes she is the most promising young warrior in his kingdom."

Thigocia closed her eyes and bowed. "Praise the Maker," she whispered.

The old man sighed again. "Yes . . . promising." He held out his hand, allowing a thin pool of water to gather in his palm. "Earthly promises are washing away, as are the lives of Adam's progeny. Life itself fades like withering grass." He patted Thigocia on her flank. "And warriors must learn other arts . . . at least for a time."

Thigocia raised her head. "Other arts? What other—"

Makaidos snorted a plume of smoke. "I sense a Watcher close at hand! Guard the Oracle!"

Thigocia wrapped up the old man again, pinning him to her side, and ignited the surrounding grass to create a ring of fire around herself and Makaidos. A mammoth-sized angel with dark red wings appeared out of the thick blanket of clouds and flew to the earth. He stalked around the blazing circle, his radiant robes reflecting the tongues of sizzling fire. "A ring of flames, dragoness?" the angel said. "Not very creative for such a wet, dreary day, but that's to be expected of a senseless beast like you."

Makaidos flicked his tail toward Thigocia. "Do not answer him. He is baiting us."

She growled. "I have fought this demon before. We must be on our guard. He is powerful and crafty."

The Oracle's shaggy head pushed through a gap in Thigocia's wing. "He is drawn to the Ovulum's power. I can feel his mind connecting with its energy field. There is no use hiding it from him."

25

Thigocia reignited a dampening arc in the protective circle. "But how could he have found the Ovulum's signal among all the decoys?"

"The question is irrelevant," the Oracle replied. "All our energy must be focused on protecting the Ovulum. Its shield must cover the refuge boat. Nothing else matters."

Makaidos lowered his voice to a faint rumble. "I will lure him away. I know a ruse he likely has not seen."

Thigocia whispered back. "Do not try it! Your father wishes that we stay together."

"He wishes that I protect the Oracle and the shield. That wish trumps all others." Makaidos unfurled his wings and rose into the air.

"Be careful!" Thigocia shouted. "Other demons might be on the way!"

Makaidos launched his body upward, beating his wings against the stormy breeze. Sharp droplets stung his eyes as he zoomed toward the billowing clouds. Then, gliding just below the dark ceiling, he watched for the demon to give chase, but the cascade of water blurred his view. He could see the meadow and the prophet's fig tree orchard, but little else. Even Thigocia was just a smudge in the center of her blazing ring.

Makaidos took in a deep breath. He exhaled slowly, pushing a narrow stream of fire into the breeze. Flying awkwardly, like a wounded duck ready to plunge to its death, he allowed the flames to sputter into weak sparks. He glanced down again and caught sight of the Watcher. The demon lifted into the air and glided over the fig trees in a low circle, rising with each arc.

Makaidos laughed to himself. What a fool this demon was to wander into the prophet's land alone! Was he a scout? A castoff? No matter. That corrupted son of God would soon fry in the abyss.

A heavy mist swirled around Makaidos. He aimed his ruby eyebeams into the fog. Where was the scoundrel now? Had he figured out the ruse and fled?

Two huge creatures in gleaming chain mail suddenly dropped from the clouds, shooting black streaks from their fiery eyes. Makaidos dodged the first volley, but the second splashed against his right flank. He collapsed his wings and plummeted headfirst. He had to get away and warn Thigocia before the darkness spell could take hold.

The burning black resin spread across his scales, climbing toward his face like acidic worms. The field below rushed toward him as a troop of towering demons stalked Thigocia and the prophet. The Ovulum's scarlet halos pulsed over them like bloody ocean waves.

Makaidos's sense of danger blared in his mind. He tried to stretch out his weakened wings. Would they be able to pull him up in time? Maybe he could plow into a row of Watchers and die in a blaze of glory. Why not? With the prophesied storm gaining strength, he was destined to die soon anyway.

His wings caught the air, leveling his body. After snorting a barrage of fiery cannonballs, he curled into a sphere and crashed into the evil squadron. As his body rolled, demon after demon toppled over. When he finally came to a stop, he looked up. Samyaza, the leader of the Watchers, towered over him, a derisive smirk spreading contempt across his face.

The Seraph laughed. "A remarkable show, young prince. Your father would be proud."

Makaidos strained to speak. "He will be proud . . . when I blow you . . . into a million blazing pieces."

Samyaza kicked Makaidos in the belly. Pain streaked through his body, radiating all the way to his tail. The black worms crawled over his eyes and drew a curtain of darkness across his vision. His ears burned as Samyaza's mocking voice pierced his brain. "When we kill the Oracle, his shield will collapse, and we will destroy the refuge boat. Now, give in to the darkness. Everything you have worked for is lost."

27

As the darkness spell swallowed Makaidos, doubt and despair flooded his mind. He moaned softly. Why had his father trusted him to protect the Oracle? He and Thigocia were too young, too inexperienced to stand against such powerful fallen angels. He had been a fool to take the assignment, too proud to have any doubt in his abilities. Samyaza was right. All was lost.

As he drifted toward unconsciousness, the sound of bestial roars and a flurry of wings sounded in his ears. He released a long sigh, perhaps his last breath. Surely the battle would be over soon. Thigocia would die valiantly. The feeble Oracle would put up a futile last stand and then be crushed by the cruel Watchers. And no one would hear their cries for help.

Heat flared across Makaidos's body, and a soothing voice awakened his mind.

"Makaidos? Can you hear me?"

Makaidos squirmed. Father's voice? How could that be? He turned his ears to listen. The voice caressed his senses like the sun's gentle beams on a spring morning.

"Awake, my son. You have fought well. Thigocia told me of your heroics, and she is now burning away the darkness. Take in her fire. Breathe the warmth through your scales. Restore your strength and renew your confidence. When I chose you to guard the Oracle, I chose well. You have made me proud."

A flash of heat melted the blackness away from Makaidos's eyes. Two dragons stood at his side. The tawny one, Thigocia, breathed a stream of fire at his body, melting away the black resin. Arramos, his father, stood at his side, his magnificent red scales reflecting the flames.

Makaidos struggled to his feet, pushing with his tail to balance his wobbly frame. The sky seemed darker, the clouds, thicker, and rain continued to pelt the meadow. The glow from the Ovulum rings had vanished. "The Oracle!" Makaidos cried. "Is he safe?"

Arramos lowered his eyes and shook his head. "Samyaza killed him and destroyed the Ovulum's shield. Clirkus is flying his body back to his people."

Makaidos slumped his wings to the ground. "Then all is lost. We have failed."

Arramos curved his neck, positioning his head directly in front of Makaidos. "Not yet. Hilidan and the others are chasing the Watchers, and I will join them. There is no time to lose, but I wanted to make sure of your safety first."

"My safety? What about the Oracle's safety? You would have done well to choose other guardians for him. We failed you."

"On the contrary, you wounded enough Watchers to allow Thigocia to fend them off until we arrived." Arramos stretched out his tail and prodded Makaidos's shoulder. "Spread your wings, Son, so Thigocia can finish her work."

Makaidos obeyed. A new surge of heat massaged the more sensitive coat under one of his wings. It stung, but each second of burning away the darkness seemed to sharpen his mind.

29

"We had been tracking them," Arramos continued, "and we were patrolling nearby, close enough to sense the danger. Now that the Watchers have come out of hiding, we can finish them off for good."

"For good?" Makaidos bared his teeth, grimacing at the pain of Thigocia's healing massage. "But the Oracle is dead, and the shield is gone! What good can possibly come from this disaster?"

Arramos thumped his tail on the ground. "Makaidos, the Oracle knew he would die today. All is coming to pass exactly as he had foreseen, and the end of the Watchers is at hand. Now that the shield is down, you and Thigocia must fly immediately to the refuge boat and protect it while we destroy the rest of the demons."

Thigocia turned off her fiery jets. "Protect the boat? Are you sure we can do it?"

"We would serve you better chasing the Watchers," Makaidos said, snorting a stream of sparks. "We are both faster than Hilidan."

Arramos spat a fireball into the air. "No!"

Makaidos backed away, trembling.

"They will split up," Arramos continued, "and we will not be able to track them all. If any demon eludes us, he will surely go straight to the boat. We need two guardians there, and you must leave now!"

Makaidos unfurled his wings again. Bowing his head, he spoke softly. "If that is your will, Father." With his gaze on the ground, he noticed the Ovulum, now dark and smeared with mud. He scooped it up in his clawed hand and let the rain wash away the grime. As the scarlet glass cleared, the image of a man's face appeared deep within the crystal, a ruddy tint blushing his wrinkled cheeks. The man's lips moved, but no sound came out. Makaidos closed his claws around it. Very strange! But it was a mystery that would have to wait.

He lifted into the air, nodding at Thigocia, and without another word the two young dragons soared into the weeping sky.

Japheth smeared a line of pitch across the joint between two planks . . . the last two planks. Checking hundreds of seams had taken all day, but it had to be done. The huge boat sat in a rocky trench, untested for buoyancy or leaks. Only water, and plenty of it, could prove if the last hundred years of labor amounted to anything more than the biggest waste of time the world had ever known. He, for one, didn't want to risk the lives of his whole family by slacking off for a single hour, especially now that the final day, the seventh day of the prophecy, was at hand.

Japheth ambled across a sagging rope-and-sapling bridge from the main deck to the rim of the trench and then into the shade of one of the dozen or so tall sycamores surrounding the ark. After wiping his hands with a fibrous rag, he picked up a flask and guzzled a long drink. *Ah!* He mopped his dripping chin with his sleeve. *Water never tasted so good!*

Taking his rag and his flask, he walked out onto the bridge again and peered down at his brother Shem about thirty feet below. The main door to the boat, which they called "Eve's Door," was wider than an elephant and as tall as a giraffe. It lay open inside the trench next to Shem, like a ramp awaiting more cargo to tromp aboard. A tense crease dug into Shem's brow as he ran his hand over the hull.

Japheth reached his flask over Shem and poured out a trickle, hoping it would . . . Yes! Right on his head!

Shem leaned back and held out his open palm.

"No, it's not raining yet," Japheth said, laughing.

Shem shook his head, running his fingers through his gray-speckled hair. "It will be soon. You'd better finish those seams." He turned back to his work, his brow once again furrowing.

"My seams are done." Japheth crouched on the swaying bridge to get a better look at the joint his brother was checking. "Will it hold?"

Shem dug his fingertip into the crack. "It's sealed underneath." He clambered up a tall ladder and hoisted himself out of the trench. Now standing on the land side of the bridge, he peeled away a shred of dried pitch from his hand. "I think that's all. We're finally ready."

Japheth scrambled off the bridge and handed Shem the rag. "Then why the long face?" He nodded toward a bank of boiling clouds spreading across the darkening horizon. "It's coming, but we'll be fine."

Shem wiped his hands, meticulously stripping pitch from each finger. "Exactly. Rain is coming." He gestured toward the boat with his head. "Inside that hull, hundreds of hooves are trampling

31

straw on a thousand cords of gopher wood." He laid the rag over his shoulder and began counting on his fingers. "We have a cantankerous camel that spits at Father whenever he walks by, a parrot that never stops shouting, 'Kill the skunks!' two dogs that shed enough hair to make wigs for all of humanity, and a pair of elephants that are always—" Shem grimaced. "Well, let's just say that I brought an extra shovel and a stack of empty bags."

"Prolific pachyderms?" Japheth pinched his nose and laughed. "But even a big stink is no surprise. We knew the stalls would get filled with—"

"Shhh!" Shem grabbed Japheth's shoulder. "Father is coming."

Noah exited a wide door in the main quarters on the top deck, "Adam's door," as they called it, and ambled across the bridge, brushing a sticky splotch of gray hair off his forehead with his sleeve. "Fool camel," he grumbled. "You'd think I'd have learned by now."

Japheth elbowed Shem's ribs and smiled, but Shem's frown deepened.

"Father," Shem said, stroking his beard, "we have a problem."

Their father's gaze lifted toward the darkening skies. "Still no dragons?"

"No sign of them," Shem replied. "I have been watching all day."

Japheth copied his brother's serious aspect, forcing himself to frown as he cleared his throat. "I have a comfortable stall ready for them on our level, better than my own quarters, but I haven't seen a plume of smoke or a scaly wing anywhere."

The old man clasped Japheth on the shoulder. "They will come. God promised at least two of every breathing creature, so the dragons will be here before the flood can sweep them away."

Japheth held out his hand. Tiny droplets moistened his palm and began to form a pool. Rain. Just as his father had prophesied. Ever since God had called out to Noah by name, he had been in close conversation with the Almighty, so why doubt him now? The dragons would come.

Japheth shook the water from his hand. "Shall we untie the bridge? The dragons could fly to the main deck."

Noah shook his head. "Your brother has not returned."

"Ham is gone again?" Japheth glanced into the trench at the cargo door's rope and pulley system, still broken from the recent gorilla incident. "Where did he go? We have to get the door fixed. We won't survive long if we don't get it closed."

"To the market for more grapes. It seems that those odd cat-like creatures"—Noah encircled each of his eyes with a thumb and forefinger—"the big-eyed ones that came from the South yesterday, are quite fond of them. And I wanted more grapes anyway for seed harvesting. When the flood ends, I want to plant a vineyard and—" The popping noise of cart wheels on pebbles interrupted him.

"Speak of the devil," Japheth whispered to Shem. "Our brother has arrived."

"And check out his two minions," Shem whispered back. "They look . . . well . . . unnatural."

Japheth scanned the ox-drawn cart, filled to overflowing with bunches of purple and green grapes. Sitting at the back with their bare feet hanging near the path, two women dressed in black glanced all around, their lips thin and taut.

When the ox halted, the shorter woman jumped off and quickly smoothed out her dress, pulling and tugging to cover as much skin as she could. Ham, his muscles flexing as he strained on the ox's harness, cast a glance at his father and nodded, then turned to unload the grapes. "I have done as you asked, Father," he said, keeping his eyes on the cart. "I have taken a wife. Her name is Naamah, Tubalcain's sister."

"Tubalcain?" Noah's teeth clenched, his face reddening. "You married in the line of Cain? Why would you bring such shame upon our family?"

Ham carried a load of grapes and stopped in front of his father, his face expressionless. "You said to find a wife for procreating. You didn't ask to approve her genealogy." He hoisted the grapes higher in his arms and lumbered toward the boat, calling without looking back. "We met the other woman at the marketplace. She seeks an audience with you."

Naamah grabbed as many grape clusters as she could and followed Ham, glancing briefly at the other female passenger before scurrying to catch up. She and Ham balanced their loads across the sapling bridge and disappeared through Adam's door.

The other woman stepped down and shuffled toward Noah, carrying a sheathed sword in her extended arms. Tear tracks stained her face. When she drew near, she dropped to one knee and bowed her head. "I come in the name of Elohim," she said softly. "I am Morgan, and I seek shelter from the coming flood. I have heard of your mercy, that you would never turn away a repentant soul. I beg you to take me in, for I am a poor sinner in search of salvation."

Japheth nudged Shem's ribs and whispered, "We could use another hand behind the shovel, if you know what I mean."

Shem kicked Japheth's ankle. "Shhh! I want to listen."

Lowering her body even further, Morgan laid the sword at Noah's feet and pressed her palms flat on the ground, her voice faltering as she wept. "An angel . . . gave me this sword to offer as my price of passage. He said to . . . to tell you that he used it to guard the Tree of Life, and it will . . . it will serve you well as a shield for the ark."

Noah picked up the sword and pulled it from its sheath. The blade flashed with light, and he gazed at it in wonder. "Amazing! It is Chereb, the sword of Eden!"

Shem stepped between Noah and the prostrate woman. "Father, you can't seriously be considering this. Elohim said nothing about last-minute supplicants." He waved his hand toward Morgan. "Besides, where was she during all the years we were building our refuge?"

"True enough, my son, but mercy covers both those who arrive early and those who arrive crying out with their last breath." Noah slid the sword back into its sheath. "Did God say I am not allowed to take a refugee who has paid for her passage with the sword of Eden and with tears of repentance?"

"He said he found only you to be righteous." Shem extended a finger at Morgan. "Not her."

Noah knelt and placed a hand on the woman's head. "Shem, are you my son? How can you be such a merciless judge?"

Shem kicked at a tuft of wiry grass and sighed. "I know I don't deserve to go with you. If not for being your son, I would soon be food for sharks. But I'm not any kind of judge. I'm just imploring you to heed God's word. If you don't, we could all be lost."

Noah straightened, nodding slowly. "Well spoken. But what of the sword and the angel's message?"

"Sword or no sword, should you heed a secondhand account of an angel, when we know fallen angels roam the earth? Shouldn't you obey the words God breathed directly into your ears?"

Noah laid the sword back down near Morgan's hands. "Maybe we can——"

A loud shriek pierced the skies. A shining creature with coal black wings swooped over their heads. Two dragons followed side by side, shooting jets of flaming gas and bursting through their own wall of fire as they gave chase. Morgan jumped to her feet but kept her face toward the ground.

"A Watcher!" Japheth yelled. "Everyone to the ark!" He dashed across the bridge to the deck and latched on to both fastening ropes. "Hurry! I'll keep it steady."

"It's Samyaza!" Noah shouted at the larger of the two dragons. "Makaidos! Beware of his eyes!"

Shem grabbed Noah's elbow and hustled him toward the bridge. Morgan followed, the sword at her side and her chin against her chest.

Japheth flexed his muscles, fighting against the jerking ropes, but when Morgan tramped onto the bridge, he almost lost his grip. He cringed, grinding his teeth in pain. Should he stop her? Father had not said for sure. But with danger all around, how could he leave her behind?

As Noah and Shem neared the ark, the shining creature landed on the deck, grabbed Japheth, and dragged him away from the bridge, locked in a vicious clench. Japheth pushed against the creature's huge, glowing arms, but they clamped down, squeezing his breath away. Shem turned around and hustled his father off the swaying bridge, nearly knocking Morgan over on his way back to solid ground. Morgan followed them to safety.

The two dragons stormed down to the boat, both bodies thumping the deck in awkward crash landings. Their claws scratched deep lines in the gopher wood planks as they scrambled to right themselves. Japheth fell lower in the demon's grip, still trapped, but at least he could breathe.

Makaidos roared. "Fight us in the sky, you coward! Are you a Watcher or a washwoman?"

The Watcher laughed. "Who is a washwoman, the outnumbered angel, or the lizard who sputters brave words when a female is guarding his flank?"

Makaidos glanced at Thigocia and spewed black smoke from both nostrils. "I am not afraid to fight you. You have my word that Thigocia will stay on this deck."

"But, Makaidos!" Thigocia said, slapping her tail on the planks, "we have been trained to fight together!"

Makaidos spat a ball of sparks that fizzled in the wet air. "Samyaza is just Lucifer's marionette. A little fire will scorch his puppet strings, and he will die, just like the Naphil."

Japheth tried to slip lower, but Samyaza hoisted him up to his massive chest and squeezed again. Japheth gasped. A popping noise sounded and stabbing pain ripped across his ribs.

Samyaza croaked, "At least this dragon speaks more bravely than his father did. Arramos whimpered pitifully before I killed him a few minutes ago."

Makaidos's scales flushed to a solid crimson. "You are a liar!"

"True," Samyaza said, nodding. "I am a liar when it suits my purposes, but I have no reason to lie about my conquests. Arramos whimpered for mercy like a beaten dog."

"Makaidos," Thigocia hissed, "do not listen to him. He twists words. He even lies about when he lies. Arramos is alive. I know he is."

Makaidos growled a whisper at Thigocia. "Whether he is alive or not, I need you to stay here and guard the refuge boat! Will you do it?"

Thigocia closed her eyes, her words barely audible. "If that is your will."

Makaidos whipped his neck back toward Samyaza. "Just let the human go. No matter how you demons fracture your promises, a dragon's covenant is never broken. I will fight you alone!"

"And if I refuse?" Samyaza replied, his brow lifting. "I could easily wait for the other Watchers to arrive. I have already signaled for them."

Japheth thrust his body upward just enough to push out a gasping shout. "Torch the devil!" he yelled. "I would rather die as this ark's signal beacon than allow it to fail!"

The demon slapped his hand over Japheth's mouth. He grimaced at the stench as pain pierced his lungs.

Makaidos nodded solemnly at Japheth. "You have your answer, Samyaza. If you refuse, Thigocia and I will grant the human's wish. You will become this boat's signal torch."

Japheth bit Samyaza's broom-handle-sized finger. The demon slammed him to the deck and shook his massive hand in pain. With his ribs in agony, Japheth sat up, and as he clutched his sides,

37

his gaze landed on Samyaza's wounded hand. Were there five fingers and a thumb? Was the legend really true?

With a flurry of black wings, Samyaza burst into the sky. "Come then, lizard! If you really dare!"

Makaidos rolled an egg-shaped orb toward Japheth. "Keep the Ovulum safe. It belonged to the Oracle." He then shot upward in pursuit of the demon.

Japheth picked up the Ovulum and struggled to his feet, pushing against the pummeling draft of the dragon's wings. Stumbling to the bridge, he shoved the orb into his tunic and grabbed the ropes again, steadying the sway while Shem hurried their father across. His aching ribs screamed in agony, but he held on while Shem and Noah hustled past him and ducked through Adam's Door.

Morgan, wrapping her arms around herself and the sword, tiptoed onto the bridge again. Japheth rolled his eyes. Now what? He couldn't untie the bridge; she would fall to her death. And there was no one left to ask about her—no human, that is.

He yanked on the rope, shaking the bridge. Morgan dropped to her knees and grasped the side with one hand, hanging on to the sword with the other.

"Stay there!" Japheth yelled. He spun to Thigocia. "Have you ever seen this woman before?"

Thigocia's eyebeams danced across the low clouds as the rain steadily worsened. Roars and rumbles sounded from above, and flashes of light painted the foggy sky. Finally, she stretched her neck over the side of the ark. "Her face is familiar." She squinted, her forked tongue darting in and out. "Hmmm."

Japheth shook the bridge again, keeping Morgan on her knees. "Well?" he asked, pain still gripping his ribs.

Thigocia nodded. "I think I know who she is, but I cannot leave the boat, so . . ." She raised her head high and roared, "Samyaza! We have a hostage who is very dear to you!"

Japheth waited, glancing back and forth between the sky and Morgan. She lay prostrate, clenching the side of the bridge with her long white fingers. The flashes in the sky suddenly ceased. Seconds later, an ear-splitting screech sounded from above. Samyaza glided toward the ground clutching a limp dragon by the neck in one of his powerful hands. Black resin dripped from Makaidos's face. He blinked weakly, his eyes glazed and his scales fading.

Thigocia stretched out her wings. "Makaidos!"

Samyaza landed on the opposite side of the bridge next to a sycamore and planted his bear-like feet. "Stay where you are," he shouted, pointing at Thigocia, "or the lizard dies!"

"If he dies," Thigocia roared, "then you will be a pile of charcoal at his side!"

Samyaza laughed. "More blustery hot air from a weak fire-breather." He turned his gaze to Morgan, still prostrate on the bridge. "What are you doing here?" he asked.

With the sword pressed under her feet, Morgan stood slowly, spreading her arms to keep her balance. She rubbed her palms together as rain plastered her raven locks to her face. "Samyaza, my love. I am here to do your bidding. Did I not tell you that I would seek passage on this ridiculous boat and sabotage their mission?"

Japheth fumed. That witch had to die! He let go of the ropes and picked at the wet knot that fastened the bridge to a post on the ark's parapet, pulling away thread after thread.

Thigocia spewed a twisting line of fire that snaked between Morgan and Japheth. She growled her words. "Give me Makaidos or my next breath turns your wife into a tallow candle!"

Samyaza waved a hand at Morgan. "Do you think I cannot find another dark-hearted wench to do my bidding? Go ahead and lick her with fire from head to toe. I'm not giving up my scaly prize so easily."

Japheth gouged out a thick strand, loosening the knot. In just seconds, the bridge would collapse.

Morgan picked up the sword and inched her way toward the land side of the bridge. "Samyaza!" she shouted through the windswept rain. "I have learned the secret of the sword's fire. If I burn, the secret dies with me."

Japheth pressed his lips together and gave the knot a final pull. "Got it!" The rope slipped away from the ark. One edge of the bridge gave way, and Morgan tipped toward the trench. In a flash of light and black wings, Samyaza dropped Makaidos and caught Morgan in his massive arms. The demon landed next to the tree again, his body glowing red as he snatched the sword from his wife.

Morgan placed her palms on Samyaza's cheeks, and her hands lit up like a pair of fiery tongs. The demon's scarlet glow seemed to radiate into Morgan's body as though he were bleeding into her fingertips. When he faded to a pale pink, Morgan released him, her own reddish tint seeming to energize her as Samyaza's wobbling frame slowly shrank.

As the demon set her on the ground, Morgan's skin returned to normal. She stood straight and set her fists on her hips, while Samyaza looked at her stupidly.

Japheth whispered to Thigocia. "The battle's over! Get him! And get that sword, too. It must be a powerful weapon."

Thigocia leaped over the side of the ark, her wings instantly whipping her body into a scaly, fire-blasting rocket. Dodging a sycamore tree, she blew a scorching wave of flames that flew inches above the demon's head. She snatched the sword out of his hands with her teeth and slapped his face with her tail as she zoomed past.

Samyaza's eyes darkened to pitch black. He toppled over, knocking Morgan down and pinning her. Thigocia arched in a wide circle, swinging around for another attack.

A loud roar sounded from above. Ten Watchers swooped toward the ground. One dragon after another darted out of the clouds, at least eight fire-breathers zooming in single-file pursuit of the demons.

Japheth clutched his ribs. All-out war was upon them, the great flood was at hand, and he could barely move! What could he possibly do to stop this catastrophe?

Feeling the bulge in his tunic, he pulled out Methuselah's Ovulum. Maybe it could help. It had power of some kind. But what?

CHAPTER

THE BATTLE
FOR THE ARK

The largest of the arriving Watchers, a square-jawed giant with red wings, landed next to Samyaza. "Make a barrier!" he bellowed. As the demons formed a ring around their fallen leader, Thigocia dropped the sword to the ark's deck, completed her turn, and flew in tight ellipses, widening her orbit as she maneuvered nearer Makaidos, who lay motionless outside the demonic circle.

The other dragons attacked, blasting streaks of white-hot flames. The Watchers parried by shooting bolts of darkness from their eyes, keeping the dragons at bay. A huge, axe-wielding human stepped into the sycamore glade. Another followed him, a scar-faced man with battle leather strapped across his torso and a club in each hand. A third, the tallest yet, his head reaching the shoulder of the biggest Watcher, tromped into view carrying a long spear. He knelt at Morgan's side and helped her to her feet.

Thigocia shuddered. Nephilim! She had to grab Makaidos before it was too late! Shooting a wall of fire for cover, she zoomed past the Watchers and Nephilim, latched onto Makaidos with her claws, and dragged him to the edge of the trench. She jerked back around, beating the wet air with her wings to keep her balance. The scene behind her was a blur of fire, steam, and black streaks—dragons, Watchers, and giants in deadly conflict. One of the streaks shot past her head, barely missing her ear. Letting out a low groan, she adjusted her grip on Makaidos's body. She had to get him to the ark, but how could she possibly carry him over the gap?

A dragon burst out of the melee—Arramos, glowing hot with splashes of black goo speckling his red scales. He landed next to Thigocia, panting. "You take his neck . . . and I will take . . . his hind quarters." Arramos gripped his son's tail and a back leg with his claws. "Now!" he ordered.

Thigocia shoved her claws under Makaidos's shoulder and draped his neck over her own. Gripping as much of his body as she could, she flapped her wings with all her might. They slowly lifted off the ground, Arramos taking the unprotected rear position as they inched toward the ark.

A black streak splattered against Arramos's side. Another slapped him in the face. The two dragons pushed forward, beating the air and scattering thousands of water droplets. As they crested the side of the ark, Japheth, clutching his ribs with one arm, guided them to a clear spot on the deck. Shem burst from Adam's Door, and the two humans, dodging flapping wings and swinging tails, helped the dragons gently lower the wounded body to the planks.

When all three dragons finally rested on the deck, Arramos bent over Makaidos, aiming his eyebeams at his son's glazed pupils. "He is alive . . . but barely. Thigocia, your mother was a healer. It is time to learn whether or not you inherited her gift."

"Should I just do what she always did?" she asked.

"Yes. Cover Makaidos with your wings and body. Quickly, now! There is no time to lose."

Thigocia crawled over Makaidos's body and lay on top of him, stretching her wings to cover as many of his scales as she could. Arramos breathed a low-power stream of fire at Thigocia's tail, then at her wings, flanks, and back, until her scales glowed with a tawny-orange hue. Warmth radiated around her body, spreading through her wings and into Makaidos.

As the process continued, Thigocia kept an eye on the battle. The dark streaks now outnumbered the streams of fire, and blackened dragon bodies littered the battlefield, lying strewn on the ground as if draped by sooty quilts. Several Watchers lay among them, some writhing, some motionless. Two of the giants smoldered in a heap, but the largest Naphil stood erect, shaking his spear in the air.

Morgan walked out of the fog. As Watchers and Nephilim gathered around her, she marched toward the ark, lifting her purple-stained palm into the air. A shimmering field of sparks formed around the evil group. When the sparks clustered, a lightning bolt shot toward the ark. The bolt missed wide to the right, but the sparks reassembled, as if recharging after the first volley.

45

Shem pulled a sling and a stone from his pocket, spun the sling over his head, and hurled the stone at Morgan, but it bounced off her shield and tumbled to the ground. As he set a larger stone in the sling, Japheth grabbed his arm and held up the egg-like orb. "If we could figure out how to use this, maybe we'd stand a chance."

Arramos snuffed his flames. "The Ovulum!" He nodded at Thigocia. "Stay on him. When your glow fades, you may get up." He lumbered toward the humans. "Speak to the Eye of the Oracle," he said. "He will give you guidance."

Japheth laid the Ovulum in his palm. "You mean talk to the egg?"

"Exactly. I do not know who or what resides there, but I have seen the Oracle speak to it with reverence."

Japheth glanced at Shem, who just shrugged his shoulders. Another bolt of lightning streaked across the deck and burned a hole in the parapet on the far side.

Arramos shot a ball of fire at Morgan's company. The flames dented the shield and rolled over the dome before fizzling out on the ground behind them. The volley made them halt, at least for the moment. "Hurry!" Arramos ordered. "If the Watchers attack, we will never hold them off! They probably do not know we are the only dragons on board, or they would have attacked already."

Japheth raised the Ovulum near his lips. "If you're the Eye of the Oracle, I assume you know what's going on out here. Please give us guidance. How can we save the ark?"

Red fog swirled within the orb and congealed into a scarlet eye. It stared at Japheth as if piercing his soul with its gaze. Shem, Japheth, and Arramos stared back at the eye, seemingly mesmerized as a translucent aura slowly grew around it, bathing Japheth's hands in crimson.

Another bolt zipped into the ark, this time striking Thigocia's tail, singeing the tiny scales on its spiny end. "Owww!" She shot up to her feet and dipped her tail in a rainwater pool. The orange glow pulsing from her scales faded. Had the healing treatment been enough to—

Makaidos raised his head, blinking his eyes at the falling rain. "What happened?"

Thigocia pulled her tail from the puddle and flicked a stream of water at him. "It is about time you woke up," she said, attempting a smile. "We are trying to figure out how to use the Ovulum to defend the ark. The sorceress is attacking, and she has new powers." Thigocia extended her neck to get a closer look at the eye. It seemed to be speaking, though the words penetrated her mind rather than her ears. The voice was sad, almost mournful, as it chanted a lament.

A stream, a flow, a cleansing flood,
The tide that sweeps away our sin,
Is not of water, nor of earth.
The flood must purge our souls within.

The aura surrounding the orb swelled, covering the two brothers in brilliant scarlet robes of light that made their bodies look like pulsing beacons.

Today begins a worldly wash,
For man has lost the Eden way,
Regarding demons as his gods,
And dark of night he calls the day.

An ark, a savior from the wrath,
Foretells of yet another flood.
A king will build an ark of faith
And purge our hearts with holy blood.

47

The red glow engulfed the entire ark, creating a massive shield, and as it expanded, tentacles of scarlet light spread over its surface, slapping at anything within reach. Morgan and company drew back, their eyes widening.

Now take the orb and with a prayer
Release it to the weeping skies.
The gates of hell will seize their souls
And earth will bleed while heaven cries.

And then arise, defend the ark,
Protect it from the lightning stroke.
The patriarch shall wave the sword
And summon heaven's shielding cloak.

The prophet's eye is never lost.
It travels now to worthy maids,
Secure within the hands of love,
Returning where a curse is laid.

While Japheth and Shem continued to gape at the eye, the orb's glow and spindly arms slowly contracted. Its aura sank below the roof of the top deck quarters. Morgan pointed at the ark and spread her arms once again as new lightning bolts formed on the surface of her dome shield.

Thigocia yelled, "Throw the Ovulum! Didn't you hear the song?"

Japheth's gaze shifted between her and the orb. "Song? What song?"

"It came from the eye! It said 'release it to the weeping skies.' Throw it now! As high as you can!"

Arramos clutched Japheth's wrist. "Thigocia, the eye is a living orb, not a youngling's plaything. We cannot afford to lose it."

"Trust me," Thigocia roared. "I heard what it said!"

Japheth and Shem stood motionless, their gazes riveted again on the Ovulum. The orb swelled, as if absorbing its own glow. As the shielding aura sank, nearly exposing their heads, the Ovulum expanded to the size of a grapefruit, red and throbbing.

The top of the ark was now exposed. A new lightning bolt zapped the roof, igniting a tiny fire.

With a quick swipe of her claws, Thigocia snatched the Ovulum from Japheth and leaped into the sky, her wings fighting heavy winds. Another lightning bolt streaked by, barely missing her head. Fighting a downburst of rain, she placed the Ovulum on the end of her tail and slung the orb into the clouds. The red glow followed, completely unveiling the ark, and disappeared from sight in the turbulent blackness above.

Thigocia hurried back to the deck. Morgan and the Watchers now stood at the precipice of the trench, a mere thirty feet from the bow of the ark. Morgan screamed a battle cry. The demons and Nephilim replied with guttural roars.

Sparks flew from Makaidos's mouth, sprinkling Thigocia's face. "What have you done?!"

"I obeyed the eye! It is not my fault you were deaf to its song."

Arramos thumped his tail on the deck. "Quiet! Do not behave like younglings!" He lowered his voice. "Thigocia, did the Ovulum say anything else?"

"Yes." She nudged the sword with her foreleg. "The patriarch is supposed to protect the ark with the sword. Something about waving it and making a cloak."

"We must—" Arramos cast a glance at Morgan. She seemed to be directing the Watchers as they flew to surround the ark. The clouds above boiled bright red, sinking lower in the sky with every passing second. Arramos stretched his neck upward and let out an ear-splitting roar. With another thump of his tail, he growled a low whisper. "Trumpet! Now! Both of you!"

Makaidos and Thigocia raised their heads and poured out a stream of blaring trumpet sounds, shaking the deck, the ark, and the earth.

"Keep it up while I give my final commands. We must make them think this ark is filled with dragons." He nodded toward Adam's Door. "Shem and Japheth, send your father out here immediately, then make sure your families are safe. Makaidos, the Watchers will know we are few in number as soon as I attack them alone."

Makaidos lowered his head. "Alone? But—"

"Trumpet!"

Makaidos trumpeted louder than ever. Shem and Japheth hustled into the quarters, Japheth pausing at the doorway, looking back at the dragons before ducking inside.

"You and Thigocia are the chosen pair," Arramos continued. "When the flood recedes, you will repopulate the earth with our kind and once again serve the race of Adam."

49

"Thigocia and me? Repopulate? But—"

"Makaidos!"

Makaidos trumpeted again, but his volume faded. The dark red clouds sank lower. Peals of thunder shook the ark, nearly knocking the dragons down.

"I know you want to fight," Arramos continued, "but the battle against the corrupters is over. It is now up to the Maker to finish the war." He nodded toward Adam's Door. "Go now."

The two young dragons silenced their trumpets and lowered their heads. New rolls of thunder replaced their blistering calls. Arramos leaped up to the parapet and looked back with a large tear in each eye. "Good-bye, my son. I am proud of you. You will make a fine king." He flapped his wings and lifted off. With a sudden turn and sweep of his tail, he dove toward the circle of demons.

Makaidos lunged toward the parapet, slipping on the rain-slicked planks. Thigocia joined him and craned her neck over the side. Blasting waves of fire, Arramos shattered Morgan's shield and slammed into the wall of Watchers and Nephilim. At least three Watchers collapsed, and the spear-wielding Naphil fell into the trench. Arramos tumbled to the ground, rolling into another Watcher and crushing his body. The other Watchers leaped toward Arramos, waves of darkness streaming from their eyes.

Makaidos jumped to the top of the parapet and unfurled his wings. "I have to help him!"

Thigocia snatched his tail in her claws and pulled him back to the deck. "Are you going to disobey your father's last command?"

"I am not going to let him die without a fight!"

"Are you so selfish that you are willing to end the dragon race because of your lust for battle?"

"It is not lust for battle! I just want to save my father!"

"Then save him by obeying him! His legacy will die forever if you don't."

Makaidos turned back toward the battlefield, stretching his neck high. Thigocia followed his line of sight. With blankets of darkness smothering Arramos, all she could see were his ruby eyes, his gaze focused on the ark, pleading . . . begging. She heard a voice in her mind, faint and trembling. "Go . . . now . . . let me know . . . you are safe . . . before I die."

She spoke slowly, dreamily, yet with firm resolve. "Makaidos. We must go . . . now!"

"I cannot leave my father!" He stretched out his wings and lifted into the air.

"We must go!" Thigocia bit his tail and yanked him from the sky.

Makaidos twisted and jerked his tail away. "Don't make me fight you!"

Red light flashed from one end of the ark to the other, casting a blood-like shroud over the deck, its glow seeming to carry a loud, bass hum that shook every grain in every plank. The dragons looked up, trembling. A ball of scarlet fire hovered just below the clouds, pulsing, throbbing like a luminescent heart. It seemed that an aging sun was sinking to the earth, blushing red and vibrating in the throes of death.

Noah ran onto the deck. "I was on the lower level. What—" He looked up at the red orb. All eyes—dragon, demon, and human—locked on the blazing sphere, every creature frozen in place and gaping in wonder. Fingers of red flame sprouted from the ball's surface. The long tendrils snaked toward the ground, and as each finger pierced the earth, a geyser of muddy water sprang from the entry point. Fountain after fountain gushed into the sky. A peal of thunder, the loudest yet, blasted across the heavens. Torrents of rain followed, sheets of cold, stinging drops that forced Thigocia to finally blink.

"Master Noah," she yelled, sliding the sword to him with her tail. "The Ovulum said to take the sword and wave it."

51

Noah pulled the blade from its sheath and lifted it over his head. The sword flashed with light, sending a bright beam into the sky, and as he waved it back and forth, the light created a wall. He swirled the sword as if stirring a spoon, transforming the wall of light into a dome that completely covered the ark. Inside the dome, an eerie tapping sounded all around. The rain beat against the shield and streamed across the boundary, painting thousands of bright rivulets on their canopy of light.

Morgan screamed, "Attack! Now!" The Watchers blasted streams of darkness at the ark, but the black jets merely splattered against Noah's dome of light.

Rushing water toppled the demons and every creature on the land, washing them toward the trench in a rampaging river. The torrent ended in a whirlpool that flushed the bodies downward into a dark, spinning hole. Morgan, flailing helplessly in neck-high water, tried to grab branches as she swept past the sycamores. She snatched a skinny limb and hung on, but her fingers began slipping as the raging water furiously beat against her body. Samyaza, having regained consciousness, swam against the current, but in his weakened state, he was no match for the ferocious river.

Thigocia draped Makaidos with her wing and shouted over the din. "Master Noah! I beg you to go inside! We no longer need the shield!"

Noah lowered the sword, and the blade's light blinked off. With rain once again beating on his head, he hurried to Adam's Door and disappeared.

Makaidos gaped at the rising water and bowed his head. As the flood hoisted the ark from the ground, it lurched to one side. The two dragons staggered toward the door, careful to avoid the sheer drop over a railing to their left. They collapsed their wings and ducked low. Thigocia entered first and found Japheth holding a lantern and standing with his feet spread apart, bracing against the rocking boat. He waved the lantern toward an interior door. "Quick! Inside! This is just the window vestibule."

Thigocia scooted toward the second door and glanced back to see Makaidos squeezing through as she made room. Rain poured in through another hole cut into the exterior wall, above and well to the right of the door, apparently an observation window with shutters on both sides.

"Hurry!" Japheth called, clutching his ribs with one arm. He picked up a bucket of thick black liquid. "I still have to seal the openings."

Thigocia crawled through the interior door and into a cavernous chamber. A solitary light shone from the opposite side, barely illuminating the wide-planked floors and dozens of dark lanterns swinging from thick ceiling beams. She could see little else, only a human shadow drawing closer. It staggered with the rocking boat for a moment, then walked more steadily as the ride smoothed out.

Makaidos followed Thigocia, pushing far enough into the room to raise his head and unfurl his wings slightly.

A voice accompanied the shadow. "That was quite an adventure!" The dark hand laid a flaming piece of wood on a lantern wick. A brightening fire cast a glow across Noah's face as he mopped his brow with a cloth. A woman stood at his side, wrinkled and white-haired and wearing a tired but satisfied smile.

Thigocia bowed low. "Mistress Emzara!" Makaidos bowed with her, though not as low.

Noah gestured for them to rise. "Welcome, my friends." He stroked Thigocia's neck three times. "Peace to you, dragoness. Your willingness to listen to the Eye of the Oracle saved the ark."

Thigocia blinked at the gentle old man. He had obviously learned the proper way for a human to greet a warrior dragon. She thumped her tail twice in response. "And peace to you as well, Sire."

"I will make sure their food is ready," Emzara said, turning to leave.

Noah bowed to Makaidos. "Hail, new king of the dragons." As he lifted his head, large tears streamed from both eyes. "It is a

53

pity that your coronation comes on a day of sorrows. Today you have lost a father, and I have lost a grandfather. While death and destruction surround us, shall we weep together or rejoice that God has rescued us from this calamity?"

Makaidos glanced at Thigocia. "With all due respect, Master Noah, she dragged me in here. I would have died fighting alongside my father."

Noah waved his hand. "Trust me. I understand. God sometimes has unusual ways to bring about his purposes." He lifted the lantern toward the rafters. "Would any human conceive of such a vessel? If I were to destroy all flesh, I doubt that I would plan to cover the earth with water and then load a stampede of goats, monkeys, and squirrels onto a monstrosity like this!" He chuckled softly. "Preposterous! Three thousand years from now, will anyone even believe it happened?"

The boat rocked again, slinging Noah to the floor. As the ark leveled, Makaidos extended a clawed hand and lifted the old man gently to his feet. "Perhaps they will believe it," Makaidos said, "if anyone lives to create the next generation."

Thigocia thwacked Makaidos on the leg with her tail. "Behave yourself!"

"Father!" Shem rushed to Noah's side. "Are you all right?"

"I am." Noah brushed a coating of sawdust from his cloak. "What about Eve's Door?"

"I couldn't believe it!" Shem ran his fingers through his hair, bouncing on his toes like a child. "It was already closed! All we had to do was seal it!"

Noah lifted a wrinkled hand. "Praise to Elohim! He watches over even the most careless of his flock!"

Japheth bustled into the chamber, still carrying the bucket and clutching his side. "Adam's Door and the window are sealed." He closed the door behind him. "Shall I seal this one as well?"

Noah shook his head. "No need. It will hold. When the rain stops, we will want access to the window."

"Before I sealed the shutters"—Japheth slowly opened the interior door again—"this bird barged in." A large, wet raven flew through the doorway and darted into the rafters. It floundered from beam to beam and scattered droplets until it managed to perch on a wide truss near the ceiling.

"Very strange," Japheth said. "It seems to have forgotten how to fly."

"Leave it be," Noah said. "It has been battered by the storm, and it's exhausted. We can leave birdseed out later."

Japheth set the bucket down and patted Thigocia's front leg. "Do you want to see your quarters? They're not much more than stalls, but we humans have the same accommodations, so we're not playing favorites with anyone."

Thigocia jerked her leg back and smirked. This human could learn a lesson or two in manners from his father. "Thank you," she said. "I would like that."

As Japheth led Thigocia into the dark chamber, Makaidos followed. "I would also like to see my quarters. I am exhausted from the battles."

Japheth glanced back. "I wasn't sure if you would need a separate room for an egg nest, but that can be constructed later."

"An egg nest?" Makaidos repeated. "Dragons bear their young alive."

Japheth scratched his head. "I guess I should have known that."

"Few humans do. We have not produced many offspring since the day of our creation."

"Anyway," Japheth continued, "the stall is plenty big for you and Thigocia, even if you have a . . . a baby. I don't know what you call a little dragon."

Makaidos halted. "We have the same stall?"

Japheth stopped and turned around. "Yes, of course. We thought—"

"My son," Noah interrupted, walking behind the group. He caught up and draped an arm over Japheth's shoulder. "Dragons have morals and rituals that are similar to those of humans, and as God's prophet, I have the authority to join Makaidos and Thigocia in wedlock. We will create their covenant veil immediately."

Japheth tilted his head at his father. "Covenant veil?"

Noah clasped his hands together. "When two dragons join, they must pass through a spiritual veil that tests their hearts' willingness to commit to their union forever. If either dragon has a shadow of deception or doubt, whether conscious or not, he or she is unable to pass, and the covenant is not complete."

"How do you make the veil?" Japheth asked.

Noah patted his son on the back. "You will find out soon enough."

Makaidos pawed the floor. "I feared this was coming."

"Feared?" Heat flooded Thigocia's eyes. "And what is wrong with marrying me?"

"We have known each other since we were younglings," Makaidos said. "We have played together, fought together, even bled together. We are best friends, not lovers."

Thigocia thumped her tail and scowled. "As it should be! I would prefer to marry my best friend over some sniveling suitor who fancies flying over romantic vistas. Give me a male like you who would rather fight in a bloody battle any day!"

Makaidos snorted. "Marrying you would be like marrying my little sister!"

Thigocia lifted her head and stared at Makaidos eye to eye, her voice pitching up. "My father married *his* sister, and I am no crybaby youngling. When we blasted that Watcher in the Valley of—"

Noah laughed so hard he could barely speak. "That's enough!" He wiped a tear from his eye and draped an arm over each dragon's neck, grinning like a proud father. "There is no other reasonable option. The existence of the dragon race depends on it. You are to be wed immediately."

A flicker of light caught Makaidos's eye. Noah's son Ham walked by the dragons' stall with the late-arriving raven perched on his shoulder. A twinge of pain pinched Makaidos's gut. He winced at the danger signal. Was it real this time?

Months on the ark had dulled his senses. He had no gems for building a bed to produce the conic shroud of light dragons needed to regain their strength. Such a regeneracy dome was crucial for a dragon's health, as his father had taught the day they first built a dome together. "Some gems give us strength," Arramos had said, extending a single red stone in his open claws, "but this one gives us identity. It represents your vision, your passion, and your sacrifice, and one day, it will be a door to freedom. Take this rubellite and wear it always. It is the key to our everlasting union as father and son."

Makaidos lowered his head and flashed his eyebeams at his underbelly. Pressed deep into a gap between his scales, a small red gem reflected his beams, his rubellite, a protective shield placed at his most vulnerable point. Even after all his battles, even after all those long days and nights on the ark, the rubellite stayed with him, reminding him of his father's gift to all his progeny. Thigocia, of course, had one, too. All the dragons of old would find a rubellite for each son or daughter, a dragon symbol for all generations.

57

He raised his head again, and a dull pain throbbed from ear to ear. With only the glow of a dozen lanterns swinging from the rafters, darkness had sapped him dry. The rain had eased several months ago, so he had hoped for a quick end to the tedious sea voyage, but it was not to be. With the ark's lower hull wedged in the peaks of an underwater mountain range, they had to withstand the constant rocking of waves splashing against the sides.

Makaidos kept his eye on Ham as he disappeared down the ladder toward the second level. It hadn't taken long to learn that Ham's brothers considered him a scoundrel. He performed his chores adequately, but there was something not quite right about him. Even as he obeyed Noah, his eyes seemed to defy every word.

Makaidos rose slowly to his feet, hoping not to awaken Thigocia. She lay near the back of the stall on a deep bed of clean straw, her head tucked under a wing. Since he kept his own pile of straw near the front, he was able to slip through the open door without a sound.

From the corridor, he glanced back at her. Thigocia's wing had moved, uncovering her noble brow and graceful snout. Makaidos couldn't help but stare. He had never really noticed before how beautiful she was. She had been a playmate as a youngling and a fellow warrior in recent years, but he had never noticed anything beyond her ability to spin a one-eighty at top speed or to scorch a Naphil with one breath. Now she looked . . . well . . . lovely. His gaze wandered to the space between her bed of straw and his own. He sighed quietly and followed Ham's path down the corridor.

The ark's frame croaked a dirge of grunts, creaks, and moans from the weakened planks, masking Makaidos's heavy steps. He passed the sleeping human families, Noah and his wife hand in hand on a pile of straw, Japheth and his wife in a smaller stall next to his father's, then Ham's wife sleeping next to a swaddled new-born baby—Canaan, they had named him. The last stall, Shem's, was empty. It was his turn to patrol the animal decks, and his wife always went with him. But why would Ham be up so early in the morning when he didn't have to be?

When Makaidos reached the ladder that led to the lower level, he peered down, stretching his neck as far as he could. Below, a flickering lantern revealed Ham sitting on the floor next to a birdcage. Shem and his wife were nowhere in sight, proba-bly on the lowest deck, the level for large mammals and non-sen-tient reptiles.

As the raven on Ham's shoulder pecked at a heap of seeds in his palm, he spoke to it in a low tone. "So what is your plan?"

The raven croaked into Ham's ear, but too quietly for Makaidos to distinguish any words.

"The air vents are too small for you to escape," Ham said. "Even after the flood subsides, Father probably won't let any birds go until he is sure they are healthy and mating."

Again, the raven answered in an indecipherable voice.

"Yes," Ham replied. "My father has already spoken about that. We will need a land scout soon."

The bird spoke again, this time loud enough for Makaidos to hear its squawking words. "Send me."

Ham shrugged his shoulders. "Why not? Since we have two other ravens, he'll think you're expendable."

Makaidos pulled his head back through the door. Although his sense of danger pinched his nerves again, the conversation between Ham and the raven seemed innocent enough. He had heard birds talk before, even ravens, and this one seemed to be trying to figure out how to escape. Who could blame it for wanting to go free? Still, something felt wrong . . . very wrong. Weren't ravens simply mimics rather than reasoning creatures? He would have to keep an eye on this suspicious crow.

59

The raven flew up through the hatch and into the rafters, carrying a dried grape in its beak. It landed on a high beam and set the grape next to another one. As Makaidos pondered the bird's strange behavior, he shuffled back to his stall and found Thigocia awake.

"Patrolling?" she asked, stretching her legs and wings.

Makaidos stayed out in the corridor and spoke softly. "It is difficult to sleep when my mind replays my father's death."

Thigocia stepped to the stall's entry and reached her wing over Makaidos's neck. "I apologize for what I said about your sister."

"My sister? What did you say about her?"

"I implied that she was a crybaby. I had forgotten that she would also die in the flood."

Makaidos cocked his head and let his voice grow a bit louder. "You said that months ago. Why do you bring it up now?"

Thigocia lowered her gaze to the floor. "I was unable to think of any other reason you might be angry with me."

"I am not angry with you! I told you I do not know why I could not pass through the veil."

"Shhh!" Thigocia warned. "The humans are sleeping."

"I *was* sleeping!" Noah stepped out of his quarters and stretched his arms. "Is there a problem?"

Makaidos grimaced. "Pardon me, Master Noah. I apologize for my outburst."

Noah walked slowly toward them, balancing against the rocking boat. "Think nothing of it, my friend. After so many months in close quarters, we are all on edge."

"Not just on edge. Thigocia and I are weak from lack of light. When we were adrift, we could absorb the rays that came in through the window, but now we are wedged at an angle that does not allow the sun to enter. The lanterns and vents in the rafters help, but we cannot survive much longer without direct sunlight."

Sympathy creased Noah's brow. "The doors are sealed. By God's command I cannot open—"

"Yes, Master Noah. I know. I did not mean my explanation to be interpreted as a complaint against you."

Ham climbed up from the lower deck. "Father," he said, bowing his head as he approached. "I overheard your conversation. May I suggest something?"

Makaidos felt a twinge of warning again. This was the most respect Ham had shown his father the entire journey.

Noah returned a head nod. "Certainly."

"Since mountaintops are visible in the distance, you suggested last week that there might be land close by in one of the directions we can't see. Why not send out a bird to test that theory. If it comes back, there is likely no place to land."

"I have thought of that." Noah pressed a finger to his cheek. "We have very few birds to spare, but I was thinking we could release one of the doves we brought for sacrifice."

Ham shook his head. "No need. We can send my raven out. She's expendable, and she can let us know if there is dry land nearby."

Noah laughed. "I heard that raven grumbling about grapes the other day. I thought I was finally losing my mind."

Ham pointed at the black bird as it perched in the rafters. "I've been talking to her for months, and she's learned quite a few words, so I trained her to fetch things, like crickets for the snakes or raisins for the monkeys. She could find something on land and bring it to us."

Makaidos gazed into Ham's eyes, searching for a hint of a lie. He had seen him talking to the raven, so that part was true enough, but the raven spoke back to him. Would Ham mention that, too?

Noah stroked his chin. "But there will be no crickets or raisins to find. Everything will be dead and washed away."

"True, but before the grapes dried out, I taught her the difference between the purple ones and the green ones. I'll just ask her to bring us something green. Maybe new seedlings have sprouted by now."

"An interesting theory," Noah said. "I think it's worth a try. We're all anxious to get our feet back on solid ground." He shuffled into the anteroom, a noticeable stagger in his step. He opened the shutters, allowing a stiff breeze to sweep through the cabin.

Ham whistled toward the rafters, and the raven fluttered down to his shoulder. "Go to my father," Ham said. He then whispered something in the bird's ear.

Makaidos snorted to himself. That whispering was more than words of comfort. Something devious was going on.

With two flaps of its ebony wings, the raven jumped to Noah's shoulder, its feathers ruffling in the wind. Ham hustled down the ladder toward the second level. "I'll be right back," he called.

"What's going on?" Japheth stepped into the corridor, rubbing his eyes. "Why are you opening the window so early?"

Noah nodded at the raven on his shoulder. "An experiment, of sorts."

"Ham's raven? What could it—"

"Here it is!" Ham said, climbing back to the top level. He held a green anole in his hand and showed it to the raven. "Green," he said, stroking the lizard's skin. "Bring me something green."

Noah turned his shoulder toward the window, and the raven leaped for the exit, its wings beating against the breeze. Noah left the window open and limped toward his quarters, his back bent. "I will pray with Emzara for the raven. Perhaps this long journey will end soon."

Makaidos lurched toward the window and extended his neck through the opening as far as he could. The ark listed to one side, clearly stuck on something beneath the white-capped waves that constantly punished the hull. To his left and only several feet below his level, the main deck's blistered planks led away from Adam's door.

From his vantage point, the deck seemed to be an observation platform where someone standing at the parapet could look out over the dark blue sea. A few distant mountaintops peeked through the endless expanse of water, too far away for any possibility of reaching them against both wind and waves. The only hope lay on the other side of the ark, but that view was out of reach, even for a long-necked dragon.

Makaidos opened his eyes wide and drank in the sun's rays. Pure luxury! His neck scales cried out for joy, but even this splendor was nothing more than a tease. He and Thigocia needed much more energy, a recharge that only a full sunbath could bring, and the rays at this angle, not quite enough to sneak into the window, provided only a glancing exposure.

He pulled his head back inside. Since the bird was nowhere in sight, there was no use keeping watch. Even if Ham's idea could work, the presence of a dragon in the window would surely frighten the raven away.

Makaidos stared into the ark's dim interior, giving his eyes a moment to adjust. His vision flashed on to compensate for the change, and the two dim beams locked onto Ham's chest as he stood next to Japheth. Both men were watching the window.

Ham swept his hand across the pair of red dots on his tunic, trying to brush them away as if they were bothersome flies. When the dots stayed put, he glanced at Makaidos, a frown taking shape on his face. Without uttering a word, he climbed down the ladder and disappeared through the hole.

CHAPTER

THE RAVEN'S PLOT

Something sharp tugged Naamah's ear. She slapped at it, making it stop for a moment, but when the tugging persisted, she opened her eyes. Shadows waltzed on her bedding, keeping time with the ark's rhythmic shifts, but little else moved in her quiet sleeping quarters. A flickering lantern hanging from a distant rafter cast a glow around a dark shape as it swayed back and forth, a bird-like phantom perched on the straw next to her head.

"Lilith?" Naamah whispered.

"Take care to call me Morgan now," the raven croaked softly. "Dawn is approaching, and the time for our plan is upon us. Are the seeds of Eden safe?"

"Yes. They're hidden in my bed."

"Good. You will be able to get them later. For now, take the grapes I put in your hand and follow me."

Naamah closed her fingers around a handful of dried grapes, checked the sleeping infant at her side, and tiptoed into the dim corridor. The raven landed on her shoulder. "Follow the moonlight to the window."

EYE OF THE ORACLE

Naamah obeyed, timing her barefooted steps to match the squeaks of the rocking ark. When she reached the window, the fresh breeze jolted her fully awake. Blinking her eyes, she angled her head toward Morgan. "What now?"

"It is time for you to take the next step."

"The next step? I already had a baby. Haven't I taken enough steps?"

"Don't worry. Having the baby was the most difficult part of your journey."

"You're telling me! He was so big, I thought I was having a whale!"

"Yes, I expected him to be larger than most. The potion I gave you saw to that. I'm sure you felt the changes it made inside you."

"You know how small I am. I could have died having a baby that big."

"I watched over you. If you had been in danger of dying, I would have taken this step immediately."

Naamah set her fists on her hips. "What *is* this step?"

Morgan fluttered to the wooden floor. "To make you immortal." The raven slowly grew, stretching into a misshapen giant of a bird. Its wings thinned into human arms, and its pointed beak shrank into Morgan's angular nose. Seconds later, Naamah's sister stood in the raven's place, her silky black dress flowing in the breeze.

"You're . . ." Naamah caressed Morgan's face, but it seemed ghostly—physical in a way, but not quite real. Her cheeks were sunken and sallow, more like a cadaver's than those of the beautiful woman who once answered to Lilith. "Are you human?" Naamah asked.

Morgan took Naamah's hand. "Not exactly. You might call me a wraith. My body died in the flood, but my spirit lives on in this world on borrowed time. I cannot last much longer without going to a new home my lord has prepared for me. There, I will be restored and live forever."

Naamah took a step back on her trembling legs. "And now you want me to be a wraith like you?"

"You will be young and beautiful." Morgan caressed Naamah's cheek with her yellowed, bony fingers. "When you see what I have in store for us, you will jump at the chance."

Naamah resisted the urge to grimace at Morgan's ghostly touch. "Jump at the chance? Why?"

"Well, let's just say you can keep your charming ways, stay beautiful forever, and you won't have to worry about having any more babies."

Though Naamah tried not to smile, her lips curved upward. "So what do I have to do to become immortal?"

"You have to die."

"Die?" Naamah's voice pitched higher. "But immortal means—"

"Silence!" Morgan glanced toward the sleeping quarters and lowered her voice to the softest whisper. "The potion you drank will restore you, then we can fly to our new home and become like goddesses."

"Goddesses?" Naamah's fear began to melt away. "Are you sure?"

Morgan spread out her arms. "I drowned in the flood, dead as any other lost soul in the wake of Elohim's wrath, and yet I stand here before you now. I assure you that my original beauty will be restored soon, perhaps enhanced with even more allure, as will yours."

"What do I do?"

Morgan nodded toward the ark's window. "You are small enough to climb through and jump. When you drown in the flood, you will be transformed into a flying creature. Then, look for me in my raven form and follow me."

This time, Naamah couldn't hold back her grimace. "I have to drown? That sounds painful."

"Don't worry. You won't feel a thing." Morgan laid her hands on Naamah's cheeks again and purred a melody.

> To Satan we will bring
> The seeds to sow and sing.
> We'll water plant and root,
> Then pluck the giant fruit.
>
> Your waking mind abates;
> The sleep of death awaits.
> Rebirth on wings is near;
> Your sleep will cast out fear.

Releasing Naamah's cheeks, Morgan blew softly into her eyes. Her breath was cold and dry, instantly evaporating all moisture. Naamah's eyelids fluttered. "I'm so sleepy," she said, yawning.

Morgan interlaced her fingers and set her hands in a cradle near the window. "Then hurry. I'll boost you before you fall asleep."

Naamah yawned again, set her foot in Morgan's hands, and climbed into the window. As she straddled the sill, she looked down from the dizzying height, her mind swimming as the ark rocked back and forth on white-capped waves. She grasped the window frame with both hands and cried out, "The water's so far down, I can barely see it. Can't we wait until morning?"

Naamah felt a sudden shove. She toppled over and plummeted headfirst toward the sea, screaming. Just before she struck the waves, blackness snuffed her thoughts.

Makaidos lifted his head. "Did you hear that?"

Thigocia's ears twitched. "A scream?"

"That's what I thought. But it was brief . . . silenced." Makaidos raised his body, his weak legs shaking beneath him. "I think it came from the window." He aimed his eyebeams, casting twin rays toward the ark's breezeway. The dim rays darted around the walls of the listing ark until they landed on the window. A gust of wind threw open the shutter. It banged against the hull, squeaked loudly as it drew back toward the window, then banged open again.

"Just the shutter squeaking?" Thigocia asked.

"No. It was different . . . louder. A human voice." Makaidos lumbered into the corridor, passing Ham's quarters. Baby Canaan lay swaddled in the hay, alone. It was Ham's turn to patrol the lower decks, so it made sense that he was gone, but Naamah only left her bed to eat and take care of personal hygiene, and she usually took Canaan with her. She had always been so possessive of her baby, even keeping him away from his other relatives, it seemed strange to see him lying there alone.

Makaidos extended his neck and gently nudged the baby with his snout. Canaan squirmed and reached his pudgy arms over his wrappings, stretching his mouth into a yawning oval. The dragon nodded. The baby seemed fine. Perhaps Naamah had thought him old enough to sleep on his own. Maybe she decided to accompany Ham this time. They did not get along well, certainly not like Noah and Emzara, or his brothers and their wives. Spending time working together with the animals might be just what they needed. But why the scream? Could she have fallen down the ladder?

Makaidos lumbered to the hole leading to the lower levels and peered down. Although his eyebeams were dimmer than usual, he could still see the deck below. A single lantern hung nearby, casting yellow flickering light on the gopher wood planks. He stretched as far as he could, but the light gave no hint of any awakened animals, except for a few birdcage tenants, including two owls that stared back at him, their eyes wide and curious.

A strange shadow seemed to crawl along the floor, like fog creeping from one cage to the next. The lantern's weak glow gave

69

only a hint of the fog's depth and color—shallow and black—as it drifted closer to the owls. The other birds seemed to take no notice, and the owls kept their gaze locked on the dragon's beams, as though the fog were invisible to their probing eyes. One of the parrots, however, shifted back and forth, bobbing its head excitedly.

A hint of danger crept over Makaidos's body. After so many months of safety, the subtle tingling that buzzed through his scales seemed like a distant memory, yet alarming all the same. He blinked at the fog. Could that be the cause? It would have to be a powerful evil for his weakened senses to pick it up.

A loud footstep clumped on the lower deck, and a pair of sandals came into view. As Ham reached for the lantern, his feet swept away the black mist. His glance landed on Makaidos, then quickly averted. "Strange fog," he mumbled.

Makaidos shut down his eyebeams. "Exactly my thoughts."

Ham waved his hand and kicked at the mist. "It's nothing, really. It's been showing up on the lower decks every morning for a week, but no harm has befallen either man or beast."

"So the animals are thriving?" Makaidos asked.

Ham chuckled. "They don't have much to do, so we're seeing more births than we expected. In fact, the elephant is about to calve. I was coming up to get Shem or Japheth to help me."

"Oh. I thought maybe Naamah was down there helping you."

"Naamah?" Ham hesitated, shifting his weight from foot to foot. "Yes, she's down there, but she's too small to help with the elephant."

"I see." Makaidos pulled his head from the hole and aimed his eyebeams into Shem's quarters. The faithful son of Noah slept soundly, nestled with his wife in their pile of straw. The soothing noises of human sleep drifted into the dragon's ears, twin sounds of contented, rhythmic breathing.

Ham climbed up the ladder and stood with his hands on his hips. "It's a shame to wake them."

"Indeed."

Ham shuffled in and nudged Shem's shoulder. "Elephant's calving. Time to get up."

Makaidos slunk toward his stall, listening to the quiet voice of Shem's wife behind him.

"Of course I'm coming with you again. Pregnant or not, I can move straw around and clean up the blood."

"Okay," Shem replied, "but be careful on the ladder rungs."

Noah stepped out of his quarters with his wife. "So," he said, "young Madeline must have been with child, er, with elephant, before she came on board."

Emzara held out her hand. "Let's go! I have never seen an elephant birth."

Stopping at the entry to his quarters, Makaidos looked back. Shem's wife walked beside her husband, one hand on her belly and the other holding tightly to his hand. While Shem descended the ladder, she looked back at Makaidos. When their eyes met, she beamed. Such a smile! It would have melted the heart of the stoniest cynic. There was no doubt. Motherhood had dressed her with sheer joy.

Noah kept a grip on his wife's elbow as she maneuvered into position on the ladder. When she was safely on her way, Noah let go, straightened himself, and smiled at Makaidos. The old man nodded. "You seem perplexed, my dear dragon."

Makaidos sighed. "Watching humans has often perplexed me. They are so strange."

Noah stroked his chin and nodded again. "Is that so?" Carefully grasping the ladder, he started his descent, but before his head submerged below the deck, he stopped, and his bushy eyebrows knitted together. "Is love really so strange, Makaidos? Even at my age, after hundreds of years of being together, my wife and I are closer in oneness every day. My heart will always be with Emzara." Noah then disappeared below deck.

Makaidos slid into his quarters and gazed at Thigocia. With her eyes wide and her ears rotating, she looked more beautiful than ever.

"Did you figure out who screamed?" she asked.

"It could have been a parrot down below. It seemed pretty nervous." Makaidos crawled to the middle of their stall and kept his gaze locked on Thigocia's eyes. "There is a dark fog creeping about. That might have spooked the parrot. I felt danger when I saw the fog, but then Ham showed up. I think I might have felt him coming."

"I see." Thigocia lay back down and scooted farther into her corner. "Are you going to sleep?"

"No." Makaidos lumbered back into the corridor. He lay on his belly but kept his head high as he turned to Thigocia. "I will wait here until Noah returns, and, if you are in agreement, I would like to attempt the covenant veil again."

A sharp chill snapped Naamah awake. She gasped for air, flailing her arms, ready to battle the pounding waves, but rather than the wetness she expected, cool dry air bathed her body. Jerking her head back and forth, she tried to sort out the blurry images. Everything seemed to bounce around, jumping and shaking, but as her senses adjusted, a view of sea waves and foam came into focus below her. Her arms continued to beat the air, each flap taking her farther away from the water.

Glancing in the direction her hand should be, she caught a glimpse of a wing, a pinion of leather that ended in a wrinkled, sharp-nailed paw. It clutched something, but she couldn't remember what might be in her grip. In fact, she couldn't remember anything after Morgan shoved her out the window. Had she really died and turned into a wraith like her sister? But the body she inhabited wasn't like a raven. Her wings were too leathery, and she had strange fingers instead of talons. What kind of animal had she become? A bat?

Naamah screeched, but her voice spurted out in a series of high-pitched squeaks that hardly resembled words at all. Cursing to herself, she searched for the raven and found her circling near the window above. The bird looked bigger than before as it straightened in flight and sailed to the other side of the ark.

Naamah tried to follow. She beat her wings furiously but couldn't figure out how to fly in a straight line. As she struggled to stay above the churning floodwaters, she continually corrected her awkward meanderings.

After a wind-blown flight that seemed to take an hour, the raven landed on a mountaintop in a patch of tender grass between two boulders. Naamah, her wings faltering, swerved left and right and finally smacked into one of the boulders before tumbling into the grass. She lifted herself and sat, flapping her wings to keep upright, but with one paw wrapped tightly around her treasure, she kept tilting to the side. She tried to speak again, and this time her squeaks sounded like the voice of a tiny child. "What . . . now . . . Morgan?"

"Patience, Naamah," the raven squawked. "Restoration is at hand."

Morgan spread her wings and wrapped them around Naamah. As they perched together, black smoke arose on all sides, penetrating Naamah's nostrils and bringing the foul stench of decaying carrion. As she closed her eyes to ward off the stinging fumes, her body stretched, her head expanded, her wings tapered, and her claws thickened into fingers. When she reopened her eyes, Morgan stood before her.

Naamah patted her side with her free hand. Something was different. Her fingers seemed to pass through her waist, but not as through smoke. Her body felt more like thick gravy. She raised her hand and stared at her palm, flexing her fingers as they melded into each other. A feeling of horror erupted and spilled out in a loud wail. "What happened to me?"

Morgan stroked Naamah's hair. "What matters is that we're alive."

"So I'm a wraith now?" She closed her hand into a fist, and it congealed into a fingerless club.

"You are more spirit than substance, but you'll learn to mold yourself into a variety of shapes. Still, neither of us can last long in this world without a regular visit to our lord's domain. He must

73

infuse us with power if the light of this world wears our bodies down."

"So I can't go back to the ark?"

"Once I explain my plan and teach you how to solidify yourself, you may return. Noah's family cannot be allowed to know you're missing."

Naamah breathed a long sigh. "That's good."

Morgan crossed her arms and squinted at Naamah. "You're not seriously worried about that baby are you?"

"No . . . it's just that . . ." Naamah's voice trailed off.

"Don't worry. If my plan works, Canaan will be yours forever." She nodded at Naamah's hand. "Were you able to bring the grapes?"

"Oh . . ." Naamah opened her fist, revealing five wrinkled grapes. "I forgot about them."

Morgan surveyed the mountaintop, a dome that flattened out into about five acres of rocky soil. The floodwaters lapped against the shoreline about two hundred paces upwind, and, beyond that, across a mile or two of arching whitecaps, the ark listed against the pounding waves. She pointed toward a flat area midway between the shore and where they stood. "We'll plant our vineyard there."

"How long will it take to turn five grapes into a vineyard?"

"Let's just say that they will grow at a wickedly fast rate, and when Noah plants his own vineyard, the same power will cause his to thrive in stunning fashion. Then, we will graft our vines onto his. The grapes from our grafted vines will be better than the rest, so he'll be sure to make wine from them."

Naamah twirled her ghostly dress. "And that's when the fun begins?"

"Yes. The wine will put him into enough of a stupor for you and Ham to get something I want."

"That's it? Get Noah drunk and steal something from him? Sounds too easy."

"Not as easy as you might think. For us to use the child, Noah must curse him and make him leave his family. I'll tell you how to do it, but it will require perfect timing and your best acting performance."

"Beguiling men is my specialty," Naamah said, grinning.

"Patience, Sister. Bide your time as a loving mother and doting wife. First, the grapes must grow, then we will speed the fermentation process. When the harvest celebration begins, wait for Noah to drink, and then . . ." Morgan smiled and raised an imaginary cup into the air as if proposing a toast.

Naamah joined her with a cup of her own. "The wine will do the rest!"

A dark mist filtered between the two uplifted arms. Naamah lowered her imaginary cup and searched for the source. A blanket of black fog hovered close to the shore just above the water. A stream of darkness extended from it, reaching out and trying to loop around their bodies.

Morgan closed her eyes. "Do you hear that?"

Naamah kept her head still, concentrating on the surrounding noise. "Just the waves. What do you hear?"

Following the mist's beckoning arm, Morgan padded her bare feet silently along the virgin grass. "Not waves. Voices. Pleading voices."

Naamah followed Morgan to the shoreline. As they stepped into the water, the black fog swirled around them, congealing into dozens of dark phantoms that pawed at their bodies like anxious dogs. Naamah couldn't feel their swiping paws, but a sense of heaviness filled her mind. "Who are they?" she asked.

Morgan smiled and cradled one of the ghostly shapes in her arms. "The spirits of the Nephilim." She closed her eyes for several seconds as the ghost caressed her ear. When she opened her eyes again, she sighed. "This one tells me that the flood killed their bodies, but their spirits had no place to rest. The human dead went to the circles of seven, and the Watchers were banished to Tartarus, but these hybrid children were prevented from entering either domain. They searched for suitable bodies in the ark, but a strange spiritual force banned their entry into the humans, and the animals in the hold were stupid beasts, unable to open their minds to allow them in. So they wander here as sea fog, unable to walk or breathe, like lost souls in an eternal nightmare."

"Isn't there some way we can restore them?" Naamah asked. "Maybe by using Samyaza's seeds of power?"

"I don't know. Our little gardening plan is designed to grow new Nephilim, not restore their wandering spirits. Still, there might be a way to find bodies for them. If not from Canaan's line, then perhaps from another source."

"Another source?" Naamah tilted her head. "The only animals left in the world were on the ark."

"Very true, yet there is one animal our lost children have not yet explored, a beast with brainpower rivaling that of many humans, perhaps even surpassing them."

Naamah tapped her chin. "They weren't in the animal hold for these spirits to find."

"And they will be at their weakest when they finally exit the ark." Morgan laid the phantom in Naamah's arms. "It will be up to you to teach them a siren's song."

"A song to tempt the heart, arrest the guardians of the mind, and open the gates of the soul." Naamah smiled. "I can do that."

"I thought so. Who has ever been able to resist your charms?"

A flutter of wings drew Naamah's gaze skyward. She pointed at a white bird flying overhead. "Look! A dove!"

Morgan followed its flight as it circled their island. "It seems that a certain raven never returned, so Noah has been sending doves out to search for land." In a puff of smoke, she transformed back into a raven and took to the air. Seconds later, she returned with her claws embedded in the dove, blood dripping from its broken neck. As she fluttered to a landing, dropping the dead bird on the ground, she cackled, "I'll let the next one live, Noah, after I plant my vineyard. Then it will be time for you to come out. And bring those lovely dragons with you."

76

The Spectral Promise

M akaidos stretched out his body on the carpet of fledgling grass. The sun's warm rays felt like the massage of strong, healing hands as each scale soaked up the delicious radiance, recharging every aspect of his dragon nature. Thigocia slept next to him, her long neck curled around the base of his. The scales on his other side begged for sunlight, but he didn't want to turn over and awaken his mate. As close to death as she had come during the months of darkness, she needed sleep as much as she needed the sun's precious energy.

A loud trumpet blast sounded from the water's edge. Makaidos lifted his head toward the ark. Japheth and Shem were leading the elephants through Eve's door, the new calf following close behind. The male trumpeted a second time, as if saluting the bright rainbow that painted the misty clouds to the west.

Makaidos sighed. The rainbow promised a spectrum of joy, each color representing a different bliss in the new paradise. The

EYE OF THE ORACLE

sun poured down warmth from a clean, clear sky, baking virgin earth that yearned to sprout new offspring from her cleansed womb. The rich soil carried no trace of footprints from either man or demon. Every Watcher and Naphil had perished, and the world now held no memory of their corruption. The weary souls on the ark seemed refined by fire, rejoicing in each moment, bouncing with every step on the newly purged earth.

Resting his head on Thigocia's abdomen, Makaidos listened for signs of life within—a gurgle, a click, a soft hum that played in Makaidos's mind like a glorious hymn. He closed his eyes and smiled. Maybe this world would be a safe place for dragon younglings after all.

As he tried to sleep, dozens of noises disturbed the quiet—parrots squawking, cattle mooing, even the buzzing of a bee in his ear. Still, one odd sound rose above the others. He perked up his ears. A haunting voice blew by, like a ghost whispering a song in the breeze.

The chill of danger swept across his scales. He raised his head again. A stream of dark mist flowed across both dragons. Curling around his snout like a translucent python, the mist wrapped his face and shrouded his eyes. Makaidos leaped to his feet and thumped his tail. "Thigocia!" he shouted. "Awake!"

The ground vibrated, and Thigocia's voice rumbled. "What is this darkness?"

"A mist. Something wicked."

"I thought I felt a presence, but I could not be sure."

"Listen," Makaidos said. "It sings."

"Shall I call for help?"

"Shh!"

Both dragons fell silent. Makaidos concentrated on the whispered aria, a lilting melody that played like a fresh breeze on tender grass.

Your heart of gold should never fear
Arrival of the dawn,
For each new day shall bring new hope
As moon begets the sun.

Erase your mind, O dragon wise,
And let your gates be breached.
The time has come to greet new thoughts
Your maker failed to teach.

For wisdom comes when laws of old
Are swept like spiders' webs,
And minds like yours discover truth
In life's new flows and ebbs.

For how can wisdom's laws be true
When taught from books to squires?
Experience stands as wisdom's tool
To guide you through the mire.

O let me in to teach you songs
That come from heaven's lights.
You'll never fail to conquer foes
And rule o'er kings and knights.

For man corrupts and soils his own;
The world will die again.
His lust for blood and gold and flesh
Destroys what dragons mend.

Makaidos clenched his eyes shut and pawed at the streaming
mist. "Do not listen! It sings foul words!"
"Too late. I heard every syllable."

"Then do not heed them!"

"I knew that much! But how do we get rid of the mist? It is blinding me!"

"Close your eyes!" Makaidos shot a blast of hot gasses in the direction of Thigocia's voice. "Can you see now?"

"Yes! Your turn!"

Makaidos kept his eyes closed while hot air, smelling of burning sulfur, bathed his face. His vision cleared, and a wisp of black fog brushed by his ear, singing one last phrase before streaming toward the sea. "I will be back for your son."

Makaidos blasted a flood of fire at the retreating blackness, but it was too late. The fog danced over the water and disappeared like evaporating mist. "If you dare come back," the dragon bellowed, "I will melt your songs into screams of agony!" He turned to Thigocia. "Any harm done?"

"No. No song could ever turn my heart from the Maker."

"Did you hear anything else, I mean, after the song?"

"No. Only the song." Thigocia nudged Makaidos's wing and snuggled under it. "What did you hear?"

Makaidos glared at the island's shore. "Just a bully's taunt. Malicious words are just noises in the wind." He extended his wing over Thigocia's body and stroked her flank. "With our danger sense getting strong again, we will be alerted if the mist tries to return."

Thigocia rubbed her cheek against Makaidos's neck. "You need not tell me about the taunt, if that is your wish, but I am curious."

"I wish not to tell. Too much information can be dangerous."

"Is the truth ever dangerous?" Thigocia asked, stretching to look into her mate's eyes. "Even too much of it?"

Makaidos avoided eye contact. "If it is more than our hearts and minds can manage, yes."

"I will remember that. Too much information can be too taxing on our brains." Thigocia turned her ears outward. "The mist sounded like many voices. Do you have any idea who they were?"

"Yes. Although they drowned in the flood, their evil spirits must have somehow survived."

"The Nephilim?"

Makaidos shifted his body toward the ark. "I have to warn Noah." He stretched out his wings and tried to lift off the ground, but they faltered and fell limply to his flanks. He sighed and raised his brow. "It seems that my strength won't fully return until we build our regeneracy domes. Will you walk with me?"

She shuffled to his side and nudged his ribs with her snout. "As if you could stop me."

Ham pushed the tent flap open and ducked inside. A single candle burned near his father's mat, barely enough light to see two elongated lumps on the opposite side of the tent. "I think I know where it might be," he whispered.

"Shhh!" Naamah warned, following him. "Just take it and leave."

As Ham's eyes adjusted, he could distinguish the shapes of his father and mother sleeping peacefully, their arms interlocked. He stopped suddenly, then stepped back. "He's . . . he's uncovered."

Naamah laid a hand on his back. "What did you expect? The wine was strong."

Gazing at Noah, Ham smirked. "The great man of God, drunk and naked. Now who's bringing shame to the family?"

Naamah pushed him forward. "Just take it."

Ham skulked to his father's side and fumbled through the clothes that lay on the ground. Ah! Chereb! He picked it up, but his father's robe came along with it. He pulled at the knot that tied the sword to the robe. "It's stuck!" he hissed.

Noah stirred, his eyes blinking. Ham froze and waited for his father to settle, hoping his drunken eyes wouldn't see clearly. When he seemed to rest quietly again, Ham tiptoed back to Naamah with the robe. "I can't unfasten it."

"Just bring it all!"

81

Ham and Naamah slipped out of the tent, but just as they turned toward their own tent, Shem and Japheth hailed them from a distance. Ham held the robe and sword behind his back while Naamah clawed at the knot. Just as Ham's brothers drew near, Naamah whispered, "I have it. I'll hide it under my robe."

Shem nodded a greeting. "Visiting Father?"

"Yes." Ham shifted his weight and glanced back at Noah's tent. "He seemed ill when he retired, so I thought I'd check on him."

"Just some bad wine," Japheth said, laughing. "He'll feel better in the morning."

Shem glanced around Ham's side. "What are you hiding back there?"

Ham pulled Noah's robe around. "I went into the tent, and Father was . . . well . . . uncovered."

"So you took his clothes?" Japheth snatched the robe away. "What are you up to?"

"Well, I was just . . ." Ham crossed his arms over his chest. "It's none of your business."

Shem grabbed Ham by the throat. "You've humiliated father for the last time!"

Ham caught Shem's wrists and wrestled his hands away. "I didn't go in there to shame him!" he said, pushing Shem back. "He was already uncovered when I went in."

Japheth shook the robe at him. "Then why did you take this?"

"Naamah was cold." Ham turned, but Shem took a fistful of his sleeve and spun him back around. Ham scowled at him. "What now?"

Japheth laid a hand on Shem's wrist. "Let him go. Father will deal with him later."

Shem jerked his hand back and raised his finger near Ham's nose. "Father told me that anyone who brings corruption back to this earth will be under God's curse. If you are the corrupter, Father will have no choice but to pronounce the curse on you and your descendants."

Ham turned again and stalked away. "Come, Naamah." Refusing the temptation to look back, he strode through a pasture and crested a low hill next to Noah's vineyard, his wife hustling to stay at his side. When he was sure they were out of earshot, he stopped and turned to her. "Where is it?"

Naamah clutched a fold at the front of her robe. "Right here."

Ham peered over Naamah's shoulder at Shem and Japheth as they approached Noah's tent. His brothers had draped Noah's robe over their shoulders, and they were walking backwards into the tent's opening. Ham shook his head. "The fools! They still believe in that old tyrant."

Naamah touched his arm. "Don't worry about them. They don't know what we really did."

"They'll know soon enough. When Father wakes up, they're sure to tell him that I had his robe, and he'll figure out that I took Chereb."

"Then you must leave before the wine wears off." She pulled the sword from her robe and laid it in his hands. "I'll follow with Canaan and our belongings later."

"You heard what Shem said. If Canaan is here, and I'm not, Father might curse him in my place."

"I will soothe your father's anger." She stood on tiptoes and kissed him on the cheek. "Now go."

Ham folded his robe around the sword. "We will meet at the third hill past the dark forest. Do you remember the glade next to the river?"

"Yes, of course. Look for me there at sunset on the third day."

Ham nodded and hurried through the vineyard.

With Shem and Japheth standing at the entry, Noah paced back and forth inside his tent, his hands behind his back. Shem pushed open the flap. "She's here," he said.

Naamah walked in, carrying her sleeping one-year-old in a blanket, her eyes darting all around. With the bundle almost too big for the petite woman to manage, she briefly dipped one knee and nodded. "What may I do for you, my masters?"

Noah grabbed Naamah's wrist. "Who are you?"

Her eyes flew open, and her voice trembled. "I am Naamah, your servant." She clutched her baby closer to her chest. "I am the wife of your son, Ham."

"No, I mean who are you really?" Noah tightened his grasp. "Where did you come from?"

"My father is Lamech of the line of Cain, and my mother is Zillah." As she stared at Noah's fierce grip on her arm, tears welled in her eyes. "Why do you ask me about things you already know?"

Noah jerked his hand away. "Don't take me for a fool," he shouted. "I have watched you ever since you boarded the ark with my son, and I know when someone is hiding a secret. Last night, as drunk as I was, I saw you bring him into my tent. You enticed him to take Chereb from me, and I want to know why."

Naamah lowered herself to her knees, her eyes pleading. "I am a servant, Father Noah. Ham asked me to be his wife, and I accepted. Since he rescued me from death, I serve him with all my heart. So when he commanded me to help him steal the sword, I obeyed, as any obedient wife should."

"He mocked me!" Noah shouted, shaking his finger. "He was pleased to see me shamed! And you saw it all."

"I do not pretend to know my husband's motives, Father Noah, nor do I know why he gazed upon you, but I am a chaste woman, and I assure you that I turned my head. I know what is forbidden to my eyes."

Noah's brow slowly relaxed, and he gestured for her to get up. As she rose, Noah looked at his two sons. "Should I believe her?" he asked.

Shem nodded. "You warned me not to be a merciless judge, Father, so I advise compassion. I know what Ham would have done to her had she disobeyed."

"I agree," Japheth said. "I have watched how she cares for Canaan. I guess I have a soft spot in my heart for mothers."

Noah sighed. "As do I. Perhaps too soft." He extended his hand toward the baby and caressed its cheek. "I still sense a dark secret in your heart, Naamah, but I will forgive your transgression."

"Oh, thank you!" Naamah rose to the balls of her feet and kissed Noah. She pulled Canaan's arm out of the blanket and guided his hand across Noah's beard. "Say thank you to Grandfather!"

Japheth leaned close, his jaw dropping open. He nudged his brother's ribs. "Shem," he whispered. "Six fingers!"

Shem shoved his way between his father and Canaan, grabbed the sleeping child's hand, and spread out his fingers. "Father! Look!"

Noah seemed perplexed for a moment, his lips moving as his eyes numbered the five fingers and thumb. "So that's your secret!" he yelled, his face flushing scarlet. "You have carried the demon seed into our refuge!"

85

Naamah backed away, her whole body shaking. "No. I am a woman. I carry no seed but what my father has passed on to me."

Noah's eyes flashed, and he pushed his hand through his white hair. "How can this be? Only a demon or a Naphil can pass on such a seed, and Canaan was born eleven months after the flood began, so Ham must be the father."

Stepping slowly backwards, Naamah gave him a quick bow. "Then by your leave, Father Noah, if you are convinced that my son is of the devil, I will go now and cast both of our bodies into the sea. Far be it from your servants to bring corruption back into our new world."

"No!" Noah gestured toward his sons. Each of them laid a hand on one of Naamah's shoulders, stopping her. "The boy must live," Noah continued. "You have spoken truly about his fate as a servant. He is cursed, and he will be a servant to Shem and

Japheth." He pointed outside. "Naamah, you must leave us. Take whatever you need for travel and sustenance, and may God have mercy on both of you."

Shem and Japheth released her. Naamah glared at both of them, clutched the baby more tightly to her breast, and backed out through the tent flap.

Shem jerked the flap closed. "She is a deceiver."

Noah sighed, nodding slowly. "I know. Yet, God will use even her to glorify his name. From the harvest of Canaan's crop will come a great evil, but the soil for his seed will carry another seed the gardeners do not expect. The crop God raises up will be as tares to the enemy's wheat, one that sets the entire field ablaze."

"A prophecy, Father?" Shem asked.

"Yes, Son." Noah lifted his gaze upward. "A prophecy . . . and a promise."

CHAPTER

UNDERBORNS

Mara held open the bottom of the scroll with her elbow and ran her finger along a line of text. The light from her lantern flickered across the page. She squinted in the dim glow, nearly swallowed by the shadows of the stony cavern, yet bright enough to read Mardon's handwriting. The story filled her with wonder—dragons, elephants, monkeys, and hundreds of other wonderful creatures all loaded on an amazing floating vessel long before she was born. She rubbed her hand along a sketch of a dragon, admiring the image of a world she had never known. What she wouldn't give to have been there!

She glanced at the hourglass perched on her worktable next to her elbow. Only a few grains of sand remained at the top. As she rolled up the scroll with its heavy wooden dowel, pain throbbed in her stiff shoulder. She grimaced at the ache. The soreness was worse than usual, but no surprise, considering all the digging she had been doing.

She hugged the scroll to her chest and closed her eyes. As a tear trickled down her cheek, she wagged her head back and forth, trying

87

to chase the beautiful images out of her mind. Seeing all those wonders was just a dream. There was no way an insignificant slave girl could ever hope to visit such a paradise, much less live there, so she might as well get back to reality, the reality of hard work, sweat, darkness, and pain.

Breathing a big sigh, she opened her eyes and admired the tall, arching alcove she had excavated in a massive wall, her rocky workplace for the past several days. Although it was fairly shallow, only about as deep as the fireplace cavities up in Shinar that she had read about, it still had taken a long time to chisel out.

She knelt at the ankle-high hearth at the base of her alcove and pulled out three loose bricks, making a low, wide cubbyhole, perfect for hiding away the scroll for a while. As she pushed the scroll inside, a clicking noise made her swing her head around. She gazed into the dimness that shrouded the massive chamber. It was probably just one of the timid rock mice that sometimes skittered through the air vents. Then again, maybe it was Mardon coming to inspect her work.

While giving her shoulder a one-handed massage, she slid a lever embedded near the bottom of the hearth, opening the magnetic field. A chorus of low hums sounded from the wall, each with a slightly different pitch that slowly rose in volume.

Taking a step back, she surveyed the bricks that lined the border of the alcove. The magneto brick at the top of the arch glowed green, just as it should. The three on the left glowed blue, indigo, and violet, while yellow and orange emanated from two of the bricks on the right. A third one remained dark.

Mara wrinkled her nose. What was wrong with the red one? The magneto should have energized by now. She leaped onto the hearth and pushed on the end of the malfunctioning brick, budging it just enough to align it with the side of the alcove. It pulsed red, then glowed steadily, adding its hum to the chorus. She brushed her hands together and smiled. Finally! The last magnet was working!

Stepping inside the alcove, she pressed her back against the rear wall. When she reached forward, her hands didn't quite pass the point where the wall was before she chiseled it away. Stretching her arms to the sides, she could barely touch the magnetized bricks with her fingertips. Finally, she reached as high as she could, but the arch was still more than twice her body's length over her head. It was perfect.

She skipped out of the alcove, jumped off the hearth, and spun around, crossing her arms as she admired her creation again. The lantern on her worktable flashed and beamed a strong yellow light that painted her shadow on the recessed wall. Shallow as it was, the grotto had taken eleven days to excavate, even with the sharpened chisel Mardon had given her, but now it was finally ready for her spawn.

As Mara retied the sash on her smock, she noticed a tiny pebble sliding toward one of the magnets. She slapped her forehead. She still had to check the balance! Reaching under her smock, she pulled a glass vial from her dress pocket and held it close to the light. She shook it, loosening the iron filings that had settled at the bottom. After setting the vial inside and at the center of the alcove, she scanned the seven magnets in turn. Each metallic brick seemed to aim its end directly at her iron filings.

Kneeling on the hearth, she peered into the vial. The filings began to dance, arranging themselves into a perfectly symmetrical crystal with tiny black diamonds sketched throughout.

Mara laughed. "I wonder if they're always that pretty." An echo repeated her words, ending with a quiet, "pretty . . . pretty . . . pretty." She glanced around the empty cavern, her gaze finally landing on the dark passageway that led out of her work area. Not a soul in sight. The voice was just a cruel joke bouncing off mindless walls through a heartless underground world. She wiped her dirty hands on her even dirtier smock. Of course no one in the hidden realms would ever consider her pretty.

89

She untied her smock and sighed. Getting banished to the growth lab was bad enough, but having to do everything alone was the worst. Sure, mining in the trenches was hard, but at least she could talk to the other girls there. Even the boy laborers on the brick level had each other . . . or so she had heard.

She shut off the magnets' lever, silencing the hum, snatched up her vial, and dropped it back into her pocket. After picking up her lantern, she sauntered toward the passageway. Time to venture to the seedling room and get the newest nursling. Maybe Naamah would be in a good mood today and tell her a story about the great giants of old.

As her bare feet padded on the warm, stony floor, she stuffed her hair back up into her coif and retied it over her head. Mardon wouldn't like it if he knew her hair had fallen loose while excavating, and even though her work was finished, it still wasn't a good time to take it off. The river lay just ahead.

The tunnel slowly brightened, and as she passed by a stone-framed window in the wall, she winced at the light pouring from it and pulled down the coif's attached veil. Although she could see through the material well enough to walk, it protected her eyes from the terror that lay beyond the window. She had seen the river of magma at the bottom of the chasm once before, and the image would never leave her mind—a bubbling and churning flow crawling toward who-knows-where. She shuddered as she passed by, nearly in tears at the thought of the underborns who had perished in the fiery stream. When she cleared the window's glow, she jerked off her coif, crumpled it up, and stuffed it into her pocket.

As she continued, the tunnel darkened again, and her lantern's flame burned green. The familiar sounds of this darkest portion crept into her ears—a chorus of squeaks from bats hiding somewhere in the recesses of the tunnel; cascading water from the stream falling into Lucifer's Pool; the tiny splashes of minnows in their never-ending pursuit of larvae; the incessant pounding of a chisel in the hands of a faraway laborer, probably one of the girls desperately trying to get her magnetite quota from the trenches; and finally . . . yes, there it was, the pleasant warble of Naamah's song.

Mara peeked into the seedling room. A trio of lanterns hung from the high reaches of the cavern, casting a blend of yellow light and crisscrossing shadows. Mara hid her own lantern behind her back. Naamah's singing meant she was probably in a good mood, but Mara didn't want to take any chances. Better to wait a few minutes and watch for signs of bad temper.

Her mistress raised a watering can over a tiny potted plant. As always, she crooned in a haunting contralto.

> To grow and live, escape the flames
> Of darkest nights and endless toil,
> O stretch and thrive my precious flower
> And drink the rain from fertile soil.

As she sprinkled the plant, it stretched out two stalks at its sides, like a man waking after a long nap. A thumb-sized pod between the two stalks turned its face toward her, two eyelets blinking as drops streamed down its green skin.

Naamah smiled and continued her song, cooing at the pod as a mother would to a baby.

> A day will come, my little child,
> When roots transform to warrior's feet
> And stalks become tight fists of steel
> To grind all men like sifted wheat.

Mara walked in, but a new shadow from the far side of the cavern glided into view. Morgan! Mara stopped and clenched her teeth. What now? She couldn't run back to the passageway. Morgan would notice for sure. She froze in place and listened.

Morgan stepped into the light and applauded. "The echo compliments your voice, Naamah. It's more beautiful than ever."

Naamah spread out her black dress and curtsied. "The male plants seem especially fond of my singing." She chucked the pod under its tiny chin. "This one is my favorite."

"Actually, the females are more important right now." Morgan waved her arm toward Mara. "The most impetuous of the girls seems smarter and more talented than any males in the land above, though she can be treacherous enough to betray even a twin sister."

Mara balled her hands into fists. She wanted to stomp her foot and shout a defense, but that would just prove Morgan's "impetuous" comment. She breathed deeply and buried the insult in the pit of her stomach along with all the others. Still, heat rose past her cheeks and inflamed her ears. She hoped Morgan wouldn't notice.

Morgan glared at Mara. "What are you doing here, anyway?"

"I . . ." Mara swallowed and took a tentative step forward. "I've come for a new spawn. My growth chamber is ready."

Morgan raised her eyebrows. "Has Mardon checked the magnets?"

"He taught me how." Mara withdrew her vial and held it up. "The magnets are perfect."

Morgan's frown slackened, but her brow stayed taut. "Very well." She turned to Naamah. "Is number four of suitable size?"

"Yes." Naamah pointed at a plant near the passageway, close to where Mara stood. "It's almost too big for the pot already."

Morgan nodded at the plant. "Get it and be on your way. I'll be by to check its growth soon enough. Your chamber had better be perfectly balanced, or you'll take the next step past banishment."

Mara tried not to flinch, but she couldn't help it. She knew what that meant. As she thought of the terror in Acacia's face, her lantern flickered weakly, as if sympathizing with her pain. She gathered the pot in one arm and hustled back into the passage, but her lantern winked out, leaving her in darkness except for the light from the seedling room behind her. Mara halted. Could she go all the way through the dark part of the tunnel without a light? Would the bats notice her? She turned back and leaned against the wall, peering at Morgan and Naamah. She didn't want to ask for light, not while Morgan was still around. Maybe she would leave soon through the other tunnel, then Naamah might help her. Naamah was always the more patient of the two, though that wasn't saying much.

Mara breathed a quiet sigh and set her lantern on the floor. Being banished had one advantage. Nabal wouldn't be waiting with a whip. In fact, no one would notice her absence until bed check. She could just watch and listen, and maybe learn more about the land above.

Morgan crossed her arms over her chest. "As I was about to say, the females will never be giantesses; at least according to Mardon's genetic analysis. But we need more laborers than Nephilim candidates right now. Once the hive is complete with thriving giants, we'll keep a few of the strongest and stupidest females for laborers, then throw the rest in the chasm."

93

Mara gulped. She probably wasn't supposed to hear that. Who would be chosen to live? She rubbed a finger along her toned bicep. She was strong, but not the strongest of the female laborers, and far from stupid. Crouching low, she hugged her plant close.

Naamah carried her pot to a dimly lit wall and set it on the end of a shelf of identical pots. Each one held a human-like seedling, some barely poking up from the soil and others as tall as the breadth of her hand. She turned the pot so the plant could see her. "I began to wonder what happened to you, Sister. You've been gone for weeks."

"Months, actually. Time shifts in strange ways between the upper and lower worlds. I'm beginning to think time is slowing down here, since the older spawns have slowed their aging."

"Did you bring more produce?" Naamah asked. "We ran out of fruit days ago."

"It's in the pantry. Nimrod's farms are producing well."

Naamah dipped her finger into the potting soil, then pulled it out, examining the mud on the tip. "Is there any other news from above?"

"Yes. It seems that Mardon has a solution to why our hybrids aren't thriving."

"They need more light, don't they?" Naamah wiped the mud on a cloth hanging on the shelf. "I always said that plants should be out in the sun where they—"

"No," Morgan interrupted. "Almost the opposite. It seems that the flood did more than simply snuff out innocent lives and scrub the planet. All light is harsher now, brighter than before, so the seeds I took from Samyaza are too pure, even when we dilute them with Canaan's genes. They make a plant that grows poorly when exposed to any kind of light, even lantern light and magneto radiance down here."

"How can Mardon fix a problem like that? Even he isn't smart enough."

"You might be surprised. Mardon and his scientists are confident they can do anything. Right now they're working on a tower that already reaches past the clouds."

Naamah's eyebrows shot up. "Past the clouds?! May I go above and see it?"

"Only if you go after dark and in your winged form." Morgan looked up at the cavern's high ceiling. "There's a full moon tonight, so you should be able to see the tower."

"Even if I can't, being a bat for a while is better than being stuck in this cave."

"Patience. Just a few more weeks. One of the craftsmen is building a home for us on the surface. It still has to be in this dimension, but at least you'll be able to go there whenever you wish."

94

"Not as a bat?" Naamah asked.

"As long as you're in the circles of seven, you can be yourself."

"Good." Naamah fanned her face with her hand. "The air down here gets stuffy, and flying makes me tired."

"Don't worry. The house will be on a lovely island, and I planted apple trees and gardenias all around. Soon the air on our island will be saturated with the scents of wisdom and life."

"Will we have any company up there?" Naamah asked.

"The circles are filling with the souls of humans who wander in the land of the dead, but the serpents I put in the waters around the island will protect us from their interference." Morgan caressed Naamah's delicate arm. "Still, we have a boat, and you will be free to stalk the shores and sing a victim into your clutches whenever you wish."

"Perfect. I've been practicing a song just for that purpose." Naamah smiled, and for a brief second, a pair of fangs appeared over her bottom lip.

95

Mara nearly fell backwards. What kind of creature was Naamah, anyway?

"If you keep your mind on your work," Morgan said, "I won't care how many men you capture. Just remember to collect what we need from them."

Naamah twirled her dress. "Have you begun to doubt my charms, Sister?"

"Not your charms, just your prudence. Our mission is more important than fun. Canaan has aged more quickly than I expected, so he's already useless."

"We have the hybrid embryos in the vault. We could always use their genes."

Morgan propped up one of the wilting plants. "The hybrids are stronger than the purebreds, but not strong enough. We have to keep experimenting until we get the right combination for survival in the world's new environment."

"What about your other plan?" Naamah asked. "Any luck finding homes for the spirits?"

"Perhaps. The dragons have birthed several younglings in quick succession. The spirits have repeatedly visited the eldest son at night, and he believes he is merely dreaming. He is already showing signs of giving in to the songs."

"You decided to use dragons as hosts, after all? I thought you decided you wanted them dead."

"I do, but I have no way to kill them . . . yet." Morgan plucked a wrinkled leaf from one of the plants, making its little green face wince. "Still, if my plan works, we will eliminate every dragon, release the Watchers from the abyss so they can live in a dragon-free land, and have an army of Nephilim to conquer the world."

"I see." Naamah stroked the stalk of the injured plant. "Home-grown Nephilim instead of dragon-born."

"Exactly. The Nephilim spirits should eventually break through the dragons' minds and secure them as hosts, but even if the spirits someday lose their scaly bodies, it will be a small price to pay to create our paradise."

"I keep hearing about this paradise. When will we get to enjoy it?"

"That's the hard part, Sister. We have to be patient. I still have to find the abyss. Then, I have to raise up a champion for our cause, a dragon slayer, you might call him. I'll mold him like putty in my hands, and place him in circles of authority. We also have to conquer the minds of the dragons one by one. Such a scheme can take millennia to accomplish, but we can afford to wait as long as necessary."

Naamah picked up a plant and gazed into the tiny eyelets of the blinking pod. Its emaciated stalk could barely hold up its oversized head, and it finally keeled over as if gasping for breath. "And in the meantime?"

"In the meantime"—Morgan strangled the plant and ripped it out of the soil—"we cultivate, sow, and water until our army is ready to uproot and march."

Mara gagged. Nausea boiled in her stomach. Still crouching as she cradled her new spawn, she picked up her lantern and tip-toed through the dim tunnel. With so little light, she could easily step on a sharp stalagmite . . . or worse. As the passage grew darker, she slowed, standing straight and probing the blackness, listening to the squeaks of awakening bats. Her spawn's prickly pod nuzzled her cheek. It was scared, too.

When she approached the magma window, she didn't bother to put on her coif; she just rushed past it as quickly as she could and slowed again as the tunnel darkened once more. Soon, a flick-ering beam revealed the oval entryway into her workroom. Clutching her spawn even more tightly, she ran the rest of the way, stopping at the opening and holding her hand on her chest as she caught her breath. She pressed her lips together, trying not to cry. She was such a failure! She had to be the only underborn in all of the below lands who was scared of the dark.

"Is there a problem?" a deep voice asked.

Mara dropped her lantern and twisted to the side. A man stood next to her, only inches away. "Mardon!" she cried, her hand on her chest again. "You startled me!"

"My apologies." Mardon's egg-shaped head tilted as he held up the scroll she had been reading. "Mara, isn't it?"

Mara sniffed and nodded. "Yessir."

Mardon cupped Mara's chin and turned her head from side to side. Under his closely cropped brown hair, a pair of thin eyebrows arched downward. His coal black pupils seemed to breathe, swelling and deflating as he probed her eyes. "Number fourteen, correct?" He released her chin and combed through her hair as if searching for bugs in her scalp.

"Yessir. Number fourteen." She hated being called by a num-ber, but at least he remembered her name this time.

"Did you cut your hair again?" he asked.

"Weeks ago, but only because it got caught between some rocks." She ran her fingers through the tangled ends. "Paili had to slice off a bunch to get me loose, and then I had to cut the rest to make it even."

"It's acceptable. Just remember to tuck it in your coif while you're working. I'm just checking for signs of biological degradation, and hair loss would be a big concern, as would loss of muscle tone." He laid his hand on her shoulder and gave it a gentle squeeze. Pain ripped through her body, and she couldn't hold back a tight grimace.

Mardon quickly lifted his hand. "Did that hurt?"

Mara squeezed her eyes shut and nodded. "Nabal's whip. It's an old wound, but it never seems to heal."

Mardon pushed the collar of her dress to the side, exposing her shoulder. Shaking his head and whispering "Tsk, tsk," he covered her wound again. "Make sure you scrub that out tonight, or it could be dangerous."

Mara opened her eyes, hoping she wouldn't cry. "I will."

"Your muscles are quite firm," he said, grasping her other shoulder. "Actually, overall, you're a very lucky girl. Have I ever told you what happened to the first twelve females?"

"Yessir." She smoothed down her hair. "But you talk to so many underborns, it's no wonder you've forgotten."

"Not so many. There are only twenty-one surviving females at my last count. Morgan has a habit of tossing the insubordinates into the chasm when she gets angry, including number thirteen, an excellent specimen." Mardon tapped his head with his finger. "Actually, I've been so busy, I seem to be getting a bit absent-minded. I don't remember everything I tell people."

"Yessir." She sniffed hard. Thinking about lost underborns was sure to make her cry, so she tried to change the subject. Steadying her voice, she nodded at the scroll. "I was just borrowing that. I hope you don't mind."

Mardon stared at the scroll, his eyes widening as if startled that it was still in his hand. "Oh, you mean this."

"Yessir. Your library isn't forbidden, so I thought it would be okay to read it."

"Of course. I was just wondering why it was in the hearth. I didn't think mice could read."

Mara pointed a thumb at herself. "But I can!" She immediately felt stupid for saying it. Being smart wasn't exactly cheered among the other laborers.

"Yes, yes, I have heard. You're the only one who can, aren't you?"

"Yessir. I kind of taught myself how."

Mardon cupped her chin again and gazed into her eyes. "Remarkable!"

Mara swallowed and lifted her plant. "My spawn is ready. Do you want to check the magnetic field?"

He tucked the scroll under his arm and headed toward the alcove. "I already have. Your workmanship is flawless." He held out his hands for the potted spawn. "Please don't ever cross Morgan. I can't afford to lose you."

"Don't worry. Making her mad is the last thing I want to do." Mara handed him the spawn and smiled. That was the first kind word she had heard in weeks. As Mardon grasped one of the spawn's stalks, she propped her hands on her knees and leaned forward. She didn't get to see implanting very often. "Is this a good spawn?" she asked.

Mardon eyed the plant from top to bottom. The face on the pod turned the edges of its thin lips upward. "I think so. The two lower stalks are thick and sturdy, the torso stalk supports the pod quite well, and the new hybridization seems to have made it more alert than the others."

"Good!" Mara rubbed her hands on her smock and scooted closer.

Mardon turned the pot over and let the ball of dirt slide out into his hand. Then, carefully extracting each root from the dirt,

99

he painstakingly cleaned them with a cotton cloth. The pod's eyelets widened with each soft rub, and its lips spread wider.

Grasping the stalk again in one hand and supporting the roots with the other, Mardon suspended the plant in the middle of the alcove. "Turn on the magnets."

Mara jumped up and slid the lever at the base, reawakening the humming choir. The colored lights began flashing on again one by one, first violet, then indigo, then blue. Within seconds, all seven magnets had lit up, each one radiating a color of the rainbow and sending a wide beam at the new spawn.

Mardon slowly released the plant. Mara barely held back a giggle when her new baby stayed suspended in midair. She clapped her hands. It worked! Her growth chamber really worked! And she had built this one without any help!

Mardon looked back at her and nodded. "Well done, Mara. Maybe this spawn won't have to go to the control room."

Mara flinched at the sound of the words. The control room—except for Morgan's quarters, it was the most forbidden zone in all of the lower reaches, the place where the weaker spawns were taken, and they never returned.

Mardon folded his cloth and tucked it into his pocket. "If I'm reading your expression correctly, you really want to know how everything works, don't you?" As he rubbed the scroll against his palm, his gaze wandered around the cavern. "Most of the laborers haven't even bothered to learn the language. A grunt is the best I can get out of some of them."

"They can talk a little bit, but Morgan punishes us if we talk too much. The smarter ones always seem to get thrown into the chasm, so why try to learn?"

He pointed the scroll at her. "You're the smartest girl here, and the oldest surviving female, yet you've avoided the chasm. She must fancy you."

Mara rubbed her shoulder and smirked. "Could've fooled me!"

Mardon stroked his chin, speaking so softly Mara could barely hear him. "You may be exactly what I need."

"Excuse me, sir?"

Mardon tapped her on the head with the scroll. "I think it's time you learned the process. I could use a personal assistant."

Mara sat down on the floor cross-legged and spread her tattered outer tunic over her knees. "I'm ready to learn!" She folded her hands in her lap and gazed up at him.

"No, not here. It would be better if no one else knew." He extended his hand toward her. "I'll show you the control room. That will make everything clear."

Mara allowed him to pull her to her feet. He picked up a lantern on the worktable, and as he marched into a passage tunnel on the other side of the chamber, she trailed close behind, drinking in his every word as his voice bounced gently off the walls.

"You've probably read stories about the world above, haven't you?"

"Yessir." She tried to keep pace, but with her shorter legs, she had to step quickly. "But I don't see how they can be true. How can a light hang in the middle of an endless sky? And is there really such a thing as a dragon? I heard Morgan talking about them. They sound awful."

"They are quite terrible." Mardon stopped at a wooden door embedded in a stone wall, but there was no latch handle, just a large wheel protruding from the center. "The stories in my scrolls are true, but not everything Morgan says is true." He grasped the rim of the wheel and turned it. "Count the clicks."

The turning wheel clicked, and Mara extended one finger for each sound.

When he stopped the wheel, he swiveled his head toward her. "How many?"

"Six," she replied.

"Good. Now count again." He turned the wheel in the opposite direction, and she counted another series of clicks.

When he stopped, she spoke up without being asked. "Nine."

"You'll need to use your toes for the last turn."

Again the clicks sounded. When they stopped, Mara sang out, "Thirteen!"

Mardon pushed the door open, releasing the familiar hum of magneto bricks from inside. "Remember that combination of numbers and tell no one." He entered and directed Mara to follow. As they walked across a smooth, stone floor, she could barely take in all the sights. At least a dozen growth alcoves, smaller than hers, had been excavated in the wall on one side. A spawn hovered in each chamber, fragile and sickly looking plants, but alive and wiggling in their suspended states. On the other wall, stacks of scrolls lay haphazardly on row after row of shelves, not as many as in the library, but they still seemed to call for her to roll them out and absorb their knowledge.

"Back to the stories," Mardon said, as he approached a large worktable at the far end of the room. "There is a sun that shines brighter than the most brilliant lantern, and it is suspended in an endless blue sky"—he nodded toward one of the spawns, who seemed to be sleeping amidst a spectral bath—"much like he hangs in his growth chamber. And thousands of people work together in peace, advancing technology at a remarkable pace."

"You mean like using a sharpened chisel instead of a hammer to dig an alcove? And carrying lanterns in the tunnels instead of glow worms?"

Mardon pointed at her. "Exactly."

"Yessir. A lot has changed just since I've been here."

Mardon laughed. "As if you've ever been anywhere else." He sighed and gazed at her, his eyes seeming to blur. "Do you know how long you've been here, Mara? Do you know how old you are?"

Mara shrugged her shoulders. "Naamah says I look about fourteen years old, but I never could figure out what the stories meant when they talked about years."

"Naamah is right, and it's no wonder you don't understand time. A hundred years ago, Morgan planted you in an older-style growth chamber, much like I just did to your spawn, and I uprooted you in your current form almost twenty years ago. But since time passage is skewed here, and you don't age as the overworlders do, it's useless to teach you about time, that is, until you visit the land above."

Mara shivered. Her throat squeezed so tight, she could barely speak. "May . . . may I?"

"If your training goes well, I should be able to arrange it."

Mara straightened her shoulders. "I'll train well. Don't worry about that."

Mardon stared at her again, this time with narrowed eyes, as if trying to penetrate her mind. "We'll see, won't we?"

Mara clutched the edge of her smock. Why was he looking at her with that strange expression? But she had enough to think about just concentrating on what she needed to learn. This was her one chance to see the upper world.

Mardon waved his arm over the worktable. "Here is where it all begins."

A collection of small glass jars covered the wooden surface, each one filled with clear liquid. She leaned over and peered into one of the jars. Suspended in the midst of the liquid, an eyeball-sized egg stared back at her. The eggshell's outer membrane was semitransparent, and a tiny creature floated at the center, acting like it was trying to swim. It looked sort of like her spawn, except much smaller and without eyelets or lips.

"This is where we plant the garden, Mara. I experiment with different combinations of eggs and seeds to find which ones make the strongest embryos. I sometimes even combine two seeds into one to make them stronger."

Mara kept her gaze fixed on the embryo. "Where do you get the seeds and eggs?"

"That lesson can wait until later. For now, I want you to see the beginning and the end."

She looked up at him. "The end?"

He picked up a jar near the middle of the table and held it close to her eyes. "Do you see anything unusual about this one?"

She squinted at the tiny spawn. "It's smaller, and it's not swimming as hard as the others."

"Exactly." Mardon walked the jar to a door on his right. When he opened it, flames shot up from within, and a hot blast of air swept into the room. He dumped the embryo into the fire and slammed the door shut.

Mara pressed her hand against her chest and stifled a gasp. Nausea boiled in her stomach again.

"No use wasting time and space with that one," Mardon said. He pointed at the spawns in the growth chambers she had seen when she came in. "These aren't thriving, so I transported them in here to extract some genetic material. Maybe I can learn what we did wrong."

"Then you'll . . ." She gulped, nodding toward the fiery room.

"Yes. They'll go into the furnace." He counted the jars on the table. "I'm not sure yet, but it looks like five out of the twenty are female. When their gender becomes clear, I'll keep one as a laborer to replace you."

"Replace me? But . . . but . . ." She couldn't even breathe.

Mardon laughed. "I didn't mean you're going to be eliminated! You'll become my assistant. Someone has to do your old job."

Mara exhaled slowly, but her relief quickly vanished. She pinched herself on the arm. How dare she feel relieved? She wasn't going into the furnace, but what about all these poor spawns? Her

UNDERBORNS

lips trembled, yet she managed to talk without squeaking. "Will I have to do both the beginning and the end?"

Mardon tapped one of the jars with his fingertip. "You're really worried about these spawns, aren't you?"

"Shouldn't I be?"

"They're just embryos, not living, breathing, hard workers like you and your friends. But don't worry. I'm not going to ask you to dispose of any. I'll do that." He picked up a fat scroll from the corner of the table and rolled it open. "I'll teach you to keep track of the genetic combinations and note the characteristics of the embryos and the growing spawns. You'll also learn to move the embryos to pots when they're ready to root in soil."

Mara tried to read the last line on the scroll, but it appeared to be just a bunch of indecipherable numbers. "Can I take care of the spawn I have now?"

"You may keep that responsibility along with your new duties." Mardon rolled up the scroll. "He seems to be a good specimen, so you can perform the daily maintenance."

"I've done feedings plenty of times."

He patted her on the head. "Why don't you feed him now? After you're done, you can consider your banishment terminated and go back to your normal labors for the rest of the day. You may tell the other girls about your new position in the control room, if you wish, but they may not join you here. You know the penalty for anyone who enters this room without permission."

Mara firmed her chin. She didn't want to utter the words. Acacia had haunted her dreams for too many nights, and she didn't want anyone else to suffer like that.

Mardon nodded toward the door. "After the feeding, go back to the quarry level. I'll see you here in the morning."

Mara walked out without a word. With the image of Acacia's terrified face searing her mind, she knew a round of nightmares would torment her again tonight.

105

The light from the control room guided her to the lantern shelf. She picked up a lantern and mechanically struck two flint stones together to light it, listening to the sound of the control room door snapping shut and the lock wheel clicking as it spun around. Plodding in a daze toward her growth chamber, she remembered to pick up a jar of plant food from the spawns' pantry as she passed by.

Her stomach grumbled. "Quiet," she scolded. "There's nothing in there for you to eat, unless you're hungry for ground-up worm guts." Her stomach churned again. "Yeah, I know. Our dinner won't be much better."

When she arrived at the growth chamber, her spawn grinned. Mara jumped up to the hearth. "Are you happy to see me?" She opened the jar and angled it toward the plant. "I have something new for you. I'm going to teach you to eat through your mouth!" She dipped her finger into the wet, loamy goop and smeared a dab across the spawn's tiny lips. The little plant moved his mouth, allowing a narrow slit to open, and Mara pushed a morsel of food in. The spawn's thin smile widened as it smacked its lips together.

Mara laughed. "This is going to be easy! You have to be the smartest spawn ever!"

When she finished the feeding, she caressed his green cheek. "Good night," she whispered. The spawn's lips stretched into a yawn, his eyelets fluttered, and he seemed to drift into sleep.

Mara kissed the top of his pod, then dashed out of the growth chamber. She bolted through the corridor and into the elevation shaft, grabbing a cudgel from the shaft's platform floor. After rapping on a metal plate that hung from the wall, she shouted into a tube that ran down the shaft. "Chazaq! It's Mara. I need to go down three levels."

The platform eased downward. As the descent paused intermittently, Mara imagined the huge giant at the bottom letting the rope slide through his massive hands, grabbing it every few seconds to keep her from plummeting all the way to the brick-making kilns, a forbidden zone for all the girls.

Sulfur fumes assaulted her nose, intensifying by the second. When she reached the third quarry level, she jumped out and swiveled her head. A glow from the nearby magma river illuminated the enormous cavern, but it flowed behind a granite wall, safely away from her sensitive eyes.

"Paili!" she called. "Are you down here?" Three girls walked by, each carrying a bucket of wet rocks, but only one turned to look at Mara. With her glazed eyes and dirty chin and sweat dripping from her stringy hair, she seemed more dead than alive.

Mara pulled her coif from her pocket and mopped her brow. The heat was more oppressive than usual. "Paili!" she called again, tying her coif and stuffing her hair underneath. "Has anyone seen Paili?"

One girl poked her reddish head out from behind a stone column. "Washing." She formed her words carefully. "Paili . . . is . . . washing."

Mara knelt and untied a cloth from the girl's ankle. "Taalah, hold still while I have a look at that cut." The girl's leg trembled, but Mara held it firm as she eyed a finger-length gash. "It's still oozing blood, but I think it's healing." She reconfigured the cloth to place a clean spot on the wound and tied it securely. "Make sure you soak your ankle in the sulfur springs tonight and wash out the bandage."

Taalah nodded and pointed. "Paili . . . come . . . now."

Mara rose to her feet. Down in the quarry, a little girl skipped along a stony path that ran between a pair of shallow trenches, clutching the sides of her too-long inner shirt as she bounced toward them.

Mara waved at her. "Paili!"

The little girl glanced up and spread out her arms. "Mara!" She ran across a narrow rock bridge that spanned the closer trench and

107

lunged into Mara's arms. "You back!" she cried, nuzzling Mara's waist.

Mara laid a hand on Paili's dark wet hair. "Were you playing in the water?"

Paili shook her head, but when Mara glared at her, her head's back and forth motion slowly changed to up and down.

"Where's your over-tunic?"

Paili pointed at the closer trench.

Mara groaned. "Oh, Paili! What am I going to do with you? It's a good thing Nabal didn't see you." She glanced around the cavern. "Where is he, anyway?"

Paili stomped once on the ground. "Brick room. He . . . back soon."

Mara fished in Paili's pocket and jerked out her coif. "He's going to catch you someday, and you'll be chiseling out growth chambers until you wrinkle up and die!" She tied the coif back on Paili's head and gestured toward the trench. "Come on. Let's dig up some magnetite."

She slid down the short slope and grabbed up the dirty, wrinkled tunic. When Paili joined her, Mara pushed the girl's outer garment over her head and tried to smooth it out, but her hand touched a sticky spot on Paili's collar. She drew her fingers close to her eyes. "Blood?" She spun Paili around, pulled her collar away from her neck, and peeked down her back. She gritted her teeth and growled. "Did Nabal do this? Did he whip you?"

Paili nodded, whimpering.

"And he told you to wash the blood to hide it, right?"

Paili nodded again.

Mara released Paili's collar and kissed her cheek. Tightening both her fists, she hissed, "Someday I'm going to kill that stupid dung-eater." She snatched up a nearby bucket and glanced at the few small pebbles covering the bottom. "Was he mad because you're behind on your quota?"

108

"No . . . find," Paili said, turning up her palms. "All gone."

Mara dug through Paili's pocket. "Where's your locater?"

Paili tucked her hair under her coif. "It . . . not work."

"Here it is." Mara pulled out a glass disk and laid it in her palm, gently swirling the metal filings inside. "It seems all right to me." She took Paili's hand. "Come on. Let's find the biggest strike ever. Maybe Naamah will give us a fig cake with dinner."

Paili grinned. "Fig cakes!"

Mara eyed the disk while slogging along the trench. As they passed by a trio of laborers digging into the slope, her leg brushed against a kneeling girl and knocked her into a pile of soot. "Oops!" Mara reached down to help the girl up. "I'm sorry!"

The other girl straightened and slapped Mara's cheek. "You are bad!" she said, pushing her finger into Mara's chest. "Acacia was good!"

Rage boiled, sending a surge of stinging heat through Mara's wounded cheek. "Qadar!" she growled, raising a fist, but when Qadar covered her face with trembling hands, Mara let her arm flop to the side. She turned and strode farther down the trench. "Come on, Paili. Let's go to the new dig area. I doubt anyone's gone there yet."

As she marched on, Paili's gentle hum lilting behind her, the trench sank into a darker region of the cavern. The air grew cold, and the light faded, almost too dim to continue, but as they rounded a curve, new light poured through tiny holes in the floor up ahead. She stooped and signaled for Paili to join her.

The little girl huddled against her side. "Cold!"

"Stay close to me." Mara hugged Paili and pointed at the holes. "I thought the light meant that the magma river flowed right under us. I guess it doesn't, or it'd be a lot warmer in here." She tapped on the rocks and listened. "Sounds solid enough."

Paili wrapped both arms around Mara's waist. "Go back. . . . I scared."

"It's okay." Mara pushed on the ground with her free hand. The rocky layer bent downward, and small cracks etched jagged streaks in every direction. "Hmmm . . . Maybe it's not so solid after all." Grunting under the Paili-sized load, Mara pivoted on her knees and headed back. "I think we'd better—"

Suddenly the floor crumbled away. "Whoooaaa!" Mara slid into a gaping hole with Paili still latched to her waist. Mara clawed at the sloping sides until her fingers snagged something solid, keeping her from sliding any farther. Pain rifled through her arms as she and Paili dangled over a seemingly bottomless pit.

"Paili!" she screamed. "Hang on!"

THE ABYSS

Paili's arms tightened around Mara's waist, nearly squeezing her breath away. Grunting and pulling, Mara inched higher. Ignoring her throbbing shoulder, she lunged upward, and her fingers groped for a new handhold until they finally found a sturdy ridge. As she dragged their bodies higher, streams of light flowed past her eyes like windblown fog, filtering into the slope and disappearing. Sounds of snapping arose from below, like hungry crocodiles vaulting to catch hold of her feet. Mara lunged again and caught the upper lip of the pit with one hand, then the other.

"Paili! Climb out!"

Paili clambered up Mara's back and jumped from her shoulders to solid ground. Dropping to her knees, she grabbed Mara behind her upper arms and pulled much harder than seemed possible for a little girl. Mara dug her feet into the slope and scrambled to safety, then rolled to the ground, puffing.

Paili laid a hand on Mara's cheek. "You okay?"

Mara rubbed her aching shoulder. "I think I'm okay." She sat up and looked her in the eye. "What about you?"

"I . . . bleeding again."

Mara scanned her body. "Where?"

Paili showed her a cut on her elbow. "Here."

Mara eyed it closely. "It's not too bad." She looked over Paili's shoulder at the pit a mere two steps away. She pushed Paili gently to the side and crawled slowly to the edge.

The ground near the pit seemed sturdy now, so she inched close and peered into the hole. Streams of light rose and fell as if something down below inhaled and exhaled radiant energy. With each rhythmic pulse, some of the light disappeared into spots on the wall, sucked in by some kind of mysterious force.

Mara slid her fingers down the side and touched one of the spots. It felt smooth and hard, like a polished stone. While probing the surface, she caught the edge, and the stone shifted. Another stream of light flowed up, weaved between her fingers, and disappeared into the stone. She pried it loose and laid it in her palm. Fitting snugly between the heel of her hand and the base of her fingers, a multifaceted jewel glittered at her, a faint beam of light emanating from one side.

Paili touched it with her fingertip. "Pretty!"

Mara closed her fist. "Yes, but what is it?"

Paili shrugged her shoulders. As Mara rose to her feet, a low moan drifted up from the pit. Both girls jumped back, clutching each other. A new chill ran across Mara's skin, and she inched farther away.

Paili hung on to her elbow, shivering, while Mara stroked her hair. "I think we'll look for magnetite somewhere else, okay?"

"Far . . . away."

After several more steps backwards, Mara turned and held Paili's hand. "If we tell Morgan about the pit and the gem, maybe we won't have to make quota today."

"Fig cakes?" Paili asked.

Mara strode forward, peering through the dimness. "Let's not push it. I'm just hoping we don't get whipped."

Mara and Paili slid into the warm spring, each girl finding a place to sit so that the soothing water covered her dirty, scraped shoulders.

With a flickering lantern at her feet, Morgan sat on a rocky ledge next to the pool, holding the gem in her fingers and examining it carefully. "A deep pit, you say? How deep?"

Mara reached for her outer tunic and pulled it into the bath with her. "I couldn't see the bottom." She scrubbed her tunic in the bubbling water. "It was strange," she said, looking up at Morgan. "Light streamed up and down, and some of it got sucked into that gem."

"Very interesting." Morgan drew the gem up to her eyes. "Did you notice anything else?"

"I did." Mara turned to Paili and examined the whip marks on her back. "Oh, Paili! How could Nabal be so cruel to a little girl?" She squeezed water from a sponge, gently sprinkling the wounds as she looked up again at Morgan. "Did you see this?"

Morgan pressed her lips together and nodded. "Nabal will be terminated. We have a new giant ready to replace him—actually a third giant we will call Nabal."

"A third Nabal?"

"I'm afraid so. The first one died the night after he whipped you. But they are identical, so I fear the new one will be just as stupid as the first two. Still, if I show him the remains of his predecessor, perhaps he will not be as cruel."

"Wow! I didn't even realize you switched them." Mara shivered, but it was a comforting shiver. "Anyway, we did notice something else, a horrible moaning sound, like someone down in the pit was terribly sad, like maybe he was lost."

Morgan clenched the gem so tightly her knuckles turned white, but her voice remained calm. "Did it speak any words you could understand?"

Mara shook her head. "We didn't stay long. It was pretty scary."

113

"I quite understand." Morgan nodded toward the tunnel that led to their sleeping quarters and held up the corners of two large cloths. "Here's a sheet for each of you. After you wash out your clothes, hang them in the breezeway and go straight to bed. Naamah will bring dinner to you later."

Paili clapped her hands. "Fig cakes!"

Morgan knelt by the pool and laid her palm on Mara's head, her voice so soft it was almost drowned by the bubbling spring. "Take care not to tell Mardon about the pit. I know how important Paili is to you"—her eyes turned fiery red—"and how important Acacia was to you."

R aising a lantern to light the way, Mara led Paili back to their hovel, a chest-high dugout in the stone wall. With her free hand clinging to her wrapped sheet, she ducked low and climbed down into their sanctum. Although their little sand-stuffed mats were no thicker than a finger, when Mara tucked herself into her individual cleft in the rock, she always felt cozy, far removed from stupid giants and their stinging whips, glad to forget about mining magnetite in stifling heat, at least for the night.

She lay on her mat and tucked her sheet around her body. "Are you warm, Paili?"

"No," came the voice from the other cleft. "Hungry."

"It shouldn't be long. Morgan promised—"

"Time to eat," a sweet voice called from the corridor. "I hear someone wanted fig cakes." Naamah squeezed into the hovel and handed each girl a bread bowl filled with orange mash. A brown fig cake floated on top like a hunk of granite bobbing in a magma river.

"Enjoy the treat," Naamah sang as she left the hovel.

Mara picked up her cake and let the mash drip from its edge. Naamah had never prepared appetizing meals, but this was better than nothing and more appetizing than a lot of the gunk they had eaten lately.

After several minutes of quiet chewing, Mara pinched the last
bite of her bread bowl and threw it toward a fist-sized hole in the
wall at the back side of their dugout. "Don't forget to save a piece
for Qatan!" she called.

Paili mumbled through her mouthful of food. "He not hungry."

"Come on, Paili. Even a mouse needs to eat."

Paili swallowed and sang out, "Story now!"

Mara drooped her shoulders. "Oh, Paili, I'm so tired tonight,
I don't think I can—" Mara suddenly lifted her head. "Do you
hear that humming?"

"Naamah," Paili said.

"Whew! Her timing is perfect again."

Their petite mistress crawled down into the dugout with layers of clothes draped over her arm. "They're dry," she said, handing each of them their inner and outer garments.

Mara slipped on her inner tunic and folded her outer dress
into a pillow.

"Would you girls like a song tonight?" Naamah asked.

"Song!" Paili chirped.

Mara searched Naamah's eyes. What could be the reason for
such a rare treat? "Sure. Why not?"

Naamah patted Mara's folded dress. "Lie down, and I will sing
you to sleep."

Mara laid her head on her dress and closed her eyes, letting her
mind relax. She might as well enjoy the song instead of questioning Naamah's sincerity. With all the new happenings of the day,
she needed something to help her unwind, and she wanted to be
well rested for her new job in the morning.

Naamah's smooth contralto crooned in Mara's ears.

Alone in caves through darkest nights,
A bitter girl is mining ore,
With pick and bucket gathering rocks,
Confined to chains forevermore.

115

No life, no love, no mother's arms,
Forever empty you will yearn.
The friends you love will fade to ash,
And you will see them fall and burn.

These caverns held the judging flow
Where floods awaited God's command
To spring into the worlds above
And drown the souls who dared to stand.

So now these caves are empty tombs
For hopeless slaves who chisel stones;
Far worse than death as on their knees
These ghosts unearth their sisters' bones.

116

Relinquish now all hope for grace,
For grace and mercy spew their scorn
At girls who live and die in caves
And those who dwell as underborns.

Naamah repeated the verses, each one filling Mara with sorrow. She couldn't protest. Every word was true. There really was no hope, and her only real friend was gone forever. Grace didn't exist. Mercy and hope were merely words in Mardon's dictionary, flat and lifeless.

As the lyrics passed through Mara's mind a third time, the song faded into oblivion, replaced by a fuzzy, dream-like voice. She knew she had begun dreaming, but as the dream progressed, it grew so real, she lost all consciousness of anything but the image before her.

"We'd better go," Acacia said. "If Morgan finds us, we're goners."

Mara stuffed a small loaf of bread into her pocket and handed one to Acacia. "I'm not leaving without enough food. Paili won't get her rations if she doesn't come to the dining chamber."

Acacia held out the loaf. "She can't eat this much."

"Who knows how long she'll be sick?" Mara pushed the loaf into Acacia's pocket. "I can't risk coming back to get more."

"The bell for roll call already rang." Acacia pulled Mara's arm. "Let's go!"

Mara pulled back. "I have to get the bread to Paili!"

"Roll call first, then we'll sneak out and feed her."

The two girls ran through the tunnel, the lantern in Acacia's hand guiding the way. After riding the platform down to the labor level, they hustled to their places in line, side by side.

Nabal glared at them and raised his whip. "Where were you?"

"Tending to Paili," Mara said. "She's sick."

Nabal, towering at least four feet taller than any of the girls, glanced over at Paili's empty place in line. He cracked the whip across Mara's shoulder, tearing her skin.

"Owwww!" Mara dropped to her knees. As she fell, her loaf tumbled out of her pocket.

Nabal's eyes widened. Acacia snatched up the loaf and took a bite from the end. "I was hungry," she said, mumbling through her mouthful.

"That was your loaf?" Nabal asked. "Where did you get it?"

"The pantry," Acacia said casually. She pulled out a loaf from her own pocket. "Want one?"

"You're not allowed in the pantry!" Nabal roared, raising his whip again. "I will—"

"Stop!" a new voice interrupted. "What's the problem here?"

Everyone turned. Morgan, her brow bent low, strode toward the line. Mara rose to her feet, trying to hide her pain.

Nabal lowered his whip and pointed at Acacia. "A food thief, Mistress."

Morgan held out her hands, and Acacia dropped the loaves into them. "You stole the bread?" Morgan asked.

Acacia nodded. Morgan walked slowly past her and touched the wound on Mara's shoulder as it bled through her outer tunic.

117

"Alone?" Morgan rubbed Mara's blood between her finger and thumb.

Acacia's eyes grew wide. She spoke quickly. "Nabal is a fool. He hit Mara when he should have hit me." She pressed her thumb against her chest. "I stole the bread. I should be punished."

Morgan brushed breadcrumbs from the material around Mara's pocket. "I see." Taking Nabal's whip, she wound it up around her hand, her gaze locked on Mara. "Nabal, dismiss the laborers to the trenches and come with me. Bring these two girls with you."

"Get to work!" Nabal bellowed. He then grabbed Mara and Acacia by their wrists and followed Morgan as she headed down a sloping tunnel. Nabal's powerful grip seemed to squeeze the blood from Mara's arm and shoot it up to her head until her brain pounded against her skull.

Morgan finally exited the tunnel through a tall, wide door. Nabal half dragged the girls through it and stood them on a spacious ledge that overlooked a deep, fiery chasm. As Mara blinked at the bright magma river below, she swallowed, hoping she didn't look too scared.

Morgan eyed them both. She tore off Acacia's coif and ran her fingers through the long tresses that fell to her waist. "If it wasn't for the length of your hair"—she yanked Mara's coif away, letting her hair fall to her shoulders—"and for Mara's wound, I wouldn't be able to tell you two apart."

Morgan hooked her arm around Mara's elbow and pulled her to the edge of the cliff. "Stand here," she ordered.

Mara bent her knees, wobbling in place and hugging herself as she kept her eyes on Acacia.

In the same way, Morgan walked Acacia to the edge, then, keeping hold of her arm, she glared at Mara. "Your friend was ready to take whatever punishment you deserved. Do you think that's a noble gesture?"

Mara couldn't answer. She trembled harder and began crying.

"I'll show you how noble it is. Watch and learn." Morgan released her grip on Acacia and shoved her with both hands, sending her over the ledge.

Acacia plummeted toward the river of fire, her arms flailing and her cries piercing Mara's ears. "Maraaaaa!"

Her body splashed in the magma, silencing her forever. Mara fell to her knees and sobbed, coughing, heaving, until she collapsed and fainted.

"Acacia!" Mara yelled, sitting up in bed. She bumped her head on the stone that covered her dugout.

"Mara?" Paili called out. "You okay?"

Mara rubbed her scalp. "I'm all right. Go back to sleep." She slid out of bed, but as she tiptoed for the dugout opening, a scratching noise arose from the wall somewhere behind her. Spinning on the balls of her feet, she faced the direction of the sound and stared into the darkness, listening intently.

Scritch, scritch.

Mara inched closer. Could it be Qatan? She had never seen the little scavenger, but the bread she saved for him always disappeared. And now, even if she could stay quiet enough not to spook him, it was too dark to catch a glimpse of either whisker or tail.

A wisp of light passed by the inside of the hole, fast and fleeting. Lowering herself to hands and knees, Mara scooted quietly toward the base of the wall. She held her breath and imagined the layout of the caverns in her mind's eye, but when she tried to draw the room just beyond her hovel, she couldn't think of what might be there. She had always assumed it was an unused cave, the kind of place Qatan might want for his home.

The light came again, and this time it stayed, illuminating the hole in the wall.

Scritch, scritch.

A pair of fingers poked out, reaching, probing. Finally, an entire hand emerged, and the index finger swept Mara's bread morsel into its grip. As the hand slowly pulled back, Mara lunged forward. "Wait!"

The hand stopped for a second, then slid back farther.

"Wait!" Mara repeated. "Who are you?"

The hand disappeared. Mara pounded her fist on the wall. "Who's there?"

A muffled male voice replied. "My name is Elam."

"Elam?" Mara laid her cheek on the floor and spoke directly into the hole. "My name's Mara. Are you one of the brick-making boys?"

"I am a brick maker," came the reply. "But I am the only one."

"I heard there were at least two. What happened to the other boy?"

His reply seeped through like a quiet breeze. "We don't need as many bricks as before, so she terminated him."

"She? Do you mean Morgan?"

"Yes. She told Nabal to beat him with his whip until he died, and they made me watch."

"How awful!"

"I still hear his screams in my nightmares."

Mara sighed. "I know what you mean." The image of Acacia flailing toward the molten river flickered through her mind again. She shook her head to expel the unwanted memories. "How did you learn to speak so well? Most of the girl laborers can hardly speak at all."

"I could talk pretty well when they brought me here, but—"

"Brought you? Aren't you an underborn?"

"No. I was taken from my parents when I was little and made a slave here, but I learned how to talk better by listening to you."

"To me?"

"Yes. I listen to the stories you tell Paili."

A strange tickle fluttered in Mara's stomach, and a smile slowly spread across her face. "You do?"

"Not every night, and I never said anything, because I didn't want you to get in trouble, but it seemed safe enough to sit and listen." He paused for a moment. "I like to hear about dragons flying through the sky."

"Me . . ." Mara swallowed hard. "Me too."

Her heart pounded through another pause. Finally, Elam continued, his voice lower and faltering. "I'd . . . I'd like to see the sky again . . . someday."

"And a dragon," Mara added.

Elam's voice perked up. "My father used to tell me about dragons. He even knew their names, and I made up stories about them."

Silence descended again, so heavy that Mara's own breathing sounded like the rushing wind in the breezeway. "Do you miss your parents?" she asked.

"Uh-huh. I miss them a lot."

"At least you *had* parents," Mara said, furrowing her brow. "I never had any, so I don't even have memories to cherish."

"Memories are a curse," Elam countered. "Losing something you had is worse than never having it at all." He let out a deep, piteous sigh. "But I guess you wouldn't know. You've never had anything, have you?"

"No . . . I haven't." Mara's lip quivered. She inserted her fingers into the hole. "Elam, please keep coming to listen. It'll be good knowing you're there."

Elam's fingers meshed with hers. "I'll come, but I can't talk until after Nabal drinks himself to sleep. That's when I go hunting for food. He eats most of my dinner."

The touch of his hand sent a wave of warmth through Mara's body, radiating from head to toe and making her heart pound. She could barely squeak. "I'll try to bring more food for you. Stay away from Nabal's whip."

"I will." His fingers withdrew, and the light faded away.

Mara rolled to a sitting position and rested against the wall, trying to slow her heart. But it was all so exciting! Elam was the first laborer since Acacia who was smart enough to communicate, and he seemed so warm and friendly. She pulled her knees up to her chest, sighing. Yes, he was friendly . . . and lonely.

She glanced toward the hole, now a curtain of blackness. She imagined the dozens of times Elam must have groped for morsels of food. She had thrown a piece of cheese the first time thinking that a mouse might find that air vent into her hovel. Now that a flesh and blood person hunted there every night, she had to find a way to get as much food to him as she could. After all, working at the brick kilns was the hardest job in the lower worlds, so he was probably always hungry.

Mara rose to her feet. She felt lighter somehow and wide awake, so there was no way she could go back to sleep. She pulled on her outer dress and crawled from the hovel. On the floor across the corridor, a weak light flickered in one of the lanterns that had been lined up for the girls to grab in the morning. Since wakeup call was only about an hour away, she might as well go ahead and report to her new job early.

She lit one of the other lanterns and traced a path to the control room. After turning the lock wheel through its combination, she pushed open the door and padded toward the embryo table.

As she passed by the growth chambers, she glanced at each sad face, pitiful spawns destined to die. When her light fell on the last pod in line, its familiar lips smiled. She lunged toward it and caressed its strong, thick stalk. "My spawn!"

Another light flashed on. Mara spun around. Mardon stood over her, his lantern rocking back and forth in his hand. "What are you doing here?"

She pressed down her wrinkled clothes. "Reporting for work."

Mardon stretched and yawned. "Is it morning already? I guess I fell asleep on the floor."

122

"Why is my spawn here? Is he—"

"Don't worry. He's not going to be terminated. I moved him so you could take care of him while you worked here."

"Oh." She laid her hand against her chest. "Thank you."

Mardon set his lantern on the worktable and rolled open the big scroll. "How many hours is Morgan allotting to this project?"

"She decided to let me come all day."

"Really? That's a surprise. I was hoping for just a few hours, but all day is even better."

"She even assigned Paili to food preparation." Mara bit her tongue. Maybe it wasn't a good idea to tell him that. She didn't want to explain the reason for Morgan's kindness. "Could Morgan be in a good mood for a change?"

"Not likely." Mardon's eyes moved toward the door, then returned to Mara. "Just watch your back. She's probably up to something."

"Yessir."

"Well," he said, waving toward the scroll, "let's get started. You have a lot to learn."

123

Mara ran her finger along a line of numbers and, with a sharpened piece of graphite, added a new one to the end. "Okay," she whispered to herself, "Mardon spliced Samyaza with Canaan for that set, and he blended those with"—she pointed to another line—"with the normal human pair, giving us . . ." She bit her tongue and scratched down a long string of numbers before setting down her graphite and wiping her brow. "Whew! This is complicated!"

After rolling up the scroll, she turned to her spawn and smiled. "I think I have it figured out . . . uh . . . what should I call you, anyway? You need a name." She rested her chin in her hand. "How about Yereq? It means green. If you like it—"

"Mara." Mardon stomped into the room, his hand cupped in a cradle.

Mara sat up straight. "Yessir?"

"I have something to show you," he said, extending his hand.

She tiptoed up to him and peeked over his fingers. A red, glassy egg fit perfectly in his palm. "What's that?"

"I'm not sure. I found it when we were digging the foundation for a fountain near the tower. I think it's a device that allows communication with Elohim."

"With Elohim? The one who flooded the upper world?"

"Exactly."

She scowled at the egg. "Isn't he the one you called a tyrant in your scrolls?"

"Shhh!" Mardon covered the egg with his hand. "Like it or not, Elohim is in control, so I want to learn to communicate with him. That's one of the reasons we're building the tower."

"I read about the tower. It sounds wonderful!"

Mardon looked up at the ceiling and sighed. "It is magnificent. The greatest accomplishment the world has ever seen. We hope the tower will get Elohim's attention, because tradition says he lives in the sky."

"What will you say to him?"

"Oh, not me," he said, laying a hand on his chest. "My father will speak to him."

"King Nimrod?"

"He wants to make a treaty with Elohim in order to prevent another disaster. For our part, we'll make whatever sacrifice Elohim requires if he will only agree to speak to the rest of us through my father. The people are bound to listen and comply when their own king gives the orders."

She pointed at the egg. "What makes you think this thing can talk to Elohim, and why are you showing it to me?"

"Listen carefully." He uncovered the egg and held it close to his mouth. "Elohim? Are you listening? Please speak to me."

Red fog boiled inside the crystalline egg, swirling until it formed the shape of an angry-looking eye. The scarlet pupil pulsed as it spoke in gruff verse.

This place accursed in demons' hands,
Where giants grow from pits of hell,
Cannot contain the prophet's eye
Until the maiden grasps its shell.

The maid endowed with nimble mind,
An oracle of fire born,
Can speak to me of toil and pain,
And I will raise the friend she mourns.

Until she comes with mind unspoiled,
Untaught in ways of God by men,
My words of knowledge silent lie;
The lips of God are sealed again.

The eye faded away, and as the fog dissipated, Mardon held the egg out for Mara to see. "That's what it says every time. Since it refers to the lips of God, I thought it might be a way to communicate with him. Imagine the effect on the people if we constructed a temple at the top of the tower and placed this as the mouthpiece of Elohim. The city would be the capital of the world, and our control over the people would be established forever."

Mara half closed one eye. "You still haven't told me where I come in."

"Well, obviously it doesn't want to talk to me, but when I realized how smart you are, I thought you might be the maid of nimble mind."

125

Mara touched the egg with her finger. A splotch of red on the inside seemed to follow her fingertip as she moved it along the surface. "What does 'oracle of fire born' mean?"

"I have no idea." He rolled the egg into her hands. "Speak to it and see what happens."

Mara brought it close to her lips, keeping her eyes on Mardon as she spoke. "Is anyone in there?"

A sense of warmth radiated into her hand. She stared at the glass, and once again, red fog swirled within the transparent shell. Halos of crimson light pulsed from the center, ring after ring of radiant energy passing over her skin, warming her whole body.

When the eye appeared, its pupil seemed awash in a softer, steady scarlet. It poured out new words that chanted in joyous rhythm, reminding Mara of a story Mardon once told of his father singing while bouncing him on his knee.

126

The maid of fire has come at last
To set the upper world aright.
Ascend dear girl to lands above
And cast the tower in holy light.

As the eye faded away again in the fog, the egg whispered three final words. "Make haste, child!" Mara gazed at the red glass, her skin still tingling from the warm radiance.

Mardon clapped his hands. "Did you hear that? Elohim wants to use this egg in the tower, just as I thought! He will speak from the tower and establish my father's kingdom!"

Mara held the egg in her fingertips. "I didn't hear it say anything about his kingdom."

"What else could it mean? Elohim wants to establish his rule through my father and protect the people from further punishment."

Mara extended the egg toward him. "Then why did it want me to talk to it instead of you?"

"We'll find out soon enough." Mardon pulled down the bottom hem of his outer shirt, smoothing the material. "Come. We'll go immediately. The sun will be too bright for you, so you'll have to wear some kind of hood to shield your eyes."

She pulled her coif from her pocket and held it up. "I have my veil."

"Oh, yes. For the magma river. That should work fine."

She tied it on and began pushing her hair underneath. "When will we return?"

"It depends on what Elohim says to my father. Could be soon; could be later."

"Will my spawn be okay?"

"Who cares about your spawn?" Mardon twisted his sandal on the floor as if squishing a bug. "He's expendable. He's nothing compared to the glory of what we are about to accomplish!"

"But I don't want him to die!"

He grabbed her hand and pulled her toward the control room exit. "Come now. Let's not play the fool! Do you have a safe place for the egg?"

Mara nodded. As she carefully placed it in her dress pocket, she pressed her lips together. The thought of her spawn being suspended in his new chamber without being fed tore her apart.

Mardon grabbed a lantern and flung open the door. "We'll have to find Morgan first and make up some kind of excuse for taking you to the top. I can't open the lower portal without her."

"Portal?"

"Too complicated to explain fully. There is no physical path to the surface, so we have to pass through a dimensional window. You see, there are multiple dimensions—" He sighed and pulled her faster. "Never mind. Since you're friends with Elohim now, just pray that my father likes you. Like all good kings, with all the pressures on him, he can be . . . temperamental."

"Like Morgan?"

127

He jerked her wrist hard, lifting her to her tiptoes. "No! Not like Morgan! My father is gentle and kind to his friends, but he has to be harsh with fools and insubordinates, or his enemies will think him spineless." He raised a tightening fist. "No king will survive for long if he doesn't crush rebellion."

The pain from his vise-like grip burned across Mara's skin. "You're hurting me!"

"Oh." He released her and brushed his palm on his shirt. "Sorry. I got carried away."

Mara rubbed her wrist. She thought of a dozen snide comments to make about the gentility of Mardon's father, but she didn't want to risk missing out on visiting the upper lands. "It's okay," she whispered.

Mardon patted her on the back. "We'll go and see Morgan first, then the endless sky."

A PRAYER FOR DRAGONS

Makaidos stood on his haunches and gazed at the horizon. Even from so many miles away, he could see Nimrod's Tower looming over the land, like a fist with a rigid finger pointed heavenward. Black smoke rose all around its base, the fires of belching kilns mixing with the foul gases of bubbling tar pits.

"Brick upon brick"—he snorted a spray of steam—"evil is growing in the city faster than I thought possible."

"A monument to the pride of men," Thigocia grumbled as she lay at her mate's side. "They are supposed to be scattering and filling the earth, but obviously even Noah has no influence over them any longer."

Makaidos sighed. "True. Most of the sons of Adam are not worthy of our service to them, but the faithful remnant still give me hope."

"We must keep praying as Noah taught us." Thigocia laid her head on the ground. "Your father would want you to keep your eyes on the Maker."

129

"The Maker is the god of men," Makaidos said, "and we are but dust of the earth, coarse pegs in a cosmic game. Why should the ever-living one care about those destined to return to dust?"

"Nonsense! What kind of talk is that from the king of the dragons?"

"Sensible talk. Down-to-earth talk. But it matters little. I am content to be his lowly peg." He bowed his head, letting his snout dip so close to the ground, his hot breath scattered the sandy soil.

Thigocia's tail moved to his brow and stroked it gently. "Are you really content, my love?"

Makaidos lifted his head and, unable to resist Thigocia's probing stare, gazed into her deep red eyes. Her powerful mind seemed to penetrate his own, as though she could read his every thought. "Perhaps not. My joy has burned like dry brush."

Thigocia sighed and looped her tail around his. "When our new one is born, you will feel joy again."

"How can I feel joy?" Makaidos pulled his tail away. "Goliath had no reason to turn against Noah. His actions defy all logic. By refusing to serve even the faithful humans, he has turned against us as well."

"You and I know that, but Goliath acts on instinct, on what he feels inside. The people of Shinar have given him reason to despise mankind, have they not? The true followers of Noah are so few now, look where they are forced to live. Rats in caves. That's what they have become."

Makaidos couldn't answer. He just lifted his chin and gazed at the sky. A smaller dragon glided down, sunlight filtering through her honey-colored wings. She landed gracefully in front of Makaidos and Thigocia and bowed her head to each of them. "Father. Mother. Greetings."

Thigocia touched the young dragon's face with the tip of her wing. "Welcome home, Roxil."

Makaidos curled his neck around his daughter's and winked at Thigocia. "Perhaps joy comes in many packages."

130

Roxil backed away. "Packages? What are you talking about?"

"A private joke between your mother and me," Makaidos said, smiling. "How was your patrol last night?"

"All was quiet. No incidents." Roxil tilted her head. "Why?"

"I was curious. I felt a twinge of danger around midnight. Something in the direction of Noah's dwellings. Do you remember seeing anything unusual at that time?"

Roxil's tail twitched and tapped the ground nervously. "Actually, I was talking to Goliath for a little while."

"While in flight?"

Roxil half closed her eyes. "No."

Makaidos thrashed the ground with his tail. "You left your patrol without relief?"

Roxil lowered her head and glared at him. "Just for a few minutes. The human village can survive for a half hour without us guarding it like winged mama bears!"

"You know they count on us for protection. Noah's people are in constant danger from Nimrod's raiders."

131

"You think I care nothing for the humans?" Plumes of smoke rose from Roxil's snout. "I will have you know that I uncovered trouble brewing in the city. Nimrod has marshaled a police force to capture more laborers for the tower construction. A dragon is his chief enforcer, one I have never seen."

Thigocia rose to her haunches. "Never seen? How can that be? You know every dragon in existence."

Roxil pawed the ground, sketching a crude dragon's body in the sand. "He is Father's size, redder, with longer spines at the end of his tail."

Makaidos locked gazes with Thigocia. "No one in our brood bears such features," he said.

Roxil scratched away her sketch. "I know what I saw."

Makaidos stretched out his wings. "I think I should visit Nimrod's Tower to see who this dragon is and what is afoot. The stories of corruption are too heart-wrenching to believe."

"I wish I could come with you," Thigocia said.

"And I, as well." Makaidos eyed the smoke rising around the tower. "If Nimrod's soldiers give me trouble, I could use a warrior at my side."

Roxil thumped her tail. "I will go with you, Father. I am not tired, and I am ready for battle."

"Nimrod's men are too dangerous." Thigocia extended a wing toward Roxil. "She is not skilled enough to fight them."

Roxil turned to her father. Her eyes flamed, but she stayed silent.

"I think a certain daughter needs an extra mission to atone for her mistake last night." Makaidos raised a wing over his daughter's neck. "A reconnaissance mission is an important part of her training, and I will be able to judge if the danger is too great."

"She has never been in battle," Thigocia countered. "The first sign of danger could be a hurled spear, and she might never see it coming."

Makaidos lifted his other wing and rested it on his mate's back. "If you had avoided battles because you had never been in one, my dear, you would never have become a warrior."

"My own past has returned to haunt me." Thigocia laid her head down again. "Would tears help me win the argument? After all, I am a pregnant mother."

Roxil let out a laugh but quickly stifled it.

Makaidos curled his neck with Thigocia's and whispered, "Dry your tears. I will take care of her. We will stay at Shem's grottoes for the night and enter the city at dawn. Surveying the tower before the soldiers roll out of bed will be the best way to avoid a conflict."

Makaidos nodded at Roxil, giving her a firm, commander's glare. "Make ready, warrior." A smile almost broke through, but he managed to squelch it.

Roxil vaulted into the air, beating her wings as she soared upward. She bent her neck toward the earth, shouting, "What are you waiting for? An invitation?"

132

Makaidos shook his head at Thigocia. "Your daughter is as funny as a spear in the belly."

Thigocia sighed. "I know. She learned her jokes from you."

Makaidos smiled and winked, then launched himself into the air. After trumpeting a shrill note, he shouted, "You're a pretty good flyer for a female."

Roxil spun a one-eighty, zoomed back to her father, and looped again to fly at his side. "For a female? Do you think you can catch me, my dear *old* father?"

Makaidos beat his wings and surged ahead. "I already did!"

Father and daughter soared across the skies, practicing dives and sharp turns as they raced toward a village built in the cliffs of a mountain range. When they drew near, Makaidos glided down to a wide ledge that skirted the mountain about halfway up its face. Shem and Japheth ran out to meet them in full battle gear, sheathed swords on their belts and oval shields resting at their hips. "Thank you for answering the call," Shem said.

"The call?" Makaidos repeated. "What call?"

"A prayer for calling dragons," Japheth explained. "Our father prayed for you to come and join us in battle. Apparently, you heeded God's call without even realizing it." He nodded at Roxil. "And two dragons arrived when we only requested one."

Makaidos dipped his head. "Your faith is strong, as I would expect from a son of Noah."

Shem and Japheth looked at each other, both men shifting uneasily. "I wish that all of Noah's sons would believe his words," Shem said, "but our brother is one of the reasons for the great evil that festers in the city. It seems that he gave Chereb to his grandson Nimrod, and now Nimrod is practically invincible, at least to pedestrian forces like ours. We endured his taxes and his robbers, but last night a kidnapper stole my granddaughter, probably for the Luna temple." He tightened his grip on his sword. "I've already lost a son to him. I will *not* lose another soul!"

"I understand," Makaidos said, gazing out over the plane, "better than you know." He surveyed the tower as it rose in the center of the vast city. "So you need an attack from the air, and you called for our help."

"Yes." Japheth stooped and assembled a pile of rocks, then used his hands to illustrate flying maneuvers. "But if you swoop low and attack his troops on the ground, he can strike you from the tower. Since Chereb shoots out flames, you won't be able to get anywhere near him."

Makaidos eyed Japheth's hands as they circled his rock pile. "So our first target is the tower itself."

"That was our thought," Shem said. "While you're distracting their main army, we'll bring our troops and crash the northern gate. My granddaughter should be easy to find, but my son has been missing for so long we might have to destroy the entire city to root out his captors."

Roxil raised a foreleg and swiped the air. "Can two dragons knock down such a large building?"

"Not likely," Makaidos said, "but if we call your brothers, I think we can destroy it in a firestorm."

Roxil's ears twitched. "Like the firestorm you told me about in the battles against the Watchers?"

"Yes. I was too young to participate, but I watched my father carefully." Makaidos nudged her flank. "Fetch your brothers and meet me back here."

"With pleasure, Father. I know they will be ready to kill the human cockroaches." Roxil beat her wings and launched into the sky.

When she disappeared into a passing thunderhead, Makaidos turned back to Shem and Japheth. "My daughter tells me of a dragon in Nimrod's forces. What do you know about him?"

Japheth rose to his feet and clapped the dirt from his hands. "I was spying on their army yesterday, and I saw him."

"Did you recognize him?"

"I know exactly who he is, though it seems impossible." Japheth glanced at his brother, who gave him a quick shake of his head.

Makaidos snorted a stream of dancing sparks. "It is not wise to try a dragon's patience. Tell me!"

Shem cleared his throat and nodded toward the cave behind him. "I think you had better speak to my father about this. He can explain what's going on far better than I can."

Without waiting for a response, Japheth ran toward the cave. "I'll tell him you're coming," he called back.

Shem swept his arm toward the gaping arch in the cliff. "Our home is blessed by your visit."

Makaidos dipped his head. "I am the one who is receiving the blessing."

"I must, however, beg your leave." Shem pointed at a dry riverbed at the base of the cliff. Hundreds of men milled about near a cluster of scrub trees. "Our troops are assembling in the valley, and they would charge into battle this very hour if I let them, so I have to calm their passions until your family arrives."

"I understand. Anger is a great motivator, but it is a poor general."

While Shem marched down a sloping path, Makaidos shuffled along the ledge and entered the dim cave, turning on his eye-beams to compensate for the depleted light. After curving around a bend and passing through a lower corridor, he followed a flicker in the distance. Finally, his twin beams fell upon Noah, sitting cross-legged on a mat and leaning back against the cave wall. With a lantern at his side, Japheth was reading from a scroll, while his father nodded his aged head. Then, when he noticed Makaidos, Japheth rolled up the scroll and handed it to his father. With a quick bow, he excused himself from the cave.

Noah lifted his gaze toward Makaidos and smiled. "How long has it been since we've talked, my friend?"

135

Makaidos lay on his belly and sighed. "Too long, Master Noah. I'm afraid that my zeal to serve your tribe has been my poor excuse to neglect our friendship."

Noah raised a gnarled finger. "Still, I have kept my eye on you and your family. As my sons report on your activities, I am able to pray for you and each of your offspring by name."

"And I have returned your kindness by guarding your offspring. Shem and Japheth and their families do honor to your name. You have every reason to be proud of them. You are a father among fathers."

Noah averted his eyes. Shining tears formed in each one. "You honor me too highly. You know that one of my sons has brought this new evil into the world, and I was unable to stop him."

"Ham would not listen to your wise counsel. That was not your fault."

"Wasn't it?" Noah shook his head slowly. "How many times have I asked myself that question? What did I do wrong? What could I have changed to steer him toward faith and righteousness?" He clutched his vest with both hands as if to rend it, but his arms fell weakly into his lap. "After all these years, I have even lost the strength to grieve."

"You have nothing to be ashamed of. You told Ham the truth."

"You're a good friend, always willing to console the bereft." Noah shook a finger at Makaidos. "But you would do well to remember your own words, for a time is coming when you will need them more than I."

"A time of grief, Master Noah? Are you prophesying doom?"

"Merely an observation. Japheth has given me details of his conversations with two of your sons and your eldest daughter, and he and I are both greatly concerned about where their hearts lie."

"Their hearts?"

Noah tapped a finger on his temple. "Actually, their wills. Their allegiances. What is the driving force that motivates their actions?"

"It is supposed to be service to the Maker, who has assigned us to help those still faithful to you. That is why Nimrod's armies have not overrun you already. We have kept the perimeter free of his invaders."

"Free of the squadrons, yes, but not free of the smaller kidnapping bands. I assume you know who was guarding us during the first of those raids."

Makaidos dipped his head toward the floor. "That was my fault. Roxil was too young and inexperienced. I should not have assigned her that task. She is much more qualified now."

"That was the most tragic night for Shem, to be sure. Losing his firstborn son brought him grief beyond description. But there were other nights, other raids."

Makaidos bent his brow. "Are you implying, Master Noah, that I have been complicit with the invaders?"

Noah waved his hand rapidly. "Not you, my friend. I do wish, however, for you to ask yourself this question. You have patrolled our perimeter yourself, as has your mate, hundreds if not thousands of times. How many of those nights have we suffered a breach?"

"There have been none, but we are more experienced. We have battled evil forces for centuries."

"It is not your experience that keeps our homes safe, Makaidos." Noah stood and laid a hand on the dragon's chest. "It is your heart, your passion. You believe in what you are doing. You feel your love for humankind in your blood; you taste it in the air; you dream about it at night; you wake up with passion spilling from the very fire in your breath, for this righteous obsession has enflamed your heart with unquenchable desire to fulfill your vision. But, although you have taught your brood to follow in your footsteps from the time they were younglings, they only go through the motions. Obedient and willing, yes, but they likely don't feel it burning in their souls."

"But they are supposed to feel it," Makaidos countered. "We dragons are made to serve humans. There is no other choice."

137

"True, but don't make the mistake of projecting your own passion on them. Just because they seem to be following, don't assume that their hearts burn with your vision for love and service." Noah sat back down and opened the scroll, angling it toward the lantern. "For I fear that their loyalty could easily be turned."

Makaidos stretched his neck toward the scroll, but not so far as to read it uninvited. "You are implying that there is something I need to know."

"Yes. May I read a summary of a conversation between my son and your daughter?"

Makaidos nodded. "Please do."

Noah's eyes shifted back and forth, scanning the text. "Here it is. Shem had just summoned Roxil to the ledge after her night's patrol." He cleared his throat and began reading. "The she-dragon seemed distracted, nervous. I asked her about the movements of Nimrod's troops, but she said they had camped quietly all night near the riverbank. I then mentioned that our own scouts had seen a pair of Nimrod's bowmen stealing through the thickets near Enoch's grove and asked if she had seen them. She grew irritated, seemingly insulted that I would imply that she had been derelict in her duties. She just flew away without another word. That's when I decided to go from home to home and check on our people and property."

Noah rolled up the journal. "That was this morning, Makaidos. We lost a girl in that raid, so we summoned a council of war. I insisted, though many were skeptical, that we call for your help. I knew you would come, but now that Roxil has arrived with you, there will be great concern among our troops."

Heat surged across Makaidos's scales. "Roxil will fight for our cause valiantly. I will see to that."

"Oh, I believe she will, as long as you are with her. My concern is for what she is doing when you are absent."

"Speak frankly, Master Noah. Do not hold back your thoughts."

"I will, my friend, but first I must give you some warning about what you are going to face, and this is a prophetic word. In the coming days and decades, you will suffer greatly, and you will suffer alone. With the exception of your dear mate and perhaps an offspring or two, everyone you love and cherish will turn against you. They will claim that no one else agrees with you, so you couldn't possibly be right. They will call you arrogant, tyrannical, and even mad. They will say that you are so obsessed with your insane version of truth, that you have abandoned all reason, that you have forsaken logic and clear thinking, that you have given up on those you love because of your neurotic fixation on a divine light that no one else can see."

Makaidos lifted his brow. "Why would loved ones do this to me or anyone else? They know my character. They have seen my integrity."

"Not just your loved ones, Makaidos. The entire world would do it, because character and integrity are not as important to them as acceptance from the masses or as comforting as the false security they receive from not examining their lives." Noah leaned back and sighed. "I know this all too well. My sons and I worked like slaves on a boat for a hundred years while people laughed at us and mocked us. Just as I prophesied concerning you, I was obsessed with obeying a heavenly voice that no one else heard. I saved the future of the planet, but in the process I lost one of my sons. I do not regret the years of coercing my sons to build that monstrosity of a boat. Though even their eyes at times seemed to question my sanity, I have been completely vindicated." He shook his head again, and a tear coursed down his weathered cheek. "But being proven right does not lessen the pain of my loss, for it seems that, in spite of all my efforts, my ark did not keep my own son from drowning."

Makaidos guided a wing tip over Noah's shoulder. "A father cannot be held responsible for the sins of his son. I have heard you say this yourself."

"Responsible?" Noah shook his head. "No. . . . But am I completely innocent just because he has free will? Seeds of rebellion cannot grow unnoticed, and I ignored them." He ran his wrinkled hands through his wispy hair, tears again filling his eyes. "Did zeal for God blind me to the rebellion of my own son? Should I have rebuked him every time he rolled his eyes, every time he grumbled when a parade of people passed by mocking us, calling us fools for wasting our lives on building an ark?" He reached for Makaidos's neck and stroked it lovingly. "Emzara died in sorrow believing Ham was lost forever. Will I go down to Sheol with the same misery haunting me? Is there any hope that a son might turn his heart back to God when he has rejected a salvation he has seen with his own eyes?"

Noah wrapped his arms around Makaidos's neck and wept, his age-spotted head bobbing up and down under the force of his sobs.

140

Makaidos hovered a clawed hand over Noah's back, hesitating to caress the dear old gentleman. Could he really comfort him with such a tough, scaly appendage? Could any dragon truly sympathize with a human? Who could know the heart of a human except for another human?

Makaidos pulled his foreleg back. "I understand," he said softly. "Perhaps I can restore the hearts of my fellow dragons to the Maker and his purpose for us."

Noah lowered his arms and wiped his eyes on his sleeve. "I believe you will, for a messiah is coming, God in flesh, who will rescue mankind. And in the same way, yet another messiah, a human in scales from the fruit of your own body will come to rescue dragonkind."

Makaidos shook his head. "Master Noah, you speak in puzzles. I do not understand your words."

"Nor do I," Noah replied, patting Makaidos's neck. "Not completely. God's ways are still mysterious to me, even after all these years."

Makaidos twitched his ears, unsure of how to continue. "In any case, losing your son is a great tragedy, and I hope to prevent this calamity with my daughter and avoid the pain you are suffering."

"Yet tragedies surround you, my friend. They lurk at the very entrance to your cave, but you do not feel the danger they threaten."

"Danger, Master Noah?"

"Yes. Japheth told me that you asked about the dragon in Nimrod's employ."

"I did. Please continue."

"Our scouts have seen Roxil and some of your sons with this dragon on more than one occasion."

Makaidos spoke through clenched teeth. "Continue."

"That dragon is Arramos, your father."

"Arramos?" Makaidos staggered backwards but caught himself before he fell. "Are you sure?"

"Arramos was a good friend of mine, so I asked Shem and Japheth to show him to me. We went to the city disguised as peddlers, and I saw him there myself."

"But how is that possible? He died! . . . Didn't he? The flood killed every breathing creature."

"God told me that it did." Noah firmed his chin and nodded. "So it must have."

"Then how do you explain the appearance of my father?"

"Until I get further revelation, I cannot explain it. I have to simply trust God that Arramos died. How is he alive? I do not know. After all I went through with the ark, I have learned a valuable lesson. Evidence that contradicts the word of God, even evidence I see with my own eyes, eventually falls and crumbles."

"But should we not revere evidence when—"

"Shhh!" Noah lifted the lantern and blew out the flame. Since they were so far back in the recesses of the cave, the chamber fell into complete darkness. "Keep your eyebeams off for a moment,

141

Makaidos, and tell me. If I were not speaking to you, what would evidence tell you? Am I here in this cave with you?"

"I know you are here. I just saw you."

"Current evidence!" Noah snapped. "Immediate evidence!"

"If not for your voice, I would conclude that you are not here."

Noah's tone softened again. "Yet you believe because of what you have learned in the past, what you saw in the light."

"That is exactly why I believe."

"Good." The lantern flashed back on, its wick blazing as Noah pinched a flint stone in his fingers. The glow highlighted every deep crevice in the old man's withered cheeks. He lifted the lantern and stood face-to-face with Makaidos, letting the orange flames sway between them. "What you have learned in the light, my friend, never doubt when it is dark."

Makaidos stared at the flame. The tongue of fire seemed to try to speak, as if it were a real tongue, carrying on its undulating glow the truth that only light can bring. After a few seconds, he bowed and backed away. "I will remember, Master Noah."

142

CHAPTER

THE WORLD ABOVE

With Morgan leading the way, Mara and Mardon ascended a winding corridor. Morgan marched quickly along the craggy stone floor, her black dress sweeping noiselessly in time with her gait. The light from her lantern danced across Mardon's face, revealing worry lines on his brow. His lips twitched on one side as his eyes stayed riveted on his dark leader.

Mara scooted closer and listened to his rasping breaths. Was he frightened of Morgan? He didn't bat an eye when he lied to her about needing his new assistant to "*observe the plants in the upper lands and learn how spawns differ from them in color, texture, and animation.*"

But now he seemed nervous as a bat. Was he worried about what the glass egg was going to say when they arrived? She grasped it through her dress pocket. It felt warm against her leg, and the heat radiated into her hand, like a polished stone from the riverbed in the hot springs. But it seemed to have its own heat source, as if it had birthed a flame in its core instead of an embryo.

As they ascended, the air grew colder. Mara rubbed her bare arms. This wasn't like the cool sensation of getting out of her bath in the springs. This felt different. It was raw, unfriendly, stark. She hoped the air in the upper world would be more inviting.

The tunnel widened into a circular room, and Morgan stopped at the center where a shaft of bright green light stood like a column between floor and ceiling. Mara gaped at it. The shaft appeared just wide enough for her to stand inside and be completely enveloped in light. Its texture seemed so thick she could scoop some into a cup and drink it.

Morgan pointed her long finger at Mardon. "You will go first. If we sent her, who knows how long she would have to wait alone for you to arrive?"

"True," Mardon said. "The time shift is unpredictable." He smirked at Morgan. "Since when do you care what happens to a laborer?"

"I don't care for her sake. I know what she carries in her pocket, and I know what your plans are. Did you think I actually believed your ridiculous story?"

In spite of the cool air, tiny beads of sweat speckled Mardon's brow, but he held his head high and stared at Morgan. "And you'll still allow us to go?"

"Yes. I am not a shortsighted woman. The Ovulum's presence will help bring about my long-term goals."

Mardon swallowed but kept his gaze locked on Morgan. "The Ovulum?"

Morgan laughed. "What a fool! You don't even know what kind of power you're dealing with." She brushed her hand along his cheek, a wry smile spreading across her face. "But you will soon see."

Morgan moved her hand down to Mardon's back and gave him a not-so-gentle push. "Enter the portal."

Mardon stepped into the bright column. The green radiance enveloped his body, seeming to swallow him until he looked like a human-shaped mass of solid light.

"Access the upper portal in the usual way," Morgan said. "I want a complete report when you return." She waved her hand over the surface of the column. "If you return."

Mardon's body elongated into a thin ribbon and burst into a flash of sparks. Mara staggered backwards, spreading her arms to keep her balance.

"Don't worry," Morgan said, extending her hand toward Mara. "Dimensional travel looks painful, but it is quite safe."

Mara inched her way back toward the column, her face and ears prickling with heat. "What did you mean by, 'If you return'?"

"Just a joke. I enjoy putting a fright into him from time to time."

Mara fanned her face. "He's not the one you scared."

Morgan leaned over and smiled a fake, condescending sort of smile. "There is no need to fear, Mara. You will return. You are the most intelligent spawn we've ever had. Even the few giants we've been able to grow have been stupid beasts, unfit to release to the world above. But I'm sure you and I can work together to create a great army of magnificent beings, strong enough to destroy the dragons and smart enough to thwart the vicious plots of Elohim."

"What about Mardon? Don't you need him?"

"I will have use for both him and his father at a later time. For now, just do what he says. But you must also perform one task for me." She reached into her pocket and withdrew a leather pouch, untying its drawstring as she held it out for Mara to see. "I went to the new dig area and found the pit you told me about, and now I know what this is." She pulled a sparkling jewel from the pouch and laid it in her palm. Radiance from the shaft streamed toward her hand, and the jewel absorbed the flow, making it pulse with green brilliance.

"The gem I found!" Mara said.

Morgan curled her fingers around the gem and slid it into Mara's dress pocket. "Don't take it out until Mardon introduces you to his father. Bow low and present it as a gift from the lady in black. Tell the king that it is a candlestone from the walls of the abyss. He will know what to do with it."

Mara patted the outside of her pocket. The two glass oddities were cushioned by her coif, so they seemed secure. "Will you please ask Naamah to look after my spawn?"

"She will be glad to." Morgan flattened Mara's hand against the pocket and guided her toward the column of light. "You must keep the gem secure while you're in the portal."

Mara paused at the edge of the column and smiled. Soon she would see the endless sky, and maybe even a dragon. She took a big step into the light. The radiance tickled, but only a little, and when she looked out, everything in the cavern, though tinged with light green, seemed clear and detailed, as though she were looking at it from inches away. She could see tiny pores in each stone and minute crystalline facets within. When she glanced where Morgan had stood, a large winged creature had taken her place. "Morgan!" she cried. "Where are you? I can't see you anymore!"

"I am here," the creature squawked. "I have never taught Mardon how to use the lower portal by himself, so don't tell him what to do. Reach up and grasp a handful of light, then pull it down as if you were climbing a rope."

Mara followed orders. The light in her hand felt like a cable, similar to the one that pulled the shaft platform up and down, only thinner, about the width of Nabal's whip. As soon as she finished a single pull, the cavern shattered into a million pieces and fell like volcanic ash, leaving a curtain of complete darkness. Then, a new scene formed, coming into focus as though her eyes were adjusting to the lighting of a lantern. As the view brightened, everything grew sharp and clear, clearer than her normal environment down below, but darker than she had expected. She blinked and drank in her surroundings, recognizing most objects from sketches or descriptions in Mardon's scrolls—buildings in the distance, trees much bigger than any spawn, and a light in the sky, a semicircle of whiteness.

Out of the corner of her eye, she noticed Mardon sitting on a log poking a long stick at a small fire near his feet. He glanced up. "Oh. There you are. It's about time."

"I thought the sun would be brighter," she said. "I don't even need my veil."

"You will very soon." He nodded toward the sky. "That's the moon, the god of the night."

"A god? Like Elohim?"

"Not really, but my father set up an idol for the moon and the sun and several of the constellations. People want to worship all sorts of objects, so he gives them temples, places to pray. It's easier to control the masses if you assimilate their superstitions into an approved, national religion."

Mara shook her head. "I . . . I didn't understand much of that."

Mardon laughed. "Don't worry. I'm just making a political speech." He picked up the burning stick and traced a line around where Mara stood. "Fire is the key to getting home. If we get separated, come to this site and take a brand from the flames. Then stand in the middle of this circle and wave it over your head as fast as you can."

Mara waved her hand from side to side. "Like this?"

"No." Mardon swung his arm in a wide circle. "Like this. The fire will energize the portal and take you home."

Mara pointed at the fire. "How do you know the logs will stay lit?"

"I have a servant who comes and tends the fire to make sure it never goes out."

Mara stared at the circle around her feet. An odd feeling seeped into her mind, a long lost sensation of grief and pain, like a mournful voice crying out in her heart. She stepped over the line, and the feeling quickly melted away.

She looked back at the circle, her vision now returning to normal. This portal was invisible, not like the column of light down

147

below. If not for the line on the dirt, how could she recognize a portal if she needed to?

Mardon reached for her hand. "Let's go to the tower. The king will be rising for the morning blessing soon."

Mara took his hand and strode beside him, passing between a pair of tall boulders that seemed to act as a gateway to the portal area. As the two gifts clinked in her pocket, she felt more important than she ever dreamed she could. She, Mara, an underborn laborer, was being taken to an audience with a king. "He lives in the tower?" she asked.

"He will live in the shrine when the tower is finished, but until then he goes there at sunrise and blesses the people from the top of the tower."

Mardon stepped up the pace, forcing Mara to jog to stay at his side. They followed a path through a stand of trees that ended at the edge of an enormous flat field. Mardon stopped and pointed at the slowly brightening scene. About a stone's throw away, a few huts lined a street that widened as it led to a huge cluster of buildings. In the center of the buildings, a gigantic tower loomed. Mara took two steps back, her mouth dropping open. Its base was so wide, just walking around it might take all day.

As they closed in on the city, details in the tower grew clear. It rose layer upon layer, seemingly without end, each layer slightly narrower than the one below it. Dozens of people scurried along its external staircases, some hustling up with armloads of timber and straw and others scrambling down empty-handed. One person slipped and fell to the next level, but no one else seemed to notice. They just kept crawling, like a thousand ants moving sand grain by grain to the top of the hill.

"They are busier than usual," Mardon said. "That means my father will be here soon."

Mardon strode ahead, and Mara followed, glancing frequently at the edge of the sky as it grew brighter and brighter. She pulled out her coif and tied it on, tucking her hair underneath and grinning as the endless sky began to reveal its lovely blue canvas. The chill of dawn didn't bother her a bit. Her own excitement pumped warmth to her fingers and toes.

As the top of the sun peeked over the horizon, Mardon approached the city gate and nodded at the gatekeeper, a bearded young man, taller and fatter than Mardon. The guard turned a wooden dial at the gate's latch, and Mara counted its quiet clicks. The gatekeeper stared at her while he worked, so she stayed close to Mardon's side. Finally, the latch clanked, and the iron-barred fence swung out with a terrible whine.

"A fresh treat for the worshippers, Mardon?" the guard asked. "She's pasty white, but the men at the Luna temple won't mind. They like the young ones."

"Quiet, fool!" Mardon pulled Mara closer and whispered. "Never mind him. He's just an ignorant commoner."

Mara spread out her fingers and compared her skin to Mardon's. His was quite a bit darker, brown instead of her pinkish-white hue. In the dimness of her home, she hardly took notice of skin color. She turned toward the rising sun, pulling her veil down as the rays began to sting her eyes. She had read about sunlight changing skin tone temporarily, but could its light be harsh enough to make everyone this brown?

They followed a path of rough-edged stones, sharp enough to prick Mara's toughened bare soles. Wearing leather sandals, Mardon ignored the obstacles and quickened the pace. Easing each foot down, she managed to keep up, and the path eventually smoothed into larger, flat stones that cooled her aching feet.

When they arrived at the base of the tower, a crowd had gathered in a semicircle around a cavernous entryway, a portico that led to the tower's main doors. A man and a woman dressed in flowing silk strode to the center of the portico and embraced. As gentle drums tapped a slow rhythm, the couple stepped elegantly to the exotic beat, moving gracefully on the polished floor from one edge of the circle to the other. Two lyres joined in, and the man twirled the woman, making her colorful dress spread out into a spinning flower.

When he caught her in his arms, Mara gasped. How beautiful! That man and woman seemed so . . . so friendly!

A hand touched her chin and pushed it upward, closing her gaping mouth. Mardon chuckled. "Haven't you read about dancing before?"

Mara shook her head, unable to speak. She had never been so mesmerized in all her life. Something about that couple sent a warm sensation into her heart unlike anything she had ever felt before, and she wanted it to never go away. Could she ever dance with someone like that, someone who would take her in his arms and make her spin in a rainbow of colors? But who could ever want to make something beautiful out of Mara, an underborn slave girl?

When the couple finished their dance, several children dashed back and forth across the portico's floor. One scurried to the huge wide-open doors that led to the tower's anteroom. From where Mara stood, she could see a ring of statues inside the first floor, all facing some kind of monument in the center. "Is that the shrine?" she asked.

Mardon shook his head. "The first floor is a museum. All the knowledge of the world, whether literature, art, or music, is collected there in scrolls. Our goal is to keep the world's people together under one authority, so they won't split up into warring factions. Having an education center here demonstrates that King Nimrod's domain is the focus of all intellectual pursuits."

The tower mound was high enough to allow Mara to gaze out over the city's endless expanse of buildings and farms. Beautiful vineyards and orchards painted the distant landscape with lush greenery, but, closer in, scars spoiled the city's marble-coated streets. Black smoke ascended from two enormous pits on either side of her view. Sweat-drenched men dressed in loincloths hauled bricks up the slopes on their bare backs. Red welts striped their shoulders as they trudged under their loads. Another man walked behind them, cracking a whip at one of the slower workers.

Mara cringed with each stroke, thinking about Nabal's whip and how he ripped the backs of girls and beat Elam's friend to death. She shivered hard and moved her gaze closer in, studying the stone columns that lined the outer courtyard. Carved with scowling faces, they seemed to watch over the people who paused to kiss the lowest cheek as they passed by. A girl with a handbasket threw flower petals at the column's base, and a woman left an object on the petals, something small that glinted in the sun.

Mardon turned Mara back toward the museum. "Look."

Three heralds carrying curved horns marched through the doors, and the children hurried back into the throng. After the horns blared a triplet of loud notes, a sword-bearing soldier led six bare-chested men onto the portico from the direction of the city gates. The six wore heavy shackles on their wrists, and chains linked their ankles.

Mardon nudged Mara. "Here comes my father."

A taller, lighter-skinned man stepped up to the portico, fully dressed, yet wearing the same kind of clothes the gatekeeper wore, an undecorated gray jacket and black breeches. Mara pulled on Mardon's elbow. "You wrote that he wore a purple robe."

"This is the solstice ceremony, a battle ritual." He pointed at the first six men. "Watch. Those are rebels the king's men have captured since the previous solstice."

After the soldier unlocked their manacles, the prisoners huddled, putting their hands together in what seemed like a child's finger game, similar to one Naamah had taught the girls. Then, the soldier unlinked one of the prisoners' ankles, and the other five bowed to the freed man and marched back to the crowd where other soldiers met them and refastened their wrists.

The king handed the chosen man a sword, then withdrew another from his belt and held its shimmering blade aloft. The rebel's eyes grew wide, and he stepped back, holding his sword in front of him. His biceps quivered, and his legs shook.

The king's sword reflected a beam from the rising sun, and the blade seemed to catch on fire. His opponent's knees buckled, and he fell backwards, dropping his weapon. The king swung his blade, but it didn't slice through the fallen man. The reflected light from the sun seemed to brush his body, radiating around his skin like a coat of fire. His eyes bugged out, and his mouth opened in a silent scream as the light transformed into sparkling dots that sizzled across his body, devouring his flesh from head to toe. Seconds later, nothing remained but his sword and a silver earring.

Mara's throat clenched. She squeaked out, "Where did he go?" But a cheer from the crowd drowned out her tiny voice.

King Nimrod bowed low, pressing his hand against his trim waist. When he rose back up, his gaze met Mardon, then shifted to Mara. He seemed puzzled at first, but he smiled broadly and shouted, "The prince has returned from his journey!" He slid his sword into a sheath that hung from a belt and extended his arm. "Come, my son. Tell us about this pale foreigner you have brought."

Mardon grabbed Mara's hand and hustled her to the center of the portico. As she stepped out of the shadow of a statue, the sun's rays shone through her veil, making her flinch. Fortunately, the roof of the portico blocked out the light again as they hurried across the cool, smooth floor.

Mardon stopped and bowed to the king, and as he rose, Mara felt his hand squeeze her shoulder. "Lift your veil," he whispered.

Mara brushed her veil up over her head and watched King Nimrod, tall and handsome, stride right up to her. He stooped and gazed into her eyes. "What kind of goddess is she?" he asked, his smile revealing a brilliant set of white teeth. "Her eyes are bluer than sapphires! I have never seen such jewels in all of Shinar!"

A low murmur arose from the crowd. Many had departed, but a hundred or so milled around the portico, apparently to get a close look at this strange visitor.

Mardon laid his hand on Mara's covered head and spoke in a low tone. "She is an underborn, Father, the oldest surviving female we have in the lower realms."

The king pinched the tie of Mara's coif. "May I take it off?" he asked.

Mara nodded, mesmerized at the king's gentle face and manner. As the covering pulled away, her hair spilled down to her shoulders. The king nearly fell backwards. "Mardon! Her hair is whiter than pearls, whiter than hailstones!"

The crowd murmured again, louder this time, as they began to press closer.

Mardon waved for the guards to push them back, then, with a gentle touch, combed his fingers through Mara's hair. "After she was uprooted, we altered the hybridization scheme, but once I learned how intelligent she was, I tried to reproduce her. Every attempt failed in the embryonic stage."

153

"You cannot repeat perfection!" The king caressed Mara's cheek and lifted a hand toward one of the columns in the courtyard that surrounded the tower. "She is a goddess sprouted from the earth, flourished in the pull of magnetic harmony, and blossomed in the light of spectral promise!"

Mara noticed splotches of dark red on the king's fingers. As he withdrew his hand, the king gazed into her eyes again. "What is your name, precious jewel?"

"Mara."

"Mara?" He looked up at Mardon, frowning. "What kind of name is that for an angel?"

Mardon pinched closed a hole at the shoulder of Mara's outer tunic, covering the bloodstain underneath. "We give all the laborers names that reflect the sadness of their lot in life. It only makes sense."

"Well, that will change." The king's gentle smile returned. "Child, you will be called Sapphira Adi, for your eyes are sparkling gems, as blue as the endless expanse on the clearest day. Even your pupils blaze like sapphires."

Mara let that name roll around in her mind. Sapphira Adi. It sounded . . . lovely.

King Nimrod stood and brushed his hands together, rubbing reddish powder onto the floor. He lowered his voice as he turned to Mardon. "We have to squelch an uprising in the mountain tribes, so I'll need more . . ." He glanced back down at Mara. "I'll need another suitable donor."

"Understood, Father. Do you have one in mind?"

"No. Just find a pregnant prostitute in the temples. They're always glad to . . ." He glanced at Mara again. "Let's just say they're willing to stay in a more profitable physical condition."

A strange smile crossed Mardon's face. "While making an embryonic donation to our cause?"

The king brushed more of the red powder from his palms. "Exactly."

Mardon laid a hand on Mara's shoulder. "Mara . . . I mean, Sapphira, is carrying something that might make further conflict unnecessary."

"Indeed?" The king's brow lifted. "What is it?"

Mardon gently nudged her forward a step. "Show him."

Mara withdrew the Ovulum from her pocket and held it up in her palm. Nimrod leaned over and eyed it closely. "And what is this?" he asked.

Mardon pushed it with his finger, making it tilt to one side. "I unearthed it when we dug the foundation for the new fountain, and I thought it little more than a trinket until I took it to the lower world. When I arrived, it spoke in odd verse, declaring that it needed the hands of an intelligent maiden if we wanted to hear from the lips of God."

"The lips of God?" the king said. "Do you mean Elohim?"

"I assumed it was Elohim, so I wanted to be sure to follow his instructions and avoid his wrath."

"Why didn't you seek a suitable girl here?" The king spread out his arms toward the surrounding buildings. "Are there no intelligent maidens in my kingdom?"

"You allow the nobles' daughters to be educated," he said, flashing that strange smile again, "but it would be difficult to discern which ones are true maidens."

The king rubbed his chin. "I see what you mean."

"But Sapphira has proven an extraordinary intelligence, and until today, I am the only human male who has ever laid eyes on her. She is a maiden, indeed."

The king picked up the Ovulum and brought it close to his eyes. "Did this trinket speak to her?"

"In an extraordinary way. I believe it is truly the mouthpiece of Elohim." He gazed up at the tower and angled his arm toward the top. "Imagine it sitting in the temple at the pinnacle of your tower. Everyone from every land will proclaim us the capital of the world. With you holding the gateway to the god of the flood, who would dare oppose you? Your kingdom will be established forever!"

The king handed the egg back to Mara. His eyes widened, and his two canine teeth overlapped his bottom lip. "Make it speak again!" he barked.

Mara stepped back clumsily. The king seemed to be a different person now, gruff, almost maniacal. She held the Ovulum close to her lips, her hands shaking. She wanted to sound like she knew what she was doing, but she had no idea what to say. After clearing her throat, she spoke slowly. "Elohim, god of the flood, speak to us now and"—she licked her lips, her eyes darting between the two men who watched with their jaws hanging open—"and grant us wisdom regarding how we might please you." She bit her tongue and glanced up at the king. His eyes were locked on the Ovulum, nearly bulging out of his head.

155

The red fog appeared again inside the glass shell, forming slowly into an eye. It gazed at her, its pupil a soft crimson hue, but when it turned toward the king, the entire eye seemed to blaze with fire. A loud, deep voice erupted from within.

> To Nimrod, hunter, ruler, king,
> The man who built a tower,
> A jackass heeds a whip and rope,
> But you heed only power.
>
> So like a jackass, you'll be whipped;
> Like straw your shrine will burn,
> For God has warned from up on high.
> But you refused to turn.
>
> Excising children, torn from wombs,
> They cry for murder's cost;
> Defiling maidens, forced to serve,
> They mourn their virtue lost.
>
> So now the justice due your deeds
> Will come in fire and smoke,
> To burn your shrine and all your wealth
> And clasp you in a yoke.
>
> For when you die, entrapped you'll be
> Within the bowels of Earth,
> Until the day the Lord recalls
> Your soul to fiery birth.

156

Nimrod's lips bent into a vicious frown, and his hand curled into a shaking fist as he raised it to the sky. "No!" he screamed. "You cannot win! I control the hearts of the people! We will fight you from the top of the tower and make heaven rain with the blood of your hosts!"

The fog had disappeared inside the egg, so Mara slipped it back into her pocket and stepped away slowly while King Nimrod raged on.

"If you send fire, I will pierce you with a spear! If you clasp me with a yoke, I will dress you in a mantle of your own blood!"

Suddenly, a stream of fire rained from the roof of the portico, and a flurry of huge wings ripped past the opening.

"Dragons!" Mardon shouted. "Guards! Get ropes and spears!"

The king grabbed a spear from a soldier and ran out to the courtyard. Lunging forward, he hurled the spear into the air. He then ran back to the portico, his face twisted in rage as he screamed toward the tower's main door. "Herald! Sound the alarm! Call out every soldier." He snatched up Mara's coif from the floor, strangling it in his fist as he shook it in front of her. His voice thundered. "You brought Elohim's curse on us! Dragons are his winged soldiers!" He threw the coif at her chest, and it fell into her hand.

Withdrawing his sword, the king gripped it with both hands and stared at the blade. As he watched it glimmer in the sunlight, the furrows in his brow deepened, and his cheeks flushed scarlet. Raising one hand, he spread out his fingers and screamed, "Mardon! I need more blood!" His maniacal stare fell on Mara, and he stalked toward her. "Yes, of course. A maiden's blood will do just fine."

Mardon pushed Mara behind his back. "There are infants in the crowd, Father. I beg you to choose any one of them. I need Mara for my work."

A blast from a horn made both men spin around. Shaking uncontrollably, Mara quickly retied her coif and pulled out the candlestone. Maybe it would distract the king. Another horn echoed the first from far away, and a third answered, even farther away.

The king shoved Mardon aside and grabbed Mara's shoulder, squeezing her wound so hard, pain shot down her spine. "I will deal with you soon enough. The temple worshippers would love to get their hands on you." He shoved her into Mardon's arms. "Put her in the stocks." He pivoted and stomped toward a mother with a baby in her arms.

Mara extended the gem in her open palm and cried out, "Look! The lady in black told me to give this to you!"

Nimrod pivoted again and marched back. Mardon grabbed Mara's wrist and snatched the gem. Both men gazed at it curiously. Light seemed to spin toward it in a whirlpool. "Could it be?" the king whispered.

Mara swallowed through her tightening throat. "Morgan called it a candlestone. She said the king would know what to do with it."

Nimrod grabbed the gem and clasped it in his fist, a wicked smile forming on his lips. "This is dragons' bane!" he yelled. "We shall see whose god wields more power, Noah's or Morgan's." He pushed Mara back into Mardon's grasp. "Lock her in my chambers. I will deal with her personally later."

FORBIDDEN FRUIT

Nimrod strode away, snatching a shield from another soldier as he jumped down the stairs to the courtyard. Tears welled in Mara's eyes. The mother with the baby had fled, so at least the king wouldn't murder that one. But would he find another? A new volley of flames struck the side of the roof, setting it on fire.

Mardon took Mara's hand and pulled her to the side of the portico. He knelt and lowered her veil over her eyes. "Hurry back to the portal. The gatekeeper will be gone, so you shouldn't have any trouble. Remember to get a firebrand and wave it in a circle over your head. I'll come back as soon as I can." He rose to his feet and nodded toward the gate. "Now make haste!"

Mara pressed her hand over her pocket to keep the Ovulum in place and ran toward the gate as fast as she could. The sun's cruel rays stung her arms, and the gravel stabbed her feet, but her eyes felt safe behind her veil. When she reached the gate, the guard was gone, just as Mardon had predicted. Standing on tiptoes, she turned the latch's dial through its combination of clicks and pushed open the iron door.

She found the grassy path back to the woods and gazed at her shadow as she ran. Though no one followed, she imagined a hundred other shadows closing in on hers, Nimrod and his people, bloodthirsty wolves who would gladly kill the weak and innocent.

When she passed between the two tall rocks, she found the stack of logs, but the fire had gone out. She picked up a long stick and stared at its charred, smoking end. What now?

She dug into her pocket and caressed the egg. Would it know what to do? If it spoke for a god, it would have to. But would it speak without Nimrod or Mardon around?

She pulled out the egg and showed the stick to it. "I need fire to go back home. What do I do?"

The eye appeared again in a soft crimson hue. Its voice was gentle, and it spoke without rhyme or verse. "You are an oracle of fire. Stand in the circle and call for flames. They will come to you." The eye then quickly faded away.

Mara squinted at the glassy shell, now dark and lifeless. "An oracle of fire? What's that?"

The Ovulum said nothing.

"How do I call for flames?"

Again, no answer.

She shrugged her shoulders and returned the Ovulum to her pocket, then stepped into the center of the portal circle. "Okay," she said, holding the stick high. "Here goes."

Closing her eyes, Mara spoke into the air. "Flames, come to my firebrand!" She opened her eyes again. Feeling a gust of wind and the sudden coolness of a mammoth shadow, she looked up. A big red dragon swooped low, its wings fanning a buffeting breeze that whipped her dress against her legs. She ducked her head, but it didn't attack. It just turned and headed toward the tower. She mopped her brow with her veil. Had the dragon seen her? Would it come back?

She brought down the stick. The end was ablaze! Had the dragon breathed fire on her stick? She pulled up her veil and searched the skies. Several dragons circled the tower's midsection, blasting it with torrents of fire. Much of the building had been set aflame, and the wind from the dragons' orbit began spinning the fire into a flaming vortex, a blazing tornado that wrapped the tower in a mantle of orange.

The tower sank heavily, a third of it dropping below the ground. As the upper portion continued to burn, one of the dragons faltered. Its wings flapped weakly, and it fell to the ground. The flaming tower followed, first leaning, then toppling straight toward Mara.

She raised the stick and waved it in quick circles. Instantly, a spinning curtain of light surrounded her—another tornado, but this one of pure green radiance. Her mind spun with it, and she felt a falling sensation, like sliding down a feeder spring into Lucifer's Pool. Seconds later, the falling stopped and the cavern appeared, still shaded in green and magnified a dozen times. She took a long step and turned back toward the column of light, the portal Morgan had used to send her to the upper lands. The bright shaft flickered, then faded to a weak glow.

161

Her eyesight returned to normal. The cave was almost completely dark—dismal and lonely. She tore the coif from her head and threw it to the stone floor, then dropped to her knees and cried. As her tears flowed, images of the glorious tower passed through her mind. She wondered at all the scrolls that must have filled the shelves of the museum—histories, genealogies, scientific journals, technical drawings—but now they all burned in the dragons' flames. Not only that, her visit to the upper world was a fiasco, and Nimrod and Mardon probably blamed her for the collapse of the greatest creation mankind had ever seen. Now she would probably never get to go back, never get to leave the darkness, the torture, the loneliness of the dismal caverns. And, really, it was all because of the dragons.

She pounded her fist on the floor. "Dragons!" she yelled. "Curse those dragons! May they all die in their own fire!"

As she continued weeping, a gentle voice drifted by her ear. "You have learned much, haven't you Mara?"

Mara leaped to her feet and spun around. A dark silhouette loomed, casting its shadow over most of the chamber. Morgan!

Makaidos poured a torrent of fire into the spinning column of flames, beating his wings to fan the cyclone as he wheeled around it in a tight orbit. Shutting off his fiery jets for a moment, he glanced back at a smaller, trailing dragon. "Aim lower, Roxil! The fire feeds upward on its own!"

Roxil blasted a volley of flames at a gap in the twisting inferno, igniting a pair of soldiers with arrows fixed on bows. Another soldier, standing on a staircase above the other two, threw a spear. With a quick reach, Roxil snatched the spear right out of the air with her claws and slung it back at its owner.

"My daughter, the warrior!" Makaidos yelled. A glimmer near the base of the tower caught his eye, and a sense of danger pulsed through his body. Feeling weaker, he pulled away from the doomed tower. It had already sunk to about two-thirds of its original height, and since the base had resettled at an angle, the whole structure leaned awkwardly. "Come, Roxil!" he shouted. "We are done here!"

Roxil's wings faltered, and she began sinking toward the ground. Makaidos banked hard and dove toward her. As he neared the tower's foundation, he noticed a man raising something shiny in his hand. Danger once again inflamed his senses. Feeling weaker by the second, he flew under Roxil and pushed up against her body, matching the beating of his wings with hers as he barked out a stroke rhythm. "Up! Down! Up! Down!"

Flying more steadily, but still descending, the two dragons glided away from the tower toward an open farm. Crash-landing in a vineyard, they tumbled and slid to a halt, plowing a deep furrow and squishing hundreds of ripe grapes. Makaidos scrambled upright and helped Roxil to her haunches. "Are you all right?" he asked.

Roxil's head wagged back and forth. "I am dizzy. Something made me ill."

"I felt it, too." He gazed back at the tower. As the flames tightened around the huge ziggurat, the remaining dragons continued fanning it toward the direction it leaned. Finally, the entire structure toppled with a thunderous crash, sending a tremor that shook the ground under their claws.

Roxil heaved a tired sigh. "We did it!"

"Yes, we did." Makaidos kept his eyes on the sky. A dragon had broken off from the troop and was heading their way. "Do you recognize him?" he asked.

Roxil angled her head toward the gliding figure. "No, and I sense something odd about him. Is it danger?"

"It is similar to danger. I am not sure what it is."

The dragon landed with a soft touch, following the dredged path the other two dragons had plowed. His powerful red wings fanned a brisk wind in their faces, forcing Makaidos to blink. When his vision cleared, he gazed at the familiar face. He backed away a step, unwilling to believe what his eyes were telling him. He sputtered a drizzle of fire as he spoke. "Fa . . . Father?"

The dragon dipped his head. "I am glad you recognize me, Makaidos. It has been many years since the day Hilidan and I fought the Watchers and the fountains of the deep erupted and swept us all away." He raised his head again and stared at Makaidos, his eyes flashing red. "But your father, Arramos, lives."

Makaidos took another step back. "How can you know about Hilidan? I have not mentioned his name to anyone since the day of the flood."

"Because I was there . . . Son."

"How did you survive? And why have you waited so long to show yourself?"

163

"It is a long story, but for now, we must be reacquainted."
Arramos bowed toward Roxil. "I want to get to know my
descendants."

Roxil bowed in return. "I am glad to meet you, Father
Arramos."

Makaidos shook his head. "This cannot be. The Maker told
Master Noah that every creature not aboard the ark was killed. The
Maker is never wrong."

"Of course the Maker is never wrong, but Master Noah has
made his share of mistakes. I am sure you have heard the gossip
that Ham spread about his drunken exposure."

Makaidos winced. "I have heard."

"And you must admit that evidence of my death is sorely lacking, for I am standing here right now."

Roxil flapped her wings, pushing her body toward Arramos.
She intertwined her neck with his and looked back at Makaidos.
"He has to be your father. I no longer feel any danger at all."

"I do." Makaidos took yet another step back. "More than
ever."

Arramos pulled away from Roxil and stretched his neck, bringing his head close to Makaidos. "My son, I fought alongside you
against the tower. I scorched King Nimrod while he held the
dragon's bane and weakened your daughter. If I had not, you
would both have fallen to the spearmen."

"Dragon's bane? What is that?"

"A gem that some call a candlestone. It weakens dragons by
absorbing their light energy."

Makaidos couldn't maintain eye contact. He gazed toward the
mountains. "Shem and Japheth told me you were on Nimrod's
side, one of his enforcers."

"I was infiltrating as a spy. The sons of Noah would not have
learned who captured the girl from their village if I had not leaked
the information to them."

Roxil thumped her tail on the ground. "Father! Why are you being so rude? He is obviously who he says he is."

"He certainly appears to be, but I sense great danger. The Maker has given me a gift that I cannot ignore, and I trust him and Master Noah before this evidence that I cannot yet fully comprehend."

Arramos lowered his voice. "Makaidos, it is important that I reestablish my leadership over our family. You know this to be true. Your sons who flew with me around the tower have agreed to join in our battle against humankind."

"But you always taught me that we were created to serve the sons of Adam."

"I did." Arramos's eyes flashed brighter than ever, but he lowered his voice even further, growling under his breath. "Time after time men have spat in the face of the Maker. Even after a cleansing flood, they have corrupted themselves again. Building a tower of pride, they have driven a fist into the Maker's nose. The time has come for dragons to take their place as rulers of the planet."

"I . . . I cannot believe what I am hearing. There is too much to think about. The danger I feel is overwhelming."

"You have already lost Goliath." Arramos waved a wing at Roxil. "Will you lose the rest of your family because of a feeling you get when I am near? Did I not teach you logic? Will you defy all reason because of your faith in a man who drinks himself to the point of shame? Where is your discernment?"

Makaidos glanced all around. As a cloud of smoke from the burning tower began obscuring the sun, a shadow fell across his eyes. "A shroud of darkness surrounds me. It would be foolish to deny what I have learned in the light. That is the chief rule of discernment."

"The time of darkness has ended my son. You may follow me if you wish, but do not make yourself an enemy." With a great flap of his wings, Arramos lifted into the sky and sailed toward the fallen tower.

165

Roxil glared at Makaidos, thumping her tail even harder. "Father! Do not be a fool! Mankind is not worth losing your own father."

Makaidos roared. "Silence! You have no idea what you are saying. You have not seen what I have seen through the centuries!"

Roxil scowled. "Living longer does not always make a dragon wiser."

Makaidos lifted his tail, ready to strike, but he let it fall. His daughter had long since passed the stage of youngling discipline. He shuffled closer to her. "Roxil, what has happened to you? You have never been so disrespectful toward me."

"I have always respected you, even when I thought your patience with the foolishness of men made you appear to be a fool yourself. Respect is why I held back my opinions for so long, but now I am of age to make my own choices." Roxil turned her head toward the sky. "Look, Father. My brothers . . . your sons . . . are following Arramos toward the mountains. Will you join us?"

"Us? You cannot be serious!"

"I am." Roxil stretched out her wings. "No sensible dragon would hang her life on the words of a drunken ark builder."

Makaidos firmed his jaw. "Your mother will be on my side."

"She is too weak to oppose you. She has always been weak."

Makaidos snorted a stream of fire at the ground near Roxil's tail. "You have no idea what you are saying! Your mother is a great warrior. Do not cast insults simply because you are too young to have seen her in action! She has spent the last century populating the world with dragons and raising up a new brood of warriors!"

Roxil flapped her wings and lifted slowly into the sky. She circled him once and dipped her head in a solemn bow. "Good-bye, Father."

A tear dripped from Makaidos's eye and fell to the ground. Roxil strayed from her path for a moment before zooming toward the other dragons as they disappeared in the growing haze.

Clasping her hand on her chest, Mara breathed a sigh. "You startled me."

Sympathy tinged Morgan's voice. "I apologize, but I wanted to comfort you."

Mara drooped her head. "How can I be comforted? My first visit to the land above was a disaster! King Nimrod got so mad at me, I thought he would kill me, and he kept talking about needing blood, so it seemed for a minute like he was going to sacrifice a baby. But then dragons came and destroyed the tower, and everything in it burned. Mardon said all the world's knowledge lay in the first floor, and now it's gone forever!"

Morgan caressed her cheek. "You have had a frightful experience, but not all is lost." She curled her finger. "Come with me."

Morgan walked toward a narrow opening at the side of the cavern opposite the one they had entered. Mara rose slowly, and, as she followed, Morgan spoke in haunting tones. "I know a great disaster has befallen the upper world. Tell me, Mara, what did you see?"

As they passed into the tunnel, darkness enfolded them. Mara slowed, but the floor seemed smooth enough. "I saw dragons. Lots of them. And they breathed fire at the tower until it burned."

"I see." Now in total darkness, Morgan's voice sounded like a sad song, like the dirge Naamah taught the girls to sing when one of them died in the chasm. "Did the fire spin like a whirlpool as it consumed Nimrod's tower?"

"It did! How did you guess?"

"And did the tower sink into the ground like a rock in a pool?"

"Part of it sank, but more than half of it started tipping over. It was so tall, I was afraid it would fall on me, so I went through the portal before it fell." A strange tingle crawled along Mara's skin. "How did you know?"

The tunnel brightened slightly, enough for her to see Morgan's eyes directly in front of her own. Sudden fear froze Mara in place. She held her breath, unable to move a muscle.

Morgan's face showed no emotion. "You fancy yourself a scientist, a lover of knowledge. Do you not?"

Mara pressed her lips together and gave her a quick nod.

Morgan swept her arm toward the source of light, another cavern that lay just beyond the end of the tunnel. "Then allow me to show you how I knew." She strode into the cavern, her black dress flowing in a swirling draft.

Feeling surged back into Mara's legs, and she rushed to catch up. When she entered the cavern, she stopped and leaned back, barely able to take in the amazing sights. The ceiling reached higher than any of the trees in the upper world, so high that she could see only a vague grayness in the upper reaches. Spinning to the side, she located the source of light, a blazing column that stretched to the ceiling's highest point. The energy in the column rotated, casting off blue eddies of light that twirled in dancing pirouettes until they fizzled into nothingness.

168

Morgan stood at the center of the cavern next to a massive circular building that stretched from one side of the seemingly endless chamber to the other. A set of broken, charred doors lay open, leading to the building's anteroom. A ring of statues surrounded something in the center, their arms raised as if saluting it with hailing praises.

Mara gasped. "The . . . the tower?"

Morgan pushed on one of the doors. It toppled over, smashing to the floor at her feet. She jumped back and waved away the dust, coughing. "What's left of it."

Mara ran to the doorway and peered into the anteroom. Now close enough to the statues, she finally recognized what the robed men and women were saluting. "A tree?"

Morgan strutted inside and motioned for Mara to follow. "Yes, a very special tree. I'm sure you read about it in Mardon's library. Adam and Eve first discovered wisdom by eating its fruit."

"I did read about it, but I thought it was destroyed in the flood."

"It was, but I am . . ." Morgan covered her mouth and coughed again. "Excuse me. I mean, one of my dear old friends is a seed collector, and she saved a few seeds from the fruit. I planted them, and this tree was the only one that sprouted."

"That must mean your friend was on the ark!"

"Yes, and you know her quite well. Did you ever read the name of Ham's wife?"

Mara drew in a quick breath. "Naamah was on the ark?"

Morgan crossed her arms over her chest. "One and the same."

Mara gazed at the tree and whistled. No wonder the statues seemed to be saluting! It was the descendant of the original tree of knowledge!

As Morgan approached the center of the room, she lifted her hands toward the ceiling, her voice echoing in the massive chamber. "The entire museum celebrates the wisdom of mankind and his pursuit of knowledge, so it's fitting that the original source of that knowledge should grow here, the progeny of wisdom's first blossom." She stopped at the tree and caressed a red, pear-shaped fruit that dangled from a low branch. "As you explore all the wonders here, you, too, will enjoy the fruits of wisdom."

Mara stopped at the statue of a tall, stately woman and caressed her smooth marble knee, a knee that seemed ready to bend at the sight of the tree, rooted in a circular planter that lay flush with the surrounding floor. Since the branches spread out ten feet in each direction, only a few paces separated the fruit from its marble-clad worshippers.

As Mara drew closer, the Ovulum in her pocket grew hot and stung her thigh. She halted. Was it angry? Giving a warning? She took three steps back. The egg cooled, but she didn't want to pull it out. Morgan probably thought she had given it to Nimrod, and it was better if her mistress didn't know where it was.

Morgan cocked her head to one side. "Is something wrong?"

Folding her hands behind her, Mara shifted back and forth on her feet. "I don't know. I just felt something strange when I got near the tree."

"Something strange?" Morgan's eyes flashed red, but the rest of her face stayed calm. "Eating the fruit is the first step toward true wisdom. The strangeness will fade soon enough." She held out her hand, her fingers beckoning Mara to come.

Mara took a step, and the egg heated up again, but not quite as hot this time. She halted and gazed at one of the statues. "I'm not hungry right now. Maybe tomorrow."

A crooked smile spread across Morgan's face. She folded her hands, and her tone became overly sweet. "If you don't eat the fruit, my dear, you will forever stay an ignorant freak of nature."

Mara bit her bottom lip. Tears crept into her eyes, but she didn't want to cry. She had to change the subject, and fast. "How did the tower get here?"

170

Morgan drilled her with a piercing stare, but after a few seconds, she seemed willing to give up on the fruit issue, at least for the time being. "It must have come through a dimensional portal," she said, pointing at the tall shaft of light outside the tower. "The only way they're created is by a vortex of light energy, so I guessed that the dragons' fire must have been swirling. Since the green portal faded and a blue one formed here, I think the path between the dimensions actually moved, shifting the lower portal to this room and the upper portal to the midst of the fire around the tower. My guess is that a lower portal's color change indicates a positional change in its exit point up above."

"How did you know that the tower sank?"

Morgan looked up at the ceiling. "Only the lowest section of the tower came through the portal, so with the foundation missing, what could the rest of the tower do but sink or fall?"

Mara followed Morgan's line of sight and saw shelf upon shelf of scrolls, hundreds of them, even thousands. Dozens of wooden ladders rose almost to the domed ceiling, close enough to each other to allow access to every shelf. Quite a number of scrolls also lay on the floor in haphazard piles. Mara let out a contented sigh. "So can I start reading the scrolls right away?"

Morgan shook her head. "Your journey threw you off schedule. It's time for your sleep cycle. When you wake up, we'll decide how to split your working hours between your control room duties and your new studies here. Mardon will be too busy to return to our world for quite some time, so I will be your primary instructor."

"But will Mardon want the scrolls back?" Mara asked. "If he has a lot of work to do, he'll probably want them."

"The fool is lucky he's still alive, and if not for the quick transport of this piece of the tower, none of the scrolls would have survived anyway." Morgan picked up one of the scrolls that had fallen to the floor and rolled it open. "Besides, the language would be gibberish to him. He wouldn't understand a single word."

171

"What?" Mara peeked around Morgan's arm and read the first few lines, an introduction to the biography of a man she had never heard of. "I can read it. Why can't they?"

Morgan rolled the scroll back up. "As soon as the new portal appeared, I went through it to see what created it. I came out in the middle of a dwindling ring of fire, apparently the center of the tower's original location. The tower had already fallen, and the people were in total chaos, babbling incoherently to each other." She laid the scroll in Mara's hands. "It seems that people speak a variety of new tongues now, and they don't understand normal speech, that is, the language of these scrolls. Since dragons were still attacking the city, I only stayed a few seconds. I came right back and hurried to the old portal, hoping you had found your way home. Fortunately, you used the pathway before it moved." She swept away a pile of broken marble with her foot. "This disaster has caused a huge displacement in the barrier between our two dimensions. In fact, the portal's shift from green to blue light tells me that it might not even lead to Shinar any longer. I haven't figured out what changes we'll experience, but it will be interesting to see how time passage here compares to the world above."

Mara unrolled a few inches of the scroll. "First a flood and now a fire. Why does Elohim want to destroy everything?"

"There will be plenty of time for questions and answers. As you read the scrolls, I'll be here to teach you. But for now, you must go to sleep."

She hugged the scroll to her chest. "May I take just this one with me tonight?"

"I didn't get to read it," Morgan said, touching the end of the scroll. "I don't want you to study something you're not ready for."

172

Mara frowned and laid the scroll back on the floor near the doorway. When she straightened, Morgan placed her hands on Mara's cheeks. "Now feel the tension of the day melt from your thoughts," Morgan said. "You have toiled in the lands above, and your mind is swimming in a flood of new discoveries. Rest, my child, and let yourself float above it all. Think only of warm springs and sweet fig cakes, and everything else will wait until morning's call."

Morgan's cool fingers felt heavenly. Mara really did feel very sleepy. She wanted to ask if Mardon was still fighting the dragons, but the question seemed too difficult to speak. "Okay," she said, yawning.

Pulling Mara along, Morgan walked to the portal and scooped out a handful of energy. After forming it into a ball of pale blue light, she placed it in Mara's palm. "This will be enough to light your way to your quarters." She kissed Mara on the forehead, an icy cold kiss. "Sweet dreams."

Mara held the ball in front of her and hurried through the tunnel. It tickled her skin, helping her stay awake as she kept her eyes fixed on the path. Finding her coif in the original portal's chamber, she grabbed it and stuffed it into her pocket, still thinking about the scrolls. Fighting sleep, she turned back toward the tower. Morgan hadn't exactly said the scrolls were forbidden, had she?

Cupping her hands around the glowing ball and letting only a little light seep through her fingers, Mara hurried back to the tower. Keeping watch for Morgan, she found the scroll next to the door, tucked it under her arm, and retraced her steps, hustling through the tunnels as they wound their way back down toward the laborers' hovels. As she neared the corridor leading to the growth chamber room, she slowed. Should she stop and check on her spawn? No. Naamah took care of him. Besides, the light wouldn't last long enough to feed him.

By the time she arrived at her hovel, the ball had dwindled to the size of a pebble, spritzing tiny blue sparks on the stone floor as she sat in her dugout. She tried to unwind the scroll, but holding the ball made it almost impossible. She only managed to reread the lines she had already seen.

173

THE WORDS OF THE BLESSING OF ENOCH, WHEREWITH HE BLESSED THE ELECT AND RIGHTEOUS, WHO WILL BE LIVING IN THE DAY OF TRIBULATION, WHEN ALL THE WICKED AND GODLESS ARE TO BE REMOVED.

Paili's voice drifted over from her own dugout. "Pretty ball!"

"It is pretty," Mara said, "but I wish it were brighter." The ball suddenly blazed, casting a sheet of radiance across the scroll. As Mara tried to read the tiny words again, the light dimmed, finally blinking out and leaving the hovel dark. She tightened the scroll and laid it close to her bed. Probing the darkness with a hard stare, she tried to see if any light trickled in from Elam's room. Nothing. He was probably asleep by now.

"Mara stay?" Paili yawned. "Mara not go away?"

"Yes, Paili. I'm here for the night." Mara took off her dress and folded it into a pillow. She curled to the side and pulled her sheet up to her shoulders. As she scooted herself into a comfortable position, a lump in her pillow poked her ear. She dug into her dress, withdrew the Ovulum, and held it in front of her eyes. In the darkness, only her fingers could identify the egg that had caused so much trouble in the upper lands.

Caressing its smooth glass brought an odd sense of comfort, soothing warmth that seemed to wash over her like a long soak in the sulfur baths. She brought the Ovulum even closer to her eyes, hoping to see a glimmer of the red light that had appeared before. What could possibly be inside that could bring both grief to a king and peace to her soul? Could a god actually live inside this thing? Why would a god even want to speak through such a small, seemingly fragile object?

Drawing it as close to her lips as possible without smudging the glass, she whispered, "Elohim?"

Paili groaned, but Mara couldn't tell if she was awake or not. She pulled the sheet over her head and whispered again. "Can you hear me?"

There was no answer. No glow. The egg felt cold and lifeless in her hand. Chilling sensations traveled through her arms and settled in her mind like unfriendly strangers following her in the darkness. Loneliness. Emptiness. Betrayal. Morgan's awful words echoed in her mind. *"Freak of nature. Ignorant freak of nature."*

Mara ran her fingers through her hair—her stark, white hair that made King Nimrod's eyes bulge. New tears emerged, and she tried to sniff them back, but they dripped down to her cheeks, her freakish pale cheeks.

Like the voice of an angry ghost, Nimrod's words came back to her. *"The temple worshippers would love to get their hands on you."* She grimaced at the thought. She had read enough to know what he meant.

Mara hugged the Ovulum against her chest. Confusing thoughts tumbled like flying ash. Whom should she trust? Nimrod seemed good for a while, but why would he want to kill her, or worse, little babies? Mardon was willing to kill the babies for him, but he also rescued her. Morgan was friendly some of the time, but she gave Nimrod something he needed to kill dragons, and the dragons were Elohim's friends. One thing was certain, Morgan, Nimrod, and Mardon all hated Elohim.

And why not? Elohim flooded the world and killed almost every creature on earth. He sent dragons to destroy the tower and the city, and now the people couldn't even talk to each other any more. But if Elohim was evil, why would he bother saving eight people on the ark? If he was good, it would make sense for him to war against Nimrod, if Nimrod was evil. Still, they could all be evil, and they'd all do anything to get power, even killing everyone by flooding the world. If only Elohim would just talk to her, maybe he could help her make sense of it all.

175

She threw the sheet off. Maybe she could warm the Ovulum up and make it work. She rubbed the glass surface vigorously with both hands, waited a few seconds, and looked again. Nothing.

Mara grumbled under her breath. Elohim had spoken to her before. Why didn't he want to speak now? Was he just too busy? Or maybe she did something wrong, and he was mad at her.

She pushed on the top of her head with her hand. There was just too much to think about! It felt like her brains were about to explode!

She laid her head on her dress and sighed. For some reason, she still wanted to hold the egg close, so she pressed its cool glass against her cheek and nuzzled her dirty pillow. As her mind wandered toward sleep, a low voice whispered in her ear. It was so soothing, she didn't want to wake up to see if it was real. If it was a dream, she wanted to keep dreaming, imagining that a gentle stranger cared enough to speak to her.

"Sapphira Adi," it sang. "You are Sapphira Adi, a gem as beautiful as the clearest sky, and your value to me is greater than any gem in all the world . . . Sapphira Adi."

Mara smiled and whispered, "Sapphira Adi," then drifted off to sleep.

CHAPTER

ELOHIM'S BARD

Sapphira closed the scroll and slid it to the edge of the table, pushing aside an embryo jar to make room. With Mardon away for so long, there was no one to dispose of the weaker plants, and she didn't have the heart to do it herself, so the worktable had become crowded with the new genetic combinations she had tried over the last hundred or so days. She set her chin on her hands and sighed. All she really wanted to do was to climb into the tower shelves and read their literary treasures, but Morgan kept making excuses and giving her more work to do.

In a sarcastic tone, Sapphira mocked her mistress's harsh voice. "Not until I find the scroll I'm looking for. If you don't have enough work to do, perhaps you would like to return to the trenches."

She blew out a loud sigh. At least she had one scroll to look at, but only a few minutes each night to read it. She couldn't risk falling asleep before putting it back in its hiding place, a narrow hole in her mattress. But those few moments of drinking in

Enoch's mysterious story were worth the risk, even though she couldn't understand most of it.

A soft, rustling sound made her turn her head. Her spawn had awakened, yawning and smacking his lips. Grabbing a tin full of plant food and her piece of graphite, she shuffled over to Yereq's chamber and knelt in front of him. "Hungry?"

Yereq gave her a short nod and grinned.

She showed him the hunk of graphite. "Do you want this?"

The little pod's brow lowered, and a tiny tongue protruded from his lips.

She laughed and dipped her finger in the food. "How about this?"

Yereq pulled his tongue back in and opened his mouth.

Sapphira stuffed the damp morsel in. "I think you're already smarter than Nabal was. I'm not even going to tell you what I saw him eating once." As she dipped her finger in again, the control room door opened, and a little girl peeked in.

Sapphira jumped up, leaving the food tin on the floor. "Paili! You're not supposed to be in here!"

Paili waved her hand frantically. "Come now!"

Sapphira ran to the door and escorted her out, spinning the wheel behind her. "How did you unlock it?"

She pointed at the wheel. "I watch you."

Sapphira set her hands on her hips. "Okay, what did you want?"

Paili waved her hand. "Come!" She picked up a lantern next to the door and ran into the tunnel. Sapphira chased her, following the bouncing ball of light through the darkness. Paili turned into a side room, and when Sapphira caught up, she leaned against the doorway to catch her breath. Inside, Paili set the lantern on a flat stone table that dominated the center of the small chamber. Atop the table, various breads, fruits, and vegetables were spread from end to end. The aroma of stew drifted through the room, wafting from a huge pot dangling over an open floor vent against the wall.

Paili stirred the pot with a ladle nearly as long as she was tall, and the light from the magma stream underneath the kitchen washed her face in an orange glow. "I cook," Paili said. She skipped over to the table and picked up a red, oblong fruit. "Morgan bring."

Sapphira took the fruit and held it in her hands. Instantly, the Ovulum in her pocket stung her leg like a hot poker. She dropped the fruit onto the table and stepped back. "Morgan wants you to put that in the stew?"

Paili nodded.

"How did you know to come to me?"

"I dream." She pointed at the fruit and stuck out her tongue, grimacing. "That bad."

Sapphira wrapped the girl in her arms. "Oh, Paili! You did the right thing! You were so brave to come into the control room and find me."

"I knock." She pushed her finger into Sapphira's stomach. "You not come."

"I'm sorry. I didn't hear you." Sapphira picked up a knife from the table and tapped it against the stone. "If you don't put it in the stew, she'll probably figure it out, and then you'll be in big trouble." She chopped down on the fruit and split it in two. Inside, a half dozen tiny red seeds spilled out from the core of the cream-colored flesh.

Sapphira snapped her fingers. "Is there another pot in here?"

Paili pointed under the table. "Two more."

Sapphira pulled out one of them and hustled it to the bigger stewpot. Transferring ladle full after ladle full, she filled the new pot about halfway with stew. "Okay," she said, grunting as she lifted the new pot to the table. "Go ahead and put the fruit in the big pot, and I'll hide this one in our hovel. We'll pass the word that

Morgan's up to something and warn them not to eat the stew tonight. If anyone listens to us, she can come to our hovel and get something to eat after baths."

Paili nodded and picked up the two halves of fruit. "I eat . . . our stew . . . later."

Sapphira patted her on the head. "Good girl." She let out a long sigh. "But will anyone else believe us?"

I n the darkness of the hovel, Sapphira slurped stew from a ladle. "Ahhh!" she said, handing the dipper to Paili.

"Good?" Paili asked.

"Excellent!" Sapphira wiped her mouth on her sleeve, then jerked her arm down. "Oops. I shouldn't have done that. Now there's stew on my tunic."

"No one come to eat," Paili said.

Sapphira nodded slowly. "I know. Not even Taalah. I guess they all ate that fruit."

Paili pointed at a light in the mouse hole. "Qatan have lantern?"

Sapphira pressed a finger to her lips and slid down to the floor. "Elam?" she whispered, "Are you there?"

"Yes," came the quiet voice.

She put her lips near the hole, hoping a whisper could make it through. "Have you had dinner yet?"

"No. I don't eat until Nabal's finished. I get whatever he leaves behind. I don't know if I'll get anything tonight, though. I haven't seen him in quite a while."

Sapphira drummed her fingers on the floor. "Listen. Even if they do feed you, don't eat the stew. Morgan made Paili put something bad in it, some kind of poisoned fruit."

"Maybe it was fruit from the tree in her room."

"No. It was from the tower museum. It's growing in the middle of—" Sapphira paused, furrowing her brow. "Did you say, 'Morgan's room'?"

"Yes. I saw a little tree growing there with blossoms and fruit. She's using our magneto bricks to give it light."

"She let you into her room!? That's the most forbidden area of all!"

"She summoned me, so I had to go."

"What did her fruit look like? The bad stuff is red and kind of oblong."

"I'm pretty sure it was white. As soon as I heard what she wanted, I told her I wouldn't do it and walked out, so I didn't get a real good look at it."

"What did she want?"

"For me to do some of her dirty work, but it's not worth talking about. Besides, I'm in big enough trouble already. Nabal killed the other brick maker, a boy named Raphah, the day after he was called to Morgan's room. Raphah never told me why he was called, but I think he refused Morgan, too."

"If Nabal's gone, he can't whip you to death."

"True, but there's always the chasm."

Sapphira nodded. "How could I forget?"

"I'm going to sneak back to her room and see if I can get some of that fruit."

"No!" she hissed. "If she catches you, she'll kill you for sure!"

"No, she won't. Before I refused her, she offered me some fruit to . . . well, bribe me, I guess. I'll just say I'm coming back to collect it."

Sapphira shook her head. "She won't believe that excuse. She's not stupid."

"I know, but the tree isn't the real reason I want to go. While I'm there, maybe I can find something that'll help me get out of this place."

Sapphira tightened her hand into a fist. Who was she to try to keep the poor guy in this awful prison? Her voice spiked with compassion. "Just don't get caught, okay?"

"I won't. I promise."

"Hey! Paili made some stew that's okay to eat, and I have quite a bit. Want some?"

"Sure, but how?"

Sapphira glanced around the dim hovel. What could she use to channel stew through such a small hole? Finding nothing, she dipped her fingertip into the lukewarm liquid. A smile broke through. "Uh . . . Elam?"

"Yes?"

"Have you heard how the spawns eat when they're in the growth chambers?"

"Uh-huh. I think so."

She plunged her whole hand into the stew. "Do you mind being a spawn for a few minutes?"

"I . . . I guess not."

Sapphira pulled her dripping fingers from the pot and squeezed her hand through the hole, pushing as hard as she could. When it wouldn't go any farther, she waited. After a few seconds, a wet, tickling sensation brushed her fingertips. Imagining Elam on the other side, she suppressed a giggle, a feeling of warm satisfaction flooding her body.

She pushed through six finger-loads of stew, trying to handle more with each attempt, but during the sixth feeding, a stern voice penetrated their hovel.

"Mara!"

Sapphira whispered, "It's Morgan!" Using her foot, she slid the stew pot behind Paili and yanked her hand through the hole. Quickly wiping the remaining stew on the back of her tunic, she stood in front of Paili.

A lantern lit up their hovel, and Morgan's face appeared in the dugout entry as she leaned in from the corridor. "Mara. You must come with me."

Sapphira didn't even glance back at Paili. She just hoped the lantern's light couldn't reach behind the girl's body. "Yes'm. I'm coming." She tried to read Morgan's expression. Could she have discovered their plot somehow?

"What's that smell?" Morgan asked, wrinkling her nose.

Sapphira blocked Morgan's view and raised her arm up near her mistress's face. "Stew. I got some on my sleeve."

"Rather sloppy," Morgan said, straightening to allow Sapphira to exit. "I expect better from you."

"Yes'm." Sapphira followed Morgan, watching the lady's long legs. It seemed strange that she always wore the same clothes, even at night. Most of the girls took off their outer dresses and slept wearing their inner tunics, while some who lived on the hot, lower level just took a sheet to bed, wrapping up in it later as the brick ovens cooled during the night. Morgan, however, seemed to be able to adjust to any temperature instantly.

Morgan stopped at the control room. The door had been left ajar, so she pushed it open and walked in. Sapphira followed, and when her eyes adjusted to the brighter light, she noticed two men examining the jars on her worktable at the back of the room. The taller of the two seemed familiar, yet not quite recognizable. The other man looked tired and battle-worn, but she knew her supervisor right away.

"Mardon!" she cried. "You're back!" She ran toward him, but he held up his hand, halting her. The other man pushed Mardon to the side and slapped her savagely across her face with the back of his hand, knocking her to the floor. Black spots speckled her vision as she laid her hand on her throbbing cheek. Warm liquid trickled through her fingers. Blood.

Too dizzy to rise, Sapphira lay on the cold stone, listening to the two men babbling in an odd language. With her cheek stinging as if on fire, she pushed up to her knees, and two strong, female hands helped her to her feet. Morgan's voice interrupted the two babblers. "Stop fighting, you fools!"

Through blurry vision Sapphira saw Mardon push the other man away, but she still couldn't tell who he was. She caressed her wounded cheek, smearing blood across her fingers. "Did I do something wrong?"

Morgan picked up a gray cloth from the table. "Oh, you won't get an answer," she said, dabbing Sapphira's cheek. "It seems, Mara . . . Oh, excuse me. It's Sapphira now, isn't it? Well, I mentioned this to you before, but it seems that Mardon no longer understands us." She handed Sapphira the cloth and set her fists on her hips. "He now speaks a crude language I have never heard before, a clucking, guttural language fit for poultry or swine."

Sapphira held the cloth over her wound and touched Mardon's arm. "Thank you for trying to protect me, but I guess you can't understand that, either, can you?"

Mardon just stared at her, blinking.

"No, he doesn't." Morgan waved her hand toward the other man. "His own father, the king, doesn't understand him."

As the lantern light flickered on the king's face, Sapphira finally recognized him. Though one cheek and his forehead were wrinkled with scar tissue, she remembered his deep brown eyes. "King Nimrod!" She dipped her head and curtsied, then looked up at him again, hoping her tears might draw some compassion. "I'm so sorry about that egg—" She covered her mouth with her fingers. "I forgot. He doesn't understand, either."

"No," Morgan said, "but apparently he remembers you all too well. What did the Ovulum do?"

Nimrod slid a ring up and down his finger. Sapphira winced at the sight of the mounted jewel that had ripped her cheek. "The egg said some things I didn't understand, and then dragons came and destroyed the tower. I guess he thought it was my fault." She nodded toward the king. "Did a dragon burn his face?"

"From what I can gather. He uses hand signals quite well, so I'm pretty sure a dragon was involved. He also draws pictures when he tries to communicate."

"Oh." Mara folded her cloth in half and laid it on the table. "Well, I guess that helps."

"Yes, and that's why I called you here. Because of your obvious intelligence, Naamah and I believe you are the one most capable of teaching these two brutes how to speak the original tongue again. In fact, with all the languages now being used in the upper world, Naamah and I also have much to learn. So, we will soon organize a language school, of sorts, and call upon your linguistic talents to make sure we are all proficient in the new tongues. Your first students, however, are Nimrod and Mardon. Even though they are men, they still have a reasonable supply of brainpower."

Sapphira shifted back and forth on her feet. "I will do whatever you request of me, of course, but may I also ask a question?"

Morgan sighed. "If you must."

"Did they notice the tower museum when they came through the portal? Were they excited to see that it survived the dragon fire?"

"They have not seen the museum." Morgan picked up a piece of graphite and handed it to Sapphira. "There are other ways to enter the lower realms, my dear, but we can discuss that later. For now, we had better get to work on something completely different. We are going to advance your spawn to mobility training immediately."

A new rush of heat surged into Sapphira's face. "How can he be ready for that? We haven't even turned down the magnetic field to test his strength."

"We'll start him off slowly," Morgan said. "But since his stalk thickness is greater than any spawn we've ever had, I think he'll be walking in less than a week."

"And then you'll replicate him?"

"Yes. We'll create a whole new race of intelligent and strong giants, and your spawn will be the leader. But right now, he is bonded to you. He cannot be the general we need until you wean him off your emotional support and release him to Mardon."

Sapphira glanced at Yereq. He grinned at her. "How do I do that?" she asked.

"I will teach him how to hate, and then you will make him hate you."

"Hate me? My spawn? I could never—"

Morgan slapped her across her unwounded cheek. "You will do what I say, or else! One more word of defiance, and my next blow will find your other cheek."

Sapphira cupped her hand over her cut. As Morgan's eyes flamed, Sapphira slowly backed away, nodding. "I'll . . . I'll do it." Blood oozed onto her fingers, and a single drop fell to the floor. As soon as it touched, the stone seemed to sizzle. A tiny string of smoke rose past Sapphira's knees. The string grew and slowly stretched out toward Nimrod, curling around his waist and then his neck.

With a sudden jerk, the string tightened into a taut gray rope and pulled Nimrod to the ground. Sapphira leaped back. Nimrod screamed, frantically reaching out, grasping for anything within arm's length. Mardon caught hold of his father's hand, but the former king sank slowly into the floor as if a sponge were absorbing his melting body. Soon, only Nimrod's terrified face and an outstretched arm remained, and Mardon finally had to let go. Within seconds, Nimrod was gone.

Sapphira fell to her seat, gaping at a black spot on the stony floor. Mardon dropped to his knees and touched the spot with his fingertips, murmuring a soft lament in his strange tongue.

Morgan glared at Sapphira, her jaw trembling with rage. "You have succeeded in cutting your teaching chore in half," she growled. "If your careless use of your power also dispatches Mardon, Paili will feel my wrath."

Sapphira cupped her cheek again, staring at Morgan as she stalked out of the room.

Morgan sat cross-legged at the edge of a deep pit, caressing a leather scabbard on the stone floor at her side. Next to the scabbard lay two gemstones—the one Mara had taken from the inner wall of the abyss and a matching stone Morgan had plucked just minutes ago.

As light streamed up from the darkness, Morgan waved her hands across the opening as if warming her fingers over a fire. Leaning closer and allowing the light to bathe her face, she spoke, her voice quavering slightly. "Samyaza. It is your wife, Lilith. If I have finally found you after all these years, I beg you to hear me and forgive my transgressions against you."

A loud growl sounded from the blackness, then a shout. "Lilith!" The angry cry echoed through the cavern.

Morgan jerked her head back, wincing.

Samyaza continued. "You black-hearted fiend! How dare you offer your sugar-coated words after betraying me with the very arts I taught you!"

She leaned over the pit again. Her voice stayed calm. "It was not a betrayal, my love. If I had not drained some of your power, you would not only be trapped in the abyss, but I would be dead and therefore powerless to help you escape. Instead, I am alive, and I have come to plan your departure from this cursed place."

Samyaza remained quiet for a few seconds. Morgan smiled, knowing she had cooled his fiery anger. "Since I am but a wraith, I have no body for you to inhabit, so even if I could climb down there, you would not be able to ride back with me. And it's possible that I could not make it back at all."

Samyaza's voice returned, quieter, yet still firm. "I know you, Lilith. You have a plan. What is it?"

"My plan has many complexities, but the ultimate goal is for you and I to rule the world. Of course, the only way to do that is to exterminate every dragon and create an army that will help us conquer our enemies."

187

"What is so complex about that?"

"As long as dragons rule the skies, in your weakened condition, you would not be able to fight them."

Samyaza's voice crackled with sarcasm. "Weakened, thanks to you."

"True, but, as I said, I was your only hope. Who else would wish to free you?"

Another pause ensued, then a quiet, "Go on."

Morgan raised a pair of her long, slender fingers. "We are trying to build an army in two ways. The spirits of the Nephilim are still alive, and they are beginning to indwell the dragon race. They will be powerful allies in our war."

"But you said you wanted to exterminate every dragon. Why make them our allies?"

"That's where the plan gets complicated." Morgan closed her fingers into a fist. "The Nephilim will make the dragon race virulent in the sight of humans, and I will personally incite war between the two species. To crown my achievements, I will raise up a champion who will ensure that every dragon will die."

"If every dragon dies, then what of our army?"

Morgan lifted a pinch of soil and let it trickle back to the ground. "We are creating another army from the earth. We are genetically engineering a race of giants, hybrids from the seeds of angels."

"Farm-raised Nephilim? Ingenious."

"Thank you," Morgan replied, waving her hands over the streams of light again. "I thought you would approve. The experimentation is tedious, but we have finally created a suitable combination, a fierce, intelligent giant who will be our model for all the others."

"How long will it take?"

"The plants grow slowly, so it will take many years."

"Plants? They are not human?"

"They are fully human. We splice a photosynthetic gene into the human genome at the embryonic stage, allowing us to grow them from the earth. It makes them more self-sustaining, able to gather light and power from their environment. Since they have a full set of human genes, they eventually slough off their plant stems and grow into a completely human form."

"So once the dragons are gone and your army is in place, how will you release us?"

Morgan paused and leaned closer, lowering her voice. "With Chereb."

Samyaza grunted a contemptuous laugh. "What good will my sword do in the hands of a sorceress?"

Morgan patted down the streams of light as if trying to quell his skepticism. "I told you I learned the secret to its power."

"So will its power destroy this prison?"

"I believe so, yet escape from the abyss might not be enough. We sit here now in the lower realms, thousands of feet of earth separating us from the skies above, but even up there we would be in one of the circles of Hades. There is no way I know for you to return to the dimension of the living. I am able to go there for a short time, because of my unusual status as a wraith, but I think that dimension would be closed to you."

"Then your plan is not complete," Samyaza growled. "We are at a dead end."

"No. I have been listening to Elohim's prophets in the world of the living. They say a king is coming who will open up the way of escape from this dimension. I will watch for this king and learn how he opens the gateway."

"What if this king is the only one with the power to make such an opening?"

"Whatever is done once can be done again. If I have to, I will find another king who will pave the way. In the meantime, I must neutralize the force that Elohim has sent to destroy my plan."

189

"What force is that?"

"The oracles of fire—two girls we spawned here. They have extraordinary intelligence and insight. I killed one of them, so I think we are safe, but I want to make sure."

"So kill the other one and be done with her."

Morgan shook her head. "It's not so easy. Whoever sheds their blood ends up dying. Even one of my stupid giants, a fool named Nabal, died before I could kill him myself. He whipped one of the oracles, and I found him dead in his hovel that very night. Something similar happened to a foolish king I know. A very powerful force protects that girl."

"Then how did you manage to kill the other one?"

"By the only method that always works against oracles sent by God. Betrayal."

"I see. A most vicious and effective weapon. But take care. Such a weapon can be turned against you."

190

Morgan sighed and nodded. "Well spoken, my love. But I have chosen my weapon, and he has already forged his way into the heart of the second oracle. He will soon be ready to plunge my final dagger into Mara's heart."

"Her name is Mara?" Samyaza chuckled. "This will be a bitter pill indeed."

"Yes, and don't be surprised if she comes here. She is the one who found you for me, and knowing her curiosity, she'll be back."

"I will be sure to listen for her. What is the name of the betrayer?"

"Elam. He is a special prize, stolen from the family of my greatest enemy. The pain his departure caused his father and grandfather was sweet to witness."

Samyaza laughed again. "Ah, Lilith! Your conniving genius fills me with confidence. We will wait patiently for your plan to unfold."

"Yes, Samyaza." Morgan rose to her feet and withdrew Chereb from the leather scabbard. "Everything has been set in motion," she said, gazing at the shining blade. "Nothing can stop us now."

The second week of language training had finally ended. As she trudged back toward her hovel, Sapphira laid her hand on her aching head, Mardon's shouts still ringing in her ears. He caught on pretty quickly, but his patience was as thin as her coif veil. Whenever a new word flustered him, he screamed louder than Nabal ever did. At least Nimrod wasn't around anymore. He would surely have made the training sessions much worse.

Exhausted, Sapphira slipped quietly back into her hovel, a dim lantern in hand. Paili snored gently, her angelic face peaceful under the glow of the flaming wick. After setting the lantern on the floor, she whispered toward the hole. "Elam? Are you there?"

There was no answer.

She pressed her uninjured cheek against the floor and whispered again. "Elam?"

Again, no answer.

The lantern's light revealed something new, an object resting in the hole to Elam's chamber. She reached in and caressed something soft and delicate. Pulling the object out, she laid it in her hand, a large flower that covered most of her palm. Though the light was too dim to tell for sure, its seven petals looked white, each one protruding from a golden center. The petals felt as soft as the pod of a newborn spawn. She held the blossom by its thin green stem, turning it in the dim glow. It had to be from the tree in Morgan's room. She pressed her ear against the cold wall. Obviously Elam got out of Morgan's room safely, but where was he now?

Feeling the sting in her cheek again, Sapphira set the blossom on her bed and stepped quietly back to the hovel entrance. The

191

oozing cut seemed to get worse and worse, even though she had washed it every evening. Tired as she was, it had to be washed again. There was probably time to hurry to the spring and still get a few hours of sleep later.

After shuffling sleepily through the corridor and into the spring's cavern, she set the lamp at the edge of the sulfur pool and gazed into the still waters. The flickering light cast waves of orange over the mirror-like surface, a glare that shimmered across her reflection. Sliding the lantern farther away, she kept her eyes on the water until she could see her image clearly. She touched her wound, feeling the ugly gash that scarred her face. Seeing her cheek made it sting even worse. It was more than a physical blemish; it seemed to expose her soul, an ugly rut in her smooth skin that undressed her wounded heart.

Sapphira pressed her lips together, trying not to cry. The empty cavern reminded her of her cruel slavery. Morgan hated her. Naamah wasn't much better. Mardon seemed to view her as a science experiment that could be thrown away whenever she was no longer useful. Even her spawn now glared at her in disgust, learning more hate from Morgan every day. And the king of all the upper realms, who once sang the praises of her beauty, had delivered a cutting blow, scarring that beauty forever.

Taking a handful of water, she dabbed the cut, tears beginning to flow as heat surged through her face, making it feel as though a bat had dug its claws into the wound and was tearing it wide open. Now, every lash, every cut, and every bruise Nabal and other slave drivers had gouged into her skin began to throb. She pulled down the shoulder of her dress, exposing the whip laceration Nabal had delivered just before Acacia died. It burned like fire.

She knelt again at the pool and gazed at her tear-stained face. Resting her hands in the shallows, she sighed. Who could ever love an ugly little slave girl, an underborn who scarred her body chiseling rocks all day in dark, lonely caverns? She wasn't a king. She wasn't a scholar. She knew nothing more than what she read in dusty scrolls salvaged from haphazard piles and squirreled away for clandestine reading during the chilly hours of the night.

While shivering at her own memories, she imagined Morgan catching her out of her hovel after bedtime. In her mind's eye, the swinging hand of King Nimrod appeared in the pool's reflection as it ripped across her cheek, pounding her to the floor in agony. As she writhed at Nimrod's feet, the sound of Morgan's haunting laughter echoed, joining a chorus of others as they chanted in mocking hatred. The pitiful girl in the pool could only gaze up at her conquerors and cry.

Sapphira slapped the surface of the water. "You deserved it! You're nobody! You're just a dirty, ugly slave!" As her reflection began to congeal again on the surface, she pointed at her rippled image. "You're not Sapphira Adi. You're just Mara, an ignorant underborn! Nobody loves you! Not Morgan. Not Mardon. I'll bet even Elohim hates you!" She spat into the water. "If you had been alive back then, he would have kicked you off the ark, and you would have drowned in the flood with all the others." Covering her face with her hands, she wept bitterly, her body heaving in wave after wave of sobs.

As her convulsions began to ease, a familiar warmth penetrated her thigh and radiated slowly across her skin. Still kneeling, she reached into her pocket and withdrew the Ovulum. It pulsed, sending crimson halos toward her that expanded into fiery rings all around her body. The rings stroked her arms, like the baking rays of the sun in the upper lands, chasing away every chill. In the pool reflection, her skin blazed with fire, flames leaping from her face and hands, as though the halos had kindled an unworldly power within.

Some of the rings passed over the water, sending ripples across the pool that deepened with every stroke of the caressing red light.

193

Soon the water seemed to dance, thousands of droplets jumping high and falling back to the pool like silvery baitfish fleeing a predator. A swirling breeze buffeted the flying waters, sending a spray across Sapphira, sprinkling her hot cheeks with soothing coolness.

She gazed at the sight in wonder, inhaling deep draughts of the fresh, cool air. As the droplets grew and began to coat her face, she spread out her arms, the Ovulum still pulsating in her hand as she whispered into the breeze. "Let the rain fall, Elohim. Let me drown and join all the others. I am Mara, a worthless slave, and I deserve to die."

The rain dampened her hair and trickled down her forehead. The Ovulum's warmth radiated through her arm, and as the heat approached her body, the sound of singing drew near, a man's voice that seemed to travel along with the warm sensation. The voice crooned in her ear.

"Sapphira Adi," it sang softly. "You are a precious gem. You are loved more than you will ever know. Bask in the warmth of Elohim's love. Feel his pleasure in the coolness of his soothing rain, for this is not the rain of floods and destruction; it is living water that will heal your heart."

Sapphira trembled. Tears flowed down her cheeks. "Who . . . who are you?"

With the cadence of a herald's proclamation, the voice resonated in the cavern. "I am the Eye of the Oracle, the prophet who first told of the great flood. I am Elohim's bard, the singer who foretells blessings and curses upon generations to come. And now I have a song for you."

Sapphira swallowed hard, barely able to speak. "A song of blessing?" Her lips trembled. "Or a curse?"

A gentle laugh flowed through her mind, then a whisper. "Listen to the words of Elohim . . . and believe." The voice sang again, this time in a beautiful tenor.

In days gone by the water fell
And draped the world in silent death;
A rain of judgment drowned the earth
Demanding life and snatching breath.

But now the raindrops fall afresh
On hearts rejecting hate and sin,
In blessings crowned with love and grace
To heal the wounds of soul and skin.

The one who loves is Elohim,
Rejoicing now in song and dance;
I shout for you to come and play,
Enjoying love, the great romance.

So dance, my child, and feel my love
In rain, the healing drops of life.
Forsake your cares, your toils and pain,
The wounds and scars of slavish strife.

O cast aside the chains of grief
And reach for heaven's grace above;
Sapphira Adi, dance with me!
Enfold yourself in arms of love.

As the song died away, the rain began pouring down, drenching her hair and clothes. The coolness penetrated her skin and seemed to wash away every sorrow, every pain, every image of slavery that tortured her mind. She peeked at her shoulder, now exposed as the water weighed down her dress. The wound had vanished without a trace. Cool drops of tingling water trickled over her cheek. She touched the spot where the wound had festered, now soft and smooth, and pain free.

Clutching the Ovulum tightly, she lifted her arms and laughed, allowing the swirling breeze to catch her body and spin her in a slow pirouette. Lights twinkled through the prismatic mist, spraying her with a dazzling splash of rainbow colors. She closed her eyes and felt loving arms taking her into a tender embrace, and she returned the favor, hugging her image of Elohim, the God of love. As the bard's song returned, repeating each phrase amidst the sounds of tumbling waters, she drank in every word, allowing her body to flow with the leading of her gentle lover.

And Sapphira Adi danced.

Book 2

Transformation

But we all, with open face beholding
as in a glass the glory of the Lord, are changed
into the same image from glory to glory,
even as by the Spirit of the Lord.

(2 Corinthians 3:18)

CHAPTER

A New Beginning

Circa AD 62

Makaidos flew high over the parched valley, buoyed by a hot, arid updraft. Sunshine energized every muscle and sharpened his vision. The conditions had been ideal—bright light and clear skies—a perfect day to satisfy his rekindled sense of purpose and fulfill this duty to which he had been called. Accomplishing such an important task had made the day complete, and the sun's slow descent into the reddening western sky gave notice that his successful mission was drawing to a close.

He scanned the landscape far below—the outskirts of the port city with its single-story huts and trading posts; scrub trees lining a dry riverbed that wound its way to the sea; and, finally, a caravan of camels, horses, and pack mules in a snaking line following what had been, before the drought, a shallow but dependable stream. Still, the sandy bed provided an unobstructed route to the docking port, making it a well-traveled path, but also a haunt for highwaymen on the prowl for easy prey.

Makaidos snorted at the thought. The only easy prey would be anyone who tried to attack Joseph and his company. The cup of Christ would be safe if this dragon had anything to say about it. A couple of days earlier, just the sight of a patrol dragon had kept a small band of human predators at bay, but now the hint of a greater danger pricked Makaidos's senses.

He circled lower and shadowed the company. Joseph rode high on the lead camel. The cup, the Holy Grail, as he called it, was probably tucked away in his saddlebag. He never let it out of his reach.

As they approached the first trading post, water muddied the riverbed pathway. The animals slogged through it, trudging closer to the sloped edge to find drier ground. A tall, bearded man at the post nodded to a stout woman next to him, a lady with a heavily painted face and at least a dozen gold and silver bangles on each wrist. She scurried down a path toward a large tent, her long gray skirts raising plumes of dust.

Makaidos's danger signal flamed. He glided toward the caravan and flew in tight ellipses around the travelers. The bearded man glanced up at him, glaring at first, but his frown transformed into a bright smile as he waved his arms. "Stop! Stop and rest! Eat! Drink! Take your leisure!"

Joseph signaled for his company to stop, and he laid the reins on his lap. "Greetings in the name of the Lord Christ. I take it that you have lodging for myself and my fellow travelers? We must board a ship for Italy just after dawn."

The man pointed at the large tent. "At my inn! The city is crowded and noisy, but out here you will find quiet and rest. The docks are not far, so you will have plenty of time to embark on your ship in the morning."

"Very well." Joseph climbed down from his camel, and the man immediately reached for the saddlebag. Joseph slapped his hand over it. "I will take care of this. You may see to the other bags."

The man slid his hand away from the saddle and nodded. "As you wish. I will signal my helpers." He glanced back at the tent and let out a shrill whistle. A man emerged through the opening, then a second, a third, a fourth, and a fifth. Ten more men joined the others and dashed toward Joseph, some waving curved swords and dark oval shields, others fixing arrows to bows.

Makaidos swooped down, his wings outstretched and his teeth bared, fire blasting from both nostrils. He aimed the twin jets at the tall, bearded man, incinerating him in a breath, then landed and turned his fire toward the attacking band. Six arrows penetrated his wall of flames and zinged into his body, five clanking on his armor and one pricking a gap between the scales on his chest. "Joseph," he shouted. "Run for cover on the other side of the riverbed!"

As the travelers dashed to the trees on the opposite bank, Makaidos cremated the remaining attackers, leaving more than a dozen heaps of ash smoldering under the baking sun.

"Makaidos!" a voice called. "Help!"

Makaidos jerked his neck around. More attackers swarmed toward the travelers on the other bank! He leaped into the air, but a rope flew his way and snagged a back leg. A second rope caught his other back leg. Clusters of men clinging to each rope emerged from the bushes and pulled against him with all their might. Snorting a quick fiery blast, Makaidos burned the lines and launched toward the new band of highwaymen. More arrows pinged his armor and fell harmlessly to the ground, but one plunged deep into his foreleg, drawing a stream of blood.

Ignoring the pain, Makaidos landed and blew pinpoint lines of fire, igniting the villains as they fought hand to hand or sword to sword with Joseph and his company. Within seconds, the battle was over. Three attackers fled on foot, dropping their weapons behind them. Makaidos stretched out his wings to follow, but Joseph grasped his foreleg, straining to hold the dragon back. "No, my friend. You are injured. It is time to rest and recover."

Joseph's arm brushed against one of the protruding arrows. Makaidos cringed and fell to his haunches.

"Those cowards won't be back anytime soon." Joseph stooped next to the wound. He pushed his thumbs against the adjacent scales, and his deeply creased face contorted. "Hmmm. It is not shallow. We will need to get it out soon. The edges of your scales are already cutting through the arrow's shaft."

"Go ahead and pull it," Makaidos said. "I heal quickly."

As his fellow travelers gathered around, Joseph nodded at one of them. "Lazarus, take Trophimus and whomever else you need and find suitable lodging." Lazarus bowed and laid a saddlebag at Joseph's feet.

Joseph stood and gripped the shaft. "I am glad God sent you, but I would like to know why you risk your life for our cause. Your faith is the most unusual I have ever seen."

"My family and I want to follow wherever you go." Makaidos felt the pressure on the arrow and spoke through clenched teeth. "You have taught me so much about the Messiah, but I need to learn more."

"Yet when will you learn that I am human, and you are a dragon?" Joseph gritted his teeth and pulled the arrow, grunting, until it finally came out. He held it up for Makaidos to see, a bloody shaft with a pointed, barbed end. He nodded at it, his white hair blowing in the dry, dusty breeze. "I have told you many times that Jesus bled and died to save human souls. Of course, it's an argument from silence, but I have my doubts as to whether the atonement includes dragons."

A woman removed her white headscarf and tied it around Makaidos's leg wound. Makaidos nuzzled her shoulder gently. "Thank you, Salome." He raised his head and twitched his ears toward Joseph. "Dragons have souls. We must. The soul of Arramos has gone to another place, for I cannot believe the evil dragon who calls himself my father really holds the true spirit of

202

Arramos. And I cannot believe the Maker would put a soul in me and not provide a way to save it."

"If, indeed, it needs saving." Joseph laid his hands on Makaidos's chest just below another protruding arrow. "Your race was not included in Adam's curse, and I have never known a soul as spotless as yours."

Makaidos braced for another round of pain. "My mistakes have cost me my eldest son and daughter as well as others in my brood. My eyes were too set on the Maker's commands, and I missed the signals that might have helped me see the rebellion before it was too late."

Joseph yanked out the arrow, but this jolt was far less painful.

"Dear Makaidos," Joseph said with a soft chuckle. "Listen to yourself. *Too* obedient to God? *Might* have helped? These are not sins; they are limitations. You cannot see and know all. Don't condemn yourself for lacking God's attributes."

Salome borrowed a headscarf from another woman and blotted the chest wound. Makaidos cringed. Now it hurt! He exhaled, trying to ignore the pain as he stretched his neck toward Joseph and lowered his voice. "You have proven that I still have more to learn. Let me come with you to the islands of the North and protect you until you find a safe place to house the Holy Grail. Then I will come back and bring my family to live wherever you dwell."

Joseph raised the second arrow, blunted on the tip and less bloody. "Of course you may come, and I welcome your protective shield. Who am I to tell you what to do?"

"My wounds are minor," Makaidos said, pushing his weight down on his bandaged leg. "I will be ready at dawn."

Joseph shook his head and laughed. "As old as you are, you still remind me of a young man I encountered in Ephesus—Timothy, a disciple of Paul the apostle."

Makaidos rotated his ears. "How so?"

203

"Well, he is enthusiastic and wishes to follow his mentor wherever he goes." Joseph raised a finger. "But he is also learning the same lesson you must learn."

"What lesson is that?"

"One that I must drive into your brain so you will never forget it." Joseph spread an arm out toward the sea. "Since we are sailing on a Greek vessel tomorrow, I want you to remember a Greek word. *Autarkeia*."

"*Autarkeia*? What does that mean?"

"It means 'contentment'." Joseph stooped, reached into his saddlebag, and withdrew a small wooden goblet. He held it in his palms as if swirling liquid inside. "A vessel that seems destined for common use can transform into a great treasure when touched by the finger of God. Whether dragon or human, we must be content with who we are and be patient as we wait to see what God will make of us." He laid a gentle hand on the dragon's long, narrow jaw. "You are not human, Makaidos. Be content with the fact that God made you a dragon for a reason. Rest in God's will for you, serve him with all your might, and he will transform you into what he wants you to be."

Makaidos lowered his head and closed his eyes. The word did pierce his brain, painful and deep like one of the arrows, yet there were no scales to blunt its penetration. He sighed and nodded. "*Autarkeia*. . . . I will remember, Master Joseph."

"Excellent." Joseph patted Makaidos's good leg. "It will be a pleasure having dragons in the northern islands."

CIRCA AD 490

Morgan bent forward and stroked the man's rugged chin, her eyes flaming red. "Are we agreed then?" she asked. "Your perfect allegiance to me in exchange for immortality?"

"Without question, my lady." The man, sitting straight on a low footstool, picked up a black helmet from his lap and tucked it under his mail-clad arm. "Although the king has outlawed dragon hunting, I trust that you will prepare the way."

Grasping the hilt of a beautiful sword, she leaned back in her throne-like chair. The dim chamber echoed every squeak of antique wood, the sounds bouncing off an open balcony encircling the airy lower floor. A dank odor of disuse hung in the air, as if neither door nor window had been opened in years.

As Morgan fingered the sword's hilt, lantern light glimmered on the shiny, etched blade. "I will prepare the way. Makaidos and his followers have had over four hundred years to endear themselves to the people of the North, but the spirits of the Nephilim are guiding another brood of dragons to our shores. Goliath and his company will repulse human hearts with their, shall we say, onerous behavior. In any case, I will personally see to Arthur's enchantment. The laws against dragon hunting will soon be only a memory."

The man rose to his feet and set the helmet next to a chess-board at the end of a long table. "And what of Merlin? He is not so easily enchanted."

"Leave Merlin to me." She ran her thumb along the edge of the blade and smiled. "There are many ways to skin an old gray fox."

The man reached for one of the chess pieces, but Morgan slammed the flat of the sword on the table. "Don't touch that!"

The man jumped back and smoothed out the banner draped over his mail shirt. "Oh! Sorry . . . well . . ." He cleared his throat nervously. "My squire has been of great service to me. Shall I tell him of our plans?"

Morgan pulled the sword back and propped it against the chair's headrest. "Only that you are ridding the world of the dragon menace. Tell him nothing of our plot to overthrow Arthur until the time comes. He will gladly fill his moneybags and enjoy unnaturally long life while keeping his questions to himself."

The man bowed. "I am confident of that, my lady, and we both look forward to serving you."

"Of course you do." Morgan stood and angled the blade toward the chess pieces. "As long as you play this game well, your rewards will be great."

The man swallowed hard and backed away. "I will play it well. I do not wish to consider the alternative."

With a deft stroke, Morgan sliced the chessboard's black knight vertically in half. "No," she said, glaring at him. "The alternative is not pleasant . . . not pleasant at all."

CIRCA AD 492

Edward shivered. Rarely had it been so cold this early in the season. He shifted his feet, trying to stay as quiet as possible while listening to the generals who surrounded the king, but the freezing rain spattering the fallen leaves sounded like a hundred slabs of sizzling bacon, drowning out the conversation. Walking on tiptoes as he strained to see the king, he wedged his way between two soldiers. They stank badly, but at least they shielded him from the cold, wet breeze.

He tightened his scabbard belt and folded his arms in behind his shield. The lining his mother had sewn into his tunic really felt good now. She had warned of an early winter, claiming that her aching bunions and arthritic elbow agreed with the forecast of the early migrating birds. She was right, as usual. Now if only he could prove himself to the king and move up in the ranks, he could afford to send some money back to her for medicines and a thicker cloak. Ever since Father died, sewing soldiers' uniforms had been their source of income, and that barely put food on the table.

He elbowed to the front line of soldiers and settled next to a burly man who smelled even worse than the others. But it was worth it. Now he could see the king sitting on a rotting stump in the center of his ring of advisors. With his arms propped on his knees, King Arthur leaned his sword against his shoulder. He spoke loudly enough to be heard over the winter storm. "I know of Goliath's evil deeds, Sir Devin, but I trust King Makaidos. He did not teach his son to murder and steal."

Sir Devin nodded with a slight tilt of his head, his pupils barely visible in his narrowed eyes. "Too much trust makes kingdoms fall, Your Majesty." His words slipped out through clenched teeth, each one tempered by the diplomacy due a knight of his order. "Your faith resides in coats of scales while you snub your nose at your own kind, which could lead to dishonorable, even rebellious, behavior." He dipped his head again. "Your Worship."

Edward fumed. How could the king put up with Devin's sarcasm? Sure, the knight had good reason to hate dragons, but his irreverence deserved a date with the ax man.

Merlin pounded the end of his walking staff on the leaf-strewn ground. "Sire, a man who breathes rumors of treachery had better back his words with more evidence than his own hot air."

Edward clenched his fist. *That's telling him, Merlin!*

Devin swept his arm toward a village on a nearby hill. "Didn't Goliath's slaughter of six orphans convince you? Isn't that enough evidence for us all to hate the very air they breathe?"

"You only hate what you fear," Merlin retorted. "If you weren't such a coward, you would learn that many dragons are trustworthy."

Devin sneered at him. "It's easy to feign courage when you hold the dragon's bane, but you won't even tell us what it is. Every dragon seems to tremble when you walk near."

"That will remain my secret, for I am bound by a covenant from Noah himself to protect what he has passed down to me."

"Merlin," Devin said with a condescending glare, "having heard you recite your pedigree too many times, we are painfully aware of your prophetic heritage." He turned to face the king. "My

207

point still stands. The seed of murder had to come from somewhere, and Goliath's father is the sower."

"And God himself created Satan and all the demons." Merlin
pointed his staff at Devin. "Where did your seed come from?"

Devin grasped the hilt of his sword. "Listen, old man, you—"

"Enough!" Arthur rose to his feet. "In a time of crisis, what
might happen must yield to what is certain to happen. We cannot
defeat the barbarian horde without help from the dragons, so there
is no real choice in the matter."

The crowd of soldiers murmured. Edward picked up the words
of the closest men. "Fight alongside dragons after so many years?
How can we know which ones to trust? And, in any case, who
would dare venture a journey near Bald Top to request their aid?"

The king waved a hand toward Devin's squire. "Palin. I will
assign another scribe for the battle. Go and ask Makaidos to
come!"

Palin lifted his quill and stared at the king, wide-eyed. "To the
dragon's cave, Sire?" He glanced at Devin, then shifted his gaze
back to the king. "I only brought my close combat sword," he said,
patting his scabbard.

Cold sweat dampened Edward's back. He took one step forward, then hesitated.

The king scowled. "You won't need a sword, Palin, just—"

Edward cleared his throat and thrust himself into the inner circle. "I beg your pardon, Your Majesty." He stepped up to the king
and dropped to one knee. "I will fetch the dragon for you, Sire."
Looking King Arthur in the eye, he tried to keep his voice steady.
"He will either come with me or die."

Arthur smiled and gestured for Edward to rise. "What is your
name, young man?"

Edward stood and nodded at the king. "Edward, son of your
servant, Edmund."

"Edmund, the orphan-keeper?"

"Yes, Your Majesty."

"He told me he named his son Edmund, after himself. Why would you disrespect him by calling yourself by another name?"

Edward nodded again. "I beg your pardon, Your Majesty, but I honor my father. I have chosen to take a similar name until I prove myself worthy to carry his."

"And what would make you worthy? Daring to enter the cave of Makaidos? He is not a danger to you or anyone in my kingdom."

"No, Your Majesty. I wish to prove myself as a faithful servant to you. A dragon killed my father as he defended the orphanage, so the thought of aligning myself with their kind is abhorrent to me. Yet, I am willing to do your bidding in spite of my hatred of dragons."

Arthur slid his sword into its scabbard. "Well spoken, young knight, but your father's murderer was Goliath, not Makaidos."

Sir Devin patted Edward on the shoulder. "It is said that the sprout never sloughs off its seed, Your Majesty. Edward is brave and honorable, as was his father. Goliath is a murderer, so his father—"

Merlin pushed Devin away with his staff. "You have spilled enough bile, Devin. Let the boy get on with it before we all freeze to death."

"And before the Saxons return for another attack," the king added.

The burly man from the circle stepped forward. "I volunteer to accompany him, Sire." He drew a long sword from his scabbard. "I fear no dragon."

"Excellent!" the king said. "No one should venture toward Bald Top alone. We will assemble at Chalice Hill as planned and await the dragons."

Edward frowned. With that huge man at his side, no one would ever give him credit for bringing back Makaidos. Besides, this wide-bodied soldier needed a bath worse than if he had been sprayed by a polecat.

After bowing to the king, Edward turned and stalked away. He could hear the soldier's heavy footsteps behind him and his deep voice. "Edward, may I suggest the more gradual slope? It makes a wide circuit around the mountain."

Marching more quickly, Edward held his shield close to his side to keep it from bouncing. "If you're too old or fat to follow, then take the easy path. I'm going the fastest way."

"I am not concerned for my sake. Goliath was seen on that slope only yesterday, and if you have never fought a dragon, you'll need—"

"The faster we get help, the faster we defeat the Saxons." Edward halted and spun around. "Are you with me, or aren't you?"

The knight's thick mustache lifted as he spoke. "I am with you, Edward, to be sure, but you are not showing proper respect to an elder soldier." He moved his shield to his other arm and peeled back his sleeve, revealing a tattoo on his hairy wrist. "And one of higher rank." The black ink was bloodstained and crude, but clearly displayed the insignia of a captain.

Edward bowed. "I had no idea. I beg your pardon, Captain, uh . . ."

"Barlow," he replied, placing a hand on his chest. "Winston Barlow of Hickling Manor."

"Captain Barlow. I apologize for my rudeness. Your manner of dress didn't match what I normally see in an officer, nor did your . . . uh . . . your odor."

"Completely understandable, young man." Barlow strode forward through the underbrush, scaling the steepening slope with ease as Edward followed. "When I go to battle," he continued, "I don't stay back and shout at my men like a prissy schoolmarm. I charge with them on the front lines. As you might expect, that can be a messy business, and we have not had time for baths in almost a month."

"I see, and again, I beg your forgiveness." Edward had to hustle to keep up with the huge man who showed no signs of slowing down as he leapt from rock to rock like a big mountain goat. "Captain Barlow, I don't mean to question your directional skills, but we just missed the path that goes around the summit of Bald Top."

"You're the one who wanted to get there quickly." Barlow grabbed a sapling and hoisted himself up to a ledge, ripping out the tree and its roots in the process. "And the shortest way to the den of Makaidos is straight over the top."

Edward scrambled up to the ledge, using his shield for leverage, and reached the Captain's side. "But we would be exposed. If we skirt the top we could—"

Barlow halted and pressed a finger into Edward's chest. "If you fear Goliath, then go around, and I'll scale the top. If Goliath accosts me, then all the better for you. At the very least, I will distract him and clear your path to Makaidos."

211

Edward clutched the hilt of his sword. "And lose my chance to slay Goliath and gain honor in the king's eyes? Never!"

"Honor?" Barlow pushed him away. "This isn't about honor." He turned and marched up the slope.

Edward ran after him, his cheeks now blazing. What a fool he had been! He sounded like a self-serving mercenary, not a humble knight! Grabbing a fallen branch from the undergrowth, he pushed the end into the ground and hoisted himself up the hill. It was time for more action and fewer words.

When they neared the summit, the forest ended abruptly, revealing a huge, grassy field that served as Bald Top's treeless dome. Flakes of snow mixed with stinging sleet, and the gusty breeze whipped the icy mix into their faces.

Barlow withdrew his sword. "Dragons can sense danger, so Goliath likely knows we're in his territory. There is no reason to dawdle." The hefty knight broke into a trot, his chain mail jingling as his feet pounded the grass.

Edward dropped his stick and slid out his own sword, balancing his body between his weapon and shield as he jogged stride for stride behind the captain. His eyes darted all around at the dreary skies, and his boots crunched a thin coat of ice pellets that salted the ankle-high grass. The clamor drowned out any hope of hearing the wings of an approaching dragon.

As the forest on the opposite edge drew nearer, Barlow stopped and raised his sword high. "Back to back!" he shouted.

Edward swung around and pressed his back against Barlow's. He scanned the blanket of clouds but could find no dragon. "Where is he?"

"Shields up!" Barlow yelled, crouching low. "Now!"

Edward crouched with him, his heart pounding. "I don't see him!"

"If you don't raise your shield, you will never use it again!"

Edward thrust his shield up over his face and tucked his body into a ball. Suddenly a wave of fire splashed around the edges of his shield, so hot, it felt like his hair had caught fire.

"Flatten!" Barlow yelled. "The tail is next."

"Flatten?" Edward repeated. "What do you mean?"

Barlow's heavy body flattened Edward face down on the slushy grass. Then, the weight suddenly lifted. Edward flipped over. Barlow was flying away, the strap of his shield caught in the spiny tail of a dragon!

"Let go of me!" Barlow shouted. "Or I'll feed your bones to my dog!"

Edward jumped to his feet, snatching up his sword and shield in one motion. With the dragon's tail swinging violently, Barlow swung with it, his arm apparently stuck in the shield's strap. The knight clawed viciously at the dragon's tail with his free hand as he continued to shout, but the wind garbled his words.

With his sword at the ready, Edward pivoted in place, his gaze locked on Goliath. The dragon swooped low and tried to slap his rider against the ground, but he only managed to dredge a Barlow-sized divot.

As they zipped toward the edge of the hill, Barlow shouted, "Complete the mission! I will take care of this overgrown butter-fly!" The dragon glided over the trees and disappeared from sight.

Edward gasped for breath, his heart pounding in his throat. Seeing Barlow's fallen sword in the slush, he grabbed it and thrust his own sword into its scabbard. Pivoting again as he scanned the skies, he puffed clouds of vapor into the chilly air. What should he do? He couldn't abandon his captain, nor could he defy his orders. Either choice seemed dishonorable.

Edward clenched the strap on his shield. This wasn't about honor.

He ran toward the opposite edge of the hilltop and found a treeless slope. Dropping his shield to the deepening ice, he sat inside it and pushed against the ground until the shield began slid-ing on its own. He plunged down the hill, pushing Barlow's sword on either side to dodge stumps and holes as he careened toward a narrow brook in the distance. When he came to a halt at the muddy bank, he jumped out, grabbed his shield, and waded across the water, exchanging swords in his scabbard, feeling much more comfortable with his lighter blade.

A muddy path on the other side led into dense forest, but, for the most part, the trail stayed clear of obstacles. He ran under the shelter of the forest canopy until he came upon a sheer cliff face, a wall of granite with mossy growth in its crevices. As he slowed to examine each dark recess in the cliff, he tried to calm himself. "Okay, the cave's around here somewhere. Just take it slow and easy. You don't want Makaidos thinking you're a dan-ger to him."

"Are you?" a deep voice called from behind him.

213

Edward spun around and swung his sword, barely missing the snout of a huge red dragon. The dragon slapped the sword away with his tail. "Has a boy come to try to slay the king of the dragons?"

Edward backed away, trembling. "Ma . . . Makaidos?"

Another voice answered from behind him. "Do not hurt him, my dear. He is harmless."

Edward spun again. Another dragon, a beige one, sat in his path. He raised his shield, first toward Makaidos, then toward the female. "I . . . I'm not here to slay you. I'm here to ask for help." He cleared his throat and steadied his voice. "His Majesty, King Arthur, requests that you join him in our battle against the barbarians from the north."

Makaidos twitched his ears, glancing at Thigocia as he replied to Edward. "With or without riders?"

"Uh . . . I don't know. The king didn't say. Does it make a difference?"

"We need riders. Ever since the fall of the tower, I have trained my sons and daughters to follow only the commands of humans when fighting in a group. They would be severely handicapped without experienced riders, and we have had no need to train any riders since before Arthur's coronation."

"Then how will we find riders?" Edward asked.

Makaidos moved his head up and down, examining Edward. "How old are you? Sixteen? Seventeen?"

Edward squared his shoulders. "Eighteen."

"Old enough. You will begin training immediately."

"Me?" Edward said, pointing at himself. "Why?"

"Because you are at hand. Do you know anyone else who is brave enough?"

"My best friend, Newman, but he—"

"Then for your first lesson, you will ride Thigocia to send my acceptance to King Arthur. After that, you will pick up Newman and return here. While the two of you are training, I will summon those who are still loyal to me."

"I am willing," Edward said, glancing around for his sword, "but won't we need more riders than just Newman and me?" Finding his weapon, he hoisted it up to his shoulder.

"I know of three retired soldiers who battled from our backs before Arthur's time. Perhaps they would be willing to relive their glory days. With them and five dragons, we should have enough to defeat a band of savages."

"Will you also summon Clefspeare?" Thigocia asked. "We could always use a sixth, especially if it is he."

Makaidos pawed the muddy ground and snorted. "How can I be sure we can trust him?"

"He is not like his father. You know that. And he will not need a rider."

Makaidos scowled. "Will not accept one, you mean."

"Let us not go over this again. Not in front of the human. Clefspeare is a great warrior, and his loyalty to you is unquestioned."

"Very well," Makaidos said, sighing. "I will ask him to join us."

Edward stepped between the two dragons. "I beg your pardon, Makaidos. Another knight joined me in this quest to find you, but Goliath captured him with his tail and flew away with him. Is there any way we can conduct a search?"

Makaidos's eyes flamed. "Captured him with his tail?"

"Yes. His shield got caught—"

"Ahem!"

Edward turned toward the sound. Barlow emerged from the trees, sleeveless and brushing a coat of thistles from his vest. "There is no need to go into details," he said, his face reddening. "I survived."

"Captain Barlow! Your chain mail came off?"

"Yes." Barlow picked a thumb-sized beetle from his undergarment and flicked it away. "The mail caught in the strap, so I stripped it off. Such a pity. That was my best shield."

"You can ride with Edward," Thigocia said. "I will take both of you home."

Barlow gave her a slight bow, apparently too sore to bend lower. "I appreciate your offer, dragoness, but after the ride I've been on, I would rather walk."

Edward pulled Barlow's sword from his scabbard and handed it to him. "What about Goliath? He's sure to be looking for you."

"I will take the long way through the forest," Barlow said, sliding his sword into its scabbard. "Fortunately, I wore my thick undergarments, so I should not be too uncomfortable."

Edward clapped Barlow on the shoulder. "Thank you for protecting me. I am forever in your debt."

"Think nothing of it." Barlow clenched wrists with Edward. "I'll look forward to seeing you and the dragons on the front lines."

As Barlow walked away, Thigocia dipped her head low. "First lesson, a neck mount. It's the safest and easiest. You will learn other methods later."

Edward stepped up close to the dragoness's neck. "Why would I need to mount any other way?"

"Well, it sounds as though Barlow very nearly succeeded with the most difficult maneuver of all, and with Goliath, no less. If I had trained him to perform a tail mount in midflight, he might not be walking home in his underwear."

CHAPTER

The Lady of the Lake

Sapphira sat at the side of the pool, gazing at the Ovulum. Even though it had been silent for centuries, she kept bringing it back to the healing waters every few days . . . hoping . . . hoping to feel love once again.

Holding it close to her lips, she whispered, "Elohim?" but, as usual, there was no answer. She dropped her hands to her lap and sighed. She didn't dream it. She really was healed. Whoever was inside really did sing that heavenly song that told her of Elohim's love.

She gazed at her reflection in the pool. The same fourteen-year-old girl stared back at her—the same smooth, pale skin and stark white hair. Morgan had warned her that the tower's dimensional rift could have altered their plane of existence, but she didn't expect not to age at all.

Still, the spawns kept growing, though very slowly, and she would have to rise early to prepare the newest candidate for mobility training. She slid the Ovulum back into her pocket and rose to her feet, grabbing her lantern on her way up. As she strolled through the corridor, she waved her hand over the flaming wick. "Come on," she said. "You can get brighter than that." The lantern responded with a flash and burned steadily, brightening the entire tunnel as she marched on.

Watching her own shadow on the tunnel wall, she pictured the humanoid plants attempting to walk on their spindly green legs, tired and wobbly as they exercised to the beat of a slave-driving drummer. But when she tried to imagine a face on the shadowy mirage, she could only see Yereq's, sad and thin as he toiled in silence.

As she slid down into her dugout, a tear formed in each eye. Yereq still came to mind every day, especially the hate-filled look in his eyes when Morgan finally sent him to the mobility room for good. What was he doing now? Could he be a fully formed giant? He had enough time to grow that much. But he had never shown up as a slave driver in the magnetite trenches or taken a shift as the lift operator. What might his job be?

Sapphira set the lantern on the floor, illuminating the two stone bunks. Paili sat in hers, her tiny feet brushing the floor as they swung back and forth. She formed her words slowly and carefully. "The lantern is very bright."

Sapphira waved her hand over the flame. "Sorry." The lantern slowly dimmed.

"If Morgan catches you doing that . . . you will be . . ." Paili rolled her eyes upward, apparently in search of a word.

"In big trouble?" Sapphira offered.

Paili nodded.

Sapphira wiggled her fingers at the lantern, and the flame waved its pointy head back at her. "I think she's already suspicious about my power, but it doesn't matter. I'm not afraid of her anymore."

"You should be afraid. If she . . . catches you trying to break into . . ." Paili glanced upward again, but this time, she just shook her head and sighed. "Too many words."

"Take your time." Sapphira stroked Paili's hair. She was still an eight-year-old in body, and perhaps even younger in mind, even after over a thousand years of training. "You've come a long way, Paili. Don't get discouraged."

Paili forced out her words as though each one tortured her throat. "I was . . . doing better. Something . . . is wrong."

"Yes, I know. I'm still trying to figure out what's holding you back." She sat on the floor next to Paili's bed, using her toes to pinch a stale morsel of bread near the "mouse" hole. A dozen or so other morsels lay strewn around the opening.

Sapphira tickled Paili's foot. "How's our food supply?"

Paili just sighed and pulled her leg up to her bed.

Sapphira winced. "Oh. Sorry. Yes or no questions." She kicked one of the morsels toward her hand and swept it into her fingers. "Do we have enough dried fruits and vegetables for another week?"

"No."

"Another day?"

"Yes."

"Is Naamah still bringing fruit from the bad tree for you to cook?"

"Yes."

"Has she said anything about when Morgan might come back?"

"Yes. Tomorrow."

Sapphira pulled her knees up to her chest. "That means tonight's my last chance to search her castle. Whenever I'm anywhere near the portal, she doesn't let me out of her sight."

Paili grabbed Sapphira's arm and pulled. "No! Don't!"

"Paili!" Sapphira jerked her arm away. "I have to find Elam."

"He is dead!" Paili moaned.

"Maybe not. Just because we don't need bricks anymore doesn't mean they killed him."

Paili spread out three fingers. "Taalah is dead. Qadar is dead. . . . Elam is dead."

219

"No!" Sapphira said, wrapping her hand around Paili's fingers. "We didn't see Elam get hauled off to the chasm like all the girls."

Paili scowled. "You . . . *never* see Elam."

Sapphira drooped her head and sighed. "I know." With a flick of her wrist, she tossed the bread back at the hole. Then, reaching under Paili's bunk, she withdrew a blossom and caressed one of its seven petals, as white and supple as the day she found her living gift centuries ago. "Elam's not an underborn," she said, laying the blossom on her bed, "so he probably died of old age a long time ago."

"Yes. So you . . . stay here tonight."

"No." Sapphira rose to her feet and smacked her palm with her fist. "I haven't looked everywhere, and I can't ignore the feeling that someone's being held prisoner in Morgan's house. Even if it's not him, I have to keep looking."

Paili grabbed her forearm. "No!" she cried, squeezing tightly. "If you die . . . I am alone."

Sapphira jerked free. "I won't die!"

The lantern's dim light reflected in Paili's tears, two long streams running down her cheeks. Sapphira sighed and sat next to her, stroking her hair again. "Paili, everything will be okay. Elohim hasn't brought me this far to let me die now. Why would he give me my power if he just wanted me to die down here?"

Paili pulled in her bottom lip and frowned.

"This will be the last time. I promise." Sapphira picked up her lantern and headed for the hovel's exit, whispering to the flame. "A bit lower, please."

As the lantern's glow diminished, she checked for the Ovulum in her pocket and climbed out into the corridor, tiptoeing in front of her own stalking silhouette. So far, so good. Morgan lurked somewhere in the overworld, Naamah was probably sleeping by now, but where might Mardon be? Since he never wanted her to leave the hovel at night, it seemed that he was hiding some terrible secret. Who could tell how late he might be working in the control room . . . or watching from the surrounding shadows?

As she approached the control room, the door swung open, and Mardon bustled out, studying a page of parchment as he strode toward her. She flattened herself against a wall and snuffed her flame with a quick wave. As he passed by, the light from Mardon's lantern brushed across her eyes, but he never looked up from his work. She waited a few seconds, then continued on, not bothering to summon her fire again. After several centuries, the winding, upward path was all too familiar, even in total darkness.

After hurrying through the old green portal chamber, she felt for the entry to the next corridor and crept through, helped by the glow in the distance from the guard's lantern and the swirling eddies emanating from the newer portal's blue column. As she neared the chamber, she tiptoed and called out her usual warning, having learned that it's never wise to startle a guardian giant. "Anak? It's Sapphira."

Just as she stepped into the chamber, the giant's deep voice echoed off the distant walls and ceiling. "More night reading, daughter of the earth?"

Sapphira cringed. No matter how many times he taunted her with that name, it never failed to sting. Firming her chin, she strode into the towering giant's shadow and crossed her arms over her chest. "At least I can read, son of putrefaction."

Anak roared with laughter, making his muscular torso quiver. "A new insult from the queen of glib tongues." He reached down and patted her on the head. "Morgan must keep you around for entertainment. I would have fed your carcass to the birds by now."

Sapphira kept a stony face under the giant's condescending hand. "She keeps me around, because I was smart enough not to teach Mardon everything I learned while he was gone. Without me, her garden of giants would produce nothing but fools like Anak and his sons." She moved her hands to her hips. "If I remember

221

the story Morgan told me, one of your sons lost his head at the hands of a shepherd boy."

"Acid-tongued wench!" Anak wrapped his huge, six-fingered hand around her face and shoved her backwards, making her flop down on her buttocks. "David and his sons rot in their tombs while I live on."

Sapphira climbed slowly to her feet and pulled out her coif. "Only by Morgan's black arts." As she spoke, she crept nearer, tying on her covering and keeping her eyes locked on Anak's. "What would happen if you passed through the portal back to the land of the living?" She began tucking her hair into her coif, slowly making a circle around the portal. Anak's gaze followed her, his body turning with his head. "If you went there, you would be a rotting corpse, because you died in that dimension, just like Mardon, and you're stuck here because Morgan uses her arts to keep you from passing on to your eternal reward."

Anak glared at her. "What do you know about eternal rewards? You're stuck in this hellhole with me."

With slow, furtive steps, she passed by him and eased closer to the swirling column of pale blue light. "I can't argue with that. But at least I have hope. I have never died." She withdrew the Ovulum from her pocket and laid it in her palm, pausing for a moment to make sure the giant moved his gaze to the egg's mirror-like surface as it reflected the portal's dancing light.

The moment he looked down, Sapphira leaped for the portal, but with a lightning fast sweep of his arm, Anak snatched her right out of the air and threw her to the ground. She tumbled head over heels and slid to a stop, scraping her elbow.

Anak extended his long arm and pointed at her. "Devious vixen! Get your scrolls and be gone!"

Sapphira rose slowly and brushed herself off, taking a second to examine the trickle of blood oozing down her forearm. It stung pretty badly, but at least she had managed to cling to her Ovulum.

She slid it carefully back into her pocket and headed toward the tower, making a wide circle around the scowling Anak. As she passed through the broken doors, she clenched her fists. She had gotten so close! Just a few more inches, and she would have been on her way back to the upper realms, to the land of the living!

Keeping well away from the tree in the center and its twelve saluting statues, Sapphira shuffled to the outer wall and grasped the sides of one of the tall ladders that lined the stacks of shelves. Putting one foot on the first step, she paused and looked back at the portal's bluish glow. What if she had made it into the column? Would it really have led to the upper world? Morgan had expressed her doubts long ago, and she was usually right about things like that. Still, it might be worth exploring if she could ever get past Anak, but would she be able to find her way home? And if she got lost in another dimension, what would Morgan do to Paili?

Sapphira slapped the side of the ladder and whispered to herself, "You should have thought of that earlier." She began climbing the ladder, skipping over the familiar weakened rungs as she scurried upward. At least with this journey, having tried it before, she knew where she was going and how to find her way back, and so far no one else seemed to know about the museum's exit at the very top.

Sitting on a hearth near a crackling fire, Morgan laid a sword on her knees. "It's time to put Chereb back into service. My dragon slayer is ready to begin his work."

Naamah, kneeling in the warmth of the greenish flames, caressed the ornate hilt. "How will you get it to him?"

"Chereb is not for my slayer." Morgan set the blade next to the hearth and rose to her feet. "It is for the king."

"Arthur?" Naamah asked, rising with her. "Why?"

Morgan kissed Naamah's cheek and whispered into her ear. "It's all part of the grand scheme Lucifer and I have been cooking up for centuries, and it's finally time to let you in on it."

Naamah set her hands on her hips. "Because you need me to do your dirty work, right?"

"Don't worry. You're perfectly suited for your part in the plan." Morgan gestured with her head toward the room's exit. "Follow me."

Morgan strode across the marble floor of the high-ceilinged room, Naamah trailing close behind. "I have experimented with this sword for centuries," Morgan said. "Even with the blood covering, it wouldn't work for Ham or his son Cush. Yet, it flashed its sacred fire for Nimrod." She paused at the entrance to a dark corridor. "Tell me, Naamah, how was Nimrod different from his ancestors?"

"He was a king."

"Yes. It seems that kings and leaders of clans, like Noah, are able to summon the sword's power." Morgan entered the corridor, walking more slowly now as she passed by a series of heavy wooden doors, each with thick metal bars in their solitary windows. "Nimrod lost his kingdom," she continued, "because he didn't bother to renew the blood on his hands before the battle at the tower. The fool relied on the candlestone to defeat the dragons. Arthur, however, won't need blood. He is a follower of the enemy."

A low moan emanated from one of the windows. Naamah longed to see the suffering of the prisoners, but even on tiptoes, she couldn't peek inside. "So, only a king can use Chereb?" she asked.

Morgan stopped at the last door in the hallway and lifted a key ring from a hook on the wall. "I don't think so. An old prophecy I once read implies that any king's heir or anyone he designates can use it as well." She slid the long, slender keys around the ring, eyeing each one. "I wanted Mardon to test the sword to prove my theory, but since he is merely a dead spirit in our caverns, my experiments were probably useless. That's why I will give it to Arthur. When he gets the sword, he will show it to Merlin, who will certainly know all about its secrets. If Merlin can use Chereb, then I will be certain about the designation theory, and my dragon slayer will make sure I get it back at the proper time."

"But when you get it back, we won't have a king or any innocent blood to cover his hands."

"I have a plan to install a new king." Morgan pinched a key, letting the rest of the ring dangle. "And we have sources for innocent blood."

"Sapphira and Paili?" Naamah raised her eyebrows. "Would you dare kill one of them?"

"No. Paili's presence keeps Sapphira in the lower realms, right where I want her." Morgan inserted the key into the lock, pausing as she gazed through the bars in the window. "And I cannot take Sapphira's blood. She is too dangerous, though she has no idea how powerful she is. Every person who spills her blood meets an untimely demise."

"Yes," Naamah said, shivering. "I know. We could really use Nimrod right now."

Morgan nodded. "In any case, Sapphira is unable to thwart my ultimate plan without her twin oracle, and Acacia is long dead, so I don't mind keeping her around. Her abilities in the control room are quite valuable."

"I follow your plan so far, but what's your source for innocent blood?"

Morgan turned the key and slid a heavy bolt to one side. "My prisoner will provide it."

"Are you sure he's innocent?"

"Since he was born before the enemy's visitation, I'm not sure." Morgan swung open the door. Naamah peeked inside, but all she could see was a tiny, empty room with an open trapdoor in the middle of the stone flooring. Morgan walked in and knelt at the trapdoor's opening. "Shem dedicated him to God at his birth, and we captured him before the normal age of corruption. He has

225

aged but a little, and since his only companion has been strife, I suspect he qualifies. But with the plan I have in mind, I won't need his blood."

"What? I thought you said—"

"Confused?" Morgan laughed. "After we talk to him, you'll figure it out."

"So," Naamah said, spreading out her hands. "Where is he?"

Morgan pointed into the dark shaft. "Exactly where I expected him to flee. The sixth circle. That's why I moved him to this cell after the Messiah cleared his followers out of the underworld."

Naamah peered into the blackness. A downward draft pulled on her hair and clothes as it swept into a chasm of apparent nothingness. "Is the village of the dead down there?"

"Yes. What's left of it."

"So he's alone?"

"Come. I'll show you." Morgan stood, and her body shrank, quickly transforming into a raven. Naamah spread out her arms. They flattened into leathery wings, and her hands molded into wrinkled claws. Within seconds, she began circling the room in the form of a bat.

Morgan jumped into the hole. Naamah dove headfirst in pursuit, plunging into the cold, black downdraft. Within seconds, the air warmed, getting brighter as they plummeted. Morgan spread out her wings and began to glide in a wide circle. Naamah followed her path, though her fluttering, jerky motions weren't as graceful.

They landed in a village that looked like a deserted copy of Nimrod's Shinar, not the marble-coated center of town, but rather the poorer outskirts. Hoofprints marred the muddy streets, and long rows of quaint stone huts stood in disrepair. A gust of wind lifted a broken piece of roof thatching and blew it across the street to a vacant marketplace, scattering straw among the empty carts of the missing vendors.

Morgan and Naamah returned to their human forms. Naamah pulled her hair back, staring into the crisp breeze. "Hades is a lonely place since the Messiah's visit."

"Yes," Morgan said, smoothing out her dress, "but the sixth circle is perfect for keeping prisoners. Elam doesn't ever seem to need food, so I can't use hunger to break his will. Yet, this circle will soon be home to spirits that will drive him mad, and Elam will finally do what I ask."

"Spirits? What kind of spirits?"

"Lucifer's spies have told me that Elohim has created an abode identical to this one, a parallel home for the spirits of dead dragons. It seems that the two dimensions will intermingle in very interesting ways." Morgan pointed toward a stack of boxes at the side of the market. "I saw him." She cupped her hands around her mouth and called, "Elam. I saw you. There's no use hiding back there."

Elam stood up behind the boxes, revealing his tall, boyish frame. He walked straight toward Morgan, a club in his hand and fire in his eyes. "I was only hiding so I could crack your head open." With the club ready to strike, he leaped at her.

Morgan raised her hands and thrust them outward. A wall of darkness threw Elam backwards, making him fly to the market. He slammed against the boxes, crushing them under his body. Slowly rising from the heap, he tightened his grip on the club and glared at Morgan. "I will get out of here. Just you wait and see. I'll make you pay for what you did to Raphah."

Naamah took a step closer to Morgan. "He still looks like a teenager," she whispered, "and he's really rather dashing."

"Yes," she whispered back. "I was hoping you would think so. It will make your job more pleasant. You will sing songs of doubt and treachery into his mind, but this isn't the time or place to explain."

Elam threw down his club. "I'm not going to stand here and be gawked at." He began stalking away. "If you have anything to say to me, I'll be at the kilns."

227

Naamah chuckled. "He's got spunk. That's for sure."

"Yes, and we'll use that against him." Morgan raised her arms and began transforming to a raven. "Come now," she said, her voice changing to a squawk. "It's time to return."

Naamah reverted to a bat and followed Morgan upward, leaving the light of the world below and plunging into darkness. As they rose, they battled the downdraft that swept air from the prison cell above, now a tiny light in the distance.

Finally, they burst through the current and landed in the cell. Naamah flittered around for a moment, then planted her sharp claws before shifting to her human form. Brushing her hair with her fingers, she watched the raven stretch upward and reshape into the tall, slender frame of Morgan.

"If you wanted Elam's blood," Naamah said, "why didn't you just take it from him instead of holding him prisoner?"

228

Morgan shook her hair back behind her shoulders. "I already told you. It's not his blood I want. He will just provide the way to get Sapphira's."

"But why don't you just get Anak to kill her? He's expendable."

"Because he is not able to kill her. Lucifer's spies learned that an oracle of fire cannot be murdered unless she is betrayed by someone she loves. Sapphira didn't speak up for Acacia when she took the bread, so Acacia lost her protection."

Naamah smiled and winked. "So you have to get Sapphira and Elam to fall in love?"

"No. Romantic feelings have nothing to do with it. We need absolute trust and sacrifice. Only complete trust generates the brutality of real betrayal."

Naamah knelt at the edge of the trapdoor and gazed into the darkness. "But with Elam down there, how will you get them to love each other like that?"

"When someone eats out of the hands of another, both the giver and the taker trust each other without reservation." Morgan eased the trapdoor past Naamah's head and closed it with a loud thud. "Don't you agree?"

"Yes. I was surprised that you let them get away with that."

"It's all part of the plan," Morgan said as she headed for the exit. "And now we need a singer of dark lyrics to break that trust, little by little."

Naamah rose and followed her. "Not a problem," she said, winking again. "The words are already forming in my mind. If this song doesn't make him doubt, then nothing will."

Edward sat uneasily on Thigocia's back, shifting his weight to keep the tough scales from pinching him. To his right, his friend Newman sat on Makaidos, looking even more uncomfortable as he adjusted his breeches while balancing his body with his shield. To his left, four other dragons waited, three of them with riders who sat tall and motionless, the trio of elderly warriors that Makaidos had brought out of retirement.

In the distance, a blanket of mist shrouded a huge swamp, and a high mound protruded from the waters like a swollen womb. A small building sat on top, a humble, thatched-roof house of worship with a rugged, stone bell tower at the front. Far to the left, a smaller hill rose above the swamp, its western slope stretching to the mainland. Weary Hill, they called it, the resting spot for Joseph of Arimathea after his long journey from Jerusalem. The bridge that once spanned the two hills was gone, destroyed by the invaders, and wood fragments still floated about the swamp, occasionally washing to shore.

The mist hovered in place, not a breath of wind to stir it, a perfect shield for the enemy troops that might approach again from the north. Edward nodded toward the water's edge. "Newman, stop pulling on your pants. The king's coming."

King Arthur marched toward the line of dragons, his sword and shield in hand. He stopped in front of Makaidos and bowed. "Your

229

presence is most welcome, King of the Dragons." As his eyes met those of the aged warriors, he smiled. "I recognize these human heroes of my childhood, but please tell me the names of your dragon soldiers so that I may properly address them in battle."

Makaidos nodded toward the others. "In order from your left to your right, the king has at his service, Thigocia, my mate; Valcor and Hartanna, twins born to us since my arrival here; Legossi, a daughter of Maven; and finally, Clefspeare, Goliath's and Roxil's only son." Each dragon bowed in turn.

"Greetings, noble dragons, and welcome." Leaning over, Arthur sketched a map in the drying mud with his sword. "Sir Devin's scout tells us that the Saxons are massing behind the great tor, and they seem to be migrating toward Weary Hill." With rapid strokes, the king drew a credible likeness of the two hills and the surrounding swamp. "We will counter them here," he said, stabbing one side of Weary Hill.

Sir Devin pointed at the map with his own sword. "But wouldn't that open up our flank to a water passage between the hills?"

Arthur scratched a line next to Devin's blade. "The dragons will be able to sense any approach, so they will guard that side."

"Your Majesty," Devin said, sliding his sword back into its scabbard, "I beg you to fortify all sides with humans. I know you do not trust the dragons as much as you appear—"

"King Arthur!" Makaidos interrupted. "I sense danger!"

Arthur straightened, raising his sword with a tight grip. "How near?"

"It is strange," Makaidos said, his ears twitching rapidly. "Somehow the danger lies between the two of us, yet there is no one here."

"An invisible enemy?" Arthur asked. He sliced his sword through the air, then back again. "If he is here, he has no body that my sword can cut. Perhaps a ghost?"

"Even as you move the blade," Makaidos said, "the focal point of danger seems to move."

Arthur held up the blade and squinted at it. "The sword is dangerous?"

"I have heard of swords that seem to have a life of their own," Makaidos said. "Where did you get that one?"

Arthur held it close to the dragon. "This is the very sword I pulled from the stone as a lad, but it is no more alive than the stone was."

Edward cleared his throat. "Sire, if I may be so bold . . ."

Arthur nodded. "Speak, squire."

"While you were scratching the mud, I think I noticed a slight quiver in the blade. Could it have been damaged during this morning's skirmish with the enemy's scouts?"

Arthur gazed at Edward curiously, then bent down and banged the sword against the ground. The blade broke cleanly away from the hilt.

Makaidos stretched his neck and sniffed the broken blade. "Yes, that must have been the danger."

Arthur shook his head. "If this had happened in battle, I would have been helpless." He rose and bowed to Makaidos, then to Edward. "I am in debt to both dragon and squire," the king said.

Edward took in a deep breath, swelling his chest. He couldn't resist the feeling of pride. He had made another step toward proving himself worthy of his father's name. Now, if he could only get another shot at Goliath.

The king threw the worthless hilt on the ground. "It seems that I need another sword."

Instantly, the sound of a dozen swords sliding out of their scabbards rose into the air. Edward thrust his forward first. "Take mine, Your Majesty." His words echoed from the lips of every knight within earshot of the king.

231

Arthur laughed. "My good soldiers, I cannot take any of your weapons. Then you would be disarmed and—"

A haunting moan drifted in from the swamp, starting with a loud hum that slowly formed a stretched-out call. "Arthurrrrrr!" The voice seemed to stir the mist with its breathy echoes. Every man and dragon shifted toward the sound, the swords swinging away from the king and toward the shadowy water.

Near the shore, a ghostly female form hovered over the swamp, her long hair and gown flowing as the mist swirled all around her. With her body veiled, she seemed a phantom, perhaps even an embodiment of the mist itself. She raised her arm, holding an indistinguishable object in her hand.

Edward shifted his weight on Thigocia's neck, trying not to tremble. The sound of murmuring filtered through the ranks.

Arthur raised his hand. "What are we? A pack of boys playing at war? Where is your courage?" He turned to Makaidos, his eyes alternately fixed on him and the phantom. "Do you sense danger from her?"

232

"Without a doubt, Sire. If she is not a demon, then she is something akin to one."

"But she bears a gift," Thigocia added, "and it is something holy."

"How do you know?" the king asked.

"I can sense it." Thigocia turned on her eyebeams and pointed them at the apparition. "Her aspect gives her away. She holds the gift as if it is abhorrent to her essence, as if its goodness invades her nature like a foreign army."

The voice drifted in again, louder and more pleading. "Arthur, I have been called to give you the ultimate weapon." With a mighty heave, she threw the object toward them, a sword spinning end over end until it pierced the ground near the shoreline.

Devin stepped forward. "Shall I fetch it for you, Sire?"

Arthur laid a hand on Devin's chest and called out to the floating specter, "Who are you, and why do you offer this gift?"

"You may call me the Lady of the Lake. You will need this sword to conquer your greatest foes. It is called Excalibur, for it can cut both steel and stone. You will also learn to use its most powerful secret, the secret of holy fire." The mist created a whirlpool of fog over the surface of the water that seemed to absorb her ghostly form. "Beware of those who call themselves friends," she said as she sank lower, "for ambitious usurpers will bide their time with smiles and bows while they await their chance to take your throne." She disappeared, and the swirling mist settled to complete stillness.

Arthur marched toward the swamp, waving his arm. "Edward," he called, "come with me. The rest of you move to the front lines, and I will join you there as soon as possible."

Edward pointed at himself, mouthing his own name.

Newman kicked his ankle. "You're the only Edward around here! Get your carcass down and follow the king!"

233

Thigocia lowered her neck, and Edward climbed down as he had been taught, stepping across the first three spines, then jumping the rest of the way. He looked back at the dragon and nodded respectfully. "I think you'd better go with the others. The king made no exceptions."

"Very well," Thigocia replied, dipping her head.

Makaidos stretched out his wings. "Leave a horse tied for each of them, and we will be on our way."

Edward hustled to join the king and marched side by side with him, trying to catch his breath. "I apologize . . . Your Majesty. I didn't . . . consider myself worthy to—"

"Exactly why I called you," the king said, clapping Edward's shoulder. "When the lake spirit said to beware of my counselors, the truth of her words resonated in my heart. I have long believed that someone is plotting to wrestle away my throne, so I need to take action to prevent it."

"Will you trust this spirit, Sire? The dragons warned that she is dangerous."

"Dangerous to them, perhaps." He stopped and looked back at the dragons as they circled low over the departing ground troops. Sirs Devin and Barlow led the way down a path toward Weary Hill.

Arthur lowered his voice. "Dragons cannot always distinguish the target of danger, and Thigocia declared that the sword appears to be holy."

Edward eyed the leading knight, clad in dark mail and marching quickly. "Do you believe Sir Devin? Are all dragons possessed by evil spirits?"

The king continued toward the edge of the swamp, slower now as the mists surrounded them. "I don't know whom to believe, so I brought you here to ask your help. I will make a formal pronouncement later, but you are now a knight. I want you to befriend both Sir Devin and the dragons. Get them to trust you. Learn their secret counsels, and report your findings to me."

Edward tried to keep a proud smile from bursting forth as he walked beside the king, but he couldn't calm his breathless voice. "And what of Merlin? He is your closest advisor."

"Merlin would never turn from me, but he would also never act as a spy. He trusts Makaidos without question, so you must make sure you hide your efforts from him."

"I will be sure to avoid him." Edward shook his head. "I have never understood his loyalty to those creatures."

With the mists now completely enveloping them, Arthur stopped again and laid a hand on Edward's shoulder. "Your distrust of dragons is warranted, but you will do well to keep your mind from prejudice. I just want the truth."

Edward glanced at the gloved hand, his smile now breaking through. "Yes, Sire. I understand."

Both men turned toward the water's edge and closed in on the lady's gift. The sword stood on its point, about a third of its length driven into the moss-speckled loam. Edward knelt close to it and examined its hilt and blade. "It's magnificent! The workmanship of a master craftsman!"

Arthur grasped the hilt. "At least this one isn't in stone." He pulled, withdrawing the blade easily. "It seems that the Lady of the Lake had no scabbard for me," he said, holding the blade high.

"Or instructions, Sire."

"Indeed. The lady's mention of secret fire reminds me of a legend I heard as a child. Such a weapon could mean the difference between victory and defeat in the coming battle." The king turned the hilt around in his hand. "But I have no idea how to use it."

"May I suggest inquiring of Master Merlin? I can fly to the castle with Thigocia and bring him back."

"No need. He will be on the front lines by now, exhorting the troops. We'll meet him there, but we'd better hurry. He won't wait to command the march if he believes God has given the word." Arthur slid Excalibur into his old scabbard. "If the sword's fire is as powerful as I have heard, maybe today will prove that we won't need the dragons ever again."

CHAPTER

THE HIDDEN PORTAL

S apphira stood on the top rung of the ladder, stretching to reach the upper edge of the highest shelf in the museum's library. Grabbing it with her fingertips, she pulled herself up and slid her feet in the usual spaces between stacks of scrolls. With a muffled grunt, she swung her body up on top of the shelf. Fortunately, Anak stood guard on the other side of the museum's wall, out of sight and out of hearing range.

Resting for a moment, she looked out from her lofty perch. Her vision had already become sharper, the first sign that a portal was near, the clue that had helped her find this one years ago when she was searching the top shelf for something new to read. For some reason, this portal was invisible, not a column of light like the others in the below lands, maybe because it originated in the world above.

Darkness veiled the distant floor, but with her enhanced vision, she could still see the ring of twelve statues saluting the focal tree. Not far above, the room's ceiling arched to a peak at the center—a dome covered with crisscrossing lattice. Two horizontal support beams intersected beneath the dome, one of them attached to the wall next to Sapphira.

Since the curved ceiling began its upward arch near the wall, she had to crawl along the beam to stay beneath the dome, but as she slid out toward the center of the room, she was able to straighten and eventually rise to her feet. Inching toward the intersection, she spread her arms to keep her balance. A sense of sadness crept into her mind, darkness and loneliness, the second clue that had helped her find the portal that lay ahead.

The feeling of sadness grew, pure despair invading her mind, images of Acacia plummeting into the chasm, Nimrod's hand swinging toward her unguarded cheek, and Morgan's twisted face as she cried, "Freak of nature!"

Finally reaching the intersection, she withdrew a stick from her pocket and looked straight up, holding it high. She whispered, "Flames, come to my firebrand." Instantly, a lively flame ignited the end of the stick. Curling her toes around the edge of the beam, she swung the torch in a slow circle and closed her eyes, imagining a swirl of warmth enveloping her as it did on that night long ago when she danced with Elohim.

As soon as the sensation of heat sank to her fingers, she opened her eyes again and watched the flame expand as it fell around her body and spun into a cone. Within seconds, the cocoon of fire enveloped her, and sparks of light flashed all around. Then, as she slowed her torch, she lowered it, allowing the flames to dissolve. Now, instead of the high reaches of an ancient tower, a castle stood at the top of a steep hill. Apple trees and gardenias grew all around, and their fragrance wafted past on a gentle breeze. Off to the right, the sun settled low on the horizon, casting her long thin shadow across the grass. She sprinted to the closest apple tree and ducked behind the trunk, away from the view of the castle, and, she hoped, away from Morgan's piercing eyes.

She laid her stick at the base of the tree and glanced at the swamp behind her, shivering at the thought of the horrible serpents lurking beneath the deceptively peaceful surface. During a previous visit, stopping to wash her face in the shallows had almost proved fatal. If not for her proximity to the portal and resulting sharp vision, she would have been a wiggling belly lump at the bottom of the swamp.

As she skittered up the hill toward the castle, she pulled her veil down and bent low. Several flat terraces interrupted the slope, like a giant's grassy stair steps. As she approached the dark building at the hill's apex, she slowed her pace. Sneaking past a pair of turrets, she imagined a watchful guard peering out of one of the tiny windows. After circling around to the back of the castle, she stopped at a heavy wooden door, painted black and speckled with mildew splotches.

The door was locked, as usual, but a barred window up above allowed a breeze to flap the inner draperies. A thick vine grew along the side of the door, leading past the window on its meandering climb over mossy stones.

239

The short steeple in the center of the castle's roof cast a long shadow over her, providing some cover for her familiar climb. She grasped the vine and began scaling the wall, poking her toes into the tiny cracks between the stones as she pulled her way up the slippery surface.

After swinging herself to the window's ledge, she pushed her head between the bars, then grunted softly as she forced her torso into the elaborate bedchamber.

Sapphira pushed her veil up and tiptoed into the corridor. The waning sunrays streamed through a stained glass window on one end, red and blue panes filtering the orange light and casting eerie colors across her path. She glanced both ways and leaned against a railing that overlooked the lower floor. No one was in sight. She had seen Morgan twice during her other visits here, and Naamah once, but she had managed to avoid them . . . barely. Getting caught meant certain death for her and probably for Paili as well.

Sidestepping the creaky boards, Sapphira scooted down the stairs, then hurried along a maze of corridors until she found a thick wooden door—slightly ajar, as usual. Picking up an unlit torch from a nearby basket, she nudged the door open wide enough to squeeze through. She descended the stone steps, and the tiny sliver of light from the doorway above faded.

Gripping the torch more tightly, she whispered, "Grant me fire to light my way." The top of the torch flickered, then blazed with light. Sapphira grimaced and whispered again. "Not so much!" The fire died down, giving just enough light to illuminate each step as she continued the deep plunge.

When Sapphira reached the bottom, she padded quietly across the hard dirt floor, following a glow of wavering lights in the distance. Twenty lanterns, some lit and some unlit, hung on each side of a pair of iron gates that blocked a rectangular entryway through a solid wall. The gaps between the black bars were too narrow even for her to squeeze through. The first time she had tried, her head had become wedged, and she spent nearly an hour freeing herself. Finding no way to get in that night, she finally gave up and went home. Since then, however, she had figured out how to pass. It had taken years of thought, but she finally deciphered the code and had since made it through the gate many times. The secret was in remembering Mardon's control room combination.

Waving her arm across the field of lanterns, she whispered, "Sleep!" and every wick fell dark. Then, pointing at the first lantern on the left, she said, "Awake!" and it flashed to life. After repeating the command to the next five lanterns, Sapphira leaned her head toward the gate's locking mechanism. A faint click sounded. She waved her hand at the lanterns again. "Sleep!" They all darkened.

She sidestepped toward the lanterns on the right and pointed at the first nine in order, commanding them to awaken. Then,

240

after listening for the lock to click, she waved them back to darkness. Finally, moving to the left again, she lit thirteen lanterns. The lock clicked more loudly and the iron frame swung open a few inches.

Sapphira quickly restored the lanterns to their original condition and entered the gate, closing it behind her, careful not to let the lock reengage. Still carrying her torch, she padded into the dungeon's anteroom, a huge chamber with rocky walls all around and a high ceiling, reminding her of the caverns in the lower world. Except for the gate behind her, three wooden doors, much like the one at the top of the stairs, stood as the only way out.

It was at this point that Morgan's sorcery and Mardon's scientific wizardry always baffled her. Every time she came, the doors led to something different—a pit that plunged into darkness; a winding path through a dismal, uninhabited tropical forest; an endless meadow with deep hoofprints as the only sign that anyone ever journeyed through the grassy expanse; and a deserted, rocky wasteland with a gorge that carried a flaming river at the bottom. Since her vision cleared as she approached a door, and sadness shrouded her mind, she knew the doors were portals to other dimensions that somehow stayed open for anyone to stumble through, perhaps to be lost forever.

Sapphira regripped her torch. It was time to choose a door, maybe for the last time. But why should the portal reveal anything new? Exploring the strange lands over and over had never turned up a soul, living or dead. Still, there was one place she hadn't searched, the dark pit. Sapphira shivered. Falling into the unknown took more courage than she had to offer.

She reached for the door on the left and opened it, revealing the huge meadow. She sighed. Nothing new there, just dried horse dung fertilizing a million acres of grass. After closing that door, she strode ten paces to the right and opened the second. A rocky ledge overlooked a deep chasm and a lava river, much like the one in her cavern back home, but this one was outside under the sun and sky in a land that held nothing more than lava pots and squealing lizards, a place an imprisoned boy could never survive. Finally, she pulled open the third door, revealing a dark hole, the pit she had never dared to explore.

She dropped to all fours and peered into the hole. It reminded her of the abyss she and Paili had dangled over, but this one breathed no streams of light and had no gems lining its walls. Still, an odd wind seemed to try to suck her downward, whipping at her dress and coif as she leaned over the precipice.

She whispered to her torch. "Give as much light as you can." As the fire blazed, she reached it into the hole, extending it to one side, then the other. Nothing. Just blackness as far as the eye could see.

Pulling up and resting on her knees, she looked back at the iron gate and the dark path home. She set her torch on the ground, allowing the fiery head to blaze over the pit. "I failed," she muttered. "I said this was my last try, and there's nothing new." She shrugged her shoulders. "Elam's probably long dead anyway, so what's the use?"

A sudden gust caught the torch and nudged it off its perch. Sapphira lunged for it as it sailed into the hole, but her hands grasped empty air. The torch fell into the darkness, a shrinking light beaten about by changing crosswinds. And then it stopped. The tiny flame flickered steadily, yet far away.

Sapphira leaned her head into the hole. There was a bottom to this pit after all, but who could ever survive such a plunge? As she studied the distant light, a strange sound entered her ears, a rough, rumbling growl. She jerked her head up and spun around on her knees. Stalking toward her, a huge dog bared its teeth, a rainbow of colors shimmering across its body from the tips of its triangular ears to the end of its pointed tail.

Sapphira tried to stand, but her knees collapsed, and she fell to her seat. She pressed her hands against the floor and slid backwards, but with the pit only inches behind her, she couldn't go much farther.

As the dog approached, taking one stalking step at a time, its growl deepened. The lanterns at the gate threw the beast's shadow over her, yet with her vision crystal clear, she could see every pulsing capillary in its bloodshot eyes.

Sliding back another inch, she teetered on the edge of the pit. The image of Paili's face flashed in her mind. Who would take care of her? Who would protect her when Morgan led her to the edge of the chasm? Would another innocent underborn suffer Acacia's fate?

A sense of heat radiated against her thigh—the Ovulum in her pocket, emanating a soothing warmth for the first time in centuries. That was all the answer she needed.

With a final push, Sapphira fell backwards into the pit.

243

Arthur and Edward stopped their horses at a low ridge overlooking the troops as they lined up only a stone's throw away. The skies had darkened, and light rain dampened their heads. The king nodded at a scarlet-robed old man standing in front of the regiment. "It looks like we're too late to ask Merlin about the sword," Arthur said. "I will have to learn to use it in battle."

As the rain grew heavier, Merlin paced in front of the soldiers, his hands behind him and his robe swishing. His powerful strides belied his wild, white hair and wrinkled face, and his resonating voice matched his vigor. "Men and dragons," he shouted, "we are not here today to cross blades with men of equal stature. Though their men stand taller and their armor repels our sharpest arrows, though their numbers make them seem as thick as rats in a latrine, in the end, they are lesser men than we."

A low rumble of thunder sounded in the distance, and large raindrops plastered Merlin's hair against his forehead. "As they have marched from village to village," he continued, "these barbarians have murdered children and committed unspeakable acts against every female, from the very young to the very old. And they have attacked at night, cowardly spearing the fighting men in their slumber and rolling their severed heads into the middle of the streets, laughing as they committed their crimes against the women and children in the public squares, thinking the God of the universe could not see their abominations or will not lift up his iron fist and smash their vermin bodies with one mighty blow."

Arthur's men shook their fists and shouted. "Smash the vermin!" The dragons thumped their tails on the ground, plumes of smoke rising from their nostrils as they clawed the muddy path.

"You are better men than they," Merlin continued, lifting his voice even higher. "You follow Arthur, the king who has given his life and rule to the greatest king of all, Christ, the Lord!"

The men shouted, "Christ, the Lord!" and began clanking their swords against their shields. The dragons remained silent, though they continued to paw the ground restlessly.

"Yes!" Merlin yelled. "With the word of God as your sword, and faith as your shield, you cannot fail!" As another loud clap of thunder echoed his shouts, Merlin stripped off his robe, revealing a suit of silver chain mail and a scabbard attached to a strap on his back. "So march!" He pulled a sword from the scabbard and lifted it high. "We will send these rats back to their latrine, and they will learn what it means to offend the heart of the living God!"

Merlin strode ahead on the path. The men followed him, waving their swords and shouting huzzahs. Barlow raised his new shield and marched side by side with the prophet. At the far end of the pack, Sir Devin walked alongside Palin, the king's scribe. The two inclined their heads toward each other as if in conversation and drifted farther back in the lines.

The dragons lifted off the ground, two without riders, one reddish and one beige. Edward blew a shrill whistle through his fingers and waved his arm. "Thigocia!" he shouted. "Over here!"

The beige dragon circled back and grabbed Edward right off his horse with her tail. With a quick flip, she slung him into the air, then dove underneath and caught him on her back, wedging him perfectly between two spines. Edward grasped the spine in front of him and hung on, unable to breathe.

Arthur shouted into the sky through his cupped hands. "That'll teach you to call for a dragon as you would a dog!"

Edward exhaled and shouted forward. "I apologize, dragoness. I am not aware of every aspect of dragon protocol."

A sly grin broke through on Thigocia's draconic lips. "Apology accepted, but it was necessary to give you an in-flight mounting lesson before the battle begins. Makaidos already gave Newman his."

"Really? How did he do?"

"Except for a spine ripping the back of his trousers, he did quite well."

As the troops marched closer to Weary Hill, the dragons rose toward the dark clouds, shielding themselves from sight in the swirling rain. Flying low enough to pierce the mists with their eyebeams, they guarded the right flank while staying out of sight.

Edward blinked at the sharp, stinging raindrops. "What do you see?" he shouted.

Thigocia aimed her beams at the ground. "Merlin and Barlow are charging. They must have spotted the enemy."

Edward mopped his brow with his sleeve, but it didn't help much. "Is anyone coming on the right? Do you sense anything at all?"

"No sign of them. The enemy seems concentrated on the direct attack."

Edward pointed downward. "Then let's help on the front lines!"

Thigocia turned off her eyebeams. "Makaidos? Did you hear the young knight?"

"Yes," Makaidos replied. "You and I will join the battle, along with Legossi, Valcor, and Hartanna. Clefspeare will stay and guard the flank." He swung his head back toward the riderless dragon. "Is that well with you?"

Clefspeare nodded. "I am at your service, my king."

As the five dragons glided toward the lowest layer of clouds, Thigocia drifted closer to Hartanna. "You know Clefspeare better than I do. Can he handle the flank by himself?"

Hartanna's ears twitched rapidly. "No one really knows him, Mother, but they say he is the greatest warrior since Arramos himself."

"Why does he refuse a rider?"

"I asked him once," Hartanna replied. "He says he works best alone, and with his dangerous maneuvers, he would prefer not to bring peril to a human."

"I see," Thigocia said, blinking away the droplets. "I have more questions, but that is enough information for now."

Makaidos surged to the front of the line. "Form an arrowhead!"

The dragons fanned into formation, Makaidos at the tip and two dragons trailing him on each side.

Thigocia flew just behind her mate's left wing, and Edward clutched her spine until his knuckles turned white. Chill bumps covered his arms, and his biceps twitched. The battle was about to begin.

Makaidos nodded at Hartanna's rider, Dirk, a bearded man with his helmet pulled low on his wrinkled brow. "The command is yours, my good knight."

Dirk raised his age-spotted hand. "Valcor!" he shouted at the top of his lungs. "Take the enemy on the left and thin their ranks. Makaidos, go for the center. Hartanna and I will blast the right. Legossi, run a torch on the back lines to prevent retreat. We will not let a single child killer escape. We will fly over the enemy in a continually cycling column, making sure that one or more of us faces their troops at all times, thereby guarding each other's blind sides."

Dirk stared directly at Edward and his dragon. "Thigocia, I have heard that you are a healer. Guard the king at all costs. Let him fight bravely, but if he is wounded, you must be there to heal him."

"I have never healed a human," Thigocia said, "but I will do what I can."

"All dragons!" Dirk continued. "Listen to your riders! They know the wiles of men better than you do."

Dirk lowered his hand and pointed toward the ground. Gradually pulling in their wings, the dragons angled downward, picking up speed with every second. Edward hung on to Thigocia's spine, but seeing Dirk clenching both fists prompted him to let go.

The rushing wind and approaching shouts of battle pumped energy through Edward's muscles. His heart beating wildly, he clenched his own fists, an unbidden battle cry bursting from his lips. As they dropped into a near vertical dive, he grasped the hilt of his sword.

While the other dragons dove toward their assigned positions, Thigocia headed straight for the battle line. Merlin and Barlow fought back to back, each man wielding his sword with perfect precision. Nearby, Arthur slashed Excalibur into a crowd of men. Each time the blade struck a shield, the silver edge seemed to flash and spark, slicing through metal and leather and cutting flesh and bone and leveling savage after savage.

Thigocia spewed a stream of bluish white fire, making a wide semicircle around the king. Dozens of enemy soldiers erupted in flames, flailing their arms as they tried to run for safety. With rain continuing to beat down, steam rose from every burning soldier, and a stiff breeze blew the vapor throughout their ranks, creating a foggy quagmire as their feet slogged through the mud. A fifth of the enemy troops stampeded back, scrambling over the slippery terrain, but they ran right into a wall of fire ignited by Legossi and the other dragons.

Edward patted Thigocia's neck. "Well done!" he shouted. "This will be easy!"

247

"Too easy. I sense grave danger. Something sinister is afoot." Thigocia landed in the space she had cleared and slapped two of the remaining savages with her tail, sending them flying. With her eyes flashing, she stormed in front of the king, her wings fully stretched as she spewed fire in a long arc toward the enemy's retreating lines.

Arthur thrust Excalibur's blade through a soldier's shield and into his chest, then pulled it out. The bloodstained blade glowed, and as he raised it high, the barbarian's blood sizzled and burned away. Arthur lowered the sword and gazed at it in wonder. "Merlin!" he called. "Do you know anything about this weapon?"

Merlin ran to the king's side and grasped his wrist. "This is Chereb!" he exclaimed. "The sword of Eden!"

Arthur turned the hilt, showing the prophet the other side of the blade. "The Lady of the Lake named it Excalibur, and it seems to breathe fire when I call upon its energy, like a dragon made of polished steel."

Thigocia extended her neck toward the king. "Your Majesty! Something wicked is coming, a horrible disaster looming in my mind like the rising of the devil himself!"

Arthur waved his hand toward the retreating troops as they burned in the dragons' fire. "But we are winning handily! Your winged wonders are cleaning up every last savage."

Merlin pointed his sword at the boiling sky. "Three dragons!" he shouted.

Edward looked up and spotted two red males and a smaller tawny female diving toward them. "More help?" he asked.

"No!" Thigocia yanked Edward off her back with her tail and dropped him next to Merlin and the king. Stretching her wings, she wrapped all three into a tight huddle and ducked her own head underneath. A wall of flames screamed past them, and the sound of beating wings whipped by, followed by a stiff breeze.

Thigocia lifted her wings and jumped into the air. "It's Arramos! And he has Goliath and Roxil with him!" She circled over the trio of humans, shooting balls of flame at the huge red dragon as he glided high above. Goliath and Roxil beat their wings in sync with Arramos, one on each side, and easily dodged Thigocia's volleys. They flew in a wide circle, Arramos taking the lead as they began to form an attack arrow.

Sir Devin rushed toward the king, Palin running at his side. Both men raised their swords. "The dragons have deceived us!" Devin shouted. "They have concocted this plan to expose us and kill us all!"

"Nonsense!" Arthur said. "They have destroyed our enemies."

Devin pointed at the charred bodies in the battlefield. "They don't care what colors a human victim wears as long as they end up in black shrouds!"

Thigocia landed and trumpeted a loud note. "Arramos is not here to kill humans," she shouted, "he is trying to draw Makaidos into battle."

249

"If that's true," Devin said, "then why doesn't Makaidos respond?"

White-hot sparks flew from Thigocia's nostrils. "Because he is busy making sure your worthless backside remains intact!"

Arramos and company angled toward them, picking up speed with every second. Thigocia sent a warning fireball that splashed off Arramos's neck but did nothing to alter his course.

"Everyone under my wings again!" Thigocia shouted, but before they could duck for cover, another red dragon zoomed into view.

Edward thrust his finger upward. "It's Clefspeare!"

Clefspeare smashed into Arramos, chest to chest, sending the elder dragon tumbling through the air. As Clefspeare passed by the other two attackers, he snaked his tail around Goliath's neck, then, taking a sharp turn, slung his body right into Roxil, collapsing her wings. Both dragons crash-landed in a deserted portion of the battlefield but scrambled quickly to their haunches, shaking off the mud as they made ready to fly again.

Merlin held up his closed fist. "Clefspeare!" he shouted. "I have dragon's bane. Keep Arramos away, and I will fend off the other two."

Without a word, Clefspeare flew in the direction he had thrown Arramos. The fierce red dragon had righted himself and was heading back toward the king. Clefspeare, his claws extended and teeth bared, crashed into Arramos again. Both dragons fell toward the ground, biting and slashing each other. At the last second, Clefspeare fanned his wings, threw Arramos into the mud, and, with a mighty flap, ascended again. Making a sharp, one-eighty turn, he dove toward his fallen opponent, shooting a blinding torrent of flames, but Arramos leaped to the side and launched into the air. He zoomed away with Clefspeare in pursuit, and the two faded into the rainy backdrop.

Goliath, now skimming the clouds again with Roxil, swooped toward the king and smacked into Thigocia, knocking her to the ground. Roxil followed with a stream of flames, but King Arthur blocked it with his shield just before the torrent could slam into his face.

Merlin held up his fist, opening his fingers slightly. Goliath and Roxil faltered, their wings out of sync. As they flew away, they alternately rose and dipped in the gusty winds. Merlin closed his fingers again.

Thigocia pushed her wings against the mud and righted herself. "I saw a new horde of Saxons swarming on the hill! They are coming this way!"

Arthur shouted, "Make your defenses!" The king's soldiers formed a wall of sword-wielding men and a cadre of bowmen behind them, their arrows bending their strings.

"Edward!" Thigocia shouted, lowering her head. "Mount! We will thin their ranks!"

As Edward climbed into position, Sir Devin stalked toward them and raised his sword. "This is more dragon treachery! The barbarians waited for their dragon allies to join them before they brought their second wave."

Merlin leaped in front of Devin and blocked the knight's thrust with his own sword. "Don't be a fool!" Merlin grunted as he pushed against the crossed blades. "Thigocia is no friend of Goliath or Roxil. She was a victim of their attack!"

"You fell for their ploy!" Devin growled. "She spawned the scaly beasts! They wouldn't kill their own mother!"

King Arthur lifted the flashing Excalibur high. "Devin! I command you to desist!"

Devin scowled at the king and backed away from Merlin, muttering something unintelligible.

Barlow's voice rose above the clattering rain. "Bowmen! Pierce those devils!" A hundred arrows shot into the downpour. Edward raised his sword and stretched to see over the wall of men. The savages were closing in, some dropping into the mud as arrows rained on their advance. Shifting his gaze to the sky, he counted three dragons sweeping the enemy with waves of fire, but he couldn't tell who they were.

Thunder boomed overhead. Rain pounded even harder. Suddenly, a spear flew in, striking Edward in the chest. He fell off Thigocia's back, but she caught him in her wing and laid him gently on the ground. As he writhed in the mud, a wave of barbarians slammed into the front lines. Arthur, Merlin, Devin, and Palin charged into the fray, Excalibur flashing in the king's grip.

Stretching her wings, Thigocia created a shield over Edward. He grimaced at her, pain crushing his words. "Break . . . break the spear. I must . . . fight."

"You cannot survive this wound," Thigocia said. "It has likely pierced your lungs."

Edward felt blood seeping into his throat. "Let me die . . . fighting . . . not wallowing in the mud." He struggled to his knees, feeling for the spear at his back.

"The point protrudes several inches." Thigocia laid her tail on his shoulder. "Stay as still as you can."

With Edward holding the front end, Thigocia chomped the shaft near the point and broke it into splinters.

Edward clenched his teeth. "Now break the other end."

Thigocia clamped her jaws around the shaft, but as she crunched the wood, Edward collapsed to the mud, faceup. The spear broke somewhere inside his body and part of it jerked out. Blood flowed freely from his chest. He arched his back, and his arms and legs stiffened.

Thigocia wrapped her wings around him and pulled him to his feet. "Battle or no battle, I will not let you die in the mud. I can try to heal you, but you have been mortally wounded. First, I have to find a dragon to breathe fire on me."

Edward stuck his head through a gap in the dragon's wings, but darkness shrouded the battlefield. Everything moved slowly, like a somber dance in a house of mourning. As King Arthur's sword swept from side to side, one barbarian after another fell to his blows. Suddenly, the blade flashed with radiance as if struck by a bolt of lightning, but instead of knocking the king flat, the bolt seemed to penetrate his body, lighting him as bright as the sun itself. A brilliant beam shot out of Excalibur's tip, and as Arthur staggered backwards, he lowered the sword. The beam slashed the ground, sending a streak of lightning along the muddy field. The glittering streak shot into Thigocia, creating a shimmering white halo all around her.

A sizzling sensation burned into Edward's skin. Everything in his vision flashed so brightly, he couldn't see at all. Blistering heat surged into his lungs, making them feel on fire. Seconds later, the light flickered off. His pain vanished.

Fighting against the dragon's leathery wings, he bounded through the opening, then laid his palm on his chest and took a deep breath. Blood dampened his fingers, but not even a twinge of pain hampered his lungs. Even the shaft of the spear had disintegrated. He grabbed his sword and gazed at Thigocia. "What happened?"

"I have no idea." Thigocia lowered her head and sniffed the hole in his vest. "A miracle?"

"I'll have to accept that. No time for guessing."

Edward saluted her and rushed into the battle. As he raised his shield, he heard the dragon call from behind him, "Praise the Maker!" An arrow thumped into his shield, then another. He glanced back at Thigocia and nodded. She nodded in return.

The king swung Excalibur's beam back into the horde. The savages in its path disappeared as if disintegrated by its energy. Arthur swept the enemy's lines. Dozens of men blew apart in splashes of sparks, their swords, shields, and helmets falling to the spots where they once stood. The Saxons began fleeing once again, many slipping and falling under the tide of trampling feet. Arthur drew the sword back, and the beam disappeared.

Goliath plummeted from the sky. Makaidos zoomed behind him, snapping at his tail. With his wings stretching wide, Goliath leveled his flight near the ground and reached down with expanded claws, seizing Arthur's clothes and jerking him upward. As the king rose into the air, his shield went flying and Excalibur fell to the ground. Arthur's bowmen turned their aim toward the sky, keeping their arrows drawn back as they awaited orders.

Scattering water droplets from his wings, Makaidos landed next to Merlin, breathless. "Do not think . . . for a moment . . . that Goliath fears killing the king. We must . . . take great care." The other dragons, Hartanna, Valcor, and Legossi, settled in next to their king. Clefspeare, however, was still nowhere in sight.

253

Goliath landed in a nearby patch of grass and threw Arthur against a large stone. Trumpeting a great roar, he planted his claws on the king's limp body and shouted at the soldiers, "Are you willing to bargain in order to rescue the human king? He is alive, but if you refuse to make a deal with me, he will be dead before sundown."

Roxil landed close to Goliath, but he pushed her away with his tail.

Merlin reached for Excalibur. The moment he snatched it up, the beam returned to the blade and shot into the sky. He angled the light toward Goliath, but when the dragon raised his claws to strike the king, Merlin pulled it back. "With Arthur in his clutches," he said, "I dare not strike the dragon."

Sir Devin drew his sword. "I will give that demon an answer he will never forget!"

Merlin pressed his forearm against Devin's chest, stopping him. He then stepped to the front of the group and faced Goliath. "What would a rebellious dragon want from the two-legged creatures he despises?"

Goliath spewed a stream of fire into the air and let the sparks sizzle for a moment as they fell to the grass. He laughed and stretched out his reply in a low drone. "War."

"Between humans and dragons?" Merlin asked.

"You catch on quickly for a human, but I do not make agreements with the lying sons of Noah. I am addressing the dragons, those who follow the so-called king of the dragons. I want them to break their alliance with the humans, so that I and my followers can freely wage war against the stupid bipeds. If they give me their word, that will be all I need."

Makaidos snorted a spray of smoke through his nostrils. "Don't give in to the demons within you, my son. They have sung lies to you, and they will bring you to destruction."

Goliath spat a ball of sparks onto the ground. "When you chose the love of humans over that of your own kind, I ceased being your son." He spread a wing over Roxil's back. "And your daughter agrees with me."

Makaidos whipped his tail down, splashing mud all around. "Roxil, was rebelling against me and birthing a youngling with this beast not enough for you? Will you now fight humans with him?"

Roxil turned her gaze toward Goliath. "We are not merely allies in war. We are mates for life."

"Enough idle chatter!" Goliath roared. He clutched the chain mail on Arthur's chest and lifted him into the air. "What is your answer, O King of the Dragons?"

Makaidos turned toward Merlin, his eyes flaming red. "I am too angry to think. Do you have counsel?"

Merlin spoke in a low tone. "We must protect the king. Tell him you'll break the alliance. A falsehood to save an innocent life is not a sin."

"You do not understand," Makaidos said. "I cannot utter words I know to be false. Goliath knows this."

255

Merlin lowered his head and folded his hands over Excalibur's hilt. "Then do whatever you must, but I advise that you make no covenant with one who uses threats of murder to gain an advantage."

Makaidos bowed to Merlin. "I understand, but Goliath is not bluffing. I must prevent him from killing the king." As he turned back toward Goliath, he lifted his head high. "We will break our alliance. I will no longer fight alongside the human race."

Goliath's toothy grin spread wide across his snout. "Very well. Meet me at your cave within the hour, and I will turn the human king over to you. Come alone."

Goliath flew into the air, Arthur's body dangling in his claws. Roxil followed, glancing back at Makaidos before turning her gaze to the skies.

Makaidos bowed to Merlin. "I regret this course I had to take, but I do not regret our long friendship. I only promised to refrain from fighting alongside you, not from being your friend. I will not forget what you have taught me over the years, how you became my mentor after Joseph died. You have given me hope for the future."

Merlin laid a hand on Makaidos's neck. "It is an honor to be your friend, noble king. As far as I know, you are the only dragon who truly understands the path we all must take. I look forward to seeing your influence spread from one dragon mind to another, for even dragons must be enlightened by the truth."

"Well spoken, Merlin." The dragon nuzzled the old man's cheek. "I will deliver your king to his throne, but, with a dangerous war looming, I cannot say when we will meet again. Farewell."

Makaidos turned to the other dragons. "You have performed admirably and defeated the enemy, but your mission is now over. Go to your caves and await my instructions. Although we will no longer battle alongside the humans, we still have a war to wage. When I return, we will plan our strategy to bring Goliath and his followers back to their senses."

Thigocia shuffled close to Makaidos. "Will you return to me safely, my love?"

Makaidos's eyes flashed. "Are you suggesting that my own son and daughter would try to harm me?"

"Roxil? She did not attack me directly, so we cannot predict her intent, but Goliath frightens me. His eyes burn with the same evil that inflamed the hearts of the Nephilim."

"I understand. But if a son I raised is willing to obey the demons within him, even if they command him to kill his own father, then perhaps I deserve to die."

Thigocia swung her head around and scanned the dozens of sets of human eyes watching them. "I will not respond to that in public. Just return to me, and we will fight together to win their hearts back."

"You have spoken well," Makaidos said. "Do you know the proper steps to take in naming a new dragon king?"

256

"I do, but I will not entertain a faithless option. Just come back to me safely."

Makaidos sighed. "You are right. I will come back to you. Just see to it that none of these loyal dragons tries to follow me to our cave. Let us meet again back at the castle hill, though I cannot be sure when I will arrive." He reared to his haunches and leaped into the air, his wings unfurling in the same motion. "I will not break my word," he called, swinging his head back around. Seconds later, he was gone.

The other dragons beat their wings and rose into the sky—Legossi, Hartanna, Valcor, and last of all, Thigocia, each one sailing off in a different direction through the dark, stormy skies.

Devin growled through his grinding teeth. "Makaidos doesn't fool me. He is in league with his son. They will form an alliance and plot the destruction of us all."

"Ridiculous," Merlin said, keeping Excalibur at the ready in front of his belt. "Makaidos said our friendship is intact, and a dragon never lies."

"Perhaps we should all trust in the words of murderers, old man." Devin lifted his sword. "But when it comes to protecting the king and his rule, I will trust in the edge of a blade." He slid his sword back into its scabbard and waved toward Palin. "Come with me. I will want a witness to record what happens."

Palin withdrew a parchment book and stylus from his saddlebag. "Yes, my liege."

Devin raised his shield, covering his chest. "We will make sure the king comes back alive."

"No!" Merlin shouted. "Makaidos was supposed to go alone. Your presence will surely inflame the dragons' parley."

"I care only for the king!" Devin turned and sprinted away. Splashing through the mud, he and Palin ran up a slope that led into a sparse forest where they had tied their horses.

As their forms blended into the trees, Edward joined Merlin at his side. "If you please, Master Merlin, may I offer a suggestion?"

257

Merlin kept his gaze fixed on the clouds. "You may."

Edward stepped in front of the old prophet and cleared his throat. "As you might know," he said, watching Merlin's eyes dart from side to side, "I don't trust any of the dragons, and I trust Sir Devin even less. It seems to me that a human loyal to the king should attend to this matter and make sure he is brought home safely."

"You are exactly right," Merlin replied, still gazing at the sky. "I am working on that already."

"You are?" Edward looked up at the empty gray skies. "How?"

"Through a prayer passed down to me by Noah the patriarch, a prayer for the assistance of a dragon."

"But the dragons have departed, and Makaidos ordered them not to help us."

"True, but there is one dragon who did not hear Makaidos's command. I would trust him with my life."

"I assume you mean Clefspeare."

"Yes." Merlin slid Excalibur into his back scabbard. "You saw him in battle against Goliath and Arramos. Is there any doubt about the heart of such a warrior?"

"He certainly convinced me. His fierceness could not have been an act."

"Indeed." Merlin gripped Edward's forearm. "I will ride Clefspeare to Makaidos's cave, and I will see if this deal between dragons is kept."

"Shall I go with you? Another witness could be valuable against the likes of Devin and Palin."

"I doubt that he would let you ride him, but even if he would, I need you to do something for me." Merlin pressed the candlestone into Edward's palm. "Take this gem to my quarters. Clefspeare might not be able to fly if I have it in my possession."

Edward gazed at the stone and tensed his brow. "Begging your pardon, good prophet, but I believe my abilities can be used more efficiently. I am a warrior, not a trinket courier."

Merlin released his grasp. "If you would stop obsessing over your honor, young man, you would easily discover what you have been commissioned to learn."

"Commissioned?" Edward chuckled nervously. "What are you talking about?"

"There is no need to pretend. I have already discerned how the king is using you as his surreptitious eyes and ears, and I am troubled by your dual purposes."

"I have no dual purposes." Edward closed his fingers tightly around the candlestone. "I am bound to serve His Majesty, and none other."

"If that's true," Merlin said, pointing at Edward's fist, "then do what I say and leave the controversy surrounding the dragons to me. I understand them far better than you do, and I have a plan to save them and Arthur. For the sake of the kingdom, stand down from this spying mission."

Edward tightened his jaw, etching his words with anger. "I will take the gem to your quarters, as you have requested, but you do not have the authority to countermand the king's orders. No one has more authority than the king."

Merlin sighed. "And that is where you lose your way." As the flurry of Clefspeare's wings sent gusts across their faces, Merlin gripped Edward's wrist again. "Don't make rash decisions while the world is dark. Wait for the light to make all things clear."

Edward didn't answer. He just glared at Merlin, every muscle in his face as taut as a bowstring.

Merlin climbed aboard Clefspeare and shouted. "To Makaidos's cave, my friend! And hurry!"

259

CHAPTER

RAISING DRAGONS

As Makaidos flew toward the entrance of his cave, danger scraped his senses. Goliath's brooding anger rose from the ground like the odor of a steaming tar pit, a heavy, simmering wrath that longed to lash out and destroy. Yet, the anger seemed to restrain itself, as if waiting for an opportune time to strike. Ever since the spirits of the Nephilim stole Goliath's mind, he had become perverted, bestial. He seemed anxious to kill anything that stood against his plan to rule the dragon kingdom. But what of Roxil? She seemed possessed by a misguided idealism, not a warped spirit.

Makaidos landed and faced the dark cave. His eldest son waited inside, and perhaps his eldest daughter as well. Was there still hope? Could they be rescued from their respective demons? Maybe. He had one last idea to try.

He folded his wings and ducked inside the cave's low entryway, turning on his eyebeams as he glanced around the inner chamber. Goliath sat next to the wall, Roxil at his side and King Arthur lying at his feet, motionless.

Makaidos focused the beams directly on Goliath's eyes. "You could not battle me yourself, my son? You had to bring your sister to help?"

Goliath blinked and lowered his head below the beams. "I will not harm you. I am here to keep my word." He rolled the king face up. "Arthur is alive but unconscious."

"I see. An unconscious king cannot bear witness to your crime." Makaidos reared up, exposing the most vulnerable part of his underbelly. "I have trained Roxil well, so the two of you should be enough to do the deed. I will not resist."

"Father!" Roxil slapped her tail against the wall of the cave. "Are you implying that I will help Goliath kill you? Have you no faith in me at all?"

"Faith in you?" Makaidos narrowed his eyes. "Did you and Goliath pass through a covenant veil?"

"You know we didn't." Roxil swung her head to the side. "Arramos joined us together. The ways of the covenant veil are the ways of the past."

"Then you have answered your own question." Makaidos lowered himself to all fours again. "Your unholy alliance with a demon-possessed mate has incinerated my faith in you. Since Goliath is against me, and you stand with him, you are against me as well."

Goliath raised a wing and draped it over Roxil. "We are not going to kill you. Roxil insisted on coming to ensure my safety from outside interference and from you. As old as you are, I still doubt that I could defeat you in single combat. Only Clefspeare is your equal in battle."

"Now I am sure it is a Naphil who speaks," Makaidos said, "for you know that my age has weakened my skills. In order to fool your mate into coming, you have chosen to lie, and lying is the fruit of the dragon prototype. His Eden curse made him a legless and wingless serpent, and I thought that ended all dragon deception forever. Obviously, I was wrong."

Roxil slapped the wall again. "How can you possibly believe what you are saying about Goliath? Our war is against the human race, not each other!"

"I believe what I am saying because I sense danger. If Goliath intends no harm, then where does the danger originate?"

Roxil's eyebeams flicked on and pointed toward the cave entrance. "I have also sensed danger ever since I arrived. A human must be near, probably someone who intends to rescue his king."

Makaidos's beams crossed over Roxil's, creating a diamond outlined in scarlet. "I should feel no danger from any human who would rescue his king. I helped save them all from the barbarians."

"They merely used you." Roxil doused her beams. "They will turn on you whenever it is convenient."

Makaidos rubbed a foreleg against his tender underside. "Humans have had convenient opportunities to strike a blow for many years, even centuries—from my days of weakness in the ark, to the nights I have slept at Merlin's side in the wilderness as he taught me the ways of his messiah, the ways of love, grace, and mercy." He flashed his eyebeams at Roxil. "Once again you have acted rashly because you know so little, yet think you know so much."

Makaidos bowed toward Goliath. "You have captured her heart, my son. Congratulations. She has forsaken all reason and will believe you no matter what you say or do." He spread out his wings, exposing his underbelly again. "Now, do what you must. Dying in your fire is better than living under your rule, especially when you have stolen the heart of my precious daughter. Following in the footsteps of the human messiah, I will not resist. I give my life gladly, hoping that Roxil will finally see the difference between a loving father and a deceiving usurper."

"Father!" Roxil growled. "Listen to yourself! Do not play the fool to win me back to your home! I stand with my mate, no matter what outrageous grandstanding you do."

Goliath snorted. "You will not die at my hand." He turned his beams toward the back of the cave. Two men leaped from the darkness. Devin plunged a sword into Makaidos's belly, and Palin thrust his into Roxil's. Both men twisted their swords, then sprang away, dodging the dragons' gushing fluids.

Roxil teetered. Her eyes widened. First glancing at Goliath, then at Makaidos, she toppled forward. Makaidos fell at her side, pressing his scaly jaws against hers.

As his vision faded, Makaidos watched Goliath. He tried to speak, but he felt his life seeping away.

Goliath pushed Arthur's unconscious body. "Take your king, Devin, and be on your way. Tell Morgan that our deal is complete. I will make no more contracts with her."

"As you wish." Devin helped Palin hoist Arthur over his back, and they shuffled out of the cave.

As Makaidos closed his eyes, Roxil's faint voice crept into his ear. "Why, Goliath? Why?"

Goliath laughed. "As our father said. No witnesses. You refused to allow the Nephilim to enter your mind, so you could not be trusted."

Darkness shrouded Makaidos's vision. As he sighed his last breath, his daughter spoke again, her voice failing. "Father. . . . I am so . . . so . . . ." She exhaled and breathed no more.

Makaidos pushed his wing over her body, then darkness washed over his mind.

Sapphira plunged headfirst through the dark, cold air in the mysterious pit, keeping the torch at the bottom firmly set in her sights. She felt no fear. The warmth from the Ovulum seemed to radiate courage into her heart.

As the torch drew closer, the darkness melted, turning the night skies into the fullness of day. Her descent slowed, and her body turned upright, as if someone had pushed an invisible hand underneath her. Finally, she landed next to her torch, both feet thudding against a hard surface, jarring her spine. Her momentum threw her into a roll, but when she came to a stop, she quickly leaped to her feet and hurried back to her landing point.

She picked up the torch and whispered to the flame. "No need for you, now."

Setting a hand on her hip, she turned from side to side. With a dry fountain to her left and the smashed remains of crates and marketplace carts to her right, this village seemed very familiar—ruined, but familiar. In her mind's eye, she painted in the missing pieces, reassembling the market and filling the fountain with gushing water. She added people, young and old, men and women in colorful clothes—

Sapphira snapped her fingers. That was it! This is Shinar! She spun around and gazed at a low rise, looking for the tower, but there was nothing at the top, just a huge gap. She scurried to the crest and peered across the empty expanse. Obviously this was where the tower stood before the museum dropped through the portal.

As she walked toward the center of the tower mound, a sense of grief grew so strong she couldn't bear to continue. Memories of Acacia again flashed into her mind—her frightened eyes, her terrified scream.

Sapphira hustled back to the edge of the crest and looked out over the city. The familiar idols and remnants of the tar pits dotted the landscape. Yet, not a soul stirred anywhere. Setting one hand on her hip again, she scratched her head with the butt end of her torch. How could this be? How could Shinar get physically moved from its place so many centuries ago and show up here? Wherever here was.

As she searched for signs of life, the sun stung her eyes, but she caught a glimpse of a shadow, a human shadow, moving far down the vacant street, back where the laborers used to pile bricks from

265

the kilns. Pulling down her veil, she ran toward a gap between two idols. The stacked stone faces that had once collected votive gifts of flowers and jewels now presided over a broken marble floor with only crushed rocks and mud to appease the goddesses.

Now back at the street level, Sapphira trotted, trying to fix her gaze on the spot she had noticed movement, but her veil flapped against her face, obstructing her vision. As she slowed to furtive tiptoeing, she straightened the veil. Whatever made that shadow had to be around somewhere. But where?

She kicked a pile of crushed rocks, scattering dust around her ankles. The high portico that had once covered the brick-making area had collapsed. Broken beams and marble lay in heaps on the dirt floor. The kilns were now punched through on every side, as though an army of invaders had marched in and ruined everything in sight. Red and gray bricks lay strewn and broken, some pieces thrown as far away as the opposite side of the dirt street. With her courage still flowing, she called out, "Is anyone here?"

A gentle breeze brushed her ears, but nothing else. "Is anyone here?" she called again.

This time, a sharp voice replied. "Who are you?"

Sapphira took a step back. Should she answer? What if this person knew Morgan? Could she risk letting him know her name? She cleared her throat and spoke in her sweetest tone. "I am a lost traveler from another land. Is there anyone here who can help me find my way?"

A head bobbed up from behind one of the kilns, a young male with ragged brown hair. When he caught sight of her, his eyes widened. "Are you a girl?"

Sapphira glanced down at her body and straightened her frumpy dress. "Isn't it obvious?"

The boy stepped out from behind the kiln. "I guess so. I haven't seen very many. Only grown women, really. No one as young as you."

Sapphira untied her coif and pulled it off, letting her hair tumble down. Shielding her eyes with her hand, she walked closer. The boy's mouth dropped open. His eyes seemed glazed.

She looked down at her dress again. "Is something wrong?"

He swallowed and retied a leather sash at the front of his dirty gray tunic. "No. It's just that . . . Do all girls have white hair and shining blue eyes like yours?"

She swept a handful of hair over the front of her shoulder. "No. Only one other that I know of, but she's dead." Taking three more steps, she closed the gap between them and stood within arm's reach. "Your voice is familiar . . ."

"So is yours."

She whispered, "Elam?"

A broad smile crossed the boy's face. "Mara?"

Sapphira laughed and threw her arms around his neck. "Yes! I'm Mara!" She hoped Elam would return the embrace, but his body stiffened, feeling cold and hard. She laid her hands on his shoulders and pulled back. "I mean, I'm not Mara anymore. My name's Sapphira now, but I'm the girl from the below lands."

He pulled back farther, letting Sapphira's hands slip away. "That's impossible," he said, squinting at her. "How could you still be alive after all these years?"

"I was going to ask you the same thing."

He picked up half a brick, his grip tight and his bicep flexed. "How do I know you're not just another one of Morgan's tricks to get me to do what she wants? You might be an imposter."

"If you remember Morgan," she said, wiggling her fingers in front of him, "I'm sure you'll remember licking stew off of these."

"I remember." His ears turned red, and he dropped the brick. "No one else would know about that."

"Speaking of stew . . ." She swiveled her head from side to side. "Where do you find food in this place?"

"I never looked for food. I haven't eaten anything for years."

267

"Years?" she repeated. "How is that possible?"

Elam shrugged his shoulders. "I never get hungry."

"Never? That doesn't make any sense."

Elam scraped his sandal along the ground. "Remember that tree Morgan has?"

"Uh-huh. Is that where you got that blossom you gave me?"

"Yes. I ate some of the fruit, the best thing I've ever tasted, and I haven't been hungry since."

Sapphira sighed. "The blossom never faded. I've been hiding it under Paili's bed for centuries."

"Paili's alive, too? I'm glad to hear that. She's a real nice girl from what I could tell."

"She is, and keeping her out of Morgan's clutches is worth all the trouble." She turned slowly in a circle. "So, what is this place?"

"It might not be the truth, but Morgan explained everything to me." He spread out his arms. "This whole place is the sixth circle of Sheol—Hades, I guess they call it now. There used to be lots of people here, dead souls who waited for the Messiah to come and take them to heaven."

Sapphira kicked a broken brick, scattering more dust across the empty path. "So I guess this messiah came, then."

"Looks that way. My grandfather told me he was coming someday. Whoever he is, Morgan hates him with a passion. She says the Messiah was vindictive and left behind a lot of souls, but they're in other circles."

Elam suddenly covered his ears with his hands and grimaced.

"What's wrong?" Sapphira asked.

He turned and doubled over. "Just stay away for a minute."

Sapphira edged toward him, reaching out her hand, but she stopped and pulled back. "Can I do anything to help?"

Breathing heavily, Elam groaned. "Just shut up and leave me alone!"

Sapphira tightened her fingers around her torch, then, as tears formed in her eyes, her fingers loosened again. "Okay," she said softly. "I'll go."

Elam spun around and held up his hand. "No! I didn't mean you!" His eyes darkened and rolled wildly.

Sapphira waved her torch in a wide arc. "There's no one else here!"

Elam covered his ears again. "I hear a voice, a singing voice. It's beautiful, but the words . . ." He clutched his vest and wrenched it in his fist. "The words stab my heart and make it bleed. I can't stand it!"

Sapphira laid a hand on his arm and squeezed. "What does it say?"

Elam pulled away and staggered into the street. He stooped, resting on his haunches with his arms draped over his knees, breathless. "Never . . . never mind. It's gone now." He flopped down on his backside and gave her a weak smile. A glimmer slowly returned to his eyes.

269

Sapphira sat down next to him, her own breaths pumping in time with his. "If you tell me the words, maybe I can help you figure out how to battle it."

He shook his head and averted his eyes. "I'd really rather not."

Sapphira shrugged her shoulders. "Suit yourself." But she didn't really mean it. Whatever that song was, it must have been pure poison, and it didn't seem right to let her friend battle it alone.

Elam nodded toward the spot where Sapphira had landed. "Morgan sometimes shows up over there, just like you did, but she glides down in the form of a raven. I guess she likes checking up on her prisoner once in a while. Not that she needs to, since there's no way to escape. No matter how far you walk or which direction you go, you always end up back here." He flicked his head toward the sky. "Now if you can teach me how to fly like you did, maybe I can get out of here after all."

"I'm not sure how I did that," Sapphira said, tapping her torch on the street, "but I have another idea that might work."

Elam leaped to his feet. "I just saw someone. A man." He grabbed Sapphira's elbow and pulled her up, keeping his body in front of her.

Sapphira laid her hands on Elam's shoulders and peeked around his head. "I see him, and a woman, too. They're coming this way."

As the pair walked slowly along the path toward the brick kilns, Elam's voice lowered to a whisper. "They're walking hand in hand. That's a good sign."

"Good enough for me." With her torch on her shoulder, Sapphira strode right up to the pair. "Do you two live here?" she asked.

The couple, a middle-aged man and a woman in her thirties, kept walking. Sapphira had to jump out of the way to keep from being bowled over. She ran in front of them again, walking backwards as she spoke. "I was just wondering if you knew anything about this place. Is there a way out or any food anywhere?"

The pair ignored her. They both looked around wide-eyed, as if they were lost or dumbstruck.

Sapphira jumped out of the way again and followed them, scratching her head. Elam joined her. "Maybe they speak another language," he offered.

"I could try another language, but they act like I'm not even here, like they can't see me at all." She sidled up to the man and tapped him on the shoulder, raising her voice. "Hello! Do you understand what I'm saying?" No response. Not even a glance. Sapphira pulled on his elbow. Again, no response. Finally, she leaped in front of him and held up both hands, but he bumped into her, knocking her flat on her back, and stepped right on her stomach. He paused for a moment, said something inaudible to the woman, then kept going.

Elam jumped to her side and helped her sit upright. "Are you okay?"

"I'm fine." Sapphira laid a hand on her stomach. "I don't get it. He didn't weigh much at all."

Elam pulled her to her feet. "Think they're ghosts?"

"I doubt it. I felt his elbow when I pulled on it, and he knocked me over." She picked up her torch and stared at the strolling pair. With all the crazy pits and portals in this place, maybe they were in another dimension. She pressed her lips together and hummed, "I wonder . . ."

"Wonder what?"

Twirling the torch in her palm, she watched the couple round a bend and disappear from sight. "I wonder if there's another way to communicate with them, maybe in a different place."

"A different place? But they're right here."

She looped her arm around his elbow. "Come on. I'll show you." With Elam hustling to keep up, she ran back to the rise where the tower had stood and marched straight toward the center. As she looked out over the city with her enhanced vision, she could see the couple back at the kilns, now with more detail than before. Worry lines etched the woman's brow and cheeks, making her look older somehow, much older. The man pointed at various objects, as though he were explaining them to the woman. His face seemed friendly and wise, but his cheeks were also etched with a criss-crossing pattern that looked more like scales than skin.

As she stood in the midst of the portal, the image of the fiery chasm flashed in her mind, this time with Paili's body falling into the magma river.

She clenched her teeth and yanked Elam close to her side. "No!" she shouted. "Not Paili!"

"Where?" Elam swiveled his head. "What's wrong with Paili?"

Sapphira gripped his shoulders. "She's in trouble! I've been gone too long, and Morgan's getting rid of her."

"How can you possibly know what Morgan's doing?"

271

"Never mind!" She raised her torch. "Flames! Now!" Instantly, a crackling flame burst forth at its tip.

Elam jumped back. "How did you do that?"

She grabbed his arm and pulled him close again. "No time to explain. Just brace yourself." She draped her arm around his shoulders and gripped him tightly. "Stay close, or you'll be in big trouble."

Moving her torch hand in a smooth orbit, Sapphira drew a blazing circle in the air. "I don't know where this portal will take us," she said, her body trembling, "but I have to try to get home." As she widened the circle, the fire began to slide down around them, creating a cocoon of flames that swirled around their heads and hissed in their ears. The heat massaged her skin, warm enough to break a sweat.

Beads of perspiration appeared on Elam's face, reflecting the torch's flickering orange flame. A gaping smile broke through as he whispered, "Amazing!"

"Okay," she said, "don't let it scare you, but this is where it really gets weird."

Suddenly, the flaming wall collapsed inward around their feet, but instead of incinerating them, the fire began transforming their bodies into particles of light, inching its way up their legs and then their torsos. The process created a loud buzzing that drowned out the hissing flames.

"When it gets to our heads," Sapphira called, "you can keep your eyes open. It won't hurt."

As the flames crawled over their faces, Elam shouted, "I love it!" Seconds later, the entire cocoon exploded into millions of pieces and scattered into nothingness. As the sparks died away, new heat stung her back, as though hundreds of tiny needles pricked her skin.

Elam spoke, his voice now quiet and steady. "Any idea where we are?"

Standing in a yellow column of light, Sapphira surveyed her surroundings. A cliff of granite stood in front of her, too sheer to climb. It rose to more than a hundred feet overhead and stretched

272

out in a wide ledge at the top that overlooked the chasm below. The portal's swirling exit column, so pale it was barely visible, seemed to dissipate as it reached toward the ceiling high above.

As she turned to face the source of heat, a bright glow blinded her eyes. The dazzling river of magma flowed a mere dozen paces away. She backed up against the cliff and clutched her chest. "We're at the bottom of the chasm!"

Elam stepped closer to the river, raising his hands to block the heat, but as he approached the edge, he lowered them again. "It's not really that hot." He inched his finger toward the surface. "In fact, I think it's—"

"Aaaaiiieee!"

The cry echoed throughout the chasm. A small, girlish body fell from the ledge, her ratty dress flapping around her legs as she dropped. Sapphira tried to scream, "Paili!" but the word barely squeaked through her cramping throat.

Paili's body splashed into the magma river and disappeared from sight in the slow-moving stream. At the top of the cliff, Morgan brushed her hands together, and she and Mardon walked away from the ledge.

273

Makaidos blinked at the dim light. "What a bad dream!" he said out loud. He tried to turn on his eyebeams, but they didn't seem to work. "Hmmm. Apparently I need more time in the sun." He yawned and smacked his lips. "Or maybe in a regeneracy dome."

As his mind cleared, he stretched his wings, but they felt strange. His foreleg touched something at his side, most likely his mate, but the sensation was different, softer somehow, more tactile. Turning his head slowly, he brought the form next to him into view.

He gasped. A human! A female human! He jerked his wing away and rolled to his haunches, but they weren't haunches, they were feet and legs! Human ones! And his wing was a human arm, clothed in a soft sleeve.

He patted his body all over, feeling his human chest, waist, and legs. What was going on? Had he awakened from a bad dream only to fall into a nightmare? Using his newly found finger and thumb, he pinched the soft flesh on his cheek. Pain. Real pain. Surely he was wide awake, but how could he possibly be human?

Keeping his hand in front of his face, he examined his new fingers. A gold ring with a mounted red jewel was fastened around his index finger. As the gem pulsed between two shades of red, he stared at it in wonder. "My rubellite is mounted in a ring, and it blinks!"

Gazing all around, he studied the strange landscape, a ruined city with broken monuments and fountains and debris scattered everywhere.

Suddenly a stream of memories flooded his mind—Goliath's mocking voice, Devin's flashing sword, Roxil's cry as she slowly passed away at his side.

Makaidos gulped. "Roxil!" He jumped to the woman and shook her body. "Roxil!" he shouted, his voice trembling. "Wake up!"

Roxil groaned. "It is too early to rise, Father, even for a warrior."

He shook her again. "Roxil! You must wake up. This is an emergency!"

Roxil blinked and gazed at Makaidos, then jerked away and shouted, "Who are you, human? Speak now, or I will torch you where you stand!"

"Roxil! Look at yourself! Look at your hands and arms!"

"Hands and arms?" Roxil lifted her hand toward her face. "What!?" she screamed. "What happened to me?"

"I have no idea. I am confused, too." Makaidos lowered himself to his knees and gazed into her eyes. "You know who I am, don't you?"

Her eyes locked onto his and widened as she whispered, "Father?"

He took his daughter's hands and pulled her to her feet. His thumb rubbed over a rubellite ring that matched his own. "Somehow we were transformed into humans." He released her and patted his body again. "We have human chests, human arms, human legs. It's amazing!"

Her body wavered back and forth, and Makaidos steadied her. "Amazing was not the first word that came to my mind."

"Do you remember what happened in the cave?" he asked.

She squinted at him, and, as her eyes widened again, they flashed. "Swords," she said softly, "and humans thrusting them into us."

"Yes! I recognized Sir Devin. He and someone else wielded swords, and I think . . ." He grasped her hand more tightly. "I think they killed us."

"Killed us? But we are alive." She pulled her hand away and wiggled her fingers. "We are as ugly as sin itself, but we are alive."

Makaidos stooped and picked up a broken brick. "It seems that we have been transported to a new environment, a shattered world of some kind." He rose and cast the brick into an empty fountain. "I expected to find a better place to rest when I died."

Roxil scanned the toppled buildings and debris-strewn roads. "This city seems familiar to me."

"It seems familiar to me, as well." Makaidos brushed dirt from his hand and extended the other toward Roxil. "Shall we look around?"

"Do I have any choice?" she asked, slipping her hand into his.

He smiled and pulled gently. "No, you do not."

As the sky brightened, they strolled along the road. Makaidos pointed at a rise in the ground in front of them. "This place in particular seems oddly familiar." He waved his finger to one side of the rise. "If I reconstruct that broken fountain in my mind and raise those two toppled idols, it starts to look like—"

Roxil pulled away and ran to the slope. "Shinar!" She beat her arms against her sides. "Ohhh!" she groaned. "If only I could fly! I could see everything so much better!"

"And Nimrod's tower is gone," Makaidos noted, "so there is no place to climb to get a good view." He joined Roxil and spun in a slow circle, his arms spread out. "This is absolutely amazing!"

275

Roxil grabbed his sleeve. "How can you possibly be happy about this? We are human now! We are disgusting, hateful, lust-filled, wine-guzzling bipeds!"

Makaidos rubbed the material on his sleeve. "How about that? God gave me a fine-looking human garment!" He stepped back and gazed at Roxil from head to toe, admiring her long cream-colored dress. "And look at you! What a lovely outfit!"

Roxil set her fists on her hips. "Father! You are impossible! We have degenerated into the worst of all the species, and just like the vainest of the lot, you are already obsessing over clothing!"

"I am not obsessing. I am marveling." Makaidos laid a hand on her back and leaned close. "Listen to me. Obviously we have entered into some sort of afterlife. God has given us a new opportunity. Maybe we can make the human condition a better one, perhaps build a city that reflects the opposite of the corruption that Nimrod foisted upon the world."

Roxil folded her arms over her chest. "What can we possibly do with this city? It is in ruins."

"The symbolism is perfect." Makaidos clasped his hands together. "As we rebuild the corrupted city, we reshape the human culture."

"But how can just two people create a culture?"

"If this is a place where dragons go when they die, perhaps new ones will join us, and other dragons are likely here already. Some perished in the great flood and others died in battles with the Watchers before the flood."

"How many?"

"Fifteen or so. We did not procreate quickly back then, so our numbers were few."

Roxil spread out her arms. "Then where are they?"

Makaidos shrugged his shoulders. "The logical approach would be to look for them."

"Logical, yes, but we are humans now. Logic never seemed to be a primary behavioral motivation for them whenever I was watching."

"True enough for many of them." He nudged her ribs. "But I also observed some dragons who ignored logic on many occasions."

She looped her arm around his elbow. "If that means, 'I told you so,' then I guess I deserve it."

"It was a gentle rebuke, my love." He caressed her cheek with his hand, letting his knuckles linger. "This enhanced sense of touch is quite pleasant, is it not?"

She nodded and rested her head against his shoulder. "It is. I cannot deny it."

"So, shall we explore this strange world and experience a new adventure?"

"I suppose so." She walked at his side, then stopped and playfully poked his arm. "But I am going to keep my eye on you. I still lack trust in the human species, and now you are one of them."

277

Makaidos shrugged his shoulders again. "Fair enough." As the two strolled hand in hand along the path, he smiled. He wanted to look at his daughter's facial expression, but sneaking a peek might tip the delicate balance of her emotions. He knew exactly what her dragon face would have looked like right now, a blend of skepticism and excitement. Although she despised humanity, she had to be relishing the adventure of living in a completely new world. Her human face probably bore a similar expression, perhaps mixed with a touch of fear. He regripped her cold, trembling hand. Maybe his confidence could cast out her fears.

They walked slowly toward the ruins of the city's brick kilns. Shinar seemed much larger than before, and somehow closer, more intimate, even in its devastated condition. Marble fragments from broken statues littered the dirt path, and a dried-out tar pit sank away to one side. Makaidos pointed at one of the broken ovens. "We can make that area into a bakery, and the tar pits can be farmland."

Roxil winced at the dark depressions in the earth. "Can you grow crops in tar?"

"I have no idea, but we will soon learn." He stopped suddenly. "Did you hear that?"

"Hear what?"

He shook his head and continued walking. "Just an impression, an image in my mind. A girl begging me to speak to her."

"What did she look like?"

Makaidos gazed upward. "It was fleeting, but I did see bright blue eyes and hair as white as wool."

"Okay, Father, you are scaring me. First, you enjoy being human, now you are getting drunk without ever touching a wineskin."

Makaidos smirked. "Shall I keep my visions to myself, then?"

"No, no. Go ahead and tell me. I have to monitor your sanity and keep you in line."

After several minutes of exploring the ruins, Makaidos stopped again and squeezed Roxil's hand. "Am I insane now?" He pointed at a pomegranate tree near a collapsed portico. "Or do I see a girl hiding behind that tree?"

Roxil whispered. "I see her, too. I cannot see her eyes, but her hair is brown, not white."

"True. She is not the girl I saw in my mind."

"Could she be one of the dragons who died in the flood? She is quite young."

"It is possible," Makaidos replied. "My sister Zera was a youngling when she died."

"Then what are we waiting for?" Roxil ran forward, waving. "Zera, is that you?"

BAPTISM OF FIRE

D riving her trembling legs forward, Sapphira shuffled toward the river. She thrust her hand into her pocket and jerked out the Ovulum. "Elohim!" she cried, her entire body quaking. "Help me! I don't know what to do!"

Elam dove into the magma. Sapphira gasped and trudged to the edge. She breathed a quick prayer and pushed the Ovulum back into her pocket. Scanning the magma's bubbling surface, she searched for any sign of life.

A head bobbed in the current. There he was! Swimming back to the side! When he neared the shore, he waded up to dry land. A thick coat of magma dripped down his tunic and instantly hardened to a crusty coat of ash, blackening his frame from head to toe. At least he was safe, but he was alone.

Sapphira dropped to her knees and cried. "She's gone! My poor Paili is gone forever!"

"Gone, yes." Elam began brushing the ash from his sleeve. "But maybe not forever."

Sapphira lifted her head, barely able to breathe. "What . . . what do you mean?"

"It was the strangest thing. I could open my eyes under there, and I could see everything clearly. Paili was sinking into a whirlpool, and I dove down to grab her, but before I could reach her hand, she suddenly disappeared. If I could survive this stuff, maybe she did, too. That whirlpool has to lead somewhere."

Sapphira pushed up to her wobbly legs and helped Elam brush the ash from his chest. "Did she look scared?"

"I think so, but it was hard to tell."

Stooping next to the river, Sapphira dipped her hand into the current and raised a sample of the magma to her eyes. It was certainly warm, but not the superheated, blistering sensation she expected. As she continued to examine it, the tiniest bubbles became clear. Each one carried microscopic bits of ash through the thick suspension. Staring at the magma seemed to raise the familiar feeling of sadness; Acacia's face, then Paili's, scorched her mind's eye.

She let the magma trickle to the ground. Each drop sizzled on the granite as it struck the floor. "It's a portal," she whispered.

"A portal?" Elam brushed both hands through his hair, breaking chunks of black crust and letting them fall to the ground.

Sapphira's legs strengthened, and her voice steadied. "The whirlpool in the river must be another portal, just like the one we used to get here. Maybe Paili went through it, and she's alive on the other side."

"You mean it's a door to somewhere else?"

"Yes, to yet another place or dimension. That last portal brought us back to the lower realms, but there's no way to tell where the whirlpool leads."

Elam waded into the magma again and extended his hand. "We'd better find her right away. There's no telling what's at the bottom of that whirlpool."

Sapphira reached for his hand and tiptoed in. As the bubbling liquid rose to her thighs, the warmth soothed her tired feet and legs. When she moved to deeper magma, she let go of Elam and paddled through the thick goop, raising splashes that found their way to her mouth. Spitting out the hot, crusty ash, she clamped her lips tight and swam after Elam, but the sense of sadness grew so strong, her arms felt weak and heavy. She bit the inside of her cheek, hoping the pain would spur her on. She had to keep going! She just had to!

Keeping afloat by paddling with one arm, Elam raised his hand and pointed at the river. "I think the whirlpool's straight down."

Sapphira nodded, barely opening her lips to speak. "Let's go!"

Elam dipped his head under and kicked to thrust his body downward. Sapphira took a deep breath and followed. Forcing herself to open her eyes, she saw Elam more clearly than if it were the sunniest day in history. He plunged deeper, and she kept following, glad she had taken so many dives into Lucifer's pool hunting for polished stones. Her lungs would hold out . . . she hoped.

A slowly swirling eddy appeared below. Elam swam inside and disappeared in the shining vortex. Her lungs now begging for air, Sapphira plunged into the center of the swirl, thrusting and kicking with all her might. As the whirlpool swallowed her, she felt the familiar transformation to light energy and a blinding sensation, then, a few seconds later, pressure on her feet as though she were standing upright.

Although her eyes were still blinded, cool air breezed past her face, signaling that she had re-embodied and was now standing on a flat surface. As her vision cleared, she saw a nearby fountain, dry and cracked. A line of broken-down shops lay beyond it, as well as another dry fountain in the distance. She drank in the air, nearly hyperventilating as her lungs slowly recovered.

"It looks like we're back where we started." Elam tightened the belt on his tunic. "At least there's no black stuff all over me this time."

"Back where we started?" Sapphira scanned the city again. This time she spotted the familiar brick kilns and tar pit. "Those portals just took us in a circle?"

"I guess so, but we're not in exactly the same place as before." He pointed at the rise on the other side of the more distant fountain. "We were over there."

Sapphira breathed a sigh. "If we made it through, then Paili probably did, too." She cupped her hands around her mouth and called, "Paili! Are you here?"

A tiny voice replied from far away. "I'm here!"

Sapphira stretched up to her toes. Excitement pitched her voice higher. "Where's *here*?"

"Right here with my two new friends." A tiny pair of hands waved in the distance behind the second fountain.

Sapphira grabbed Elam's wrist. "I see her! Let's go!"

They ran past a carpenter shop, a seamstress boutique, and a spa, all with broken columns and entryways, then across a patio that led to the fountain. Letting go of Elam, she surged ahead, jumped into the fountain's cavity, and dashed to the other side. She leaped over the low parapet and swept Paili into her arms.

After swinging Paili in a full circle, Sapphira set her down and combed her fingers through the little girl's hair. "You're okay! I'm so glad you're okay!"

"Me, too!" Paili chirped. She turned and pointed. "I have new friends!"

Sapphira took a quick breath. A man and a woman stood at the base of the fountain, the same couple she had seen by the brick kilns. She dipped her knee in a brief curtsy. "Uh, hello."

The man ascended the few marble steps leading to the fountain. "It is the girl from my vision!"

Elam stepped in between the man and Sapphira. "Who are you?"

The man stopped and extended his hand. "Makaidos is my name. What is yours?"

Elam lifted his hand slowly, his eyes revealing deep suspicion. "I've heard that name somewhere before."

Makaidos gripped Elam's hand and shook it, then looked back at the woman and smiled. "This is my daughter, Roxil."

Elam's brow lifted. "I *have* heard your names! Those are dragon names. My father told me lots of stories about dragons."

"Your father?" Makaidos released Elam's hand. "Who are you?"

Elam squared his shoulders. "I am Elam, son of Shem, grandson of Noah."

"You are Shem's missing son?" Makaidos stared at Elam. "You must have died over a thousand years ago!" He glanced back at Roxil and scratched his head. "But now I am confused. We died as dragons and awoke here, so I thought this was a place for dragons to rest after they died. Why would a dead human be here?"

"We're not dead," Sapphira offered. "We can travel from one dimension to another. We came here looking for Paili, and we're planning to leave as soon as possible."

283

"Do you know how to leave this place?" Roxil leaped up to the fountain level. "May we come with you?"

"I don't know," Sapphira replied. "If some of these dimensions are meant for the souls of the dead, would it make sense if they could leave? I mean, wouldn't they all just leave if they could?"

Makaidos took Roxil's hand. "It could be dangerous. I think we should stay right where we are."

"Listen to you!" Roxil said, turning to face him. "The one who loves adventure!"

"A well-placed stroke." Makaidos shook a finger at her. "But there is adventure, and there is foolhardy risk."

Roxil tapped her foot on the ground. "Would you prevent me from trying?"

"Would I be able to stop you?" Makaidos sighed and gazed at every face in turn. "We have only been here a short while, and I suspect that other dragons are hereabouts in the guise of humans, perhaps my father and mother or my siblings." His gaze lingered on Sapphira. "Would you care to assist us in a search?"

Elam cleared his throat sharply. "I don't see any dragons, and we have Paili, so we should—"

Sapphira squeezed Elam's arm. "I'd love to help! Just because we can't see the dragons doesn't mean they're not here."

His eyes glazing, Elam raised his hands toward his ears, then lowered them quickly. He jerked his head back and forth as if shaking water from his hair.

Sapphira caressed his arm. The voice must have been tormenting him again. "When I'm standing at a portal," she said, "I can see everything. Maybe if I—" Sudden warmth radiated over her thigh. Sliding her hand slowly, she reached into her pocket and withdrew the Ovulum.

Makaidos stepped closer, his eyes bulging. "The Ovulum! Where did you get it?"

He reached for it, but Sapphira pulled it away. "I've had it for centuries," she said. "The Eye of the Oracle said I could keep it."

Makaidos pushed his hand through his short reddish-brown hair. "The Eye speaks to you?"

"Yes . . ." She pulled the Ovulum closer to her face. "Or he used to. It's been a while since the last time. But the egg got pretty warm just now, so I thought he was going to speak again, maybe to help us find your dragon family."

"So," Roxil said, "what do you do? Ask it a question?"

"Yes, but he doesn't always answer." Sapphira raised the egg to her lips and spoke slowly and clearly. "Are there any more dragons here, and if there are, can you help us find them?"

"That's two questions," Elam said. "Maybe you should ask one at a time."

"Don't worry. He's smart enough to—" The egg suddenly grew red hot. Sapphira juggled it for a moment, passing it back and forth between her hands as she lowered it to the marble skirt around the fountain. It rocked to the side for a second, then stood upright on its larger end.

Red halos pulsed from the glass, creating vertical rings of light that dimmed and thinned out as they expanded. The frequency of the pulses increased. Ring after ring flew from the Ovulum, so quickly that the gaps between them vanished, leaving a shining red half oval that feathered into pink hues at the edges.

Sapphira reached out and touched the flat oval with her finger, making the surface ripple. She leaned close and gazed through the translucent screen. Elam and Paili stood on the other side, bathed in a wrinkled red shroud, but Makaidos and Roxil appeared as dragons. She jumped to the side and peeked around the edge. Four humans stood agape next to the fountain.

She looked through the screen again. Two humans and two dragons stared back at her.

Elam pointed at her from the other side of the screen. "Sapphira! You're covered with fire!"

M erlin rode on Clefspeare's back through the clearing skies and gazed at the terrain below. A stream wound through a forest, leading away from a cliff that housed Makaidos's cave. A rough path followed the stream through dense forest and undergrowth, but few now ventured its dangerous trek. With Goliath on the warpath, this area attracted only the ignorant or suicidal.

Clefspeare circled lower. "I fear we are too late, Master Merlin. The sense of danger peaked and now wanes with every second. If I had not been such a fool, I would have realized that Arramos was leading me away on purpose."

"Don't fret about the past," Merlin said, patting the dragon's neck. "Just get us to the cave." He pointed toward the path. "I see two people carrying a third. Is that the king?"

"Yes," Clefspeare said. "Devin and Palin are carrying him. Hold on!" He angled into a dive, taking Merlin almost straight down.

As they approached, Devin and Palin laid the king on the ground and withdrew their swords. Making a sharp turn, Clefspeare avoided the blades and slapped them away with his tail. He landed with a rough bounce, and Merlin scrambled down his back.

"Fools!" Merlin shouted. "Couldn't you see me riding on the dragon?"

Devin picked up his sword and pointed it at Clefspeare. "If you had seen the heroics we had to accomplish to rescue the king, you would have done the same. No dragon can be trusted!"

Merlin squeezed Excalibur's hilt but kept it in its sheath. "Speak quickly. I am in no mood to listen to your idiotic boasts."

Devin kicked the other sword toward Palin. "When we sneaked up to the cave, we overheard Goliath and his mate conspiring with Makaidos. They planned to kill the king and blame it on our allies. Inciting war, they said, would ensure more human deaths and distract us from hunting dragons." He nodded toward his squire who now stood next to him, his sword raised in a similar defensive posture. "Palin and I had to rescue the king from their clutches."

"Your story smells like a nest of rats," Merlin said. "The dragons would have sensed your approach."

"Who can say what they sensed?" Devin waved his arm toward the cave entrance. "The carcasses are in there, so feel free to judge for yourselves. Unfortunately, Goliath got away. When faced with two warriors in closed quarters, he showed his true cowardly stripes and fled. But he cannot hide forever. Even if I do it with my last dying breath, someday I will slaughter that beast, just as Palin and I killed his mate and his father, Makaidos."

Heat surged into Merlin's cheeks. "You killed the king of the dragons?" He yanked out Excalibur, and the beam shot into the sky.

Palin stumbled backwards, his eyes wide, but Devin held his ground. "Makaidos was a traitor!" Devin shouted, a vein bulging at the side of his head. "Palin is my witness. We had to rescue our king!"

"Rescue me?" Arthur pushed himself up to a sitting position. "What need have I to be rescued?"

Devin dropped to his knees next to Arthur. "Your servants, Palin and I, rescued you from the clutches of three dragons, Your Majesty."

Clefspeare roared. "You are a liar! My grandfather would never harm the human king!"

"But what of your father?" Devin helped Arthur to his feet, keeping his stare fixed on the dragon. "Will the son of Goliath defend him as well?"

"Defend him?" Clefspeare roared. "To the likes of you? You killed my mother and my grandfather. I should roast you and your little pageboy where you stand."

"Perhaps not to me," Devin said, nodding toward Arthur, "but I think the king would like to hear why he was unconscious in the cave of Makaidos."

Arthur massaged the back of his head. "Yes, I would like to know. I remember nothing after my sword flashed."

Merlin shoved Excalibur back into its sheath, extinguishing its light. "Goliath captured you and threatened to kill you. As a ransom, he demanded that Makaidos give up his war alliance with humans. Makaidos agreed and flew to his cave to meet Goliath and restore you to us."

Devin pointed his sword at Clefspeare. "An obvious excuse to join forces against us in war. Makaidos saves face while plotting our demise in the recesses of his cave. I heard the conspiracy with my own ears."

Palin waved his sword. "I heard it as well, exactly as Sir Devin has described."

"Merlin," Arthur said, "I cannot ignore two eyewitnesses. This is a most chilling accusation."

"Your two witnesses are a lying snake and a conniving parrot." Merlin strode in the direction of the cave, shouting over his shoulder.

"I will see the carnage for myself. Clefspeare, I doubt that these two cowards would be brave enough to attack you in the light, so please stay here and represent my interests."

"Gladly, Master Merlin."

Merlin girded his robe and hustled down the muddy path. Within a few minutes, he arrived at the cave's yawning entrance. In the dim recesses, two nebulous lumps took shape, quiet shadows that rose from the floor in uneven mounds. Stepping lightly on the pebble-strewn threshold, he avoided streams of dark blood trickling around his shoes and climbed to higher ground inside. As his eyes adjusted, the dusky outlines became clear, two dragons, his old friend Makaidos with his wing draped over his beloved daughter Roxil.

Merlin fell to his knees and pressed his hand against his stomach. As bitter nausea boiled within, tears flowed and dripped to the ground. Rocking back and forth through convulsive sobs, he grabbed two handfuls of pebbles and squeezed them in his shaking fists. "God!" he cried out. "O God, my Father! Why must the valiant bleed while the devious plot treachery against the innocent? Why must the noble among us lie silent in a bed of blood while murderers whisper treachery and death into the ears of a king?" He threw the pebbles against the wall and rose slowly to his feet, lifting his head and spreading out his arms. "But I cannot see what you see. I see only shadows, while you see everything unveiled. Grant me hope in these dark days, for I feel the dread of evil coming upon this land like a swarm of locusts, yet I know that you can blow a horde of wickedness out to sea with a single breath. Let me feel a hint of that breath while I await the deliverance you always bring to those who follow your path."

As he lowered his head, a glint of light caught his eye, a red flash near Makaidos's body. He walked in that direction, again high-stepping over bloody streams. Stooping next to the tiny red strobe, he touched it with his finger. "A gemstone?" he murmured.

He lifted the knuckle-sized stone, mesmerized by its hypnotic oscillation between two shades of red light. He curled his fingers around it. "This must be the rubellite he kept between his scales. It probably popped out when Devin killed him."

He crawled over Makaidos's body and lifted his wing off Roxil, then, pushing with his feet on Roxil and his back against Makaidos, he rolled her to her side. After wiping the blood away from her belly with the hem of his robe, he searched her cold exterior shell. There it was. A pulsing red gem lodged between two scales.

Taking a deep breath, he pried the tiny stone free and gently placed it in his left pocket while sliding Makaidos's gem into his right. Then, resting a hand on each dragon's body, he heaved a sigh. "Father, I know very little about the spirits of dragons and their eternal destiny, but I do know that you are both just and merciful, so I trust that you will take these souls to the place you have prepared for them. Wherever that is, I pray that you will grant peace and everlasting justice to these noble leviathans. Makaidos showed his undying faithfulness to your purpose for dragons, his unflinching loyalty to serve humans at the risk of his own life and the loss of his family, and his hope in your plan for salvation, for, although he was a dragon, he trusted in the human messiah for his deliverance. I ask you to honor his obedience and give him the desire of his heart."

Merlin rose and shuffled out of the cave, looking over his shoulder briefly before girding himself again and hurrying back to the king. When he arrived, Devin was gone and Palin stood next to Arthur, his sword drawn.

"Where is Devin?" Merlin asked. "I want to have a word with him."

Arthur pointed down the path. "I sent him to call a council of war at noon tomorrow. We agreed that we must eliminate Goliath and his followers as soon as possible."

289

Merlin spread out his arms. "I beseech you, my king. Do not allow this maniac free reign in his quest. A dragon slayer, once he savors the aroma of dragon's blood, will always lust for more, and he will not care if the dragon is a follower of Goliath or Makaidos. The good dragons will also be targets."

"During the council we will draw up safeguards to protect your so-called"—the king eyed Clefspeare suspiciously—"good dragons."

"Do not denigrate a soul you know so little about simply because its appearance frightens you." Merlin laid a hand on Clefspeare's neck. "If humans, kings or otherwise, could elevate their virtue to the level of this noble creature, they would not have to battle hordes in the wilderness, and they would not doubt the counsel of their prophets."

Arthur's face reddened, and he spoke through his teeth. "Just make a list of the dragons you want me to protect, and I will forget your careless words."

290

Merlin bowed his head. "Although I fear such a strategy, we will make your list." He climbed up on Clefspeare's back and looked down at Arthur. "May I assume, Your Majesty, that you do not want a ride to the castle?"

The king averted his eyes. "You may assume."

"Then I will meet you in the throne room for this council." Merlin sighed and shook his head. "May God help us all."

As the king and Palin departed, Merlin grasped the tallest spine on Clefspeare's neck. "I fear that this war against Goliath will not stop at the boundary of his influence."

"Nor at the boundary of his species," Clefspeare replied.

"What do you mean?"

A low growl created a tremor across the dragon's scales. "I believe Devin has more on his mind than the conquest of dragons, but time will tell."

apphira walked to the edge of the pulsating red screen and patted her dress with her palms. "Fire? What are you talking about?"

Makaidos closed in on the screen from the opposite side. "When we view you through the light, it appears that you are aflame from head to toe. Do we appear the same way?"

"No," Sapphira replied. "You and Roxil look like dragons, and Elam and Paili are human, but no one is on fire."

Makaidos stepped to Sapphira's side of the screen and looked through it. "Amazing! Elam is taller and more muscular, while Paili is smaller and emaciated."

Sapphira lowered herself to her knees and touched the Ovulum. It was no longer hot. Carefully lifting it, she carried it and the entire screen in her palm. The half oval expanded below her hand into a full ellipse, exactly as long as Sapphira was tall and more than twice as wide as her narrow frame. As she gazed through it, dozens of new details appeared. The fountain gushed; the statues stood erect, polished with a pristine shine; and the brick kilns puffed gray smoke from iron stacks on top. Yet, no one attended the ovens or strolled the immaculate streets.

291

"I'm going to try something." Sapphira walked slowly back toward the portal near the broken fountain. The screen of light added no weight, and it shifted with the slightest turn of the egg, making it easy to keep the viewing screen in front of her. Elam, Paili, and the two "dragons" followed, but they kept silent.

When Sapphira arrived at the dimensional doorway, she held the Ovulum out as far as she could and gazed at the city. All of Shinar seemed coated in crimson, yet clear—a hundred times clearer than before. She could count the sparkling crystals in every marble statue and distinguish between the tiniest leaves on a distant sycamore tree.

She turned the screen toward the rise where the tower once stood. Her hand trembled. The tower was there in all its glory, an enormous ziggurat, stretching so high, it extended beyond the edge of her screen and out of sight. As she gazed at it, the screen enlarged and seemed to expand over her head and swallow her body, making her feel like she was inside the scarlet halo. The tower grew, and she could see its very top, a tiny point in the midst of the clouds. Looking down again, the tower's entry portico began magnifying, as though she were flying toward it at blazing speed. The force against her body rippled her muscles, making her arms and legs cramp, and the stiff counter-breeze dried her eyes until they ached.

The tower's doors swung open, and she zoomed inside, the sudden turns twisting her body. The planter swung into view along with the dozen surrounding statues, but the tree itself was no longer there. Her body swept into the middle, and her feet settled where the tree once rooted into the soil.

Now that her journey had stalled, she looked around, expecting to see the saluting forms, but they were no longer statues; they were tall lanterns with flaming wicks. Each flame swayed like a writhing ghost.

On the museum wall, huge letters burned into the marble, spelling out a message that nearly encircled the entire chamber. Sapphira read it slowly, letting the words sink into her mind. "When a maid collects an egg, she passes it on, giving it to the one she feeds."

"It's a riddle," she whispered. Suddenly, her body jerked backwards, and she flew in the opposite direction. The tree, the lanterns, and the doorway all shrank, and the screen itself came back into view, as though the halo had spat her out onto the ground. Then, the entire screen flashed off.

Sapphira's arms fell limp at her sides, but she managed to hang on to the Ovulum. She was back where she had started, or maybe she hadn't really traveled at all. The whole city spun around her, so fuzzy and confusing, her legs wobbled beneath her.

"What did you see?" Makaidos asked. "Your face is as white as your hair!"

Sapphira could barely whisper. "I know where they are."

She felt her body falling and the Ovulum slipping from her fingers. Strong hands lifted her back to her feet. "Fear not, child," Makaidos said. "I have you, and I picked up the Ovulum as well."

Sapphira blinked at a circle of helpers, four lovely, concerned faces. "Help me get to the tower," she whispered.

"The tower's gone," Makaidos said.

"No. Where it used to be."

With a quick sweep, Makaidos lifted Sapphira into his arms and marched toward the rise. Sapphira laid her head against his shoulder. His powerful muscles felt secure and stable, like the arms of Elohim when he danced with her at the pool. Even though Makaidos bounced up and down with his gait, she knew he wouldn't drop her.

"We're here," he said softly.

His voice seemed to awaken her from a dream, and as he set her gently on her feet, her mind snapped to attention.

"I think this was the center of the tower's foundation," Makaidos said.

Sapphira's vision magnified all her surroundings, and the familiar sorrow draped a sad curtain across her mind. "It is the center." She pivoted slowly, trying to see beyond the emptiness that surrounded her. There were supposed to be statues, or maybe lanterns, but nothing appeared.

Elam stroked his chin. "Something's here, right? You sense something that we can't see?"

"I think so." She waved her arm in a wide arc. "Statues. Twelve of them, I believe, and they make a circle around where I'm standing."

"What makes you think they're still here?" Roxil asked.

"I saw them through the Ovulum's screen, but they looked like lanterns instead of people."

Elam raised his hand as if holding a lantern. "You mean like cavern lanterns?"

"Yes. I think—"

Paili piped up. "Light them!"

"Light them?" Sapphira repeated.

Paili bounced on her toes. "With your fire . . . like at home."

"How can I light lanterns that aren't there?"

Elam lifted her hand. "Light the lanterns with these," he said, spreading out her fingers. "They feed the hungry and bring light to the darkness."

"Okay," Sapphira said, "I'll give it a try."

She raised her other hand and closed her eyes, imagining where the statues once stood. In her mind, she fixed twelve spots in the space around her. Then, opening her eyes again, she pointed at one of the spots and shouted, "Give me light!"

A flame burst to life and floated in midair. The fire burned downward, creating a blazing human frame. Without fuel or wick, the flame burned on, its human shape writhing as if in the bonds of torture.

Makaidos shielded his eyes and leaned back. "What now?"

Sapphira heaved breathlessly, her hands still raised. What should she do? Light up eleven more people and let them suffer in flames?

Paili tugged on her dress. "Five more!" she shouted.

"Five more?" Sapphira looked down at her. "Why?"

"To make six! Like the wheel!" Paili turned an imaginary wheel.

Sapphira gasped and cried out, "Of course! The control room wheel!" She pointed at the spot to the left of the first statue. "Give me light!" she yelled. Another flame erupted, again creating a human form with its light. She moved to the next—"Give me light!"—then the next, until six human-shaped torches blazed in orange brilliance.

Breathless again, Sapphira lowered her hands. Suddenly, a gust of wind blew the flames out, and six men stood limply atop the blackened marble. As their bodies collapsed to the floor, Sapphira's companions rushed to help them.

294

"Time for nine more!" Sapphira said, waving her arms. "Move those six over here!"

Groggy and groaning, they shuffled or crawled toward the center. Makaidos gazed carefully into the eyes of the first one, a young man who seemed to be in his late teens, and touched a ring on his finger. He nodded at Roxil and whispered, "It's Hilidan."

Sapphira lifted her hands again and pointed at the next spot in the circle. "Give me light!" Another statue of fire erupted. She repeated the process, this time moving around the circle in the opposite direction. Finally, the ninth fiery form appeared. She lowered her hands, and a new gust of wind snuffed the flames. Eight women and one girl, all dressed in white silk, crumpled to the floor. The four helpers rushed to guide them toward the center.

A stiff breeze kicked up, swirling around and buffeting Sapphira's hair. She raised her hands once more, this time closing her eyes.

"We have all the dragons!" Makaidos shouted. "You did it! You can stop."

"We're not finished!" Sapphira shouted back. "There's still the number thirteen."

She pointed next to the spot where she had ignited the previous lantern. "Give me light!" Yet again, a human-shaped column of fire ignited.

"One!" Paili called out.

Then, going completely around the room, Sapphira lit the other eleven, Paili counting out each new lantern as it burst to life. Finally, when Paili's shrill "Twelve!" was carried away by the gentle breeze, Sapphira opened her eyes and lowered her arms. This time, no gust of wind came to blow the flames out.

"We need a thirteen!" Paili cried.

Sapphira spread out her arms. "There aren't any more places in the circle!"

Makaidos pointed at one of the flaming forms as it writhed in place. "I think they're suffering! We have to do something!"

Sapphira closed her eyes. The portal center once again flooded her mind with grief. Acacia's terrified face blazed across her inner vision, and her best friend's muffled splash in the magma river echoed in her mind. As she opened her eyes, she whispered, "There is one more lantern!" She wrapped her arms around herself and, her eyes filling with tears, shouted as loud as she could, "Give me light!"

Sapphira's hair erupted in flames. Streams of fire poured down her arms and chest, like magma rivulets coursing their way to her feet. She lifted her arms, and her whole body burst into an inferno, enveloping her in a spinning vortex of fire. When she lowered her arms, a new gust of wind, the strongest yet, nearly knocked her over.

As the tongues of fire ripped away into the breeze, a heavy weight grew against Sapphira's chest, a girl leaning on her, completely covered in white, her dress, her skin, even her hair.

Sapphira draped her weary arms around the girl. "Acacia?" She ran her fingers through the girl's thick white hair, barely able to breathe a whisper. "Is it really you?"

Acacia groaned, her face buried in Sapphira's dress. "Where am I?"

Sapphira helped her sit down and lifted her chin. "Look. It's me, Sapph . . . I mean, Mara. Don't you remember me?"

Acacia's lips formed the first letter, "M . . . M . . ." Then, her eyes suddenly brightened, tears glistening in each as she whispered, "Mara?"

Sapphira grabbed her and hugged her close. "Yes! Yes! It's Mara!" She rocked Acacia back and forth. "Oh, I missed you so much! I thought you were dead! I thought you were lost forever!" She pulled back and wiped tears from her eyes. "Do you remember what happened? I mean, what have you been doing all these centuries? Or have you been unconscious?"

Acacia pushed against the floor and rose to her feet. Sapphira rose with her and brushed the grit away from Acacia's sleeves. "I remember falling and being sucked into something, then"—she gestured toward the other twelve girls who were also rising to their feet—"I saw my sister spawns all sitting around listening to an old man."

"Sister spawns?" Sapphira tilted her head. "I don't recognize any of them. I don't see Taalah or Qadar."

"You and I didn't know these sisters. They were the first twelve."

"Explain later." Sapphira took her by the elbow. "Let's get away from this place. It affects my mind in weird ways."

"Me, too." Acacia followed Sapphira's lead down the tower mound's gentle slope. "It feels dark and sad. Does that mean we're not in heaven?"

"I'm not sure where we are, and I don't know much about heaven, only what I read in Mardon's scrolls."

Acacia pushed her hair out of her face. "I don't think heaven feels so depressing. My teacher told me it would be wonderful."

"Who is your teacher?"

"He never told us his name." Acacia shrugged. "We just called him Teacher."

"Well, I hope he's right about heaven. I wish I could be sure. Every place I've been is pretty depressing."

The entire group gathered at the bottom of the slope. Makaidos stood at the center and lifted his hand in the air, twisting the ring on his index finger. "Our rings hold the traditional gem of the dragons, so I believe they are a symbol of the new life our Maker has given us in this place. Many of the dragons who died in or before the flood are here." He waved for a young girl to come close. She wrapped one arm around his waist and leaned against his side. "Zera, my sister, made it." He nodded at a young man who was straightening his clothes and another man wearing a bowler hat. "Hilidan and Clirkus, my two young warrior friends, as well." He nodded again, this time at an older woman. "My mother, Shachar, is here, too."

Roxil laid a hand on Shachar's back and rubbed it tenderly. "But your father is not here. That proves Arramos is still alive."

"Arramos could very well be alive." Makaidos's jaw tensed. "But that evil dragon who masquerades as my father is not Arramos."

Shachar slid her arm around Makaidos's waist, overlapping Zera's grip. "Arramos is alive, my son. I do not know how long I have been floating in a senseless limbo, but I always felt his presence, and that made my wandering existence tolerable. If an evil dragon says he is Arramos, rest assured that he is a liar. My mate would never succumb to Lucifer's song."

"And on that truth, I will take my stand." Makaidos brushed his lips across Shachar's cheek, ending the gentle caress with a kiss. "Somehow, I will find him."

"So what do we do now?" Hilidan asked. He quickly covered his lips with his fingers. "How strange. What kind of accent is that?"

Makaidos laughed. "You sound like one of the Celts."

"I am fond of it," Hilidan said. "It has the quality of song."

"Indeed it does!" Makaidos clapped him on the back. "It seems that the Maker has given us unique human characteristics, including unique voices, body shapes, and personalities."

"Unique?" Roxil grimaced. "That was not the word I had in mind."

"Roxil, the Maker has given us this destiny, so we would be wise to make the best of it. We should forget the past, rebuild this village, and live as humans until the Maker sees fit to send us elsewhere."

The other former dragons nodded their agreement, but Roxil's face hardened as she stared at the ground. "Have you already forgotten my mother?" she asked. "Have you forsaken Thigocia?"

Makaidos's face turned pale.

Roxil crossed her arms over her chest. "So you *have* already forgotten her!"

Makaidos nodded slowly. "Why would that be? How could I forget the love of my life?"

"Is it because you reject the Maker's plan?" Roxil asked. "He made you a dragon, and now you want to forget everything about your dragon life, so he stripped away your greatest love."

"I reject nothing!" Makaidos spread out his fingers and showed them to Roxil. "Did the Maker not also choose this form for me? I accept any form my creator shapes around my mind!" With the Ovulum resting in his palm, he gazed at it and walked back toward the tower portal. "I have to think."

When Makaidos passed out of earshot, Roxil glared at Elam and the underborns, her eyes flashing. As she crossed her arms again, a barely perceptible smile grew on her lips. Her voice altered to a slow, Morgan-like cadence. "If this is a place for dragons to rest, then perhaps the humans ought to find another home."

Sapphira called up the innocent voice she often used to answer Morgan. "Well, I'm not sure exactly how human we are," she said. "We're called underborns. At least most of us are."

Roxil held up her ringed finger. "There will be no mixing between dragons and humankind, underborn or otherwise. As long as we have to dwell here in these human disguises, we will keep ourselves pure."

Elam strode up to Roxil and looked her in the eye. "Don't worry, dragon lady. I'll leave on the fastest camel out of here, but if you get sick of this place in a thousand years or so, don't be surprised if no one, human or underborn, comes to rescue you."

Roxil kicked at the ground, raising a cloud of dust. "Even if this place were to crumble beneath my feet, I would never take aid from a human! Never!"

"Suit yourself." Elam turned and waved for Sapphira to follow. "We're leaving."

Without looking back, Elam marched up the rise. Sapphira took Paili's hand, then Acacia's, and hurried to follow. The other girls huddled into a group behind them and began walking up the slope toward the portal.

When Elam reached the top of the rise, Makaidos met him with a raised hand. "Please! I beg you to wait!"

Elam halted. Sapphira tightened her grip on Acacia's hand and waited near the crest. Makaidos held the Ovulum in his palm and waved at Roxil. "Come. All of you. I want to tell you something."

Roxil lowered her arms to her sides, her face softened by a hint of fear. She and the other dragons ascended the rise and gathered at the top.

"I must give clear instructions before the humans leave," Makaidos said. "When they return, I will be gone."

"Where will you go?" Sapphira asked.

"I wish I knew." He handed the Ovulum back to Sapphira. "You see, as soon as I walked into the old museum area, the Eye of the Oracle spoke to me. He told me that I must complete my work here and God would grant me the greatest desire of my heart."

Sapphira took Makaidos's hand. "What is the desire of your heart?" she asked, caressing the pulsing gem on his ring.

Makaidos stroked her hair. "I dare not presume. I would not jeopardize the possibilities for all the world."

She gazed into his soft brown eyes. "Then can you tell me what you're supposed to do?"

"Yes." He waved his arm across the city scene. "We are to raze everything that would remind us of Shinar's evil past and use the materials to build a new, peaceful village. We are to forget what lies behind and live and act as humans until God sends someone to deliver us to a better place."

Sapphira twisted the ring on Makaidos's finger. For some reason, touching the gem soothed her mind, the opposite feeling the portals evoked. "You're supposed to forget everything?" she asked.

"About being dragons, yes. The Eye explained that God will grant us forgetfulness so we can survive here while we wait. Otherwise, we would go insane."

"I wish we could stay and help." Sapphira glanced down at his ring. As her thumb rubbed the gem, the pulsing stopped and its surface faded to pink, then to white. When she pulled her thumb away, it changed back to red and resumed its pulse.

"It would be best," Makaidos continued, "if we dragons—"

"How odd!" Sapphira whispered.

Makaidos looked down at her. "Odd? What is odd?"

"May I try on your ring?" she asked.

Makaidos glanced at Roxil. Her sour expression had deepened. "I suppose it would be all right," he said.

Makaidos pulled the ring off and pushed it over Sapphira's finger. Since it was several sizes too big, it slid easily down to her bottom knuckle. The gem turned snow white. He lifted her hand close to his eyes and whispered, "Amazing!"

She slipped it back off and returned it to Makaidos's finger. "Look!" she said, "it's red again."

Roxil raised up on tiptoes and craned her neck, but she said nothing.

Makaidos twisted the ring back in place. "Perhaps a dragon's touch keeps it red."

"Or maybe the touch of an Oracle of Fire turns it white." Sapphira set a finger on her chest. "That's what I am. At least that's what the Eye told me."

"That reminds me." Makaidos pointed at her. "I need to tell you the rest of the Eye's warnings. This dimension is reserved for the spirits of dragons, so everyone who is human will have to leave at once. The Eye said that a new king of the dragons will arise to set all dragons free and lead them to a better world. The two Oracles of Fire will have the power to open a portal to allow him in, but if they open it before the proper time, this place will burn with fire. And even when the king comes, the very hour he departs with his followers, all of Dragons' Rest will be destroyed."

"So we have to go right away?" Sapphira asked.

Makaidos lowered his gaze to the ground. "You have no choice."

Roxil stepped forward and hooked her arm through Makaidos's and pulled him away. "Father, I think we should get right to work and let these humans"—she glared at Sapphira—"and underborns obey the Eye's commands."

Makaidos began walking with Roxil toward the brick kilns, but he glanced back at Sapphira. "Godspeed, my child. I hope the Maker allows us to meet again."

A tide of sadness washed through Sapphira's mind. She sniffed, then waved, not wanting to turn and leave this lovely man . . . or dragon . . . behind.

Acacia whispered. "We'd better go. We don't belong here. And besides, we have a thousand things to talk about."

The joy of having Acacia back overwhelmed her sadness. She grasped her twin's hand. "And all these other girls to get to know."

"Do we have to swim up through that whirlpool?" Elam asked. "It's no fun, believe me."

"We came through the portal down near the fountain, so going back that way will likely put us back in the magma river. I'm not sure, but the one where the tower used to be might lead us to the bottom of the chasm, like it did when Elam and I used it. I'm kind of confused, because I don't think we're in the same dimension as when we used it before, so going back might take us somewhere else, like maybe the top of the museum." She winced at her own words. "Does that make any sense at all?"

Elam shook his head, while Acacia nodded. "Perfect sense," she said. "I vote for the tower portal. I don't think anyone wants to fight that whirlpool."

"That part makes sense," Elam said, "but if the other portal takes us anywhere near Morgan, the magma whirlpool might start looking like a fun swim."

302

COUNCILS OF WAR AND PEACE

M erlin skulked into the enormous cave, laying his hand against the side wall as he crept forward. This had to be the place. Valcor's directions were exceedingly precise. As the cavern dimmed, he ducked under a spider dangling from the ceiling and slowed even further. Although he was more acquainted with dragons than was any other living human, the thought of attending a council of a dozen or more in an unfamiliar cave wasn't exactly comforting. Some would be strangers, and if he failed to adequately explain why their king was killed by humans like himself, they might be inclined to use him as a torch for their council of war.

As he entered the darker inner cavern, Merlin slowly withdrew Excalibur from its sheath. The blade began to glow, lighting his way. Although he couldn't see any dragon faces yet, he sensed a presence in the distance. He called into the void. "I am only carrying this for light. I assume you sense no danger from me."

A deep, gentle voice replied. "You are most welcome here, Master Merlin. There is no malintent in your heart."

Merlin increased Excalibur's glow, illuminating the craggy walls of the vast chamber and a knee-high, flat stone at his feet. At least thirty dragons encircled him, several of them breathing loud, spark-filled snorts. His legs suddenly unsteady, he turned and located the female dragon who had greeted him. He bowed. "Hartanna, thank you for sending for me." He swung back, noting several dragons he didn't recognize, and nodded briefly toward Valcor, then to Thigocia before returning to Hartanna. "Your brother's summons seemed urgent, so I came as quickly as I could."

"It is urgent, dear prophet. Thigocia has asked me to gather Makaidos's followers and inform them of our present distress. I summoned you for guidance concerning the affairs of the humans."

"A wise decision." Merlin sighed and turned to Thigocia again. "I assume you located the bodies of your departed mate and daughter."

"I did." A large tear trickled down Thigocia's cheek. "I will take care of them. Perhaps Valcor will help me."

Valcor dipped his head solemnly. "It would be an honor, my queen."

Merlin sat heavily on the flat stone, wiping his teary eyes with his robe's baggy sleeve. Taking a deep breath, he lifted Excalibur and gazed around the room. "Perhaps I am not as familiar with dragon customs as I ought to be, and my question might be premature, but will you choose a new king or will the queen assume the leadership role? In this time of crisis, the dragons will need a clear chain of command."

Thigocia lowered herself to her belly, and the other dragons settled to the ground with her. "We have had only one succession," she said, "and Arramos designated Makaidos as king before the flood. In other situations, we females assert ourselves boldly when no male will step to the lead, but without Makaidos, I would not be able to lead this noble group. I believe both genders are necessary for such guidance."

"Then will you choose successors, or will you find another mate?"

Thigocia turned on her eyebeams and rested them on Merlin's robe. "After thousands of years with my beloved, I cannot bear the thought of taking another. I will choose successors, one for Makaidos and one for myself." Her scarlet beams drifted from one scaly body to the next until they rested on Clefspeare, who promptly scooted back a few inches. "If I may be so bold," she continued, "I believe Clefspeare and Hartanna are best suited to take our places."

"Clefspeare!" Hartanna cried. "He is—"

"Hartanna!" Thigocia's beams flashed.

"Yes, Mother." Hartanna closed her eyes, and her head dipped low. "If that is your will."

Merlin rose to his feet and approached Clefspeare. "I will finish your sentence, dragoness, with my own opinion, if I may." He laid a hand on Clefspeare's neck. "He is a courageous and noble friend. There is no dragon, or even human, with greater integrity."

A gentle smile broke through on Thigocia's face. "No one can deny your words, Master Merlin. I believe Hartanna's concern is that Clefspeare has always been such a loner that we only know of his heroic battle exploits, not whether he could lead the dragons or be a proper mate."

Clefspeare made a rumbling sound within his chest and bowed. "Then let my service to your departed mate, my one and only king, be your guide. If it were my choice alone, I would continue in my life of solitude, but if your will is that I should be betrothed to Hartanna, then I humbly accept, for I know that your will is equal to that of Makaidos." He raised his head and nodded toward Hartanna. "I do, however, request the traditional, five-year betrothal period. Before we pass through our covenant veil, a time of separation is essential for me to prepare myself for this duty."

"Duty?" Hartanna snorted. "Does not marriage involve more than duty?"

Clefspeare slid farther back. Shadows covered his face.

"Hush!" Thigocia spread a wing over Hartanna. "My dear, words of warmth will encourage a reluctant male far more quickly than will the slap of a tail."

Merlin angled the sword's glow toward Thigocia. "I am not familiar with this covenant veil that Clefspeare mentioned. May I ask its meaning?"

Thigocia extended her neck, bringing her head close to Merlin. Her eyes glimmered with several reddish hues, as though replaying past wonders. "It is the most holy ceremony in our culture. When two dragons come together in wedlock, they must affirm a covenantal vow. Although uncorrupted dragons cannot knowingly utter false words, it is possible that they might not know their own hearts. So, in order to guard against self-deception or ambiguous intent, the dragons must have at least two witnesses present. These witnesses collect in front of the dragons, divided into two groups that stand about two tail lengths apart. The witnesses speak our traditional vows in unison, and this creates a spiritual covenant that hangs like a veil between the groups. The dragons then pass through that veil. If either one of them does not have the vow firmly entrenched in his or her heart, he or she will not be able to pierce the veil. We call it the Great Key, for it unlocks the secrets of a dragon's heart."

Merlin stared at her, chills running across his skin. "Remarkable! That is a great key, indeed!"

"I only wish Roxil had not rejected our tradition," Thigocia said, her fiery eyes fading. "Goliath would not have passed through, and her tragedy would have been avoided."

"A tragic mistake, indeed," Merlin said. After pausing in silence for a few seconds, he raised a finger. "Can this veil be created for vows other than a marriage covenant?"

"I have been told that it can, but I have not witnessed it. I assume any sacred confession can be made into a veil."

"I see." Merlin raised the sword upright and rested it on his shoulder. "Now that you have settled the matter of succession, I am ready to offer my advice."

"Speak, then," Thigocia said. "We are listening."

Merlin paced in the midst of the circle of dragons. "King Arthur has summoned a council of war. With Goliath on the rampage, I fear that he will heed Devin's call to kill every dragon who follows that renegade."

"And what would be wrong with that?" Valcor asked. "With Goliath and his ilk out of the way, the people would no longer fear us."

"Quiet, Valcor!" Hartanna scolded. "They are our brothers and sisters! Do you care nothing for their souls?"

Valcor swung his tail around and flicked her on the ear. "Are you still my twin sister, or are you already queen?"

Merlin chuckled. "Thigocia, have they always been like this?"

"Even in the womb," Thigocia replied. "I do not wish twins on any dragon mother."

"Yet, they illustrate our need for unity against our common foe." Merlin interlaced his fingers over his chest. "After today, we can only be united in purpose, not in physical fellowship. I don't trust Devin to keep his war against dragons within the confines of Goliath's followers, so all of you should go into hiding. Gather gems and build the best regeneracy domes you can. Rest and gain strength until you hear from me again. Your danger sense will alert you if Devin's war expands and approaches your cave."

"And if the war comes?" Hartanna asked. "What then?"

307

"I am formulating an idea that will radically alter everything you have come to know, even those of you who have lived for thousands of years, but it will save your lives and your future. Because the plan is so drastic, I will not deploy it unless Devin's bloodlust spreads. Even then, I will reveal the strategy only to the new king and queen, and they will prepare you for what will come to pass."

"Master Merlin," Thigocia said, her eyes shifting from one dragon to the next, "I want to reassure my descendants, for I sense their anxiety." She closed her eyes for a moment, then reopened them, displaying new tears. Her voice trembled. "Each dragon here . . . has its ultimate origin . . . in my womb . . . and I care for them beyond measure. I have lived for thousands of years, and I have known humans from every generation in the history of the world. Merlin, with the possible exception of Enoch himself, there has been none with more integrity than you. I trust you without reservation, and I am convinced that you are the new oracle. The spirit of Enoch and his son Methuselah rests on you like a mantle from above."

Merlin brushed his sleeve across his eyes again. "Your words are kind, dear dragoness. I only hope that we will not have to pursue the measures I have in mind. If the plan bears fruit, however, I hope you will continue to trust me, for it will test your faith like nothing you can possibly imagine."

He nodded toward Thigocia, Hartanna, Valcor, and finally, Clefspeare. "When you see me again, my friends, I fear that your lives will change forever."

Holding her lighted torch, Sapphira stood next to Acacia at the center of the tower portal. The brood of twelve girls surrounded them, wearing the typical worker tunics, worn and ratty in places, yet cleaner and whiter than usual. "Just in case this portal leads to the top of the museum," Sapphira said, "we should go one at a time. If we all pop onto the ceiling crossbeams, there's no way they will hold us, and we couldn't possibly sneak past Anak if we're all together."

Paili pulled on Sapphira's sleeve. "Anak is gone."

"Gone? Why?"

Paili closed her eyes and spoke slowly. "Morgan said she found your blood on the floor, so Anak went to hell." She exhaled loudly and opened her eyes, a hint of a smile breaking through.

Sapphira covered her mouth and gasped between her knuckles. "To hell?"

Elam extended a finger. "That's one obstacle out of the way." He raised a handful of straw he had gathered. "Can I go first, you know, to check it out? I don't want any of you to get hurt if Morgan's around."

Acacia took Elam's free hand in both of hers and held it close to her chest. "Where did you find this gentleman, Mara? Our teacher told us that unselfish men were rare."

Hot prickles dotted Sapphira's neck. "My name is Sapphira now." She shifted uneasily from one foot to the other. "I guess we kind of found each other . . . but, sure, Elam can go first."

Elam laid most of the straw on the floor and tightened his fist around the small handful he kept. Sapphira touched the torch's flame to the ends and stepped back. "Now wave it above your head in a circle."

Elam swirled the small fire around, but the wind he created snuffed the tiny flame. Sapphira yelled, "Ignite!" and the flame shot up, quickly burning down toward Elam's hand. "Faster!" she shouted.

Elam whirled the flame so fast, it looked like a single line of orange. The line expanded and dropped like a falling curtain until it reached the floor and covered Elam's body with a flickering veil. Suddenly, he vanished, leaving only a few scattered ashes on the floor.

Acacia took Elam's place. "I should go next," she said. "The girls know me, so I should be there when they arrive."

Sapphira chewed on her lip. "Okay," she said, shifting on her feet again. "Get some straw."

Acacia took a handful from the floor and copied Elam's actions. After she disappeared, Sapphira instructed the others to follow—Paili first, then the twelve new arrivals. Each one gave her name, and Sapphira tried to lock them into her mind. The girls seemed to come in matching sets of three, and within each trio, the spawns looked so much alike it would be impossible to tell them apart later. From trio to trio, they ranged from the darkest human skin she had ever seen to complexions as light as her own, and the hair of the dark girls seemed thick and crinkly, while the fair-skinned girls had light, baby-fine hair.

When the last spawn disappeared, one of three olive-skinned girls with carelessly cropped short hair, Sapphira shuffled into place. All the amazing events of the day confused her thoughts and chased the new names from her memory. She gazed down at the former dragons. Makaidos had found a mallet and was swinging it at the base of one of the remaining idols. Obviously, he wanted to get his job done in a hurry, but, although several idols already lay crumbled, this one seemed to defy his most powerful blows.

Sapphira raised her torch. In one sense, Makaidos had it easy. He knew exactly what to do. If only Elohim would give *her* straightforward commands, she would be glad to obey them, wouldn't she?

As she swirled the torch in a wide circle, sadness again swept across her mind. She would soon be back in Morgan's world, now a fugitive who would have to avoid the dark mistress at all costs. But how? Morgan seemed to know so much more than anyone.

The torch's light grew into a wall of flames and descended toward her feet. As her legs began to transform, a familiar warmth caressed her thigh. She pressed her free hand against the Ovulum and smiled. Maybe someone knew more than Morgan did. Maybe soon, when she needed him most, he would prove it.

As Merlin strode toward the throne room, a guard pushed the doors open and shouted into the inner chamber. "Merlin, prophet of the Most High and advisor to His Majesty, has arrived."

Merlin entered, shaking his head as he tromped across the newly installed red carpet. Ever since Devin had been accepted as one of the king's knights, he insisted on all this silly pomp and heraldry. Merlin had the urge to spit something nasty on the floor. Devin should sweep up all this nonsense and take it with him to—

"Hello, Merlin!"

Merlin jerked his head up. Devin smiled, pretentiously friendly, as always, when preening for an audience. The knight, dressed completely in black, stood next to the king, who was seated at his usual place, centered near the front of the platform. Although he rested comfortably on his newly installed throne, his eyes stared straight ahead. They seemed glazed . . . distant . . . as if his mind wandered elsewhere.

The loyal knights—Lancelot, Gawain, and the others—stood at floor level facing the king, each one dressed in typical finery, though most of them flinched and shifted, as though aching to scratch themselves.

Two women huddled close on a two-person bench next to Arthur's throne, both draped in black and seated with their hands folded on their knees.

Merlin eyed the taller of the two—beautiful, with flawless raven locks that meandered down her back, and sharp, angular facial features framing piercing eyes that promised an equally sharp mind. When her eyes locked with his, a cold chill penetrated his heart.

He bowed to the king, then to the two ladies, before finally acknowledging Devin. "Have you brought two new witnesses for the prosecution?"

311

"Merlin," Arthur chided, "your manners are sorely lacking."
He gestured toward the women. "They are sisters of mine—
Morgan and Elaine, by my mother and her first husband."

Merlin gave them the slightest of bows. "Clearly they are not
quite as dead as you had heard."

"No. They were—"

"Merlin," Morgan interrupted, rising in front of her bench,
"obviously my dear brother hasn't had the opportunity to inform
you of our rescue from the dragons. Even though my mother, Lady
Igraine, gave us up as lost, Sir Devin never abandoned the search.
With God as his guide, he found us in Makaidos's cave when he
killed the beast and his demon witch daughter."

Merlin raised his brow. "It's odd that Sir Devin neither
escorted you home nor informed us of your rescue when
Clefspeare and I found him and Palin near the cave."

A hint of sarcasm spiced Morgan's tone. "For your information, Sir Devin and Palin acquired horses for their journey, and as
soon as they rescued us, they, in their most chivalrous manner,
beseeched us to ride to Camelot while they walked home with the
king." She gestured toward Devin. "Regarding the honorable
knight's lack of boasting, such humility is in keeping with his
unimpeachable character."

Merlin glanced at Devin, catching a brief smirk on his face.
"Oh, I see. I'm not surprised. I expected Devin to cook up a
scheme to gather all the dragons into his murderous net, and this
one has a foul recipe, indeed."

Arthur shot to his feet. "Merlin! Are you accusing my sister of
lying?"

Morgan sat down, her nose uplifted. "How rude!"

"Your sister?" Merlin pointed at Morgan. "I am accusing *this*
woman of lying, whoever she might be."

Sir Devin gripped the hilt of his sword. "Your Majesty! Allow
me to silence this reviler forever."

Merlin withdrew Excalibur and held it high. It blazed with brilliant white light. "Whom do you trust, King Arthur?" He waved his arm at the three dressed in black. "This foul beast of a knight who tickles your ears with songs of praise? These two dark women who suddenly appear on the eve of a council of war against dragons with an amazing tale of rescue from 'evil' dragons?" He took a step closer to the king and allowed the sword's radiance to pass across his face. "Or do you trust a prophet of God, who tells you the unmixed truth, who awakens your conscience and undresses your soul, who has guided your steps from the very first one you took until this present day of sorrows?"

Morgan scowled. "A prophet of God?" she asked, her voice laced with venom. "Did you not disguise Uther as my father so he could deceive and take advantage of my mother?"

Merlin swung toward Morgan, letting the blade's glow sweep across her body. A slight flinch wrinkled her face, but she quickly recovered. He lowered the sword and rested the flat on Morgan's shoulder. She recoiled, her brow furrowing, and her cheeks paled.

313

"Now I finally know who hatched that lie about me." Merlin turned his head toward the knights and nobles gathered before the king. "Morgan's father, Gorlois, perished mysteriously, and Arthur's father, Uther, always denied her mother's accusation that he arranged Gorlois's death. Yet, Uther loved Igraine and took her as his wife, begetting our future king, a child born of love, not of deception." He raised the sword and arced it toward Elaine. The petite woman glared at him, unflinching. "I have heard stories of nymphean deceivers and their seed-collecting ways," he said. "For how many centuries have you two been planning this wicked scheme?"

"Merlin!" Arthur shouted. "Have you gone completely mad? I command you to withdraw!"

Merlin backed away and resheathed the sword, but he kept his gaze firmly fixed on Morgan. "As you wish, Sire."

Devin thrust his finger toward Merlin. "Your Majesty, I object to this vile accuser's profane impeachment of your sisters' honor. In his mad, misguided attempt to save his demonic allies, he has chosen to slander your family! In order to clear his own name, he has indicted your mother as a liar!" He swept his arm toward Morgan and Elaine. "This insane prophet has turned a celebration of your lost sisters' joyous return into a shameful display of self-exoneration and embarrassing insults against the virtue and reputations of these impeccable ladies. I insist that he be censured and removed from this council!"

"Merlin!" Arthur shouted, his face blistering red. "I am persuaded to heed Sir Devin's counsel. What do you have to say for yourself?"

Merlin kept his voice calm and quiet. "Remember that I speak from times gone by, before you ever breathed the air of the kingdom you now rule and before Sir Devin breathed his first lie. Before you ever saw scale or claw of your first dragon, I rested in the crook of Clefspeare's leg, in the very shadow of his fiery snout. In the cold night air of his drafty cave, I slept unmolested under the cover of his gentle wing. Take heed to what you are about to do. The way of death is irreversible. Do what you must to the bloodthirsty followers of Goliath, but leave those faithful to the teachings of Makaidos alone."

The king sat down and took a deep breath, stroking his chin while gazing at the floor. Merlin eyed Morgan closely and caught her giving an almost imperceptible nod to Devin. Devin winked at the entry guard, who quietly opened the door.

Palin burst into the room, red-faced. "Clefspeare," he said, panting, "has killed Andrew . . . the horse merchant. He burned him like straw . . . in front of witnesses!"

Arthur jerked his head up. "Clefspeare? Are you certain?"

Palin nodded, still breathless. "Witnesses, Sire. We have witnesses."

Merlin set his hands on his hips and sighed. "Well done, Sir Devin. I should be ashamed of myself for not predicting that you would sink to such depths."

Arthur pointed at the exit, his voice shaking. "Merlin, I ask you to leave on your own accord. I honor you too well to have you escorted under armed guard."

Merlin bowed. "As you wish, Sire." He walked slowly toward the door, trying to catch Morgan's eye, but she averted her gaze. Near the exit, he stopped and raised a finger. "There is one request I wish to make, Your Majesty. May I have an audience with Morgan? It is obvious that I have offended her, so I wish to converse with her privately to ensure that our relationship is"—he rolled his eyes upward, searching for the right phrase—"mutually understood."

"Granted!" Arthur said. "I'm sure my sisters would both like to repair this unfortunate first impression."

Morgan finally looked Merlin's way. Her eyes flashed red. Merlin nodded at her and, without turning back again, walked out the door.

315

Sapphira jumped from the final ladder rung and gazed at the many pairs of eyes staring at her. The girls seemed winded after the long climb down the museum's bookshelves, and their somber expressions mirrored those on the twelve statues surrounding the tree. Sapphira caressed the face of one of the darker-skinned girls. It was no wonder they were tired. The portal from the dragons' dimension had led to Morgan's scary island, and the eerie howling of a dog had set them all on edge. It didn't take long, however, for Sapphira to find the portal near the apple tree that led back to the museum.

Elam smacked a heavy scroll against a shelf. "No sign of Morgan anywhere. She's probably in her castle or in the true upper realms."

"The true upper realms?" Acacia asked.

Elam jerked his thumb upward. "The dimension where I come from, the land of the living. I guess since I was her prisoner, Morgan didn't mind telling me what's going on. You see, she's really dead . . . well . . . sort of dead, so she has to stay in what she calls the circles of seven, a place my father called Sheol. We're underneath one of the circles, but we still can't go from here to there without some kind of portal, because there's no tunnel all the way to the top."

Acacia looked up in wonder. "Then can we block her from coming back somehow?"

Elam pointed the scroll at Sapphira. "You're the portal maker. What do you think?"

Sapphira tapped a finger on her chin. "I suppose if we could somehow move the portal she uses, she couldn't get in here. At least then we'd be safe."

Paili shivered. "Not with Mardon and giants here!"

"She's right," Elam said. "We would still have to deal with them."

"I'd rather face a hundred giants than one Morgan." With the others following, Sapphira exited the tower's museum and crept toward the shining blue column, perhaps the only remaining portal Morgan could use to enter the lower realms. "Morgan can find portals when she's down here, because most of them are lit up, but they're not visible up above. I can just sort of feel them when I'm up there."

"Then how does Morgan find them?" Elam asked.

"I think she just remembers where she appears in the land above." Sapphira gazed at the swirling blue light. "Morgan comes here through this portal, so if I move the spot where it comes out up above, she won't be able to get here, because she probably doesn't know about the portal on her island that leads to the top of the museum." Sapphira touched the edge of the column of light, making it sparkle at the tip of her finger. "But it's pretty risky, because I'm not sure where this one leads, and I don't know if I can create a firestorm big enough to move it. I watched the dragons make one, and that was more fire than I've ever seen in my life!"

"A firestorm?" Acacia took Sapphira's hand. "If we're both oracles of fire, maybe you can teach me how to make fire, and we can try to do it together."

Sapphira let out a long sigh. "Anything to keep Morgan away from these girls." She squeezed Acacia's hand and pulled her toward the column. "Let's go before I change my mind."

"We'll wait here." Elam picked up another scroll and clacked them together. "I can probably take on Mardon, but the giants are a different story. I learned that from fighting Nabal for my dinner."

Sapphira and Acacia stepped into the portal together and hugged each other close. Sapphira raised a hand and reached for a fistful of blue light, catching it like a rope and pulling down. In a blinding flash, the museum chamber crumbled away, and, seconds later, a million pieces of multicolored light flew together and bonded seamlessly into a new mosaic, a dim sky framing the dark turrets of Morgan's castle. An orange hue on one side signaled the breaking of dawn.

Sapphira set a hand on her hip and whispered, "I thought we might come out in the land of the living where the tower fell, but this is pretty close to the portal we used to go home just a little while ago. I guess this one really did move from Shinar, like Morgan guessed."

"How did the firestorm move the portal here?" Acacia whispered back.

"I don't know. The dragons moved it to the tower from another place first, but Morgan told me that everything shifted around after that, so I guess it moved again." Sapphira nodded toward the swamp behind them. "She keeps snakes back there and a big dog inside the castle, so we have to be extra quiet."

Acacia pointed at a nearby apple tree. "She probably recognizes the portal site by landmarks like this tree, so we have to move it to a place where she would never find it."

"Right, but if an entire first floor of a tower can sink into a new portal, we'll probably take some stuff with us, too. We don't want to do it where she's likely to miss something that gets swept up in the storm."

"Good point," Acacia said. "We can't leave any evidence."

"But where could we possibly go?"

Acacia turned toward the swamp. "Are you afraid of snakes?"

"Well, take away the fact that some can squeeze you to death and swallow you whole, and the fact that some can inject venom that will eat your flesh or shrivel you into a prune . . . no, not really."

"Same here." Acacia tiptoed into the swamp.

Sapphira tugged on the back of Acacia's dress. "I was kidding. We can't go in there." The sun's dawning rays illuminated the dark water. A mere two arm lengths away, a long, slender body broke the surface, its scales reflecting the sunlight. It quickly disappeared again, and the water stilled.

Acacia backed up a step. "Do you have a better place? Somewhere Morgan won't notice?"

"No, but even if we don't get eaten, do you want to take a bunch of swamp water and deadly snakes down where the other girls are?"

"What are you afraid of? We can make fire, can't we? We can burn them to a crisp."

Sapphira pointed at herself. "I can make fire, but I haven't taught you how yet."

A dog barked in the distance, then howled loud and long.

"You'd better start teaching me. That dog's bound to alert someone."

Sapphira picked up two sticks at the base of the apple tree and handed one to Acacia. "You just kind of think fire onto the wood,

318

but you also have to speak to it to make it happen." Sapphira stared at her stick and said, "Ignite!" A small flame immediately erupted on the end.

Furrowing her brow, Acacia focused her eyes on her stick and whispered through tight lips, "Ignite!" Nothing happened.

The dog howled again, this time louder.

"Concentrate!" Sapphira urged. "Give it everything you've got."

Acacia gripped the stick so tightly, it trembled in her hands. "Ignite!" Again, nothing happened. She lowered the stick and frowned. "What am I doing wrong?"

Sapphira felt a familiar warmth on her thigh. The Ovulum was signaling for her attention. "You're supposed to get your power from Elohim, the God of Noah. You haven't danced with him yet, so I guess he hasn't given it to you."

"Danced? You have to dance with someone to get power?"

Sapphira withdrew the Ovulum and showed it to Acacia. It glowed red and warm in her palm. "Well, the first time I did it, the Eye of the Oracle told me to command the fire to appear, but I never really felt the power was my own until I danced with Elohim. He's the one who speaks through the man in the Ovulum."

Acacia laid a hand on top of her head. "Okay, you're making my head hurt. You danced with a god, and there's a man in that egg?"

"Yes." She handed the Ovulum to Acacia. "Just look inside and see if you can find—"

The dog howled once more and bounded into sight, a huge, long-legged beast with a multicolored coat that shimmered in the glow of the rising sun. His shining eyes locked onto them, and he loped their way, closing the gap quickly.

Sapphira spun and held out her stick, shouting, "Blaze!" A bright flame shot up, and she waved it at the dog. "Get back!"

The dog halted and growled, baring its long, sharp teeth.

Acacia gazed into the Ovulum. "I see him! He's my teacher!"

Sapphira thrust the firebrand toward the dog, making it back away a step. She twisted her neck toward Acacia. "Is he saying anything?"

Acacia, now standing in ankle-deep water, cradled the Ovulum in her palm. "Yes! He's talking to me." She held her firebrand up and spoke to the glass shell. "Like this?" The Ovulum seemed to nod as it wobbled in her hand. Acacia lifted her head toward the stick and shouted, "Flames, come to my firebrand!" The stick immediately flashed with fire.

Sapphira backed toward the water, still thrusting her firebrand at the dog. With each step she took, the dog took its own step closer, staying low. When her feet touched the cold swamp, she gave the dog a last lunging thrust, then lifted her stick high and spun it in a fast orbit. She yelled, "Give me a firestorm!"

The dog lunged. A twisting wall of flames encircled the two girls, throwing the dog back. A yelp and a splash followed, then silence.

Sapphira peered through slender gaps in the orbiting wall. The dog crouched at the edge of the swamp, as if waiting for the slightest opportunity to pounce again. She hooked her arm around Acacia's elbow and edged farther out into the mire. There was no going back now.

The wall of fire dipped into the water and raised thick plumes of steam. The wall fizzled, becoming thin and transparent as it cooled. Three snake bodies humped over the water's surface about four paces in front of them. The dog crowded the bank and growled, his lip curling away from his teeth. A trio of scaly heads popped up from the swamp, their mouths open and fangs bared.

Sapphira waved her stick faster, nearly knocking it into Acacia's tiny flame. Sapphira slid her arm around her sister's waist. "We need more power! Call for a firestorm!"

The chilly water seemed to consume their dwindling wall. The dog waded toward them, closing in. One of the snakes swam through a gap in the flames and slithered around Acacia's legs. As it traveled up her body, it wound her in tight coils, and when it reached her chest, its head swung around to the front, ready to strike.

Nearly blinded by steamy vapor, Sapphira grabbed the snake's neck and wrestled it with one arm while trying to keep her fire-brand rotating. The struggle jostled Acacia's arm, knocking the Ovulum into the water.

The other two snakes swam around them in a slow orbit, drawing closer with each revolution. Pushing with all her might, Sapphira wrenched the snake's neck toward the swamp's muddy bed. She shoved her toe into the wet sand and nudged the Ovulum onto the top of her foot, raising it to the water's surface, but with neither hand free, she couldn't grab it.

321

Acacia reached for the egg, but the snake's thick coils kept her from bending. She grunted, her voice breaking. "I . . . can't . . . reach it!"

The other two snakes turned toward them and broke through the fire. Sapphira screamed at the Ovulum as it rocked precariously on her foot. "Elohim! Help us!"

CHAPTER

THE PRICE OF BETRAYAL

T he Ovulum slipped off Sapphira's foot, and its splash erupted in a gigantic spray that wrapped around the girls in a tight waterspout. As the other two snakes spun away, the swamp dried at the girls' feet. The Ovulum sat next to Sapphira's toes, pulsing crimson halos that seemed to spin the water around, making a vacuum that drew everything upward, including the girls' hair and their drenched clothing.

Sapphira's arms ached, but she kept her grip on the serpent, still coiled around Acacia as it snapped with its needle-like fangs. Lifting her firebrand higher, Sapphira shouted, "Give me a new firestorm! I need all the power I can get!"

Tongues of fire leaped from her hand, and the stick exploded in a shower of streaming flames. The fire expanded into a new spinning wall that circled around them inside the waterspout. Sapphira's vision suddenly sharpened. Sadness crept through her mind. There was no doubt; a new portal window was taking shape, but, with her arms throbbing, could she keep the writhing snake at bay?

Air rushed upward, and the sunlight winked out. They zoomed down, the whole world plunging so fast their bodies seemed to lift off the ground and hover in midair. The walls of fire and water blended together into billowing clouds of vapor. Then, in a splash of fire and steam, they crashed into a shallow bed of water that cushioned the blow of the rocky ground below. Sapphira lunged for the snake, but it had slipped from her hand. Now crawling on all fours on wet stone, she groped for its neck. When she finally found it, she jerked it up, but its limp body lay loose within her fingers. The snake's head had been crushed.

Sapphira glanced around. Elam stood next to her holding a thick scroll. "That snake won't bother anyone," he said, smacking the scroll's heavy dowel against his palm.

The portal's column of light flickered between blue and orange and finally settled on a muted orange hue. Acacia stirred next to Sapphira, trying to push the serpent's coils down to her ankles. With her soaked white hair plastered against her pale face, she looked like a frazzled ghost.

At Sapphira's feet lay the Ovulum, cold and dark, but unharmed. She breathed a long sigh and gazed at Elam, barely able to whisper, "Thank you." She reached over and helped Acacia unwind the snake's coils. A dozen more hands joined in, one pair wringing out Sapphira's dress, another combing through Acacia's hair.

Acacia pulled her clinging sleeve away from her skin. "We need to get out of these wet things."

"You know," Elam said, pointing his thumb at the exit corridor, "with Morgan gone now, I think it's safe to explore. There are quite a few rooms I was never able to see."

Sapphira smiled. Elam's chivalry never seemed to falter. She nodded toward a lantern near the museum door. "Give me light!"

she called out. The lantern's wick ignited. "There. Come back when the fuel's about half gone and tell us what you find."

Elam winked at her and draped the dead snake over his shoulder. "Got it." He strode to the corridor and dropped the serpent's body at the entrance. "I'll leave it here. It shouldn't stink too bad this far away." He smiled and disappeared under the arch.

Sapphira pointed at a pile of scrolls stacked against the museum's outer wall. "Could some of you girls bring about ten of those scrolls over here? That's my throwaway pile, and they'll be good for building a fire." She pulled her outer dress over her head and stuffed the Ovulum into its pocket.

Acacia stripped her outer dress off as well. As she rung out the excess water, her eyes followed the three girls who began building a stack of scrolls. "Why would you want to burn scrolls?" she asked.

"If you knew what was in them, you'd want to burn them, too." Sapphira nudged a scroll with her toe. "One is Nimrod's account of his temple activities, and another describes how to prepare human sacrifices for the idols in Shinar. The others are just as bad or worse."

Acacia picked up one of the scrolls and scowled at it. "Ignite!" One end burst into flames, and she threw it back into the pile. The fire quickly spread to the other scrolls.

Sapphira laughed. "I think you're getting it!"

Acacia pulled off her inner tunic. One of the girls removed her own outer dress and handed it to Acacia, then helped her stretch it over her head.

Acacia smiled. "Thank you, Yara."

Yara, now wearing only her inner tunic, spread Acacia's wet clothes over two broken ladder pieces. She grinned bashfully at Sapphira. "Your turn."

A taller girl, also dressed only in an inner tunic, presented Sapphira with an outer dress. Sapphira peeled off her underclothes

325

and slipped on the dry outer tunic, letting the bottom hem drop to her ankles. "Thank you, uh . . ."

"That's Awven," Acacia said.

Sapphira nodded at her and smiled as sweetly as she could. "Thank you so much, Awven." Awven smiled back and hung Sapphira's wet clothes next to Acacia's.

The two oracles of fire faced each other, sitting cross-legged with the crackling scrolls between them. The other girls gathered in a circle around them and sat quietly.

Sapphira rubbed her hands in front of the fire. It flashed orange, matching the portal column's new color. "Well, I guess moving the portal worked. This place will be a lot more peaceful knowing Morgan won't be sneaking up on us."

Acacia laughed softly. "Right. No more plunges into the chasm. That was no fun at all."

"I can believe that. Your scream haunted my nightmares ever since it happened." Sapphira nodded toward one of the other girls. "Do you know their stories? I don't remember seeing any of them before today."

"You wouldn't. We were still in our growth chambers when Morgan decided these girls were too smart for her purposes. She threw them into the chasm not long after we were uprooted. Yara overheard Morgan telling Mardon to keep you and me so he could learn why we were so different and to try to"—she glanced at Paili—"uh . . . alter the next brood, I guess you might say. Then, Morgan caught her listening and threw her into the chasm."

"So," Sapphira said, tapping her fingers on the stone floor, "Yara made it through the whirlpool along with the other eleven who came before us. But I wonder what happened to Taalah and the spawns who came later. And what about the little embryos that Mardon incinerated?"

"Before you came and freed us, the man we listened to told us that some girls burned in the magma, and some burned elsewhere.

He said their souls traveled to other destinations, but he wouldn't tell us where. He pretty much said, in a kind way, of course, that it was none of our business."

"Your teacher is the person inside the Ovulum? And you listened to him for centuries?"

"It sure looked like him, but we didn't listen to him all the time. He would tell us stories for a while and then we would sleep. I think we slept for very long periods of time, but I'm not sure. I never dreamed, so it was hard to tell. It never got boring, and we never got hungry or sick."

Sapphira nodded at Yara. "The only difference between these girls and the ones who didn't survive the magma is when they were spawned. Why would that be?"

"That couldn't be the reason," Acacia said. "Paili survived, and she was spawned after we were."

Sapphira raised her knees and propped her chin on them. "Well, then Paili is the real key. Why is she different from Taalah and Qadar?"

327

Paili leaned forward and whispered in Sapphira's ear. "They ate Morgan's fruit."

The words echoed in Sapphira's mind and dredged a painful trench in her heart. She swallowed through her tightening throat as tears welled in her eyes. The truth behind "They ate Morgan's fruit" rang like a clear bell.

"Is something wrong?" Acacia asked.

Sapphira nodded. Her lips quivered, and her voice cracked. "It's my fault! I shouldn't have let Paili use that fruit in the stew. I should have thrown it all in the river."

Paili laid her hands on Sapphira's back. "You told them," she said softly. "They not listen."

Sapphira shook her head and kicked a protruding scroll farther into the fire. The flames leapt up and crackled louder, masking her squeaking voice. "I could've stopped them. I really could have."

Acacia squinted at her. "What are you talking about?"

After taking a deep breath, Sapphira related the story about Morgan's fruit from the tree in the museum. She added most of her other significant adventures, from the tower collapse to the amazing midnight dance with Elohim. As she spoke, Acacia paid close attention, glancing at the tree in the museum from time to time and stoking the fire whenever one of the girls brought a new scroll for fuel.

When Sapphira finished, she exhaled loud and long. "There's a lot more to tell, but I'm getting tired."

"Don't worry," Acacia said. "I'm sure we'll have time later. I don't think we're going anywhere for a while."

Sapphira raised her eyebrows at the drying clothes. "We'd better get dressed before Elam gets back."

The girls hurriedly changed clothes, giving back the outer dresses to their owners. As Yara continued to feed the flames, Acacia ventured into the museum library and browsed through the scrolls that lay within reach, picking up a few and blowing dust off their yellowed exteriors. "Are there any maps that show the layout of this place?" she called. "We could use one for exploring."

"Yes," Sapphira replied, pointing. "Check the third shelf up, near the back, over by the ladder with the broken first rung."

"I think I see the shelf." Acacia grasped the ladder and began climbing.

Sapphira strode to the corridor, stepped over the dead snake, and peered into the dark hall. Elam should have been back by this time. Could Mardon have found him? Knowing Elam, he probably tried to get into every forbidden room he could find.

"Sapphira," Acacia yelled from the ladder. "I found it. It shows everything—"

"Wait!" Sapphira held up her hand. "I hear something." Slaps of sandals on stone echoed in the tunnel. Light appeared, drawing rapidly closer. Sounds of heavy breathing mixed in, then a shout.

"Sapphira!" Elam's face glowed in the bouncing light of a lantern. He stopped at the end of the corridor, his cheeks red and streaming with sweat. "You won't believe what I saw!"

"Try me." She kicked the dead snake's body. "At this point, I'm ready to believe anything."

"I found the mobility training room for the spawns. It's amazing!"

"How did you get in?"

Acacia walked up, an open scroll in her hands. "Through the ceiling, I'll bet."

Elam mopped his brow with his sleeve. "How did you know?"

Acacia held up the scroll. "This is a map to the layout of this place. There's a heat release vent and tunnel above the mobility room ceiling."

"Did they see you?" Sapphira asked Elam. "They're all giants now, right?"

"They're huge!" he replied, spreading out his arms. "But, no, they didn't see me. I just peeked in from above and closed the trap-door real quick."

"Was Mardon in there?"

"Uh-huh. He was showing the biggest giant how to train the others."

Sapphira shook her head. "I'll bet that was my spawn, Yereq."

"Yes!" Elam pointed at her. "That was the name he called it. Yereq."

Acacia took the scroll closer to the firelight and rolled it out on the floor. "Here," she said, pointing to the upper right portion of the map. "This one's labeled the mobility room."

Elam pressed his finger on a room at the bottom left. "We're way over here."

"That's strange," Acacia said. "The room we're in isn't labeled."

"I remember looking at this a few years ago." Sapphira tapped her finger next to Elam's. "I think this was an empty chamber before the museum dropped in. Mardon probably drew this map long before that happened, and he still might not know about it. Morgan never told Mardon anything he didn't need to know, not even about the abyss."

"The abyss?" Acacia tilted her head at Sapphira. "What's that?"

"Something only Morgan, Paili, and I know about. Paili and I found it while mining and almost fell in, but we had no clue what it was." Sapphira scanned the map. "Where's the mining level?"

Acacia rolled it out farther. "Let's see. . . . Laborers' quarters . . . Ah! Mining level."

Sapphira slid her finger along dark lines that represented the trenches. "This is an old drawing. We mined past the end of this before I got promoted to the control room." She pointed at a spot off the map. "If you extended the drawing, the abyss would be about right here. It's a deep hole, so deep I couldn't see the bottom."

"Then I guess you wouldn't know what's in it," Elam said.

"Not for sure. We heard someone moaning, and I read something in a scroll that told me what might be down there. I assumed the scroll was right, so I never went back. One thing's for sure; Morgan seemed interested in it."

"Well, I don't know about you girls," Elam said, "but if Morgan's interested in it, I want to know what's going on."

"What's your hurry?" Sapphira asked. "It seems safe enough where we are."

"Until we learn everything that's going on here, I won't assume we're safe." He picked up the lantern. "Anyone want to join me?"

Sapphira sighed. "I guess I should. I know exactly where it is."

"No!" Paili shook her head and grabbed Sapphira's hand. "Not the deep hole!"

Acacia gently pulled Paili away from Sapphira and hugged her close. "I'll stay with the girls. If Mardon doesn't know what's in this chamber, maybe we should set up a home here."

Elam nodded. "That sounds perfect."

Sapphira picked up a scroll from the fire and tapped out the flames. "I'll use this if the lantern fuel runs out."

Sapphira and Elam hurried along the corridor, Elam staying a step or two in front. They passed the original portal chamber and wound through the meandering corridor that led to the laborers' hovels. When they reached the lift platform, Elam paused and stared at the cudgel and metal plate hanging on the wall. "We don't want to wake Chazaq, that's for sure, but he might not be down there, anyway."

Sapphira touched the warped plate, making it swing like a pendulum. "So we're stuck?"

"Looks that way." Elam tugged the pulley rope, but it wouldn't budge. "It's probably tied at the bottom."

"Do you know another way to get down?"

"Sure. If you can climb down a rope."

Sapphira tapped her foot on the platform. "You mean there's room to squeeze between the wall and this board?"

"I'm not sure. I've never done it before. But once you get past the passenger platforms, there's probably lots of room, and going down should be pretty easy."

"True, but we also have to get back." Sapphira laid the scroll down and grabbed the rope with both hands. She pulled herself off her feet and dangled in the air. Her arms weren't as strong as when she was digging for magnetite and chiseling out chambers, but she felt pretty confident she could lower herself to the mining level. Dropping back to the platform, she pointed at the lantern. "What about our light?"

"Not a problem." Elam unfastened his belt and looped it through the lantern's handle, then tied it in place. "As long as we get down before it burns a hole in my clothes." He pulled his sleeves over his hands, latched onto the rope, and began sliding down with his back against the side wall, but the lantern bumped against the platform, keeping him from descending.

Sapphira pushed against the side wall to make the gap wider. "Good thing you're going first."

After sliding down farther, he paused, his face now the only part of his body above the platform. As a breeze from below blew his hair into a frenzy, he smiled. "Don't worry. If Nabal's down there, I'll chase him away with his own whip."

He slid out of sight, and the lantern's glow faded, leaving Sapphira in almost complete darkness. She groped for the scroll and tied it in her own belt, then copied Elam's descent. Being smaller than Elam, she managed to squeeze herself and the scroll between the platform and wall without help.

When she slid into the gap between levels, only the glow from Elam's lantern colored the darkness, providing just enough light to illuminate the rope that stretched between them. With a cool draft breezing up from below, she felt like a dim island in a blowing sea of blackness, following a guide she really barely knew at all. Of course she could trust him, couldn't she?

332

Feeling exposed and helpless, she continued sliding, concentrating on a mental image of Elam's noble face and chivalrous manner. This young gentleman wasn't anything like the bestial monsters in Nimrod's lust-filled temples. He would never entertain the idea of taking advantage of a girl.

Elam pushed each succeeding platform out of the way with his feet. When he finally reached the mining level, he swung off the rope and held out his hand to her. She took his hand, and when she planted her feet on the board, she kissed him on the cheek. "Thank you," she said softly.

He untied the lantern and gazed into the mining cavern. "For what? Taking your hand?"

"That's part of it." Sapphira pulled the scroll from her belt. "It's hard to explain."

Without looking back at her, Elam nodded and walked out into the cool chamber. "I think I know what you mean."

She pulled up alongside him and breathed at the lantern. "Time to sleep for a while," she said. The wick immediately darkened, leaving only the billowing glow from the nearby magma river. She strode ahead and waved for Elam to follow. "No giants in sight. Let's go."

The two hustled along the trench, probing deeper into the dimmer recesses of the chamber. The coolness of the stale air chilled Sapphira's hands and cheeks, and just when she thought about relighting the lantern, the distant radiance of the abyss caught her eye.

Sapphira slowed to a creeping tiptoe, Elam at her side. When they neared the edge, he laid a hand on her shoulder and took the next two steps alone, craning his neck forward to peek down into the strangely illuminated hole. Sapphira edged to his side again and peered down with him.

The streams of light that swirled to the surface looked like a morning mist caught in a gentle eddy. When the gemstones on the walls of the abyss absorbed the streams, the crystalline facets seemed to exhale them in a more consistent, static glow that rose toward the ceiling.

333

Elam whispered into Sapphira's ear. "Only one way to find out what's down there."

"Talk to it?" she asked. The Ovulum began to warm in her pocket. "Are you sure?"

"Why not? If whatever is down there could get out, wouldn't it have escaped a long time ago?"

"Good point." The Ovulum grew so warm, it began to sting her leg. She took a step away from the pit. "But if it's what I think it is, I'm not sure we should talk to it at all."

Elam glanced back at her. "What do you think it is?"

"A bunch of evil spirits called Watchers. I read a scroll that said they would be sent to the abyss in the lowest realms."

"How do you know they're evil?"

"The scroll said so."

Elam looked down at the ground for a moment, a pained expression on his face.

"What's wrong?" Sapphira asked. "The song again?"

"I'm not sure." Elam covered one ear with his hand. "It's like the song's stuck in my mind. I don't know if it's a voice or just a memory, but the words keep coming back."

"And you can't ignore it?"

"I'm trying to." He uncovered his ear and stared at her, giving her a weak, forced smile. "Anyway, can you trust who wrote that scroll of yours? I mean, if Morgan told me something was evil, I would think it was probably good. How do you know what to trust?"

"I've thought about that too many times to count. I think—"

A low moan sounded from the abyss, growing in volume as voices of varying pitches joined in. One of the moans transformed into a string of words, lament streaking its tone.

"Does a valiant warrior from above seek to rescue the downtrodden? We are wretched creatures who have been condemned to eternal torment, and we have suffered for century after century in this cold, desolate hole. Without trunk or limb, we cannot climb the walls to freedom. Without a savior to hear our appeals for forgiveness, we lie here doomed forever."

Sapphira took another step back, but Elam leaned closer. "What's your name?" he asked.

She jumped ahead and latched onto his arm. "Elam, don't."

The swirling light collected at the top of the hole, white at first, but it split into multicolored streams that rose above ground level and formed into a vertical, elliptical aura. "We have many names," the voice continued. "Come and help us."

With each word, the rainbow colors shimmered across the aura's surface, making it look like a dimensional viewing screen, much like the one the Ovulum had made except more lovely to behold, with dazzling colors waltzing in its ghostly glow instead of a flat, dull red. It also seemed deeper, richer, more captivating as its allure drew them closer, step by step.

The Ovulum stung Sapphira's leg again. "Ow!" She jumped back. "The Eye of the Oracle doesn't want us to listen."

"Ah!" the voice continued, now without a lamenting tone. "There are two of you, and a young female doubts our words." The colors in the aura formed into the image of a face, a noble-looking man with a strong chin, flashing eyes, and flowing silver hair. Its lips moved in sync with the voice. "I am a Seraph, an angel of Elohim and king of the watching guardians. My kind fought with the dragons, and our battle brought about the great flood that plunged us here to Tartarus. All I need is a courageous young man who is willing to forsake timid, female counsel and climb down to carry us to freedom."

As Elam turned toward Sapphira, his eyes darted wildly.

Heat surged into Sapphira's cheeks, and she backed away another step. "No, Elam. He's lying. I know he is."

Elam grimaced. He lifted his hands toward his ears, then jerked them back down. "How can you be so sure? My father believed in Elohim and his angels. Maybe the voice in the abyss is telling the truth."

Sapphira held up the scroll. It trembled in her hand, matching her quivering voice. "I believe Enoch. He was a prophet who warned the Watchers about their evil ways. They were Seraphim who made war against Elohim and his dragons."

Elam stared at the scroll. "Does Enoch say that Elohim had dragons?"

"I don't remember!" She waved it in front of him. "But you won't find the stories in this scroll! Enoch's is a different one! It's still hidden in my dugout."

The voice in the aura spoke again, the lamenting tone returning. "Alas! It is true young Elam. Enoch warned us about fighting against the dragons. We thought they were allies of the first dragon,

Lucifer, the prince of rebels against Elohim. Go and read Enoch's scroll. You will see that we are angels who did not join Lucifer's prideful quest to unseat the Holy One. To our shame, however, we followed an ill-advised course that brought about our banishment. Now, in our sorrow and contrition, we beg for escape so we can fly to the mercy seat of Elohim and plead for forgiveness."

Sapphira balled her hand into a fist. "I don't believe a word he's saying, Elam. He's lying. I can feel it."

The voice grew louder. "Elam, you have heard the song of truth in your ears. Why trust the ever-fluctuating feelings of this little girl? Read Enoch for yourself. Gather your own strength and wisdom and follow the course set before you by trusting your heart of gold."

Elam stared at the noble face, then at Sapphira. With each glance, his expression stayed the same—stern, cautious, maybe carrying a hint of fear. He stalked away from the abyss, and as he passed Sapphira, he wiggled his fingers in front of her face. "Stay here," he ordered, nodding at his fingers. He then broke into a jog through the trench, calling behind him. "I'll be back."

As Elam's sandal thumps died away, a chill passed across Sapphira's skin. He had acted so strangely! What did the wiggling fingers mean? But she couldn't ask now. She was alone with a demon, or maybe a bunch of demons. Who could tell how many? And knowing that they probably couldn't escape did little to ease her mind. She edged back into the darkness, letting her feet pad noiselessly from toe to heel. She didn't want that . . . that thing to know she was still around, but as its light cast a glow over her retreating body, she couldn't shake the chilling fear.

A loud click sounded from somewhere beyond the abyss. The angel's image vibrated. "Is someone still here?" he asked.

Sapphira halted. The angel probably couldn't see her at all. That face was just a projection of some kind, and the eyes were really blind.

The click sounded again. "Someone *is* here," the angel said. "Who is it?"

Sapphira held her breath. Elam had gone the other way, so he didn't make the noise, and she had never gone farther than the pit, so she had no idea what could be beyond it. Bats, maybe? Something worse? She took another quiet step backwards.

A coarse, female voice crashed through the silence. "Well, if it isn't little Miss Mara!"

The chill pierced Sapphira's heart and made her freeze in place. Morgan! Sapphira scanned the chamber in the direction of the voice, but the pit's brilliant aura blinded her.

Framed by the angel's shining profile, Morgan's familiar silhouette sashayed around the abyss, her face shadowed. Still, Sapphira could imagine the evil smile on Morgan's lips just from the crackling sarcasm in her voice. "So nice of you to greet me at the back door, Mara dear. You must have known the front door was locked, so you rushed down here to form a welcoming party with Samyaza."

That name sounded familiar, but Sapphira didn't want to let Morgan know. She twisted her face in mock curiosity. "Samyaza? Who's Samyaza?"

Morgan turned her sarcastic tone to its maximum setting. "Do you mean to tell me you haven't been properly introduced?" Her shadowy hand rose to her mouth. "For shame! Samyaza is such a friendly angel. I wonder why he hasn't told you who he is."

The name finally clicked in Sapphira's mind. Enoch listed Samyaza as one of the Watchers! She squeezed her scroll tightly and slid her free hand into her pocket, groping for the Ovulum. It was growing warm, a soothing kind of warmth. Maybe Elohim was ready to help her battle this witch.

Sapphira held the scroll high and waved it. "Maybe Samyaza didn't introduce himself because he knew I learned his name from a certain book you've been looking for."

337

Morgan's voice pitched up. "You found Enoch's scroll?"

Sapphira stared at the tightly wound parchment. "Ignite!" she shouted. A vigorous flame burst forth at the upper end, growing larger by the second.

"No!" Morgan lurched toward her, but Sapphira leaped out of the way. She dashed to the abyss and held the scroll over the edge, poking Samyaza's image in the nose, but he didn't seem to notice. "Leave this place forever," Sapphira said, "and I'll give you this scroll."

Morgan set her fists on her hips. "What good will it do me if it's just ashes?"

Sapphira nodded at the scroll. "Enough," she said, and the flames dwindled away. She rolled it out a few inches and studied the text. "Hmmm. I can still read it."

The angel's image vibrated once again. "She is not holding Enoch's scroll. I sent Elam to get it. He is preparing to play the role of Judas, just as you had hoped."

Morgan's face lit up. "Ah! Excellent!"

"Judas?" Sapphira asked. "What are you talking about?"

"Elam is putty in my hands," Samyaza continued. "Naamah's song has broken his will, and his temptation to yield to Lucifer's call is strong. The girl will soon be out of our way forever. Now we merely have to paint the proper portrait of our little oracle of fire."

Sapphira kicked a pebble and shouted, "What are you talking about?"

Morgan pressed a finger over her lips. "Hush now. Fits of impatience are so unbecoming. Little slave girls like you need to learn their place. You're just an overgrown plant, a freak of nature without a soul. You might as well get used to the idea"—she smiled wickedly and poisoned her final word with sarcasm—"*Mara.*"

Scorching heat surged through Sapphira's body. The scroll burst into flames again, burning downward until it concealed her hand in fire, but she ignored it as she raged at Morgan. "I am not

Mara! I am Sapphira Adi! I am not a freak of nature! I danced with Elohim, and he loves me!" The soothing warmth of the Ovulum caressed her thigh, calming her down. The scroll continued to burn, though not as brightly.

Morgan cast a glance along the trench. "It is time, Samyaza," she said softly.

"Understood," Samyaza said.

The scroll's flames weakened further, and Sapphira's mind swam in a spinning whirlpool of anger and confusion. "Time for what?"

"For you to learn the truth." Morgan shook her head slowly. "Poor, deceived, little Mara. I personally planted your seed, Naamah watered you and sang to you, and I uprooted you and placed you in a growth chamber until you were strong enough to stand. I even helped you take your first step in the spawns' mobility room. Shouldn't I know that you're just a mutant plant who has been created to battle against the sons of Noah? Didn't you think it odd that I chose you over Acacia? You deserved to die in the chasm, but I sent Acacia to her death instead, because I had a special role in mind for you." She took a step closer to Sapphira and extended a hand toward her. "Come back to the hovels with me, and we will continue our quest to eliminate what remains of Shem and Japheth. You were wise to turn Elam over to me so I could keep him a prisoner for so long. Now, let's finish the job."

Samyaza laughed. "You used Mara to imprison Elam? How clever of you!"

"What?" Sapphira glanced back and forth between Morgan and the aura. "What are you talking about?"

"But," Samyaza continued, "by your own code, all traitors have to be cast away. If Mara would betray Elam, she would certainly betray you."

Morgan stroked her chin. "Of course, you're right, my love. I had forgotten about that."

339

Sapphira massaged the Ovulum in her pocket. "But I didn't betray Elam! You kidnapped him from his people." The flames on her scroll vanished, leaving only a rising string of smoke.

"I did have him kidnapped," Morgan continued, "but I would not have known about his trespassing into my room if not for the blossom you left for me to find." She walked slowly toward Sapphira, her hands swaying hypnotically. "It is time for you to go now, Mara. Your life cycle is over. You betrayed a friend, so no one can trust you."

Dizziness swirled Sapphira's vision, and sleepiness weighed down her eyelids. "But I didn't . . . leave the blossom for you . . . to find. I hid it . . ."

"Under a bed? Come now, Mara. I found the blossom but never Enoch's scroll. You obviously wanted me to find one and not the other." Morgan grabbed Sapphira's shoulders. Her icy fingers radiated sheer cold through her tunics, jolting the fog from her brain. Morgan turned toward the trench and smiled. "Did you hear our conversation, Elam?"

Elam stepped out of the shadows, but the pit's dim light illuminated only his face. His lips were taut, almost invisible. "I heard it."

Morgan shuffled Sapphira to the edge of the abyss. "Did you bring it?"

He glanced behind his back. "I brought it."

"Now you finally know that the songs are true. Sapphira has lied to you and used you." Morgan kept one hand on Sapphira and extended the other. "By giving me Enoch's scroll, you will be signifying your rejection of this traitor and condemning her to the abyss. Agreed?"

Sapphira could barely breathe. Nothing she could say now could possibly outwit Morgan. She was too crafty, too devilish. Would Elam be able to see through her deception? The Ovulum kept getting warmer. Sapphira slid it out and tilted her head upward. *Elohim! Give him wisdom!*

"I don't trust you," Elam said. "I don't want you to get close enough to grab me."

"Very well. You may leave it there, and I will pick it up." Morgan started toward him, pulling Sapphira with her.

Elam raised his hand. "No. Don't come anywhere near me. I'll throw it to you."

Morgan halted, still near the edge of the abyss. "If you insist." She held out her hand again. "You may throw it."

An urgent call pierced Sapphira's mind. *"Run, child! Run!"* She wrenched free from Morgan's grip and bolted for Elam. Elam reared back and threw something at Morgan, something long and flexible that whipped around and around. As it flew, a pair of fangs glistened at one end. A thick, scaly body slapped Morgan across the face, twisted around her shoulders, and slung her down. She lay motionless inside a huge coil that pinned her to the ground, trapped by her own dead serpent.

The Ovulum pulsed in Sapphira's hand, sending hundreds of red rings toward Morgan and the abyss. The halos built up into a crimson screen, a translucent divider that spread from wall to wall and floor to ceiling, separating Sapphira and Elam from the sorceress.

341

Holding the Ovulum away from her body, she let it pour layer after layer of red across the new wall. She draped her other hand over Elam's shoulders and pulled him close. Sobs punctuated her cry. "I'm so glad you believed in me!"

"She's a really good liar," Elam said, "but I never really thought about getting the scroll. I just saw that pit as a good place to toss the snake and shut that demon up."

On the other side of the thickening screen, Morgan threw the snake's body to the side, rose to her feet, and kicked it savagely into the abyss.

Elam grinned. "I should have attached a message to it. 'To the Watcher. With love, from Elam.' "

Sapphira laughed. "Too bad he can't send you a thank-you note. I think we won't be seeing him again for a very long time."

As the Ovulum continued to pulse halos, the voice entered her mind again. *"Perhaps you will not see him, child, but first you must send the abyss to the lowest of all realms. Prepare to generate the greatest portal you have ever made."*

Sapphira laid the Ovulum on the ground, took a deep breath, and lifted the scroll high. "Give me light!" she shouted. Flames instantly leaped from the top, jumping and dancing as they consumed the scroll. She waved it in a circle, slowly at first, then faster and faster as the flames expanded into a wide curtain that enveloped Elam and herself as well as the entire chamber. Within seconds, all they could see was the inside of a fiery tornado. The vortex spun so fast, the orange tongues blended together into solid streams of blazing light. The Ovulum's red pulses mixed in, deepening the orange and tingeing the entire cyclone with bright crimson highlights.

The voice from the Ovulum shouted out loud. "Now, Sapphira Adi! Shine forth the light of love! Show Elam the joy that only Elohim can give!"

A rising tide of ecstasy rose in Sapphira's heart, filling her mind with song, the same song the Eye sang when Elohim led her in holy dance. The words began to pour from her lips unbidden, more beautifully than she ever imagined she could sing.

> In days gone by the water fell
> And draped the world in silent death;
> A rain of judgment drowned the earth
> Demanding life and snatching breath.
>
> But now the raindrops fall afresh
> On hearts rejecting hate and sin,
> In blessings crowned with love and grace
> To heal the wounds of soul and skin.

The flames exploded in brightness. Intense heat nearly blistered her skin, but she didn't care. She just closed her eyes and sang on.

The one who loves is Elohim,
Rejoicing now in song and dance;
I shout for you to come and play,
Enjoying love, the great romance.

So dance, my child, and feel my love
In rain, the healing drops of life.
Forsake your cares, your toils and pain,
The wounds and scars of slavish strife.

Droplets of water sprinkled her cheeks, and the sizzle of cooling stone breezed past her ears. She tossed the remnant of the scroll to the ground and embraced Elam, her eyes still closed, her body still swaying with her song.

343

O cast aside the chains of grief
And reach for heaven's grace above;
So son of Shem come dance with me!
Enfold yourself in arms of love.

This time, Elam returned the embrace, and as cool water poured from above, the two spun slowly with the whirling breeze. Elam's head nodded in rhythmic spasms as he wept on Sapphira's shoulder.

She patted his back and drank in his wordless song of joy. Elam had found Elohim. Though Elam had not seen his beloved father in centuries, he had witnessed the truth of his father's stories about God as he endured the injustice and torture of Morgan's prisons. Now he stood in the presence of the holy, finally feeling the loving caress of Elohim. The same God who scrubbed the world's filth with a cleansing flood was now bathing him in a shower of mercy.

As the melody in her heart played on, new words drifted into her mind, sung in the rich voice of the Eye. She listened, wondering if Elam could hear them as well.

A day will come when you will speak
My name anew in sacrifice,
The day you set your heart afire
And give me all, the only price.

The voice faded away, and the fire settled to the earth and vanished. In its place stood a steep grassy slope rising to a high promontory overlooking a valley. Rain poured down from a dismal sky, the sun obscured by a curtain of dark, thick clouds.

Elam pulled away from Sapphira. He gave her a shy smile and nod, then turned his gaze upward, blinking at the sheets of rain. "Any idea where we are?" he asked.

Sapphira took in a long breath. "No clue, and I really don't care." She picked up the Ovulum from the mud, wiped it on her sleeve, and slid it into the pocket of her dampening dress. "I have Elohim's prophet with me, so I have a guide." She took Elam's hand. "And I have a warrior with me, so I have a protector."

Elam kept his gaze focused on the ground. "If you say so," he said, shrugging his shoulders. He looked up at her, his face shining in spite of the gloomy skies. "Even though I'm not the strongest guy around, or the bravest, I'll be the best warrior I can be." As his glistening eyes locked on Sapphira's, he raised his hand and wiggled his fingers. "But, no matter what happens, I won't ever betray the girl who risked her life to feed me. That's a promise."

CHAPTER

Abandoned

erlin swung his oar at the serpent, gashing its throat as its body lunged over his dugout canoe. He kicked the snake back into the water, thrust the oar against the muddy bottom of the swamp, and shoved the boat toward shore. Now at a depth of only a couple of feet, he jumped into the water and sprinted toward the grassy beach, splashing through the shallows. When he neared the shore, he vaulted toward the bordering grass and rolled to a stop next to a lush apple tree.

He clutched his chest and took in long, slow breaths, hoping his heart wouldn't leap out of his throat. He glanced back at the swamp. The roiling snake bodies had submerged, and the surface was once again calm. Fumbling with the folds of his robe, he uncovered his scabbard and pulled out his sword. He wouldn't be caught with only an oar in his hand again.

Merlin sat up and gazed at the castle on the hill, wondering at the familiar constellations riding above the twin turrets. Why would the stars of the living world be in the skies over Hades? He shrugged his shoulders. At least he had finally found her. Tracking

Morgan had been much more difficult than he had imagined. It had been a big enough surprise when she transformed into a raven, but when she vanished through a dimensional portal, he couldn't believe it! A wraith, a sorceress of old, had invaded England with her ancient black magic.

He rose to his feet and began trudging up the slope. The days of tedious research had finally paid off. Yet, learning who this woman really was proved to be a curse. With her prowess at the dark arts, every inch of his journey could bring a new puzzle to solve . . . or another dangerous trap to avoid.

After coming under the shelter of a high portico that led to the main doors, he halted. A shadow, small and fleeting, like a child's frightened ghost, scurried for cover behind a marble column. Merlin watched the column for any sign of movement. It wasn't just his imagination. In this domain of wraiths, who could tell what evil might be lurking in the shadows?

Keeping his sword clearly exposed, he strode confidently to the door. If the mysterious ghost had plans to attack, it probably would have done so by now. He grasped the ornate knob, and the force of his hand swung the door noiselessly, opening it about a quarter of the way. He peered into the dim anteroom, then, allowing the sword to lead the way, he squeezed through the gap. When he cleared the door, he pushed it with his backside, but not far enough to engage the latch.

As he passed under an archway, a single torch hanging on a side wall flickered brightly, allowing Merlin to scan the enormous chamber, perhaps a ballroom or a meeting hall. Dozens of candelabras dangled from a high ceiling, and a huge rectangular table adorned the center.

Shifting his eyes back and forth, Merlin walked slowly toward the table. Tall chairs surrounded the dark wooden surface, each with padded headrests and elaborate trim. Near the head of the table, a marble chessboard sat at an angle, as though the master of the house had planned to play someone at the adjacent seat. Tall, wooden chess pieces stood around the board in mid-play, awaiting their marching orders. The white king, dressed in a purple-trimmed robe and carrying a rugged cross, sat on a muscular white horse. On the other side, the black king, dressed in red-trimmed mail and a turban of intertwined snakes, rode on an armored black dragon.

Something moved—a shifting shadow seated at the tallest chair. A voice, soft and sultry, rose from the shadow. "Welcome, Merlin."

Merlin nodded. "Morgan Le Faye, I presume."

She gestured toward the seat next to hers. "You survived my serpents. I'm impressed." A black cobra-shaped pawn advanced on the board by itself, threatening an opposing rook, but a white knight jumped to the pawn's space and crushed it into dust.

Eyeing the enchanted pieces, Merlin slid the chair out and sat, keeping his legs swung to the side. "I prefer to speak without pretense, Morgan. I know who you really are."

347

"Of course you do." Morgan pulled close to the table and propped her folded hands. "You saw right through my façade in the king's throne room, yet you refused to give away my identity. Why?"

A black knight jumped in front of its queen. The orange-eyed horse pawed its square, snorting viciously.

"You give me too much credit," Merlin said. "I knew you were not the king's sister, and I suspected that you were not fully human, but I didn't guess that you were once called Lilith until I found an ancient scroll that described two wraiths who stalk the righteous in winged forms."

"Ah! So in Arthur's court you only suspected my true identity, did you?" Morgan leaned back in her seat and smiled. "Still, it would have been easy for you to prove my lack of normal humanness, but you chose to suffer embarrassment instead. I must know your reason."

The white king advanced one square, slashing in front of him with a gleaming blade. The black knight leaped back to its previous space.

Merlin tightened his grip on his sword. "The king would have demanded Excalibur from me and executed you on the spot. He suffers no sorceress to live in his domain."

"The king would have demanded nothing of the sort. A potion I gave him saw to that. He was so strong, it took a triple dose, but his brain was sufficiently muddled in time for the council of war."

Merlin sighed. "I thought he seemed rather confused that day."

"Still," Morgan continued, "you sacrificed your standing to keep me safe. Why do you care if I live or die? What am I to you?"

He glanced between Morgan and the chessboard's black queen. Both flashed shining red eyes. "According to my research," he said, "you could be more human than you realize. You still have a soul—a dark, corrupt soul, but a soul, nonetheless."

"And you, in your vacuous perception of the higher moral ground, want to save my soul." Morgan sneered at him. "How noble of you."

Merlin folded his hands on the table. "I'm not seeking nobility, but if you wish to learn how to be redeemed, there might yet be a way. First, however, you would have to obtain a new body."

"Why would I want to do that?" Morgan stood and rubbed her hands along her hips. "I can mold this body into any shape I choose."

"Shape without substance is a mere shadow. I know you want more."

She stood and slinked toward him. "Of course I do. I always want more, and I always get what I want." She touched the top of his head and swirled his hair around her finger.

Merlin shot to his feet, toppling his chair as he stepped back. "You cannot have what belongs to another."

Morgan laid her hands on his shoulders and pouted. "Why can I not be your Gwendoloena, at least while you're here?" Her hands slid toward his cheeks, and she pursed her lips. "After all, what happens in the circles of the dead remains a secret forever. No one needs to know what you do here."

He grabbed her wrists and glared at her purple-stained palms. "My wife's name is Gwendoloena only in my songs, for I would never tell you her real name, and no power-draining spell is going to make me betray her."

Morgan's arms melted into wisps of smoke, and she backed away, laughing. "Everyone has a price of betrayal, Merlin. I just have to find what your thirty pieces of silver is."

Merlin banged his fist on the table, toppling half the chessmen on the squares. "I am no fool, Morgan. It is not my wife you seek to betray."

"And that is why I will let you live." Morgan waved her hand over the board, and the pieces aligned themselves in their beginning positions. "You are the only one wise enough to gain the full trust of the dragons and help me eliminate them from the face of the earth. That would be the ultimate betrayal."

"You dribble the drool of an imbecile. No price would tempt me to betray the dragons."

"Oh, but you do have a price, Merlin." Morgan laid her hands on her chest. Her body slowly softened into a gel-like state and reshaped itself into a slightly shorter woman with wider hips, a careworn face, and graying hair. She slid her hands slowly from her chest to her hips. "Does the image of your wife please you?"

Merlin blinked rapidly, but he forced himself to stay calm. "What are your intentions?"

"My intentions?" She withdrew a gold ring from her pocket and held it out to him, her eyes flashing redder than ever. "For you to join me in my battle against Elohim and the dragons. With my power and your intimate knowledge of the enemy, no

349

one could stop us. Just say, 'I do,' and we will be united in purpose forever."

Merlin glared at the ring. "And what are the consequences when I refuse?"

She drew a dagger from her belt and plunged it into her chest. It sank into her jellied skin, fell through her body, and clattered on the floor. Waving her arms, she quickly changed back into her original shape, laughing again. "Need I say more?"

Heat scalded Merlin's cheeks. He curled his hands into fists but kept his voice in check as he spoke slowly and clearly. "I found what I came here for. Now that I know for certain who you are, I will inform my king." He tightened his belt with a quick tug. "That is, if I am able to leave this God-forsaken place."

"You may already know the law of passage in the circles of seven. Since you willingly entered, you may willingly leave. You will be a valuable tool for me, so I will not prevent your departure."

Merlin cocked his head toward the exit. "The serpents in your swamp and the beast that lurks in the shadows might have other ideas."

"Beast?" Morgan chuckled. "Oh, that's just Naamah, or Elaine, as you know her. She always inspects the men who stumble onto our little island. She won't bother you, and I'll make sure my serpentine pets are asleep during you journey home. I'm looking forward to this new adventure, and I'm confident that you will do what I'm asking. Your dear wife is too young to die."

Keeping his eye on the chess pieces, Merlin picked up the toppled chair and set it back on its feet. "I get the impression that you desire a battle of prophetic foresight."

She picked up the black king and twirled it in her fingers. "Yes, Merlin, but more than that, a battle between your god and mine, a chess match that allows for no stalemates."

"Understood," Merlin said, lifting the white king into his palm. "Till death do us part."

With the rain diminishing to a light sprinkle, Sapphira scanned the grassy slope, her vision again crystal clear. "This must be a new portal, so I guess we should be able to use it to get back home. The scroll's gone, so I just need to find something that will burn."

"I *am* back home." Elam spread an arm toward the misty valley. "See the glow from the fires? This is the real world, the land of the living." He took in a deep breath and let out a long, satisfied sigh. "Even the cattle and goats smell good."

Sapphira closed her eyes and breathed deeply. "It's an odd smell," she said, opening her eyes again. "It makes me feel warm inside."

He pointed at the small building behind them on top of the hill, a thatched-roof structure with two boards nailed to the wall—a vertical board about as long as Nabal was tall, and a horizontal one crossing over the vertical about two thirds of the way up. "I saw a lantern in that window. People must live there. Real people."

"Do you want to stay?" Sapphira asked. "I mean, where would you go? Everyone you ever knew has to be long dead, and the people here won't even speak the same language you did."

"I know, but . . ." Elam shifted his weight from foot to foot. "I don't want to sound mean or anything, but I don't belong down there with the underborns. Besides, I'd be the only male, and that would be . . . well . . . difficult."

"Not with you always being such a gentleman. We would all trust you."

"Trust me or not, it would still be difficult." He retied his belt, though it didn't seem to need it. "I guess you wouldn't understand."

Sapphira folded her hands in front of her and lowered her chin. "I think I do."

Elam lifted her chin with his fingers. "That's actually a compliment, you know."

She gave a slight nod and whispered, "I know."

Turning to the side, Elam nodded toward the valley. "Besides, Elohim gave me an important assignment here. Now that you and the other girls are safe, I can do it."

"Elohim gave you an assignment? When? How?"

"When we were dancing, he sang a song, and the words keep repeating in my mind.

> O son of Shem, so brave and true,
> Come learn of love's fulfilling vow.
> The land of life calls out to you,
> The blood of Christ your refuge now.
>
> 'Tis dragons you will find and serve,
> But first take care of what you need,
> To root and sprout and grow and bloom,
> And Lazarus provides the seed.

352

"Whew!" He wiped his sleeve across his brow. "That's a lot better than the other song I kept hearing."

"You're right," Sapphira said, nodding. "You have to stay here."

Elam lowered his head. "It sure looks that way."

"And I'll stay with you." She hooked her arm around Elam's. "At least we'll have each other, and I might know the language here. After the tower fell, I had to study a long time to figure out Mardon's, so Morgan used me as a sort of translator over the years for all the new languages she came across."

"What about Paili? Who'll take care of her?"

"Acacia and the other girls are there, and I could go back and visit whenever I wanted to. It's not like I would be abandoning them."

"You can't live up here." Elam set a finger under her chin again. "I mean, look at you! With your hair and eyes, if the people are anything like what they were before, they'll think you're some kind of angel."

Sapphira touched the ends of her hair. "An angel?"

"Or a demon. Most people I knew were superstitious. They attacked anything they didn't understand, and they would never understand how someone so different can be . . ." Elam chewed on his lip and shifted his weight again.

"Can be what?"

"Can be . . . so kind . . . so thoughtful." He lowered his gaze to the ground. "So perfect."

Sapphira took Elam's hand. "As long as you're with me, I don't think I have anything to worry about."

A man's voice shouted from behind them in an odd language.

"What did he say?" Elam asked.

Sapphira whirled toward the source. "He said, 'Who's there?' "

Elam stepped in front of Sapphira. "Can you translate for me?"

"Yes. I know this language. Morgan made sure we trained especially hard for this one."

As Elam whispered to her, Sapphira spoke the translation in a loud voice. "Sir, if we are trespassing, we are very sorry and will leave immediately. Allow us to go our way in peace."

353

Lantern light flashed across Elam's eyes, and the voice calmed. "There are no trespassers in Christ's courtyard. All true seekers are welcome." The shadowy form of a man ambled down the slope, keeping one leg stiff to brace against falling. The light revealed a generous smile on his narrow, aged face.

As Sapphira quickly translated, Elam pulled her close beside him. "Hide your eyes," he whispered.

She jerked out her coif and tied it on, pushing her hair underneath and veiling her eyes.

"Two of you, eh? We can make room. Are you two married?"

Sapphira shook her head, then Elam did the same.

The man pointed at his face. "I was wondering, with the veil, you know, maybe she was a new bride. Are you brother and sister?"

Sapphira whispered the words to say. Elam tried to parrot them, but they came out skewed. "No," Elam said in the man's language. "We are just . . . together."

"Oh. . . . I see. Well, I can't say that I approve, but I guess you foreigners have different customs. You're welcome to stay the night, but I'm a Christian man, so we'll have to separate you. The girl can sleep with my wife, and you and I can push some bedding together on the front room floor. It's not the most comfortable place to sleep, but we'll be warm and dry." He extended his hand. "My name is Lazarus. What's yours?"

Elam jerked his head around to Sapphira. "I didn't understand any of that, but I thought I heard him say Lazarus."

"He did." Sapphira stepped up and curtsied. "His name is Elam, and mine is Sapphira." She nodded toward the building. "What is this place, if I may be so bold?"

Lazarus gestured toward the boards on the wall. "See the cross?" he said, pulling a smaller wooden replica from under his belt. "It's a church, dedicated to Michael."

Sapphira translated for Elam, then asked Lazarus, "Michael, the archangel?"

"Yes, indeed." The man leaned toward her and blinked his friendly old eyes. "Obviously you have heard of him in your country."

Again, she translated, then, as she readied another reply, Elam pulled off her coif. Her hair spilled to her shoulders, and she stepped back, wincing at the lantern light.

"An angel!" Lazarus dropped to one knee and bowed his head. "What do you request of your humble servant? I am ready to do your bidding."

Elam pointed at Lazarus. "Sapphira, tell him you're a special messenger called an oracle of fire, and now that you have brought me here to his church, your work is done."

Sapphira shielded her eyes with her arm. "But—"

"Tell him!" Elam ordered, stuffing the coif into her pocket.

Sapphira translated the words and lowered her arm. "What now?"

354

He pointed at Lazarus's cross. "Ask him if I can use it."

Sapphira asked.

Lazarus laid the cross in Elam's palm. "By all means!"

Elam wrapped Sapphira's fingers around the cross and covered them with his own. "Go home, now. We'll see each other again. I know we will." He helped Lazarus to his feet and stepped back, pulling him along.

Sapphira drew in her bottom lip and bit it hard. She yearned to be with Elam, but he was right. This world would never accept her. No matter how much love a precious few people showed to her, she would still be a freak of nature in the eyes of everyone else. And who was she to expect Elam to live buried in dark hopelessness, trapped in the dimension of the dead, with a bunch of plant girls, no less? He had a vision from Elohim, and she should spur him on, not drag him back.

As she gazed at Elam slowly climbing the hill with Lazarus, she looked past him and, with her sharpened vision, read a sign on the church's wall. *Jesus saith unto him, "Feed my sheep."* The riddle on the museum wall came back to her mind: *"When a maid collects an egg, she passes it on, giving it to the one she feeds."* Sliding her hand into her pocket, she felt the Ovulum, now cold and lifeless. She knew it was time to obey.

"I'll go," she called, withdrawing the Ovulum, "but . . ."

Elam pivoted and stood on a flat terrace several paces up. "But what?"

She held the Ovulum in her palm. "But only if you take this. I think you'll need it more than I will." She tossed it to him, not wanting to give him a choice. He caught it with both hands and pressed it close to his chest.

Keeping her eyes fixed on his, she raised the cross high in the air. As tears blurred her vision, she shouted, "Give me light!" The cross ignited, burning with lively yellow flames from an inch above her hand to the very top. She began to swirl it in a slow orbit.

355

Lazarus lowered himself to his knees again and lifted his hands. "May God be praised. I have seen another miracle!"

Elam nodded at Sapphira, the glow of the cross shining in his eyes. "Go on, now," he said softly. "I'll learn the language soon enough."

Swirling the cross faster, she steadied her voice and spoke as clearly as she could. "I love you, Elam, son of Shem."

Tears rolled down Elam's cheeks. "And I love you, Sapphira Adi, sparkling gem of perfection."

As the flames danced in a curtain all around her, Elam, Lazarus, the grassy slope, and the church incinerated in her sight, like a painted canvas burning from top to bottom. When the fire died away, the mining trench appeared. Competing shadows criss-crossed the dark furrow, some cast there by a column of purplish light spinning around her, the underworld exit point of the new portal. Dimmer shadows tripped around the flickers of the lantern Elam had left behind next to the corridor's new dead end—a stone wall the Ovulum had erected with its layers of crimson light, blocking Morgan's entry into the girls' home.

Sapphira tightened her grip on the smoldering cross and stepped out of the column. After picking up the lantern, she shuffled back toward the elevation platform, kicking black pebbles all along the way. Why hurry? She had all the time in the world to climb that long rope and rejoin her spawn sisters, then years and years to sit and wonder what Elam was doing up in the land of the living.

When she reached the platform, she stared at the rope and the black void above. Everything seemed so empty, so hopeless. Elam was far away up there, separated from her by much more than space. He was in a completely different dimension, probably happy now to be away from this God-forsaken hole in the ground.

She leaned against the wall and slid down to her seat, staring at the trench, the pathway back to the world above. Setting down the cross and lantern, she slid her hand into her pocket. She felt only her coif. The Ovulum was gone.

She grasped a handful of dust and threw it toward the trench. God-forsaken was right. Now everything and everyone from the living world had escaped, and they were all probably glad of it. This was a place of torture and sorrows, and those born here were destined to live here alone, separated from God forever.

Now she knew what Elam had meant. Having something and then losing it was a lot worse than never having it at all. At least now Elam could find new parents or maybe somebody else to show him love and care.

Sapphira pressed her trembling lips together. She had nothing, and what she had lost would never return.

She scrunched up her face, trying not to cry, but tears flowed anyway. Her voice quaking, she looked up at the dark, blank ceiling. "I guess you got what you wanted out of me, didn't you? You destroyed the tower, you rescued Elam, but you left me here to rot."

Lowering her head, she let her tears drip into the dust. "Why didn't you just let me be Mara, the slave girl? Why did you have to show me so many wonders of the living world, only to trap me down here again?" She rose to her knees and, balling her fists, she screamed, "Why didn't you just leave me alone?"

She fell prostrate and wept, sobbing and heaving, not caring how dirty, ugly, or ridiculous she looked. Who would ever come around to see her? Nobody cared . . . nobody.

After a few minutes, something soft touched her head. "Sapphira?"

Sapphira jerked up and stared at the female form, a girl with white hair, sparkling sapphire pupils, and a burning torch in her hand. Sapphira rubbed her eyes with her filthy knuckles. "Acacia?"

Acacia extended her hand. "Let's get you back to the museum room. There's something you have to see."

Sapphira took Acacia's hand and pulled herself to her feet. "Did you leave Paili and the others alone?" she asked, brushing the grime from her dress.

"They'll be okay. You were gone all night, so I had to look for you." Acacia nodded at the cross on the floor. "Where did you get that?"

"From the land of the living." Sapphira picked up the cross and tucked it under her belt. "I'll keep it to remind me of Elam."

Acacia leaned into the elevation shaft and looked up. "Come on. It's a long climb. We'll stop by the pool and clean up when we get to the top."

"What's going on in the museum room?" Sapphira asked.

"You have to see it to believe it." Acacia dropped her torch and pointed at it. "Lights out!" Then, picking up Sapphira's lantern, she extended her hand again. "Let's save our stories for when everyone's around."

Sapphira intertwined her fingers with Acacia's and followed her into the elevation shaft. The warmth of her touch fed her soul with comfort. At least she had one friend left in the world. She grabbed the rope and looked back at her twin. "Better put out the fire."

Acacia smiled and nodded at the lantern. "Lights out for you, too."

Now in total darkness, Sapphira pulled on the rope and inched her way up. She knew the rest of her journey would be a long, hard climb.

CHAPTER

THE TRANSFORMATION

CIRCA AD 495

Merlin climbed the rocky bed, grunting as he scaled the incline. This journey had been a lot easier the first time he attempted it, but that was at least thirty years earlier. Now the slope seemed steeper, the jagged rocks, sharper.

He set down a large, leather saddlebag and pushed his long robe out of the way, then, steadying his feet on two stable rocks, cupped his hands around his mouth. "Hail! Clefspeare!"

As he waited, his spindly shadow loomed on the face of the cliff, a phantom in the full moon's glow. Above him, another dark shape yawned as if stretching to swallow his silhouette—the entrance to a familiar cave, the home of his lifelong friend.

He cupped his hands again. "Hail! Clefspeare!"

Again, no response. He turned and looked down the rugged slope. The king stood on a smoother path below, somewhat over-dressed in his fine riding attire, now coated with dirt and sweat.

"Come, Your Majesty," Merlin said, holding out his hand. "I can support you."

The king, using both hands to steady himself, climbed the rocky embankment, and as soon as he approached Merlin, he grasped the outstretched hand and pulled himself the rest of the way. "Master Merlin," the king said, "your strength amazes me."

"I have climbed many hills in my time," Merlin replied.

Arthur gazed down the slope. "I'm not comfortable with this ruse. Devin is nowhere in sight."

"He will come," Merlin said, following Arthur's gaze. The moonlight revealed scraggly trees and an empty path far below, but little else. "We don't want him here too early. As long as he stays away from Bald Top, the plan will work."

"I respect your courage and wisdom, Master Merlin, but would you have me march right into the dragon's mouth? How can I be sure that he has forgiven my rash decisions?"

"You have to trust me. In spite of that trumped-up story about Andrew, you must believe that Clefspeare is not a danger to us." Merlin hoisted his bag and continued the climb for a few more yards before stopping to wait again. When the king joined him, the two proceeded on level ground, Merlin again leading the way. After passing a few bare, stunted trees, the travelers faced the entrance of the cave. A gentle breeze blew from within, and then, seconds later, the breeze reversed, and the cave drew the air past their bodies.

"The cave breathes," the king said, his mustache twitching, "but I smell no rotting flesh."

"Nor will you." Merlin filled his lungs and bellowed once again. "Hail! Clefspeare! It is I, Merlin, Prophet of the Most High. With me is His Majesty, King Arthur."

Again he waited but received no response. Merlin squatted, picked up a pebble, and tossed it down the slope. "He must be in regeneracy."

"Regeneracy?" The king stooped next to Merlin and peered into the shadows. "What is regeneracy?"

"You will see." Merlin rose and walked straight into the darkness. As his eyes adjusted, he looked back. The king had fallen behind. "We must hurry," Merlin warned. "The others will be assembling very soon."

The king quickened his pace and caught up. "The others?"

"I will explain soon enough." A strange glow from deeper in the cave illumined the path, dimly at first, but ever more brightly as he proceeded. They passed together under a high archway and into an interior chamber. In the very center, a shimmering, inverted funnel of pure light pointed toward the cave's ceiling, its circular base resting a few inches from the rocky floor.

Within the swirl, a dazzling array of flashing glitters flew like buzzing bees from one side to the other, bouncing and dancing until they struck the huge, heaving body at the center.

The king drew closer. "Master Merlin, am I beholding a holy sight or an accursed demon? I don't know whether to bare my head and feet in reverence or pluck out my eyes in shame."

361

Merlin placed a strong hand on the king's shoulder. "Perhaps you should save your artful speech for your diplomatic meetings. It isn't necessary in the company of dragons." He waved his hand at the cone. "This light is neither accursed nor holy; it's a natural process called regeneracy. This is how a dragon prefers to sleep. You see, a dragon's scales and eyes breathe the light as you and I breathe the air. He absorbs energy and expels the light he doesn't need. If a dragon were subjected to darkness for a long period of time, he would be overcome by weakness. Without at least a candle to feed his body, he would eventually die."

Merlin set his bag down, approached the glowing dragon, and stretched out his hands over the cone. "At night he rests on a bed of silver and gold, and the power of the day flows into his bed. The energy grows into a shroud of luminescence around his body, and he reabsorbs the light as it passes over his scales." He pointed at the base of the dragon's bed and moved his finger around as if stirring.

"Intermixed in the precious metal pieces are polished gems. They reflect the light, making it rebound within the shroud, so that more of the light strikes his body."

The king took a step closer. "You say that he is asleep?"

Clefspeare snorted and stretched out his leg. The king placed his hand on the hilt of his sword, but Merlin jumped back and grasped Arthur's forearm. "You have nothing to fear, but if you think or act aggressively, he is likely to sense danger."

Arthur returned the grasp but kept watching the dragon. "When will he awaken?"

"That's unpredictable. I don't understand the process completely, but the light eventually fades, and the dragon awakes."

"Is he vulnerable to attack while he sleeps?"

"Not likely. Many have come upon dragons in their lairs, but a dragon can sense danger and always awakens. Since I am his friend, and you have come as his new, albeit suspicious ally, Clefspeare senses none. But I must awaken him now."

Merlin unfastened a string from around his neck and used it to pull a strangely shaped object from beneath his vest, a pendant stone dangling at the end of the string, small enough for his fingers to fully envelop.

"This is a candlestone, a kind of anti-prism," he explained. "You see, a normal prism bends light and splits the colors. This stone does the opposite. It arrests fractured light and straightens it out. The light passes into it as excited energy and is dispelled as a simple beam. If I place it at the base of Clefspeare's shroud, it will interrupt the circuit and disperse his shield. It also interrupts a dragon's photo-respiration, and therefore his energy flow. It can actually absorb light, and with it the life force of his body."

"Then could it be used as a weapon against dragons?"

"Most definitely. I wear it around my neck for defense against the evil, fallen dragons. One of my ancestors found it in Shinar after the destruction of Nimrod's tower, and it was passed down to me through the centuries. I believe I am the only one alive who knows how to use it, but after today it will matter no more."

Merlin placed the stone on the ground and slid it into the base of the shroud. Instantly the dancing light radiated toward the candlestone, and a brilliant, steady beam poured forth from its opposite side. The shroud vanished, and the candlestone glowed with an eerie, flat light.

After a few seconds, the sleeping dragon stirred. With a great stretch and a mighty yawn, Clefspeare rose to his haunches, his enormous tail acting as a balance. Smoke and sparks belched from his open mouth. The king drew back and once again gripped the hilt of his sword.

Clefspeare spied his two visitors. His deep gravelly voice erupted. "Master Merlin! I have been expecting you, though I did not expect to see the Sovereign." Clefspeare gave him a clumsy bow and nearly fell on his face, but with a flap of his wings, he righted himself. "Master Merlin, would you be so kind as to remove that accursed stone from my sight before I become violently ill?"

Merlin picked up the candlestone and covered it with both hands. "Are you sure the stone made you lose your balance, or are you still overcome by sleep?"

"I assure you that my eyes are clear. I recognized the king, did I not? Now please put that wicked jewel under a pile of rocks. Covering it with your hands does little to blunt its evil effects."

Merlin walked to the cave's edge, guided by a dim, flickering light. He found a flat rock and placed the candlestone underneath.

With a great snuff from his nostrils, Clefspeare blew a stream of flame at an iron stand on the wall, igniting a rag-topped torch. "Aaah! Now we have better light." He looked back at Arthur and this time merely bowed his head. "Your Majesty, welcome to my humble abode."

King Arthur bowed in return, much more gracefully than did the dragon, but his voice carried a slight tremble. "After fighting alongside you in the heat of battle, I am honored to visit the home of the greatest of the dragon warriors."

Clefspeare nodded again. "Your words are overstated, yet still treasured."

"How long has it been since the battle?" the king asked. "Three years?"

"Three years and six months, to be precise. Forty-two months of fleeing Devin and his band of slayers."

Arthur drooped his head. "Yes, it took quite some time for Merlin to convince me of the truth. My apologies seem shallow in the wake of so many dead dragons."

"Heartfelt apologies are always deep, and perhaps yours are not too late." Clefspeare turned to Merlin. "Am I to understand that your presence signals the coming transformation?"

"Yes, Clefspeare."

"How many are assembling?"

Merlin shook his head. "I'm not sure. The slayers have been busy, so very few of you remain, I'm afraid. Hartanna is gathering the dragons who still honor the memory of Makaidos."

Clefspeare let out a long, spark-filled sigh. "The corrupted ones have been our downfall, Merlin, as you prophesied. A fallen dragon is the most detestable beast on Earth."

"And who can know," Merlin added, "whether corruption hides in the hearts of the remnant? Hartanna is wise, but she cannot always detect the seeds of darkness that spread evil shadows within. She has examined them to the best of her ability, but even a dragon's senses can be fooled."

"True enough." Clefspeare blinked at Arthur. "And the king? What is his role?"

"We will need his help after we are finished. I can trust no other."

"But will the other dragons trust the one who commissioned the slayers to eliminate our race?" Clefspeare turned on his eyebeams and aimed them at the king. "We know of his deeds, and we have seen his valor in battle, but how can we know his heart?"

King Arthur strode boldly forward and stood directly in front of Clefspeare. "How else can a man's heart be known, or even a dragon's, if not by his deeds? To me, you look very much like the dragon that murdered my brother and sister right outside the very walls of Camelot, the beast which Sir Devin slew only last week. Against my earlier judgments, I was persuaded by the wise prophet to come to your lair in order to help the race that stole the lives of my beloved siblings. He has recounted your many deeds, deeds that have been explained away by your enemies as mere selfish desire for treasure. I learned why you accept the gifts of the wealthy after you do your mighty works. I also know of the appearance of these treasures in the homes of the poor, ben-efiting widows and orphans who now have good food on their tables and warm clothes on their backs. Your deeds have set you and your friends apart from the evil dragons, Clefspeare, and I have come to grant Merlin's request and aid you in your time of need."

Clefspeare bowed once again, this time with more agility. "Well spoken, wise king. I was wrong to dwell on your past mis-takes. Forgive me for not accepting your earlier apologies."

Arthur returned the bow. "All accounts are now clear between us, good dragon."

Merlin picked up his bag, threw it over his shoulder, and placed a hand on Clefspeare's flank. "I have summoned all the remaining noble dragons to Bald Top. Come, now. We must fly to the meeting place."

"Master Merlin!" Clefspeare's beams shifted toward the cave entrance. "You and the king must climb on my back. Make haste. I smell danger."

Merlin squinted at him. "You will allow the king to ride?"

"No time to argue!" Clefspeare growled.

Merlin reached for the torch and stamped it out, then, with the scales' luminescent glow guiding their way, he and Arthur scrambled up the dragon's scaly flank, stepped to his spiny middle ridge, and seated themselves at the base of his neck.

Merlin held on with one hand while gripping his saddlebag with the other. "Do slayers approach?"

"Most likely." Clefspeare straightened his tail. "Heads down and hold on!"

"Wait!" Merlin shouted. "The candlestone!"

"No time! And I will not fly if you carry that cursed dragon's bane!"

With a great flap of his wings, Clefspeare rose from the ground and hovered in the midst of the cave. After taking in a deep breath, he blew out a raging river of fire. Then, slowly at first and still breathing fire, he moved forward into the stream, floating easily on the cushion of flaming air. As they passed through the tunnel, accelerating as they traveled, Merlin peered through the passing inferno. Flames bounced in all directions, and two shadows dove for cover in the rocks. Within seconds, Clefspeare burst into the open and launched into the clear, night sky.

Arthur gripped Clefspeare's spine with both hands. "Amazing!"

"Hang on!" Merlin called. "We have to get higher than their arrows can reach."

When their angle of ascent tapered off and they reached a safe altitude, Clefspeare snorted a final puff of smoke. "I apologize, Your Highness, for the rough ride."

The king took a deep breath in the cold, thin air. "It was exhilarating! A masterful escape!"

"Could you tell if Sir Devin was among the attackers?" Merlin asked.

Arthur shook his head. "I saw only shadows."

"I saw him," Clefspeare said. "His lust for my blood is stronger than ever."

Merlin looked out over the scene far below, a shifting gray canvas with firelight speckling the shadows cast by the ghostly moon. "The drug I slipped into Devin's mead wasn't timed as well as I had hoped, but at least he will be far from Bald Top while we take the next step in my plan."

The light of two flashing torches filled the cave, and a pair of shifting shadows crawled along the walls. With every step of the dark images, an echoing clop replied, but there was more silence than echo. The wary travelers made their way ever so slowly toward the center of the main chamber.

"There is no hint of fresh kill to guide us," Sir Devin said.

Palin sniffed the air. "No, my liege. In fact, the air is very clean, but I am sure his bed must be right in front of us. I see flashes of light."

Palin stooped over a pile of gems and swung a pair of saddlebags to the ground. "All is not lost. We have the treasure."

Devin knelt and scooped up a handful of glittering stones. "It is much smaller than Goliath's." He grinned at Palin. "May his dragon soul rest in peace."

Palin opened the saddlebags. "It was so kind of him to designate us as heirs to his fortune."

Devin let the gems spill back to the ground. "Split it up in my presence and reserve the proper portions for God and for the king."

"Of course, my liege." Palin deposited the stones into the saddlebags piece by piece, cycling through the bags to make an even disbursement. "You are most gracious to give equal shares to us all, even though the others wait outside in fear."

Devin held his torch close to the ground and surveyed the cave floor. "What does the census say now?"

The squire pulled a scrap of parchment from his tunic and studied it for a moment before looking up again. "After your

367

valiant conquest of Maven last week, and your extraordinary slaying of Goliath this morning, I know of only ten remaining. The Demon Witch, Hartanna, is next. She will pay for wounding you."

"All in good time, my friend." He stalked across the floor, kicking the pebbles in front of him. "By our count, only ten of the devils are left, and now that the king knows of Merlin's conspiracy with them, I shall have the old wizard's head by noon tomorrow."

"What if Morgan is right? What will you do if the king betrays you and sides with Merlin?"

"Then we will proceed with Morgan's rebellion plan. I don't like the idea of the unusual marriage arrangement she proposed, but having that kind of power would be worth putting up with her." After sweeping more rocks to the side, Devin stopped suddenly and stooped close to a flat rock near the wall. "Palin, what is this?"

"Where, my liege?"

"This glowing pebble." Devin picked up the stone by its attached string. As the surrounding light grew dim, he drew the stone closer to his face.

"Our torches are going out," Palin said.

"No. The flame lives; only the light dies. It is drawn to this gem."

Devin closed his hand over the stone. Instantly, the light from the flames scattered throughout the cave. "I have heard legends about such a gem, but why would it be here, in a dragon's lair?"

"What have you heard about it?"

"An ancestor of mine told a story of Nimrod, the king of Shinar, and how he used a light-absorbing gem as a weapon against dragons."

"A weapon? How?"

Devin slipped the gem into his vest. "I'm not sure, but I intend to find out."

Clefspeare circled over Bald Top, casting a shadow over a pod of dragons milling about on the summit. As the dragon flew lower, Merlin gestured toward the rear. "Your Majesty, prepare to slide down. Remember, find the clearing and watch the proceedings from the woods. The dragons will not sense you because you pose no danger, but until all is complete, it is best if you stay in hiding."

The king nodded. "Agreed."

"He's slowing down over a clear spot. Go!"

Arthur slid across the scaly hindquarters, then dropped and rolled in the soft turf. Clefspeare rose over the tree-filled mountain and hurried toward the summit's clearing.

Before descending, Merlin caught a glimpse of Arthur hiding behind a tree a few yards inside the edge of the woods, far enough away to stay out of sight, yet close enough to see the dragons and hear their booming voices.

As Clefspeare settled to the ground, he beat his wings rapidly and lowered his head. Still carrying his bag, Merlin descended the ridges and jumped to the grass. After letting the bag drop, he counted the dragons in attendance, three males, reddish and standing tall, and nine females, smaller and tawny in color.

One of the females stepped forward. "Master Merlin, all are present, as you requested."

Merlin bowed. "Thank you, Hartanna. You have been a great help. And are all in agreement?"

"Yes. We have discussed the final preparations, and we are ready." Hartanna shifted her body toward Clefspeare. "Has Master Merlin prepared you?"

Clefspeare bowed his head. "Yes, Hartanna. Diving into the human condition is an adventure that none of us covets, but we dragons do what we must do."

"Well said." Hartanna touched Merlin's shoulder with the tip of her wing. "We await your instructions."

369

From his deep pocket, Merlin pulled out a skin flask and placed it in the middle of the semicircle of dragons. Then, standing in front of the solemn assembly, he called out, "The flask contains only wine, but those who drink it in faith will receive what God has promised. All who have their hearts prepared will be transformed, and when the fullness of the time has come, you will be restored to your desired state. The slayers will eventually die out. Once they believe that dragons have become extinct, they will no longer train to battle your kind, and the poisoned hunger for dragon killing will cease to exist. When you return, there will be no fallen dragons to make the people fear you again."

Hartanna stepped forward. "Then let us proceed. I volunteer to go first."

"No one will change until all have tasted," Merlin warned. "Otherwise, faith would be made sight before its time."

Merlin picked up the wineskin and lifted it toward the sky. "Heavenly Father, King of the Universe, bless this wine. Fill it now with the seed of Adam so that these will bear his likeness, both in his glory as the image of God and in his shame as reflections of a fallen race. They understand that the benefit of your presence will depart from them as they share in the human curse. They also understand that should they fall after the likeness of Adam's sin, they must find their salvation through the Light of the World."

Extending the flask in front, Merlin walked toward the line of dragons. Hartanna lowered her head and opened her great mouth. Merlin raised the opening of the skin over her teeth and tipped it forward. At first it came out too quickly, spilling a bit over her jaws, but he pulled back before he lost too much.

Hartanna lifted her head and swallowed with a loud gulp. "Be brave, my friends. The wine goes down without harm."

One by one, Merlin gave the drink to the dragons. A few seemed tentative, but they took it without much hesitation. When

370

he came to Clefspeare, the last in line, the great red dragon bowed his head. "I look forward to shaking your hand."

Merlin bowed in return. "And I, yours."

Clefspeare followed the ritual, and after he swallowed, the twelve waited in silence. For the first torturous minute, nothing happened. Merlin took a seat on the ground, while the dragons gathered in a circle.

Several more minutes passed. A few dragons lowered their hefty bodies to the cool grass. Hartanna and Thigocia whispered to one another while Valcor and Legossi tested their wings. Merlin crossed his legs and bowed his head in prayer.

After what seemed to be an hour, one of the dragons broke the silence. "He's a fraud!"

Merlin looked up. A male dragon backed away from the rest of the council, his head low.

Hartanna beat her wings against the ground. "What did you say?"

"He's a fraud! Merlin has made fools of us all. There was a second man riding on Clefspeare's back. I saw him. He must be a slayer, and he will bring the others while we wait for this traitor's potion to fail."

Hartanna roared. "Silence, Gartrand! Will you destroy the faith of the others with your own infidelity?"

"This is not faith," Gartrand said, thumping his tail. "I, too, want to survive. Who ever wants to die? But we have stepped into the humans' trap. Let us kill this evil sorcerer and fly away to safety."

Gartrand lunged toward Merlin. In a flash of wings and glistening red scales, Clefspeare blocked Gartrand's path, but when he opened his mouth to attack, only hot air spewed forth. He turned, as if trying to slash his foe with his tail, but when he swung, the tail shriveled and vanished.

Edging backwards, Gartrand trembled. "This must be one of Merlin's tricks. The rest of us are still in dragon form."

Clefspeare's scales melted into smooth skin, his claws reshaped into fingers and nails, and his giant mouth shrank into the jaw and lips of a human male. Gartrand let out a piercing scream and took to the skies, still completely in dragon form.

Clefspeare pressed his hands together and interlocked his fingers. Hartanna shuffled toward him, and as she moved, her spiny top transformed into long, silky blonde tresses and her scales smoothed into milky white skin. Soon, the other dragons began the meta-morphosis, and within minutes, all eleven had the appearance of fully mature adults, perhaps in their early to late thirties. When the process was complete, they gathered together in excited laughter.

Merlin rose to his feet and carried his leather bag to the hud-dle. He pulled out bundles of clothing—dresses, shirts, and breeches—and tossed them to the ground. "Get dressed," he said, in a matter-of-fact tone. "You are naked, and the king is watching."

"Oh! Yes, of course!" Hartanna picked up one of the dresses and smiled. "Come everyone! Here is another new experience. Clothes!"

The former dragons picked through the garments, offering pieces to one another and helping each other figure out how the fasteners worked. Soon, all were dressed in the garb of middle-income commoners.

While Thigocia buttoned the back of Hartanna's dress, she peered at Merlin over her daughter's shoulder. "Master Merlin, what of Gartrand? Surely this was unexpected."

Merlin dropped his bag to the grass. "Unexpected, indeed, and unfortunate."

Thigocia fastened the last button. "How so?"

"He may be the only dragon left in the world. He will feel abandoned, frightened. He will not take the usual care, so Sir Devin will have no trouble finding him. Gartrand is extremely vul-nerable, and since he knows what has happened, all of you are vul-nerable as well."

372

"What shall we do?" Hartanna asked.

"While I was in prayer, the Lord spoke to me. His purpose remains unchanged, but with the departure of the traitor, God will accomplish what he has set out to do in another way."

"Traitor?" Clefspeare tied a leather belt around his waist. "Will Gartrand betray us?"

"Yes, but only at the point of a sword. Devin will extract the information he needs by force."

"Then the slayers will pursue us always," Hartanna concluded.

"I fear you are correct. They will continue to sharpen their swords, and the scent of your blood will never leave their nostrils."

Arthur walked out of the woods and approached the gathering. "Hail, great council," he said, bowing. "I salute you who were once clothed in the majesty of your race. As long as I live, I will protect you. I cannot take the slayer's thirst for your blood out of his soul, but I can deprive him of the means to pursue his quest."

Hartanna curtsied, clumsily at first, but with her second effort, as gracefully as any princess. "I trust that you will prove your promises, my king." She touched Merlin's elbow. "Master Merlin, if the slayers are unable to destroy us in their lifetimes, they will surely teach their bloodlust to their descendants. How, then, will we ever become dragons again?"

Merlin took her hand. "Hartanna, it's possible that some of you will never be dragons again."

A rumble of murmurs sounded from the gathering. Hartanna waited for the noise to subside, then clasped Merlin's hand firmly in both of hers and gazed into his eyes. "How will our race survive? How long shall we live? Shall we procreate? And if we do, what kind of creature shall we beget?"

Merlin signaled for all the dragons to come close, and when they were within a whisper's distance, he looked around at the circle of concerned eyes. "You will not be able to procreate with each other," he said softly, "but you will live long on the earth. I know of no dragon who has ever died of natural causes, but death is part of Adam's curse. I cannot say how you will be affected."

"No progeny?" Hartanna said. "Then all is lost?"

Merlin shook his head. "No, Hartanna. All is not lost. Listen to a new prophecy." He lifted his hands toward the sky and began to sing, his voice low and sweet.

> When hybrid meets the fallen seed
> The virgin seedling flies;
> An orphaned waif shall call to me
> When blossom meets the skies.
>
> The child of doubt will find his rest
> And meet his virgin bride;
> A dragon shorn will live again
> Rejecting Eden's pride.
>
> A slayer comes and with his host
> He fights the last of thee,
> But faith alone shall win the war
> The test of those set free.
>
> A king shall rise of Arthur's mold,
> The prophet's book in hand;
> He takes the sword from mountain stone
> To rescue captive bands.

374

Merlin lowered his hands. During his song, the former dragons had settled to their seats, and now they waited in silence. After a minute or two, Hartanna gazed up at Merlin. "What does it mean?"

"I don't know, dear lady, but I think the passing of time will disclose every secret." He sighed and kicked his nearly empty saddlebag. "Now that we have to go to Camelot on foot, there is no need to carry unnecessary baggage." He bowed to Arthur. "Are you ready for another adventure, my king?"

Arthur bowed in return. "Lead the way. I will guard the rear."

Merlin headed for the woods, marching with Clefspeare on one side and Valcor on the other. "Because of Gartrand's treachery," Merlin said, "I must take an extraordinary step in order to oversee the salvation of the dragons. Soon, I will have to depart for a very long time."

"Where will you go?" Valcor asked.

"I only know that somehow I will guide the paths of those God has chosen to fulfill his prophecy." When they entered the forest and began descending the slope, Merlin grabbed a sturdy stick and leaned on it with every second step. "While we are awaiting my departure, the two of you must prepare. Clefspeare, in order to help me preserve the king's life and rule, I will ask him to make you a member of his court and family. Valcor, you must go into hiding, in case Devin figures out who Clefspeare really is. A male dragon must be preserved at all costs."

375

"Into hiding?" Valcor asked. "Where?"

"Do you know where Blood Hollow is?"

Valcor pointed westward. "The glen in Bowman's Forest."

"Exactly. Meet me there at midnight at the next full moon, and I will show you a place you can stay. I don't want to mention your hideaway now, because it would be best if Clefspeare doesn't know where you are."

Valcor nodded. "I understand."

"I will arrive at Blood Hollow with the king," Merlin continued. "There is something I must show you and Arthur before I go on my journey."

"I trust that you will return soon," Clefspeare said. "We have few friends besides you."

Merlin handed his walking stick to Clefspeare, then draped an arm around each former dragon. "Don't worry. I will eventually return . . . in one form or another. The dragons will not be left without a friend."

CHAPTER

DRAGONS' REST

As the king paced in front of the throne, Merlin's cheeks burned, but he kept his voice in check. "A day will come," Merlin said, "when Morgan will pay for all her sins. I didn't expose her identity to you at first, because I had hoped that she could be redeemed. I even told her about finding a hostiam, her only path to salvation, and how did she repay my kindness?" He paused, swallowing to control his emotions. "She poisoned my wife with her devilish fruit!"

The king stroked his chin and strolled in a slow circle around Merlin. "Has it already been three years since that tragedy? I remember very little from my days under Morgan's spell."

Merlin took a deep breath. "Yes, it has been a very long three years to me. I sent my son and his wife into hiding to protect them, so I am alone during the dark, quiet hours."

"I can't imagine the torture," the king said, pausing to lay a hand on Merlin's shoulder, "but why do you bring it up now?"

"Because of what I must show you tonight. You see, Morgan's food robs both life and soul. The meat and meal of devils chokes

377

out life and empties the soul of its vitality. And now I've learned that my wife wanders in the so-called Dragons' Rest, like one of the dragon spirits without a heaven for a true resting place . . . or a hell to reap the bad seed they have sown."

The king peered from under his downturned brow. "Dragons' Rest?"

Merlin sighed. "So much to tell you and so little time." He stood slowly, bracing his back as he straightened, and strode toward the corner of the chamber. "Come with me on a short journey. It has been one lunar month since the transformation of the dragons, and the time has come to begin the next step in my plan."

He pushed on a panel at the back of the throne room, opening a door that blended perfectly with the surrounding wall. The two ducked under the low doorframe and stepped cautiously on a craggy stone floor. Only a tapered shaft of light from the chamber illuminated the room, revealing a narrow passage under a low ceiling. A musty odor filled the corridor, a reminder of abandonment—melancholy, but not unpleasant.

After lifting an unlit torch from a metal wall bracket, Merlin closed the door, shutting out the light from the throne room. His voice echoed in the darkness. "Your Majesty. If you please."

A glowing sword suddenly appeared, Excalibur shedding its royal glow, its hilt firmly grasped in the king's hands. Merlin set the end of the torch against the blade and whispered, *"Eshsha."* First as a tiny spark, then spreading across the torch's fiber and fuel, a flame came to life.

The two tramped down a slippery stone slope for several hundred yards before leveling off and beginning a climb back to the surface. The ceiling and floor drew closer together until both king and prophet had to stoop to continue. By the time they finally reached a dead end, they crouched on their haunches.

Merlin handed the torch to the king. With both palms flat on the low ceiling, he pushed up on a wooden panel and placed it on the ground outside. Pressing his hands on each side of the opening, he lifted himself out of the tunnel and stretched.

The king followed, his sword still in hand. Merlin put the hatch back in place and covered it with dirt and leaves. "I tamped out the torch," the king said. "We can use it again on our return."

The full moon's glow framed a dark forest, shedding light on phantasmic oaks that stretched out their branches as if to snatch up unwelcome wanderers. Merlin nodded toward a thin line of dirt that weaved a narrow path through the darkest part of the forest. He took a deep breath, his chest rattling slightly. "This way."

As the two stole through the woods, Excalibur's light leading the way, Merlin whispered, "Remember this path. It is the way to Blood Hollow, a place Devin likely doesn't know. It is also a meeting place I have designated for one of the former dragons, one with whom I have recently gained a close bond."

They waded across a knee-deep stream, then followed a deer path, descending once again through thick brush until they came out into a clearing, an elliptical, rocky space that resembled a miniature amphitheatre.

Merlin stood at the center, lifted his head, and whistled a nightingale's call. He then stooped and signaled for Arthur to join him. "The stench of discord taints the wind," Merlin said. "I believe Devin will soon launch a rebellion, and in order to quell the uprising, I will conduct my greatest, and my last, experiment." He bent close to the king. "Valcor will be here momentarily. When he comes, you will learn a secret about dragons even the dragons themselves do not know."

Bushes rustled. King Arthur rose to his feet, Excalibur at the ready. A man emerged from the darkness with his hands raised. "I am Valcor, unarmed and at His Majesty's service." He bowed low.

The king returned the sword to its sheath and touched the man's head. "Arise, Valcor. I have not forgotten you so soon. You seem more fit than ever."

"Enabling me to serve you with more vigor, my king."

Merlin laid his hand on Valcor's shoulder. "You have learned diplomacy well, my friend."

"Not recently, good prophet. Makaidos instructed his offspring in the protocol of human royalty long ago."

"I shouldn't be surprised." Merlin waved his hand across the depressed clearing. "I have chosen this place because the dividing wall between this world and the world to come is as thin as papyrus. Here, creating a portal to that world requires only the paltriest skill."

Merlin knelt and placed a gem at the lowest point of the depression. Its crimson glow pulsed, like a dragon opening and closing its eye. "This rubellite belonged to Makaidos. As you know, the gem itself represents the essence of a dragon's soul, beautiful in form, as is the dragon, yet scarlet, the color of the unredeemed. What you may not know is that when a dragon takes the stone as his own, his soul becomes tied to it, and it transforms into his gateway to the dragon afterlife, a place where humans are not meant to go.

"If a dragon has one, as long as there is the slightest glimmer of a dragon's soul remaining, his chosen rubellite will be red, and when he passes through the gateway into Dragons' Rest, the gem becomes a pulsing beacon, indicating his presence there."

Merlin laid his hand on the rubellite, capping its glow for a moment. Then, as he raised his hand, the glow seemed to follow underneath, growing into a vertical column, a rising scarlet pedestal that finally stopped when it reached the prophet's height. Merlin drew an oval around the pedestal with his finger, and the glow seemed to bleed in all directions, filling up the frame he had drawn until it formed a scarlet ellipse.

He backed away and joined the king and Valcor as they gaped in silence. He waved his hand at the flaming halo and spoke in a resonant tone.

O make the passage clear to men
Who wish to see the gate,
The path no dragon deigns to cross,
For death is not their fate.

From top to bottom, the halo's red hue faded to pink, then to white. A straw-laden path took shape, and as people crossed from one side of the road to the other, they trampled the straw into a maze of muddy footprints. The scene appeared to be a marketplace. Two young women stood in front of a hut, displaying their handmade wares on the tops of wooden tables; a burly man carried a pole with a deer carcass hanging by its hooves; and a matronly woman bore a fruit basket in each of her meaty arms.

Merlin took two quick steps forward. "There!" He pointed near the top of the ellipse. "See the woman standing next to the nobleman? The one carrying the scrolls?"

The king leaned closer. "The gray-haired lady handing him a scroll right now?"

"Yes! Yes! She's the one!"

The king stroked his chin. "She is familiar to me, Merlin. Very familiar."

"She should be. She's my wife."

"Your wife? So are we looking upon Dragons' Rest?"

Merlin's fingers hovered over the image of his wife, caressing her face from afar.

"Merlin?" The king shook the prophet's arm. "Is that Dragons' Rest?"

Merlin tore himself out of his trance and stepped back from the oval. "Yes." He took a deep breath, now keeping his gaze on the king. "As I told you, Morgan's food not only kills the body, it drains vitality from the human soul, and this dungeon is reserved for the dead who enter into eternity without a vibrant, human

381

soul. Now my wife languishes in that hopeless village, not knowing who she really is or why she is there."

The ellipse suddenly shifted to gray, then black. Darkness seeped out of the oval like a night fog. Billowing smoke crawled along the ground and rose into a column, slowly solidifying into a human form, slender and feminine—the shape of Morgan Le Faye.

King Arthur drew his sword, but Merlin raised his hand. "Not here," Merlin said. "Not now. She has yet to fulfill her purpose."

Morgan, dressed in her usual silky black gown, waltzed up to Merlin, laughing. "I saw you mooning over the gateway. Do you miss your sweet wife, my old friend?"

Merlin clenched his fists. Serrated words slipped through his grinding teeth. "Leave it to you to attack a man by killing his defenseless wife."

"Oh, but Merlin," she crooned, "there is no more effective tool. Taking a man's woman is the same as ripping out his heart and pouring his life's blood on the ground." She patted his cheek, pursing her lips as though speaking to a child. "And watching you wither over the past three years has been such a joy. It seems that checkmate is at hand." She turned and gave the king a mock curtsy. "Your Majesty. It is an honor to see my brother again."

King Arthur drew back his sword. A brilliant ray erupted from its tip and shot into the sky. "Merlin, step aside, and I will slay this foul witch where she stands."

Merlin stayed put. "She is a wraith, more dead than alive. In your hands, the sword would do nothing more than reveal her nature. Killing her requires much more."

The king shoved Merlin aside. With a wild swipe, he sliced through Morgan's waist. Her body absorbed the sword's light, and her face transformed. A sultry, painted mask melted, replaced by a bloody raven's head, its red eyes aflame and its mouth locked open in a raging scream.

382

Arthur fell to his seat, and the sword's light died away. Valcor rushed to his side and slid his hand behind the king's shoulder. Morgan returned to her female form and glowered at the king. "You are all such fools. Knowing about my strategy will not protect your wives now or in the future. All who oppose me will feel my wrath, and no loved one is safe—man, woman, or child."

Morgan sublimated to black fog and disappeared into the ellipse. Seconds later, the portal cleared to a pulsing red glow.

King Arthur jumped to his feet. "That sorceress from hell will not kill my queen." With the sword lighting the way, he sprinted down the narrow path.

"Your Majesty!" Merlin called. "What of my plan?"

Arthur halted and spun around. "You have proven your words once again. Bring Clefspeare and Hartanna to me. I will adopt them, as you requested."

Timothy brushed on a final stroke of paint and read the sign out loud. "Brogan's Flowers," he said proudly. He turned and addressed the young man standing next to him. "What do you think?"

"I think my mother will run the shop," Brogan said, his Celtic accent breezing through his words, "but it will do. Still, I am not accustomed to my new name. After being Hilidan for so long, Brogan seems foreign to me."

Timothy laughed and set the sign on a wagon. "I understand. We had our dragon names even before the great flood." As he wiped his hands on a paint cloth, he gazed at the new huts that lined the straw-laden path. Two young women bustled around their pottery table, setting out their wares for trading. A matronly woman carrying a fruit basket ambled across a walkway that passed through a garden in the middle of the village square. She smiled and tossed a yellow apple toward the two men.

383

Catching the apple with one hand, Timothy returned her smile. "I think the marketplace is complete. With all the new arrivals, we will have a thriving community in no time."

"Jasmine is coming," Brogan said, nodding at the path. "Does your daughter ever smile about anything?"

"I heard you," Jasmine's sharp voice rang out. "How can I smile? New arrivals can only mean that more dragons are being murdered by humans."

Timothy took a bite out of his apple. "Are they reporting details?"

"Only sketchy stories," Jasmine replied, her tone calming. "They are quickly forgetting their dragon past, just as you hoped they would. They do know that Devin has committed most of the murders, and one reported that Goliath has also been killed."

"Goliath?" Timothy nearly choked as he swallowed his mouthful. "Dead?"

As Jasmine lowered her gaze, her voice dropped to a whisper. "Yes. He should have been here by now."

Timothy rubbed her back gently. "Perhaps he is here and has forgotten who he was."

Jasmine stepped away from his caress. "I have matched every citizen with the name of a dragon, and neither Goliath nor Arramos is here. With the exception of one woman, all the arrivals knew who they were, though they forget everything quickly. It seems that the three of us are the only ones who still remember most of our past."

"I am beginning to forget, too," Brogan said. "I barely remember what it was like to fly."

"I will never forget being a dragon." Jasmine crossed her arms tightly. "I refuse to forget."

Timothy pointed at her. "Remember if you must, but do not torture the others. It would be better for them to live at peace here."

"On that issue, I do agree." She breathed a long sigh. "In fact, I will encourage them to forget, but at least one of us has to keep the memory of our species alive."

Timothy held up his hand, displaying his pulsing rubellite ring. "These rings are surely a sign that the Maker has not forgotten who we are. Horses and other animals have appeared out of nowhere, as did a crop ready for harvest. God knows we are here, and he will not abandon us forever."

Jasmine rubbed her ring's gem. "That woman I mentioned doesn't have one. She also has white hair, so I thought she might be an underborn."

"Many humans have white hair," Timothy said, "especially the older ones."

"She is older, to be sure, and she is also very intelligent, though she remembers very little of her past. I put her in charge of archiving scrolls until I had an opportunity to ask you about her." Jasmine nodded at the path. "Here she comes now."

An elderly woman with a sweet smile extended a scroll to Timothy. "Here is the harvest inventory, Captain Autarkeia."

"Captain?" Timothy laughed. "Am I now a Captain?"

"My designation for you as king of the dragons and founder of this town," Jasmine explained. "I am establishing a hierarchy using a military system. I thought it best to maintain an orderly governing body."

"I see." Timothy bowed his head toward the newcomer. "What is your name?"

"Sarah." She dipped her knee. "Pleased to meet you."

Timothy leaned over and studied her face. "We have met before, have we not?"

Sarah rearranged the stack of scrolls in her arms and smiled again. "Not that I can remember, Captain."

"I know we have," Timothy said, tapping his forehead, "but memory loss seems to be affecting me."

A popping sound made Timothy pivot. A red glow, an elliptical aura, much like the one created by the Ovulum, arose from the garden in the town's central circle. Bordered by the only two idols remaining from Shinar's ruins, it vibrated a tune as if strummed by a skillful hand. Entranced, Timothy walked slowly toward it.

"Where are you going?" Jasmine called.

Timothy pointed. "To the red glow."

"What red glow?"

He stopped at the edge of the garden and spread out his arms. "Right here. Right in front of me."

Brogan ran up to his side and whispered, "Timothy, perhaps you have been working too hard. There is nothing here but tulips and daffodils."

Timothy pointed again. "Look! I see Merlin on the other side. And there is King Arthur. I also see a third man, but I do not recognize him."

"Father," Jasmine said, sliding an arm around his elbow, "you need to rest. Come with me."

Timothy pulled away and tromped right into the flowers, reaching for the aura.

"Father!" Jasmine called.

Timothy touched the crimson surface, raising a splash of sparks. The radiant energy crawled along his hand, then up his arm, and covered his skin with vibrating red embers. When the energy reached his eyes, a dazzling flare of scarlet enveloped everything in his field of vision.

Jasmine screamed. "Father! Do not leave me!" Her voice sounded distant and warped.

Timothy felt himself being drawn into the aura, swallowed whole, as if becoming part of its pulsing red field. The town disappeared in a foggy sea of scarlet, leaving only the two idols intact as they seemed to join him in the sparkling radiance. Distorted words drifted past his ears, like a woman's desperate cry blown about by the wind.

"Father!" the voice called. "I love you!"

Merlin strode to the portal and set his hand on top. Pushing down, he squeezed the aura into the rubellite on the ground below. As it compressed, a stream of energy popped out. It spun around Merlin and Valcor three times, then shot into the sky like a frazzled lightning bolt. Two balls of energy followed and launched over the trees in a high arc.

"What were those?" Valcor asked.

Merlin laid his hand on top of his head. "I have no idea!"

"Is it a sign? Part of the prophecy?"

"I will seek wisdom on this mystery, but for now"—Merlin picked up the gem—"I want you to take this rubellite. Keep it safe. When I have set the plan of redemption in order, I will make sure the way to use this gem is added to the king's chronicles." He laid the stone in Valcor's palm. "I will call it the Great Key, for through it the dragons will be able to leave their prison and find a true resting place."

Valcor drew it closer to his eyes. "Master Merlin! The rubellite is no longer pulsing."

Merlin rocked the gem with his finger. "Makaidos! His spirit has either died, or . . ." He gazed at a vapor trail vanishing in the sky. "He has escaped."

"My father? Escaped?" Valcor lifted his head upward. "What will happen to him? Where will he go?"

"I'm not sure. He died before the transformation, so he has no body in which to reside. Unless he finds a way to reanimate his dragon carcass, he will be a wandering spirit."

Valcor held the gem in his fingertips. "Shall I tell Clefspeare and Hartanna about this? After all, Makaidos was Hartanna's father and Clefspeare's grandfather."

"Yes," Merlin said, "but guard what you say. Tell Hartanna that the rubellite once belonged to her father, that it reflects the vitality of a dragon's mortal essence, but keep the rest to yourself. Since we don't know what really happened to Makaidos, speculation about his fate would be foolhardy."

Valcor peered into the gem. "What about the village we saw inside? And what about the other dragons? Should I tell Hartanna about that?"

Merlin shook his head. "Until the dragon messiah comes to set the dragons free, the gateway to Dragons' Rest must remain a secret from everyone else."

"To keep the dragons safe from Morgan?"

"Morgan cannot harm those already dead. What's important is that the dragon messiah finds his way to Dragons' Rest, and, according to the word God gave me in a dream, he must do so only through a special messenger whom God will prepare at the proper time."

Valcor closed his hand around the rubellite and gazed at the moon, now hazy behind a veil of thin clouds. "May God bring that messenger soon!"

"Perhaps you will have a hand in his coming." Merlin patted Valcor on the back. "Walk with me to the place where you will hide until I summon you again to Blood Hollow. You and Sir Gawain must organize the king's knights. I am certain now that a rebellion will soon arise, and I will need Arthur's loyal soldiers to help me put it down."

Stooping low, Elam smoothed the dirt on top of the grave, picking out each pebble and fleck of debris. As the headstone's speckled crystals shimmered in the rising sun, he admired the block letters and rugged cross he had carved with his own hand. "Lazarus VII, descendant of Lazarus of Bethany. Rest in Peace." Following the outline of the etched cross with his finger, he whispered, "Thank you for teaching me. I know we'll be together again someday."

He stood and clapped the dirt off his hands as he counted the graves in the family plot—the original Lazarus with his tombstone that read, "Lazarus of Bethany, in Heaven to Stay"; Lazarus's wife, passed away two years earlier; Joseph, father of Lazarus VII; an unnamed girl who died at birth; and a boy named Elam.

The last grave carried no body. Elam had carved the cryptic marker, "Elam the Wanderer," to answer neighbors' questions. Whatever happened to that wandering waif who showed up over three years ago? Now they would know. He had moved on to another life.

Elam slung a knapsack over his shoulder and looked behind him at the towering hill, the tor of Glastonbury and the tiny church at its apex. Yes, it was time to leave for good, and best to do so without answering all the well-intentioned questions of the villagers. Firming his chin, he marched around the bordering swamp and followed a damp, muddy trail that led into a forest. Camelot lay ahead, a new home atop a new hill, and this one promised adventures unlike any he had ever known.

As he passed under a lush canopy, he reached into his knapsack and withdrew the Ovulum. The egg was dark today, but that wasn't unusual. It seemed to warm up and glow only when it had a mind to talk, and that wasn't very often, maybe a half dozen times over the last three years, and most of those had come when Lazarus was holding it.

Elam rubbed his thumb over the glassy surface. Still, it had spoken directly to him once since that wondrous song during the rainy dance, and he would always remember its short, but passionate plea.

389

A lad of faith will never fail
Beholding truth and light.
So keep me close and never doubt,
And I will be your sight.

In the dimness of the dense forest, the Ovulum glowed ever so slightly. Elam halted and looked around. There had to be a reason for its illumination, but everything seemed in order. Nothing but trees and undergrowth lined his narrow path. No sounds arose in the woods except a soft rustling from a light breeze announcing the wakening day.

The rustling grew louder. The wind kicked up dirt and leaves and spun them in a tornadic dance. Trees waved back and forth and littered the ground with twigs and moss. Dark clouds rode the wind, drawing a blanket across the sky and sending acorn-sized raindrops in sporadic intervals, sometimes just two or three, then a cascade that quickly dampened the path.

Elam reached back to store the Ovulum, but a lightning flash made him cover his head. The bolt sizzled into a tree, splashing embers in high arcs. One of the streams collected in an elongating arm that reached toward him. It orbited his body once and plunged into the Ovulum, igniting a burst of scarlet within.

Elam clung to the pulsing egg, his fingers clenched around it, his muscles contracting uncontrollably with every colorful, rhythmic throb. His whole body shook. His teeth chattered so hard, his jaws ached. Finally, his fingers relaxed, and the Ovulum fell to the ground, still pulsing.

With large raindrops splashing on his head, he dropped to his knees and touched the Ovulum. Although it still pulsed red, its surface was cool. "What . . ." He swallowed painfully. "What happened?"

The red glow slowly faded away. He scooped the egg and wiped it clean with a dry corner of his tunic, then broke into a quick march, keeping his head low as he continued his journey toward Camelot. According to Lazarus, there was only one man who could solve the mysteries of the Ovulum, and he served the king within the walls of the castle.

Elam accelerated, running as fast as the slippery path would allow. He had to find Merlin as soon as possible.

CHAPTER

THE CONSPIRACY

E dward tramped up the dark slope, following Barlow's lantern as it swung a few paces in front. Well ahead of Barlow, another lantern swayed back and forth in the hands of a short, old man. "Come, come," the man sang gleefully. "This place of sadness is now a place of joy. I will never fear Bald Top again."

Barlow picked up his pace on the steepening grade, while Edward stayed close behind, glad his battle-hardened legs had become equal to his captain's. He grabbed a branch and pulled up to the top of a boulder. "Captain, did the old man say why he was up here that night?"

"Yes." Barlow stopped and turned around. "He was supposed to meet Goliath at the summit to pay a ransom for his daughter. He didn't know Devin had already slain him."

"Ah! I heard about Devin rescuing a maiden. With all the accolades, his head must be more swollen than a pumpkin by now."

Barlow marched again and gestured for Edward to come alongside. When they were walking abreast, Barlow lowered his voice. "I don't like Devin, either, but we must admit that his zeal to protect the kingdom is unsurpassed."

"Perhaps, but this gypsy's story is too unbelievable to be true, just the mad ravings of a highwayman."

"Shhh!" Barlow nodded toward the dark figure in front of them. "He'll hear you."

"Here we are," the old man said, dancing on the grassy plain. "Follow me!"

Barlow and Edward ventured out onto the vast summit. "It's a good thing Goliath is gone," Barlow said. "Battling him at night would be difficult indeed." He held the lantern low and began searching through the grass.

"Over here!" the old man cried from about thirty paces away. "Here it is!"

The two knights hurried to the spot. The old man shone the lantern light on a pile of clothes.

Edward picked up a shoulderless dress and held it at arm's length. "Ugly as a mangy cur's coat. No wonder it was left here to rot."

The old man picked up a pair of men's trousers. "The dragons took the rest. Naked as a rat's tail, they were, so Merlin gave them clothes. I saw them with my own two eyes."

Barlow pointed at a splotch of dried mud. "Dragon tracks." He knelt and set his lantern on the mud, his eyes close to the ground. "At least three different dragons, two females, one male." He crawled on all fours, then stopped suddenly. "They become human footprints!"

"I told you!" the old man said. "I told you! Merlin transformed them. I saw it with my own eyes. And one of them looked exactly like the king!"

Edward bent down and picked up a saddlebag. "Sir Barlow, what do you make of this?"

Barlow got up and examined the bag. "It's Merlin's." He pointed at a waxy emblem. "See. Here is his signet seal."

The old man jumped up and down, chortling, "He was here! He was here! I knew it! Merlin performed his black magic right on this spot, just like I said!"

Edward threw the bag to the ground. "You're starting to annoy me, old gypsy."

The gypsy pointed at Edward with a long, bony finger. "Because I was right. Say it. I was right. Merlin loves dragons so much, he replaced the king with one. Say it. You know it's true now."

Barlow clamped his huge hand over the old man's mouth. "As much as I hate to admit it, I think we have to believe Devin's story. Merlin's love for dragons has apparently driven him mad."

Edward furrowed his brow and nodded. "So what do we do?"

"What choice do we have?" Barlow replied, shrugging his shoulders. "In order to be true to the king, we have to join Devin in opposing Merlin."

Edward let a smile break through. "Exposing the fraud and rescuing the true king would be quite a feat, wouldn't it?"

"Yes, but don't forget," Barlow said, wagging his finger. "This isn't about obtaining honor. It's about loyalty to His Majesty."

Edward shook his head. "You're right, as usual. Keep reminding me."

Barlow released the gypsy. "If you breathe a word of this to anyone else, you will die a traitor's death. Understood?"

"Oh, yes," the old man cackled. "Not a word."

Barlow tromped toward the summit's edge. "Come then. We have to meet with Sir Devin."

Edward followed, but the gypsy stayed put. "Aren't you coming?" Edward asked.

The gypsy pointed toward the other side of the summit. "My family is that way. Mustn't keep them waiting too long."

Barlow stopped and raised a finger at him. "Don't forget. Not a word."

The old man lifted his lantern in front of his wrinkled, leathery face. "My lips are sealed!"

Barlow and Edward turned and headed down the slope. "So how does one expose a powerful wizard?" Edward asked.

"I have no experience in that area, so we'll just leave it up to Sir Devin."

"I'm sure I can get Newman to join us," Edward said. "Do you have friends you can count on?"

"A few. My nephew Fiske is sure to do whatever I ask."

A loud flapping sound breezed by them. Barlow whipped out his sword. "What was that?" he asked, raising the blade high.

Edward pointed into the air. "A bat! The biggest I've ever seen!"

Keeping his sword in front of him, Barlow marched ahead. "We shouldn't dawdle in haunted places. Bald Top still holds dark secrets, and we'd best get off its slopes."

The two men hurried down the hill, staying quiet for the rest of their journey.

Clefspeare, I dub you Jared, son of Arthur." The king tapped the bowing man's shoulder lightly with a gleaming sword. "By this decree, I name you my son, though you have already become closer than any of my natural offspring." He turned and tapped the lady's shoulder, touching the flowing blonde hair that draped her sparkling white gown. "And you, dear Hartanna, I dub Irene, for your very presence brings peace to my soul. You are now my daughter, a treasured princess, who, I hope, will always find peace within the walls of my palace."

King Arthur lifted Excalibur from Irene's shoulder and handed the blade to Merlin who stood with him on the platform. The sword maintained its faint white glow, strong enough to illuminate Merlin's wrinkled hands, yet it seemed no more than the brightest candle among the dozens that lined the throne room. When Merlin slid the sword into its sheath, the ornate scabbard swallowed the glow.

Arthur picked up a scroll from the table at his side. "For your protection, I have entered your names as Reginald Bannister and Tabitha Silver in the official records as my adopted son and daughter. Hide your identities well, for if your enemies discover them, you will be chased by bloodthirsty hounds for centuries to come. I suggest choosing different surnames for yourselves for the time being, though you may return to Bannister and Silver to protect your inheritance when the time comes."

Jared lifted his eyes toward the king and slowly stood. "Sire, I humbly accept the gracious bestowal of your good name. May I always bring the name of Arthur honor and a blessed heritage."

Irene stood at Jared's side. "I, too, am honored, Your Majesty." She rubbed her hand across her bare forearm. Her skin seemed to radiate silvery white. "Having shorn my scales, and with them the dignity of a dragoness, I now feel clothed once again with the integrity, nobility, and heritage your deeds have inspired. May I wear this livery well."

Arthur's solemn face broke into a proud, fatherly smile. "Well spoken, my friends. I trust that I will be able to live up to my duty and keep you safe in your new skins. Have the other dragons taken the necessary steps to secure their safety?"

Jared glanced at Irene. "The ladies have chosen new names and blended into life in the nearby villages or secluded themselves elsewhere, as you instructed. We do not know, however, what has become of Valcor."

Arthur's brow lifted. "I was with him in Bowman's Forest only a few weeks ago. I assume he has gone into hiding."

"We have assumed the same," Jared said. "At least Devin will never be able to learn his whereabouts from us, even through torture."

The king took off his formal outer robe and handed it to Merlin. "Speaking of Devin, now that our ceremony is complete, we must make haste."

"Indeed." Merlin placed Excalibur and the robe on his chair. "Devin's traitorous band could attack at any moment. I have arranged for your knights to secretly assemble at Blood Hollow, so I suggest that you leave through your escape route at once to convene with them. Gawain will meet you at the tunnel exit and escort you to the other knights."

Arthur strapped on his armor and reached for his sword on Merlin's seat.

Merlin grabbed Arthur's wrist. "But you must leave Excalibur."

Arthur pulled away from the prophet's grip and lifted the sheathed sword in his palms. "Go into battle without the sword?" He strapped the scabbard to the belt on his back. "I should say not!"

"I have more need of it," Merlin said, holding out his hands. "Devin's tiny army is counting on surprise to win. When you arrive, your forces will crush him like a shoe on a cockroach. Should you come late, Excalibur is my only hope for survival."

Arthur placed his hand on Excalibur's hilt and hesitated. Outside the door the distant sound of clanking steps shattered the evening's quiet meeting.

"There is no more time," Merlin urged. "Trust me! Leave Excalibur and fly to Blood Hollow. Gawain will have a sword for you."

Arthur unfastened the sword from his belt, scabbard and all, and handed it to Merlin. He then scrambled to the secret panel in the corner and shut it behind him.

Merlin picked up Arthur's robe and helped Jared put it on. "Should I wear the crown?" Jared asked.

Merlin helped him straighten out the sleeves. "No. Your hair is a close enough match, so the robe should be sufficient. Just keep your back to the door. I expect Devin to enter at any moment." He turned to Irene. "You may face the door and kneel before our 'king.' Can you make yourself cry?"

Irene shook her head. "I have not yet learned all the ways of women. I have shed many tears, but I cannot force them."

"Then try to look sad, as though entreating the king for some-one's life."

Within seconds a servant came to the throne room's doorway. "Sir Devin to see His Majesty."

Merlin nodded to Jared, who spun toward the back of the room. Irene dropped to her knees and extended her folded hands toward him, twisting her face in counterfeit pain. Merlin stepped to the entryway to intercept the quickly marching Devin. "His Majesty has a guest, Sir Devin. May I give him a message for you?"

Devin looked over Merlin's shoulder. "Is the lady ill? She seems to be having intestinal distress."

"Not sickness; her entreaty is a private matter. We will be in prayer for her for the next half hour, and then I shall escort His Majesty to his chamber."

Merlin noted a hint of a smile in Devin's otherwise stoic expression. Devin bowed and spoke in his most formal and rever-ent voice. "Please give His Majesty my blessings, and I will spend the entire half hour on my knees as well." The knight gave Merlin a polite nod. "Good evening to you, Master Merlin." He left the court with the same quick march that brought him in.

When the door closed, Jared turned around. "Do you think it worked?"

"I think so. A man who is not trustworthy rarely trusts any-one, yet, I believe that our ruse has convinced him that King Arthur is in this room."

Irene stood and brushed her knees. "Then how soon will he attack?"

"He believes he has a half hour, so I would guess we have only half of that before he strikes." Merlin pulled Excalibur from its sheath. A blinding beam of light shot from its tip and burned a hole through the ceiling. "I will have to use Excalibur to extinguish the enemy, and in the process, I will conduct my greatest experiment."

"Experiment?" Jared asked.

Merlin cast his gaze on Jared and Irene. "I have tested the sword at length. Excalibur does not merely cut; it transforms. It changes matter into light energy; it transluminates. If I wield it to kill, its radiance will shatter a man's bones into shards of flashing luminescence, and his remains will be absorbed into a candle's breath. And his soul? If it is not somehow trapped on the earth, it will be sent straight to the judgment seat of God.

"Jared," Merlin continued, "you and Irene must enter the tunnel door for safety. When Excalibur's power fills the room, all who remain will be transluminated. Although I bear the sword, even I will be changed."

"Changed into what?" Irene asked.

"As with the rest, my body will likely become light energy, though I think I will survive. Whether I will ever regain a body, I cannot say."

A sudden clanking of soldiers' weapons and marching footsteps echoed in the outer hallway. Merlin pushed Jared and Irene toward the corner door. "Go! Go!"

The pair of former dragons hurried across the room and disappeared into the secret passage, drawing the access panel closed behind them. Seconds later, two armed men broke through the main entry door and stretched loaded bowstrings back to their ears. Merlin held Excalibur in both hands, its point straight up. "Barlow and Edward, you should know better than to distrust a prophet of the living God!"

The soldiers raised their forearms to shield their eyes from the blinding light. Six others poured through the door and halted as they beheld the sword.

When a full dozen had arrived, Merlin waved the sword in a great circle. The soldiers seemed rooted to the stone floor, their legs trembling like saplings in a storm's fury. A single beam from Excalibur's tip multiplied into hundreds. The beams flashed in all directions until they joined together in a massive curtain of light.

Merlin gazed upward. "Now, my Lord Christ, take me on this great adventure to find the dragons' messiah." The moment he waved Excalibur, a luminescent surge washed through the court, and particles of sparkling light buzzed through the traitors. As their bodies melted away, shields and armor clattered to the floor to mark where men had once stood.

The surge splashed back at Merlin. Dazzling light blinded his eyes, a tingling sensation covered his body, and a loud buzzing vibrated in his ears. He floated above the platform, his sense of sight transforming. Somehow everything looked like competing sources of light, some brilliant, some almost dark, and others in between.

Looking at himself, he saw his body as a stream of sparkling light, barely recognizable as a body at all. Other similar streams, maybe a dozen or so, floated around the room.

A human form dashed across the floor of the throne room, its light flickering between bright and dim. It looked like Jared, anxiously searching through something on the floor, apparently the remains of the armor the treacherous soldiers had left behind when they dissolved.

Another man marched into the room, a shadow that emanated no light at all. Merlin willed himself closer and saw the image of Devin outlined on the shadow's face. Jared's light shimmered as it hid in the drapes behind the throne.

Devin suddenly leaned over. When he stood again, he held a bright object in his hand, long and sleek. Seconds after Devin picked it up, the object darkened, becoming just a sword-like extension of his shadow.

For a moment, Devin disappeared from the room. Jared's form emerged again, and he seemed to shout, his voice warped. "Devin, you son of a leprous jackal! You recreant thief, plucking treasures from dead men's bones! Come back here and fight like a man!"

Devin reappeared, this time with a bright object in front of his chest, some kind of pendant that sparkled against his dark

399

silhouette. Merlin felt drawn to it, as though it pulled his weight-less body with a strange, tractive power.

The other sparkling masses streamed toward the pendant and vanished. Merlin fought against the flow like a fish struggling upstream. It was no use. The force elongated his body and slurped him toward the pendant.

He tried to watch the confrontation between Devin and Jared. They seemed to be fighting. Jared fell to the floor, but that was all Merlin could see before the room vanished. He tumbled down an avalanche of pure light, hurtling toward a black sphere. He plunged into it, feeling no pain, only a sinking sensation as dark-ness enveloped him. His body seemed to settle and stop, as though he stood on an endless floor. Twelve masses of sparks stood nearby, huddling close and flashing green, yellow, and red.

Merlin tried to sort out all the amazing images and evaluate his situation. He and the traitors had been transformed into light energy and absorbed into the candlestone as it hung around Devin's neck. Now they were trapped inside a crystalline prison, riding within the candlestone's walls as the dark knight's prison-ers, though Devin likely had no idea they were there.

When Merlin tried to speak to the others, a stream of light energy carried his thoughts. "Barlow?" His voice seemed to buzz through the darkness. "Edward?"

"I am Barlow," one of the sparkling masses replied. "Edward is next to me . . . I think."

"Yes." Edward's energy field turned bluish white. "I am here, a young fool at your service. May I ask who addresses us?"

Merlin decided to keep his anonymity, at least for the time being. "You are, indeed, a fool. What helped you learn your les-son so quickly?"

"As soon as Merlin raised Excalibur and its holy light passed over my body, it was as though I could see everything—the prophet's integrity, Devin's plot, and my own stupidity." Edward's energy shrank to a quivering ball of purple light. "I am but a fool. My dear mother will die in disgrace, and I will never be able to wear my father's name. He deserved better than the stooge who masquerades as his son."

Merlin's mass of sparks grew bright white. "Hear me, Edward, son of Edmund. Remember what you learned in the light and never doubt it even if you have to spend years in the dark. Heed my words, and you will eventually earn a place of honor and regain your father's name." His energy dwindled back to normal, and he willed himself into motion. "Think about what I have said. I will see you again."

Elam scooted back into a dark cleft of the secret passageway, watching the beautiful lady as she stooped low, peering out of the slightly open panel. He had already learned her name by listening in on her adoption ceremony—Irene, the king's new daughter. Quiet and cautious, she spied on the happenings in the throne room.

A man shouted, "Devin, you son of a leprous jackal! You recreant thief, plucking treasures from dead men's bones! Come back here and fight like a man!" The sound of evil laughter followed, then, seconds later, the clashing of swords and loud grunting.

The woman gasped. She kept opening the panel farther, then closing it, as if fearing someone might spot her. Finally, she threw it open and dashed into the throne room. Elam leaped to the panel and peeked out. Several knights were carrying a bleeding man and hustling him toward the passageway.

As the group burst into his hideout, Elam ducked back into the cleft and crouched low. Irene led them down the tunnel, a lantern swinging in her hand. "Follow me!" she cried. "We have to get Jared to Thigocia." In less than a minute, the lantern's light faded away.

Elam crept into the open and pulled out the Ovulum. "*Fiat lux,*" he whispered. It glowed red, just enough to guide his way

401

through the tunnel. Though it had been hard to believe, Merlin's amazing stories were all true—the coming rebellion, the former dragons, even the secret to calling for the light of the Ovulum.

After quietly closing the panel, he picked up his knapsack and tiptoed in the direction Irene had fled. Now it was time to fulfill the sacred duty Merlin had charged him with, a secret mission he could reveal to no one, at least until the Eye gave him permission. He lowered his head and sprinted. He couldn't get too far behind, not if he was to find the former dragon named Thigocia.

CHAPTER

In Hiding

Jared and Irene huddled around a flickering candle. A tent draped across three short poles acted as their only break against a chill wind. As they rubbed their fingers in the candle's fragile warmth, their breaths troubled the flame. Jared sat cross-legged on a threadbare gray blanket, watching the changes in her expression—the anxiety in her furrowed brow, the fear in her wide eyes, and the pain in her tight bluish red lips. He glanced from time to time at the tent's entrance, wondering if the occasional snaps of twigs or hoots of owls signaled coming danger.

With his hands clenched over his mouth, Jared took in a deep breath and whispered between his thumbs. "If he is not here soon, Irene, we have to assume the worst. Valcor is no match for Devin."

Irene placed a gentle hand on his forearm. "He is no match in battle, but my brother is wiser by far. Do not give up hope. I would not have arranged our meeting had I thought this a fool's errand."

Jared raised his head. "I heard a nightingale."

Irene whispered, "It is the signal." She pursed her lips and blew a warbling bird whistle.

Within seconds, the tent flap flew open, and a man with water dripping from his sleeves bustled in.

Irene grasped the man's arm. "Valcor! Are you hurt?"

Valcor, stooping under the low ceiling, shook his head, panting. "Devin . . . Devin tracked me to the river's edge, so I swam . . . swam upstream as far as I could." He took a deep breath and continued. "I ran the rest of the way. It will be some time before the dogs pick up the trail again, but we must hurry." He pulled a scroll from his vest, sat beside Jared, and rolled it out on the blanket. "I found the letter, and I managed to keep it above water."

Irene glanced upward and clasped her hands together. "Thank the Maker!"

Wrapping his arms around himself, Valcor shivered. "Yes. It is a miracle that I escaped. My bribe must not have been rich enough to keep the guard quiet." He rolled up his wet sleeves and ran his fingers across the parchment. "But this information is worth all the trouble."

Jared eyed the letter. "It is lengthy. Please give us a summary."

Valcor held the letter close to the dancing flame. "It is clear that Devin is now more dangerous than ever."

"But he failed," Irene said. "Arthur and Merlin squashed the rebellion."

"Devin did not fail completely. He took Excalibur, and now Merlin has vanished. Who can predict how powerful Devin and Morgan will become?"

Valcor slid the candle closer to the letter. "This explains what I believe is an even greater danger. You see, Merlin promised to tell Morgan how to restore her wandering spirit to a body. The promise, it seems, has been fulfilled in this letter, which I recently learned was in Devin's possession."

Irene shifted to Valcor's side and draped her shawl across his shoulders. She eyed the letter's exquisite penmanship. "Why would Merlin make such a promise to a witch?"

Valcor took his sister's hand. "I asked Merlin that very question before he disappeared. He said the plan is of divine origin and extends well beyond his vision, but we should not worry; God knows what he is doing. In any case, as you may already know, Morgan is not a common variety witch. She is the wife of a Watcher. Her original name was Lilith, a wretched enchantress who lived before the flood. Her husband taught her the evil arts of the fallen angels, but she did not know that practicing these arts would cause her to become a wraith. She actually took on the nature of the Watchers and has no hope of redemption without regaining a body and giving herself in obedience to the Christ."

A peal of thunder rolled across the sky. Valcor's gaze flashed toward the tent entrance as he rolled up the letter and thrust it back into his vest. "There is much to explain, and time is short." He held his hand over his vest pocket. "Merlin told Morgan she needs a *hostiam viventem*, a living sacrifice, in order to shed her ghostly cowl. That sacrifice has to be a legal, female relative of the king. Morgan had her evil eye on Guinevere, but not even the Watchers' arts could persuade Arthur to give up his wife. So, it seems that she changed her plan, hoping Devin could take the throne during the rebellion."

"But how would that further her cause?" Jared asked. "Devin has no wife and no female relatives that I know of."

"Who would have him?" Irene sliced her hand across her throat. "I would kill myself before I let that piece of filth touch me!"

Valcor smirked. "Even dead, you might still be a target, Irene. Merlin wrote that a deceased woman can be a hostiam providing, of course, the body has not been dead for very long. But Devin would have no need to hunt for corpses. If he had succeeded in

405

usurping the throne, he would have had his choice of women. Morgan would have entered his wife and become queen, and Devin would have the power to rule the world. I believe Devin would have put up with a witch of a wife for a prize like that."

A distant howl drifted into the tent. Valcor pushed the entrance flap to the side and leaned out for a moment, then ducked back in. "So Devin and Morgan had an understanding. She would provide him with power, with influence in high places, and he, in turn, would use that power to become king, get married, then provide Morgan with a woman to possess. But since his rebellion has failed, Morgan might not wait for him to try again."

Irene raised a finger to her chest. "But if any legal female relative can serve as host, then I really would be a candidate, would I not, since I am an adopted daughter?"

Valcor nodded. "You would be, yes."

"Then why does Devin seek to kill me?"

"Because," Valcor replied, stroking his chin, "he has merely identified you as a former dragon. He hasn't yet made the connection that you are also in the royal line. So you have peril either way. If you are a dragon, Devin wants you dead. If you are an heir, Morgan would prefer to take your body alive, yet in such a way that you would be better off dead. I believe, however, that Devin's bloodlust will override his desire to search for Morgan's hostiam, so he will likely try to kill you until the day he dies."

"If he ever dies," Irene added.

Jared lifted his brow. "If? Why do you say *if*?"

"Haven't you noticed his new youthfulness?" Irene brushed her finger across her calf. "He shows no sign of the leg wound I gave him when I fought with him. If Morgan's evil handiwork has given him healing power, then who knows how long he might live?"

"So," Valcor said, "the presence of a seemingly deathless stalker means that we must go into hiding permanently. The farther apart we live and the less we communicate with each other, the more difficult it will be for Devin and Morgan to find us all."

Valcor began to rise, but Irene pulled on his sleeve. "Wait. I have something for you." She opened her palm. Two spherical red stones rolled to the edge of her hand, looking like a pair of polished cranberries at the peak of harvest. "When you gave me Makaidos's rubellite, it reminded me of its meaning to the dragon race, so I went back to Bald Top to search for other rubellites. I assumed they fell to the ground when we were transformed, so I thought they might still be up there."

Irene seesawed her hand, letting the gems roll from side to side. "I found two in the grass, the lighter of these gems and another one I put away in a safe place." She plucked the darker of the two stones from her palm and gave it to Valcor. "Dear brother, this is our father's, the one you gave to me, and I ask you, as his son, to take it back." She handed the other stone to Jared. "Always remember what we once were. If you ever procreate, pass yours along to your progeny at the appropriate time."

Closing his fingers around his rubellite, Jared nodded. "I will. You can count on it."

Valcor's lips parted as if to speak, but, as his face reddened, he just lowered his head.

Irene's blue eyes sparkled. "As these gems reflect the vitality of your mortal essence, may you always reflect the nobility of our race through your courage, your integrity, and your sacrifice."

Valcor stood and bowed, tears streaming down his cheeks. He rolled a tear onto his finger and held it out for Jared and Irene to see. "How rare were the tears of a dragon. We once lived in Paradise, and because of the corruption of an angel disguised as a dragon, all the world was cast into darkness. Now, as humans, we shed many tears—for what was lost, for what might have been, and for the end of friendships. Good-bye, my true friends." He bowed again and hurried from the tent.

Jared held the tent flap open for Irene. "We had better go, as well."

She raised a finger. "We must wait for his signal that all is clear."

Jared paused, listening so intently he could hear a faint sizzle from the candle's wick. Another howl pierced the night. He wet his fingers and snuffed the flame. "That is a good enough signal for me." He and Irene shuffled from the tent and folded it with the blanket.

After tucking the bundle under his arm, Jared inhaled deeply. "It is a new world, Hartanna, if I may call you that one last time. We will now be alone and friendless, perhaps for many years."

"Before I go into hiding," Irene said, "I must tell my mother what has happened. She will surely be Devin's prime target."

Irene turned to leave, but Jared grabbed her hand. "I have one regret," he said softly.

She tilted her head. "Regret? What regret?"

He sighed and caressed her fingers with his thumb. "That I was never able to become Hartanna's mate."

As Irene gazed into his eyes, her tears glistened in the dim light. "You would have made a magnificent king, Clefspeare."

He kissed her hand tenderly. "May the Maker grant you safe passage." He bowed and marched quickly into the forest.

In the gloom of night, Elam sat in front of the hut, watching the undulating glow of firelight as it danced inside the open window. Cautious voices from within drifted to his ears.

"Do not tell me where you are going, Irene. It is better that I do not know."

"But you are my mother. How will I ever find you again?"

"Have faith. The Maker will see to our reunion . . . someday."

"At least choose a new name and tell me what it is. Thigocia will not serve you as a proper name in this land."

Elam scooted closer to the window.

"At first I chose Emzara, because, like Noah's wife, I am the mother of all who remain of my kind, but I decided it was too uncommon and obvious. Devin would guess it easily. So, I have chosen to answer to the name of Hannah."

"Hannah is a fine name. It is easy to remember and not conspicuous at all."

"You should go now, precious daughter. The longer you stay in this country, the more danger you will be in."

Elam rose to his feet, picked up his knapsack, and tiptoed to the edge of the surrounding forest. Leaning against the wide trunk of a tree, he slid back down to his seat and watched Irene leave the tiny hut. She and Hannah embraced, then, after holding her mother's hand for a moment, Irene strode into the shadows and disappeared.

Elam pulled the Ovulum from his bag and whispered, "*Fiat lux.*" A faint glow emanated from the glass. He smiled and spoke softly to it. "Thigocia seems to be safe for now, so I guess I'll just sleep here until she decides to go somewhere else."

The orb pulsed but gave no reply.

Giving the smooth surface a gentle rub, Elam continued. "Sometimes I wish you'd talk to me more. I want to do a good job watching over Thigocia, but I feel like I'm just guessing what I'm supposed to do."

The Ovulum's glow brightened, and its pulsing frequency increased, but it stayed quiet.

Elam let the Ovulum rock back and forth in his palm. "I believe Sapphira gave you to me for a reason, and I guess I'll figure it all out as I go, but maybe it would help if I knew how long I'm supposed to keep track of Thigocia." He drew the Ovulum closer to his face. "Will you tell me when the slayers die?"

The eye slowly congealed inside the glass. Its crimson-coated image pulsed in time with the orb's glow. "For the sake of your curious mind, Elam, son of Shem, I will reveal what I know." The

409

eye seemed to retreat, and the entire face of an elderly man appeared. "I am Enoch, the first oracle. When God took me up from the earth, he gave me the task of overseeing a certain portion of his redemption plan. I reside in a spiritual realm, and my window to your world is the humble egg you hold in your hands, a dimensional viewer that is passed from oracle to oracle. Methuselah inherited the oracle title from me, but the flood created the need to pass the Ovulum to Sapphira Adi, a special kind of oracle whose true mission has not yet begun. Now that she has been set on her path, the Ovulum is yours, and as my descendant, you are the rightful heir."

Elam pointed at himself. "So am I an oracle?"

"That mantle is yours to be grasped, but time will tell if you are able to wear it with authority." Enoch's face seemed to back away even farther. Robed in scarlet, he sat on a stool next to a table. "For now, I will address your immediate question, but there is no simple answer. Morgan's arts could keep the slayers alive for many years, so the time of fulfillment of your task is uncertain. Just stay close to Thigocia and stay hidden."

"That shouldn't be too hard. I don't eat, and I don't get older. All I need is some sleep now and then."

"It may be harder than you realize. The mother dragon is stalked by a monster who will stop at nothing to murder her. Guard her well."

Elam nodded. "I will. You can count on that." He breathed a sigh. "Good night, Enoch." After pulling the knapsack under his head, he held the Ovulum close to his chest and drifted off to sleep.

Sapphira stepped back from the rectangular screen of light and waved her hand across it, dimming it to a soft glow. "That's enough for a while. Elam's just going to sleep." The screen shrank from a dragon-sized aura back to a spinning orange column, the portal to the snake-infested swamp up above.

Paili bounced on her seat in the center of a pile of straw. "More!" she chirped.

Yara, sitting next to her, wrapped her arms around Paili's neck and pulled her into a strong hug. "You need to sleep, too."

Sapphira sighed. "We all do. Elam's so busy, just watching him makes me tired."

"It was so strange," Yara said. "He looked right at us when he said good night to Enoch."

"I saw that. It's almost like we've been looking through Enoch's eyes ever since Elam left."

Paili rubbed her stomach. "Can we eat before bed? I'm hungry."

Sapphira laid her hand over her own stomach. "Did Acacia bring more food?"

"A couple of hours ago," Acacia called, waving from the museum.

Sapphira walked toward her sister and peered through the doorway. "Looking for something new to read?"

411

Acacia held open a scroll. "I'm studying the map again. When I was sneaking back with the food, I overheard Mardon talking about the digging project."

"Any idea if the giants are getting close to the surface?"

"That's why I'm checking the map." She pointed at a drawing of the uppermost floor. "I think they started here, and the legend says that point is about two thousand feet below the surface." She rolled up the map. "But I have no idea how long it will take. If they hit bedrock between here and there, it could take a thousand years."

Awven brought each of the twins a jar. Acacia opened hers, dipped her fingers in, and pulled out a gob of black gunk. "But as long as the worm farms hold out, we'll have their yummy guts to eat for years to come." She pushed the gob into her mouth, then grimaced as she swallowed. "Not a good batch. Must have had a grub worm in the mix."

As the two girls walked back toward the portal, Sapphira opened her own jar. "Everything's going to change when they finally break through," she said, "but if they don't do it pretty soon, and if we don't figure out how to open a portal"—she pinched a clump of worm guts and winced at it—"I might just choose to starve."

"Elam never eats," Paili said, wormy gunk spilling down her chin.

Sapphira stared at her. "What did you say?"

"Elam never eats," Paili repeated. "Haven't you noticed?"

Sapphira set her jar down, not bothering to recap it. "I already knew. He ate the fruit from the other tree." She ran back to the museum, rushed past the statues, and knelt where Morgan's tree once grew. It had taken days to uproot the awful thing and burn it, and the smoke had filled their chamber with a putrid odor for weeks, but it was worth it. As soon as Paili stopped handling the fruit, her speech improved dramatically.

"Paili," she shouted. "Do you know where I keep my blossom?"

Paili appeared at the museum's doorway. "Under my old bed?"

"No." Sapphira pointed at a bookshelf near the door. "I moved it to that shelf I cleared out. Please bring it to me."

Finding the blossom, Paili cradled it in her palms, and carried it to the bed of soil.

Sapphira wrapped her hands around the petals and folded them up into a ball. She gouged the soil with her fist and laid the blossom in the hole. "We'll make a growth chamber right here. There ought to be enough magnetite bricks lying around." Scooping dirt from around the blossom, she covered it up under a mound.

Acacia strolled into the museum, her arms crossed over her chest. "How do you know it will germinate? It can't have seeds yet, can it?"

Sapphira looked up at her. "Do you remember hearing Merlin's prophecy when the dragons transformed?"

"Remember!?" Acacia laughed. "You woke me up, screaming, 'Look at the portal! Look at the portal!' I was kind of groggy, but I remember watching."

Sapphira got up and grabbed a scrap of parchment from a nearby shelf. "I wrote down the prophecy." Pressing her finger on the parchment, she read the poem.

> When hybrid meets the fallen seed
> The virgin seedling flies;
> An orphaned waif shall call to me
> When blossom meets the skies.

Sapphira raised her eyebrows expectantly.

"Well," Acacia said, "we're all hybrids, virgins, and orphaned waifs." She shrugged. "I guess it's worth a try. Maybe that blossom will somehow sprout and touch the sky."

Sapphira smiled. "Good rhyme, Acacia."

Acacia smiled back at her and slid a scroll from one of the lower shelves. "Speaking of poetry," she said, her mouth stretching into a yawn. "I think I'll read some. It's time for us all to get to bed."

"Great," Sapphira said. "I could use a good bedtime story."

"Then you'll join us?" Acacia asked.

Sapphira nodded. "I'll be there in a minute."

Acacia gave her a worried-mother look. "You okay?" she asked.

Tightening her lips, Sapphira nodded again. She leaned against the museum doorway as her twin oracle walked back to the girls, who had gathered in a circle around a small pile of scrolls near the portal. Although the museum had once housed thousands of documents, the modest heap represented a precious share of their diminishing fuel supply.

Acacia pointed at the pile and ignited it, then jumped back in mock alarm. The other girls laughed, and as Acacia squeezed in between Paili and Awven, she glanced back at Sapphira, smiling in a

413

sad sort of way before unwinding the scroll and settling down to read.

Sapphira strolled back to the planter and lowered herself to her knees in front of the mound she had piled over the blossom. She gazed up into the dark reaches of the cavernous library. The portal at the museum's upper crossbeams no longer worked. The orange portal where the girls gathered probably still led to the nest of vipers in the swamp. The whirlpool portal at the bottom of the chasm was now unapproachable. The magma had become so hot, it scalded their faces even as they stood on the ledge, warning them that a plunge into its current now meant certain death. And the portal down in the mining trench where the abyss used to be had fizzled soon after it was created.

Still, any untested doorway could lead somewhere worse than their present location. She couldn't go to the dimension of dead dragons and risk destroying their new home. Dwelling in the land of the living was out of the question; the people would think she was a freak and put her on display. And showing up at Morgan's castle would be the worst idea of all.

Sapphira sighed. She and Acacia would just have to be content watching the upper lands from afar, cut off from everything that really mattered—from Elam and his dangerous task, from the dragons and their new adventure, and, worst of all, from Elohim and his loving embrace. They would have to consider, however, what to do with the other girls. Since they looked like normal humans, they could find homes up above, and they would be a lot more comfortable there, having access to beds and blankets and something better to eat than worm guts. Of course, getting them there safely would be the hard part. Maybe she could somehow reopen the trench portal. Since it likely led to the hill near the church of Michael, she could find homes for the girls and then go back to the lower realms.

She leaned over and smoothed out the dirt on top of the planter's hopeful womb. She felt as though she had entombed herself, Sapphira Adi buried alive in a God-forsaken hole. The girl

414

Elohim had used and thrown away had died, and Mara the slave girl had come back to life, a girl trapped in a dismal prison with no rescuers in sight.

She rocked back and forth on her knees, her hands folded tightly in her lap. Maybe, just maybe, that blossom would root and grow. Who could tell? If dragons could become humans, maybe a freak of nature could become something beautiful, something that could be loved, not just used for a while and cast back into the darkness, but loved and treasured forever.

Sapphira lifted her head and gazed at Lazarus's cross, nailed to the wall next to the shelf where she kept Enoch's scroll. The dark-grained wood, burnished by the flames that spun her back to the lower realms, sparkled from afar, reflecting a lantern hanging near the museum door. The dazzling gloss seemed to flicker in rhythmic flashes, reminding her of the Ovulum's pulsing cadence, yet radiating white light rather than red.

Bowing her head again, she raised her clasped hands under her chin. "Elohim," she whispered. "I hope you'll give me another chance. I . . . I guess there's still something I don't understand, or maybe I did something wrong, and that's why I have to stay down here . . . but that's okay. I know Acacia and the other girls need me right now."

She tucked her lips in, trying not to cry. "I didn't really mean what I said about wanting you to leave me alone. I was tired and scared, and losing Elam and the Ovulum made me feel awful. It was like I died inside, twice in the same day." She looked up at the cross and blinked at its dancing glitters. As the sparkles rode the grain from top to bottom and side to side, it seemed to laugh with joy. She fixed her gaze on the dazzling display and sighed deeply. "I hope you'll come back someday and show me how to dance with you again."

BOOK 3
Refiner's Fire

But who may abide the day of his coming?
and who shall stand when he appeareth? for he
is like a refiner's fire, and like fullers' soap:
And he shall sit as a refiner and purifier of silver:
and he shall purify the sons of Levi, and purge
them as gold and silver, that they may offer unto
the LORD an offering in righteousness.
(Malachi 3:2-3)

When thou passest through the waters, I will be
with thee; and through the rivers, they shall not
overflow thee: when thou walkest through the fire,
thou shalt not be burned; neither shall
the flame kindle upon thee.
(Isaiah 43:2)

CHAPTER

New Homes

Circa AD 1924

C rouching low, Sapphira peeked into the open trapdoor. With her flaming cross in one hand and a coiled rope draped over her thighs, she shook her head and whispered to Acacia behind her, "I can't see a thing." She grimaced at her own voice. The secret tunnel above the spawns' mobility room always seemed to be a sanctuary of quiet, but now even a shushed tone sounded like a rushing torrent.

"I found a thick stalagmite," Acacia whispered back.

Sapphira tossed one end of the rope to her. "Make sure it doesn't rub on anything sharp. I don't want it to snap on my way down." As the rope tightened, she reeled out another loop.

"It's secure." Acacia crawled toward her along the stony floor but bumped her head on the ceiling. "Ow!"

"Shhh!" Sapphira warned.

Acacia rubbed her scalp. "I don't think anyone's down there to hear us. It's been quiet for months."

"Silence worries me." Sapphira unwound the remaining coils into the open hatch and breathed on her cross. "Lights out for now." When the flames died away, she pushed the cross behind her belt buckle and grasped the rope. "I'll see you at the bottom."

As she slid through the cold pocket of darkness, a chorus of sounds arose from below—the familiar hum of magneto bricks; a persistent tick, tick, tick from an unseen source; and the rapid thrumming of her own heart. She clenched the rope more tightly. The silence above now seemed a lot friendlier than the noises of the forbidden room.

The long slide stung her hands. The fibers were coarser than those on the rope in the elevation shaft, but this had been the only one she could find in the land of the living. Ever since she finally opened the portal in the mining shaft and began foraging for supplies in garbage heaps, she had to make do with whatever people had thrown away or would give her out of pity. This rope wasn't the best, but it would hold . . . she hoped.

When her toes finally reached the rocky bottom, she breathed a sigh of relief, and, pulling out her cross, she whispered for its light. "Just a little for now." Low flames crawled along the wood like bright orange worms. Though set on fire hundreds of times over the years, not a grain was ever consumed or even scorched.

She raised the torch high, signaling her safe arrival. Waving it slowly back and forth, she tried to imagine what lay in the shadows beyond her light's reach. Could the giants be sleeping somewhere? Might a sudden noise awaken them? And where was Mardon?

Acacia finally came into view, first her bare feet, then the skirt of her tunic, soiled and wrinkled from the crawl space above. When she settled to the floor, she pulled a scroll from her belt and whispered, "Give me light," and a gentle flame sprouted at the top.

With their torches casting a flickering glow, Sapphira and Acacia tiptoed side by side. The rocky floor smoothed out into a flat, almost glass-like surface, and the hum of magneto bricks grew to a crescendo, like a million locusts buzzing their afternoon chants. As the shadows on the walls sharpened, the sisters slowed to a halt. Acacia's mouth dropped open. "These growth chambers are enormous!"

Sapphira reached her torch close to the chamber's inhabitant and shone the light in his gruesome face. "It's a giant. I think he's asleep."

Acacia skulked alongside the wall, raising her voice as she called back. "They're all over the place! Napping like little babies!"

Sapphira moved her light to the next giant and grimaced. "Like big, hairy, monkey-faced babies. I doubt if even a mother could love these freaks of—" She stopped and bit her lip hard.

"What did you say?" Acacia asked.

Sapphira slinked to Acacia's side and kept pace with her. "Just that they don't remind me of any babies I'd like to snuggle." She joined her light with her sister's, trying to see the face on each bowed head. "Yereq must be around here somewhere."

"Do you think you'll recognize him? They all look pretty much alike."

"They do." Sapphira firmed her chin. "But I'll recognize him."

Creeping past each chamber and peering at each hideous expression took several minutes, but Sapphira finally stopped and studied one face more carefully, a much more pleasant face. The giant's brow arched over his closed eyes, and his firm, square jaws supported a smooth, rounded chin. His thin lips carried the delicate smile of a contented sleeper.

Sapphira pointed at the giant with her cross. "This is Yereq. I'm sure of it."

Acacia propped a hand on her hip and gazed at the sleeping giant. "Okay. Now that we've found him, what do we do?"

"Figure out what's going on." Sapphira pivoted and reached her light toward the center of the chamber. "If I know Mardon, he has a worktable around here and probably a scroll for recording what he's been up to."

Sapphira ventured ahead, slower now as she passed over a rougher part of the floor. A shadow loomed in front of her, and as the cross's glow shifted toward it, the dark form sloughed its shroud, revealing a high, square table. Sapphira laid her hand on the smooth surface. There were no glass jars with struggling embryos, only a large scroll perched at one corner.

She swung her head around. "I found it!"

"I'll be right there."

Sapphira rolled open one side of the scroll and held it in place. Since most of the revealed portion was blank, the data entry that led up to the empty space likely represented Mardon's last work. She squinted at the smudged cacography. It had been many years since she had read Mardon's data, and now his handwriting was worse than ever.

Acacia joined her and held the scroll open. "You found the record?"

"Uh-huh, but it's a mess." She pointed at the top of one entry. "I think he's complaining about hitting bedrock while digging for the surface." Sliding her finger down the parchment, she read on. "The giants don't have enough food, and they're getting tired and cranky, so instead of continuing the dig, he makes them carve out growth chambers for themselves."

Acacia pulled the scroll open a few more inches. "Hunger is a good incentive, I suppose."

Sapphira pointed again. "He says that right here. In fact, they don't have room to make chambers for all of them, so he poisons the least productive ones and leaves them outside of the mobility room to rot."

Acacia nodded. "That explains the bones in front of the door."

"But after they finish digging the chambers"—Sapphira moved her finger to the top of the next section—"he invents a new kind of magneto brick, something about a timer built inside it, a counter of some kind. It's supposed to wake them up when it counts down to zero, but there's a way to wake them up earlier in case he figures out how to get them out of here."

"Well, not that I want to wake them up, but does he tell how?"

Sapphira tapped her finger on the paper. "There are seven lines of numbers. It must be some kind of code, but I have no idea how to break it."

"Any clue where Mardon is now?"

"This is the messiest part of all, but I think he found an air shaft through the bedrock that's too small for the giants." Sapphira slid her finger to the bottom of the entry and shrugged her shoulders. "And that's the end."

"But he's not really alive. How can he get out?"

Sapphira raised her cross as high as she could, but the glow still wouldn't reach the ceiling. "The land above us is still in the dimension of the dead, so if he made it out, he should be fine, but he'd probably need help to open a way big enough for the giants to escape."

The girls locked gazes and nodded at each other. "Morgan," they said together.

Sapphira rolled up the scroll and tucked it under her arm. "Let's take this back to the museum."

"What about the counters he mentioned?" Acacia stooped and looked under the table. "Should we be able to see them?" she asked, rising again.

Sapphira nodded toward the scroll. "Mardon said they were built into the bricks."

"Then how could he tell how far they've counted down? Wouldn't he want to keep track of that?"

"Good point." Sapphira strode toward the wall, much more confident than before. Mardon was likely nowhere around, at least for now. "If he has external counters, they're probably near the bricks."

Arriving at Yereq's chamber, she squatted and set her torch near the magneto's control lever. "There *is* something here. It looks like a candy bar with numbers on it."

Acacia's light flickered on the meter. "It says, '9856.' What do you think it means?"

"Like Mardon wrote. When it counts down to zero, they'll wake up."

"I guessed that, but is it 9856 years, months, days?"

Sapphira shrugged. "Who knows? Maybe if we come and check every once in a while, we'll figure it out."

Acacia rubbed her arm with her free hand. "Okay, but let's get out of here. It's cold and creepy, and Paili's bound to wake up soon. She'll need more herbal tea and a cold compress."

"Okay. Awven's going to need it, too." Sapphira swung her torch to the side. "The main door should be over there. I don't think we'll need a combination to get out."

Acacia pointed toward the center of the room. "What about the rope?"

"I'll go up the back way and reel it in. We might as well make it look like we weren't here. You never know when Mardon might return."

Acacia tapped the scroll under Sapphira's arm. "Then you'd better leave that here."

"But how am I going to study the code?"

"Come back with your own scroll and copy it."

"Of course!" Sapphira rapped her forehead with the heel of her hand. "How dumb of me!"

Acacia grinned. "*I* didn't say that!"

Sapphira lifted her torch close to Acacia, catching the mirthful glimmer in her sister's flashing blue eyes. As the flames warmed her skin, Sapphira winked. "I know. *I* said it. Sometimes I can't see the answer to my question even if it's staring me right in the face."

CIRCA AD 1929

With the dusk of evening just beginning to fade to darkness, Sapphira stopped at the doorstep and crouched in front of Paili. Combing through silky strands of dark hair with her fingers, Sapphira whispered, "We want to make a good first impression." After several more sweeps, Sapphira lowered her hands and smiled. Though tossed and tangled from walking two miles in a stiff breeze, the bedraggled mop of tresses wasn't as bad as usual.

After retying a scarf over Paili's head, Sapphira lifted the little girl's chin. "Are you ready?"

Paili just nodded, a tear forming in her eye.

Sapphira pointed at the growing tear. "Don't cry. We want them to like you. Don't you want a comfortable bed and good food, maybe even fig cakes?"

"I don't want fig cakes." Paili threw her arms around Sapphira. "I want you!"

Sapphira patted her lightly on the back. "We've been over this. I'll visit you whenever I can. I promise."

Paili looked up at Sapphira, her eyes glistening. "Tomorrow?"

"I'll check on your progress in a couple of days. Everything will be fine."

Paili squeezed more tightly. "But what if they don't like me?"

"How can anyone not like you? You're loving, you work hard, your speech is normal now, and you'll probably age right along with the other girls here in Glastonbury." Sapphira pushed her gently away. "Trust me. The local gypsies told me these people take in hungry strangers all the time, so I'm sure you'll be all right. But you must never, never tell anyone about where you're from, even if you think they might already know. Got that?"

Paili nodded meekly and turned toward the modest home, a noticeable tremble in her hands. Sapphira pulled the wooden cross

425

from her belt and knocked on the door. After a few seconds, the door swung open revealing a stout, red-haired woman holding a lantern. With soft, round cheeks and chin and bright shining eyes, she seemed just as friendly as she had been during the evenings Sapphira had spied on her.

"Well, who have we here?" the woman asked, probing the darkness with her lantern. "Another pair of lost gypsy girls?"

Sapphira backed away a step into the darkest shadows and lifted her cross. "We are not gypsies, dear lady, nor are we lost."

The woman waved toward the inside of the house. "Well, lost or found, you are welcome to our supper. My husband's not home yet, but he won't mind."

Sapphira whispered to the cross. "Give me light." Fire sprang forth, illuminating everyone on the porch.

The woman staggered but caught the door frame before falling. She seemed ready to drop to one knee, but she hesitated and stared, wide-eyed. "Are you . . . an angel?"

Sapphira deepened her voice and added a solemn cadence. "What I am is not important. You have been watched from afar, and because of your goodness and mercy, both to your fine husband and to your fellow citizens in this village, your childless state has come to an end."

The woman covered her mouth but made no sound.

"This girl needs a home," Sapphira continued, laying a hand on Paili's shoulder. "If you are pleased to take her in, she will become your daughter."

The woman set her lantern down and gathered Paili into her arms. "Oh!" she cried. "Oh, yes! Yes! Yes!" She hugged Paili close, tears streaming down her cheeks.

"Very well." Sapphira stepped back a few more paces. Then, wrapping her arms around herself, she whispered, "Give me light." Her entire body exploded into a human torch. The woman lifted Paili into her arms and lurched back through the doorway.

426

Sapphira commanded the fire to cease and dashed into the dark road.

The gloom of a cloudy night draped the outskirts of Glastonbury. Sapphira shuffled toward the city's famous towering hill and the monument that had replaced the church of Michael, the same portal location where she had left Elam years before. Another descent into the dismal world below lay ahead, then another reemergence at the ghostly mining level. Finally, she would climb up the elevation shaft and wind through the corridors leading to the museum room where Acacia would be waiting . . . alone.

Sapphira plodded forward, hoping to delay her return to the lower realms. She took a well-trodden path that promised no obstacles to a traveler who knew its twists and turns. With tears flowing, she counted her slow, careful steps out loud while struggling to conquer her tortured thoughts.

"Nine . . . ten . . . eleven. Seven more until I turn. . . . Of course Paili will be fine. Thirteen . . . fourteen . . . after all, now she can eat good food instead of old cabbages and dried beans . . . sixteen . . . seventeen . . . and that woman is so sweet . . . eighteen . . . Turn here." She pivoted to the left and continued. "One . . . two . . . All my other sisters are happy now. Four . . . five . . . six . . . so Paili will be happy, too . . . seven . . . eight. And Acacia and I won't have to worry about her getting so sick again. . . . nine . . . ten . . . That fever nearly killed Paili and Awven, and now that Penicillin's been discovered, it doesn't make sense to risk their lives . . . twelve . . . thirteen . . . so now Acacia and I can concentrate on . . ." She halted and tapped her finger on her chin. "Concentrate on what? Staring at each other for several more centuries?"

She turned back toward the little cottage in the distance, barely able to see two lanterns now glowing brightly at the front door. A man and woman stooped together, embracing Paili warmly.

A tear trickled down Sapphira's cheek, but she didn't bother to wipe it off. It didn't matter. Nothing else mattered. Even if she and

427

Acacia had to live under a billion tons of rocks forever, giving such a glorious new life to someone so precious was worth it all. Her sweet little sister finally had a home . . . and people who loved her.

Sapphira ignited her cross and ran the rest of the way to the portal.

APRIL, 1935

Elam slung his knapsack over his shoulder and slid a silver coin across the counter. "Will that cover it?" he asked.

"Quite well, laddie." The innkeeper tipped his beret. "Come back again."

Elam nodded at the floppy-eared old man, then pushed open a heavy oaken door and strode out into the misty dawn. Glasgow smelled worse than usual, oilier somehow, certainly more sulfurous than the day before. He pulled a beret from his trousers pocket and pressed it over his head. Or maybe he just noticed the odors more. When he worked in the Clydebank shipyards, the stench of tar and sweaty men masked everything else, and now that he had been out of a job for a couple of months, his sense of smell was probably more sensitive.

Elam turned back toward the one-story flat he had called home for the past two years. Although he had shared his ratty suite with a family of eight, this hostel was more than adequate in such tough times, and the innkeeper was fair and friendly. He laid his hand on the lintel, and, using the Scottish accent he had picked up over the years, whispered, "May the Lord bless the keeper of this house, and may he and his wife live long and well on the earth."

He dug into his pocket again and felt his leather purse, fingering the few coins that still weighed it down, enough for a brick of soap now and then, but not enough for lodging. He pulled his beret low over his brow and marched toward the road leading out of town. It was best to go back to camping in the woods, at least until hard times lifted. Ever since they finished building the *Queen Mary*, jobs had dropped off at the docks like ailing old men in the TB sanitariums.

As he strode past his church, dozens of people streamed from the sanctuary. He stopped for a moment and enjoyed the sea of smiling faces. The sunrise service had been resplendent, filled with wondrous choruses for the risen Savior, but Elam had slipped out right before the benediction. While hardly ever missing worship, he couldn't risk partaking in fellowship. There were always too many questions and never enough answers.

Elam marched on mile after mile. Once he passed the outskirts of the city, he took a side road, a familiar dirt and pebble path that wound its way through sheep pastures on its hilly course to Hannah's cottage. It had been at least three weeks since he last checked on her, so making camp in the woods behind her boarding house seemed a good choice for the night.

As he strolled by a pasture of grazing horses, he reached into his pocket and felt the Ovulum. Since it had been cold and quiet for decades, his delay in visiting Hannah probably hadn't mattered. The slayers were likely chasing down one of the hundreds of misleading clues he had left for them in London.

He stopped in front of the cottage and lowered his knapsack to the path, imagining Devin and Palin conducting their search. In his mind, they leaned over to hunt through a dustbin in a foggy London alley and bumped heads so hard they fell back on their posteriors. Elam laughed out loud.

"May I help ye, laddie?" a sweet voice called.

Elam gulped. Hannah! She had come outside, and he hadn't noticed! Why wasn't she working the charity breakfast lines? He tipped his beret and tried to squeeze out some intelligible words through his narrowing throat. "Uh, yes. I, uh . . ."

"Are ye sick?" Hannah stepped off her porch and walked straight up to him, her long dress seeming to sweep her petite body gracefully forward. "Do ye need a place to stay?"

Elam grabbed his beret and wrung it with both hands. "Uh, yes, but I'm running short on money."

"Atween the wind and the wa, are ye?" Hannah snatched up his knapsack, hooked him by the arm, and pulled him toward the cottage, her long auburn hair bouncing in rhythm with her gait. "Don't let it ever be said that Hannah MacKay turned out an impoverished laddie."

Elam gave in to Hannah's persistent tug and followed her into the cottage's front room. As the door swung closed, the rusty hinges squawked a loud complaint. Elam glanced around casually. Having sneaked in through the quieter back door several times to check on her, he was already familiar with the layout—a small but tidy dining area to the left, a cluttered little kitchen to the right, and, lining a short hallway straight ahead, four perfectly square bedrooms, three for tenants and one for Hannah. During those visits in the wee hours, Elam sometimes crept into her room, feeling the need, as a faithful shepherd of dragons, to stand and gaze at her as she slept. Still unmarried after all these centuries, she always slept alone.

She stopped at the first bedroom on the right and peeked inside. "You're in luck. Mr. Logan took his chimney brooms. He and his boy won't be back until at least tomorrow night." She laid his knapsack on the floor and pointed at a washbasin. "Water's there if ye wants a cat's lick before supper."

As she turned to leave, Elam laid a hand on her shoulder. "Wait!"

Hannah spun back, her friendly smile growing and her brow rising again in anticipation. "Are ye not throu?"

Elam shuddered. Hannah's Scottish accent was forced, and her idioms were slightly off-kilter. If the slayer ever heard her speak, he'd unmask her right away.

"What's the matter?" Hannah asked. "Short o' the Greek?" She stared at him with her wise old eyes, nearly as ancient as the earth itself, yet framed by a smooth, narrow face. Her gaze seemed to attach to his mind and absorb information.

He tried to shake off the brain lock, but it was no use. Something was up, and Hannah knew it. The Ovulum suddenly grew warm in his pocket, a good warmth, a prodding warmth. The prophet within the glass shell didn't always need words to let his will be made known.

Elam let out a long sigh. He had to tell her everything.

Devin pulled Excalibur from its scabbard and lifted it in front of his face. The shining blade divided his view, slicing the image of Palin in half as the squire donned the final garment in his battle array, a dark leather surcoat with a red dragon emblazoned on the front. Five hundred years had passed since he last strapped on his scabbard, but everything still seemed to fit.

431

Devin pointed the sword at Palin's head. "Does your new helmet suit you?"

Palin sat on his bed and rocked the domed helmet back and forth over his mop of black hair. "Yes. It's not the same style as my old one, but it will do."

Devin resheathed Excalibur and leaned out of their second-floor window. A fresh breeze blew streams of mist across a triplet of castle turrets rising from the adjacent wing. He breathed in the moist air and smiled. "It seems that your old model isn't fashionable with the mannequins in the Scottish museums. The first two castles had nothing but full body armor costumes. Can you imagine going into battle in one of those?"

Palin took off his helmet and laid it on his lap. "Maybe you should inform the museum curators of proper battle attire in the sixth century." He rapped the top of the helmet with his knuckles. "Or perhaps *we* need to be informed of proper, twentieth-century battle attire."

Still gazing out the window, Devin pulled up a necklace chain and let the candlestone dangle in front of his surcoat. "I know you think my obsession rather odd, but we are hunting dragons who are disguised in human skin, wolves in sheep's clothing. Our integrity would be in question if we were to appear as anything but slayers when we confront one of the devil lizards." He smoothed out the emblem on his vest, a screaming dragon with an arrow protruding from its belly. "I am not about to bow to hypocrisy just because our raiment is out of step with the vagaries of this century's fashions. Unpretentious and unmasked, we have stripped the dragons' disguises with the point of a sword, and we will continue in that sacred tradition."

"As you wish, my liege." Palin drew his sword, his eyes scanning the blade as it emerged from its scabbard. "It is freshly sharpened for the ceremonial undressing of the queen of the demon witches."

"Excellent!" Devin raised the candlestone in front of his eyes. "If this Logan fellow speaks the truth, Thigocia will soon be ours. The witch who whelped the entire coven will finally be exposed."

"And then only two more," Palin said, shoving his sword back in place.

"Yes. I will repay Hartanna for wounding me, but"—Devin clenched a fist around the candlestone's chain—"I want Clefspeare's blood more than any other. To use his power to extend our lives would be the ultimate victory."

CHAPTER

REUNION

Still facing Hannah, Elam reached back into his mind and recalled the ancient Hebrew he once spoke so well. Now the language seemed foreign, but the words came quickly enough. "I know who you are," he said.

Hannah's mouth dropped open. She sputtered, also speaking Hebrew. "What . . . what did you say?"

Elam slowly withdrew the Ovulum from his pocket and lifted it in his open palm. "I know who you are."

Hannah grabbed Elam's arm, pulled him into the bedroom, and slammed the door. "Who are you? How did you get the Ovulum?"

Elam raised a shushing finger to his lips. "Are any other boarders here?"

"None who speak Hebrew!" She gripped his wrist so tightly, pain shot along his arm, making the Ovulum tremble in his palm. "If you are a slayer, you were a fool to come with neither sword nor shield." She squeezed even harder, revealing a strength that belied her petite frame. "Now, I will ask again, and you will answer. Who are you, and how did you get the Ovulum?"

"I am Elam, son of Shem," he said, laying a hand on his chest. "The Ovulum came to me by the will of Elohim. Since Noah was my grandfather, and Methuselah was his grandfather, it rightfully belongs to me."

Hannah gasped. "Noah was your grandfather? How is that possible? You are not more than sixteen years old, eighteen at the most!"

Elam extended a hand and gently placed his palm on her cheek. "How old are you, Thigocia?"

Hannah released his arm and backed away, her voice spiking with alarm. "Where did you hear that name?"

He stepped toward her, but when he noted the anguish in her eyes, he halted and spoke in a soothing tone. "I have kept watch over you for fifteen hundred years. I prevented Devin and Palin from finding you at least a dozen times."

Hannah backed up against the bedroom's far wall and flattened her palms against the plaster. "You"—she swallowed hard—"you have been following me around for centuries?" She glanced at an open window, just an arm's length from her hand. "Why should I believe a word you are saying?"

Elam raised the Ovulum onto his fingertips. "Because I bear the dwelling place of the Eye of the Oracle." He drew it closer to his face and said, "*Fiat lux*." The glass began to glow, and a nebulous crimson cloud took shape within.

A look of curiosity swept across Hannah's face. She took a half step forward, craning her neck. "Can you see him?"

The cloud congealed into the shape of an eye, bright and clear. Dozens of reddish hues painted the pupil, the iris, and every serpentine capillary. Elam nodded at the pulsing egg. "Yes, but he rarely speaks, he—"

A squeak sounded, the whine of the front door's rusty hinges. Elam spun around and laid his ear on the bedroom door, whispering, "Are you expecting someone?"

Hannah shook her head and began inching toward the window. A slow creak drifted in from the hallway, a bending floor plank on the other side of the door.

The Ovulum's temperature spiked hotter in Elam's hand, and an urgent whisper hissed from the shell. "Fly! A dark knight is coming quickly!"

Elam rushed to the window. Hannah had already straddled the sill. Grabbing her wrist, he lowered her to the ground, then scrunched low and leaped out. They backed away from the cottage, watching for any movement in the room. Suddenly, Devin vaulted through the window frame. Before the dark knight hit the ground, Palin followed. As Devin straightened, he faltered for a moment, clutching his leg in pain.

"He's hurt!" Elam said, grabbing Hannah's arm. "Run!"

435

Hannah jerked free. "No! I am through running!" She snatched the Ovulum from Elam and held it in her outstretched hand. "Thousands of years ago, I saw the Ovulum protect the ark of Noah from the most powerful demons in the world. I am sure it can hold off two of their stupid lackeys."

Devin withdrew his sword and stalked toward them with Palin at his side, his sword also at the ready. As the Ovulum pulsed bright rings of red, Devin stopped and sneered. "You would battle two knights with a glass bauble?" he asked in an old English dialect.

"It is enough for the likes of you," Hannah snapped, using the same dialect.

Devin swiped his sword over Hannah's palm, slicing through the Ovulum. The top half fell to the ground and spun in the grass. He flashed a mocking smile. "Sorry to crush your hopes, dragoness, but your faith is fatally misplaced."

As Devin drew back his sword again, the lower part of the Ovulum spewed a towering fountain of scarlet sparks that streamed in every direction. Hannah jerked her hand away, dropping the broken egg. The half shell rocked back and forth and continued gushing until the streams coalesced into two cyclonic columns that spun like crimson tornados between the pairs of opponents.

One of the columns lifted off the ground and soared into the sky, while the other drilled downward and splashed a huge cloud of dust into the dark knights' faces. Devin and Palin covered their eyes, coughing and gagging as they backed away.

Elam lunged for Palin and threw him down. Wrapping his arms around the knight's sword hand, he slammed the mail-clad arm against the ground, then pried the sword free and jumped up with the hilt in his grip. Setting his feet, he pointed the blade at the pair of slayers as they continued to cough uncontrollably.

More dust erupted from the lower end of the spinning column, blending russet streaks into the crimson cyclone until it looked like a swirling pinwheel of flesh and blood. The streaks solidified and coiled into a tight cylinder. As the spinning slowed, a man's body took shape, his hands at his sides and his eyes tightly shut.

The turning stopped. The man gasped a deep breath, then opened his eyes and looked around frantically. Spotting Hannah, he swept her up and began to run.

Still holding Palin's sword, Elam rushed after them. Hannah thrashed in the man's arms, screaming, "We can run faster if you will let me go!" She jabbed her elbow into his ribs until he stumbled and dropped her. After toppling over her body, he flopped face first into a patch of dandelions.

Elam hustled to the man and rolled him over. He seemed familiar somehow, and since he had come out of the Ovulum, he likely wasn't an enemy. "Are you all right?" Elam asked in modern English.

"We have to escape," the man replied in Old English. "The effects of the gas on the slayers will not last long."

Elam and Hannah each grabbed one of the man's arms and helped him to his feet. Elam glanced back at the two knights. The slayers were slowly rising, still coughing, but not as vigorously. "We must make haste," the man continued. "Are there any rapid conveyances?"

Hannah nodded. "Yes, I have horses."

"In the pasture down the road!" Elam swept his arm forward. "Come on!"

The trio dashed away from the cottage, scaled a low fence, and sprinted across a grassy field. When the horses came into view, Hannah pulled on Elam's sleeve, slowing him down. "Careful, or we will frighten them."

With Palin's sword still in hand, Elam walked briskly, alternately glancing at several horses grazing about fifty paces in front, then behind him at the slayers who followed at a distance. "Can you ride bareback?" he asked Hannah.

"Yes. Can you?"

"I think so." Elam turned to the stranger. "Do you ride?"

The man nodded. "Yes, but never in this world."

Elam propped the sword over his shoulder. "What's that supposed to mean?"

"I will explain soon enough."

"Wait here." Hannah strode ahead. As she approached the horses, she held out her hand toward a bay mare and spoke as though she were addressing another human. "Legossi," she said, returning to her Scottish-soaked, modern dialect, "we are in great danger. I need you and Hartanna and Clefspeare to carry us to safety. Will you do it?"

The mare replied with a lengthy bob of her head. Two other horses, a dapple-gray mare and a chestnut stallion, both nodded in the same way. Hannah sidled up to the stallion. "I will take

437

Clefspeare," she said, switching back to old English. "Elam, you ride the bay mare. You"—she pointed at the stranger—"you can ride the dapple gray."

Elam checked the slayers' progress as they crossed the field. Palin, now brandishing Excalibur and running ahead of his injured master, would be at their throats in seconds. Elam dropped his captured sword and set his hands in a cradle near the ground. "Hannah! Quick! I'll boost you!"

"No need for boosting!" Taking a running start, Hannah leaped over his hands and vaulted onto the stallion. Then, snatching Elam's collar, she hauled him to the bay mare and lifted him high. Elam grabbed the horse's neck, swung his leg over her back, and righted himself. The stranger leaped onto the dapple-gray mare and slid deftly into place.

Now only a dozen paces away, Palin charged toward them, Devin's sword in one hand and a dagger in the other.

Giving Clefspeare a firm kick, Hannah shouted. "Let us fly!"

The stallion bolted, and the mares galloped after him. Elam squeezed the mare with his knees to steady himself, but sudden pain made him lurch. He clutched his upper arm. Palin's dagger! The jagged blade had penetrated deeply, probably to the bone. He jerked the dagger out and slung it to the ground. Pain ripped through his neck and down his spine. Blood flowed freely, coating his arm in seconds.

He glanced back. Palin was pointing at the ground with the sword Elam had left behind. Elam grimaced. A blood trail! But he couldn't stop to make a bandage. Hannah and the stranger were already too far ahead. Leaning forward and hanging on with his good arm, he could only watch the tall grass zip by underneath while blood dripped from his fingers. He might as well make a sign that said, "This way to the dragon!"

He tried to pull the mare to the right, hoping to steer his pursuers away, but she stayed on course behind the pair in front.

Closing his eyes and laying his head on the horse's mane, he focused on enduring the escape. The mare's hoofbeats rattled his brain, and each jolt brought a new stab of agony.

Soon, the thunder of other hoofbeats grew closer, so close they seemed to hammer the ground in a stride-for-stride gallop next to him. Elam clutched the horse's mane. Was Devin about to grab him? Too groggy to sit up, he tried to kick his horse, but he lurched to the side and fell. Strong arms caught him, lifted him into the air, and set him in place again on a different mount. A gentle male voice drifted into his ear. "Hang on, young man. Keep your courage. I will let you rest in a moment."

When the horse finally stopped, another pair of hands grasped his uninjured arm as he slid slowly downward. Hannah's voice lilted in his ears, her Scottish accent spicing her Old English. "I will lay him down! Move the horses away! Quickly now."

Elam fluttered his eyelids, catching glimpses of tall blades of grass next to his cheek, Hannah's worried face on one side of his body and the stranger from the Ovulum on the other. Every image seemed filtered by a dark screen. Even the sun wore a basaltic mask that coated the skies with gray. With pain roaring from arm to arm, he clenched his teeth, unable to put his torment into words.

The man's voice drifted by, soft as a phantom's whisper. "Can you stop the bleeding?"

Hannah's sharp reply drilled into his ears. "Give me your shirt!"

New throbs shot through Elam's brain, shocking him to a more wakeful state. He peeked through his partially closed eyelids. Hannah, dim and blurry, wrapped a shirt around his injured arm. After tying it in place, she pressed her hand on the wound.

Elam moaned. The pain was worse than the sting of Nabal's cruelest whippings.

Hannah's voice returned, now more soothing. "Shhh. I have to put pressure on it or you are likely to bleed to death."

439

The stranger, now in a singlet undershirt, knelt at Elam's other side and mopped his brow with a torn sleeve. "My dear lady, you seem to have experience with healing fallen warriors."

Hannah kept her head turned toward Elam. "And you seem to have experience with heroic rescues. You remind me of a very dear friend of mine, an old friend from long ago."

"How kind of you to say so. Was your friend a hero?"

Hannah's eyes misted. "To me, he was much more than a hero—much, much more."

"I see." He angled his head toward Elam but kept his eyes fixed on her. "Was this hero a former flame?"

A sad smile wrinkled Hannah's lips. "You have no idea how well you have described him."

The man's eyebrows lifted. "Perhaps I do."

"No," Hannah said, sighing deeply, "you do not."

The man turned his cloth over and dabbed Elam's forehead again. "Have other flames come to warm the embers this love left behind?"

"What?" Hannah glared at him. "I would expect better manners from a man who sprang forth from the Ovulum!"

The man lowered his head. "Forgive me, dear lady. The Eye of the Oracle commanded me to ask that very question."

As Hannah's glare softened, she sighed. "Well, if the Eye bids me to answer . . ." She shook her head slowly, and her voice pitched slightly higher. "My embers are cold, and they are slowly crumbling to dust." She yanked a blade of grass away from Elam's cheek. "I do not allow even a spark to approach them. No one will ever rekindle my coals."

"May I venture to describe this lost flame of yours?"

Hannah sniffed, her chin trembling. "If you must."

The man took a deep breath and spoke with a poetic cadence. "Embodying the spirit of a paladin, he ignited the passions of your heart. Flashing the courage of a warrior, he burned away all your fears. Massaging with the gentleness of spring sunshine, he warmed your scales on cold, anxious nights."

"Well done. It almost seems that you—" Hannah clenched a handful of grass. "Did you say, 'scales'?"

"Yes. And if he is the fiery romantic that I suspect, he probably told you that he would eventually come back." He gazed directly into Hannah's eyes. "Is that true . . . Thigocia?"

Hannah's lips quivered. Still keeping her hand on Elam's arm, she leaned closer to the stranger and gazed into his eyes. After a few seconds, a tear trickled down her cheek as she whispered, "My . . . my husband?"

He took the ends of her fingers into his hand and guided her around Elam. "We said, 'till death do us part,' but even death could not keep our love apart forever."

"Makaidos!" Hannah leaped into his arms. "My darling husband! It is you! It is really you!"

Holding her close in his lap, he stroked her silky hair. "My human name is Timothy, but I will answer to any name you wish to give me." He gently pushed her toward Elam. "You had better tend to your patient."

"Oh! Yes! Of course!" She stepped over Elam and pressed down on his arm.

Elam grimaced, but the pain wasn't quite as bad as before.

"How did you do it?" she asked, a broad smile stretching her cheeks. "I mean, how did you come back to life?"

Timothy mopped Elam's brow again. "God preserved my spirit in the Ovulum, and I spent over a thousand years there learning from Enoch. He said that someday God would create a new body for me from the dust of the ground. When the Ovulum broke open, Enoch closed his eyes and said, 'It is time.' Then, he disappeared." Timothy laid a hand on his chest. "And now I am here, back with my beloved."

441

Hannah reached across Elam and took Timothy's hand, drawing it close. She kissed his fingers and rubbed the back of his hand across her cheek. "What happened to Enoch?"

"I am concerned about him," he said. "God took him from the earth long ago, and he resided in the Ovulum as a prophetic eye for thousands of years. But he knew he would be leaving, and he said he did not know where God would take him next."

Hannah released the pressure on Elam's arm and slowly peeled the blood-soaked shirt away from the wound. "It is just oozing now." She patted Elam on the cheek. "You are certainly a fast healer."

Elam forced a smile. "Must be from clean living." He rose to a sitting position, blinking at the beams of sunlight filtering through the high treetops. Two horses stood in a shallow stream that trickled over their hooves, while the third nosed through a patch of clover next to a nearby oak tree. He raised his good arm. "Help me up. Devin will follow my blood trail, so we have to keep moving."

"There is no hurry." Hannah rose and pulled Elam to his feet. "With that bad leg of his, he could not possibly keep up."

"He was a knight," Elam countered. "He and Palin know how to mount and ride horses."

"An excellent point." Hannah brushed off her dress. "We will follow the stream to the River Clyde. If we can make it there by nightfall, we should be able to erase our trail in the water under the cover of darkness. Then we can follow the river to Uddingston."

While Hannah gathered the horses, Elam picked up the drenched bandage and wadded it into a ball. A drop of blood slowly gathered at the end of a sleeve and dripped to the ground. "I have a better idea." He forked his fingers at Timothy and Hannah. "You two can go to Uddingston. I'll lead Devin away with a trail of blood."

"No," Hannah said, now riding on Clefspeare. "If he catches you—"

"The boy is right." Timothy turned to Elam. "You must separate from us. Now that Thigocia and I are together, you are finished here. Enoch told me that your next assignment is to find Valcor, another dragon turned human. Although he fled from Europe for a time, he now lives in Glastonbury, England, under the name of Patrick Nathanson. You will learn how you must aid him as you so faithfully aided Thigocia."

"My name is Hannah now," she corrected. "And you will need to learn the new tongue quickly."

Elam shook his head and chuckled under his breath. "Both of you could use a lot of work with your speech. Just relax, and don't try so hard. I mean, you sound as stiff as dragons' armor."

Timothy smiled. "Is that so," he said in modern English, his words lilting with the rhythm of a perfect Scottish accent. "You'd be surprised at what a man can learn trapped inside a glass egg for hundreds of years. I just breathed the Scottish air for an hour, and I'm already a Scotsman!"

443

"Excellent!" Hannah clapped her hands and laughed. "You even used contractions. I always found those difficult to master."

A low rumble vibrated the ground. Elam strained to listen. Hoofbeats? If so, they were still far away, but closing fast. He waved toward the gray mare. "Timothy! Hurry! Whichever way you go, I'll ride in the opposite direction."

Timothy boosted Elam onto the bay mare, then leaped aboard the dapple gray's back. "I trust we will see you again, Elam."

"If it is in my power." Pressing the horse's shoulder with his good hand, Elam steadied himself and nodded to both former dragons. His throat caught, and tears welled in his eyes. "It has been an honor to serve you. May the Lord Christ be with you always."

Hannah rode to his side and patted Elam's horse. "Legossi, stay with him and keep him safe." Legossi gave her a horsey snort and nodded.

Hannah pulled Elam's sleeve. "Farewell, brave warrior." She kissed him on the hand. "Thank you for watching over me."

With a firm kick into Clefspeare's side, Hannah rode into the creek and galloped downstream.

Timothy guided his mare next to Elam's. "You recognized me all along, didn't you?"

Elam shrugged. "It's been a long time. I wasn't sure enough to say anything."

"I understand." He lowered his head briefly before returning his gaze to Elam. "Pray for me. I must tell my beloved about Roxil. As far as I know, she is still trapped in that God-forsaken town. And I also must search for the spirit of my father. I refuse to believe he is really that deceiver who indwells the body of Arramos."

"I will pray." Elam nodded downstream. "You'd better get going."

He gave Elam a military salute and chased after Hannah. As his horse disappeared into the thick forest, Elam waited, listening to the approaching hoofbeats. He let the bloody bandage dangle over the ground for a moment, then rode along the creek's muddy shoreline, following it upstream as he squeezed more blood onto the ground.

"That should do it," he said out loud. "We'll see if Devin takes the bait, and then we'll try to find Valcor." After patting the mare's neck, he gave her a gentle nudge with his heels. "Okay, Legossi, let's make tracks!"

Sapphira bolted upright in bed. Sweat dampened her nightgown and plastered her sleeves against her skin. The dream was awful. A man jumped out of a window with a sword and swung it at Elam and Hannah, but the dream suddenly ended. She never saw what happened.

Sapphira focused her bleary eyes on the portal screen, now just a vortex of fuzzy orange light. How strange! Had she shut it down and not remembered? Waving her hand at it, she whispered, "Expand," but the dim eddies just swirled like deaf pixies, dancing on without a care.

Sapphira stared at a stubborn rash that had recently invaded her palm. Could the irritation be hampering her power? She touched it with her fingertip, reinflaming its awful itch, but she resisted the urge to scratch.

She pushed gently on Acacia's back. "You'd better get up. Something's wrong."

Acacia rose to her elbows, barely opening her eyes. "What? What's wrong?"

"The screen is off, and it won't come back on."

Acacia lifted an eyebrow. "Didn't that happen once before?"

"Yes. Elam got a bunch of tar on the Ovulum. But it's not black this time. It won't expand at all."

"Don't worry about Elam. He's been around for a lot of centuries. He knows what he's doing."

"Maybe you're right." Sapphira scratched her head and yawned through her reply. "I'm going to get ready for the day, and if the screen's still blank, I'll start worrying about Elam."

"You do that." Acacia turned over and nestled into her pillow. "It's Easter morning, so we're allowed to sleep in."

"But we still have to eat." Sapphira shoved her again. "And it's your turn to get food today."

Acacia sat up and frowned. "It *is* my turn, isn't it?"

"I'm afraid so." Sapphira rose to her feet and, with her vision still blurry, stumbled toward the museum, ready to step through her routine—wash her face from the basin, measure the tree's growth, pick out the new books she would read, and sit in front of the portal to watch Elam for a few hours before kicking back for a quiet afternoon of reading.

After splashing in the basin and drying her face, she picked up a measuring tape from a shelf and set one end on the ground near

445

the slender trunk. Then, pushing her face in among the lush green leaves, she unraveled the tape against the trunk, moving it upward until it reached the top of the growth core, a height that roughly equaled her own. She pressed her thumb on the mark, and, after extracting herself from the foliage, read the tape and sighed. "Still sixty-three inches."

Gazing at the surrounding shelves, she located the magneto bricks she had installed and counted the bright rainbow colors. All seven seemed to be working, but whether or not they did much good from so far away was impossible to tell.

She grabbed a pencil and a nearby scroll and marked down the tree's measurement. "You haven't grown an inch in three years now." Rolling back to the beginning of her records, she tapped the pencil on the parchment. "I almost forgot! If I'm marking time correctly in the upper world, today marks one thousand years since you sprouted!"

Sapphira closed the scroll and put it away, smiling as she turned back to the tree. "Shall we have an anniversary celebration, or—" She stopped and stared. Something new hung at the end of one of the branches, something white and spherical.

Sapphira sang out her sister's name, extending the syllables. "Acacia! You need to see this!"

"Coming!" Acacia called.

Sapphira set her palm under the fruit and slowly lifted. It was light, much lighter than she expected. Caressing it with her fingers, she marveled at its tactile surface, more like the lumpy buds of cauliflower than the slick peel of an apple or a pear.

Acacia hummed a lively tune as she entered but suddenly stopped and smiled. "We have fruit!"

"Yes." Sapphira rubbed the fruit with her thumb. "It's kind of strange, though. It feels sort of fibrous, like it might be soft and flaky."

"So, shall we have it for breakfast?" Acacia asked, reaching for the fruit.

"Wait!" Sapphira grabbed Acacia's wrist.

Acacia pulled back. "Wait for what?"

"If this is the tree of life, it might make us live forever without ever getting hungry."

"Right. I thought that was the idea."

Sapphira cocked her head to the side. "Well . . . do you really want to live forever? I mean, this isn't exactly heaven. I know we're not aging now, but maybe we will someday, and from what I've read about heaven, I'd like to get there eventually."

Acacia scratched her scalp through her tangled white hair and laughed under her breath. "All this time we've been begging the tree to produce fruit, and now that it's here, are we going to change our minds?"

"Sometimes you have to when reality kind of smacks you in the face."

Acacia tapped the fruit with her finger, making it swing back and forth. "So what should we do with it?"

Sapphira laid a hand over her heart. "Let's promise each other that we won't eat it unless we're truly starving, like if for some reason we can't get any food from the upper world."

"That doesn't make sense. Even if we were starving, we still wouldn't want to live forever, would we?"

"I don't know what I'd do if I were starving." Sapphira caressed the fruit with her fingertip. "But it can't be a coincidence that it showed up after exactly a thousand years, can it? It has to mean something."

"True, but we don't have anything but guesses."

Sapphira leaned to the side and peeked at the portal screen. "Maybe we'll see something today that will make it all clear. We always seem to get messages from the Ovulum whenever we really need them."

Acacia leaned with her. "I don't think we're going to learn much from it. It's still just a column."

447

"I noticed." Sapphira crossed her arms and began tapping her foot.

Acacia wrapped her fingers around Sapphira's wrist. "I can read your mind, Sister. You're not going to traipse over to Glasgow to see what's going on."

Sapphira stopped tapping. "Why not? With our disguises, we could get there without anyone noticing us. We'll be wearing our sunglasses."

"Oh, sure," Acacia said, rolling her eyes. "I can see the people on the train, pointing at us. 'Look at the poor little blind girls all dressed up in their frilly bonnets. Aren't they cute?' "

"But today is Easter, so no one will think anything's unusual. And maybe we won't need bonnets at all. I read about a new hair dye that might work."

"Another one? Those chemicals did nothing but give you a rash, and, besides, we can't color our eyes. Wearing sunglasses might raise a lot of pity, but it's not going to get us to Glasgow." Acacia took Sapphira's hand. "Look. Even if you could get there, how would you ever find Elam?"

Sapphira heaved a big sigh. "I guess you're right, but when I can't keep an eye on him, I just—" She pulled her hand slowly away from Acacia. "My palm! The rash is gone!"

Acacia touched Sapphira's clean, healthy skin. "It healed overnight?"

"No, it itched terribly this morning." Sapphira swung her head toward the tree. "The last time I remember scratching it was right before I touched the fruit."

"How could fruit heal your rash?"

Sapphira caressed her palm with her finger. "Maybe it has medicinal properties."

"And maybe it was a miracle." Acacia touched the cross resting behind the waistband of Sapphira's long gray skirt, part of the dreary outfit she had scavenged from a charity box. "After all the miracles you've seen," Acacia said, "I don't understand why you get so jumpy about Elam."

Sapphira pulled out the cross and gazed at its seemingly invulnerable surface. "I guess you're right."

"I know what we can do!" Acacia whirled around and marched toward the exit corridor, her own mousy skirt spinning around her legs. "Let's go visit Yereq. Maybe the screen will be on by the time we get back."

"Wait for me!" Sapphira hustled to catch up, whispering to her cross, "Give me light!" Instantly, a bright flame danced across the slender wood, smokeless and reaching tiny yellow limbs toward the cave's ceiling. As the two walked silently through the tunnel, Sapphira reflected on the cross's eerie glow and repeated the words to herself, *"Give me light."* Though she hadn't spoken them out loud this time, the command seemed to echo in her ears. *"Give me light. Give me light."* She blinked at the undulating flames and shook her head. If there was a deeper message hiding behind those simple words, it wasn't ready to show itself yet.

449

Now accustomed to the once forbidden path to the mobility room, Sapphira took little notice of the empty growth chambers lining the final corridor that led to the massive vault-like room. Even the bones of dead giants were easy to skip around. The stench of their rotting flesh had long since diminished, so they were just a morbid collection of stones the girls could easily dodge.

Now, marching right into the room seemed easy, almost too easy. The once prohibited journey had become like a stroll to the library, a way to pass the time. Sapphira raised her cross near Yereq's growth chamber, illuminating the ten-foot-tall giant floating within the recess of the stony wall. "Hello, Yereq," Sapphira sang. "It's me."

The sleeping giant's face remained stony at first, but slowly, ever so slowly, a weak smile appeared.

"Someday I'm going to wake you up," she continued, "but I can't yet, not until I figure out the code in Mardon's journal." She turned to Acacia and let out a heavy sigh. "Do you ever get tired of hearing me say that?"

"I got tired of it after the tenth time." Acacia nodded at the chamber. "But Yereq seems to enjoy it."

Sapphira lifted the cross higher, sending the light over Yereq again. His smile spread across his face. She lowered the cross and gazed at her twin but didn't want to ask her burning question for the hundredth time. Though it remained unspoken today, Acacia answered it anyway with her usual gracious tone. "Don't worry. If we ever wake him, he'll love you."

Sapphira knelt at the base of the growth chamber. The counter now read "8550," just a few ticks lower than the previous reading. She tapped the counter with her finger. "I think it's still dropping at the same rate."

"It's moving so slowly," Acacia said, "we'll have to wait till the twenty-first century to see it hit zero."

After rising to her feet, Sapphira waved the burning cross at the seven or eight chambers within reach of her light. "Maybe, but if Yereq and these giants wake up in a foul mood, I don't want to be around."

Acacia raised her finger. "If we take a meter, we won't have to be anywhere near them. We'll know when they're about to hatch."

Sapphira knelt in front of the chamber's hearth again and pried the meter loose. "That's strange." She turned it over and examined the back. "No connection wires."

Acacia crouched low. "So it doesn't do anything?"

Sapphira flipped it to its digital side. "Maybe it's just a visible timer that matches controlling timers embedded in the magneto bricks themselves."

"How do you know so much about magneto bricks?"

Sapphira slid the meter into her pocket. "I helped Mardon with his experiments a lot more than I care to talk about."

Devin stooped next to the stream and pinched a clump of blood-stained mud. "Only one set of tracks follows the trail."

Palin guided his horse into the stream. "The other two might have stayed in the water. The bed is solid enough."

Rising to his full height, Devin shook his head. "If they wanted to throw us off that way, all three would have stayed in the creek. The blood trail was meant to steer us away from the demon witch."

"Shall we separate, then?" Palin pointed upstream. "The boy is wounded. It won't be hard to catch him."

"He is of no consequence, and I will need your help until my next infusion of power." Devin limped toward his horse, a muscular roan gelding with a cropped mane.

451

Palin jumped down and gave Devin a boost onto its back. "When will you perform the next infusion?" Palin asked. "Your limp is getting worse every day."

"Do you think I haven't noticed?" Devin pulled out the candlestone's chain and dangled the gem at his chest. "The blood we have is getting old. I want to wait until we can use Thigocia's blood."

"I see. New life from new blood."

Devin guided his horse into the water and pointed downstream. "The witch will probably head for the River Clyde. She's a crafty devil, so we'd better hurry or we'll lose the trail."

"Any more ideas about the man who came out of that egg?" Palin asked.

"No, but if he tries to stop us"—Devin wrapped his fingers around Excalibur's hilt—"his head will be looking up at his body from a pool of blood."

CHAPTER

GABRIEL'S GIFT

JANUARY, 1949

Elam fastened a pin on the diaper and poked the baby's fat little belly. "Feel better now?" The baby made a splurting sound from underneath his diaper and giggled.

"Rupert!" Elam moaned. "Not again!"

A woman's voice sang from across the room. "I'll do it, Elam."

Elam smiled at Mrs. Nathanson as she crossed the enormous nursery, sidestepping coloring books, a plastic baseball bat, and three toddlers snuggling blankets on the soft carpet. He nodded at the snoozing children. "Except for Rupert and those three, all the under-twos are changed and in their cribs."

"You really are a gentleman!" Mrs. Nathanson said, taking Rupert from Elam. "Just like"—she suddenly turned her head—"just like always."

Elam wondered about the strange hesitation but chalked it up to her frequent state of emotional upheaval, the longing for a child that she and her husband had never been able to have. He watched

453

her loving hands as they laid the six-month-old boy down—her fingers tender as she caressed the wiggling body, deft as she kept the pins from sticking soft flesh, and playful as she tapped Rupert's nose and cooed at him.

He let out a quiet sigh. Had his own mother been so loving? Had she protected him from pain and exposure? How many years did she weep for her lost son? Did she die in grief, never able to break free from the pain of a mother's empty arms?

After four thousand years, only a shadow of his mother's image remained. Still, this childless woman's care for orphaned babies brought a familiar warmth, something he longed for that had gone wanting for too many centuries. Even her eyes somehow seemed familiar, like those of a friendly stranger who had smiled for no reason and then walked away, disappearing into the passage of time.

Mrs. Nathanson patted his hand. "Don't worry about checking the escape tunnels tonight. I don't think it will rain, so they should stay dry."

"I'll check them anyway. I'm trying to memorize all the paths in the maze."

She gazed toward the ceiling, and her voice changed to a dreamy whisper. "I memorized them a long time ago. It's fun to explore."

"You memorized *all* of them? Why? They're only for emergencies."

"I sort of feel at home down there. It's so peaceful." She shook her head as if casting off her dream, but she kept her smile. "You'd better hurry to the meeting now. Patrick will want to begin on time."

"Oh, yeah. Right!" Elam bolted toward the door. "Thank you!"

"Dress warm!"

"I will!" He grabbed a sweater from the back of a chair and rocketed from the room, sprinting down a long, high corridor as he slid his arms into the sweater's sleeves. Although the mansion seemed designed by a stuffy aristocrat, with marble floors, brass doorknobs, and sculpted columns, neither the master of the house nor his wife would ever scold him for his mad dash down a hallway. After all, with about sixty orphans of various ages, shapes, and sizes living in a human beehive, the house always seemed abuzz with activity. No one would take notice of a multi-thousand-year-old teenager breezing by.

Elam slowed and turned down another corridor, a narrower one with a low ceiling and rough walls. Grabbing a lantern and a matchbook from a shelf along the way, he stopped at an entry to a dark hall. A heavy oak door, usually closed and locked, stood open, probably in anticipation of his arrival.

Striking a match, he touched the flame to the lantern's wick. The fire crawled across the braided cotton and leaped upward into the glass chimney, giving rise to a beautiful image in his mind—Sapphira Adi, her white hair igniting and the flames spreading down her lithe body just before she brought Acacia back to life. Though tears filled his eyes, he smiled. He would find her again someday . . . somehow.

455

He stepped through the doorway·into another corridor. Its ceiling was so low, he instinctively ducked, though he knew he could stand erect without scraping his scalp. A few of the ceiling's ancient, wooden beams bent toward the floor, and a musty odor hung in the dank air.

The corridor ended at another open doorway that led to a much larger room. He soft-stepped in and found Patrick seated where he expected him to be, in one of seven chairs at a round table set precisely over a circular compass etched into the floor. Two lanterns sat on the table, their wicks burning brightly.

As Patrick tapped his finger on a scroll he had rolled out in front of him, a cold pocket of air filtered through a ragged-edged rectangle in the stone ceiling high above. Several large ravens fluttered from one side of the opening to the other, apparently longing for the relative warmth of the humans' abode.

Bathed in the eerie glow of moonlight, Patrick buttoned his thick gray sweater, then brushed his hand through his short reddish brown hair. A shadow, stenciled on a green curtain covering a ten-foot-by-ten-foot section of the wall, mimicked his actions.

After blowing out his lantern, Elam approached the table. "I am here, as you requested."

Patrick rolled up his scroll and motioned toward the chair next to him. "Please sit. We have a lot to talk about."

Elam slid into the chair and set the lantern at his feet. "Your wife told me you had news from other dragons."

"I do." Patrick opened a folded note. His thick eyebrows angled downward as he scanned it. "This is a translation. The original was written in a mixture of Hebrew and an old English dialect. Unfortunately, I have forgotten much of both languages, so I took it to Charles, who translated it for me."

"Charles? Who's he?"

"You met him a couple of years ago at an archery tournament. We congratulated him for winning his division. He was a high school senior then, and now he is an extraordinary linguist studying at Oxford, but even he had to dust off some old books to complete the translation."

Elam leaned closer and tried to read the note, but the handwriting was too scribbly. "Can you trust him?"

"I trust him as far as I need to at the moment. If my investigation of his character proves him worthy, I hope someday to invite him to join my circle of knights at this very table."

"So, does Charles know about the dragons now?"

"No. The message was in symbolic language, so he wasn't able to interpret the meaning of the English words, but the project made him extremely curious. I am tempted to explain it to him, but he is young and inexperienced, so I have decided to wait a while."

Patrick flattened the note on the table and pointed at the first line. "Let me read it to you. I had to embellish it a bit to fill in the gaps."

As Elam leaned back in his chair, Patrick cleared his throat. "The king and queen are still in play, though the two dark knights have lurked through a fortnight. A pawn emerged from the queen's skirts, enraging the evil pursuers. When the knights finally found the king and queen, the royal pair flew to a new world to mark a trail, leaving the pawn to hide under the shelter of the white knight's home."

Elam blurted out his interpretation. "So Hannah and Timothy are alive! And Devin and Palin have been chasing them for fourteen years."

"Exactly." Patrick gestured for Elam to continue. "And . . ."

"And they had a baby, so, in order to protect him, they flew to the States, hoping Devin would follow him, and they left their baby here with you."

Patrick clapped his hands. "Very good! Charles was completely baffled."

457

"Well, it's not so hard when you know the history." Elam glanced toward the hallway that led back to the main house. "So, does your wife have the baby?"

"Oh," Patrick said, chuckling, "he's hardly a baby."

Elam pointed at him. "Right. Hannah could've had the baby years ago."

"Timothy told me earlier that even though they believed they were already husband and wife because of their dragon ritual, he and Hannah decided to have a legal human wedding before reuniting. As I understand it, the baby was born almost exactly nine months later."

Elam counted on his fingers. "So if he was born in January of 1936, now he would be . . ." He rolled his eyes upward. "Thirteen?"

"Precisely! Timothy's and Hannah's getaway to the States occurred only very recently, so one of my colleagues fled with the child from Glasgow and brought him here." Patrick slid out his chair and turned toward the green curtain. "Gabriel, you may come out now."

The curtain moved, parting in the middle. A boy peeked through the gap. "Did you tell him about the"—he gestured with his head as though someone were behind him—"you know what?"

"Oh." Patrick winced. "How could I forget?" He turned back to Elam. "Gabriel doesn't want to frighten you. He has a unique gift passed down to him by his mother, so be prepared for a shock."

"Uh . . . okay." Elam folded his hands on the table. "I'm ready."

Gabriel stepped out from behind the curtain. As he strode toward Patrick, a set of wings unfurled behind him, huge reddish brown canopies that stretched out to each side farther than the boy was tall.

Elam leaned back. He wanted to yell "Dragon wings!" but that seemed too awkward. Instead, he just crossed his arms and nodded. "Those are amazing! Can you fly?"

Gabriel pulled a wingtip forward. "Since I was ten, but I only fly at night when nobody can see me."

Elam forced himself to maintain a cool aspect, in spite of the strange sight—a teenager, half human and half dragon. He pointed at one of the wings. "I'll bet you have a lot of fun zipping around the sky, right?"

Flexing his lean muscles, Gabriel shrugged. "It's fun hopping from roof to roof and bombing cats with water balloons, but it gets pretty boring when you can't show anyone your flying acrobatics."

"Can't show anyone?" Elam repeated. "Why not? Do you keep your wings a secret?"

Sadness clouded Gabriel's face, belying his painted-on smile. He pointed with his thumb. "I stuff them in a hiking backpack like a pair of huge socks. My mother cut holes in the panel that goes next to my back to let my wings fit through, but they're always trying to escape."

Elam rose to the balls of his feet, stretching to get a look at Gabriel's back. "So do you have holes in your shirts, too?"

"Yeah, but it's a real pain. I have to—"

"Gentlemen." Patrick gestured toward the table. "Please sit. We can talk about dragon-wing accessories another time, but right now we have more important matters to discuss."

Elam and Gabriel took seats across from each other. Patrick withdrew a velvet jewelry box from his pocket and opened it as he set it on the table. Inside, a red gem sparkled at the center of an octagonal pendant. "The gem," he said, lifting it by its chain, "is a rubellite. And not just any rubellite; it belongs to Timothy, Gabriel's father."

Elam reached over and tapped the swaying pendant, making it twirl. "But since Timothy is Makaidos, isn't he your father, too? And wouldn't that make Gabriel your brother?"

Patrick nodded. "Makaidos was my father, but whether or not Gabriel could be called my true brother, I cannot say for sure. You see, I was born to dragons, and he was born to humans, one of whom was transformed under Merlin's prophecy and one who was apparently generated, if you will, from scratch. Although the transformed dragons never intramarried, knowing they could not procreate with each other, Makaidos was exempt from that incapacity since he was not part of Merlin's prophetic group." He let out a long sigh. "So, as you can see, Gabriel and I have extremely peculiar genealogies, and our relationship is uncertain."

Elam nodded toward Gabriel. "You said he inherited the wings from his mother. How do you know that? Both his parents had wings."

"From blood tests. Timothy has no traces of dragon blood in him, while Hannah and I show some unique cellular structures that I don't yet understand."

"Why is Timothy different?" Elam asked, but when he saw Gabriel's gaze tip downward, he regretted his question.

"I wish I knew," Patrick replied. "I can only deduce that God removed his dragon nature and gave him a human soul."

Gabriel's head perked up. "Don't you have a soul?" he asked Patrick.

"I do, but not a human one. At least that's what Merlin told me."

"Merlin told me the same thing about the transformed dragons," Elam said, glad to turn the examination toward Patrick. "You're somehow both dragon and human, but without a human soul."

"Merlin told you?" Gabriel asked, swinging his head toward Elam. "He lived over a thousand years ago, and you can't be older than a couple of hundred."

Patrick raised his hands, laughing. "As you both can see, there are many questions to answer, and I will allow the two of you to converse at length some other time. For now, however, we must plan our strategy." He reached under his chair, pulled out a briefcase, and withdrew a ragged scroll of yellowed parchment. Carefully unwinding it, he laid it across the breadth of the table, giving Elam one of the rollers and Gabriel the other.

Patrick ran his finger along the text. "This is a missive from Merlin to Morgan that I . . . well . . . intercepted from Devin. As you can see, through about two-thirds of the scroll, the lettering is in the old style, but from there until the end, it is written in modern English."

Elam leaned forward and gawked at the parchment. "Did you write the new stuff?"

"No. When I first read this letter centuries ago, Merlin had not used the entire scroll. I would guess about one foot of parchment was blank. I only discovered this new entry a week ago while I was deciding what I could show to Charles to help him translate the letter from Timothy and Hannah."

Patrick tapped his finger on the first line. "If you please, Elam."

Elam nodded and read the new text out loud.

A spawn conceives to bring new birth;
Then lays her hybrid down to rest.
The king's own son must sacrifice
To purge the dragon in your breast.

Beware of Morgan's hidden plot
To find an heir to Arthur's throne.
She lusts to dwell within the veil
And reap the harvest you have sown.

For as Hartanna's age-old twin,
The seed you sow implants an heir.
A daughter sprouts in walls of flesh
And grows in secret, cloaked in prayer.

Now Morgan learns where Valcor dwells;
She lurks in shadows, patient, still,
Awaiting blossoms from the sprout
To cut and capture, then to kill.

Beware the snake and hide the girl,
But let her live a carefree life.
Instill in her a faithful heart
For only faith endures the strife.

Above all plans, protect the gem,
The key that opens Dragons' Rest,
For Arthur's seed must find his way
To rescue captives in his quest.

Take care to learn this secret path
To fertilize the barren land,
For dragons die to shed their scales
And bow before the Son of Man.

461

Elam breathed a low whistle. "I hope that doesn't mean what I think it means!"

Patrick smiled, but it was a weak, sad sort of smile. "What do you think it means?"

Elam folded his hands and pressed his thumbs together. The part about the hybrid being laid to rest and the king's son sacrificing seemed to point to Gabriel, but should he mention something so morbid right in front of him? Had Patrick already figured it out? Maybe it was best to focus on another part of the prophecy, at least for now. "Obviously," he said slowly, "Morgan's out to get a girl, and . . . uh . . ." He shifted his gaze to the roof where only a single raven remained, preening its feathers. "Is Mrs. Nathanson . . . expecting?"

Patrick tapped a finger on the table. "The exact question I immediately asked myself. You see, we had always thought Ruth was unable to bear a child, so, to soothe her empty arms and fill her great desire to care for abandoned children, we established our orphanage. Yet, when I saw this prophecy, I urged her to get a blood test."

"And . . . um . . . did the rabbit die?" Elam asked.

"No." Patrick's weak smile returned. "I'm afraid the little hopper is alive and well." He took a deep breath and let it out in a long sigh. "I was hopeful, but Ruth is not expecting."

Elam picked up the rubellite and peered into its crimson center. "Then how can this prophecy be fulfilled? Who's the daughter Merlin's talking about? And how can this gem be a key? And what was that stuff about barren land?"

Patrick opened his palm, and Elam laid the pendant in his hand. "As you have so aptly demonstrated," Patrick said, "there are many questions, and I can answer only one with confidence. The prophecy will eventually come to pass, but it seems that the fulfillment might come in ways we do not expect."

The raven suddenly swooped down and snatched the pendant's chain. In a flurry of black wings, it took off toward the hole in the ceiling with the pendant dangling underneath.

462

"Noooo!" Patrick lunged at the bird but missed.

Gabriel unfurled his wings, leaped onto the table, and launched himself upward. Folding his wings slightly, he squeezed through the hole without missing a beat. One second later, he was gone.

Elam held his breath. Patrick's gaze locked on the ceiling. After about half a minute, Gabriel dropped through the hole, his wings letting him drift gently to the floor. With his brow furrowed, he shuffled back to the table.

Patrick gasped. "You . . . you didn't get it?"

Gabriel held up the pendant. "Oh, I got the gem."

Patrick clutched his chest. "Don't frighten me like that!"

"Yeah," Elam said. "You looked like you were mad."

"I am mad. I grabbed that little buzzard by the neck and yanked the chain from its beak, but when I turned back, a huge bat latched on to my wrist." He held up his arm, displaying a stream of blood. "It hung on until I let the bird go."

Patrick cradled Gabriel's arm and examined the wound. "We can't take you to the hospital, but we have a nurse on staff who is well versed in these matters."

"Can we trust her to keep my wings a secret?" Gabriel asked.

"Certainly. She's my wife." Patrick took the pendant and laid it back in its box. His brow knitted a trio of deep creases as he sat down at the table. "Elam, have you figured out who the raven is?"

Elam stared at the ceiling's hole and sat next to Patrick. "Morgan? After all these years?"

"Can there be any doubt?" Patrick shook his head. "Now she knows about Gabriel, she knows who I am and where I live, and she likely recognized you."

"Do you think she'll bring Devin here?" Elam asked.

"Perhaps to kill you and Gabriel, but if I understand the prophecy correctly, she's hoping for me to generate a hostiam for her, so she won't soon seek my destruction or Ruth's."

463

"A hostiam?" Gabriel repeated. "What's that?"

"I will explain later. For now, we must get your wound cleaned and find a place for the two of you to hide."

Elam clenched his fist. "I'm not hiding. I stopped being afraid of that witch thousands of years ago."

"I appreciate your courage," Patrick said. "I didn't expect you to cower behind any skirts. If, however, my wife and I are blessed with a child, I must protect both of them at all costs, and keeping Devin far away is item number one on my priority list."

Elam drummed his fingers on the table. "Since Mrs. Nathanson isn't expecting, I say we draw the slayer here now. Get it over with. It's either him or us."

Gabriel clapped Elam's back. "I'm with him. Maybe I'm not as old as the hills, but I've been hiding ever since I can remember, and I'm tired of it."

"I am of a mind to agree," Patrick said, "but if we summon Devin, all our lives will likely be in jeopardy." He nodded toward the exit. "Elam, please ask Ruth to come here with her medical bag. Then I would like you to retire for the night. It has been a most stressful evening for all of us."

Elam laid his palms on the table and rose slowly, eyeing Patrick and Gabriel as he picked up his lantern. "Okay. . . . I can do that."

Patrick gave him a formal nod. "Thank you, and good night."

As he marched to the doorway, Elam glared at the shifting shadows. Something was wrong. Patrick had dismissed him too abruptly. He had treated a grown man like a child, literally sending him to bed without his supper. But why? Was he planning to discuss some kind of secret with Gabriel?

As he strode through the corridor, Gabriel's sad eyes took shape in his mind. Somehow they were too sad, like a . . . a . . . Elam shook his head. He wasn't sure what Gabriel reminded him of, but it wasn't good. He mentally kicked himself into gear and ran the rest of the way to the main nursery.

Patrick drew one of the drapery panels to the side and tied it back, while Gabriel pulled the other. With the curtain out of the way, Gabriel backed up to take in the sight. The wall behind the curtains framed a strange window. Without a single streak or reflected image, it looked like a rectangular hole in the wall, an escape hatch to a forest he could leap to without smashing any glass.

He approached the hole and laid a palm on the stone surface. It wasn't a window at all. The scene on the other side, with its equatorial trees and low-hanging vines, was unlike anything in Patrick's estate or all of England. Not only that, dozens of lush, fern-like leaflets trembled under a drenching downpour in the dimness of a cloudy day. Of course, that didn't make any sense, not in the middle of a cloudless night on this side of the window.

"So," Gabriel said, "it looks like a good day for frogs in there."

Patrick touched the window lightly. "It seems to rain frequently in that dimension, which, I think, is appropriate for what we have in mind."

"You mean, send the slayer to Hades so he can soak his hot head?"

"Precisely. And now that Elam has indicated his willingness to fight the slayer, all of the pieces are in place."

"When are you going to tell him our plan?"

"Tomorrow morning. But first I want to make sure you and I are of the same mind concerning the prophecy. Do you understand what it appears to be saying about you?"

Gabriel shrugged his shoulders. "If you mean that line about the hybrid and the king's son, then, I guess I do."

"If you are the hybrid to be laid to rest, then inviting a battle with Devin could mean your death."

"I know." Gabriel turned away from the window. "I just want to do what I have to do and get it over with. If Devin dies, then we'll celebrate. If I die, that's okay, too. I'm ready to go."

Patrick crossed his arms over his chest and nodded respectfully. "You have a heart that reflects the selflessness of your savior, but we will do whatever it takes to protect you. Although it seems clear that we must take this step to bring our conflict to some kind of resolution, Merlin's words frighten me. His prophetic utterances have never been wrong."

"I know what you mean." Gabriel pressed his hand against his stomach. "It makes my dinner want to come back up and smack me in the face."

Patrick clasped Gabriel's shoulder. "You could go into hiding. God might use a different son of a dragon king. Your mother and father, or another dragon turned human might have another child. You don't have to—"

"I'm not a coward!" Gabriel said, slapping his wings together. "Why should I risk someone else's life?"

Patrick stepped back. "Of course you aren't a coward. I was merely pointing out your options."

Gabriel sighed and spread out his hands. "I'm sorry. It's just that Devin's the reason my parents are always on the run. I'm not missing this chance for anything."

Patrick lifted a finger. "I have one further concern. Since you are, shall we say, somewhat of a unique species, I'm not sure where you would go if the worst should occur. That is, I am not confident your soul will go directly to heaven. You might spend some time in Dragons' Rest."

Gabriel steeled his jaw. "It doesn't matter. Whether I ascend to heaven or make my bed in hell, God will be with me."

"Yes, yes," Patrick said, nodding, "I know the psalm. Still, you are not a normal human. Such promises are rather vague in your case."

"Then it's a new adventure, isn't it? I'd rather go to war than cower in shadows all my life. My parents think Devin's hiding in every alley—he's the bus driver; he's the balloon man at the fair;

he's the principal at my school. The way he gets around, you'd think he was Superman. No one can be that powerful."

Patrick's brow creased deeply. "Don't underestimate someone who has survived for centuries. According to the last word I have, his morbid tally stands at six dead dragons since the transformation. With Morgan giving him power, his prowess likely far exceeds your estimation."

"Maybe, but he hasn't found you or my family yet, so I'm not scared of him. If I have to spill my blood to protect the people I love, then I'm ready."

Patrick laid his hands on Gabriel's shoulders. "You are a true warrior. I shall not try to dissuade you any longer."

"A warrior?" Gabriel turned his head to the side. "If you say so. I just hope I have the guts to back up my hot air."

"I understand." Patrick slid his hands away and strolled to the table. He picked up the pendant and let it dangle by its chain. As the rubellite twirled at the bottom, its facets glimmered, sending red flashes all around. He caressed the gem with his fingertip. "Why the path to salvation must be coated with blood, I'll never understand, but of this I'm sure—it is the sacrifice of love that will draw the faithful to the Great Key's threshold."

Merlin floated along one of the candlestone's crystalline hallways, his body's radiant light casting just enough glow to guide his path. Learning how to change the shape of his energy field had made it easy to disguise himself when he stopped by to see the rebellion conspirators. He usually spoke only to the six who had since repented of their crimes. Barlow, Edward, Newman, Fiske, Standish, and Woodrow now professed fealty to the king, though Arthur had been dead for centuries. They were good men—unwise to allow themselves to be deceived, certainly, but their basic motivations had been noble.

Merlin gazed at his shining body. Now a spiritual entity, bearing no more weight than a flame, he had far more control over his mind and greater clarity of vision. He looked up and concentrated on a tiny light in the distance, the entry hole that drew him into the candlestone yet still prevented any escape because of the gem's tractive power. He peered through the opening, willing his vision to enlarge the window—ten times, a hundred times, a thousand times—like a telescope expanding its light-gathering mirrors. Within seconds, it seemed that the entire outside world had enveloped his body, though he merely stood in place, still trapped in a gemstone prison.

On this particular day, since the sun shone so clearly, Devin had to be wearing the gem on the outside of his vest, a perfect time for opening a viewing port. Merlin guided his radiant hand over the surface of one of the crystal's inner walls. It flashed with light, showing a bouncing panorama of an English road, the scenery in front of Devin as he walked.

With his enhanced spiritual perception, Merlin peered intently through the wall and gazed toward multiple horizons, taking in the sights and sounds of millions of happenings throughout England and even over the northern border in Scotland. Quickly orienting himself to the landscape, he soon located Patrick and listened in on his conversation with Elam and Gabriel.

Merlin shook his head and sighed a stream of energy. They were trying so hard, yet they knew so little. Bound by their physical bodies, they could only comprehend as far as their senses could reach. And Patrick, though he was reasonably wise, had no teacher to guide him past the more difficult obstacles to spiritual maturity. The man who had served so gallantly as Valcor, a noble dragon for a thousand years, would soon face a mind-bending challenge that would stretch every strand in his moral fiber, call into question everything and everyone he had ever loved, and possibly alter his life forever. The future of the dragon race depended on the choices he would soon make, and he had no idea that such a test was coming.

Merlin whispered in the air, breathing a tiny line of twinkling sparks that rose toward the gem's entry. "Father, what can I do to help? I have left them only scattered scraps of wisdom in an artless song that begs to be translated into coherent speech. Were I to read it, knowing what they know, I would be pulling my hair out in frustration. When I wrote the song, I knew so little of what I was writing. You spoke through me in mysteries too deep for my limited mind to fathom, and now that I no longer see through physical eyes, I can plunge those depths and uncover mysteries so great, my flesh-bound mind would have burst with joy as it tried to grasp your incomprehensible love, wisdom, and goodness.

"Yet, now that I know the answers to my own rhyming parables, I cannot turn the hearers to the path of salvation from ruin, nor dissuade them from the snake-filled pits that lie under indiscernible cover. They need a guide, someone with more knowledge than they possess, someone who can see what has been hidden from their limited perception. Even in my current state, I cannot see what spirit rules their hearts, so I ask you to provide whatever they need, within or without, to allow Valcor to complete his holy mission."

Merlin's energy field flashed with a blue tint. Who could possibly fill this massive void? Every potential helper was either dead or—

"Merlin!"

Merlin searched for the source of the voice. It couldn't have come from any of the conspirators. None of them knew who he was. He glanced up at the entry hole. A shining human shape floated down and gently landed in front of him. Surrounded by a radiant red aura, the elderly man smiled. "You seem surprised to see me, Merlin."

"Surprised, indeed, and the fact that I don't recognize you does nothing to diminish my surprise."

469

The visitor laughed. "We are both prophets, my friend, so I will not hide my identity. You know that Moses and Elijah were able to make appearances from the spiritual realm. Who else among the prophets might be able to pierce the veil?"

Merlin stroked his chin. "If you are one of those whom God himself buried, whether by earth, by fire, or by air, I suppose you must be Enoch."

"An air burial is an intriguing metaphor," Enoch said, "considering the fact that I never really died."

"Nor did Elijah, but God ended your stays on the earth, so I thought the word choice appropriate."

"Ah! I see what you mean now." Enoch's glow shimmered from head to toe. "In any case, God sent me here in response to your prayer. You asked for a guide for Valcor, and you and I are going to provide one."

"Then are you setting me free from this prison?" Merlin asked.

470

"No. You must stay for a little while longer. A prince and princess will arrive here one day, and they will need you to guide them through the valley of the shadow of death, but you will learn about that in due time. For now, you must expand your vision and allow your perspective to follow me. I will take you where your sight has not yet been able to travel and show you how to reach beyond the physical horizons you have already surveyed. Ours is a world of spirit, a sphere of invisible influence, where the forces of light and darkness do battle day and night. As I did through the Ovulum for many centuries, you must provide a window to the world of the living for a God-seeking soul who longs to see the realm of lost loves."

Merlin bowed. "Although I cannot see how I am to fulfill this great commission, I am at your command, good prophet."

"I expected you to be willing," Enoch said, "and I now advise you to be ready for a fight unlike any you have ever seen. In order to complete the creation of the Great Key, we will step into the midst of a climactic battle."

"The rubellite in the pendant is ready to serve as the Great Key, but who will be the two witnesses?"

Enoch spread out his glowing fingers. "One who will come in a disembodied state similar to ours as well as another witness who is flesh and blood. A number of years must pass before the culmination of that plan, for the dragon king has yet to arrive, and the second witness has yet to find her way."

Merlin melded his fingers with Enoch's scarlet wrist. "Is Valcor in as much turmoil as it appears?"

"Without a doubt. He wishes to shelter everyone in his protective wing, yet he knows that God has not called him to cower in the shadows. While Valcor struggles in his mind, the destiny of all dragons hangs in the balance." Enoch laid his hand on Merlin's forehead. "Close what is left of your physical eyes and follow me. Since the Oracle of Fire will count on the lessons she has learned through the centuries, our timing must be perfect."

471

After poking her head through the neck hole of her fuzzy blue nightgown, Sapphira let the hem drop to her knees. She laid her cross next to Enoch's scroll at the edge of her floor mat and curled up close to Acacia. Her twin snored lightly, tired from her turn in the village scrounging for food—the usual potatoes, cabbages, and beans—as well as for books, clothing, and firewood.

All the other scrolls had burned long ago, and the cross's flames never seemed hot enough for cooking. So if they ever wanted warm food, they had to get fuel, and hauling an armload of wood up to the portal on the steep hill proved to be quite a task. Still, taking turns kept the burden manageable, and the townsfolk thought the same blind girl visited the alleys and dustbins every day probing for castaway remnants. Although they never begged, sometimes their accessories—sunglasses, a ragged bonnet, and a walking cane—coaxed a bit of monetary sympathy from a few kindhearted souls.

The money they collected came in handy for an occasional bar of soap or a newspaper.

Sapphira pulled her blanket to her shoulder. The cavern seemed to get a bit colder every decade, but sleeping had become much more comfortable since the people in the living world began throwing away such treasures as mats and blankets. With only a tiny hole punching through the material here and there, her new bed had provided many nights of comfort without the soreness that her old sand mattress had inflicted, and the threadbare blanket was just enough to ward off the chill.

Still, a mattress alone couldn't bring complete comfort. Sapphira closed her eyes, trying to shut out the pain of a thousand haunting thoughts, but visions of Elam kept flashing in her mind. What was he doing now? Did he get away from Devin back in, what was it, nineteen thirty something? Or was it only a dream? Was he even alive? If he was, had he forgotten about her?

Over the years since Elam stopped appearing on the screen, every time Sapphira surfaced in Glastonbury to hunt for food or other supplies, she took note of every young man she passed. Strangely enough, many of them smiled at her, though they believed her to be blind, giving her opportunity to study their faces. Hundreds of smiling faces later, no Elam. Images of Paili also haunted her. How old would she appear to be now? Twenty-five? Thirty?

As Sapphira drifted into a dream, her age calculations jumbled together into a mass of battling numbers—the *fives* using their little hats as swords to stab the helpless numeral *ones*, and the *zeroes* coming to the *ones'* defense by bowling over the *fives*. The *eights* joined the *fives* and pounced on the *zeroes*, breaking them like fragile eggs. More *zeroes* rolled in and flattened the *eights* into lopsided infinity symbols.

The digital war raged on and on until, finally, a few surviving numbers lined up into a neat row, creating "6913," but there seemed no reason for the sequence. Then, the battling numbers crumbled and blew away in the wind, leaving only darkness.

As Sapphira squirmed toward wakefulness, the portal viewer flashed to life in her mind, showing Paili sitting at a table. She appeared in her eight-year-old body, not as the grown woman she had to be by now. With a long dagger, she sliced one of Morgan's evil fruits and raised a section to her lips.

Sapphira pitched off her blanket and ran to the screen. "No, Paili!" she cried. "No!"

Paili put the wedge into her mouth and chewed. Blood dripped from her lips, and her face wrinkled into a hideous, mummified mask.

"Why, Paili?" Sapphira wailed, as she sank to her knees. "Why did you eat it? You knew better!"

Paili spat out a red seed. As soon as it hit the table, it grew, stretching into a saltshaker-sized red dragon that stood tall and proud. She spat out another seed, then another, until the tabletop was filled with miniature dragons, each one trumpeting and vying for position near Paili.

473

A final seed passed through her lips, a red-and-white-striped one that fell to the table and grew into a boy with dragon wings. The dragons spewed fire on him, turning him into a spinning column of flames. A dozen tongues of fire erupted from the column and slurped the dragons into the vortex. Seconds later, the table was clear except for one dragon standing at the center.

The dragon molded into the shape of a man and jumped toward Paili. His body merged with hers, leaving Paili by herself again. A moment later, a girl sprang from Paili's bosom, a beautiful young lady with sparkling blue eyes and blonde-streaked hair. She sat in a chair next to Paili and folded her hands on the table.

Paili cut out a second wedge from the fruit and handed it to the girl. As the girl studied the wedge, Sapphira cried out again.

"No! Whoever you are, don't eat it!" She closed her eyes and wept, unable to look.

When she finally peeked between her fingers, the scene had cleared again, and an image of Elam appeared, then a boy with wings, then a man who oscillated between being human and a dragon, and finally, Morgan. Although she was in human form, Morgan, using talon-like feet, carried Paili high over a huge estate toward a driveway guarded by two of Shinar's idols. After landing next to Elam and the dragon man, a sword flashed out of Morgan's mouth and stabbed the winged boy. Suddenly, a little girl appeared, and Morgan flew away with the child locked in her talons.

Acacia groaned. Sapphira opened her eyes. They were both still in bed. Now throwing off the covers for real, she hopped up and spun toward the portal. As usual, its dim orange light whirled in a stoic column, slow and silent.

She snatched up her cross and gazed at Acacia for a moment. No use putting her in danger. Besides, even after all her practice, Acacia still wasn't as adept at opening portals, and portal manipulation might be the only skill that could rescue Morgan's potential victims.

Sapphira grabbed her upper-world disguise and hurried silently out of the room. If she failed, she didn't want to risk losing Acacia again.

CHAPTER

MORGAN'S VICTORY

Elam stood on a driveway leading to Patrick's mansion and leaned against one of two stone columns that supported an open, wrought iron gate, the entrance to the expansive manor. Standing in front of him, Gabriel fidgeted while Patrick unfastened his backpack. "I apologize for my clumsiness," Patrick said, pulling the pack away, "but you're free now."

"Thanks." Gabriel spread out his wings and shook each of them in turn. "That's a lot better. It felt like two elephants were hopping on pogo sticks back there."

Patrick withdrew a small handgun from the pack and slid it into his pocket. "Perhaps they were jumpy because of my revolver."

"Could be. More likely because I'm as jumpy as a cricket in a frying pan."

Elam pointed an unlit torch at the backpack. "Are your wings always uncomfortable when you stuff them in there?"

"You get used to it." Gabriel lifted each shoulder in turn. "Well, sort of."

Elam backed away from the gate's supporting column. Chiseled with eight vertically stacked hideous faces, it looked like a prop from a bad horror movie. He had recognized these remnants of Shinar's idols when he first saw them bordering the driveway, but he hadn't remembered to ask Patrick about them. He poked one of the faces with the torch. "How'd these get here?"

Patrick pointed toward his mansion. "The portal we plan to use to get rid of Devin is the very same portal from which Makaidos escaped Dragons' Rest. It was in a depression called Blood Hollow, and I bought this property with the sole purpose of protecting that point, which now happens to be at the back wall of the compass room. When Makaidos emerged, it seems that these columns came with him. The force of their expulsion apparently propelled them all the way from the back of the property grounds to the front entry. Since I found them to be practically indestructible, I decided to keep them as souvenirs. They make excellent sentries, don't you think?"

476

"It's a great advertisement." Gabriel held his hands out as if displaying a sign. "Wanted: Ugly guards. Apply within."

"You're quite the jester today." Patrick rubbed his finger across a narrow, engraved plaque wedged in the lips of one of the stone faces. "But they actually do carry a sign. As you can see, I managed to embed my home's address in the mouth of this particularly ugly woman."

Elam touched the numbers with his fingertip. "Sixty-nine thirteen? Why do you have such a high number? Yours is the only house in sight."

"I picked it myself," Patrick replied. "Six is the number of man. In order to get the second number, add three, the number of God. That represents the union of God and man in the Messiah. Finally, the thirteen honors both the Messiah and Merlin. The Messiah, of course, guided twelve unruly disciples and transformed all but one into holy saints. Merlin brought twelve dragons to Bald Top to be transformed, and stood as our ally, a thirteenth dragon, if you will, and transformed all but one into new creatures. The number thirteen has long been considered a symbol of transformation from one state into another, a dying to an old way of life, and many leaders of twelve have walked this earth to deliver that transformation, promising to return to their followers someday. I still trust that both the Messiah and Merlin will return at exactly the time we need them."

Gabriel winked at Elam. "That's exactly what I thought it meant."

Elam laughed and popped Gabriel on the arm with his fist. "I thought of it first."

"Yes, gentlemen, and I am a monkey's uncle." Patrick withdrew a pocket watch from his trousers and checked the time. "I expected Devin to arrive an hour ago. My sources must have inaccurately estimated his position."

As Elam scanned the dark, cloudy skies, damp gusts swept through his hair. Somehow, the dismal weather seemed a perfect backdrop for the looming battle. Fortunately, the slayer had agreed to come alone. Boldly daring him to face his enemy without his little lackey was a stroke of genius on Patrick's part, and picking this hill that overlooked the entire estate proved to be a perfect rendezvous point. The slayer had to show himself long before he could attack.

Elam firmed his chin. It was better this way—out in the open and face-to-face. The only question now was how Devin would arrive. On foot? In a car? Dropped out of the sky? Whichever way he chose, he was likely to have a few tricks up his sleeve.

Gabriel pushed his hands into his pockets and angled his head upward. "I'll keep watch overhead, just in case that raven shows up."

"Sounds good to me." Surveying the horizon, Elam tried to pick out the great tor in the haze. The steep hill's dim outline protruded from the surrounding plane, slightly darker than the blowing fog that veiled its summit. As misty droplets thickened into a steady drizzle, something moved in the foreground of the gray countryside. Tiny and nebulous in the distance, a human figure trotted up the long driveway. Elam waved his hand. "Someone's coming!"

"Stand ready, men," Patrick said. "Have courage, Gabriel."

Elam lowered his hand to his side. "Wait! I see a skirt. It's a woman . . . or a girl."

"I see her," Gabriel said. "Unless Devin's hiding Excalibur in his bloomers, we should be safe."

"Yeah, but it might be Morgan. Devin's got the fangs, but she's got the poison." Elam shielded his eyes from the rain. "It doesn't look like her, but Morgan can disguise herself as a toad if she wants to."

Gabriel smirked. "Would she even need a mask for that?"

"Actually," Patrick said, lifting a chain necklace over his head, "she bears a striking, even bewitching, beauty." He dangled the pendant from his fingers. "Gabriel, take the gem and be ready to fly to the portal window, just in case."

Gabriel hustled back to Patrick and closed his fingers around the pendant. He locked gazes with Patrick for a moment, then tightened his fist. "Let's do it."

As the female drew closer, Elam focused on her frilly bonnet, dark sunglasses, and white walking cane. Though her most striking features were covered, he could never mistake her pale skin, her slender, girlish form, and her distinctive, frantic trot. Sapphira was back!

Fighting the slick incline, Sapphira hurried up the long driveway. The hike from the tor's portal had been long and wet, and asking for directions based on fleeting images and an obscure number from a dream had proved an embarrassing chore. "Why would a blind girl need such information?" one woman had said. "You shouldn't be out on such a frightful day." Yet, she finally gained the favor of an old newspaper deliveryman who answered her questions kindly, and now that she had reached the last turn in his rather convoluted directions, she knew she had found the right place. The two idols were exactly where she had seen them in her dream.

She stopped and pulled Yereq's digital timer from her pocket. Just as she thought it might, the numbers now matched the address she had been looking for, "6913." She slid it back into her pocket and drummed her fingers on her thigh. So many coincidences! Something big was about to happen.

At the top of the hill, three male figures watched her—an adult, a boy with wings, and another young man, a very special young man she had longed to see for many years. Her legs trembled so hard she could barely stand. Elam was there, and he had spotted her. She was sure of it.

She waved, but Elam didn't wave back. He just spoke to the man standing next to him. She took off her sunglasses and waved again. Maybe now Elam would recognize her.

A rumbling drone sounded from above. Sapphira glanced up at a low-flying airplane approaching the estate, but it caught her attention only for a second. She turned back to Elam, who was now waving frantically. "Hurry!" he called. "Get up here!"

Sapphira dropped her cane and broke into a mad dash, slipping at first before her bare feet caught the driveway's blacktop. Spreading her arms to keep her balance, she sprinted up the slope. "Elam!" she cried. "You're alive! Thank God, you're alive!" She leaped into his embrace. As Elam spun her around, she bent her knees and lifted her feet into the air. When he let her down, she gripped his shoulders. "Elam, I just had to come and find you. Last night I dreamed what would happen today, and it was so real, I knew it had to be true. You're in great danger."

"I know." Elam pointed toward the sky. "We think a dragon slayer's in that airplane. But don't worry. Patrick and I have it under control."

Sapphira put her sunglasses back on and nodded at the winged boy. "Morgan wants him dead. We need to get him out of here."

Elam squinted at her. "How could you dream about Gabriel? Do you know him?"

"Just from the dream. I also saw Patrick and his wife, and she's in trouble, too." Sapphira regripped his shoulders. "You have to get Gabriel away from this place!"

Patrick pointed upward. "A parachute opened. We can expect Devin to arrive in about a minute."

Elam pulled a lighter from his pocket and set fire to the oil-soaked torch. "Gabriel is our bait. We're going to get Devin to follow him and me to the portal, and I'll send him to Hades."

Sapphira laid a hand on Patrick's back and pushed him toward Elam and Gabriel. "I'll take care of the dragon slayer." She pulled the cross from her waistband. "But you three had better get inside before Morgan shows up. Knowing her, she's likely to kill your wife."

Patrick shook his head emphatically. "We cannot leave you with Devin on a wild hunch that Morgan might be in my house. Ruth is not in danger from her."

The cross slipped out of Sapphira's hands. "What name did you call her?"

"Ruth." Patrick picked up the cross and handed it back to Sapphira. His eyes focused on hers, lingering for a moment. "I take it you know her by another name . . . perhaps a much older name."

"When I see her, I'll know for sure." Sapphira pointed the cross at the mansion. "If I'm right, as soon as Morgan lays eyes on her, she'll figure out the truth and kill her!"

"Morgan won't kill her. She needs her to produce an offspring."

"But Ruth isn't normal. I learned in my dream that the only way she'll ever conceive by you is if your dragon genes get altered into human ones, and when Morgan figures that out, she won't mind killing her."

Patrick waved his hand at Sapphira. "Yes, I know all that, which is exactly why I set up this confrontation." He patted the outside of his pocket. "And don't worry about Devin. I have a backup plan if our primary plan goes awry."

"But Morgan will—"

"Stay behind me!" Patrick spread his arms, making a shield in front of Sapphira and Gabriel. "No time to explain! Devin is upon us!"

As the slayer neared the ground, Elam stepped out in front and waved his torch, but it seemed a feeble weapon against a trained knight bearing the sword of swords.

With a deft swipe, Devin cut his parachute lines just before landing. After rolling to the wet grass and then jumping to his feet, he brandished Excalibur and glowered at his opposition. "An unarmed man, a winged mongrel, a boy with a torch, and a skinny, blind girl. How pitiful! Killing you four would hardly be sporting."

481

Elam pointed his torch at the slayer. Its fire sizzled in the growing rainstorm. "Does a true knight threaten a girl? Let them go and follow me to the mansion's ancient grounds where we can fight one-on-one in a hallowed arena."

"Oh, it's you!" Devin grunted a contemptuous laugh. "Don't you ever grow up, little boy?"

Elam waved the torch toward the mansion. "If I'm such a little boy, you should take my offer. Unless, of course, you're nothing more than a yellow-bellied mama's girl."

Devin slapped Elam's wrist with the flat of Excalibur's blade, knocking the torch to the ground. He strode forward and pricked Elam's throat with the point. "I'm not here to kill a bleeding Scotsman, but I don't think my mistress would mind if I add your head to my collection."

Elam's eyebrows arched up, but his voice stayed calm. "It's a simple concept, even for you. I'm challenging you to a duel. Are you man enough to accept?"

"Elam!" Sapphira called. "Don't! I'll handle him!"

Lowering his sword, Devin glared at Sapphira. "Who *is* this plucky blind girl?"

Elam ran over to Sapphira and put his arm around her waist. "My friend from down under. She's always been overly confident."

Devin bowed dramatically. "Young lady, I am bowing in honor of your fiery spirit."

Puckering her face, Sapphira muttered under her breath. "You don't know the half of it, you coward."

Elam picked up his torch. "So, Devin, are you coming with me?"

After straightening his body, Devin rested Excalibur on his shoulder and snorted. "I am not here to be baited into your trap. I am merely waiting for my mistress to arrive before I skewer the mongrel."

"Patrick!" Gabriel shouted, pointing upward. "Look!"

A huge raven flew toward them carrying a woman in its talons. As her long dress flapped in the wet breeze, she cried out, "Patrick! Help me!"

Patrick stared at her, his mouth agape and his arms and legs stiff.

Sapphira gripped the cross so tightly, it stung her palms. Suddenly, the crossbeam ignited on its own with a pale yellow blaze. She gaped at its sizzling flames and whispered, "I didn't call for flames. Am I supposed to do something now?"

Gabriel leaped into the air and met the raven in mid-flight. With his wings beating wildly, he grabbed the bird's throat and forced it toward the ground. "Let her go, you stupid turkey, or I'll tear you drumstick from drumstick!"

The raven screeched and dropped the woman. Its feathery body suddenly vaporized into a column of smoke and slipped through Gabriel's fingers. The raven's victim slid between Patrick and Devin, and the smoke column settled over her crumpled frame. Within seconds, Morgan appeared, straddling her hostage.

Sapphira gulped. Those cheeks! That hair! It really was Paili! Sapphira shushed her cross's fire and returned it to her belt. Maybe it was best to keep quiet and wait for a better chance to save her.

Gabriel landed next to Patrick, panting and coughing. "That bird's more . . . more slippery than a greased eel."

His face ablaze, Patrick jerked a handgun from his pocket, fired at Devin, then lunged toward Morgan. She spread out her arms and launched a sphere of darkness that blasted Patrick in the chest, knocking him on his back and slinging the gun far away.

Devin jerked to the side and laid his hand on his sword-bearing shoulder. Blood oozed between his fingers. He switched the sword to his other hand and charged toward Patrick. "I'll teach you to—"

"Stop!" Morgan commanded.

Devin halted and scowled at his mistress. "Let me kill that fool, or I'll . . ."

Spreading out her arms again, Morgan glared at him. "Or you'll what?"

Devin lowered his sword, his eyes flaming with murder. "Beware of pushing me too far. I will not be your toy soldier."

"You'll be whatever I tell you to be." Morgan swung her head toward Patrick, who had managed to push up to a sitting position. She cackled. "When you were a dragon, you might have stood a chance against me. But look at you now—a wet, weak human without a prayer."

Patrick shook his fist at her. "Get away from my wife, you monstrous hellcat."

"Oh, don't be so dramatic, Patrick. She's not in danger . . . yet." Morgan flashed a wicked smile at Sapphira. "Mara! So nice of you to come! How is living in an eternal grave suiting you?"

Sapphira crossed her arms over her chest. "It's better than any place you stink up with your presence."

"Pleasant as always, I see." Morgan turned to Patrick and gave him the same devilish smile. "It was so kind of you to bring the sacrificial lamb. I expected as much."

"Sacrificial lamb?" Patrick shot up to his feet. "What are you talking about?"

"Oh, Patrick, you are such a poor liar. You knew Devin was coming, yet you allowed his young victim to stand as an easy target. You didn't seriously think you and Elam could stop Devin and Excalibur, did you? Even your bullet hardly fazed him."

Elam smacked his torch in his palm. "If your all-powerful slayer didn't need any help, then why did you show up?"

"I heard that little Mara was on her way, and her power would tip the scales in your favor." Stooping low, Morgan withdrew a dagger from her belt and pressed its edge against Paili's throat. Her eyes opened and darted from Patrick to Elam to Sapphira, but she didn't breathe a word.

"I have come," Morgan continued, "to ensure that Mara doesn't interfere. If she does, this daughter of the earth will die."

"Daughter of the earth?" Elam repeated. "Is she a—?"

"Yes, an underborn spawn." Morgan winked at Sapphira. "Your little Paili's all grown up now, a mature flower ready to be plucked. If she were not an underborn, I might have tried using her as a hostiam, though I doubt that Patrick would have allowed it."

Sapphira pointed at the dagger. "Ignite!" The hilt burst into flames. Pinning her hostage under her foot, Morgan sprang up and threw the dagger to the ground. Sapphira leaped at her and clawed at her face, but her fingers just sank into the witch's jelly-like skin. Morgan grabbed Sapphira by the hair and slung her onto the driveway.

Sapphira skidded on the wet pavement and rolled to a stop. Too dazed to stand, she pushed her palms against the pavement and tried to crawl, but her head bumped into something solid. She blinked at the object in front of her, one of the two guardian idols. She swung her head around and saw the other idol on the opposite side of the driveway. Her vision slowly sharpened, and a feeling of calamity weighed her down. Still dazed, she looked back at Morgan. Elam and Patrick were both lying on the ground, and Devin stood over them with Excalibur poised to strike.

Morgan raised her hand. "Don't kill them!" She snatched up her dagger and again pricked Paili's throat with the edge. "Patrick, I know the prophecy depends on this spawn's survival, but don't think I won't kill her if you and her mutant sister continue to interfere. I would find another hostiam eventually."

Patrick and Elam struggled to their feet. Patrick clenched his teeth and shook both fists at her. "I swear to you that you will never possess my wife or any of my progeny, so help me God!"

Morgan laughed. "Such a feeble oath from a dragon who lost his armor and now uses children as his protectors!" She pressed the dagger into Paili's skin, drawing a trickle of blood. "You have no idea how much I can make you suffer. This blade is nothing compared to the torture I have in mind for you."

Gabriel beat his wings and slid closer to Patrick. "Don't risk her life. I'm willing to die."

Sapphira stumbled over to Elam. She leaned against his shoulder, hiding her lips from Morgan's view. "Listen," she whispered, "there's a portal between the idols. If we can lure Devin there somehow, I can transport him out of here."

Hiding his own lips, Elam kissed her on the forehead. "Then Morgan would kill Paili."

Morgan pointed at Devin. "Slayer, strike the mongrel through the heart. His courage has earned him a quick death."

Sapphira cringed. Her tortured whisper rose to a squeak. "Do you have an idea?"

"Maybe. Merlin told me something about Excalibur. It's a long shot, but it's better than nothing."

With blood still oozing from his wound, Devin stalked toward Gabriel and pulled back his sword.

Elam waved his arms and dashed between Gabriel and the slayer. "Wait! It won't work unless Patrick does it!"

The slayer paused and glanced at Morgan. "Shall I kill them both?"

"Let him explain," Morgan said, her eyebrows lifting. "I am intrigued."

Elam patted Gabriel on the chest. "Patrick has to kill him. It's the only way."

"Elam!" Patrick's cheeks flushed scarlet. "Have you gone mad?"

"It would be mad to let him die in vain! We have to do it right or the prophecy won't be fulfilled!" Elam glared at Morgan. "Or maybe you don't know anything about ancient prophecies."

Morgan nodded at him. "Please enlighten me."

Elam laid a hand over his ear. "I once had a song in my head that kept playing over and over. It told me that I had to betray the one I loved so she could sacrifice her life for me. It said she loved me, and if I really loved her, I would turn her over to you. I didn't believe it at the time, but now that I see a sacrifice happening right in front of me, I finally understand. The one who benefits from a sacrifice should play a part in the execution. Otherwise, the sacrifice won't work."

"I see what you mean." Morgan eased the dagger's pressure on Paili's neck. "Betrayal has long been the instigator of redemptive sacrifice."

"So"—Elam pulled on Gabriel's arm and began leading him toward the idols—"Patrick should do the job over here, right between the idols."

Morgan narrowed her eyes. "Why there?"

"You know why," Sapphira said as she hustled to Elam's side. "The ancient scrolls say that many human sacrifices were made between these idols when they stood in Shinar. What better place is there?"

"No tricks!" Morgan pressed the dagger's edge under Paili's nose, drawing more blood. "Or I'll carve this pretty little face like a pumpkin on Halloween."

Sapphira shuddered. Her voice pitched up again as she shook her head. "No. . . . No tricks."

Gabriel pulled the rubellite pendant from underneath his shirt and let it dangle in front. "Let's do it and get it over with."

Morgan nodded at Devin. "Give Excalibur to Patrick."

"After he dispatches the mongrel," Devin said, glowering at her, "he will turn the sword on me."

"You fool! Haven't you figured out that he is paralyzed while I hold his beloved at the edge of a blade?"

Devin grumbled and laid Excalibur in Patrick's hands. As soon as Patrick wrapped his fingers around the hilt, its beam shot out from the tip. Patrick's eyes bulged, and Devin jumped back.

487

A smile spread across Morgan's face. "Ah! The king's heir reveals his pedigree."

His arms trembling, Patrick frowned at the sword. "And now he wields it in shame."

"Get on with it!" Morgan shouted. "Disintegration will be clean and quick."

With his shoulders slumped and the beam angled toward the sky, Patrick marched slowly to the driveway.

Elam nudged Sapphira and whispered, "Light your cross, but try not to let Morgan see it."

Now standing about ten paces in front of Gabriel, Patrick raised the beam straight up. When Morgan's eyes lifted to follow the brilliant shaft of light, Sapphira slid the cross out and whispered, "Give me light." A low flame rippled across the wood.

Patrick swiped the beam downward but halted it just above Gabriel's head. His face twisted in agony. "I can't do it!" he cried. "I just can't do it!"

"Do it now!" Morgan screamed. "Or I will slice your wife into pieces!"

"Patrick!" Gabriel extended his folded hands, his face pleading. "In the name of all that is holy, don't let that witch hurt your wife! Strike me down! Better you than the slayer!"

Patrick's stare burned into Sapphira's. Tears flowed down his cheeks. "What do you two say?"

Sapphira wiped away her own tears. "You have to, Patrick. We all agree."

"Trust us," Elam said, nodding. "You have to do it now, before Morgan sheds any more of Paili's blood."

Patrick tensed his muscles and swung the sword the rest of the way. The beam sizzled through Gabriel, and he dissolved into a column of sparks.

Elam barked a low whisper. "Now, Sapphira!"

Sapphira waved the cross in a broad circle over her head. A wall of flames began edging downward from her hand, wide enough to envelop herself, Elam, and Gabriel's field of sparks. The rubellite pendant floated in midair and absorbed Gabriel's energy along with a stream of flames from the wall.

"Elam!" Sapphira shouted. "What's happening to Gabriel?"

"I don't know! Maybe he'll be okay on the other side!"

Sapphira peeked through the vortex of flames. The fiery stream rushing into the rubellite suddenly reversed and spewed out in a lightning streak of dazzling crimson. The cross's wall of fire shattered into a million jagged pieces and crumbled away.

488

CHAPTER

THE GUARDIAN ANGEL

When the pieces from the fiery vortex cleared from view, Sapphira dropped to her knees, exhausted. Lifting her head slowly, she peeked up at the surrounding shadows. Two human figures stood next to her, alive and well. One unfurled a set of beautiful dragon wings.

Sapphira leaped up and hugged Gabriel. "You're alive!"

"I guess I am," Gabriel said, patting his torso. "What happened?"

Elam clapped Gabriel on the shoulder. "Merlin told me that Excalibur's beam doesn't necessarily kill; it just changes physical matter into light energy. I was hoping Sapphira could bring you through to this dimension, but I didn't know you would be physical again. Looks like it worked better than I expected."

"Your plan was brilliant!" Sapphira tucked her cross into her waistband and hugged Elam. "It's so good to be with you again!"

"Brilliant, yes, but did we fulfill the prophecy?" Gabriel slashed his finger across his throat. "Will Morgan believe that I'm dead?"

"I think she will." Elam caressed Sapphira's cheek and pulled away. "It looked like you dissolved before everything disappeared."

"I guess we can hope so." Gabriel kicked at the ferns at his feet. "So where in the world are we?"

Elam crouched and peered down a narrow path that wound through the forest. "We're probably in another dimension, but I'm not sure which one. I've never seen this place before."

Sapphira plucked a fern leaflet and twirled it in her fingers as she studied the landscape—nothing but tall trees and dense undergrowth as far as the eye could see. "I was in a place like this, but I don't think I've been to this exact spot."

Gabriel grabbed a thick vine hanging over his head and pulled it down to eye level. "The trees look sort of like the ones I saw through the portal window at the back of Patrick's mansion."

490

"So," Elam said, scratching the ground with a stick, "if the window leads to this dimension, Sapphira can find where it comes out here and get us to Patrick's house. Then we'll sneak back to the idols." He looked up at Sapphira. "What do you think?"

"It's better than popping right into Devin's clutches." Sapphira dropped her leaflet and picked up a long stick. "We'd better hurry. If Morgan's not convinced that Gabriel's dead, then Patrick and Paili are both in trouble."

"Wait! What's this?" Elam pushed his stick under a chain and picked up a dangling pendant. A dim glow emanated from the gem in the center. "Looks like the rubellite came through with us."

"Super! I was worried Morgan would find it." Gabriel took the chain and draped it around his neck. "Any idea why it's lit up?"

Elam and Sapphira both shook their heads.

Gabriel peered at the gem for a moment, then shrugged his shoulders. "Okay, which way do we go?"

Sapphira pointed her stick at a massive trunk. "If we're still near the idols, then in the world of the living, the mansion would be over there, past that big tree, so I'll head in that direction."

Gabriel beat his wings and leaped into the air. "I'll check out what's ahead." He zipped up through the trees, deftly avoiding every branch. Soon, he was circling high above.

Sapphira strode ahead, slashing ferns with her stick and hopping over protruding roots. Now that she had stepped out of the portal, her vision had faded to normal, so she kept her gaze on the ground and studied the passing leaflets and tufts of thick-bladed grass, hoping to see them suddenly magnify.

After guessing the approximate location of the mansion's portal room, she marched through the jungle-like undergrowth. She counted fifty paces, then, shifting a few feet to the side, she marched right back. Dodging tree trunks and ducking under low-hanging vines, she kept watch for a change in her vision or a plunge in her mood.

Elam scurried in front, tossing aside sticks and warning her of stones and roots. He suddenly halted. "Look at this!" he called, picking up a long white rod. "It's a bone of some kind!" He leaped ahead and stooped. "A whole skeleton!"

Sapphira raced toward Elam and crouched at his side. As she laid her hand on the bony remains of an unfortunate human, her vision clarified. The eye sockets in the skull widened, and its gaping mouth seemed to pour out a silent scream.

A gust of wind and a flapping sound announced Gabriel's return. He settled to the ground next to Sapphira. "What did you find?"

"A skeleton." She dropped her stick and fingered the tattered clothing that still clung to the ivory ribs. "We're at the portal. Maybe this poor guy was trying to get through it somehow."

"Let's get out of here." Elam straightened and swiveled his head from side to side. "This place is spookier than any dimension I've ever been in."

Sapphira stood with him and pulled out her cross. "Gather together."

Gabriel extended a wing and draped it around Elam and Sapphira. "Okay. Let's see what happens."

Sapphira lit the cross and circled it over her head. The familiar cylinder of flames encircled them, and the forest scene vanished. Seconds later, Sapphira fell through a flexible wall of thick material and tumbled to a hard floor. After dousing the cross, she grasped the material and pulled herself up, drawing it to the side as she rose. "A curtain," she whispered.

"The portal covering," a hoarse voice replied.

Sapphira searched for the source of the voice. Darkness obscured a human figure nearby. She raised the cross again and commanded light. A gentle flame rippled across the wood, illuminating Elam's reddened cheeks.

"What's wrong?" she asked.

492

He cleared his throat. "Gabriel's not here. He must not have made it through."

"How can that be? The fire surrounded all of us." Sapphira raised the cross higher. "More light, please." Instantly, a new surge of flames brightened the room. Just beyond Elam, an eerie profile glittered, like crystals reflecting sunlight. The silhouette of a winged boy moved, more like a shining ghost than a living human.

Sapphira clapped her hand over her mouth and spoke between her fingers. "Gabriel!"

Elam pivoted. "Where?"

Sapphira crept toward Gabriel's sparkling frame. He extended his hands as if trying to communicate, but no sound emanated from his radiant face.

She moved the cross closer to his body. "Look. He's trying to say something."

Elam spread out his arms. "Where? I don't see anything."

She reached out and touched one of Gabriel's glowing hands. "He's right here. I guess my vision is sharper than yours."

Elam laid his hand on top of Sapphira's. "He must still be disintegrated in this dimension."

Sapphira closed her eyes, and the portal's soul-sinking influence weighed down her mind. "Will he die?"

"I don't know." Elam pointed at the window. "Can we send him back in there?"

As a flood of pure sadness drowned her spirit, Sapphira could only shake her head. "He doesn't want to go."

"How do you know?" Elam asked. "Is he speaking to you?"

Sapphira shuddered, trying to fight off the gloom. "In a way. It's like a stream of thoughts or feelings. He says he doesn't want to be trapped in there."

"He'd rather be out here without a body?"

"He says he planned to sacrifice himself to fulfill the prophecy, so he'll just wait to see what happens. It's better than being trapped all alone in the world of the dead." Sapphira spied something on the floor. The pendant! She scooped it up and showed it to Elam. "It came back through with Gabriel, but it stayed physical. And the gem's white now."

"How could that be?" Elam touched the gem with his fingertip. "It's still glowing."

Sapphira drew her fist close to her mouth and bit her thumb. "We . . . we have to get outside and see if we can help Patrick and Paili, but we can't just leave Gabriel here!"

Elam took the chain from Sapphira and draped it around his neck. "We don't have much choice." He took a step and stood between her and Gabriel. "I guess you're in front of me somewhere, and I hope you can hear me. We'll try to come back with Patrick as soon as we can. Maybe he can figure out what's going on."

EYE OF THE ORACLE

Elam took Sapphira's hand. "Come on." With the fire of the cross lighting the way, they dashed out of the room, sprinted through the maze of corridors, and burst out the front doorway into a drenching downpour. Sapphira extinguished the cross and tiptoed behind Elam as he crept toward a rhododendron shrub. Hunching over, they both peered through the breaks in its foliage. The pounding rain smothered every other sound.

Across a wide expanse of grass, Paili knelt on the driveway, cradling Patrick in her arms. Morgan and Devin were nowhere in sight.

"Let's go!" Elam whispered. He leaped out into the open and sprinted toward Paili. Sapphira followed, her bare feet splashing through the squishy lawn. As they approached, Paili looked up. Pain warped her face, and a trickle of blood oozed from under her nose and dripped onto her lips.

Elam fell to his knees at Patrick's side. "Is he . . ." He swallowed hard, unable to finish.

Paili shook her head. As tears and raindrops poured down her cheeks, her pain-streaked voice barely penetrated the wall of rain. "He's . . . alive. I think . . . he's asleep."

"Asleep?" Sapphira knelt next to Paili and clasped her hand. "What happened?"

"You disappeared." Paili nodded toward the idols. "Then a stream of red fire came out from your flames and . . ." She mopped her brow with her trembling fingers. "And it went right into Patrick's chest. He lit up for a few seconds and then fell to the ground."

Sapphira pushed Paili's hair out of her eyes. "What happened to Morgan and Devin? Where did they go?"

Paili took a deep breath. "Morgan picked up the sword and said, 'Only one more step on my stairway to heaven,' and they both disappeared in a puff of smoke."

APRIL, 1949

Holding a dim lantern at his side, Elam tiptoed into the ancient chamber at the back of Patrick's mansion. As he neared the central table, the lantern's weak flame twirled in the cool draft descending from the hole in the roof, giving just enough light to cast a glow over a figure sitting in a high-backed chair. Patrick's crumpled outline hunched over the table, his head buried in his arms. Elam reached to touch Patrick's shoulder, but just before his fingers alighted, Patrick lifted his head.

Elam backed away a step, his voice low. "Sorry. I just wanted to check on you."

Patrick's lips spread out in a frail smile. "You heard the news, I assume?"

"Yes," Elam replied, his tone like the gong of a death knell. "Congratulations."

"Thank you." Patrick's smile abated. Tears glistened in his eyes. "Morgan will wait until the child is older, perhaps a teenager, before she makes her move, but we have to begin preparations now. Of course, we're assuming the baby will be a girl, but I have little doubt."

Elam pressed his palm against his chest. "Just let me know what to do. I'll do anything you ask."

"Of that, I am certain." Patrick's gaze wandered, finally settling on the lantern in Elam's hand. "We will have to be extremely creative if we wish to fool Morgan. In order to keep her searching elsewhere, I'll begin spreading the news that my cousin Stanley will take over the orphanage, and my cohorts will plant stories of Patrick Nathanson, his wife, and Elam moving to various towns in England. Paili and I will change our names and relocate to another house, but we'll likely stay near Glastonbury so Paili can keep track of the children."

495

Elam watched the lantern's flame waltz in Patrick's eyes. "So Stanley will take care of them?"

"Yes. He is not my natural cousin, of course, but I adopted his last name after becoming good friends with his family. In any case, he and his wife will move into this house. They have four children of their own, so they are well versed in the practice of child rearing."

Elam pulled out a chair and sat next to Patrick. "Do you want me to stay here and help? I know this place inside and out."

"I was hoping you would volunteer." Patrick clasped Elam's shoulder. "I'm sure Paili would be comforted knowing you're here. Since Morgan has her evil intentions set on our child, I don't think she will bother you."

"True," Elam said, setting the lantern on the table, "but I wouldn't mind changing my name, at least to use for business matters. *Elam* isn't exactly common anymore."

"Certainly. Do you have a preference?"

Elam folded his hands on the table and pressed his thumbs together. "My shipyard manager in Glasgow died to save my life. I'd like to take his name."

"You would do well to honor him that way. What was his name?"

"Markus." Elam patted his chest. "I even have a shirt with Markus embroidered on it, so I'll wear it when I'm in public."

"Well, then, Markus," Patrick said, clasping Elam's shoulder again, "I hope you live as many years with that name as you've lived with your previous one."

Elam adjusted the lantern to expose more of the wick. "What will your name be?"

Patrick folded his hands next to Elam's. "I chose Robert. It's a simple name that won't raise eyebrows. We can't use Ruth any longer, and Paili couldn't decide on a new name, so I chose Sarah for her."

"Sarah? Why Sarah?"

"It was Merlin's wife's name. Merlin seemed to die inside when Morgan poisoned his wife, so I wish to honor them by resurrecting her memory. It's a small token, but it's meaningful to me."

"I understand." Elam leaned back in his chair and sighed. Pain and sorrow had visited the homes of prophets and dragons all too often—Merlin's lost wife, murdered dragons, a threatened pregnant mother and unborn daughter, and now he had to raise another troubling issue that promised more heartache. Elam drummed his fingers on the table. "I met with Sapphira today."

Patrick's gaze seemed locked on his folded hands. "You did?" His reply was halfhearted, as if he hadn't heard Elam's comment.

Elam pushed the lantern closer to Patrick, trying to awaken his attention. "She saw Gabriel."

Patrick lifted his head higher. His eyes seemed to flash with a burst of hope. "She saw Gabriel?"

"Well, she didn't really see him face-to-face." Elam positioned his fingers to make a frame. "It's really weird. There's this portal where she lives. While I had the Ovulum, Sapphira's portal stretched into a viewing screen, and she could watch me through it. Then, after Devin broke the Ovulum, the screen disappeared. But now the screen is back, and she can see glimpses of Gabriel's feet and hands and sometimes the tips of his wings."

"Glimpses of just his extremities? How odd!"

"It's sort of like she's able to see what Gabriel sees, like she's looking through his eyes. Sometimes his extremities come into the picture."

Patrick flopped to the back of his chair. "Amazing! His eyes have become a cross-dimensional camera!"

"That's what we guessed, too. But how could it happen?"

"I cannot fathom the reason," Patrick said, stroking his chin. "I know very little about disembodied spirits."

"Disembodied? You mean, like a ghost?"

"Certainly not," Patrick replied, shaking his head. "The ghosts you see in horror movies are an absurd warping of reality. Although every spirit rises from its body, very few are ever seen on the earth. Gabriel is far from a haunting, morbid presence."

"Do you think he's dead?" Elam's voice squeaked. He cleared his throat and took a deep breath. "I thought maybe he survived, that he's just in another form."

"Excalibur transformed his body, to be sure, but he still moves about in our world, so I think writing an obituary is premature."

"But didn't the prophecy say he had to die?"

"The prophecy does not use those words." Patrick withdrew a folded piece of paper from his pocket and flipped it onto the table. "I have read it a thousand times since that fateful day, and there are many ways to interpret its morbid verses. By learning from other events in history, however, I believe we can hope that Gabriel survived. When God directs a sacrifice for the sake of others, isn't it reasonable to assume that he has also paved the way for a resurrection? God used Gabriel's sacrifice and the energy from the rubellite to make me human. I believe that such love and power could never end in death."

Elam slid the paper close and slowly opened it. "So, what do you think Gabriel will do? I mean, he can't just wander around, can he?"

"When it comes to willingness of heart, Elam, you and Merlin are the only humans I have ever met who come close to Gabriel's stature. I am sure God will use him somehow."

"Maybe Sapphira will figure it out. She'll be watching what he does."

Patrick wagged his finger at Elam. "It could be dangerous for you to continue meeting Sapphira. Morgan is always vigilant and will track Sapphira to her portal. For her safety and the safety of the children, you should stay in the house as much as possible and only come out through the tunnel exits."

Elam spread the note out on the table but didn't bother reading it. The words were already etched in his memory. "I guess you're right. I'll meet with her once more and let her know."

Patrick raised the pendant from underneath his shirt and caressed its pearly white gem. "Ever since I became fully human, I have felt more alone than I ever had before. It's as though my emotional connection to my dragon heritage departed hand in hand with my dragon soul. With the exception of you and my faithful wife, I feel I have lost everyone I ever loved."

Elam gazed at the lantern's flame as it danced atop the wick. "I know exactly what you mean. I still have Sapphira as a friend, but I can't risk seeing her anymore. You're the only person I can really talk to, and now we have to part company." Blinking away tears, he turned to Patrick. "I'll help you out in the orphanage as long as you need me."

Patrick clasped wrists with Elam. "May God go with you, Markus. I am glad to have a friend I can trust."

499

Gabriel floated in front of a hotel room door and read the numeric script at the side. Room 1178. This was it. After weeks of searching for the slayers, he had finally tracked them down. Maybe now he could end the nightmares his parents had faced for so many years.

He collapsed his body to a flat layer of energy and crept through the crack under the door. After expanding to his normal height again, he stalked toward a pair of typical hotel beds. Each mattress carried a gently heaving lump, two sleeping men with only drapery-filtered moonlight illuminating their forms.

Gabriel hovered for a moment over the first bed, peering at the shadowy profile—a dark mustache, a swarthy complexion, but not familiar at all. As he floated toward the next bed, the shadows shifted away from the second man's face. This was Devin. No doubt about it. Sleeping with his torso exposed, Devin snored lightly, apparently without a care in the world. Attached to a chain and resting on his hairy chest, a sparkling gemstone seemed to inhale wisps of moonlight.

Gabriel edged toward the gem. Somehow, it pulled on his body and drew him even closer. He tried to will himself backwards, beating his wings to create an electrostatic countercurrent, but even as his upper half moved away from the stone, his lower half stretched toward it, stringing his body out in a narrowing line of radiance.

His wings collapsed, and the gem slurped his entire energy field. He plummeted down a rivulet of light, sliding faster than if he were freefalling out of the sky. Tiny pricks stung his elongated body, and the sound of a rushing torrent surged through his mind, numbing his senses. After a few seconds, he pierced a soft black sphere, a jelly-like membrane that slowed his plunge. While floating downward through a chamber of blackness, his body retracted to its original shape and size, and when he finally stopped, all pain vanished, and a gentle hum replaced the noisy torrent.

He looked around the strange dark world and set his glowing hands on his hips. What had just happened? How could a gem absorb his body like that? Slowly willing his feet forward, he tried to move, but with only blackness all around, it seemed impossible to tell if he was making any progress.

Stopping for a moment, he focused his eyes in one direction, hoping to adjust to the lack of light and get his bearings. As he began to recognize the borders of a dark hallway, a glimmer appeared at the end of the corridor, growing quickly. Gabriel tried to back away, but he bumped into a wall.

The approaching light took shape, an old man with a friendly smile. Like his own body, this man seemed completely composed of energy.

"Ah! Gabriel!" the man said. His voice rippled along a thin current of radiance that passed between them. "I'm glad to see you!"

Gabriel floated a few inches to the side. "Uh, how do you know me?" His own voice sounded garbled and strange, like a static-filled radio broadcast.

The man chuckled, jiggling the edges of his field. "A friend of mine told me to expect a boy with dragon wings and that his name would be Gabriel. You're the first visitor who has fit that description."

"Really?" Gabriel spread out his arms. "How many visitors do you get in this place?"

"Very few, to be sure, but I would like to dispense with the banter, if you don't mind." The man bowed his head. "I am Merlin, prophet of God and former advisor to King Arthur."

Gabriel shuddered and clumsily returned the bow. "And I'm Gabriel, but you already knew that."

"You will be surprised at all I have come to know. But before I get to that, I would like to ask you a question."

"Okay. I'm ready. . . . I think."

Merlin stretched his arm upward, elongating it to twice its normal length. "According to my estimation, it is around two o'clock in the morning, so since you found Devin, I assume you came upon him while he was sleeping." He shifted his arm toward Gabriel and draped it over his shoulder. "What did you intend to do?"

"To kill him. He wants to kill my parents, so I was trying to stop him."

"I see." Merlin stroked his chin. "How could you kill him in your disembodied state?"

Gabriel lifted his glowing hand and splayed his fingers. "I've been experimenting with channeling electricity. I've only done it with batteries, and I shocked a couple of cats, but I think I can hook up to an outlet and deliver a lethal jolt."

"Assuming you were able, what do you think the jolt would have done to you?"

501

"I really don't care." Gabriel rolled his fingers into a fist. "Even if it scattered my atoms to kingdom come, it would be worth it if I could protect my parents from that murderer."

Merlin nodded. "A reasonable motivation, to be sure, but do you think killing an unarmed man in his sleep is a noble act?"

As Gabriel tightened his fist, it flashed with a crimson hue. "I wasn't thinking about nobility. I was just thinking about getting rid of a fifteen-hundred-year-old sewer rat."

"I understand. In cases like this, strong emotions always seem to trump chivalry, so I won't argue the point." Merlin raised a sparkling finger. "Instead, I will tell you about your assignment."

"Assignment?" Gabriel stretched out his arms and wings. "In this place?"

"Oh, no. You will soon be leaving, but I will explain that in a moment." Merlin melded his hand with the tip of one of Gabriel's wings. "Because of your status as a disembodied humanoid dragon, for the lack of a better term, you have been chosen to be the guardian of others like you."

"Are there other disembodied humanoid dragons?"

"I mean other offspring of former dragons. A new one has recently come into the world. Patrick and Paili have had a daughter."

"How am I supposed to be a guardian?" Gabriel clasped his radiant hands together. "I can't even use a slingshot."

"You have already figured out how to manipulate electrical fields. Perhaps you will learn other ways to alter your environment. The key is to figure out how to warn someone of approaching danger."

"Maybe, but it seems like everything's against me. My body passes right through the things I'd like to touch, like people or tools or weapons, but I can't seem to penetrate most walls or doors. That would come in handy."

"Ah, yes," Merlin said, nodding. "God's ways are mysterious, indeed. He seems to erect just enough boundaries to force us to

502

seek the paths he wishes us to find. Experience, however, has taught me that every unexpected wall we slam into has a purpose, though we often cannot fathom it. Even we prophets find the limitations severely taxing at times."

"But if you're a prophet, and you're still stuck in this place, how do you expect me to get out?"

Merlin pointed at a darker area of the chamber. "This gem has an exit channel. If I were to go through it, my atoms might diffuse, but your energy frame was welded together by the Great Key. You see, as the son of Makaidos, you became, in one sense, Patrick's messiah. Not his human messiah, of course, but you were the sacrificial lamb who purged Patrick's dragon nature. Because of that, you were able to live again, not in your old body, but in a nearly indestructible new body."

Gabriel basked in the sparkle of the prophet's dazzling eyes. They seemed to radiate sincerity and truth. "It all sounds pretty crazy, but I believe you."

"As well you should." Merlin laid a hand on his chest. "It is not often you find yourself inside a gemstone talking to a disembodied prophet."

Gabriel shook his head and laughed. "I can't argue with that."

"Now," Merlin continued, "although you have been a fine conversationalist, I must see you to the gem's back door and ask you to be on your way. When you leave through the exit channel, you will have to fight against the candlestone's pull or you will just be reabsorbed."

"Yeah. I felt like a fly on a frog's tongue when I came in here, but I'll see what I can do."

Merlin raised a finger and stepped closer. "One final exhortation, and I am telling you this as a prophet of God. Since you are a body of light, your greatest enemy is darkness. If darkness envelops you, it will gnaw away at your sanity and threaten your

503

very essence. You will know it is upon you when your body dims or shrinks. If you seek the light, you will have the power to overcome the darkness."

As the prophet's eyes pulsed with brilliant light, Gabriel let the words sink in. Finally, he nodded. "I will remember your warning."

Merlin spread out his arm toward the darkest region of the bleak chamber. "Come now; you must be on your way."

CHAPTER

ACACIA'S JOURNEY

OCTOBER 31, 1964

Gabriel swooped low over the Glastonbury Tor and scanned its grassy slopes. Only a few tourists lined the path that ascended the famous hill, making it easy for him to check every face closely. Any one of these sightseers might really be a predator stalking Shiloh, Gabriel's young ward, as she made ready for a celebratory picnic in a nearby copse.

He guided his energy field in front of a tall, slender woman plodding up the hill and hovered a foot ahead of her, floating backwards at her pace. He gazed into her eyes, searching for a sign of an indwelling evil witch. With all of Morgan's disguises, she could be any female, maybe even a male—the grade school boy with the pea green knickers who trudged behind this woman, perhaps, or the hulking brute holding the boy's hand.

Gabriel groaned. It seemed hopeless. Morgan could even fly in as a raven, and he couldn't possibly search for a hint of unusual intelligence in every black bird fluttering in the trees. Even if he could identify the dark sorceress lurking nearby, the only electrical device he could use out in the open was the flashlight Shiloh had packed in her basket. Would lighting it up be enough to warn her in time?

He floated down to a small cluster of trees near the base of the hill. Carrying a folded blanket, his young protectorate searched for a suitable place to sit with her parents. When she found a place under the shade of a lush oak tree, he eased close and checked the basket dangling from a handle on her arm. The flashlight lay inside nestled against an apple and a wrapped sandwich.

As she spread out the satin-trimmed blanket, Shiloh's gold-streaked hair shone in the setting sun, and her sparkling blue eyes flashed. She seemed like an angel, so innocent and pure. Even her gentle laugh as she sat next to her parents revealed a forgivable naïveté. To her, they were Robert and Sarah Nathanson, not Patrick and Paili. Though she knew about Patrick's former life as a dragon, she had no idea that her mother was really an underborn almost as old as the civilized world. Yet, because of the stealthy relocating Shiloh had suffered through in her young life, including a recent, month-long visit to the U.S., she knew they were potential prey for a stalker of some kind.

Gabriel lifted into the air and hovered over their heads, watching the boundaries of their tree-filled haven. The magnificent tor towered above them like a protective sentry and cast a shadow that crept closer to the blanket as the minutes ticked by.

Patrick lifted a camera and pointed it at Shiloh. "Smile, birthday girl!"

Shiloh spread out the edges of her white party dress and flashed a cheesy smile. After the shutter clicked, Patrick laid the camera in Shiloh's basket and all three settled on the blanket in a tight circle.

Paili set a double fudge, two-layer cake in the center. Fifteen candles lined the frosted perimeter. "I know you didn't ask for a cake," she said as she struck a match, "but what's a birthday without cake and candles?" She cupped her hand around the match to keep the cool breeze from snuffing out her efforts.

As soon as the last candle came to life, Patrick and Paili sang a hurried version of "Happy Birthday." Shiloh then leaned forward and blew out the candles.

Patrick clapped his hands. "All fifteen in one blow!"

Shiloh pushed back her hair and smiled. "I think the wind helped me."

A twig snapped. Gabriel floated higher and gazed at a nearby thicket. Nothing moved. Maybe the breeze had knocked down a limb. He edged close to the thicket and peered through the leafy branches of a head-high bush. A man crouched behind it, and a raven perched on his shoulder.

Gabriel zoomed back to Shiloh and swirled his energy over the blanket. The flashlight was still in the basket! He dove inside, stretched his energy into a thread-thin line, and penetrated a tiny hole in the flashlight's casing. He bridged the battery's current to the bulb several times, making the light flash repeatedly, but how could they possibly notice? He streamed out again and wrapped himself tightly around Shiloh. Maybe somehow he could communicate the danger from mind to mind.

507

"And now for your gift!" Patrick withdrew a small, velvet-covered box from his jacket pocket, and, carefully lifting the hinged lid, presented it to Shiloh.

As she pulled out a delicate gold chain, a wide smile spread across her face. An octagonal bronze pendant dangled at the bottom of the chain with a marble-sized white stone glimmering at its center.

"Shiloh!" Gabriel shouted. "You have to hear me! Morgan is coming!"

Paili ran a finger along the chain's links. "Do you like it?" she asked.

Shiloh leaned over and kissed each of her parents. "I love it! Thank you!" She settled back and examined the gem in the pendant's center. "What is this? A pearl?"

After draping the chain around her neck, Patrick hooked the fastener. "It's a rubellite, the rarest kind. It was once red, and it suddenly turned white almost a year before you were born. It's a family heirloom my sister gave me a long time ago."

Gabriel laid his hands on Shiloh's cheeks. His fingers flashed like scarlet beacons. "Danger is near, Shiloh! You have to run! Now!"

Shiloh's eyes widened, and her lips parted slightly.

"Is something wrong?" Patrick asked.

Shiloh lowered her brow. "I'm not sure. I have a funny feeling, like someone's calling me."

"Really?" Paili touched Shiloh's hand. "Is it an audible voice?"

Shiloh closed her eyes for a moment, then shook her head. "It's nothing. I'm probably just tired." She rubbed her thumb across the smooth stone. "So you got this from Irene? The lady in your stories about the dragons?"

"Yes," Patrick replied. "It represents our life essence. Irene—"

The man burst out of the thicket. "Stay where you are!" He drew a sword from a scabbard and ran toward the birthday gathering.

Gabriel unfurled his wings in front of Shiloh and flashed his energy field with all the power he could muster, but how would that stop a charging swordsman? Without electricity, he was nothing but an invisible ghost! He scanned the skies. The closest electrical line hung at least a hundred yards away. Too far to tap into its power!

Leaping in front of Paili and Shiloh, Patrick spread his arms. The intruder halted and pricked Patrick's throat with the point of the sword. Paili jumped up, but Patrick lifted his hand, signaling for her to stay away. He angled his head back. "Palin!" He swallowed hard. "What is the meaning of this?"

508

A female voice answered Patrick. "You know the meaning, Valcor."

Stepping aside, Palin lowered the sword. A slender, dark-haired woman appeared from behind a tree. Her ghostly form seemed to float, though her legs moved in a normal cadence. "You didn't send me a card with your change of name and address," she said. "I was worried that I would never find you again or meet your lovely daughter."

Patrick glared at her. "Morgan. How typical of you to pollute the pristine meadows like a walking weed."

A scowl flashed across Morgan's face, but she quickly replaced it with a broad smile. "Poetic, as always, my old friend, but your insults are misplaced. I have a wonderful birthday gift for Shiloh, and I would like for her to come with me to receive it."

Gabriel tried to shove Morgan with his hands, then with his wings, but to no avail.

Shiloh stood behind her father and wrapped her arms around his waist. Patrick grasped her hands in front and intertwined his fingers with hers. "You'll give her a gift when pigs fly, Witch!"

Morgan's smile melted into a thin horizontal line. "I thought you would come up with a more original quip, but your denial was expected."

"Where is your other pet gorilla?" Patrick asked, nodding toward Palin. "Has Devin finally given up hunting for your hostiam?"

Morgan reached for Palin's blade and pricked her finger on its tip, drawing a bead of black fluid. "Because of your little shooting incident the last time you two met, I thought Devin would not control himself as well this time. If you decided to reject my demands, as I expect you will, Devin would kill you, and all would be lost." She held out her hand, allowing a drop of thick blood to fall to the leaf-strewn grass. A wiggling brown sliver crawled out of the ground, like an earthworm squeezing up from a narrow hole. As it emerged, it lengthened to the size of a man's foot, then doubled, constantly growing in girth, and, as it continued to stretch, one end morphed into the head of a snake.

Gabriel tried to grab the snake, but his fingers slipped right through it. He clenched his fists and screamed, "Help me! I don't know what to do!" But his cry fizzled, unheard. Even the giant hill refused to reply with an echo.

Morgan grasped the snake and wrapped it around her shoulders and torso. Cradling its neck in her hand, she brought the hissing head closer to Patrick as he edged backwards. "So when we finally tracked you down," she continued, "I sent Devin to make sure the place I prepared is ready for your daughter's arrival." She took a quick step toward Patrick, and the snake lunged and latched its fangs onto Shiloh's forearm.

Shiloh screamed and shook her arm until the snake finally released her and dropped to the ground. Patrick stomped on its head with the heel of his boot, pounding it flat. Paili yanked Shiloh away and hustled her to the nearby oak tree.

Morgan shook her head in mock lament. "What a shame! Now I'll have to take Shiloh with me." She picked up the dead snake by the tail. "You see, I have the only cure for the serpent's venom."

As Paili tended to Shiloh's wound, Patrick spat at Morgan's feet, his face red and taut. "What good is she to you?" he shouted. "She can't be your hostiam without my approval!"

Morgan wound the snake's body into a ball and slung it into the thicket. "Don't worry. I will keep her safe in the sixth circle until you change your mind. I'll let you decide which is better for her. Will you let me take her body, or will you condemn her to live an eternity of tortured loneliness? For now, though, you have to answer a more urgent question. Will you allow the serpent's venom to rot her flesh over the next three days until she suffers an excruciatingly painful death, or will you give her to me?"

Patrick shot her a threatening glare. "For healing only. Not as your hostiam."

Morgan smirked. "I will accept that for now. It will amuse me to see how long it takes you to change your mind."

Patrick ran to the tree and scooped Shiloh into his arms, whispering as he carried her back to Morgan. "Will you trust me, dearest angel?"

Amid dripping tears, Shiloh nodded. "Yes, Daddy."

As Patrick gazed into her eyes, his own tears fell onto her dress. "Will you remember what I've taught you? Never lose faith, no matter how long it takes. Above all, never eat Morgan's food. God will provide for all your needs."

Shiloh shook her head. "I won't forget, Daddy! I'll never forget!"

Sapphira pointed at the screen. "Palin's carrying Shiloh up the tor. Do you think Gabriel will be able to follow her?"

"To the sixth circle?" Acacia pinched her chin. "I doubt it. He'd have to cross dimensions again."

"But Shiloh's got the pendant with her. Maybe Gabriel can use it somehow to get through a portal."

"Good point, but we'd better hush and listen. It's hard to hear them."

In the viewport, Patrick and Paili charged up the hill behind Palin. Morgan halted, waiting for the pursuers to close the gap. She knocked Patrick flat with a wall of blackness, then shoved Paili with her foot, sending her tumbling to the bottom. Patrick scrambled down and helped Paili to her feet. Now separated by the entire slope of the towering hill, Patrick yelled up at Shiloh. "I'll send someone to find you. I promise!"

"I know you will, Daddy!" she called back. "I'll be waiting!"

With Shiloh still draped across his arms, Palin crouched low in front of Morgan as the dark sorceress waved her hand over her head. A blinding light flashed across the viewport and covered the hill with a sparkling blanket of white.

A lump grew in Sapphira's throat. Was Gabriel close enough to Morgan to follow her through the portal? Would the scene change to the other dimension? After a few seconds, the flash's glow faded away, revealing the familiar sloping grass of the Glastonbury Tor.

Sapphira stamped her foot. "He didn't follow!"

"Shiloh's in big trouble." Acacia turned to Sapphira. "Why did her father tell her not to eat Morgan's food? Does he know about her poisonous fruit?"

Sapphira folded her hands in front of her lips. "Probably, but I don't think Morgan would give it to her. She wants Shiloh to live."

"So now, if she doesn't disobey her father, she'll starve."

"Not if I can help it." Sapphira withdrew the cross from her waistband. "I know how to get to the sixth circle."

"How? When we go through the portal Morgan just used, we come out at our mining level, and the rest of the portals here are closed."

Sapphira waved her hand across the screen, and it rolled up into a spinning orange column. "Not this one," she said, nodding at the portal.

"That leads to Morgan's swamp. I know you love wrestling with serpents, but it's still not the sixth circle."

Sapphira tightened her grip on the cross. "I got to the sixth circle from Morgan's island. I can do it again."

"Will you be able to get home?"

Sapphira stared at Acacia. The deep lines in her sister's brow mirrored her own concern. Could she return? To get to the sixth circle, she had plunged through that strange hole in one of the three doors, so there was no way to climb back up. And she left the sixth circle through a portal that led to the floor of the deep

512

chasm, but, even if it still worked, climbing the sheer cliff would be impossible. The only other option was to dive into the boiling magma river, but going through that portal would destroy Dragons' Rest, if it didn't destroy her first.

Acacia laid her hand on Sapphira's cheek. "You don't know how to get back, do you?"

"No," Sapphira said, lowering her chin. "I don't."

Acacia leaned over and picked up a stack of folded denim next to her sleeping mat. "I guess we should wear blue jeans, shouldn't we?"

"For what?"

Acacia handed Sapphira a pair of jeans and kept another pair for herself. "For our journey to the sixth circle. Our skirts aren't exactly suitable for tromping through snake-infested swamp water."

"Right, but we don't know how—"

"To get back. I know. A minor detail." Acacia slipped her jeans on. "We'll just create a new portal somewhere and see where it goes."

Sapphira pulled up her own jeans. "But what if it's dangerous? We can't risk Shiloh's life."

"Easy." Acacia pinched the snap closed. The faded jeans hung loosely on her narrow hips. "We'll return by ourselves, and then, if it's safe, we'll go back to get her."

"Okay." Sapphira fastened her own baggy jeans, castaway pants from a beggars' bin. "But in case we can't get back," she continued, tucking away the cross, "I want to bring her some food that'll last a long time." Sapphira ran to the museum and plucked one of the smallest white clusters from the branches, now plentiful in the midst of the lush greenery, some as large as a small melon. As she hustled to the portal, she carefully slipped the fruit into her jeans pocket.

"Do you think you can keep it dry in the swamp?"

"It won't matter," Sapphira said. "If she's hungry enough, she'll eat it."

513

"I'll be right back." Acacia hurried to the museum and returned with a thick scroll tucked under her arm.

Sapphira pointed at it. "Is that for opening a portal or bashing snakes?"

"Both." Acacia opened the scroll a few inches. "It's one I've been saving for portal travel, but if it breaks on a snake's head, I won't mind. Besides, we have lots of modern books now."

Sapphira took Acacia's hand. "Let's get going."

The two oracles walked into the column. As usual, Sapphira's vision sharpened, enabling her to distinguish the tiniest slivers of radiant energy as they swirled around her head. Fighting the sadness, she grasped a stream of light and pulled. Instantly, the cavern dissolved, and they zoomed upward. A heavy, wet wind buffeted their heads. Sapphira pulled out her cross and shouted through the gusts. "Ignite!" Wind-beaten flames covered the cross and sizzled in the moisture-laden air.

Suddenly, they blasted through the surface of the swamp. Flying upward within a spewing cylindrical geyser, Sapphira wriggled around to get her bearings. The swamp lay about twenty feet below, and she and Acacia were still soaring higher, though their acceleration seemed to be slowing.

Acacia readied her scroll. "Flying is pretty cool," she said with a deadpan tone, "but I think we're going to fall now."

The two girls linked arms and plummeted toward the water. Sapphira pointed her cross downward and shouted, "Give me all you've got!"

A narrow fountain of flames roared from the cross and sizzled into the swamp, creating a thrust that slowed their plunge. Erupting from the water's surface, a dense column of steam struck Sapphira's buttocks, soaking her jeans with scalding moisture.

Sapphira and Acacia splashed into the swamp and immediately lunged toward shore through its scummy, waist-deep water. "Hurry!" Sapphira yelled, holding her still-flaming cross high.

Acacia trudged at her side with the scroll clenched in her fist. Behind them, the water began to stir. Serpentine scales broke the surface and glinted in the sunlight.

Sapphira slogged through the muddy bottom. Every step seemed an eternity as they waded to thigh-deep, then knee-deep water. Finally, Sapphira began to sprint, but as she splashed toward shore, a horrible scream made her spin around. Close behind her, Acacia limped toward shore dragging a huge serpent that had latched on to her ankle. She fell to her knees and smacked its body with her scroll.

Snatching the scroll, Sapphira pounded the snake's midsection. When it finally let go, she grabbed it by the tail and whipped it out into the swamp. Pushing her arms under Acacia's shoulders, she heaved her sister onto dry land.

Acacia's face twisted in pain. "My leg's on fire!"

Sapphira brushed a strand of hair from Acacia's forehead. "It's the venom. I can see red lines crawling up your skin."

"My heart!" Acacia gasped. "It's jumping like crazy."

Sapphira whispered for the cross to darken and laid it on Acacia's chest. "Don't die on me, now. Just hang on."

Acacia's voice fell to a whisper as she labored through convulsive breaths. "Morgan said . . . she has the only cure."

"Morgan's a liar!" Sapphira dug into her pocket and retrieved the fruit. "Maybe this will help."

"But we said . . . we weren't going to eat it unless . . . we were starving."

"You're not going to eat it." Sapphira squeezed the fruit between her palms. Now that it was wet, it smashed easily into a thick, pasty poultice. She held the mash in her palm and picked up her cross again. "I'm going to rub this stuff in, but first, I'm going to open up the wound a bit more to make sure it gets into your bloodstream."

"What makes you think . . . this will work?"

515

"It healed the rash on my palm, so I think it's worth a try." Bringing the cross near Acacia's ankle, she whispered, "A small flame, please, right at the tip." The top of the cross ignited with a conical flame. "Okay," she said, looking back at Acacia. "This is really going to hurt."

"Go ahead. It can't hurt more than it already does."

Sapphira pushed the tip of the fire into one of the puncture wounds on Acacia's ankle.

"Aaaauuugh!" Acacia gritted her teeth. Her words barely punched through. "Okay . . . I was . . . wrong."

"Shhh! The dog might show up." The flame sliced a nearly bloodless gash, the heat cauterizing most of the vessels as they blistered open. With the wound now raw and gaping, Sapphira rubbed in the poultice, hoping she could massage it into Acacia's bloodstream.

Her entire body trembling, Acacia bit her shirt and let out a muffled scream.

Sapphira grimaced. "I'm sorry. I have no idea if I'm doing this right. I'm no surgeon, you know."

"No kidding." Acacia shook even harder, but after a few seconds, her tremors subsided, and she let out a long sigh.

Sapphira kept her hand over the wound. Heat radiated through the mash and stung her palm. "Is it feeling better?"

"A little. Now it's more like Nabal's whip hitting me on the ankle about a thousand times."

Sapphira lifted her hand. The goop had turned pink, but a small white spot stood out in the mixture. She plucked out a tough, yet flexible bead about the size of a baby's tooth. Tiny red stripes encircled the bead three times.

"The fruit had a seed in the middle," Sapphira said, stuffing it into her pocket. "I'll save it for later."

"So what are we going to do now? We don't have any food to give Shiloh."

"I guess I'll tell her I'll come back once I create a safe portal."

"Okay." Acacia folded her hands over her waist. "I'll wait here for you."

"No. If Morgan doesn't find you, that dog probably will."

Acacia pushed up to a sitting position. "Then I'll go with you."

Sapphira touched Acacia's leg just above her wound. "You have to drop through a hole and land pretty hard. I don't think your leg could handle it."

"Okay," Acacia said. "Do you have a plan?"

"I thought of a way you might be able to go home without fighting those snakes again."

"Go on. I'm listening."

Sapphira nodded toward Morgan's castle at the top of the hill. "Remember the three doors I told you about in the dungeon up there? Usually one of them opens to a dimension I've been to before. Elam, Gabriel, and I went through a portal we found there and ended up at Patrick's mansion."

"So you think I can find the exit portal?"

"It's easy. A skeleton marks the spot."

"A skeleton?" Acacia rolled her eyes. "Wonderful. Sounds like a safe place."

"Don't worry. It seemed safe while we were there, and I'll help you." Sapphira stood and held out her hand for Acacia. "Think you can walk?"

Acacia pulled up on Sapphira's hand and tested her ankle. "Maybe. We'll see."

Sapphira helped Acacia sneak up to Morgan's house. Sapphira had to climb into the window by herself, but since no one seemed to be home, she unlocked the door from the inside, and the two of them took their time descending the dungeon's staircase.

As darkness flooded their surroundings, Sapphira reignited the cross. When they arrived at the lantern gateway, she illuminated and extinguished the lanterns in the usual numbered sequence,

517

and the gate creaked open. Acacia leaned heavily against Sapphira as they passed through. Every few seconds, she breathed a muffled groan.

"Are you going to make it?" Sapphira asked.

Acacia sat down in front of the trio of doors and extended her sore ankle. "I'll rest while you open the doors."

When Sapphira swung open the first door, the endless field of grass appeared. Stepping over to the second, she turned the handle and opened it more slowly. Behind this one, she found the hole that led to the sixth circle. "Here's my door," she said.

As she crept toward the third door, her hand trembled. This had to be the forest! It just had to be! She reached for the knob and slung the door open. Tropical trees arched over a winding dirt path that slipped under dozens of low-hanging vines. She spun around and dramatically swept her arms toward the doorway. "Acacia, I give you the path home."

Acacia rose slowly to her feet and hobbled toward Sapphira. "Well, it's not the wardrobe to Narnia, but it'll do."

Sapphira helped Acacia limp along the path until she got her bearings. Running ahead, she located the portal and searched through the ferns until she found an extra long bone. She plunged it into the earth next to the skeleton and hustled back to Acacia.

"Okay," Sapphira said, catching her breath. "When you pass the fifth tree on the right, turn ninety degrees and you'll see a grassy mound. The portal is about fifty paces on the other side. I stuck a bone in the ground to make it easy to find. Just open the portal and you'll fall into Patrick's house. You can take your time, but I want to hurry back and find Shiloh."

Acacia embraced Sapphira, then pulled away and pressed her finger into her sister's chest. "Don't take any chances. If I don't see you by tomorrow, I'm coming to find you."

"Fair enough," Sapphira replied. "Did you bring your sunglasses?"

"No. I don't have a hat, either."

"I guess you'll have to go anyway." Sapphira combed her fingers through Acacia's white locks. "With the styles I've seen in Glastonbury lately, no one's going to say anything about your hair. If you keep your head down, maybe no one will notice your eyes. Just walk slowly."

Acacia grinned. "Yes, Mother."

Sapphira turned and headed toward Morgan's dungeon, frequently glancing at Acacia as she limped down the path.

The doorway back to the dungeon seemed to hang in the air, suspended a foot or so from the ground by an invisible force. Sapphira jumped into it and hurried to the middle door. Standing at the edge, she gazed down into the darkness. "Okay," she said out loud, grasping the cross. "Don't think about it. Just jump." Closing her eyes, she leaped in.

Squatting low, Acacia rubbed her finger across a jewel mounted in the skeleton's belt. How strange that the man's flesh would rot, while the leather in the belt showed no signs of decay.

A deep voice pierced the silence. "There are many mysteries in the land of the dead."

Acacia gasped and rose to her feet, keeping her weight on her good leg. A tall, tuxedo-clad man with a pair of umbrellas tucked under his arm stood next to her. "Welcome to the first circle," he said.

Acacia shuffled to the rear until her heels bumped against the bones. She teetered backwards, her arms flailing, but the man grabbed her wrist and pulled her upright. She pressed her palm against her chest. "Thank you."

The man smiled and nodded. "You're quite welcome."

She slipped her arm away from his grasp. "Who are you?"

"I am Joseph," he said, bowing. "I am a guide for lost souls in this place."

519

"Well, it's nice to meet you, Joseph." Acacia extended her hand. "But I can't stay. I have to get back to the land of the living."

Joseph took her hand and gave it a gentle shake. "Indeed you do. A terrible tragedy is about to befall a very old friend of yours, and, after it happens, you must bring her to me."

She jerked her hand back. "Who? Sapphira?"

"Her identity will be revealed in a very short time, but you must bring her the moment you learn of her trouble, or an even greater calamity will result."

"So you'll be right here?" Acacia asked, pointing at the ground. "I should come back to this spot?"

"Yes." Joseph lifted an umbrella. "Dark clouds are rolling in, far darker than you can imagine, but I will be your guide as you and your friend embark on a long journey."

Acacia glanced at the stormy sky. "Okay, I'll do my best, but my ankle's pretty sore, so it might take me awhile."

"You will have time." He pointed the umbrella at the skeleton. "But you must go now. The portal's glow will indicate that it is still open, so you will not need your scroll to return. But make haste. Every portal leading to these circles will soon be closed to all but a select few, and the oracles of fire will be powerless to break through the seal that God will set on the portals. They will remain closed until the new dragon king comes."

As Elam clopped into the ancient chamber, his footsteps echoed from the distant walls. Ever since Patrick's adopted cousin moved the round table, no obstructions lay hidden in the darkness, so he marched ahead until he stood directly underneath the hole in the ceiling. A moonbeam shone on his head as he called out into the shadowy chamber. "Robert. Are you in here? It's me . . . um . . . Markus."

"Over here." The voice was sad and low. "But you can call me Patrick again. Morgan has taken my precious daughter. What more can she do to me?"

Elam stepped out of the moon's glow. "I heard about Shiloh. Is that why you returned?"

"Yes, Paili and I will take the orphanage back immediately. She needs the children's company to ease her pain."

"Aren't you going to fight to get Shiloh back?"

"Fight?" A derisive laugh punctuated Patrick's tone. "What can a man do against a sorceress? How can a living human track down a prisoner in the land of the dead? If the great Merlin could not retrieve his wife, how can I expect to ever find Shiloh?"

"Paili told me that you promised to send someone to search for her. Who will that be?"

"I made that promise in haste." Patrick's voice trembled. "I have no idea what to do. I am confused, and I cannot think straight. I am lost in a wilderness, and darkness has enclosed me. There is no hope at all. None."

Elam pulled a flashlight from his belt and turned it on. Aiming the beam in the direction of Patrick's voice, he searched the wall until he found his old friend sitting on the floor next to a cross mounted on a stand. Elam strode up to him and set the beam just under Patrick's eyes. "Send Sapphira and me," Elam said. "We'll find her."

Patrick squinted at the light. "How? Won't she be hidden?"

"I've been in Morgan's prisons. I know how to get to them."

Patrick picked up a lantern and climbed to his feet. Striking a match, he lit the lantern's wick. "Where are they?"

"You have to go through portals, but I'm not sure which ones lead where anymore." Elam turned off his flashlight. "We'll have to experiment."

"I will go." Patrick's tears glistened, reflecting the lantern's flaming wick. "Just show me what to do."

Elam shook his head. "It's too dangerous."

"I don't care about danger!" Patrick clenched Elam's shoulder. "This is my daughter we're talking about. She's my only child, a child of prophecy."

Elam laid his hand on Patrick's and gently loosened the former dragon's grip. "If she's a child of prophecy, she'll be protected. That's why I'm more concerned about your safety than about hers." He lowered Patrick's hand. "Let me do it. I have a lot of experience."

A loud grunt sounded from behind Elam. He spun around and caught a glimpse of a female stumbling through the portal window's drapes. As she pulled the curtain aside, an eerie glow brightened her outline. She carried a fiery torch and waved her hand at it. "Lights out!" she commanded, and the fire disappeared.

Elam relit his flashlight and pointed it at her. The beam illuminated her white hair, and her eyes reflected the beam, bouncing it back with a blue tint. She lifted her hand, shielding her face.

"Sapphira!" Elam redirected his flashlight and strode toward her. "What are you doing here?"

"I'm not—" She winced at the glow from Patrick's lantern as he walked up to her.

Elam stepped in front of the lantern, casting a shadow across her face. "Why were you in there?"

"First of all, I'm not Sapphira. I'm Acacia. Second"—she pulled up her pant leg, revealing a red, oozing wound on her ankle—"I'm hurt, so I'd like to sit."

"By all means." Patrick helped her down to the floor. "I'll fetch Paili and our medical bag."

She sat cross-legged, obviously favoring one of her ankles. "I hope he hurries. I have something important to ask him."

Elam stooped next to her. "Ask me. Maybe I know."

"A tragedy is imminent. Do you know of anyone besides Shiloh who might be in danger?"

"No . . . No, I don't." Elam sat down and gazed at Acacia. In the glow of the portal, her white hair shimmered, and her eyes sparkled bluer than even Sapphira's. "So," Elam began, "uh . . . do you know where Sapphira is?"

"Sapphira and I were trying to find Shiloh." She extended her wounded leg and rolled up her pant cuff. "One of Morgan's serpents bit me, so Sapphira had to clean out the wound and send me home."

"That looks nasty! You're lucky to be alive!"

Loud footsteps closed in, followed by rapid breathing. Patrick rushed through the doorway, his lantern swinging in one hand and a medical bag dangling from the other. "To be visited by one oracle of fire is amazing enough," he said, "but two in the same evening is quite a surprise."

Acacia squinted at him. "Two?"

"That's why Paili is delayed." Patrick nodded toward the hallway. "She is speaking with Sapphira in the front den. Sapphira was just leaving, so Paili will be along shortly."

"Sapphira? How can that be?"

"She said she heard about Shiloh being kidnapped, so she baked some fig cakes for Paili. Apparently they were her favorite treat many years ago."

Acacia's eyes flashed. "Don't let her eat them!"

"What? Why?"

"That couldn't have been Sapphira! She was with me! She didn't bake any fig cakes!"

Elam leaped up and grabbed Patrick's arms. "Paili's in the front den?"

"Yes! Hurry!"

Elam sprinted from the room, his legs pumping so fast, he felt like he was flying. Careening around corners, he dashed down one hall, then another. Finally reaching the front of the house, he threw open the door to the den. There was Paili! Sitting by the fireplace! He lunged across the hardwood floor and slid on his knees up to her side.

He scanned her body. No sign of the fig cakes. Trying to slow his breathing, he gazed into her eyes. "Paili . . . I mean, Mrs. Nathanson. Are you all right?"

Tear tracks smudged her cheeks. She drooped her chin to her chest and shook her head. "Not all right," she said, her voice low and thin. "Shiloh gone."

"I know. I don't mean that. I mean . . ." He lifted her chin. "What did you say?"

A new tear trickled down her cheek. "Shiloh . . . gone."

Elam covered his face with his hands. "No! Tell me you didn't eat the fig cakes!"

She raised a finger. "Only one. But I sick now." Her eyes closed and her head lolled to the side.

Elam lowered his head to the floor and banged it against the wood as he let out a mournful wail. "Noooo!" He nuzzled her limp hand and kissed her fingers tenderly.

"Paili!" Patrick called.

Elam jerked his head around. Patrick stormed in and scooped Paili's limp body into his arms. "Come, Elam!" he said as he headed toward the door. "There is still hope!"

Blinded by tears, Elam leaped to his feet and stumbled behind Patrick.

"I'm taking her to the ancient chamber," Patrick said, grunting as he struggled along the corridor. "Acacia said she might be able to save her."

"I left my flashlight in the chamber." Elam surged in front of Patrick. "I'll get another lantern!" After sprinting down the hall again, he stopped at a table that held two lanterns. He snatched one up, lit it, and waited for Patrick. When he came in sight, his cheeks puffing in time with his grunts, Elam strode ahead, adjusting the wick to provide a strong, vibrant glow.

When they arrived at the chamber, Acacia pushed up from the floor and held out her arms. "Give her to me."

"Are you sure you can carry her?" Patrick asked as he transferred Paili's body to Acacia.

Acacia groaned under Paili's weight. "I'll do whatever I have to do." She limped toward the portal window. The glow bathed the two female forms, dissolving their bodies, and absorbed them into the ghostly wash.

The portal suddenly darkened, leaving Elam's lantern as the only light in the room. He fell to his seat and covered his face with his hands. "Why is this happening?" he cried. "Why would God allow Morgan to kill someone as innocent as Paili?"

Patrick's trembling grip massaged Elam's shoulder. His voice quaked. "I . . . don't know. . . . I just . . . don't know."

Elam lowered his hands and looked up at Patrick, who was now sitting on the floor. "I feel like the whole world is coming to an end," Elam said. "Is Morgan going to win this war?"

Patrick's face, now as pale as Sapphira's, seemed old and worn out, like a ghost weary of haunting a troubled home. He firmed his chin, pain and determination stretching his words. "She . . . will . . . not . . . prevail!"

525

SEARCHING FOR SHILOH

S apphira threw an empty crate to the side. Nothing behind that one, either. Setting her hands on her hips, she surveyed the stacks of crates that lined the alley, groaning at the number. Searching every one of them would be a huge pain, and, besides, Shiloh wouldn't have any reason to conceal herself, would she? Then again, fear of being alone in the sixth circle might drive a teenager into hiding. The eerie remnants of Shinar could give anyone an urge to cower in the shadows.

She sauntered back to the deserted road, shuffling her tired feet. When she reached the middle of the cobblestone paving, she cupped her hands around her mouth and shouted, "Shiiilohhh!" She waited a few seconds. A distant echo responded, but no other sound interrupted the quiet evening.

Sighing loudly, she hopped up to a raised, planked sidewalk and forced her legs into a trot. "Shiiilohhh!" She repeated her name over and over as her bare feet slapped the boards.

Stopping at the center of town in the shadow of a clock tower, she gazed at a tall statue in the main square—a sculpture of a man riding a horse. As she crossed the street and approached the statue, she blew a low whistle. The village had changed so much! Makaidos and the other dragons, working in another dimension, had altered every building and garden in Shinar. But, of course, they weren't around for her to congratulate. Still, she might see some of them, as she had seen the images of Makaidos and Roxil the last time she visited.

Sapphira followed the berm that formed the perimeter of the village's central garden until she came upon a pitcher pump. With its spout poised over a patch of bare dirt at the edge of the street, it seemed a likely place for anyone in town to come for water.

Cinching up her loose jeans, she sat on the berm and worked the handle. After several repetitions, a stream of water trickled out, then a gush. She thrust her hands under the flow and splashed her face, gasping in the chilling refreshment.

After slinging the droplets from her fingers, she sat with her elbows on her knees and gazed at the deserted town. Maybe Shiloh wasn't here after all. Or maybe she was delayed. Since Morgan wanted Shiloh to live, she couldn't just dump her in Hades without making sure she would survive the snake bite.

Sapphira looked up into the gray sky. "Elohim?" she whispered. "If you're keeping an eye on things here, I could use some help. I have no idea what to do."

As she wiggled her feet in a little puddle, she rubbed the outside of her pocket. At one time, the Ovulum used to warm up when she was going in the right direction or sting her thigh when danger was near. Now that she needed help more than ever, the strange egg wasn't around to give her guidance.

Her fingers passed across a tiny lump. She stood and dug out the bead she had plucked from the fruit and laid it in her palm. Gazing up into the sky again, she half closed one eye. "What do you expect me to do? Plant it somewhere? It took a thousand years to get fruit down below." A new trickle of water dripped from the pump's spout and splashed over her toes. She scooped up a handful of the muddy water. If Shiloh ever came to the circle, she would eventually find the water supply and use it, wouldn't she?

Sapphira let the water spill between her fingers. What could it hurt? She knelt and dug into the mire with her fingers, gouging a two-inch-deep hole in just a few seconds. After dropping the seed inside, she breathed a quick prayer and covered it up, patting the mud firmly with her hand.

She pushed the pump's handle again until a turbid puddle swirled over her tiny garden. Then, straightening her body, she wiped her hands on her already-filthy jeans and turned to leave. Shiloh might take days to arrive, so why stick around? Finding a way out made more sense than waiting. She could always come back once she found an exit.

Too tired to run, she strolled back to the spot where she had landed. After finding the scuff marks in the dirt where she had touched down, she set her feet over her prints and gazed into the sky, hoping to find the entry hole high above. Her vision remained normal, providing no obvious sign of a portal. Still, it was worth a try, and maybe she was close enough to the old portal to create a new one at this spot, but would it lift her back to Morgan's dungeon and its three doors, or would it lead somewhere else?

She ignited her cross and swirled it over her head, faster and faster until the wall of fire crawled down and surrounded her with its usual blanket of warmth. When the wall touched the ground, she began to float and rise slowly into the sky. After a few seconds, the air thinned and grew cold, very cold. Now barely able to breathe, she tilted her head upward and caught a glimpse of light.

Gasping for breath, she swirled her cross even faster, hoping it would propel her upward, but her speed stayed constant. Her lungs ached. Her head pounded. The light above drew nearer and crystallized into the shape of her entry hole. She stretched her neck, hoping to draw in the first hint of oxygen. Finally, a breeze flowed from above, and her lungs greedily drank the delicious air. When she emerged in the dungeon, her momentum carried her at least three feet above the hole before dumping her into a head-long fall. As she tumbled and rolled, her wall of fire dwindled away.

She pushed up to her hands and knees and stared at the gate in the distance. The lanterns on each side began winking out, one by one. Within seconds, half of the lights had darkened. She scrambled to her feet and jumped through the doorway. The three doors simultaneously slammed and began to warp and swell. Tongues of fire licked through the cracks at every side.

She ran to the gate, finding it unlocked, as she had left it, but as soon as she passed by the iron bars, the gate slapped closed and latched. Two more lanterns blinked off, and their glass containers shattered. The three doors, now dim in the distance, suddenly burst open and spewed fountains of lava. Three flaming rivers rampaged toward her.

Sapphira tucked her cross away and sprinted. Reaching the stairs, she leaped over three steps, but her foot slipped, and she sprawled over the steps, banging her shins and forearms. Rolling face up, she pushed with her hands and clambered backwards, stair by stair. The rivers of fire surged against the stairway, sloshing around the base and spitting globules of magma that spattered over the first step, then the second.

Her shins aching, Sapphira pushed herself higher. The step above the magma burst into flames. Snaking tongues of fire crawled toward her, bending and cracking the wooden stairway.

Finally, ignoring the pain, she turned and ran, the blistering fire licking at her heels. When she reached the top step, she lurched into the upper corridor and slammed the door.

Breathless, she sagged against the wall, barely able to stand on her throbbing legs. She paused and listened to the sounds of splintering wood. After a few seconds of quiet, she laid her palm on the door. Cool. Not a hint of fire. She opened the door a crack and peeked through. The stairway had collapsed, piled in a burning heap at least a dozen feet below. The fiery river seemed to be receding, but it still covered the stony floor.

After latching the door, she leaned against the wall and closed her eyes. The only way to the sixth circle was gone. How could she get Shiloh out now? How could the tree possibly grow quickly enough to do any good? Was there any other way to help her?

Sapphira blew out a long sigh. Staying in Morgan's house to ponder everything didn't make any sense. Acacia was hurt, and she needed someone to look after her. That wound could get infected. Maybe she was already home and waiting for help.

She withdrew her cross, grasping it in a tight fist. It was time to fight the snakes again.

531

Patrick knelt at the side of a bent oak tree. With a miniature tombstone cradled in his hands, he gazed up into the branches. The knobby limbs seemed to invite him into their embrace, calling for him to journey upward, just as he had done so many times with Shiloh. He turned away from the trunk. There was no joy remaining in that old tree, only painful memories of carefree, girlish shouts that teased his tortured mind. *"Come, Daddy. Let's climb higher! One branch higher!"*

He plunged a trowel into the frozen ground and unearthed a wedge of leaf-rich soil. As he let the dirt spill, he noticed a tiny white button and plucked it with his fingertips. The smooth ivory coating sparked a stream of memories, an Easter bonnet on a towheaded Shiloh, tree climbing after church, and a lost button that brought tears from the little angel's eyes. Could this be the same button, now drawing tears from his own eyes?

A voice drifted into his ears. "Oh, Paaaatriiick!"

He swiveled his head. Sashaying toward him, a slender woman dressed in black sighed with exaggerated sympathy. "Does a ghost from the past haunt your memories?"

He thumped the tombstone into the divot and squeezed the trowel. Redness blurred his vision. "Morgan! How dare you come to this place!"

She stood two arms' lengths away. "Just as I dare many bold steps, my old friend. I fear no one."

Patrick hurled the trowel at her. The sharp edge pierced her chest for a moment, but then eased back out and fell to the ground. She picked it up and shook off the remaining dirt. "I have come to see if you have changed your mind about Shiloh."

"Never, you foul witch!" He stood and faced her toe-to-toe. "When you burn in hell, I will laugh at your torment!"

"I prefer to laugh now, for your promised dreams of heavenly bliss are merely words uttered by dead prophets . . . like Merlin." She tickled Patrick's chin. "And where is Merlin? Where is his wife? Both swept away in the wind. Still, they are likely not suffering as much as Shiloh is suffering now."

He knocked her hand away. "Begone, devil! I will never give you Shiloh. It would be better for her to die a miserable death than to live in torture as your hostiam."

"As you wish." She handed him the trowel. "But remember that I am quite capable of taking away everyone you have ever loved. Until you give me Shiloh, you will never have a moment's rest."

"There isn't anyone else!" Patrick roared.

"Oh, no? How about young Markus? Or should I say, Elam? Without him, you would truly be friendless."

Patrick clenched his teeth. A dozen retorts popped into his head, but any one of them could bring more danger to Elam. He pointed at the tor with his trowel. "Just . . . leave . . . me!"

"I'm going, but I'll be back again with a report on Shiloh's suffering. I'm sure you'll want to hear all about it." Morgan transformed into a raven and flew away, croaking as she circled overhead. "Your little tombstone will do no good, Valcor. The memory of Paili and Shiloh will fade into oblivion. They were little sparrows that no one cared for. . . . Just little sparrows." The raven straightened its course and flew away.

He dropped to his knees again and dug frantically around the concrete marker. He sank it deep and packed dirt tightly around it. "Someone will remember Shiloh," he said, grunting with every shove into the earth. "This stone will see to that."

When he patted down the final clump, he read the inscription out loud. "Shiloh Nathanson, beloved daughter of Patrick and Paili Nathanson. Born—1948. Last seen at this tree on October 31, 1964." He squinted at the carved numerals. "Nineteen forty-eight?" Moaning softly, he rolled his eyes upward. "The engravers got it wrong," he whispered, shaking his head. "They got it wrong."

533

Patrick laid a trembling hand on the tombstone. Hot tears welled in his eyes. Rubbing them away with a grimy knuckle, he sniffed hard and gritted his teeth. He couldn't cry. Not yet. The battle for Shiloh had just begun.

CIRCA AD 1986

G abriel glided through the maternity ward, eyeing the numbers on the doors as he passed. Finding room 1545, he slid under the door and re-expanded. With the lights dimmed, shadows obscured the faces of the two adults in the room, but it didn't matter. Gabriel knew them immediately. Hannah and Timothy. Mother and Father. Twenty years of searching had led him to this hospital, and the computer in the basement pinpointed the room and included details about their baby—Ashley, a daughter of drag-ons, a chance to redeem himself as a guardian.

He drifted toward his parents. Hannah lay in bed, nuzzling a swaddled infant with her smooth, ageless cheek. It made sense that her dragon genetics would keep her young. Easing closer to his father, Gabriel studied his wrinkle-free face. How had he main-tained his youth? Becoming fully human should have started a normal aging process, but he didn't look a day older than when he left for the States almost forty years ago.

Timothy leaned over the railing and gently pulled the baby's slender arm from underneath her pink blanket. Cooing at his daughter, he placed his finger in her grasp. "Ashley!" he cried in mock pain. "What a strong grip you have!"

Lifting his energy field, Gabriel glided over the bed and gazed down at his new sister. "Ashley," he said in his electrostatic voice. "I'm glad to meet you."

Ashley's eyes locked on his. Gabriel drew back. Did she hear his greeting? Could she see him now? No one but Sapphira had been able to see or hear him before. He floated to one side of the bed. Ashley's gaze followed. He floated to the other side. Ashley followed him again.

Timothy cocked his head upward. "Is she looking at something?"

Gabriel shrank his energy field to the size of a baseball and drifted higher.

"That fly on the ceiling is all I can see," Hannah said.

"Isn't that unusual?" Timothy asked. "I thought babies couldn't see so far away. Gabriel didn't follow objects with his eyes until much later."

Hannah sighed. "No . . . he didn't."

"I'm sorry." Timothy shook his head. "I'll try to remember."

"It's okay. Hearing his name doesn't hurt quite as badly as it used to." Hannah turned Ashley's face toward her and chirped in a suddenly cheerful voice. "You're just a smart little girl, aren't you?"

"Smart, yes," Timothy said. "But . . ." His voice faded away.

Hannah took Timothy's hand in hers. "Say what is on your mind, my husband. I will not be angry."

Timothy squinted at her. "You sound like you did in the old days."

"I spoke that way intentionally." She rubbed her thumb along his knuckles. "Let us retrieve our dragon courage and speak plainly."

Timothy's gaze followed the buzzing fly as it flitted from ceiling, to wall, to bedpost. "I heard from Patrick this morning. I risked contacting him because it had been five years since we'd heard from him." He shook his head sadly. "Still no sign of Gabriel. No one has seen him in almost forty years."

Clenching her eyes shut, Hannah covered her mouth and bit her finger.

Gabriel surged down to her side and stroked her hair with his radiant hand. He glanced at the door. The courier was late. The computer should have sent the telegram over two hours ago. Gabriel gazed at his fingers, each one etched with jagged lines of energy. Using those clumsy digits to manipulate a computer through electronic impulses was a new skill. His earliest experiments had often failed, and he had to cut his message short before he ran out of power. Still, it would do, at least for now . . . if the courier ever showed up.

Timothy clasped Hannah's hand with both of his. "Gabriel was old enough to hide on his own. Maybe he's—"

"He was only thirteen when he disappeared!" Hannah countered.

A knock sounded at the door. "Telegram for Hannah Drake."

Gabriel breathed a radiant sigh. Perfect timing.

Timothy returned from the door, opening a Western Union envelope. Deep creases etched his forehead. "It's a telegram from Glasgow."

"More bad news?"

535

He shook the page in front of her. "It's good news! Excellent news! But I'm not sure how to interpret it."

"Don't just stand there!" Hannah cried, trembling. "Read it to me!"

Timothy raised the paper to his eyes and cleared his throat. "Congratulations on the birth of your daughter. May she live in peace and learn the secret behind the Oracles of Fire. Signed, Gabriel."

Hannah slapped the bed rail. "Gabriel? Then he's alive!"

Timothy leaned over and kissed her with a loud smack. "Yes!" he shouted, rising again with her hand clasped in his. "He must be!"

Hannah made a shushing sound, but her laughter washed it away.

Timothy laid a hand over the baby. "Careful," he said, "you'll jiggle Ashley."

With a wide smile still gracing her lips, Hannah pointed at the telegram. "Do you know what he meant by the secret behind the Oracles of Fire?"

"I told you about meeting Sapphira in Dragons' Rest." He folded the telegram and stuck it in his shirt pocket. "I never saw her again."

"Could the secret be how to get her to open the portal to Dragons' Rest without destroying it? Maybe there's still a way to save Roxil . . . or, Jasmine, I guess I should call her now."

"And save all the others, for that matter." He tapped his finger on the note. "But if he knows the secret, why wouldn't he just tell us?"

"Maybe he knows there *is* a secret, but he doesn't know what it is."

Timothy wrapped his fingers tightly around the bed rail. "If there was only some way to contact him. He must be in terrible danger if he won't come out of hiding to explain."

Hannah hugged Ashley close. "But he's alive!" she said, tears streaming. "After all these years, he's alive! And since he knows we're in Montana, maybe he'll join us and help us look for Irene. He might know where she is, too."

"Let's not go too far." Timothy rubbed her forearm. "It's not like he's that fly on the wall."

Hannah laid a finger over her lips. "Right. One step at a time." She took a deep breath and let it out slowly. "Too much information will make your brain choke."

Gabriel expanded again to his full size and let his radiance glow brightly. He shared their ecstasy, rejoicing with them the only way he knew how—silently, invisibly, yet with all the joy he could muster.

He lowered his glowing hand to Ashley's cheek. As he caressed her pink skin, she turned back toward him and gazed directly into his eyes. She smiled and gurgled.

"Did you hear that?" Timothy said. "She's happy Gabriel's alive, too!"

Hannah laughed again. "Maybe she'll get to see him someday."

Gabriel joined their laughter. He *was* that fly on the wall, an imperceptible listener who learned the secrets of the room's quiet conversations. But one secret whispered more loudly than all the others. He had a new sister, and he loved her. Nothing would ever harm her. Not Devin, not Morgan, not even the devil himself could come between him and this precious baby.

Sapphira sat in front of the portal screen. She tried to smile at the lovely sight—a new baby, a rejoicing mother and father, good news of lost loved ones. But she couldn't smile, couldn't shake the unbearable sadness that weighed her down.

Being alone for over twenty years seemed to make good news crumble to the floor. If Acacia had been there, they would have joined hands and danced in a circle. If Paili had been there, they would have embraced and squealed, feeding and watering the good news with hugs and kisses.

But now two of her dearest friends had disappeared to who knew where? Her only clue was a brief conversation she had heard between Elam and Patrick. Apparently, Paili ate Morgan's fruit and had somehow vanished, but Gabriel, her eyes and ears to the world of the living, couldn't pick up any more information. And she couldn't leave to get any news on her own. The screen wouldn't roll up into a portal column, so it was now impossible to go anywhere.

Sapphira stood up and wandered toward her bed. Everyone had forsaken her. Even Yereq no longer responded to her verbal prodding. No matter how much she chattered or sang, he just slept on and on. And loneliness led to her bigger problem—boredom. With nothing to do but sit and watch others enjoy life, she could only reread the books she had memorized long ago. She had no slumber party friends giggling over shared secrets, no birthday guests singing around a frosted cake, and no family sitting at a table filled with steaming dishes of delicious bounty.

Not that she needed a meal. After nearly starving, she had finally eaten the fruit from the tree of life and never felt a hunger pang again. But watching families happily clinking glasses and passing laughter from place to place instilled a craving for their glorious joy.

Sapphira sat cross-legged on her mat, worn to a thin pad from hundreds of nights of tossing and turning. Acacia's mat lay beside hers, its blanket pulled back for her should she ever return. Between the two mats lay her cross. She picked it up and stared at it. Why didn't it work anymore? Had it lost its power?

She pointed it at herself. "Have *I* lost *my* power?" she asked out loud.

She cringed at the sound of her voice. It had been months since she had spoken, months since she had vowed never to speak again until she could be reunited with Elam and tell him . . . tell him . . .

She flopped down on her back. Not *those* words! They were too sad to utter, even in her mind.

Holding the cross upright on her chest, she gazed at its dark wood, now weathered and worn. Strange that it had always stayed smooth when she used it to open portals. As she traced her finger along its edges, an image from long ago appeared in her mind—Elam walking into an Easter service at a church in Glasgow, and a cross decorating the front of the sanctuary. One of the songs played like an enduring echo, a song of death, resurrection, and victory.

Sapphira winced at the lyrics. The song didn't make any sense. There was no joy in getting mocked and abused, living a life of torture, then dying a cruel death. So what if a messiah died and rose again? What good did it do? Elohim didn't resurrect Gabriel's body after he sacrificed it for a friend. He didn't whisper in Paili's ear to warn her when the devil's mistress gave her the food of death. And he didn't seem to care any longer about a freak of nature buried alone under thousands of feet of rock.

539

She sat up and slung the cross at the portal screen. It agitated the light as it passed through and bounced across the rocky floor on the other side. She flopped back down and, sliding her hands behind her head, squeezed her eyes closed. She sniffed and spoke out loud, her words pouring forth in a lament. "Elohim, please tell me you're not just another Nimrod. Tell me you aren't a king who just uses people for what you can get out of them." She extended her open hand upward and shouted through her sobs. "You danced with me! Don't you care about me anymore?"

She rolled over and stuffed her blanket into her mouth, biting it hard as she cried on and on.

Circa AD 1988

Gabriel floated high over the Drake residence, surveying the dim, moonlit landscape. The remote cabin sat alone at the top of a rural mountain, so strangers had no reason to venture the long, narrow road that ascended the steep incline. From his vantage point, he would be able to see any car headlights as far away as Flathead Lake at the base of the tree-filled slope. So far, no one was in sight.

Since Hannah and Timothy had gone to a movie in Kallispell, leaving Isaac Stalworth, Timothy's "adopted" father, to babysit Ashley, Gabriel paid closer attention to his job than ever. Isaac was a trustworthy old man, but could he handle an attack by a slayer? Vigilance was in order for other reasons as well. Ever since he had created that telegram, it seemed that his parents had been shadowed by a mysterious stalker, making that form of communication too dangerous to continue.

Gabriel flew lower and peered in through the window. Isaac bounced little Ashley on his knee, making her straight brown hair sway across her back. She pointed at him, apparently saying something, but her voice didn't penetrate the glass.

After filtering in through a narrow slit under the window, Gabriel drew close. Isaac rested his leg and patted his chest, wheezing. "I'm getting tired. Can't we do something else?"

Ashley slid closer and laid her hand over his. "Do your lungs hurt, Dada?" she asked.

"Strange." Isaac lifted his palm. "They did hurt, but they feel better now."

She crawled back out on his knee and slapped his thigh with her little hand. "Then one more ride before I tuck you into bed."

"Tuck *me* into bed? Don't you want me to read to you?"

"No!" She crossed her chubby arms over her chest. "You never want to read what I want to read!"

"Look, young lady," he said, shaking a finger at her, "I endured *Lord of the Rings*, but I'm not cracking open *War and Peace*. I'd be asleep before the second page."

She spread out her hands, and her smile dug a dimple into each of her cheeks. "Then you go to bed, and I'll read it to you."

Isaac nudged her chin with his finger. "You're only two years old! You shouldn't be filling your head with all those war stories."

"Why not?"

He tapped her head. "You know what your mother says."

"Don't say it!" Ashley covered his mouth with her hands. "I won't let my brain choke."

"If you're not asleep when Mommy and Daddy get home," he said, mumbling between her fingers, "I'll be in big trouble."

Ashley pressed a fingertip on his nose. "You're too big to spank!"

A sudden popping noise pricked Gabriel's senses. He peered out the window. A car rolled into the gravel driveway, its headlights dark. The car's doors opened, and two shadows skulked toward the house.

Gabriel flew up to the ceiling and jammed his finger into an empty socket in a hanging light fixture. The shock sent him flying into the hallway, and the bulbs in the other sockets exploded.

Isaac scooped up Ashley and hunched over her, protecting her from the shower of glass. "Not a sound!" he said. "You know the plan."

Ashley pressed a shushing finger over her lips and nodded.

Isaac scrambled to the back door, but when a beam of light flashed through the adjacent window, he pivoted and ran toward the hall, whispering to Ashley. "Remember how we practiced jumping out the window?"

Ashley nodded again. Isaac stomped right over Gabriel, and the two disappeared into a bedroom.

The front and back doors flew open. Bright beams slashed the living room, each one finally landing on the other's source and illuminating the intruders' faces. Dressed in chain mail and draped with surcoats, Devin and Palin drew out their swords.

Devin, the candlestone swinging over his chest, pointed his sword at the hall. "That's the only way he could've gone!"

541

Palin resheathed his sword and ran. Gabriel plugged his fingers into a nearby outlet. Instantly, pulsing energy swelled his body. Palin set his feet, but his momentum carried him into Gabriel's glowing field.

Palin's face lit up, and streaks of electricity spewed from his mouth. Devin grabbed Palin's hand and pulled. The current arced into Devin's body, but with a backwards lunge, he yanked Palin free.

Lying on the hallway floor, Palin pointed at Gabriel. "Who is that winged boy?"

"It must be that mongrel I hunted back in England." Devin rose slowly to his feet. "I think his name was Gabriel. Morgan told me he's Thigocia's son. It seems that he survived his execution."

Gabriel unplugged himself. His energy field collapsed, but jolts of electricity continued to sizzle across his body.

Palin rose slowly, wobbling on shaky knees. "What is he made out of?"

"It looks like electrical sparks of some kind." Devin kicked at Gabriel's dwindling energy. "But whatever he is, he doesn't appear to be physical, and it doesn't look like he can move."

As the sparks dissipated, shadows enveloped the two slayers. Only the moonlight from the living room window illuminated their dim frames. Palin nodded toward the bedroom. "Should we try to find the old man?"

"He was alone, wasn't he?"

Palin flicked on his flashlight and ran its beam along the hallway floor. "I didn't see anyone else."

"As soon as we prepare Thigocia's welcome home surprise, we'll look around, but he's not likely to be able to warn her from out here in the middle of nowhere."

Palin limped toward the front door. "I'll get the gas."

As the last of Gabriel's sparks winked out, his outer extremities stretched toward the candlestone. He tried to resist, but his confused atoms did little to defy the gem's power.

Devin turned on his own flashlight. Some of the beam's particles seemed to break away and trickle in the opposite direction. "Your mother hid her tracks well, but not well enough."

After returning with a gasoline can, Palin splashed the contents over the furniture and rugs. Pausing for a moment, he set the can down and picked something up from the floor. The clump of material draped over his hand looked like one of Ashley's rag dolls.

Gabriel cried out in his mind. Now they would know about Ashley, and they would comb the forest until they found her!

Glancing at Devin, Palin stuffed the doll under his surcoat and continued his morbid job. When the last drops drained out on the hallway carpet, he handed Devin a glass bottle with a rag sticking out of the top.

As Gabriel stretched toward the candlestone, Devin stomped on the carpet. "I know you're still around here somewhere." He raised the bottle. "Ever heard of a Molotov cocktail? When your mother returns, Palin and I are going to propose a toast, thanking her for donating her blood to our cause. If our little explosion doesn't kill you, then I guess nothing will."

Gabriel strained against the candlestone's relentless pull. With the slayer standing right over him, the gem seemed to lasso his body and drag him upward. He finally gave in. As he flew toward the glittering crystal, the room stretched out into warped colors and disappeared.

543

CHAPTER

BONNIE CONNER

AUGUST, 1995 A.D.

G abriel? Can you hear me?"

The eerie voice seemed unearthly, yet familiar. Gabriel opened his eyes but could see only darkness. He turned his head to one side. With a veil of blackness in view, he couldn't tell if he was standing, sitting, or lying down.

"Over here, Gabriel."

He swiveled his head to the other side. A bright humanoid shape reached a shimmering hand over his brow.

Gabriel whispered, "Merlin?"

"Yes. It's time for you to wake up."

Gabriel stood and shook his head, clearing his foggy mind. "Wake up? How long have I been sleeping?"

"Ever since you reentered the candlestone seven years ago."

"Seven years? How could I sleep for seven years?"

"Because of necessity and mercy." Merlin pointed a radiant finger at him. "Your energy was nearly spent in your battle with Devin and Palin, so you needed to recharge. Sleeping was also an act of mercy, for wandering here for years on end is not exactly a pleasant experience."

"I remember shocking the slayers, but—" An image of Palin drenching furniture with gasoline flashed in his mind. "Merlin!" he shouted with his static-filled voice. "Did they kill my parents?"

"I'm afraid so." Merlin laid a hand on Gabriel's shoulder. "Yet, there is still hope for them, and we must work together to salvage what we can."

"There's hope?" Gabriel rolled his fingers into fists. "What do I do? Where do I go?"

"Patience. The path to their restoration is not straightforward. First we must take care of the dragon offspring."

"Like Ashley? She got away, didn't she?"

"Ashley is in no danger. Her grandfather adopted her and changed her last name to his own. Since her dragon traits are not easy to detect, she will not attract the slayer's attention."

"That's a relief." Gabriel relaxed his fingers. "So do I get to guard her again? I managed to save her, didn't I?"

"There is no doubt that you saved Ashley's life." Merlin's bright silhouette paced in front of Gabriel. "After losing Shiloh, you rebounded well as a guardian angel."

"Thanks. I know I'm not a real angel, but sometimes I felt like I was supposed to be. It's hard when you can't always figure out what to do."

"Intelligence must mingle with wisdom and shrewd planning." Merlin stopped and touched Gabriel's chest with his glowing finger. "You cannot rely on your physical field alone. Electricity manipulation is limited and dangerous."

"I know. It's sort of shocking, too."

Merlin's energy field flashed red. "Very funny. You almost disintegrated, and now you're making jests."

"Right." Gabriel bowed his head. "Sorry."

Merlin slowly faded back to dazzling white. He floated to the darkest part of the chamber and knelt next to a fissure in the floor. "I awakened you, because you are likely now strong enough to leave the candlestone."

"I feel strong." Gabriel knelt beside him. "Trust me. I'll get out somehow."

"And you must. Your next assignment awaits."

"Next assignment? Do you mean I can't watch over Ashley?"

"You may visit her from time to time, because your new charge lives within a reasonable distance. But you must not let your concern for Ashley distract you from focusing on Bonnie."

"Bonnie?"

"Yes." Merlin rose to his feet. "Bonnie Conner is the daughter of Irene, formerly Hartanna. She has a wonderful dragon trait that has only recently become obvious, and her parents will now have to hide it to keep the slayers at bay."

"What trait does she have?"

"You'll soon find out." Merlin gestured for Gabriel to stand. "Come, let us expand our vision, and I will show you where Bonnie lives. Then, you must leave this place and become her guardian angel."

547

Gabriel glided up to the two-story Victorian home, flapping his wings as he ascended the three wooden porch steps. Although his movements did nothing to propel him, changing his energy boundaries made him feel more alive and less like a floating cloud of invisible gas.

Pausing at the front door, he read the address, 377, each calligraphic numeral illuminated by the rays of the rising sun. He glanced around for a way inside. Weather stripping blocked the crack under the door, so he drifted to the side of the house and focused on a vent, possibly leading to a kitchen stove. Traveling past soot and hot air wouldn't be fun, but he had entered Ashley's new home that way.

Shaking his head, Gabriel floated back to the porch. Ashley's home was where he really wanted to be, and it was only about eight or nine miles away on the other side of Missoula, about an hour's journey at the pace his thought-induced locomotion provided. This assignment would be so different. Bonnie and her parents were strangers. What if she turned out to be a brat? Or a stuck-up princess, smug and proud as she strutted about in her latest fashions?

Gabriel peered in through a window that abutted the door. Standing beside a coat rack in the foyer, a woman helped a little girl adjust a backpack, checking the zippers multiple times and smoothing out the wrinkles in her sweatshirt. The woman grabbed a jacket from the rack, and the two headed for the door.

548

As Gabriel backed away, the door flew open. Swinging a Winnie-the-Pooh lunch box, the girl bounced out and ran right through Gabriel. The woman followed, laughing. "Bonnie! Wait! What's your hurry?"

Bonnie spun around and backpedaled toward the street, her blonde hair streaming in the stiff breeze. "If I'm late for my first day, the teacher might not like me!"

"Who wouldn't like you, silly girl?" Her mother caught up and took her hand. "Anyway, the bus won't be at our corner for another five minutes. There's plenty of time."

As mother and daughter walked hand in hand along the sidewalk, Gabriel followed close behind. Bonnie seemed nice enough, far from what he had feared. No bratty princess could ever produce her smile—so pure, so genuine, the image of youthful innocence. Her mother, of course, had to be Irene, the former dragon who once bore the name Hartanna. She seemed dutiful and friendly, another welcome discovery.

He zoomed ahead, then floated backwards in front of Bonnie, matching her pace. He gazed into her bright blue eyes—so much like Shiloh's, it was amazing! In fact, her hair, the shape of her nose, the way she walked, everything about her reminded him of Shiloh. How could cousins look that much alike?

When the two stopped at the corner, Irene pulled Bonnie's hair back into a thick ponytail and wrapped it in an elastic band. "Remember," she whispered, stooping to meet her eye to eye. "Don't take off your backpack and no one will see your . . . um . . . growths." She pulled the hem down on Bonnie's sweatshirt and kissed her forehead. "It's very important that no one finds out about them."

Bonnie nodded, her smile unabated. "Okay, Mama. I won't take it off."

"Good. You were right to tell me about those growths. We'll talk more about them later."

Bonnie adjusted the strap on her backpack. "Will I have to go to the doctor?"

"We'll see." A diesel engine clattered in the distance. "Here comes the bus." Irene kissed Bonnie again. "You'll be fine. I'm sure you'll make lots of friends."

The bus pulled to a whining stop. When the doors swung open, Bonnie hopped on board and waved to her mother. Gabriel drifted in behind Bonnie and waved with her, though, of course, Irene had no idea he was there.

Bonnie turned and smiled at the bus driver. "Hi! I'm Bonnie! What's your name?"

"Pearl." The middle-aged woman frowned under her tightly pulled hair bun and pointed toward the back. "Now sit down."

Bonnie's smile faded. She walked slowly down the aisle, her eyes shifting from side to side. One girl laid a notebook on the seat next to her and gave Bonnie a nasty glare. Another whispered with her neighbor and giggled as Bonnie passed by. When she approached

549

the rear of the bus, a boy tossed a wad of paper that bounced off her cheek. "No first graders back here!" he called.

"Look at her stupid lunch box," another boy said. "Only babies watch Winnie the Pooh!"

Blinking rapidly as she retreated toward the front, Bonnie hitched up her backpack and slid into an empty bench in the middle section. She wiped a tear from her eye and leaned her head against the window, her lips tight and her chin quivering.

Gabriel sat next to her. He scooted close and wrapped a wing around her whole body. Of course she couldn't feel it, but maybe he could somehow relay a bit of sympathy. The very first stab of rejection always bled profusely, a shedding of innocence he knew all too well.

Bonnie glanced at another little girl sitting alone across the aisle. With her chin pointing at her chest, the girl's gaze wandered Bonnie's way, and the hand in her lap gave Bonnie the slightest hint of a wave.

Keeping her head against the window, Bonnie waved back.

The girl flashed a gap-toothed smile. "Do you want to be my friend?"

Bonnie nodded, her lips still tight.

"My name is Carly." She patted the seat next to her. "You can sit by me if you want to."

Bonnie glanced at the driver, then hopped across the aisle. "I'm Bonnie," she said as she slid in next to her new friend.

Carly pointed at Bonnie's lunch box and whispered. "I watch Winnie the Pooh. Tigger's my favorite."

"Me, too!" Bonnie smiled and bounced in her seat. "Can you tell?"

Carly pulled a lunch box from under her shoes. A bouncing Tigger decorated the front and back. "Shhh!" She glanced toward the rear. "Don't tell those boys."

"Who cares what they think?" Bonnie looped her arm around Carly's. "As long as we stick together."

"Yeah," Carly said, tightening their clutch. "Who cares what they think?"

Gabriel floated close to the two girls. As they chatted happily, it seemed as though the gentle power of pure love streamed into his energy field, strengthening him with every second. What a perfect assignment! Being with this little angel would be like heaven itself.

As the bus rolled to a stop, Gabriel surveyed the passersby on the sidewalk. It was time to go to work. His duty had transformed from a chore to a labor of love. No one would dare lay a finger on Bonnie, not if he could help it. This time, he would not fail.

Sapphira sat with her arms wrapped around her legs. Since Gabriel awakened and emerged from the candlestone after all those years, she finally had something to watch. With the viewing screen dark for so long, she had barely noticed it after a while, just glancing at it from time to time as she pored over her finger-worn books. Now, the new adventures that flashed before her eyes awakened her imagination and filled her with new hope.

As Bonnie and Carly laughed together, Sapphira smiled. What a sweet little girl! She seemed to dance through life like a waltzing flower. Even after enduring the nasty glares and verbal barbs, her faith in love and kindness seemed unearthly.

Sapphira wiped a tear from her cheek. Bonnie Conner was definitely worth watching.

Gabriel peered into Bonnie's bedroom and spied her sitting in the midst of a circle of rag dolls. Good. She had finished changing into her nightgown. He breezed in and sat in front of her. As she dressed one of the dolls for bed, he let his gaze wander. On the walls, hand-painted pastel balloons floated in the midst of a pale pink sky, and bright green grass near the floor partially hid a mouse, a rabbit, and, peeking out from behind a bookshelf, a wide-eyed raccoon. A Tigger blanket covered a youth bed in one corner, and a white three-drawer dresser filled the opposite corner,

551

but most of the room seemed dedicated to a host of small, hand-made Raggedy-Ann-and-Andy-type dolls.

Sitting cross-legged, Bonnie set one doll on each knee, animating the one on her right with a gentle shake. "Carly," she said, her voice pitching high, "You're my best friend." She gave the other doll a shake. "And you're mine, too, Bonnie."

As Bonnie continued playacting with her dolls, Gabriel focused on a new pair of voices filtering into the room in hushed tones. The name Carly, however, came through clearly.

Bonnie's head perked up. She leaned over and pulled the door fully open, and the voices clarified.

"Well," a man said, "I'm glad to hear she found a friend, but I have work to do and—"

"Wait," came a woman's reply. "There's something else. Remember those growths I called you about?"

"Yes. Did you figure out what they are?"

"When she got home, I studied them carefully. They have scales."

"Scales? Like dry skin scales?"

"No. Like armor scales. And there are two sharp points that remind me of claw hooks."

Bonnie tightened her grip on her two dolls and leaned closer to the door. The few seconds of silence seemed to last an hour. Finally, the man blurted out, "Wings? We can't have a daughter with wings!"

"Shhh! Not so loud! We have what we have, and there's no way to change it."

"But," the man continued, "we won't be able to show our faces in public, not with a mutant for a daughter!"

"She's not a mutant. You understand genetics well enough to know that."

"Then she's a freak, a freak of nature. No human has ever grown wings before. We'll have to—"

The conversation stopped. Heavy footsteps pounded in the hallway. Irene leaned into the bedroom.

"Mama!" Bonnie cried. "Why did Daddy say—"

Irene raised a finger to her lips. "We'll talk in a few minutes." She gave Bonnie a brief tight-lipped smile, and closed the door. The footsteps, quieter now, retreated.

Bonnie stared at the door, her mouth open and tears streaming down her cheeks. Covering her face with her dolls, she drew her knees up to her chest and wept. As she rocked back and forth, her head bobbed, and tiny, shrill cries seeped between her two raggedy friends.

Gabriel tried to cover her with his wings and lay an arm over her shoulders, but it was useless. She couldn't feel the slightest bit of reassurance from an invisible, massless comforter.

He straightened to his full height and spread his wings as he gazed upward. "What can I do?" he called out in his electrostatic voice. "If you want me to guard her, at least let me do my job! I know exactly how she feels! I can help her!"

He looked at Bonnie and yelled as loud as he could. "Bonnie! Can you hear me?"

Bonnie's red, tear-stained face peeked out. Her eyes widened. She laid her palms on the floor and slid back toward the wall, trembling.

Gabriel lowered his voice slightly. "Don't be afraid," he said, holding out his hand. "I won't hurt you."

Bonnie swallowed. "Who . . . who are you?"

"My name is Gabriel."

"Gabriel?" Bonnie pointed at her bookshelf. "Like the angel in the Bible?"

Gabriel noted a child-sized Bible lying on top of the shelf. How should he answer? He certainly didn't want to lie. He took a half step closer. "What do I look like to you?"

Bonnie wiggled her fingers. "Like a sparkly ghost with wings. I can see right through you."

"It's fair to say that I am *like* a guardian angel, for I have been assigned to watch over you."

"Why?" Bonnie pointed at herself. "I'm not important."

"You are far more important than you realize. You heard about your wings, didn't you?"

Bonnie's eyes teared up again. "Daddy said I'm a freak."

"Look at me." Gabriel flapped his wings. "Do you think I'm a freak?"

"No." Bonnie wiped a tear with her finger. "But you're an angel."

Gabriel knelt next to her and caressed her hair with his hand. "And so are you, the sweetest angel I have ever met."

Bonnie raised her hand and set it on Gabriel's arm. "I can't feel you at all."

"No, and you couldn't see me earlier, even though I was with you all day."

"All day?" Bonnie sniffed and smiled. "Really?"

"Yes, I saw that sour bus driver and those mean boys, but I also saw your new friend Carly and her Tigger lunch box."

Bonnie took in a quick breath. "You really *were* there!"

"And I will stay with you as long as I can. Even if you can't see me or hear me, I'll be there."

Bonnie drew back her hand. "You're disappearing! Don't go!"

"I won't go. I'll stay here all night."

"I can barely hear you now."

"Then hurry to bed, and I'll sing you to sleep."

"Oh, please do!" Bonnie jumped up and turned off her light, then, throwing back her blanket, she nestled into her bed. "I'm ready!" Her eyes darted around. "But I can't see you anymore."

Gabriel knelt at her bedside. "Can you still hear me?"

"Yes, but like a whisper."

"Okay. Close your eyes. I'll sing as loud as I can."

Bonnie closed her eyes tightly and drew her blanket up to her chin. Her delicate lashes still sparkled with leftover tears.

Gabriel stroked her hair again and sang.

*Whither shall I go from thy spirit? Or whither shall I flee from
thy presence?*
*If I ascend up into heaven, thou art there: If I make my bed in
hell, behold, thou art there.*

Bonnie smiled. Her eyelids began to relax, and she sighed
deeply.

*If I take the wings of the morning, and dwell in the uttermost
parts of the sea;*
*Even there shall thy hand lead me, and thy right hand shall
hold me.*
*If I say, Surely the darkness shall cover me; even the night shall
be light about me.*
*Yea, the darkness hideth not from thee; but the night shineth as
the day:*
The darkness and the light are both alike to thee.

555

As light from the window faded, Bonnie opened her eyes
again. "Are you still here?"

"Yes, I'm still here."

"Gabriel?" She reached out her hand. "Are you here?"

"Yes, sweet angel," Gabriel said, laying his hand on hers. "Can't
you hear me?"

Bonnie's eyes darted around again. "Gabriel?"

Gabriel tried to hold her hand, but his fingers passed right
through hers. "I won't leave you, Bonnie. I would give my life to
protect you."

Bonnie straightened out the wrinkles on her blanket and laid
her arms on top. "Gabriel, I guess I can't hear you anymore, but
you said you'd stay with me, so I know you must be here." She
closed her eyes again and smiled. "Angels never lie."

November, 2002

Elam carried a lantern through the corridor that led to the ancient chamber. He glanced back at the man walking behind him, a tall, older gentleman who had to duck to make his way under the low ceiling. It had been hundreds of years since he had seen Merlin, but this new arrival looked so much like the old prophet, it was frightening.

"Almost there, Professor Hamilton," Elam said. "The ceiling gets higher in a few seconds."

"It's quite all right, my good fellow. The anticipated meeting is well worth such trivial unpleasantries."

When Elam passed the final doorway, light from within the chamber washed out his lantern, so he lifted the glass and blew out the flame. Beside him, Professor Hamilton ran his fingers through his wild, gray hair. "Remarkable!" he said, gazing all around.

Elam smiled. "You ain't seen nothin' yet."

A voice beckoned from the far end of the chamber. "Charles! Welcome!" Patrick waved at them from the round table in the back. "Come here and join us."

Elam led Charles over the compass design on the floor in the center of the room. "The table used to be here," Elam said. "I'm not sure why they moved it."

Professor Hamilton slowed his pace as he passed over the design. His eyes locked on one of the sketches. "Astounding!"

When they reached Patrick, Elam stopped for a moment to allow his eyes to adjust. Three bright lanterns formed a triangle at the center of the table, illuminating Patrick's face and the faces of four other men. Their eyes followed Charles as he drew close to one of two empty spaces.

Patrick nodded at the chair. "Please sit, my friend."

Elam strode to Patrick's side, taking his place as the oldest errand boy who ever lived.

Professor Hamilton slid out the chair and cleared his throat. "May I say, Sir Patrick, that I am honored by your selection of me as a new member of this distinguished body, and—"

"Oh, cut the squash!" one of the men boomed. He then laughed and patted the man next to him on the back. "We're about as distinguished as rubber socks! Aren't we, Kaplan?"

Kaplan glared at him. "Rubber socks? What's the connection?"

"Nobody knows we exist!" The man burst out with a series of belly laughs.

"I know rubber socks exist," a third man protested.

"Quiet!" Patrick raised his hand. "Let's not give our new designate the wrong impression."

Kaplan drummed his fingers. "It seems to me that he is getting exactly the right impression. All we ever do in our meetings is crack jokes and tell tall tales. When McCorkle died, maybe we should have just propped up his body in his chair, then we wouldn't have needed a replacement."

557

The first man piped up again. "McCorkle's corpse would be funnier than he ever was. That's for certain."

"The point is," Kaplan continued, "that waiting for Arthur's heir to arrive has been like sitting in the maternity ward waiting for fifteen hundred years of labor to finally end. It's no wonder we expectant fathers are getting a bit punchy."

"Fathers?" the first man rejoined. "I feel like the poor mother!"

Patrick rapped his knuckles on the table. "Gentlemen! Please!"

The men murmured for a few seconds, and when all was quiet, Patrick again gestured for Charles to sit.

Professor Hamilton nodded and sat down. "Thank you, Sir Patrick."

Patrick folded his hands. "Since we consider ourselves equals, Charles, we normally dispense with titles that indicate superiority. I realize my knighthood is significant to you, but I am merely called Steward. You will learn the others' titles in due time."

"Very well. What shall I be called?"

Elam leaned over and whispered in Patrick's ear. "Merlin."

Patrick's face brightened. "Of course. Merlin!"

"Merlin?" Professor Hamilton repeated. "Why Merlin?"

Patrick glanced at Elam but quickly returned his gaze to Professor Hamilton. "It seems to me that you are as gifted in spiritual matters as anyone I know. Your heart for God reflects the legends of the great prophet of old."

Professor Hamilton's face flushed. "I am grateful for your confidence in me," he said, fidgeting in his chair.

"Merlin," Patrick continued. "As you know, we are the protectorate of the Arthur legacy, and we wish to make his heir's ascendancy to the throne an easy path. Since you are the newest member, it is your privilege to investigate the latest report of a possible heir and either verify or falsify his pedigree."

Professor Hamilton bowed his head. "I am honored."

"Not if he sends you to Alaska," Kaplan said. "That's where I went on my wild goose chase when I joined."

Patrick rapped his knuckles again. "Not Alaska, but you will have to visit the States—West Virginia, to be precise."

"Very well." Professor Hamilton folded his hands and nodded. "What information do you have?"

Patrick withdrew a small map from his jacket and spread it out on the table. "Our intelligence is based on the movements of our enemies, and one of their prominent agents has set up residence in Castlewood, West Virginia." He pointed at a spot on the map. "Our spy believes the agent is seeking information about a young person, perhaps a pre-teen or teenager."

Leaning close, Professor Hamilton touched the edge of the map. "Then securing a position at a local school would be an optimum plan of action. My credentials should suffice."

Patrick touched a ring on the professor's finger. "The officials might wonder why an Oxford professor would want to teach there, so you should prepare a convincing explanation."

Elam edged to the table and tried to read the emblem on the bejeweled gold band. It appeared to be etched with Latin words signifying the professor's achievement in college—*Philosophiæ Doctor*.

"I would simply tell the truth," Professor Hamilton said. "I have always been interested in Arthurian legend, especially the stories surrounding Excalibur, and my research has led me to Castlewood. I doubt that anyone would question me beyond that."

"True enough, I suppose." Patrick folded the map and returned it to his jacket. "If you find the heir, and you are convinced of his authenticity, bring him back to me. There is a test he must pass to prove that he is worthy in mind, body, and spirit. I won't divulge the nature of the test at this time so that you can honestly say you don't know what it is."

Professor Hamilton withdrew a pocket calendar and opened it to the current date. "Is there a suggested timetable?"

"You are to leave immediately and bring him back as soon as you have him in hand. Since our opposition seeks to thwart Arthur's return, their agent will not have the heir's best interests in mind."

Kaplan stood at his place. "Merlin, all jesting aside, I, for one, welcome you with open arms. Our jocularity has no real reflection on our sincere wish to fill our empty chair with the one true king. If you should find him, we are willing to lay down our lives to assure his ascendancy."

"So say we all!" the first man shouted, now standing next to Kaplan.

The other two men stood with them. "Hear, hear!"

Patrick slowly rose to his feet and nodded at Professor Hamilton. "What say you, my old friend?"

Professor Hamilton slid back his chair and stood with the rest. "If Arthur's heir is in West Virginia, then I will not rest until I bring him to this very room."

CHAPTER

BLOOD AND LIGHT

DECEMBER 30, 2002

Gabriel followed Bonnie as she tiptoed down the stairs. When she neared the bottom, she peered over the banister, her hiking backpack shifting with the movement of her hidden wings. With no one in sight, she skulked toward the front door.

All was quiet. Gabriel zoomed down the hall to the laboratory and sneaked a look through the open doorway. Just as Bonnie had feared, Dr. Conner sat at a table next to a collection of glass vials and a set of hypodermic needles. He marked one of the vials with a Sharpie, then scratched down an entry in a logbook. Gabriel glided back to Bonnie and mentally shoved her toward the exit. Maybe she would be able to get away before her father had a chance to find her.

As her hand touched her coat on the wall rack, the telephone rang. Bonnie froze in midstep. Dr. Conner breezed into the front room, holding a mobile phone to his ear. "Yes, Dr. George." He pulled out a desk drawer and withdrew a thin stack of paper. "I have the test results right here. There is no doubt about the find-ings. My wife's blood definitely has the allele we discussed." He nodded and dropped the stack on top of the desk. "That's right. An anthrozil. . . . Yes, I'll bring the samples to you tonight. . . . That late? . . . Sure. I guess I can do that." He glanced at Bonnie, and the color in his cheeks suddenly drained away. "Dr. George, I have to go. I'll see you at my office."

Bonnie lifted her cell phone. "Daddy, Mama called. I'm sup-posed to meet her downtown. She's taking me shopping for my birthday."

"Oh. Your birthday. Right." Dr. Conner ran his fingers through his short nap of red hair, keeping his eyes from direct contact with Bonnie's. "That can wait. I just need a couple of minutes."

Bonnie shuddered. "But you said you'd never—"

"I know what I said." He grabbed her wrist, tightly at first, but his grip slowly eased. "This really is the last time. I promise."

Bonnie pulled in her bottom lip and stared at her father. A tear welled in her eye. Finally, she whispered a shaky, "Okay," and fol-lowed him toward the laboratory.

Gabriel stalked behind them, his energy field flashing. Bonnie was no guinea pig! If only there was a way to stop this madness! He could plug himself in somewhere and short circuit the lights, but that wouldn't last longer than the time it took to flip the cir-cuit breaker, and the shock would paralyze him for hours. What else could he possibly do?

When they reached the lab, Dr. Conner picked up a hypoder-mic needle. "You know the drill, Bonnie. It's just a prick."

As Bonnie pushed her sleeve up, her hand quivered. She picked up a rubber ball from a letter basket, laid her arm on the table, and squeezed so tightly, her forearm muscles bulged.

Dr. Conner tied a rubber band around her upper arm and swabbed the tender flesh in the crook. As the needle drew near, she closed her eyes and turned her head, her whole body trembling.

562

Gabriel caressed her skin at the needle's entry point. It poked a tiny hole in the midst of a dozen or more minute white scars. Dr. Conner attached a collection tube to the needle, and as blood began to flow, he unfastened the band and tossed it to the lab table. "Just a few more seconds, and I'll be finished."

Bonnie kept her head turned, panting as she whispered something to herself. Gabriel moved closer to listen to her feeble, halting voice.

"Yea, though I walk . . . through the valley of the shadow of death . . . I will fear no evil . . . for thou art with me . . . thy rod and thy staff they comfort me."

Dr. Conner pulled out the needle and pressed a ball of cotton on the wound. "I have what I need. You can go now." He turned away and began entering numbers on a log sheet.

Tucking her head low, Bonnie hurried out of the lab. After grabbing a coat off a rack, she ran to the front door. Gabriel zipped alongside her, but, of course, he could offer no comfort, only a sympathetic embrace with his wing, another hug she couldn't feel.

Bonnie threw the door open, ran outside, and banged it closed. As she stuffed her arms into her sleeves, trying to fit her coat over her backpack, she slipped and almost stumbled down the porch steps. Stopping for a moment on the lawn, she heaved in a couple of deep breaths and mumbled to herself. "Okay, Bonnie, get a grip. You don't want Mama to know you've been crying. She'll just get upset again."

She took a final deep breath, and a thin smile grew on her lips. Combing her fingers through her hair, she hustled to the open garage and snatched a helmet from a shelf next to her bicycle. After strapping it in place, she straddled her bike and guided it onto the driveway. Overhead, tiny flakes of snow floated silently down from the gray sky.

She pushed a pedal and rolled out onto the street. Gabriel rushed ahead of her and hopped onto the front, attaching his

energy field to the metal handlebars. Bonnie pumped the pedals hard until the bike reached a brisk cruising speed, then relaxed and pedaled more easily.

Amidst a flurry of snow, girl and guardian raced through the neighborhood and onto the main thoroughfare's bike path. Having left her gloves at home, Bonnie raised a hand to her mouth from time to time and blew on her fingers. As a thin dusting of snow coated the street, she slowed her pace and guided the bike toward the clearer pavement. Traffic dwindled, and with it the danger of colliding with a car, but she maintained a tight grip on the handlebars to keep from losing traction and taking a spill.

After several minutes, they reached a two-story white building at the edge of downtown Missoula. As the snow thickened, Bonnie parked her bike next to a hedge in front of the building and jumped over the two steps that led to the entrance. Blowing on her cupped hands, she pushed open the front door with her elbow and slipped off her coat. As she unhitched her helmet, she scanned the spacious lobby, then smiled. Her mother sat on a cushioned bench just outside an office.

Tucking the helmet under her arm, she ran to her mother's side and kissed her cheek. "Mama," she whispered, "what's going on? Why here instead of the mall?"

Irene combed back Bonnie's mussed hair. "I heard from my brother. He believes that a slayer has moved into our area. That means he's probably on my trail."

"How could a slayer find you?"

"My brother gave me no details." Irene unfolded a telegram and began reading. "A dark knight is coming quickly." She lowered the paper and looked at Bonnie. "That's a coded message all dragons are supposed to know." Clearing her throat, she continued. "Go to the surrogate nest. Your daughter's passage has been arranged." She refolded the telegram and put it into her purse.

"What does it all mean?" Bonnie asked.

"My brother is concerned that something might happen to me, so he arranged for a safe hiding place for you, just in case. He is well-connected with adoption and foster care services in England and in the U.S., so he can make sure you are buried in the system where no one can find you."

Bonnie gripped her mother's forearm. "But nothing's going to happen to you, right?"

"I don't think so." Irene patted Bonnie's hand. "But we have to be ready, just in case."

"So why did you call me here?"

"I wanted to show you where to go." Irene nodded at the office door next to the bench. "If something awful happens, get here as quickly as you can. Mrs. Lewis works in this office. She knows what to do. I wanted to introduce you, but she's in a meeting right now."

"I . . ." Bonnie turned her head away. "I don't want to think about it."

Irene stood and lifted her purse strap over her shoulder. "You don't have to dwell on it. Just remember this place and this office. It might never happen, but we have to face the possibilities."

Bonnie kept her head turned. Her lips trembled as she whispered, "Okay, Mama. I'll remember."

Irene laid her hand on Bonnie's cheek and gently turned her head back toward her. "Bonnie, I love you very much. That's why I'm telling you these things."

Bonnie wrapped her arms around her mother's waist and laid her cheek on her shoulder. "I know. I'm just scared."

Irene kissed the top of Bonnie's head. "There's one more thing. If the worst does happen, you need to find another dragon. My brother thinks he lives in Castlewood, West Virginia. His human name was Jared at one time, but I don't know what it is now. I did hear, though, that he has a son about your age, so that might help you find him."

"If you're gone," Bonnie said, still leaning on her mother's shoulder, "how will I get there?"

She nodded at the office again. "Since you can't get past airport security, they will arrange to transport you to Castlewood by train. It might take a while, and you might have to endure quite a few transfers, but you'll get there eventually."

Bonnie pulled away and looked her mother in the eye. "You want to hide me from Daddy, don't you?"

Irene turned away, her voice barely audible. "He can't protect you from a slayer."

"*Won't*, you mean. He's in love with his research, not you or me. He thinks we're lab rats." Bonnie took her mother's hand and extended her arm. "He's stuck you even more than he's stuck me."

"You know I can't stop him." Irene pulled her hand away. "Not without revealing our secret."

"I know." Bonnie stuffed a hand into her pocket and lowered her head. "You're right."

"If something happens to me, you'll be safer in foster care than you would be with your father. They'll change your name, so he won't be able to find you."

"I'd better get going," Bonnie said, taking her helmet from under her arm. "It's starting to snow pretty hard."

Irene tapped the helmet with her fingertip. "If we can't fit your bike in the car, we'll just leave it here until tomorrow. I'm sure they'll let us."

Bonnie wiped the water droplets from the shiny surface. "So, are we really going to the mall like you said?"

"Of course." Irene hooked her arm around Bonnie's elbow and led her toward the door. "Thirteen is a special birthday. Have you decided what you want?"

"That pen set I told you about, and maybe a new journal. I'll probably fill my old one up in the next couple of weeks."

Irene pushed the door open. "Don't you need anything else? Books? Music?"

Bonnie dipped her head. "Do you think it's weird to just want pens and journals?"

"I didn't mean that at all," Irene said, waving her hand. "You have a writing talent that amazes me! You write with a fiery passion that I could never hope to equal. In two thousand years I have never seen anyone your age who comes even close."

Bonnie let a thin smile break through. "Thank you."

"And do you know where your talent comes from?"

"From being a dragon?" Bonnie guessed.

"You might have inherited it from a dragon. I'm not sure. But I do know this; your talent comes from God. However you choose to use your writing, make sure every word honors your maker. If you do that, I'll be delighted to give you all the pens and journals you'll ever want. I was just wondering what else you need."

As they descended the front steps and pierced the curtain of falling snow, Bonnie looked up at the dark sky, blinking at the thousands of flakes. "As long as I can write prayers in my journal, I have all I really need."

567

Gabriel floated near the ceiling in Bonnie's room, admiring the new wallpaper—wide vertical purple and pink stripes that matched the purple blanket and pink sheets on Bonnie's poster bed. Ever since they moved to this new house, her father had promised to decorate her bedroom, mostly to assuage her pain at leaving Carly and all her friends at her old school across town. Finally, after four years of her father's promises and excuses, a pair of handymen came in and slapped the paper up with little care for craftsmanship.

Using his glowing finger to trace a narrow gap between two sheets of wallpaper, Gabriel shook his head. At least the worst spots were up near the ceiling where no one else would notice.

He drifted slowly down toward the bed. With the thick blanket pulled up to her waist, Bonnie reclined on her side, propping her head on a stack of pillows and gazing at a spiral-bound notebook that lay open on her sheet. One wing rested on her arm and leg, while the other extended beyond the edge of the bed and touched the floor, her usual sleeping position since the age of ten when her wings truly blossomed.

She had just finished retacking her posters to the wall—a unicorn with a long, flowing mane, and, adjacent to that one, a girl kneeling at her bedside in prayer while a winged angel watched over her. She chose that one years ago, a week after her first day at school.

Tired from her strenuous day, and with snow spoiling her plans for a walk, she had decided to go to bed early, opting for her short-sleeved nightgown in spite of the cold. Of course, Gabriel had excused himself to the hallway while Bonnie dressed for bed, and when he returned, he wanted to scold her for her selection, but, as usual, he had to complain in silence. Still, Irene had turned the heat up, and the blankets would likely keep Bonnie warm if a chill draft seeped in around the window. She would be fine.

Gabriel chuckled to himself. After only a few years, he had become a mother hen, yet without an audible cluck to nag his little chick. Sinking closer to the bed, he peered at Bonnie's journal. She often left it out on her night table, and Irene came by now and then to read her latest entry even while Bonnie was in the room, so it seemed that she didn't consider her daily missives to be private, at least to friendly eyes.

As her silver Papermate flowed across the page, leaving behind a beautiful blue script, Bonnie's thoughts came to life. Gabriel read them slowly, pondering each phrase, hoping to feel the emotions with the same passion the young author poured into her words.

Dear God,

I descended into the shadowlands today. A specter of fear wrapped his cold, cruel fingers around my heart and led me into his chamber of treachery, a sanitary cube of torment that once again enclosed my mind in darkness. Can any instrument of torture deliver cruelty as savage as love betrayed? Does a dungeon's rack stretch a body as sadistically as betrayal stretches trust? Can faith endure a traitor's sinister hand as it turns the wheel, each notch testing conviction until the sword of despair separates peace from its rightful habitat?

He bared my skin. He pierced my flesh. He robbed more than my life's blood; with his brazen face and callous dismissal, he robbed my innocence. He shattered my image of a father's love.

Once upon a time, a tall, strong knight took my little hand and led me to the edge of a cliff. Comforted by his powerful grip, I felt no fear, for this valiant knight would never let me fall. Below lay the jagged rocks, the raging river, and a thousand feet of cold, empty air. As I leaned over the precipice, the joy of beholding danger with unflinching eyes flooded my soul. I have an anchor. I have a sure hold in the land of promise. My father would never let me go.

Yet, he did let me go. Nay, he pushed me over the side. And now I fall, staring up at him as he coldly walks away. The wind chills my heart, and the certainty of eternal torment rushes at me with no savior in sight.

God of wonders, catch me now in your loving hands. Fly down on your stallion and rescue me from this plunge into despair. Let us ride together, buoyed by wings of faith and energized by the love that delivered your only begotten son, for he is the king who catches his falling sparrows. Let us waltz together in this dance of death, for you have called me to suffer with you in willing sacrifice and to burn the image of your crucifixion in my heart. Let us live together in the light of your resurrection, for I cannot survive this walk of faith without the comfort of knowing that you will never let go of my hand.

569

You are Jehovah-Jireh, my provider in times of trouble. You are Jehovah-Shalom, my peace in the midst of turmoil. And above all, you are Jehovah-Shammah, the God who is always there, a true father who rises to my aid when the specter has taken off his fatherly mask and exposed his treacherous heart.

Ask me for my blood, and I will give it freely. Yea, ask me for my life, for you have already crucified me on Calvary's hill and raised me from the dead, purging the life of sin I left behind. Ask me for my soul, for you have already paid for it with your own precious blood, the holy blood of Jehovah-Yasha, my savior.

And now I see it. I can give you nothing that you have not already given to me. I am purchased, a slave of love. I am your vessel to be used in whatever way you wish. If you make me an urn for ashes, a common earthen jar to bear incinerated bones, leaving me to collect dust in a forgotten tomb, even then, I will be content. For just as you would not leave your son forever in the ground, I know you will raise me up from the land of the dead. You have not ignited this fire in my heart to be wasted in Sheol's pit. Though dead, buried, and forgotten, I will rise again.

No matter what happens, I will never forsake you, for you will never forsake me. You are with me, no matter where I go.

Love,

Bonnie Conner

Bonnie nestled her head into her pillow and stared at the window. Snow cascaded across the screen, some of the flakes dusting the glass with powdery splashes. A lamp on a table cast a dim glare on the surface, but it suddenly vanished in a shadow.

"Bonnie?"

It was her father's voice. Bonnie slid her journal under her blanket. "Yes?" she replied without turning.

His outline shifted back and forth in the window. "I have to meet someone at my office. Your mother's taking a bath, so I thought you'd like to know in case the phone rings."

Bonnie cleared her throat. "Can you make it to the campus in this weather?"

"The radio said the main roads are clear. Once I get out of the neighborhood, I should be fine."

"Okay." Bonnie threaded her pen between her fingers. "Um . . . Be careful."

His shadow seemed to come a step closer, but it halted. "I'm . . . I'm sorry about today. That really was the very last time. I promise."

Bonnie closed her eyes and bit her lower lip.

"Do you . . ." He paused, and his voice lowered to a whisper. "Do you forgive me?"

Bonnie's eyelids clenched tightly, and a pair of tears squeezed through. For a few seconds, it seemed that she wouldn't answer, but she finally nodded, and her voice squeaked. "I forgive you."

The shadow disappeared, and the lamp's light returned. Bonnie opened her eyes and dabbed her tears with the edge of her pillowcase. Pulling out her journal again, she set her pen next to the page as if ready to write, but, after a wide yawn, she closed her eyes. Seconds later, her breathing settled into deep, rhythmic pulses.

571

Gabriel eased over to the window. Dr. Conner's SUV pulled out of the driveway, sliding more than rolling, but once the tires grabbed the snowy road, he seemed to have no more trouble as he crawled toward the neighborhood's exit.

As soon as the SUV's taillights disappeared in the flurry of white, a Cadillac parked at the side of the road started its engine. Leaving its headlights off, it rolled forward and stopped in front of Bonnie's house. Two men in trench coats jumped out and jogged toward the front door, one of them favoring a leg. Even through the curtain of falling flakes, Gabriel recognized the sinister face. Devin!

Sapphira dropped to her knees and wept. Bonnie's words stabbed deep into her soul. This dragon girl, another freak of nature, mistreated and betrayed by her father, had torn Sapphira's heart in two.

Lifting her head, she stared at her portal screen. Now the slayer lurked right outside Bonnie's door! There had to be a way to help her! There just had to be!

She jumped up and ran to the other side of the screen. Finding her cross, she lifted it off the rocky floor and cradled it in her hands. "You haven't ignited in a while, but now I think it's time to try again." She licked her lips and shouted. "Give me light!" Flames leaped from the wood. Each weathered sliver seemed to pop and sizzle as if laughing with joy.

She strode from the museum room and rushed to the elevator shaft. Snuffing the flames for the time being, she pushed the cross under her belt, grasped the rope, and shinnied down.

After swinging out to the mining level, she reignited her cross and followed the forbidding path that she had seen Morgan trod on so many occasions, leading condemned little girls to a fiery fate. This time, it was finally Sapphira's turn to face the chasm, but it wasn't Morgan who led her to the executioner, it was a flaming cross.

Sapphira turned through the final passageway leading to the ledge overlooking the chasm. Marching right up to the precipice, she gazed down at the boiling magma river. Hot air blasted upward, instantly drying her eyes and stinging them mercilessly. Although the liquid torture was far hotter than when she trembled at its sight so long ago, not a shred of fear tingled her skin.

She planted her feet firmly. Raising her cross high, she shouted into the upper reaches of the enormous dark chamber. "I was born Mara, a slave girl of the earth!" Her call echoed as if shouted back at her a hundred times. "And I once knew you as Elohim!"

The echo repeated, *"Elohim! Elohim!"*

"But now I call you Jehovah-Yasha!"

"Jehovah-Yasha! Jehovah-Yasha!"

"I finally know what you want me to do!"

"To do! To do!"

"You want me to die!"

"To die! To die!"

"And to be raised from the dead as Sapphira Adi!"

"Sapphira Adi! Sapphira Adi!"

She waved her cross in a circle. A spinning cylinder of fire dropped from above and met the flames rising from the cross.

Sapphira stepped to the very edge of the overhanging rock. "Now take me where you want me to go, whether to heaven or to hell, to England or to Montana, or keep me here in this tomb forever. I will be content to serve you no matter what you decide . . . Jehovah-Yasha."

Sapphira pulled the burning cross down and pressed it against her chest. The cross melded into her skin, her entire body burst into flames, and she leaped into the chasm. As she fell, she looked up, bracing herself for the impact. The cylinder spun down with her and wrapped her up in a fiery coil. Within seconds, everything vanished.

573

Gabriel zoomed toward the bedroom exit and flew right through Irene as she peeked in. He paused at the top of the stairs, drumming his radiant fingers on the banister.

Dressed in a long bathrobe, Irene whispered, "Are you asleep, dear?" When no answer came, she reached in and turned off the lamp, then padded quietly down the steps. Gabriel rushed ahead and zipped straight to the window at the side of the front door. Palin, standing next to Devin, raised a crowbar and slammed it against the glass, smashing a hole the size of a bowling ball. Reaching in with his gloved hand, he turned the deadbolt, and the two burst inside.

A ceiling light flashed on. Irene ran into the front hall and laid a hand on her chest. "Matt!" she called, angling her head toward the stairs, "get the shotgun! Hurry!"

Devin shed his outer cloak, revealing his chain mail and the red dragon on his surcoat. The glittering candlestone dangled in front. "The good doctor just left for an important meeting on campus." He withdrew a long, silvery sword from a scabbard. "You do remember me, don't you? You slashed my leg and fled like a coward, and about fifteen hundred years ago, you knelt before the king with a bogus plea."

Resisting the candlestone's pull, Gabriel glided toward an electrical outlet. He might have only one chance to zap Devin, so he had to avoid the candlestone and time his attack perfectly.

"Fifteen hundred years!" Irene tightened the sash on her robe. "Do I look that old to you?"

Devin took a step closer, wincing as he set his foot down. "Let us not play games, Mrs. Conner. Your dear husband told me about your dragon blood, so I am here to collect a healthy sample of it. Do you have a gallon or two to spare?"

Stripping off his own cloak, Palin dashed around Irene and stood behind her. As he drew his sword, his dark mail shimmered in the light.

Devin spread out his hands. "You may now reenact your pleading posture, and perhaps I will let you die quickly."

"Do your worst," Irene said, crossing her arms over her chest. "I'll never kneel to you."

Devin drew back his sword. Gabriel stretched out to grab him, simultaneously plugging himself into the outlet. As the current buzzed through his energy field, he latched onto Devin's ankle. Sparks flew up the slayer's leg and sizzled across his mail. Devin's limbs stiffened, and his fingers locked around the sword's hilt. Light bulbs popped in the ceiling fixture, and the room fell dim. With the current no longer streaking through him, Gabriel collapsed and released his grip.

Palin stood transfixed, as if hypnotized by the glow of streetlights illuminating the room. Irene jerked away his sword and charged at the slayer.

Devin toppled forward, and with a stiff jab, thrust his blade into Irene's stomach, slashing downward as he fell. He thudded prostrate to the hardwood floor, covering the candlestone.

Irene dropped Palin's sword and grasped her belly. Blood oozed between her fingers. Her legs buckled, and she dropped to her knees, her eyes wide and her mouth agape.

Gabriel could barely crawl. His energy field sizzled as he willed his way toward Irene.

She fell to her side, her eyes still open. Palin jumped over her, retrieved his sword, and knelt beside his fallen leader. He shook Devin's body. "My liege! Can you hear me?"

Devin stayed flat on the floor. "I hear you. . . . But I can't see anything . . . except a lump on the floor. Did I kill the demon witch?"

Palin glanced at Irene. "A mortal stab, my liege. If she's not already dead, she will be soon."

Gasping for breath, Devin lifted his head. "An electrical shock. That mongrel . . . Gabriel . . . must have done this."

"I see him," Palin said. "Just a few glitters on the floor near your feet, and he seems paralyzed, but he's definitely here."

"No use . . . worrying about him." Devin nodded toward the stairs. "Check the house. . . . See if the witch whelped any mongrels. Conner said he had no kids, . . . but make sure."

"And if she has?"

"Kill them. But save . . . some of their blood."

Palin turned and, stepping over Irene's deathly still body, headed for the stairs. Gabriel followed, slithering along the thin planks like a dribbling stream of sparks.

Pointing his sword upward, Palin climbed the stairs slowly. Devin pushed up to his hands and knees. The candlestone again dangled from its chain, swaying back and forth as the slayer struggled to right himself.

Gabriel strained against the relentless pull. He had beaten the evil gem before, but would he be strong enough to get away this time? Stretching and clawing, he attached his energy to the heads of the nails holding down the wooden strips. Like scaling a sheer cliff, he grabbed one nail after the other and slowly edged toward the stairs.

Finally, the drag from the candlestone eased. He crawled faster and reached the carpeted stairway just as Palin stepped up to the top landing. Gabriel plodded upward, trying to float, but his energy field seemed mired in sticky mud. At least his sparks had faded. He would likely be invisible to the slayers now.

Palin disappeared into the master bedroom. Gabriel lurched forward. The slayer wouldn't find anyone there, but Bonnie's bedroom was next in line.

As Gabriel reached the final step, Palin poked his head out of the master bedroom and gazed down the hallway in the opposite direction. Gabriel slid into Bonnie's bedroom and settled next to the outlet that fed the lamp, close enough to the door to grab Palin before he could reach Bonnie.

Palin stepped into the room. With every light off, he seemed more phantom than human. Gabriel plugged his fingers in again, but this time no painful buzz rocketed through his body. He yanked his hand back. That last jolt must have knocked out the electricity!

The slayer reached over to the lamp and turned its switch. Nothing happened. He leaned back into the hall. "Sir Devin! Are you up?"

"Yes," came the reply. "Did you find anyone?"

Gabriel cringed. Would their conversation awaken Bonnie? Would she groan or cry out?

"Not yet," Palin said. "The electricity's off. Can you see well enough to find the circuit breakers?"

"Maybe. Hold on."

Gabriel forced his energy field to stand up, but he fell backwards, right through the lamp and into the wall, flattening himself against Bonnie's poster of a little girl praying. He draped his fingers across the girl's twin ponytails. Looking toward Bonnie in the darkness, he imagined her head lying on the pillow, her own ponytails draped across her neck.

Gazing at the angel who watched over the girl, Gabriel lifted his hand and cried out in the buzzing, electrified tongue that only gods and gifted children could hear. "I am no guardian angel, and I never have been. Please don't let this monster kill my precious lamb. Don't let my failure cause her death."

Suddenly, Gabriel's energy field began to glow. Although the lamp's bulb stayed dark, the entire poster lit up as if painted by a phosphorescent brush. Palin glanced back. "Thank you, my liege. I can see now."

"No!" Gabriel screamed. "Now he'll kill her for sure!"

Palin spied Bonnie as she slept peacefully in her bed, her wings easily visible in the soft light of the poster's luminescence. Leaning toward her, Palin flexed his muscles and drew back his sword.

CHAPTER

THROUGH THE STORM

Pressing his cheek against the poster, Gabriel cried out, "Dear God, I beg you. Protect her! I am helpless!"

Palin swung his sword, but just before the blade reached the bed, he flexed his arms and drew it back. Taking a step closer, he gazed at Bonnie for several seconds. Gabriel lumbered to the bedside and stood next to the evil slayer, so weak he could barely keep his energy from crumbling to the floor. What could he do but stare alongside the slayer?

The poster's glow highlighted Bonnie's radiant face—peaceful, serene, angelic. The tender skin on her bare arms displayed an innocent vulnerability, as though she were a gentle lamb who knew nothing of the wolf poised at her throat. With her eyes still shut and her mouth stretching into a quiet yawn, Bonnie pulled her knees closer to her chest and nuzzled her pillow.

Palin peered at the door for a moment, then at Bonnie. Lowering his sword, he tiptoed back to the hall and leaned out. Finally, he left the room, and the sound of creaking steps faded in the distance.

As Gabriel backed away from the bed, the poster's glow disappeared. With a surge of strength, he floated down the stairwell and found Devin and Palin standing close to the front door, both putting on their cloaks.

"Can you see well enough to drive?" Palin asked.

"My vision's coming back slowly, but I couldn't even find the breaker box."

"You couldn't?" Palin glanced back at the stairs, but only for a second.

"No mongrels in the house?" Devin asked.

Palin shook his head. "And no sign of Gabriel. I guess he disappeared again."

"In future slayings, we'll be sure to stay clear of electrical outlets, but I'd still like to kill that mongrel. I'll ask Morgan if she has any ideas."

"At least we finally got Hartanna," Palin said, pointing his sword at Irene.

Devin fumbled for the doorknob and patted a pocket in his cloak. "And I have her blood. Just the medicine for a wound inflicted by the witch's claws."

He opened the door, and as they passed into the snowy breeze, Palin laughed. "Hair of the dog that bit you, huh?" The door slammed heavily behind them.

Gabriel knelt at Irene's side. A pool of blood surrounded her body and streamed along the lines between the hardwood strips. He laid his head on her side and wept.

A sleepy voice sounded from the top of the stairs. "Daddy? Is that you?"

Gabriel spun around. "Oh, dear God!" he moaned. "Don't let her see this carnage!"

As Bonnie padded down the stairs, she draped a bathrobe over her wings and shoulders. When she reached the bottom, she stopped and squinted. The streetlights cast a dim glow over Irene's curled body.

"Mama?" Bonnie called. "Are you okay?"

Gabriel raised his hands to stop Bonnie but to no avail. She scooted across the floor and ran around to Irene's head.

"Mama!" Bonnie screamed, dropping to her knees. "What happened?"

Irene's pallid face gave no reply.

Bonnie lifted her mother's hand from the floor. Blood dripped from the ends of her fingers. She grabbed the limp arm and screamed again. "Mama! Can you hear me?"

Irene's hand suddenly latched around Bonnie's wrist. Her mouth opened, but no audible words came forth.

"What, Mama?" Bonnie leaned close. "Say it again!"

"Your father betrayed us," Irene whispered. "Go to the agency. . . . Just like our plan. . . . Don't let . . . let them find you."

Bonnie clutched her mother's hand, her arms and voice quaking. "I can't leave you like this! You'll die!"

"You must find . . . the other dragon. . . . Don't come back here . . . unless I call you."

581

A loud clump sounded from the garage at the side of the house, then heavy footsteps. Irene's eyes widened, and a sudden surge of energy strengthened her voice. "Now run, dear child! You know where to go. Don't look back! Just run!" With a final, gurgling gasp, Irene stopped breathing, and her eyes slowly closed.

Bonnie shot to her feet. Wiping blood on her nightgown, she swiveled her head from side to side. She clenched both fists and tiptoed toward the back of the house. Still barefoot, she opened the door quietly and disappeared outside.

As the door swung closed, Gabriel waited at Irene's side. Bonnie wouldn't go far in such a storm. If the slayer was coming back, it would be better to stay and find a way to keep him from following her.

Dr. Conner's voice pierced the dreary scene. "Irene? Are you sitting in the dark again?" The footsteps drew closer. "I should've known Dr. George wouldn't show up. The weather was so bad—"

He flipped the light switch, but no lights came on. "I forgot. The electricity's out. I had to open the garage door myself."

Squinting into the dim room, he called, "Irene?" He dashed to her side and fell to his knees, sliding in her blood. "Irene!" he cried out. "Talk to me!" He tore off his muffler and pressed it against her wound, then laid his ear against her chest. "C'mon! Give me something!" After a few seconds, he sighed. "Okay, you're still with us." Keeping a hand on Irene's stomach, he shouted toward the stairs, "Bonnie! Come down here!"

Gabriel rushed to the rear of the house and slipped through the crack between the door and the jamb. When he emerged on the back porch, swirling snow encircled his energy field like a white cyclone. Bare footprints marred the walkway's powdery blanket, blazing a path to the access alley beyond an open gate. He zoomed out to the street, but tire tracks swallowed the trail. In the midst of blizzard-like winds, he scanned the snowscape, desperately hoping to spot a hunched-over girl cowering in a bush.

As a gust of wind whistled a mournful tune, he realized the awful truth. Bonnie was nowhere in the area. Setting his sights on her most likely path, he glided toward the main road, scanning the mounting blanket of snow. Of course, she would try to get to the foster care agency. What choice did she have?

Finally, in the distance, he spotted a trail of footprints and floated toward them. The streetlights suddenly blacked out, and the neighborhood fell into darkness. Gabriel roared. Now how would he follow her trail?

Flashing his energy field with every ampere of current he could muster, he crawled close to the ground and followed the outlines of narrow, bare feet as though he were a sniffing hound. The going was slow, but somehow he would find the lost and frightened little lamb.

Bonnie pushed uphill against the hammering gusts, ducking her head to keep the wind-driven snow from stinging her eyes. Still trudging barefoot, she could no longer feel her toes. Her robe had blown away with the first chilling blast, exposing her wings to anyone who might peek out of one of the warm, cozy homes lining the street. Bitter cold sent a pulsing throb into her aching calves, but she kept wading through the drifts—one bare foot in front of the other, again and again. The storm was too fierce for flying, and she had to keep moving, had to fight the urge to surrender to hopelessness and grief. Mama was dead, and there was nothing she could do about it except to obey her last wish, to survive and somehow find a former dragon and his son.

A gust of snowy wind slapped her face and sent her tumbling into a drift. Biting cold stung her body like a swarm of bees plunging icicle stingers into her exposed flesh. Exhausted, she lay on her stomach, half buried and peeking out into the darkness of the city as streetlamp after streetlamp winked out under the burden of failing power lines.

Yet a solitary light glittered at the top of the hill, growing brighter by the second. It looked like a beacon sending out a warning to passing shipmasters or a lantern carried by a lost traveler seeking shelter in the storm. As it drew closer and closer, the light transformed into the shape of a girl. From the bottom of her bare feet to the top of her head, she glowed, as if sunshine leaked out through every pore. Gentle ivory flames rippled along her hands and forearms.

She knelt next to Bonnie and laid a warm hand on her cheek. The girl's hair, already white from the falling snow, glittered in the firelight. "Bonnie," she said softly, "can you get up?"

Bonnie's teeth chattered so hard, she couldn't answer. She pushed her stiff arms against the snow, and with the help of the girl, rose to her feet, barely able to feel anything in the blistering cold.

The girl waved her hand in a wide circle over her head. A towering flame burst from her palm, and a wall of fire cascaded around them, surrounding them in a cocoon of warmth.

583

"There's no portal here," the girl explained, "so I'd have to make an even bigger firestorm to send us to another dimension."

Bonnie rubbed her eyes. "Huh? What are you talking about?"

"Oh." The girl laughed. "How stupid of me. Of course you don't know who I am."

"You look kind of familiar." As her vision cleared, Bonnie focused on the girl. Her hair wasn't covered with snow; it was actually white, and her eyes sparkled with an unearthly blue radiance. "Are you an angel? Did you come to take me to heaven?"

As the girl laughed again, the fiery cocoon trembled. "My name is Sapphira, and I have come to escort you to safety." She took Bonnie's hand, and, as they walked, the cocoon of fire moved with them. "It's a good thing I found you. You would have frozen to death before too much longer."

"Thank you," Bonnie said, her teeth chattering. "The storm's so bad . . . I couldn't even see . . . the street signs. . . . I'm glad . . . you found me."

"Well, once I saw Gabriel, I knew you would be around somewhere."

Bonnie glanced around at the wall of flames. "Gabriel's here?"

"Oh, yes," Sapphira said, her arm still waving above her. "He never leaves you."

Bonnie smiled for a moment but let it melt away. "Oh. . . . I see."

"You see what?"

Bonnie's chattering teeth slowed, and she drooped her head. "He couldn't be with my mother . . . to keep her from dying."

"She died?" Sapphira raised her hand to her mouth. "Oh, I'm so sorry!"

As tears filled her eyes, Bonnie sniffed and cried out, "I'm so confused, I don't know what to do! I thought maybe you were an angel, and you were going to take me to my mother!"

Sapphira draped her arm around Bonnie's shoulders. "I'm not an angel, Bonnie, but Jehovah-Shammah sent me to guide you through the storm."

"Jehovah-Shammah?" Bonnie sniffed again and wiped a tear away from her cheek. "That's what I sometimes call God, too!"

"Jehovah really is always with us, and he'll help us through this storm. Just keep your eyes straight ahead and we'll eventually get to the place he wants us to go."

"Okay." Bonnie glanced at Sapphira's bare feet and matched her pace. "I'm glad you know where we're going."

"Oh, I have no idea how to get to your agency, but Gabriel does. I can see through the gaps in the flames, and I'm following him."

Bonnie laid a hand on top of her head. "Maybe this is all a bad dream. Maybe I'll wake up, and Mama will be there."

"If that's what Jehovah wants you to think, then so be it. He will teach you what you need to know at the proper time." Sapphira lowered her arm, and the wall of fire began to fade. "Gabriel has stopped. We must be at the agency."

"Already? That was fast."

As the wall of flames vanished, the steps leading to the building slowly came into view. Sapphira nodded at the office window. "I see a candle through the window. It looks like someone's still working."

"That's the office I'm supposed to go to," Bonnie said. "It must be a miracle."

"I think you'll be seeing a lot more miracles, Bonnie, but it might be best to keep Gabriel and me a secret."

Bonnie shook her head and sighed. "Nobody would believe me if I told them."

"Probably not. At least not yet." Sapphira raised her hand again. "I will be watching you. Don't ever forget what you wrote in your journal. Jehovah-Shammah will rise to your aid." The wall of fire reappeared, brighter and more vigorous than ever, and swallowed Sapphira in its spinning vortex. In a splash of sparks, she disappeared.

Bonnie stared at the spot where Sapphira once stood. The vision of her blue eyes and white hair already seemed to be a fleeting

585

memory, an impossible dream. She trudged up the stairs and pounded her fist on the door. Seconds later, a woman flung it open, her eyes wide. "Bonnie? Bonnie Conner?"

The brisk wind brought a new chill to Bonnie's bare arms, and her teeth chattered again. "Yes."

The woman guided Bonnie through the doorway. "I'm Mrs. Lewis. Hurry inside where it's warm! We don't want anyone to see your wings."

Bonnie shuffled across the anteroom's warm carpet, rubbing her arms. Mrs. Lewis stopped and placed a hand on each of Bonnie's shoulders. "Your being here can only mean bad news. Is your mother . . . dead?"

Bonnie nodded. New tears welled in her eyes.

"I'm so sorry!" Mrs. Lewis embraced her for a moment, but Bonnie was too cold to hug her in return. "Come into my office," she continued. "We have a lot of work to do. Is it safe to go to your house?"

"I don't think so." Bonnie entered the candlelit office and sat in a chair. "When Mama died, I heard a noise and ran out."

Mrs. Lewis picked up her telephone and punched in a number. "I'll arrange to get the essentials from your room. Do you need anything besides your backpack and some clothes?"

"I'd like my journal." As the tears trickled down her cheeks, Bonnie's voice cracked. "It's . . . it's all I really need."

DRAGONS IN
OUR MIDST

Sapphira basked in the warmth of the portal's fire as it spun dancing arcs of orange across her view of Bonnie. The foster care agency faded away, and, seconds later, the familiar surroundings of her home reappeared—the enormous museum, hers and Acacia's bedding, and stacks of books waiting to be read for the hundredth time.

She stepped out of the swirling column of brilliant white light, the dimensional portal that once led to the snake-infested swamp around Morgan's island, and turned toward it. As dozens of white eddies twirled independently within the larger vortex, she lifted one in her palm and gently guided it out of the column, staring at it in wonder. What were these amazing portals made out of, and what did the loss of color mean? Could she now travel wherever she pleased and return to this spot?

She stepped back from the column and whispered to it. "Expand, please." The portal slowly widened into her viewing screen, and the sound of a train clacking across steel rails filled the chamber. Light flooded her view, and vague shadows congealed into shapes—cushioned seats lining the inside of a railcar, a uniformed steward checking paperwork on a clipboard, and a girl with blonde-streaked hair stuffing a bag into an overhead bin.

Bonnie slid into a window seat, leaning forward to make room for her backpack. She pulled the hem of her thick sweatshirt down over the waistband of her jeans and settled her head against the window. As she bounced in time with the train's rhythmic clatter, she gazed at the scenery that graced the beautiful state of Montana.

During a stop at a small depot just outside of Missoula, Bonnie watched each person who climbed aboard her car. Whenever a female entered, she brushed off the seat next to her, yet, no one took her up on her silent invitation. No one even looked her way.

Finally, a girl Bonnie's age walked in with her head bent low. Her gaze brushed quickly past Bonnie, and she sat in the window seat across the aisle. After fumbling with the zipper of a duffle bag, the girl opened it just far enough to reveal a colorful blanket, a Tigger blanket. She pulled out a book and zipped her bag back up.

Bonnie moved into the aisle seat and leaned across. "Carly?" she whispered.

The girl jerked her head around. Her eyes grew larger, and a beaming smile spread across her face. "Bonnie?"

Bonnie jumped into the seat next to Carly's and hugged her friend close. Neither one laughed or squealed. They just held each other quietly for nearly a minute.

Carly sniffed and gazed at Bonnie through teary eyes. "Bonnie, I've thought about you every day for four years. I've never had another friend like you, and when I found out I had to move to Pittsburgh, I thought I'd never see you again."

"I thought about you a lot, too." Bonnie pulled a pack of tissues from her pocket and gave it to Carly. "Why do you have to go to Pittsburgh?"

Carly pulled the last tissue out of the pack and dabbed her eyes. "Well, my parents have been fighting for years, so they decided to—"

"No." Bonnie laid a hand on Carly's shoulder. "Don't tell me any more."

"Why not?" Carly pinched the empty tissue pack and dangled it in front of Bonnie. "They said it happens all the time."

Bonnie took the plastic and crinkled it into a wad. "I . . . I don't want to believe it happens all the time. I want to believe that maybe someday I'll find . . ." She stopped and pressed her tightened fist over her lips.

"It's okay," Carly said, laying her hand on Bonnie's. "I understand."

Bonnie lowered her hand and smiled weakly. "Let's talk about something else."

"Okay. How about where you're going?"

"Me?" Bonnie cleared her throat, and her face reddened. "My first stop is Charleston, West Virginia." Her voice slowed and cracked. "My mother died . . . so I have to . . ."

Carly gasped and covered her mouth. "Oh, Bonnie! I'm so sorry!" She rubbed Bonnie's arm tenderly. "You don't have to talk about it."

Bonnie gave her a trembling smile. "Thank you." After a few seconds, she reached into the bin above her seat and withdrew a spiral journal from her duffle bag. As she sat back down, she flipped through some of the dog-eared pages near the front. "Tell you what. I'll show you some of the prayers I prayed for you."

Carly craned her neck to get a closer look. "You prayed for me?"

"See here?" Bonnie pointed at the top of a page. "I prayed that we'd see each other someday, and now look what happened."

"God answers prayers for little things like that?"

Bonnie leaned against Carly. "Friends getting back together is not a little thing. I wasn't allowed to write to you before, but now I can, so we'll write to each other and be pen pals for life."

As the girls hugged again, Sapphira stepped farther away from the screen and turned toward Acacia's bed. The top blanket was still folded back for her eventual homecoming.

She let out a long sigh. Maybe Bonnie was right. Maybe praying for Acacia to come home would be the answer. She had returned once before, even after she had given her up for dead. Maybe it could happen again. And what about Paili? Could she somehow be brought back from the dead, too? And she could never forget Elam. If only they could reunite, maybe she could finally tell him what she had been thinking for thousands of years.

She sat down in front of the screen and hugged her knees close to her chest. The train scene zipped by, and, as the images accelerated, the details melted away. Days in the land of the living passed as only minutes ticked away in Sapphira's chamber. With another promise to write to each other, Bonnie and Carly went their separate ways. Bonnie arrived in Charleston, West Virginia, and transferred from foster home to foster home until she moved to Castlewood. There, she met a young man named Billy Bannister, the son of Jared, who was once the great dragon, Clefspeare, still alive centuries after his transformation by Merlin.

Adventure after adventure swept before Sapphira's eyes. The viewport displayed an animated montage of highlights that followed the lives of Bonnie, Billy, a wise gentleman named Professor Charles Hamilton, and a funny, yet heroic young man named Walter Foley, as they battled Devin, Palin, and Morgan.

Bonnie soon met Ashley Stalworth, the daughter of Makaidos and Thigocia. With the help of Ashley's technological genius, Billy and Bonnie rescued Barlow, Edward, and the other loyal knights from the candlestone, and the destruction of that prison allowed Merlin to escape, as well. Edward reclaimed the name of Edmund, finally honoring his father with his heroic efforts in a great battle against Devin that followed the candlestone's demise.

Then, guided back to England by Professor Hamilton, Billy and Bonnie ventured into the portal in Patrick's ancient chamber. Bonnie found Shiloh in the sixth circle of Hades, where she had lived for forty years without aging a day. Shiloh survived because the seed Sapphira had planted sprouted and produced a fruit every morning, keeping her from starving. During her rescue, the spirit of Clefspeare was cast into the abyss and absorbed into Dragons' Rest through the Great Key, the gem in her pendant, causing it to change from white to red again.

Billy and Bonnie reunited Shiloh with her father, Patrick, though their efforts brought about the release of Samyaza and his demonic followers. In the seventh circle, Billy discovered the bones of the dragons who had turned human, those who were murdered by Devin after their transformation. He revived them, restoring their dragon bodies, and they all burst out of Hades to battle Samyaza.

When the viewport revealed Billy as the new dragon king, the rapid succession of scenes finally slowed. He and Bonnie prepared to enter Dragons' Rest through the gem in Shiloh's pendant. Professor Hamilton held Excalibur, making ready to slash its disintegrating beam through the two dimensional travelers so they could enter the rubellite.

Sapphira stood and drew close to the screen. She hovered her fingers over the images, awed by the miraculous way everything had fallen into place. The prophecy the Eye of the Oracle revealed to Makaidos so long ago had finally come to pass. Now it was time for an oracle of fire to open the portal and allow the king entry into the domain of dead dragons.

While focusing her mind on the pendant's gem, Sapphira laid her hand on the screen. "Collapse!" she ordered. The screen rolled up into a column. She jumped in and grabbed a stream of swirling light. Instantly, every image around her shattered, and a new scene took shape, empty crystalline walls flushed with scarlet hues. In front of her, veiled in red by a glassy screen, Professor Hamilton pulled back the sword. She gulped. Obviously the portal had transported her inside the gem, just as she had hoped, but what should she do now?

"Hurry, Sapphira!"

Sapphira spun around. A man holding a foot-tall hourglass stood in the midst of a red fog, but even the dense mist couldn't hide his identity. She clasped her hands and smiled. "Master Mer—"

"Ignite your fire," Merlin shouted, "and command the portal to open!"

Sapphira raised her arms. "Give me light!" A raging flame sprouted in her palm and swallowed her hand with fire. "How do I command it to open?"

Merlin pointed at the red glass leading to the outer world. "Lay your hand on the wall of the rubellite and shout, 'Ephphatha.' Give it all you've got."

592

Sapphira pressed her palm on the glass. Just as Professor Hamilton began to swing the blade, she shouted as loud as she could, "Ephphatha!"

The flames spread out in a wide circle, fading the red glass to pink, then to white. Professor Hamilton sliced the beam through Billy and Bonnie, and the sword's shaft of light wrapped around their bodies. The two teenagers dissolved into sparkling silhouettes that meshed together and swirled toward the screen like a silvery ribbon.

Sapphira pulled back her hand. The white hole continued to widen, and the energy swirls poured through.

Breathing a sigh, Merlin set his hourglass on the gem's floor. "You did it!"

Sapphira whispered to the fire. "That's enough." When the flames died away, she laid her hand on her chest. "Whew! That was close!"

Still recognizable in their energy form, Billy and Bonnie stood in the midst of the red gem, blinking rapidly as though they couldn't see anything.

Merlin nodded at Sapphira. "Excuse me for a moment." He reached for Billy's hand and laid a ring in his palm. The ring dissolved into the boy's sparks. "Take this," Merlin said, "you will need it later." The prophet leaned closer and whispered something else to Billy, but Sapphira couldn't hear his muffled words.

Billy and Bonnie passed through another screen on the opposite side of their entry point and disappeared.

Merlin wiped his brow. "The dragon messiah has now entered Dragons' Rest."

Sapphira pointed at each side of the gem. "So the way they came in leads to the land of the living, and the way they left leads to Dragons' Rest?"

"Your powers of observation are right on the mark!" Merlin bowed. "I am glad to finally meet you formally, Sapphira Adi."

Sapphira dipped her knee. "And I'm glad to finally meet you, Master Merlin."

Merlin's aged face flashed a proud smile. "You recognized me!"

She straightened and grinned. "I've been spying on you."

Merlin laughed. "Apparently we've been watching each other." He pointed at their window to the living world. "Here comes the other witness!"

A new swirl of radiance streamed through the same hole Billy and Bonnie had entered and coalesced into the shape of a boy with two flapping canopies on his back.

Sapphira clapped her hands. "It's Gabriel!"

As the sparkling shape thickened, its glow faded. Within seconds, Gabriel appeared, looking the same age and wearing the same clothes as the day he stood to face his executioners at Patrick's estate. He raised each leg in turn. "I feel like I weigh a ton!"

"You're solid again!" Sapphira lunged and wrapped her arms around his torso. "I'm so glad to see you!"

Merlin embraced both of them in his long arms. "In a few moments, Billy will lead the faithful dragons out of Dragons' Rest and into this rubellite." He pulled back and pointed at Sapphira and Gabriel. "You two have been chosen to bear witness to a covenant the dragons must make in order to pass through to the other side. As they enter, Gabriel will try to identify his father. If Makaidos doesn't come, Gabriel will enter Dragons' Rest and search for him there. But he will have to make haste. According to Enoch, that dimension's annihilation will be swift and complete."

Sapphira stepped up to the glass leading to Dragons' Rest and peered inside. "So you don't know who's in there?"

"Only a few that I recognized from the outside. My window to their world is quite limited."

"Should we do anything while we're waiting?" Gabriel asked.

"No." Merlin picked up the hourglass and gazed at the trickling sand. "Time is passing far more quickly in Dragons' Rest than it is in here, so Billy will finish his work shortly."

Gabriel huffed on the glass and wiped it with his sleeve. "Is that him coming this way?"

Merlin waved them back. "I must speak to him alone. Ponder what you have heard, and I will return in a few moments."

Sapphira and Gabriel strolled to the glass wall on the other side of the gem, the barrier that separated them from the land of the living. Sapphira leaned against it and nodded toward the opposite wall, now veiled by a curtain of red mist. "Did someone tell you to look for your father in Dragons' Rest?"

"Yes. Merlin says he's not in heaven, hell, or any of the circles of seven." Gabriel shrugged. "We couldn't think of anywhere else to look."

Sapphira rubbed his arm tenderly. "If he's in there, he'll follow Billy. Don't worry about that."

"You're probably right." Gabriel's wings lifted and stretched out. "But if I don't see him, I'm going in. I'm not taking any chances."

Sweeping his arms back and forth, Merlin parted the curtain of fog. With his head bowed low, he pointed at the Dragons' Rest screen. "Behold. The messiah comes in the arms of the virgin."

Sapphira dashed through the fog and peered through the glass. Veiled by the crimson barrier, Bonnie shuffled toward the gem, carrying Billy in her arms.

Gabriel joined her at the screen. "Did someone kill him?"

"I'm afraid so." Merlin wiped a tear from his withered cheek. "He knew this fate was possible, yet he went there willingly to save the dragons from doom."

"If he's a messiah"—Sapphira paused through a throat cramp— "will he rise from the dead?"

Merlin pointed at the world of the living through the other screen. "It depends on two teenagers out there who are doing everything in their power to battle against death. I think you will meet Ashley and Walter soon enough, but theirs is a story that must wait."

As Bonnie drew closer, Sapphira stepped back from the glass. "Can we do anything to help?"

"Exactly what God has called us to do, what he has spent centuries preparing us to do. It is time for the two of you to create a covenant veil and complete the Great Key."

"How do we do that?" Gabriel asked.

Merlin pressed his hand on Sapphira's shoulder. "You stand here." He pulled Gabriel parallel to the glass wall, separating him several paces from Sapphira. "And you stand here." He raised both hands. "Lift up a hand toward each other, and as witnesses to this covenant, you will shout the vow all dragons must believe in order to pass through to the other side."

"Vow?" Sapphira wrinkled her forehead. "What vow?"

"The name you so recently learned. The name that imbedded the fire within your soul. Then Gabriel will answer with the same words."

Sapphira and Gabriel lifted their hands. A stream of flames shot from Sapphira's fingers to Gabriel's, creating a fiery arc.

Bonnie, her glittering silhouette carrying Billy's, passed through the Dragons' Rest screen and shuffled into the foggy chamber. Red sparks dripped from Billy's side and splashed on the gem's floor. She paused and looked around, as if lost.

"Now, Sapphira! Now!"

Sapphira took in a deep breath and shouted, "Jehovah-Yasha!"

"Jehovah-Yasha!" Gabriel echoed.

The shouts pushed the mist inward, producing two scarlet sound waves that collided under the center of the arc. At the point of impact, tongues of fire stretched out in all directions and licked up the fog. When every trace of mist disappeared, a wall of red light congealed between Gabriel and Sapphira and pulsed like a beating heart.

Bonnie's face suddenly brightened, and she walked through the shimmering wall and out of the rubellite.

"Stay steady!" Merlin said. "Here come the dragons!"

Another human entered and instantly transformed into a mass of sparkling energy. As he passed by Sapphira, his bright blue eyes met hers.

"Hilidan!" She smiled so widely her cheeks hurt. When Hilidan pierced the throbbing veil, his energy field melded into it and passed through on the other side in the shape of a dragon, shining more brightly than ever. Then, with a sizzle and a pop, he penetrated the screen to the world of the living and disappeared.

Several more figures passed by, and Sapphira called out the names of the ones she recognized—Zera, Shachar, and Clirkus—but they didn't seem to hear her as they penetrated the covenant veil.

When the parade of escapees came to an end, and the last sparkling form exited through the screen, Merlin sighed. "It is finished. You can lower your hands now."

Gabriel and Sapphira rested their arms, but the arc of fire remained suspended in the air. The covenant veil continued to pulse, radiating a steady beam of light toward the living world. The gem's interior, now clear of fog, seemed to glow with a light of its own as if the walls had been brushed with a million glowing crystals.

"My father didn't come through." Gabriel slumped his shoulders. "I'm sure of it."

Sapphira peered through the gem's entry into Dragons' Rest. Inside, a solitary man stood on a stage that faced dozens of rows of chairs. He stuffed his hands in his pockets and paced in front of the screen.

"Could that be Makaidos?" Sapphira asked.

Gabriel cupped his hands around his eyes and peered in. "Dad's not that tall, and his jaw is more rounded."

"Roxil didn't come through, either." She clutched Gabriel's sleeve. "We need to find both of them."

"We?" Gabriel shook his head. "I don't think you should go. If that place is going to blow up—"

"Enough talk." Merlin waved both hands at the screen. "You may both go, but you must hurry. And remember, Roxil cannot leave through this passage unless she believes the covenant you declared."

Sapphira turned to the translucent veil. As it continued to throb, somehow it seemed inviting yet forbidding at the same time. "Isn't there any other way?"

"For a dragon to gain eternal salvation?" Merlin shook his head emphatically. "No."

Sapphira laid her hand on the glass, and her fingers passed right through. "Are you going to stay here and wait for us?"

"I must attend to a very important matter in the world of the living. You see, Morgan has yet to reap the harvest of destruction she has sown for thousands of years. I am going to send her to her final resting place. Then, since the gateway to Dragons' Rest has been torn open, I will rescue my wife, and we will ascend into heaven together." Merlin passed through the covenant veil and disappeared.

Tears welling in her eyes, Sapphira backed through the barrier and whispered, "I didn't even get to say good-bye."

Gabriel followed her. "Me, either. He seemed to be in a hurry."

When she emerged on the other side, a cool wood floor greeted her bare feet. "Is this a theatre?" she whispered.

"I think so. I've only been to a couple of movies, though, and it's been a long time, so I'm not sure."

"Same here. People looked at me funny. Blind girls don't go to movies very often."

"Or boys who refuse to take off their backpacks." Gabriel nodded toward the side of the stage. "There's that tall guy we saw. He's talking to two old ladies. Let's scoot."

"Shouldn't we warn them?"

"Since they're here, they've probably already been told." Gabriel took her hand. "If this place is going to get nuked, we'd better hustle."

"I guess you're right." Sapphira's foot nudged something that slid across the floor.

"What's this?" Gabriel asked, stooping. "A knife?"

Sapphira rubbed her finger along the wooden hilt. A hint of dark blood stained the rough stone blade. "I've seen it before. I think it's Morgan's."

He slid it between his belt and trousers. "It might come in handy."

As he led the way down the stage steps, Sapphira noticed his back, his wingless back. "Gabriel! Your wings! They're gone!"

Gabriel never broke stride. "Yeah. Dimensional travel rocks. Maybe they'll show up at baggage claim."

After they exited the theatre and ran out to the village streets, Gabriel stopped and swung his head from side to side. "Any idea where to go?"

"Probably the town square. I've been to a reflection of this place in the sixth circle, so I know it pretty well." She nodded toward a clock tower that rose above the tops of the other buildings. "It's that way."

Gabriel marched toward the tower. "I'll recognize my father, but do you know what Roxil looks like?"

"I know what she used to look like, but we can ask around for Jasmine. That's her name here."

The ground trembled. A window in a nearby feed store shattered, and a crack split the road between Gabriel and Sapphira. Gabriel leaped over the widening rift and grabbed Sapphira's arm. "Hurry!"

599

Running side by side, they followed dusty cobblestones that led to a broader road and then to a city square. In the central garden, a statue of a man riding a horse stood watch over an array of colorful flowers, and a rope lay over his outstretched arm with a hangman's noose dangling underneath. Several people milled about, and a woman knelt next to a body lying on the road.

Gabriel let go of Sapphira. "I guess they didn't feel the quake here."

She ran up to the corpse—the body of a petite female. A gash in the front of her dress revealed a gaping wound in her bosom. Sapphira gulped. "Naamah!"

The kneeling woman stood and faced them. Her stern, angular features hadn't changed in the slightest. "So, you have come to bring our destruction, have you?"

When Gabriel joined them, Sapphira latched on to his wrist and squeaked. "It's good to see you again . . . uh . . . Jasmine."

Jasmine glared at Gabriel. "You're not an oracle of fire, are you? The prophecy said that there would be two oracles, not one."

Gabriel pointed at her. "Listen, Roxil, or Jasmine, or whatever your name is now, I may not be an oracle of fire, and I don't know about any prophecy, but this place is about to blow, and I need to find my . . . I mean, your father."

The ground shook again. Two more windows cracked, and a chimney toppled, spilling broken bricks down an angled roof. Sapphira stooped to keep her balance, and Jasmine dropped to her knees. The people in the streets scrambled in every direction.

When the tremor settled, Jasmine rose slowly to her feet. "You won't find my father here. He left a long time ago, and he never came back."

A fountain of fire erupted in the city hall building, spewing wiggling ribbons of flaming debris onto the street. As sparkling ash rained down, the three backed toward the statue to avoid the embers.

600

"Merlin predicted this," Sapphira said, swatting at the ash. "We have to get you out of here before it's too late!"

Jasmine sneered. "I should have known Merlin had something to do with this. He has been plotting to kill dragons all along, and now he has arranged our apocalypse."

"Merlin set up the way of escape!" Sapphira grabbed a fistful of Jasmine's sleeve. "This place is about to burn! What's it going to take to get you to change your mind?"

"Truth!" Jasmine shook away Sapphira's grip and pointed at Naamah's body. "She killed that so-called dragon messiah with the same dagger that took her own life. A dead messiah cannot save anyone from this God-forsaken place. It is hopeless. There is no way out."

"Really?" Sapphira narrowed her eyes. "Then how did your father leave?"

Jasmine nodded at the statue in the garden. "He wandered over there in sort of a daze, saying something about a red glow, but Brogan and I never saw anything. Then, he just vanished."

"And he became human." Sapphira clasped her fingers together. "He rejoined your mother, who also took a human form, and they had two children, Gabriel and Ashley, your brother and sister."

Jasmine's expression softened, and her voice lost its sharp edge. "So, they're a happy family now, I suppose."

Sapphira shook her head. "A slayer killed your father and mother, but Billy risked his life and resurrected your mother from a dragon graveyard."

Jasmine glanced at the hangman's noose. "Billy resurrected her?"

"Yes. She's alive now and is a dragon again, but your father's spirit is missing." She nodded at Gabriel. "That's why your brother is here looking for him, and we were hoping you'd want to help."

Jasmine's lip trembled slightly, but she quickly firmed it. "Of course I want to help, but there are a couple of important obstacles." She extended a finger. "First, I'm dead." She extended another finger. "Second, apparently you have to trust in a human to get out of here, and I haven't seen any good reason for doing that."

Gabriel stepped up to Jasmine and stood toe-to-toe. "I've been listening to you jabber long enough." He extended his own finger. "Our father was dead, too, and that didn't stop him from coming back to life." He flashed all four fingers and began lowering each one as he continued. "This Billy guy is human, and he died trying to save you. Merlin's human, and he sent Billy in here to save all the dragons. I'm human, and do you think I'm going to gain anything by risking my own life to argue with a stubborn dragon?" He lowered the last finger and formed a fist. "And Sapphira's human, and she has more love than all of us combined. Without her, I would have been dead, Billy couldn't have come here to rescue dragons, and you wouldn't be getting another chance to crack your cold heart of stone."

The ground suddenly lurched. Sapphira fell on her seat, and Jasmine toppled backward into the garden. Gabriel kept his balance, flailing his arms as he rode out the bucking cobblestones. When the quake settled, Gabriel helped Sapphira up, but the entire garden area broke away from the street and began to sink, taking Jasmine and the statue with it.

Gabriel dove for the edge and reached down into the growing chasm. "Jasmine! Grab my hand! I'll pull you up!"

Jasmine struggled to her feet and jumped, but her fingertips merely brushed against Gabriel's. With her second jump, her hand passed several inches too low.

Sapphira dashed along the chasm's perimeter, jumped down toward the statue, and landed in the rider's lap. Grabbing the hangman's rope attached to the horse's neck, she screamed up at Gabriel. "Catch the noose!"

Gabriel reached both hands. "Toss it!"

Sapphira slung the noose upward. The rope smacked Gabriel in the face, but he managed to latch onto it before it slipped away. "Got it!" he shouted, wrapping it around his wrists.

Sapphira clambered down to the pedestal and extended her hand. "Up here, Jasmine! We can still climb out from the top of the statue!"

Jasmine bent her knees, but the ground suddenly crumbled. She fell forward and grasped the bottom of the statue's pedestal as it dropped, and her momentum drove the pedestal against the sloping wall, wedging it there.

The weight dragged Gabriel's body farther out over the pit. He strained against the load, every muscle in his face quivering, and he let out a roar. "The rope's cutting my wrists!"

"Hang on!" Sapphira yelled.

As Jasmine dangled over a deep pit, purple fumes rose from the blackness, smelling of camphor and garlic, then a voice filtered upward. "Roxil. Come and join me. I have been waiting for you."

Jasmine twisted her neck and looked down. "Goliath?"

"Yes. Just let go. I will catch you, and we will live together in the true Dragons' Rest."

Jasmine spun her head back toward Sapphira, her wild eyes darting all around. The statue lurched down a few inches, jerking one of Jasmine's hands loose, but it suddenly halted, teetering over the black pit.

Gabriel slid farther. Puffing and grunting, he let out a loud, wordless moan.

Stooping carefully, Sapphira grabbed Jasmine's wrist. As she pulled, her vision sharpened. Far below, the skeletons of several dragons lay scattered in the midst of a black fog. A huge red dragon stood among the bones and called out, "Please do not abandon me!"

"Don't listen to him!" Sapphira reached for Jasmine's flailing arm. "Give me your other hand!"

Gabriel screamed. "I can't hold on much longer!"

The voice erupted again. "Roxil, I need you! Do not trust the humans. If you climb into Makaidos's arms, you will be in his clutches forever."

Sapphira glanced up at the statue's horseman. Its open arms seemed ready to welcome the company of another rider. As the pedestal tipped further, she reached her free hand down as far as she could and shouted. "You have to make your choice right now!"

Jasmine looked down one more time, then swung up and grabbed Sapphira's hand. As Sapphira pulled, tongues of fire erupted from the pit and swirled around Jasmine's feet. With a final grunt, Sapphira hoisted her, and they scrambled up to the side of the rider. With their feet planted on top of the pedestal, they clung to one of his arms.

A huge plume of twisting fire shot up from the depths and swirled around the statue, creating a tall, spinning cylinder of flames. The hangman's rope ignited and burned to a charred thread, and the statue slid down the side of the chasm wall.

Pushing her snowy hair from her eyes, Sapphira looked through the circular opening at the top of the fiery cylinder. Several feet above her head, Gabriel clung to the lip of the chasm, digging his shoes into the slope.

Sapphira cupped a hand around the side of her mouth. "Gabriel! Jump! It's your only chance!" As hot wind from the whipping fire snatched her words into the cyclone, the cylinder's opening squeezed shut. With a loud crack, the statue plunged downward.

Suddenly, Gabriel burst through the wall of fire. He caught the horse's head and swung up to its back in one motion. Now riding in front of the soldier, he took Sapphira's hand. "Are we in a portal?"

Sapphira squeezed his fingers. "I think so!"

"Did you make all this fire?"

"No! I have no idea who did it!"

Dry air and streaming flames flowed upward all around. Jasmine locked an arm around Sapphira's waist, and Gabriel slapped the thigh of the sculptured rider behind him. "Ready to hunt for our father?"

As Jasmine held her dress down with her free hand, a trembling smile broke through, and her voice cracked. "You humans . . . have a strange way . . . of beginning a new adventure."

Gabriel grinned. "Hang on tight, Sister. You ain't seen nothin' yet!"

The downward plunge slowed to a gentle drift. A rectangular hole opened in the fiery wall, revealing a screen similar to the museum room's viewing port. It displayed Merlin standing at the edge of a precipice with his hand wrapped around the neck of a huge raven. At the bottom of the chasm, a river of magma churned, bright orange and steaming. Merlin struck the bird's head with a glowing sword, and its feathers burst into flames. He released the raven's neck, and it immediately attacked him, pecking and clawing his head. Tongues of fire lashed his shoulders and ignited his clothes. Merlin transformed into a glittering lion, snatched the raven in his great jaws, and dangled it over the chasm. With a mighty shake, he cast the raven downward, and it morphed into Morgan's dark silhouette. Screaming and flailing her arms, she plunged into the boiling river of fire. The splash ignited a towering blaze, and Morgan's face melted into the stream.

Merlin gazed down at the river and whispered, "Checkmate." Then, with a turn and a bow of his sparkling lion head, he smiled. "Sapphira Adi, your tormentor is no more. May you live the rest of your years in peace and joy. I will see you again in Paradise."

Sapphira sniffed and waved. "Good-bye, Merlin. Thank you . . . Thank you for everything."

Merlin faded away. The screen disappeared, and the hole in the fiery wall closed. The cyclone's spin suddenly accelerated, whipping the hot air into a frenzy. Sharp pain dug into Sapphira's arm. A set of claws dragged across her skin and scratched down the side of the statue. A pair of wide red eyes flashed in the center of a scaly brow as a dragon's face slowly shrank into the darkness below.

Sapphira bent over and grasped a foreleg. "Roxil! Hang on!"

Wings sprouted from Roxil's back and spread out toward the spinning fire. When the tips brushed against the flames, she pulled her wings tightly against her body.

Sapphira looked upward. "Jehovah-Yasha!" She grunted as she strained against Roxil's growing weight. "Help me! I can't hang on much longer!"

The wall of fire contracted and spilled over them. The statue burned away, and all three plunged into a black void. Sapphira's

EYE OF THE ORACLE

body erupted in flames. Gabriel, falling next to her, also burst into a fiery column.

The surrounding darkness crumbled and blew away. Sapphira pressed her feet down on a cool stone floor. The flames crackled and shrank into dwindling sparks that scattered around the familiar museum chamber. Standing at her side in his winged form, Gabriel batted away the remaining sparks as if they were pesky gnats. The portal column swirled in front of them, white and shining.

Sapphira clasped her hands together. "We made it! Thank God!"

Gabriel smiled and flicked his thumb toward the rear. "Our hitchhiker made it, too!"

Sapphira spun around. Sitting on its haunches, a tawny dragon stretched its wings and shook off a coat of ashes. It wagged its head back and forth and groaned. "I hope that was just the longest nightmare in history!"

Sapphira laughed. "Wake up, sleepy dragon! It's time to search for your father."

"Yeah," Gabriel said, giving his wings a vigorous shake. "We need you to heat up the coffee."

Roxil breathed a steam-filled sigh. "Very well. I can put up with a couple of humans for a while."

Gabriel shook a finger at her. "Listen here. You might be a powerful, fire-breathing dragon, but to me you're just my overgrown, scaly sister. I should—"

"Shhh!" Sapphira grabbed Gabriel's wrist and whispered. "Just be patient. At least she didn't go with Goliath, and we might have a long journey ahead of us, so we have to deal with what we've got. Besides, sister or not, you shouldn't argue with a fire-breathing dragon."

Gabriel firmed his chin and nodded. "Good point. Don't stoke the dragon."

Sapphira patted him on the back, and the two walked together to the dragon's side. "Roxil," she said, pointing back at the spinning portal, "are you ready to carry a couple of riders to another dimension? I'm not sure what Gabriel's going to look like when we get there, but we'll figure out a way to work together."

"If I must." Roxil lowered her head to their eye level. "Where will we begin?"

Sapphira pressed a palm against her chest. A fiery glow spread from her fingertips down to the heel of her hand and radiated pulsing white light in a soft elliptical aura. "We'll begin wherever my dance partner leads me."

Waving her hands around a spinning column of fire, Acacia guided the vortex down toward a book that lay open on a wooden table. Inside the column, a miniature boy and girl clung to a statue and descended with the flames. Acacia clapped her hands over the top of the column, and the vortex collapsed, setting the pair inside on fire. The two burning figures hovered above the book for a moment, then crumbled into glowing embers that fell onto the pages.

607

Another pair of hands, larger and wrinkled, closed the book. The hands belonged to a white-haired man who sat across from Acacia. His bushy eyebrows rose high on his broad forehead. "Well done, my child. You have saved the lives of your friends, and you have given a dragon a second chance, an opportunity not normally afforded anyone, whether human or dragon."

Acacia took the hand of a little girl who sat on the bench next to her. The girl's eyes gleamed in the dim light cast over the table by a flickering lantern. With only a stack of books piled against one of the stone walls, the stuffy chamber raised memories of her long, pain-filled days in the stark caverns of the underworld. "What happens now, Father Enoch? Will Paili and I go home?"

"I do not know for sure." Enoch rubbed his hands across the weathered cover of the book. "Time is not like a story. You cannot turn to the back and discover the end of the tale. You have to suffer through life one page at a time."

"But aren't you a prophet? Can't the Eye of the Oracle see the future?"

Enoch shook his head. "I speak only what Jehovah commands me to speak. Whether he writes the final page, reads every page from front to end at the same time, or perfectly predicts what we will write there ourselves, I do not know. It is a mystery far too great for me to comprehend." He lifted the book's cover and flipped to the back. "But this much I do know. No matter what happens, Jehovah-Jireh will provide for all your needs, Jehovah-Shammah will be there from the first to the last, and Jehovah-Yasha will deliver you to safety, whether at home with Sapphira or at home with him. You will never be forsaken."

608

Paili slid closer and clutched Acacia's arm. Acacia smiled and laid her hand on the book's final page. "Then the Eye of the Oracle has spoken?"

Enoch laid his hand over Acacia's. "Yes, my child. The Eye of the Oracle has spoken."

EPILOGUE

I am now a daughter of light, and the path set before me is blazed by the glow of Jehovah-Yasha—bloody footprints imbedded in a trail of tears, yet leading to a glorious kingdom set on a shining hill. Though trials stand in the way—a search for lost friends, the awakening of sleeping giants, and the uncertainty of Mardon's looming specter—I know the path will never lead to a place of desolation. The shining city will always guide me home.

I now look forward to what lies ahead. New friends will mingle with those familiar. Ashley, the daughter of dragons, and Walter, the descendant of a king, will grace the path with their presence, riding on the wind atop the great warrior Thigocia.

My story continues. The joy of discovery awaits. And I hope that my path somehow, someday, crosses the path of another ageless seeker, the receiver of the only blessing I had to offer so many years ago—a handful of stew that quelled a boiling hunger. Yet, it was more than simply a pottage of sustenance; it was my compassion, my humility, my submission. When I gave him the fruit of my hands, I also surrendered my heart.

When I see him again, I will tell him so.